THE THIRD TESTAMENT
FOR THE THIRD MILLENNIUM

SPIRIT

I0660730

Kevin Carey

Sacristy Press
PO Box 612, Durham, DH1 9HT

www.sacristy.co.uk

First published in 2011 by Sacristy Press, Durham

Sacristy Limited, registered in England & Wales, number 7565667

British Library Cataloguing-in-Publication Data
A catalogue record for the book is available from the British Library

ISBN 978-1-908381-01-9

www.perpetua.tv

I. PASTORALE

1.

This is the story of how the word of Perpetua, the fourth person of the God-head, began to spread in rural England.

Nigel Bourne made his way labouriously across his yard on an unseasonably cold Easter morning, only vaguely aware, as a former hard drinking prop forward, of the effect of the previous evening's sparkling wine at the customary post Vigil gathering—the event at the Rectory had never blossomed to the extent that it could even loosely be called a party. "Lamb of God," he said, conversationally, "you take away the sin of the world." They were all routinely anxious and competitive as he distributed their food. "You're lucky you're not a Paschal lamb," he said playfully to a male, too young for the next cull. "I don't know how long we can go on with this," he said, as he returned to the lonely house for his bath before going to church. "I don't want to give up the sheep but it gets harder every year."

Clement Sutcliffe, a few miles away in the centre of Walmbury, put the customary pinch of Earl Grey into the Darjealing, opened the last full bottle of milk, nearest the hinge, warmed the pot, poured the water and addressed the radio only slightly less combatively than he would on a week day. Bad Morning annoyed him because it was too aggressive and superficial but Faith annoyed him because it was unshapely and bland. "Why isn't somebody angry about the Perpetua story?" he asked the radio as he turned it off, carried the tray of tea into the bedroom, and turned another radio on.

Father Mark Price, the Rector of Walmbury, listening to the same item, wondered whether to bring Perpetua into the eight o'clock sermon but decided it was pointless. He was satisfied if the grim attendees, all in their special and widely separated places, could be coaxed into smiling. "Christ is risen," he thought "but it doesn't seem to touch them. I really wonder why they come to church at all."

Bishop James Hall of Alchester was not sure either, as he wearily followed the final item of Faith in his car on the alleged temporary 'banishment' of Archbishop Hawthorne to North America, supposedly to keep him from intervening in the Perpetua affair; but, then, he was rarely sure of anything. He was both humble and indecisive, with a penchant for over-elaboration. Like Hawthorne, he was addicted to the subordinate clause, but whereas the Archbishop gave the impression of subtlety and even profundity within his commas, dashes and brackets, the Bishop conveyed tediousness and muddle. Indeed his administration and pronouncements might best have been described by Bill Shankley when he bemoaned a poor Liverpool performance by saying, "The lads over elaborated in the middle of the park." "Of course he wasn't in North America because of the Perpetua crisis—if it was a crisis—because he was there long before the dreadful climax of her mission. He was there because of the dispute over gay clergy. Thank God we handle things more delicately here", he thought. "Well, I mustn't delude myself, it isn't thanks to me that Aleford isn't an issue, and now it is all over the media because she has died in very strange circumstances—if you can call a death from drug-induced violence strange—and, as usual, they are more interested in her now she's dead than when she was alive—but I suppose you could say that about Jesus. And this is bound to lead to the usual muddying of the waters so that those who are against women bishops will somehow be unscrupulously implicated in this unfortunate and bizarre—if it was bizarre—death."

"Christ is risen!" said Father Mark in a 'church shout' to the 9.45. "He is risen indeed, alleluia!" they replied, with the well trained choir making almost as much noise as the 270 (215 Communicants) in the body of the church. "I'll try it again at odd moments throughout the service, to check that you are still awake and to see if you can do any better." They smiled. The old ones certainly were the best ones.

Even though she had prepared Scott thoroughly, Marie still looked anxious as the Penitential Rite finished and so she was relieved when Mark began the spoken Kyrie without interruption. Nigel could not suppress his customary irritation that the Kyrie was only sung in Penitential Seasons and was, therefore, said before the Gloria. Scott began the play-over at a cracking pace but then, as usual, slowed down radically so that the choir could not possibly come in together. Father Mark sometimes thought that he would be better off without the choir which, in spite of its shortcomings, pretended to cathedral habits. His High Anglican upbringing and post Vatican II inclinations were frequently at odds.

"Christ is risen!" he said, in something approaching a real shout, at the beginning of the sermon. "He is risen indeed, alleluia!", the congregation shouted back, warming to the permission it had given itself to demonstrate a little joy. "You should have been here last night," he thought as he always did at this point in the Easter Family Eucharist, "then you would know why you are rejoicing. I wonder how long I can go on saying the same things and having precisely the same regrets every year. The place is packed at Christmas but there were only 32, including fourteen choir, at the Vigil.

"In the name of the One God, Creator, Redeemer and Sanctifier. Amen.

"Some of you will have heard the dreadful news of the death of Perpetua on Good Friday. Indeed, some of you may have seen the events leading up to it if you watched The Cutting Edge Channel. I am sorry to mention such a sad event on this most joyful of mornings but I hope you will soon see why.

"Perpetua, our fellow believer in God our Creator Parent and in Jesus our Redeemer Brother, said she was trying, sustained by Her Sister the Sanctifier, to bring new life into the worship of God and to bring new hope to all the people of God. This message was not welcomed by our Church authorities; although Archbishop Hawthorne, in his customary spirit of open-mindedness, refused to condemn her claim to be a special person of the Godhead, the Petrans and the Torans and even most of the Medians have attacked her as a blasphemer.

"But picture a street in Jerusalem when Mary Magdalene, the first human being to see Our Risen Lord (never forget it was a woman who first saw him) says that Jesus, not just a teacher or a prophet, but the Son of God, has risen from the dead and she has seen him. As we will see in the next few weeks as we read through Acts, the followers of the risen Christ did not receive a friendly reception from the religious authorities; and ought this not to be a warning to us? Not that I expect for a moment that Perpetua will 'rise from the dead' in any way; I simply want to make the point that we should have treated her the way we would have liked Jesus to be treated when he was challenging the religious authorities with his unconventional theology, the way we would have liked stephen to be treated. Remember, Stephen, a good Jew, given a new perspective by his encounter with Jesus, was stoned without dialogue.

"And so, on this happiest of days, we should thank God for sending the Holy Spirit and ensuring that the Good News, the new hope, which Jesus brought, was not snuffed out by the establishment; and, in like manner, we must see what we can learn from what Perpetua had to tell us.

"One thing we might learn is what remarkable twists and turns the story of the relationship between God our Parent and all the children of earth can take. Think of that short span of time in which Jesus was sent to us in the Incarnation—God's intervention in history—then died for us—God's intervention in our relationship with Creation—and now, today, has risen from the dead, under-writing our individual and collective hope in eternal salvation. If you had sketched this train of hope for any great religious leader of the Chosen People, they would have greeted it with incredulity. We, who re-live these great events every year, must not go to the opposite extreme and take the Resurrection for granted. This is our Day! Christ is risen!" "He is risen indeed!", the well practised congregation roared back, "Alleluia!"

"I will write to the Bishop," muttered Lady Marianne Gowers, as she usually threatened without every giving it effect. "I know there is latitude in the Church but he takes it too far." Many others took what he said with a pinch of salt—it was just Mark being Mark—but most were simply washed over with a feeling of mild joy. They had not partaken in any Lenten fasts nor Holy Week rites. They were getting their religion on the spiritual—and financial—cheap so they cheerfully accepted that the quality would not be all that high. A few were aware of the dispute between Torans and Petrans about the primacy of the Crucifixion or the Resurrection; and most of them had an inkling of the disputes over women and gay clergy, although they resented the yoking of the two issues. They had largely been opposed to women priests until one had stood in for Mark when he was on holiday and they were delightfully surprised. But they were definitely against gay clergy even though the fact that their Area Bishop was gay, though avowedly celibate, barely registered. Clement, standing in his place in the back row of the choir next to the Sanctus Bell, was so preoccupied with what Mark had said that he almost missed a phrase of the Creed, which he always said with meticulous intonation as part of the choir's role in leading the worship. Either Perpetua was going to be a massive factor in the Church or fade away almost immediately, the choices Gamaliel had advised. Veronica, who would make an ideal priest in any other Diocese but Alchester, read the Prayers of the Faithful (Mark and Clement both hated the shorthand term "Intercessions"), interpolating the set text, on which Mark insisted, with a reference to Perpetua. The generosity of the sentiment and Mark's love for Veronica meant that she was forgiven. Clement knew this because after Mark proclaimed the Easter Peace he greeted Clement with the customary: "Christ is risen!" and allowed him to return: "Christ is risen, indeed, Alleluia!" instead of grumbling about the prayers or giving an instruction about the ringing—or not—of the Sanctus Bell. Although they were identical (some parishioners said telepathic) over many things, Mark did not appreciate that Clement needed his sympathy, after Helen's, more than that of anyone in the world to sustain his emotional and spiritual life. During the Peace, Helen transformed herself from her chorister into her Churchwarden role and arranged the carrying of the gifts of bread and wine up to the altar. Helen saw her mission as bearing witness to God in a multitude of small acts of care. On this occasion she found the two smallest and poorest children from the social housing to carry the gifts rather than the over-anxious Walmhursts from the Tudor Manor House. Mark noticed this detail with true appreciation and noted the number of communicants (up 35 from last year) and prepared himself for the Great Prayer, which he always said with almost exaggerated care so that every phrase would tell.

"On the night before he died he had supper with his friends ...". He saw her standing on a dais on Christmas night, handing out food and drink to all kinds of people. "... and taking bread, he broke it ...". He saw her lying in the mud, almost dead. "... This is my body ...". Whose body? "... Do this in memory of ...". He faltered. He only just stopped himself saying "her." Clement, poised to ring the Sanctus Bell, noticed the faltering and almost mis-timed his pull which generated the usual puff of sandstone dust and a triple single note that sounded more funereal than joyful. He knew precisely what was going through Mark's mind. "And taking the cup ...". He saw her blood, caked on her broken face. "... This is my blood of the New Covenant ..." Which Covenant? He tried opening his eyes, and shutting them, and opening them again to banish the vision of her final moments, just for now. Scott gave him the note for the Acclamation and he got through to the Our Father where he had time to pull himself together.

After one of the most harrowing days of his year, he relaxed after he closed the church door on Good Friday, enjoying a traditional early fish pie supper with his bachelor and gay clergy friends. Scanning the channels for something to watch after they left that would take his mind off the Vigil, which always made him tense, he came across the Cutting Edge Channel and watched in horror as Perpetua died in front of him. Was she the fourth person of the Godhead or a sham? He could not tell but the imprint of her death was all the deeper for his liberal outlook.

"Lamb of God," he sang under his breath, as usual glancing over his left shoulder at Nigel. Then he broke the bread as the choir finished off the Agnus.

He wholly regained his equilibrium as he distributed bread and blessings. He retained his capacity as a former teacher to take a complete register as he gave absolute attention to each person in front of him. He noted the absentees, not with censure but with a sense of loss. He was so intent that he did not notice the Choir singing the anthem. To celebrate Easter, when the distribution of Communion and blessings was long enough to allow the only long anthem of the year, Marie had chosen the choir's favourite party piece, "Steam Ship" Wesley's Blessed Be The God And Father. Marie enjoyed her solo and her dialogue with the ladies; Nigel enjoyed the booming bass notes; and Clement enjoyed hitting the tenor entry in the fugue just right and keeping everyone together during the final passage which was always in danger of breaking into a ragged canter. As it was: the choir dropped almost a semitone before the organ crashed in on "From the dead", Marie's nerves almost ruined her solo entrance; the ladies, as usual, were late on their entries, and in spite of Clement's best efforts, Scott was the culprit in the fugue. Nonetheless everyone was pleased. Mark noted that there was time for the child-friendly hymns he had set. The choir thought it had got through honourably enough, and the congregation was proud to have a choir of twenty that could still tackle such a grand anthem and generate such an impressive noise when so many churches had no choir or, worse, a pop group. Mark, trusting to his faulty memory, had to be reminded by Helen of the Banns. He then blessed the congregation and Nigel took up the cross to lead the recession to Thine Be The Glory before the exchange of ornate but slightly insecure Alleluias at the dismissal. For some reason Clement could not work out, Mark insisted on the organ playing at full register after the dismissal instead of allowing Scott a gentle introduction so that the choir could complete its vestry prayer. Marie, who chose somebody special to blow out the candles—the marking of a birthday, the reward for a Psalm well led—was pushed forward to blow them out herself. Then there were cream eggs all round and the satisfaction of a job well done, disrobing at the end of a week which had started with the Palm Sunday procession. "I don't see how people can get very much out of today unless they have gone through the whole week," said Clement, sincerely enough but drawing attention to his own annual 100% Holy Week attendance. In spite of a yearly gentle reminder from Helen, Mark only ever thanked the flower ladies on Easter morning, forgetting everyone else, including the choir, for a week's hard work but now it was over nobody seemed to mind. At the back of the church Mark went through his usual, almost subconscious calculations: "Communion was longer but his sermon had been shorter so the lamb would go on in in time for a 1.45 p.m. main course; there were more for coffee but they would go sooner, so that would balance out." He thanked the Skett children for bringing up the gifts and made a special fuss of the Walmhurst children who had been overlooked in spite of their enthusiasm. Like an actor at the end of a run he was passing from the actual stress to what might even be the main point, the enjoyment of looking back at a job well done. Clement and Helen helped the affectionately known "Dyson Girls", who were both above 70, to finish the washing up and then they went down the High street towards home.

As usual they had a discussion about buying a paper. It had started as a specific antipathy to Murdoch, but had extended to all so-called 'quality' newspapers. "There won't be anything in it worth having," said Clement. "What about the Perpetua story?" "It will have been overtaken by events, if there are any. I spent yesterday afternoon on the net in between listening to the football." "What about teachers?" "I can't bear the thought of yet more stories about teachers threatening to strike, saying their morale is at 'rock bottom', accusing the Government of not caring. But it's a cliche: the morale of teachers, the police and nurses is always 'at rock bottom'. The Government might be only passably competent, but it does care. The media deliberately confuses complexity with uncaring when the complexity results from over scrupulousness. Every time a general rule is shown to be unfair to some sector, an exception is made and the rule book thickens. When the Government, pendulum-style, then goes to simplify it is accused of harming some sector or other. The trouble is that papers like the Toxic Times deliberately indulge in a paradox where they can always flay the Government: the post code lottery and Whitehall doesn't know best, why the Government doesn't do something, and the stupidly termed 'nanny state'." I know all that," said Helen, patiently. "Every easter we have the same thing with the teachers and the Government." "Anyway, I don't have time to bother. There is more writing to finish." "Yes, I suppose it's those Harvest prayers. I don't know how you think of Carols in a heat wave and Lent during Christmas." "Retailers have to do the same sort of thing." "Why do you have an answer for everything? I just wish you would accept the compliment gracefully. You can alternate so rapidly between the serene and the grumpy."

When they got home they enjoyed a bacon and egg brunch, which would see them through to dinner. Clement put on a CD of the Easter Oratorio and filed away all the Holy Week music—Gesualdo, Byrd, Charpentier, Frank Martin but, above all, Bach—and was slightly annoyed when the phone rang. "Christ is Risen!" "He has risen indeed, Alleluia!" "Is. Is risen. Not has risen. Just as the Prime Minister has an audience of the queen and not with the Queen." "Yes. Sorry." "Anyway, I thought you would like to know that Perpetua has been on television. After the Urbi Et Orbi of the Bishop of Rome, she suddenly appeared on all channels, all over the world, talking to everyone in her or his own language." "I wonder how the lip readers got on." "I'm serious. She has taken over the world in a Pentecostal echo." "I wonder what you could mean by that." "Look, Clement, be serious for a moment, you are the theologian who reads all the books I don't have time for and don't have the inclination to take on holiday with me. You tell me what it means. There is this woman and she says she is the fourth person of the Godhead. She promises her followers—let's call them Disciples for argument's sake—that she is going to be killed but will never desert them. Duly, she is killed, right before the eyes of millions of people, but when Cutting Edge wants to sell the footage and re-mix it for future programmes, there is no extant copy of the filming anywhere. Not on its machines, not on the machines of any of the thousands who recorded it. Then the body disappears—and you know I went to Saint Stay's College with Bill Midway and he wouldn't do anything underhand or bizarre—and then she appears to every person in the world, speaking directly in the appropriate language. What do you make of that?" "It does seem to be a telescoped isomorphism of the Passion to Pentecost Chronology, but whether the days on which it took place or the actual events are having an effect on your discernment, I don't know. It does look to me like a contemporary but telescoped ..." "Quite, even without the fancy words ... good heavens, there's Varnish walking through what looks like an Easter Market with a Roman Parish Priest." "What is remarkable about that?" "No, it isn't the two of them together that's remarkable—although I used to share an office with Varnish and he didn't seem very ecumenical to me, more architectural, really—it is that they are actually on television. I mean television isn't interested in news unless it is represented in pictures, but these pictures aren't news." "There's a rumour that Varnish's son and a Catholic Priest's nephew were mixed up in the Perpetua affair so they might be trying to sort things out, though the last thing they would want would be to be on television." "Look ... I'm sorry, I wonder why I'm talking to you instead of letting you watch for yourself." "Because you enjoy talking," thought Clement. "The pictures are being shown under the god4u logo even though I am tuned to the BBC." "I will switch on immediately. Enjoy the rest of your day. Christ has risen." "Is risen." "I know, just teasing. Alleluia!"

Tony Blair reached Gwyn Edwards, the head of DIM (The Directorate for Independent Media) just as he was lining up an approach shot at the tenth. "Christ is risen!" "What?" "I said 'Christ is risen!'" "I know you did. Are you a religious nut or something?" "Maybe, maybe not, but it's Tony, you know, the Prime Minister." "Sorry, Tony. I was concentrating on a shot, and I'm not religious." "I know but that does not excuse your ignorance. The common civility is for me to say 'Christ is risen' and for you to reply 'He is risen indeed, Alleluia!'" "Yes, Tony, I'll remember next time, but you didn't ring me up to test my sacred etiquette, did you?" "No Gwyn, I'm far too frightened of your, er, towering intellect." "And I don't suppose you rang me to flatter me, or was that ironic? It's hard to tell with you." "That's the point, Gwyn. That's why I'm Prime Minister and you're an ex-Number 10 policy adviser put out to grass at DIM. Sorry, that was indelicate." "Yes, you're too fond of reminding me." "Anyway, I rang because something very odd has happened. Do you remember that Christmas midnight incident when Perpetua somehow appeared on all channels?" "Yes. We never did get to the bottom of that. Bloody BBC arrogance, saying it was only accountable to its paper tiger Trustees and not to us." "Well, it's happening again, now. I got back from church and switched on to watch the Pope and when he'd finished there was Perpetua, on all channels." "Well, at least she waited for the Supreme Pontiff—that's right, isn't it?—to finish." "Was that a joke?" "Please yourself. So what do you want me to do?" "Well, first of all, stop being so belligerent. Then I think you need to see for yourself what's going on." "Do you mean the technical phenomenon?" "Of course not. I mean this historic event—there's been nothing like it since Jesus. But you also need to be on the technological case. I think people were prepared to overlook an event which took place in the middle of Christmas night, but this incident is in broad daylight. Thank God ..." "... Do you mean that?" "Of course I do. Thank God there's no Premier League football this afternoon or there really would be trouble." "All right, Tony. What are you going to do?" "Watch as long as it lasts. Let me know later today what you decide, but by the time you report fully, you'll be up against Gordon, so enjoy the humour while it lasts. Incompetence and bullying enjoy a direct relationship." "Well ..." "... I know what you're going to say but you're wrong. There's a difference between sticking to a line, no matter how difficult, and bullying. I've never blamed anybody else for a line I've taken. You wait for Gordon. It won't be argument—and, er, charm, you know—but bullying, and It will always be somebody else's fault." "I can't wait." "They never love you until you've gone." "No. Prime Minister."

As he walked briskly back to the club house, Gwyn weighed the options. He could call the Situation Monitoring Committee and risk hysteria and accusations of over-reacting or he could call his 'kitchen cabinet' and risk the accusation of being too laid back. As usual, it was a lose/lose situation. Porter, his predecessor would have gone the informal route where his charm would have been more lethal. Gwyn could not even feign charm so he opted for the Committee.

Bishop Hall valued his quiet Easter lunch with Doris after his Baptismal and Confirmation exertions, which had taken him the length of the Diocese in the past sixteen hours. It was also customary for his Suffragans to dine privately after their own respective exertions, made more exacting by their recent adoption of total emersion as somehow more spiritually authentic and uplifting than the use of a jug and font. On the one hand, he wanted to build up his strength before the next bout of civil war but, on the other, an invitation to Aleford and Castlegate to lunch with him might just stave off that next episode. He could no longer talk to them in his office, nor on official occasions so he hoped that a less official approach might work. The appointment of Aleford had been straightforward enough. He had been something of an episcopal prodigy with his fresh good looks, his love of ritual combined with his penchant for evangelical preaching and his unusually good rapport with children. For this reason his—admittedly fleeting and exaggerated—gay lifestyle and his complete lack of administrative ability had been overlooked. Bishop Tony had only had one concern and that was to preserve Alchester as an anti-women priests Diocese. Matters had been complicated, however, when Tony, whom Hall loved above all other, had made a deal with the then Toran archbishop of Canterbury to put Castlegate, a member of Return, on to the bench of bishops. The Archbishop had his man and the Diocese had a Petran and a Toran Suffragan, each equally opposed to the ordination of women as, of course, was Hall himself. The price, however, was high as Castlegate would not talk to Aleford because he was gay and, therefore, horrendously unscriptural. Aleford tried to smooth over the disagreement by becoming ever more outwardly Toran in spite of the Petran which still lived inside his slowly deteriorating skin. As for Castlegate, he had never wanted to be a bishop nor now did he have any intention of behaving like one and he, even worse than Aleford, ignored administration completely. He could not even preach a decent sermon, for all his fanatical Toran credentials, as Aleford never failed to remind him.

"Christ is risen!" said Hall. "He is risen indeed, Alleluia!" replied Aleford while Castlegate remained ostentatiously silent. "How did your Easter ceremonies go, Bruce?" asked Hall, looking unsuccessfully for safe ground. "Too many unbiblical ministers—who call themselves Petran priests, like the Romans do—with Roman habits, fires and candles." "Well, that's the price—if it's a price at all, given the overall situation where you have to see the pros and cons even if the cons of every pro seem more weighty than the pro itself and vice versa—the price you have to pay unless you want me to fill some of your too long vacant parishes with liberals. After all, the Medians will take anything, as we have shown by placing—I suppose I have to use that word though there are others which might tend to down-play an undue degree of pressure on parishes—liberals like Mark Price. Would you like him for one of your parishes instead of an outright fire and candle merchant?" "He's fire and candle enough. It's just that he's betrayed your Saint Stay's Romish tradition by supporting women." "So you will have to pay the price—if it's a price, it's always very difficult to calculate these things if you can calculate them at all and then it depends what you mean by calculate—if you want the Diocese to be safe for our kind of alliance. How about you, Hilary?" "The immersions are very popular even though they are expensive and a little time consuming. However, they do provide people (and me) with a little theatre and variation. The trouble is, people are beginning to think I'm like Castlegate just because I proclaim the Scriptures. They say I'm no longer a proper Petran." "He's not a proper anything," interrupted Castlegate.

"Your extra large glass of sherry, Hilary," said Hall, offering Aleford a wine glass, "and I'm terribly sorry, Bruce, but Doris has forgotten the fruit juice, so I'm afraid you'll have to make do with the soda water next to the whiskey. "Now let's start at the beginning. We three are in an alliance against the ordination of women to the Priesthood—or, to be more realistic since there are already ordained women—we are against women priests here and against women bishops wherever they are as they would, in my view, destroy the Church. So we have come together to try to make a safe space for conservatives of both sorts, Petran and Toran. But we can't go on like this—if you can call the current situation going on which is, well, a moot point given the way we are limping along—if we are to be viable. Alchester has become a byword in the Church for incompetence and dithering, we are openly ridiculed, even by those who agree with us. Hawthorne tries to avoid talking to me, most senior people don't know whether to ridicule or condescend and inside the Diocese we are regarded as mad. You should see the letters I get. Now we are about to lose our long-suffering, scrupulous, workaholic, and astute Secretary due to his declining health and then we will be left to it because, after all, we are now going nowhere. I have blotted my copybook by appearing to make simple things complex, by seeing all sides of everything and failing—if it is a failure which I think it is not, though many would disagree—to establish a clear position on anything but the women issue. People think I am too 'muddled', as they call it, and even though I follow my even handed approach faithfully, I seem to be getting nowhere. As for you, Bruce, you were appointed in very unique circumstances and even if you denounce Return you won't be moving to another Diocese, as nobody would have you. And as for you, Hilary, your, er, past life makes it impossible for you to be promoted. It would be taken to mean acceptance of your, er situation. I notice that even your best friends in Faithful Foundations don't want to be seen with you. We have to live together or we will simply suffer corrosion and bitterness. As an orthodox bishop I have to be the focus of unity in the Diocese. What is your solution, Bruce?"

"Three things. Firstly, we need to ensure that all clergy, particularly bishops, conform to a Biblical standard. Secondly, we need to become the simple church of the Acts of the Apostles. Thirdly, we need to take the Church out of the hands of the exclusivist clergy and approve lay Presidency at the Eucharist." "He's mad," said Aleford, unable to contain himself. "Just a moment," said Hall, "you will have your turn. Now, Bruce, the first suggestion is completely impractical. Technically, the appointment of a Suffragan is nothing to do with anyone, not even Hawthorne, but me. However, things are never that simple. If Hilary resigns, which I take to be the essence of your first point, he will almost certainly be replaced by a liberal Suffragan. Although we have a tight grip on the Diocese in terms of the Petran/Toran alliance, there are other factors. Firstly, we are seen to be a failing Diocese in need of strong external intervention, but that can't happen as long as we stick together. Secondly, even though Hilary's departure would perhaps be seen as a win by the Nigerians and Ambrose, Bishop of the Southern Cone—whose line on the, er, gay issue is, I think, technically right, but whose abridgment of Provincial protocol within the Communion is regrettable. Perhaps the way to put it is to say that it isn't subtle enough—it would also create a chance for the liberals who, thirdly, are by no means dead, even in this Diocese. Clement Sutcliffe is proving to be a nuisance, even though he is the only Member of the Great Synod on our Group who is not on one of the two more 'orthodox' wings represented by the three of us. He used to work with Smoother, Hawthorne's Press Secretary, on Humanity and you know what that means. By standing for the Appointments Commission, and organising the re-distribution of second and lower preferences, he has got two liberal radical women onto it. I know that the gift of Suffragans is entirely in my hands, but look what happened with Bruce. In the end, Bishop Tony didn't think he had any choice once Lambeth insisted. Furthermore, there seems to be some truth—though how much it is always difficult to gauge in such a minefield—in Sutcliffe's belief that the media matters. He is forever going to the papers and he loves telling that story about you, Hilary, when he made the presentation on the need for the Diocese to have a media policy based on information technology and you responded with a eulogy on the fountain pen and that one about you, Bruce, giving a whole sermon on why incense is Biblical and candles aren't, as if most of our people care." "It's just sour grapes because you and I agreed to halt his ordination discernment process." "That might make him more rather than less dangerous, Hilary. Remember, we turned him down—well, of course we didn't, as we were discerning in the power of the Holy Spirit so, effectively, it is the Holy Spirit that turned him down—because he is too driven and that very drive might be coming straight towards us unless we are very careful."

"As to your second point, Bruce, you know how much I dislike the complexities of the modern Church, but I question where the balance lies between the burden of Establishment and the disadvantage of being just another Christian sect. You will argue—I've heard you do so before but I have failed to be convinced although you do it very well—that I should not sit in the House of Lords, but if you prefer to be in a sect you can always choose that option. Nobody is forcing Torans like you to stay in our reformed—though not Protestant— Church, let alone be Bishops. As to your third point, you know I will not accept lay Presidency. Now I accept there are those—I might not always be clear in my conclusions but I take account of every position—who say that we cannot survive with my policy. I oppose the Ordination of women, I don't want Locally Ordained Ministry, and I'm not keen on retired clergy. That leaves very few candidates for Priestly Presidency, but extension or lay Presidency is no solution. After all, Bruce, if you support lay Presidency you might as well abolish the clergy." "Yes, you might." "So why doesn't he just resign?" snapped Aleford. "I will if you will," sneered Castlegate. "Now then, Brothers in Christ," said Hall, almost ironically. "You next, Hilary. Can you do better?"

"Firstly, reverse the woman priests legislation. Secondly, restore discipline and good order, particularly in ritual. Thirdly, issue an ultimatum to the liberals." "Yes, Hilary, you know how I agree with your first point, but even I have to admit—trying to see all sides of the issue and looking for any possible way to keep the issue of 'reception' or, rather, non-reception open—that women Non-Stipendiaries are very handy in a rich but niggardly diocese like this. I don't see larger contributions from the Parishes that are against women to help pay for more high cost men. True enough, Bruce—before you chip in—the Torans pay most per head for the costs of a church they don't really want to support—which is very strange—but the issue of women priests is already settled. I must say, Hilary, I do admire you for failing—well, in the context of what I'm going to say it can hardly be described as a failure though plenty of other people, including bishops, would call it a failure of sorts—to make a reciprocal alliance which many liberals support with the pro woman lobby because, as they rightly point out, supporters of the Ordination of women have always supported, er, gay clergy. So your first suggestion, though I agree with it in theory, is a practical non-starter. I fear the agrement to Consecrate women as Bishops will ruin any prospect of an agreement with Rome. It almost drives me away from the Church that Tony loved so well. Were it not for the consolation of the Eucharist—though of course I would enjoy that in the Roman Church—I somehow wish I was a humble Roman Catholic Parish Priest." "You would hate it," said Castlegate. "I am not sure. That's the trouble. I'm just not sure. Anyway, Hilary, your second point is admirable enough, but I don't see what difference it would make. Bruce won't wear a mitre because it's not Biblical and many of the people on his patch complain that they don't have a Bishop. However, the Church of England has passed from gentle, mutual tolerance to an organisation in which everybody pleases himself." "Including bishops," said Doris, tartly, as she summoned them to lunch. "If I insisted on ritualistic discipline, Hilary, you and I would lose many allies, including Bruce. The question you have to keep asking is whether there is any more important issue than keeping women out, and I think you and I agree that there is not. Your third point is also very valid in its way, but what else can I do except set out my own orthodoxy and encourage others to follow. As the instrument of unity I have to talk to Inclusive Catholicism even though I can't stand its people. It's even worse now that Sutcliffe pretends to as much theological discernment as me. The problem is—again trying to see all sides—that my stance appears to make everybody who disagrees with me unorthodox." "Quite," said Aleford. "Rubbish," said Castlegate. "Well, Bruce and Hilary, you have to see that insisting on some kind of uniformity cuts both ways. It depends who has the power and whose heterodoxy can be weakened." "That sounds suspiciously like power politics," said Castlegate. "Yes, Bruce, but you can turn your back on people like Clement Sutcliffe who keeps sending me awkward letters about you and who makes speeches against me at the Great Synod, but I can't do that. The Petrans have the sticking power to resist change, the offended gravity, the victimhood, the betrayal. The Torans have money, organisation, and—forgive me Bruce— a MacDoctrine approach, as if the Alpha Course can confront the mystery of God, but the liberals have the zeitgeist, the ability to make us look foolish and old fashioned and, much worse, unjust." "So what would you do about it, then?" asked Castlegate, almost aggressively. "Well, that is a very interesting question which does not permit an easy answer, but I think I would put it like this. First, we need people to understand what it means to be an orthodox Anglican. We are, after all, a reformed church and we claim to be 'Catholic' which means we can't make unilateral decisions about doctrine." "Which makes a nonsense of the Reformation," said Castlegate. "I thought the point of it was to free ourselves from the tyranny of Rome." "I wish you would not be so coarse, Bruce. There were some over-reactions in the sixteenth century, but we need to recognise that, facing a secular world, our destiny lies in ecumenism not factionalism. Like Hilary, I believe that the tolerance of the Church of England has just gone too far." "True, James," said Castlegate, "but it depends in which direction." "Be that as it may—and that is both the glory and the suffering of the Anglican tradition, although I grant that others understand it—or at least express it, whether they understand it or not—differently. A Bishop as a focus of unity needs to impose." "A strange idea," said Doris as she chivvied them into the dining room. "My second point is that we are losing sight of the essentials, but that depends on what you think is essential. Some people tell me that I lose sight of the New

Testament essentials by concentrating on the fight against women and gay bishops but you tell me that these are essentials. In your different ways you refuse to
rank issues, insisting that the acknowledgment of the mysteries of the faith—or
refusal of acknowledgment—is in the same category of sin as living in—what
do they call it?—a loving, stable and monogamous gay relationship between
two consenting adults who claim that they are part of God's creation. Again, I
find myself unable to sort out what kind of principle this amounts to. Finally, we
need to get rid of the Dean." Doris flinched and left the room. "What?" Aleford
and Castlegate responded together. "We know he's the arch liberal, James, but if
you got rid of him he would be replaced by another liberal. Even the Conservatives under Cameron are liberal in Church matters. Just leave him be." "I can't,
he's an affront to the unity of the Diocese." "As I have said before," said Doris as
she came in and handed out the soup, "you need to learn from Alchester instead
of just enjoying it. Leave well alone, James. As for you two gentlemen, I will say
it because James is too soft hearted. There's a risk to be assessed between getting
rid of awkward suffragans and getting unhelpful replacements. The best way is
for all three of you to say as little as possible outside your homiletics, get a new
Secretary as good as Simon Taylor and give Clement and his sort as little room
to complain as possible. He can't help being aggressive because you stalled his
ordination discernment process—don't wince, James, everybody knows it had
nothing to do with the Holy Spirit, but simply suited your own convenience
and temperament to turn him down—but there is no reason why this Diocese
should have a high profile. It never has before and it shouldn't have now. Leave
the Dean alone! Furthermore, throughout the time you have been talking while
I have been present you haven't mentioned God or Jesus so the less you say as
churchmen, the better."

She left them in silence as she went to carve the lamb. She glanced up at the
television in the corner, strategically positioned so that the overworked Bishop
could watch the news while he ate a hurried evening meal. The picture looked
strange. She saw a man apparently preaching an impromptu sermon, but she
could not work out why this might be being broadcast. Easter was over for the
general public. The lamb was being eaten, the eggs would not last the day. She
noticed the god4u logo. She was about to re-enter the dining room when the
phone rang. "Christ is risen!" said the Dean. "He is risen indeed, Alleluia!"
said Doris, somewhat mechanically. "I just wanted to tell James that Perpetua
is risen." "Has risen," interrupted Doris. "No, is risen from the dead. I thought
James would like to know that the Inclusive Catholics welcome Archbishop
Hawthorne's rumoured open response." "I've got lunch to serve. What rumour?"
"Smoother is said to be advising an open response." "I'll tell them." "Them?"
"Yes, James has foolishly invited Bruce and Hilary to lunch in the hope of brok-
ering a ceasefire." "Well, Doris, as we both know, if he achieves that their whole
artillery, for what it's worth, will be turned on me." "Don't worry, Mr Dean,
there's no chance. Bruce and Hilary are too certain of what they want, James not
certain enough. Anyway, what do you mean, 'risen'?" "She was killed, as you will

recall, and then the body disappeared and now she's been on television. Dexter, her right hand man, is proclaiming her resurrection and the dawning of a new age for the Godhead." "That will put James into a terrible flap before he comes down in favour of the Trinity." "Yes. Try to keep him calm. You know how much I love him even though he can't stand me. It's the liberal burden." "Shut up, Mr Dean. I'll carve the meat and tell them."

Doris bided her time until they had all finished circulating serving dishes. Hilary had a bottle of good Claret planted in front of him. James, as usual, opted for a rather insipid half of Anjou rosé and Bruce was drinking warm Coca-Cola which, Doris thought when she found it at the back of a cupboard, was totally inappropriate with meat or anything served at a dining table. When they were all settled she said, "The Dean rang to say—and just because it's him it's not wise to assume that the information is less reliable than it would be from any other source—that Perpetua has apparently risen from the dead and is being proclaimed by Dexter." "Unbiblical," said Castlegate. "Feminist claptrap," said Hilary. "Oh dear, I thought it would get messy," said Hall. "The liberals will make hay. It's bound to be troublesome, I mean whichever way you look at it, whether she is or she isn't, things will be turbulent for a few weeks at least." "Hawthorne is inclined to welcome the news with an open mind," said Doris. "Yes, well there's open and open. I don'tt think for a moment that anyone would doubt that I have an open mind, even to the virtues of individual women priests—it's the principle that's against them—but Hawthorne's kind of openness is to allow just about anything that the Church will let him get away with. The trouble with clever theologians—and of course I'm not classifying Hawthorne with them as such— is that they always sail too close to the heretical wind. We orthodox bishops will have to stick together."

The lunch then passed off quietly with some soul searching as each digested the Perpetua problem.

By the time Gwyn Edwards reached the DIM headquarters, there was a general global panic and, as the pioneer of converged self-regulation, DIM was flooded with enquiries about how to act. The Committee consisted of the externally affable Chair, Lord Robert de Ville, his Vice Chair, Jeremy Wroth, Gwyn's Director of Operations, Dick Cable, and his Director of Communications, Emelda Bright. The Government had proposed to send a representative, which was an affront to an independent regulator, but Gwyn had no choice. Conversely, the BBC had refused to send a representative as it claimed total independence, even though its spectrum allocation was determined by DIM. De Ville, with his usual smooth bonhomie, told his opposite number at the BBC that if it did not come into line he would issue an injunction, citing it for broadcasting pirate channels on its frequencies and so it reluctantly caved in. "As I see it," said, Gwyn, "we are in uncharted territory. The Christmas episode was never resolved because we couldn't do it without the necessary co-operation." He looked meaningfully at the BBC representative. "We could not get an all-round picture. But this incident has now been going on for more than five hours. What have you heard from god4u, Dick?" "I talked with a man called Max Silver, apparently a disgraced ex-banker acting on its behalf. He claims it is legitimately operating under a Community Television Licence and has done nothing unusual or wrong. He says it's Perpetua controlling the world's media." "Could we pull the licence?" "Yes, but only with the use of emergency powers exercised on behalf of Blair." "What do you think, de Ville?" "I doubt he would want to intervene. His emergency powers cover war or an extraordinary natural disaster and, since Iraq, sentiment has gone against using these powers." "Emelda, what do you think?" "Our problem is admitting that we don't know what's going on. We might have trouble if we use emergency powers, but our biggest problem is looking foolish rather than decisive. We are in a state of siege from the print media, and the broadcasters are approaching hysteria. It's credibility, revenue, a feeling of being out of control." "In those circumstances we ought to call Tony. I talked to him earlier in the day and he seemed a trifle, er, excited and intrigued rather than really worried, so you better try him, Mr Chair."

"Tony, it's Robert de Ville. ... Yes, Gwyn opted to call the situation Monitoring Committee. ... Yes it is a pity he has, we have, to work on Easter Sunday of all Sundays. ... I agree it makes interesting viewing, but ... well I realise we're an independent regulator, so it's up to us to decide but, between you and me, the independence is more theoretical than practical, isn't it? ... Granted the public won't see it that way. Yes, like the Bank of England being independent. ..."

"Damn." "What?" "He just said, 'if it comes to a confrontation between God and humanity, you know who's going to win', and then he said, 'Christ is risen!'—I'm a Jew, for God's sake—and put the phone down." "Well he might be a religious nut," said Gwyn "which is why I persuaded him to keep his religion separate from his politics when I was at Number 10 but blaming him won't help us." "What about asking for a voluntary switch-off for a couple of hours to see if it straightens out?" asked Dick. "Possible," said Wroth, who never liked to be caught on either side of an issue, "but that won't work unless the big boys play ball." "We won't," said the BBC man, grimly. "Being independent of you lot is more important than suffering from what appears to be a universal, inexplicable phenomenon." "Try switching on again," said Emelda. "Still the god4u logo on the BBC frequency. It looks as if the ceremony in—where is it?—yes, Grunge Park, is coming to an end. Look, there she is in studio shot." "I am sorry if some of you have been disappointed by missing your favourite programmes, but sometimes we all need to be reminded of the power of God. Enjoy the rest of this Easter Day. Christ is risen. I am risen. Alleluia!"

Clement had not watched so much television since the Sunday of Princess Diana's death. In fact, apart from the subsequent General Election Nights he hadn't watched it at all. As the afternoon wore on he became more worried and excited, worried about his comfort but excited about the theology. As a recent Systematic Theology graduate he had less of a problem than the average non-believer with ideas such as the non-existence of shepherds and kings at the birth of Jesus or the questionable reality of the empty tomb. He thought that the

Creeds being used by Christians had been concocted under political pressure to solve some thorny Greek or, more specifically, neo-Platonic problems and so the extension of the Godhead did not disturb him unduly. After all, we had to consider how God might intervene in the affairs of his creation on other planets, so the Trinity might be artificially limited. His faith was firmly rooted in incarnational theology and its crystallisation in Karl Rahner, not the compulsory nods towards Rome to keep him publishable, but his essence. He was honest enough to know that much of what he loved was a matter of upbringing and temperament and therefore, as a preacher, he was scrupulously careful not to stray into urging adherence to what he did not hold to be essential.

In her own way, Helen was equally unconcerned by what had happened. She had enthusiastically welcomed Perpetua's intervention as a breakthrough for women in religious life, but she knew that her own form of ministry would not change whatever the theologians said. There would still be rotas to fill, readings to be distributed, money to be raised, and special arrangements to be made while the church roof was being repaired. Wherever he ended up in the controversy she would still have to keep Mark on an even keel, no matter how much it hurt her when he struck out, even though he was always full of remorse.

"There are—one wishes we could mentally get away from the Greek, for if there's one thing worse than dichotomy it's insisting that there are three reasons for everything as it's only a cultural number—three problems," said Clement, "for the Church as I see it: Firstly, she's a woman and that will only aggravate the current controversy. Secondly, she has challenged the ecclesiastical power structure. Thirdly, we don't know where she will 'strike' next." "What are you going to do?" asked Helen. "Well I see no fundamental objection to her theology that her sacrifice was in some way identical with that of Jesus, but at a different time and place. I don't see any reason for falling out with people over theology which is simply a set of human metaphors." "Yes, I know all that, but what are you going to do about Mark?" "Nothing. He's the Priest, I'm the Reader. It's for him to take the lead publicly, no matter what we say to each other privately." "What about dinner?" "Well, I'm entitled to say what I like at my own dinner table but, again, if there's no point arguing with people who disagree with you about, say, politics, there's certainly no point arguing about metaphors." "Well, be careful. You know what you're like; quiet for hours, listening, and then you get caught up in something and you get very definite, particularly after a couple of large glasses of red."

During their work they kept the television on. The BBC switched its main channel from regular scheduling to running news or, rather, now that Perpetua had disappeared and her followers had dispersed, to running chat which, Clement thought wryly, they had the cheek to term 'analysis'. There had been some speculation as to whether the recordings of the day's events would survive. The Perpetua broadcast was not extant, but all the footage of her followers had been safely captured. They worked contentedly and efficiently through the arrangements for dinner. They liked entertaining as Clement didn't much like other

people's cooking or wine. In spite of his warmness towards people he was a bit
of a snob. He gone through the list by the time Nigel arrived, as he always did,
first, bringing a couple of beers for himself and a consignment of cheese as his
customary contribution. Indeed all the contributions were customary.Marie arrived next with a bottle of chilled Australian white wine and a pudding, Scott arrived with two bottles of slightly better than average Rioja, and Meg arrived—as
always, last, having seen her mother, Iris, settled down for the night at Godfrey
House—with the starter. Clement briefly wondered why Marie couldn't bring a
better bottle and why Meg, who always came last, was charged with the starter, but he dismissed the thoughts as unworthy. For the only time since he had
stopped taking football seriously, Clement wanted to keep the television on but,
as a matter of principle, he would turn it off at the first knock on the basis that
people were more important than television. They sat in their customary chairs
with their drinks and started, as they always did, under Marie's leadership, by
dissecting the morning's 'performance' but, completely against the usual pattern, this broke down almost before it had begun when Nigel—in his usual form
of a series of statements—asked Clement what he thought about the Perpetua
phenomenon. "The consensus at The Oak is that it's some silly prank, the sort
of thing that happens with computer hackers and virus generators. As for the
content, they think it's just Web 2.0 junk. I'm not so sure. It worries me a bit, but
on the other hand, although I'm a traditionalist, Perpetua's crew might get this
lot sorted out. I mean Hawthorne's all right but our bunch are a shower." "The
television thing was a puzzle, though," said Marie. "I like a bit of junk to help
me with my Sunday afternoon snooze, but it was all Perpetua." "Iris, who always
knows more than anybody could possibly guess," said Meg, "says that this will
totally rejuvenate Christianity." "Well, Meg," said Helen gently, "your mother is
a wonder for her age." "I don't know what it all means," said Scott, "but things
can't get worse. So many traditional values have been swept away." "But won't
this sweep away even more?" asked Nigel. "Yes, I suppose it will," said Scott. "If
this house group movement takes off the way she wants it to, it will kill choral
music," said Marie. "Well Clement," said Scott, "you're the theologian. What do
you think of it?" "I think that it won't go away and we have to find ways of understanding what Perpetua meant and means." "On the fence, Clem," said Nigel,
affectionate but slightly aggressive. "That isn't like you." "Well I only argue about
politics when I've had too much to drink and only about religion when I've had
even more." "Well, what does Mark think? He certainly sounded very supportive in his sermon." "He was using her life as an example rather than saying he
believes what she says." "He's always at odds with Hall." "I'm not sure, given your
opening remark that Perpetua might get things 'sorted out', whether you think
it's a good or a bad thing for Mark to be in disagreement with the Bishop." Helen
saw Nigel's contradiction and Clement's inability to let pass any kind of incon-
sistency so she said, "Well, at least Mark had the courage to part company with
all those pseudo-Romists at Saint Stay's and stand up for women in the Church.
It's ruined his career and I'm amazed he isn't bitter. He still loves Hilary dearly as

a friend even if he thinks he's an absolutely hopeless Suffragan."

Although he didn't see clearly how to continue the discussion without giving rise to sharp differences, Clement was nonetheless surprised—Helen knew he should not have been—when the conversation slowly drifted to a series of personal anecdotes which were shot into nowhere rather than at any individual. It was like a Pinter, but not so intense. They were all friends and the four guests lived alone and needed plenty of time to indulge in mild conversational competitiveness. Clement listened and Helen steered. They all sat in their usual places and did their usual things: Marie worked the hatch with Helen, Nigel poured wine, Clement ran his list, Meg saw that vegetables were handed round, and Scott mourned the passing of tradition. During the cheese—served before dessert—Nigel tried to goad Clement into a discussion about the relative merits of Gordon Brown and Tony Blair, but Clement knew that if he favoured Brown Nigel would argue for Blair and vice versa. Brought up on that kind of 'devil's advocate' political controversy, Clement now hated it as it solved nothing. He liked arguing about ideas, particularly speculating about connectivities, but he thought argument for the sake of it was a waste of time. "My mother says that Perpetua will be coming here before long." "Well, her followers will have a lot of ground to cover, but here's as good as anywhere," said Helen, encouragingly. "That will put Mark on the spot," said Marie who counted herself as almost one of his family. "That depends how the bishops react and I suspect that it will be a mess. If we're lucky—if that's the word I'm looking for or perhaps I might say if we are able to formulate some sort of consensus acceptable to a majority of those concerned, as Bishop James would put it—there might be a motion before Diocesan Synod in the middle of May, but that is more than a month off."

Mark had to miss the bulk of the god4u coverage to welcome Jane's extensive family which came to a lunch which always lasted well into the early evening. He managed to watch the closing events of the day in the kitchen and then settled down with Jane to watch the highlights and the 'analysis' although he kept getting up to look a what the Open Anglicans website was saying. To his horror, but not surprise, Aleford and Castlegate had both signed statements on behalf of their respective extreme wings of the Church of England. "Why can't they just shut up!" he blazed. "They can't exercise any degree of self-control. If there's anything unhelpful to sign, they sign it." "Well at least James hasn't said anything yet." "Just the dither before the deed, I suspect. O look, there's Brandon. I haven't seen him since he fainted at Walsingham. Whether it was devotion or drink was never definitively established! As an ordinand he was very pro Women—that was at the time just after vatican II when you could say anything—but he's changed his mind now he's a Bishop." "What are you going to do about Perpetua, darling?" (Jane was one of the very few people who addressed her husband in private as "darling", without the slightest degree of irony). "I already know that our three bishops will be against Perpetua's attempt to renew the Church, but I suspect they won't do anything, other than sign damaging letters, except hitch it to their anti-woman obsession. Honestly, somebody challenges the Holy Trinity and all they can do is think about women bishops! It's crazy!" "What if one of her people comes down here?" "I will do everything I can within the strict letter of Church law. I don't know how I manage to be a liberal and a stickler at the same time, but Helen never stops telling me that's what I am." "What will Clement do?" "He is a deep one and his theology is very inventive and, from my perspective, very sound. However, he was brought up a Roman and always behaves like a Roman towards his Priest. He will think what he likes, but he always submits his draft sermons to me and he won't say anything in public to embarrass me. I think ... goodness me, look there. It's Varnish, what's he saying? Boasting that he was the first ever to appear on television with Perpetua. He's lucky, by all accounts, that there's no footage of the final hours of her life because his son was implicated. ... and there's Smoother. He's a bit of a smarm, but he's standing by Hawthorne, as he should." "Wasn't his daughter involved in the Cutting Edge Perpetua scandal?" "Yes, openanglicans says that she had a deal with Sneer of the TT, but he'll work his way out of trouble, he always does. ... and there's Damian whatshisname whose father was Vicar of All Fools until he ...". "Mark, look!" "Good Lord, they've got James. He looks a bit distracted. Turn it up."

"And now we turn to The Right Reverend James Hall, Bishop of the Prestigious Diocese of Alchester and a senior Church Peer. Bishop, what do you think of today's events?" "Well, it depends what you mean by events. I mean at one level we have all seen what has happened, but at quite another level we don't really understand its significance. The Church of England has to try to see all sides of the questions that Perpetua has raised, but in the end I will be standing up for orthodoxy." "And what does that mean in this context?" "Well, it means sticking to the Creed and the 39 Articles and the Formularies, you know and ..." "But what will you do in the unlikely event that the Pope recognises Perpetua?" "Well, as you know—or you wouldn't have asked the question, I'm not so much of a fool as you think, I have a strong attachment to the Catholicity of the process of formulating doctrine—but that is a highly unlikely scenario." "Well what if Archbishop Hawthorne pursues the course which he has publicly initiated today of calling upon the Church to view Perpetua's teaching and the meaning of her life and death with an open mind?" "I will stay loyal to the Archbishop as long as he continues to be orthodox." "Well, that was Bishop James Hall of Alchester threatening to resign as a bishop so we are likely to see some fireworks from senior figures in the next few days as well as from some of the usual suspects like Aleford and Castlegate." "Oh God!"

"Now we turn to one of Perpetua's followers. Wayne, what does all this mean?" "It means that Perpetua has taken Christianity to a new stage just as Jesus took Judaism to a new stage in Christianity. We are not denying Jesus, we are building on his work." "Yes, very nice, but what about the gross interference with free speech when your people completely took over the world's broadcasting networks?" "The power of the Holy Spirit is beyond measure. We cannot understand what happened, we just have to accept God's power instead of trying to belittle it or argue it away." "But what about free speech?" "Atheists, agnostics, non-believers, advertisers, liars, charlatans, show-offs, cheapskates, trivialisers, pornographers, and so-called pundits have the airwaves to themselves almost all the time. This was just a mild counterweight." "Mild?" "Well, Christ is risen and Perpetua is risen and if it had been left to you to celebrate the first and report the second, God's power would have been almost completely overlooked by the media." "Good for you," said Jane, "but I bet Trina is a bit nervous of this line." "Don't worry," said Mark. "this is no time for prevaricating. If they are right—and of course I don't know—they have to behave like Peter and the Apostles on Pentecost Day. ... Oh look, there's Hawthorne looking haggard."

"I am sorry to say," said the Archbishop, "that on a day of such great moment for the Christian Church and possibly of great moment for our future with what we have heard of the mission, life and death of Perpetua, that many in the Anglican Communion have opposed my encouragement to consider these matters with an open mind and have seen this massive challenge through the lens of gender politics. This is no time to make hasty judgments and I am sorry that many Bishops in England and elsewhere have been precipitate in their responses. Here in America I am sorry to say that I was detained for much of the day in discussions which are trivial alongside today's events. I have therefore decided to abandon any attempt to reach any consensus over the gay bishops issue and to concentrate on prayerful consideration of God's will for us all."

"At least," said Doris, "he mentioned God which seems to be a rarity amongst bishops these days."

2.

On Easter Bank Holiday Monday Kylie arrived at London Paddington Station before nine and caught a Western Train. After the overwhelming events of the day before she ought to have felt tired but she was elated by the prospect of her first day on her solo mission. She did not know what she was going to do or say, but she was absolutely convinced that she would receive guidance; just as the Holy Spirit had led the Apostles of Jesus after Pentecost, She would lead Perpetua's disciples. Kylie had only gained four GCSE passes, but Saint Peter himself only had Sabbath Day training in the Jewish Scriptures. The man opposite her on the train was reading the back page of his newspaper so she was able to see the front:

MYSTERY FORCE GAGS TV

Scanning the same story in his morning press digest, Tony Blair smiled as he read the litany of culprits in the Toxic Times: the (liberal) BBC had shown total failure to take control of its own operations, the (nanny) DIM was (paradoxically) toothless, and the (arch liberal) Hawthorne had signally failed to uphold Christian tradition. If the events could be connected with Perpetua the influence was malign as the gang that had been shown on all channels were a shady bunch. Blair noted that all the tabloids had more or less forgotten the brutal murder and its strange circumstances and had failed to deal with the theology of death, Resurrection and Pentecost which the events suggested. The 'quality' papers were not much better, with even the Religious Correspondents—a dying breed in spite of the resurgence of religion brought about by Islamic and Christian immigration and a plethora of stories connected with the conflict between tradition and liberalism—claiming that they could not understand what had happened. Blair wondered how they could justify their salaries if they could not see the New Testament parallels. After almost ten years in office and fourteen as Party Leader, he could not help the reflex of assessing how the front pages—he placed comparatively little importance on obvious editorial comment compared with editorial comment masquerading as front page news—might affect his Government. He had been right to say nothing. Gordon, who wore his religion more heavily but less deeply, Blair thought, might have problems later on if the Roman Catholics in particular but, in the English context, Hawthorne, reacted unwisely. Rome would almost certainly follow the Torans into outright opposition. It was being outflanked all over the world, even in Latin America, by an aggressive evangelism which shared Catholic moral values, but denounced its hierarchy. He did not think that Hawthorne's reaction would be critical to the history of Christianity in the long run, but he loved the man dearly and cared both for his personal suffering and his brave subtlety in a crude era. Very few people had understood his decision to appoint somebody whom he knew would disagree with him emphatically on Iraq. His job was to be Prime Minister, Hawthorne's job was to be Primate and it was wrong for the head of the Government, on behalf of the Queen, to fail to appoint the best person just because he would make life more difficult for the person giving the advice. Cynical journalists might think that politicians invariably acted in the expected venal way, but Blair knew, better than any politician of his generation, that political cynicism was the road to ruin. Not because the media would fasten on it but because people could spot it a mile off. They had never believed he could walk on water and now they did not believe he was a total failure. Between the two points in time they had disagreed with him over Iraq but did not doubt his sincerity. Having decided the date of his departure, he would have more time to follow the Perpetua story. He would even have time for a little fun.

"Gwyn, Christ is Risen!" "He is risen indeed, alleluia! Prime Minister." "Very good, Gwyn." "But that was yesterday." "No Gwyn, we are in the Octave of Easter; Easter Sunday lasts for eight days and the season of Easter lasts for forty days." "You are saving me the cost of a distance learning course, Tony, but I doubt that's why you rang." "It's my way of thanking you for your loyalty and compensating you for all the sins you committed in my name." "Thank you, Tony, for being so sensitive to my moral danger." "That's all right; but I rang to assess your regulatory danger. Am I right in thinking you did nothing yesterday?" "Correct. Before we had finished considering our options the situation righted itself." "You're almost as lucky as me." "I agree, the BBC was being obstructive as usual, deliberately confusing its independence of output with its obligations to DIM over spectrum." "Yes, that must be a problem for you. I know this is being recorded. but history must take its course. In spite of its priggish and bombastic insistence on doing Cameron's job of holding us to account instead of undertaking its noble but, as it perceives it, humble, even demeaning, task of reporting the news, its general left of centre stance is a steady force in favour of our kind of liberal decency as opposed to Mrs Thatcher's liberal brutality. So I am hardly likely to do anything about it's awkwardness." "So, other than for my religious instruction, why did you call?" "To enjoy myself—it's always a pleasure sparring with you, Gwyn—but also to warn you. Even if there is no further divine interference with the networks—and my guess is that Perpetua has said her last word—which raises important issues over freedom of speech, people like you who are simply indifferent to, or dismissive of, religion will tend to under-estimate the importance of the issues which Perpetua's people are likely to raise. There will be an almighty row in the Church of England, a slow burning row in the Roman Catholic Church, which is likely to break out in all kinds of unlikely places, like volcanic forces finding weak points in the earth's crust. But, above all, Perpetua's people are going to say their piece and their lives are likely to be threatened. I advise you to do two things: read the Acts of the Apostles, and get your standards people to look at current rules on impartiality and freedom of speech. I will have a quiet word with the DG at the BBC—there's no point talking to the Chairman of Trustees—to give him a similar warning. Perpetua's people will challenge the ignorance and sneering which characterises journalism in general and religious reporting in particular. Christ is risen!" "You will have your joke! He is risen indeed, Alleluia!" "You rather spoiled that valedictory echo, Gwyn. It isn't a joke."

"Commissioner, forgive me for calling you at home on a Bank Holiday, and I don't want to tread on the Home Secretary's toes nor, for that matter, numerous other toes I could mention. I ask your forgiveness because I am not clear how you might proceed with a possible murder enquiry when the body is missing." "That is not unusual in itself, you know." "Yes, but what I was going on to ask is how do you proceed if the body returns in a manner of speaking? Can it still be murder or only attempted?" "I think you will have to ask the prosecution people about that, but we are not anxious to proceed. Look at it this way: we accepted the proposal to create a non-interference zone in the public interest. Something apparently went wrong as we were told, never officially, that a murder was committed. If that is true we gather that the victim's friends removed the body, rather than the perpetrators but, in any event, for reasons we don't understand, all the film evidence seems to have disappeared. Now matters are more complicated for

us because the victim appears to be alive and might even be liable to prosecution under the Broadcasting Act for her Easter and Christmas 'pranks'. It's up to
the prosecutors, Prime Minister, but there's no body and no evidence." "Quite,
Commissioner. Thank you for the informal briefing which, as I say, should not
be confused with any official approach from my Ministers. By the way, do you
intend to keep Perpetua's followers under surveillance?" "No, Prime Minister.
We are over stretched already, as you know, and these people show every sign of
keeping themselves in the public eye rather than out of it." "True. I just want to
be sure that we are even handed in dealing with all religious activity. We don't
want to be seen to tail Muslim extremists and leave Christians alone." "Point
taken, Prime Minister."

"Christ is Risen, Mr Smoother!" "He is risen, indeed, Alleluia! Prime Minister." "I have read the Archbishop's, may I say admirable, statement." "Thank
you." "You weren't supposed to say that, really." "No. Sorry. The Archbishop did,
however, have the goodness to say that I anticipated his sentiments in almost
every respect." "As I know, from your record beginning at Humanity, that you
would. Anyway, I didn't really telephone to discuss the statement, which would
not be proper, but simply to ask how the Archbishop is, given the pressures." "As
you know, he has cut short his trip to the United States." "A trip, I gather, that you
strongly supported." "Yes, in the circumstances at the time, I admit I did. I was
wrong." "That's handsome of you, just don't admit it. The press are forever saying they want public figures to apologise and when anyone does he's destroyed
in a day. Anyway, you were saying?" "The Archbishop will be back tomorrow
morning. In the meantime, he has asked me to say as little as possible." "Very
wise. People make two charges against me: firstly that I invented 'spin' which
is clearly a Tory falsehood, and secondly that it has destroyed my Government
when what has actually damaged it most is lazy journalism. They just won't read
official documents. In the circumstances, the less you say the better. I can't get
away with that but you can. Paradoxically, when you're dealing with theology
it's all—forgive me—spin, but when you're dealing with politics, particularly on
the Government side, there's a huge amount of paper, mostly non-controversial,
behind everything you say. The Archbishop, as a shepherd of the Middle East
sort, can lead from the front but I have to behave like a contemporary shepherd
by pushing the flock along with the help of highly trained dogs. Anyway, send
my love to the Archbishop. I will pray for him, for what it's worth, as I know he
prays for me."

Rather than reading about it, Kylie prayed for the world until her train
reached Greenhalt where she got off and walked Westwards, with a river on her
left, until she arrived at Walmbury. It was a grey day and the High Street was
almost deserted. She had walked almost the whole length of it before she was
greeted by Meg. "Hello, you look a bit lost. Can I help?" Kylie did not calculate,
but relied, as Perpetua had advised, on the Holy Spirit. "I have come to advance
God Our Parent's cause amongst the Created," she said. Meg, who was one of
the few people in the whole village who would not be surprised by such an

forthright statement, said, "Are you a Toran or a Seventh Dayer, or a Mormon or something?" "No, I am a follower of Perpetua." "Oh, lovely! I'm not sure about all the ins and outs, but she seemed such a lovely person and I'd like to hear more. Are you planning to stay?" "Yes, for as long as our leader asks." "Look, my house is tiny"—it was indeed the tiniest cottage in the whole large village—"but you are welcome to stay." "Thank you." They walked back to Meg's little house while she crammed Kylie with information of a most unusual sort about the village. Because she was totally free of malice, she occasionally thought people might do better and sometimes carefully said so. Although she was very poor and exploited by employers and her family, she rarely complained. When they reached the house and shared a sparse lunch, Meg simply treated Kylie as a welcome guest, but at least Kylie persuaded her to take a little money. "It isn't quite like the time of Jesus when you could expect people to be accepted in a house indefinitely, until the wind changed for sailing, or something", she said. "Anyway, if you don't want the nominal bed and board you can give it to your church or a charity." Again, unusually, because Meg had family connections from the self-appointed genteel to the rougher end of social housing, she was comfortable with Kylie's personality. Not long after lunch, Kylie asked if she might go for a walk alone, to think things through. She wandered around the village until she reached the social housing. Nobody stared as she fitted in with her cheap, ill fitting clothes on her overweight body, her scuffed handbag, and her slightly vacant, uncalculating expression. "You looking for someone round here?" asked a man, helpfully, as he tinkered with his motorbike. "I've just arrived and I'm looking for people to talk to." "Like who?" "Nobody in particular. I tried to talk to the Rector, but he's away now Easter's over." "Who?" "The Vicar." "Oh him! We don't have anything to do with him. Religion's to do with posh folk." "Why do you say that?" "The people who go to the church at the top of the hill, Holy Trinity, keep themselves to themselves. They don't come down here except when they want us for something: electioneering, surveys, using us to get money for village projects, that kind of thing. Though I must say when we had a bit of a disaster with a fire they sent loads of stuff, but you somehow think the stuff is in place of real conversation." "But how good are you at receiving a friendly approach when it's offered? It can't be all one way." "It's a fair point, but as they're better equipped to do the talking than us, they should make the first move." "How?" "By asking us up there; and then helping us when we get there. I went once for a wedding—she didn't want to get married, but they made her because her dad was going to beat her up if she didn't—and although the Vicar was really nice to them, considering they were just going through with it, I didn't understand most of what was going on, the words and that." "So if I'm coming now to make friends with you and your neighbours, what am I supposed to do?" "Tell us why you want to be friendly." "For the sake of it." "Nobody is friendly for the sake of it. People usually want something out of being friendly and when they say they don't we get even more suspicious. The Government keeps sending people here to do something about 'Community', but it's rubbish.

What makes us a community, the thing we share, is that we can't get out of here because we're poor. Instead of scattering us among the well off and educated we're left to suffer from each other's ignorance. The first thing people do when they have money is get out of this so-called community, and the first thing even richer people do is that they buy privacy." "Well, what if I came to say I was bringing you good news?" "I'd say you were some kind of religious person. We have them. They've started coming here lately with pop music and American style coffee and doughnuts. I know I have been critical of the vicar, but at least those people don't pretend to do anything for us. All this religion and cake is just condescending, as if we'll believe in God according to the amount of jam." "Well, I'm bringing nothing except me. Have you heard of Perpetua?" "Yes, she was done in, wasn't she? And there's some story she's paranormal and my morning paper—I get it for the football really—says her followers sabotaged the telly, which was a bit of a laugh." "I'm one of her followers." "Now I see." "What?" "You want us to join something." "Yes." "What's in it for us, apart from joy in the next world?" "There's no such thing as joy in the next world without responsibility in this one. What's your name?" "Keith." "Well, Keith, I'd like to talk to some people here about what I am bringing. I'm only asking for your time. I'm certainly not asking for money." "It's a bit difficult with soap operas and football, but if you come to our club on Friday night we'll listen for a few minutes. At least you took the trouble to come."

Even though it was Bank Holiday Monday, Clement hardly varied his morning routine except that he shouted less vehemently at a Bad Morning programme. It was less provocative than usual, with a smattering of lighter items. He peeled, stripped the pith from, and then unencased grapefruit segments, not so much because he liked eating grapefruit most mornings, but because he enjoyed the act of preparation—just as he liked preparing pomegranates for Helen even though he found the fruit too sweet. The challenge was to produce as many perfect segments as possible and since he began in the new year his performance had been steadily improving so that today he only broke two segments. He put them in the fridge to chill as he was very particular about the hotness of hot food and the coldness of cold food, disliking warm or mixed hot and cold dishes. He took tea to Helen and they got up before nine. As a Bank Holiday ritual, Clement ate boiled eggs and soldiers. It was just dry enough for Helen to mow the lawn and Clement said his prayers and read the Bible until she finished. Then they sat companionably at their desks for the day's work. Clement took a handful of Bach Cantata discs and a box of Mahler from his CD shelves and put on his latest version of Cantata 82; he would play the Mahler if Helen went to do something else. She was working on the annual Walmbury Arts festival known familiarly, even though it had only been going for four years, as the Walmbury Weeks. Clement was writing a series of special prayers to back his recent proposal that September should be devoted to Creation. He thought that Jesus had far too much prominence in contemporary Christianity and that the Father and the Spirit were under-considered. With the rise in ecology he thought this was an excellent time to revitalise the Creator. They had a light lunch and went on with their work until mid-afternoon when Clement broke for a cigar, a beer, and a little radio sport. Helen turned to some Churchwarden duties and then worked on her beloved photographic collection in her computer. They both loved days like this when they could take care of unpaid work and create. They were beginning to think about one of their long, slow dinners when Meg Rang. "I've got somebody I think you should meet; one of Perpetua's people. She's tried to see Father Mark but he's having a day off, so I think you two should meet her." "No problem," said Helen. "That sounds interesting."

Meg brought Kylie to the door and then tactfully said she wanted to see Iris was all right, fed, and ready for bed. Kylie was a little awkward, but showed no signs of being overawed by this odd shaped house crammed with 5,000 CD's and almost as many books. It was not difficult: Clement was fierce with people in authority and with people whom he considered to be or who considered themselves to be, his equals and that often gave the impression, not least to Bishop Aleford, that he lacked a 'pastoral heart'. With those who needed help or who were less capable, less well read or confident, he was the perfect shepherd. Because he was so emphatic when he said anything, people mistakenly thought that he spent most of his time talking, but he actually talked very little and spent most of his time listening. "Welcome, Kylie, we've followed the Perpetua story with great interest and I know that Clement is sympathetic to a great deal of what she said." "That's unusual," said Kylie, encouraged. "One thing to bear in mind," said Helen, making her comfortable, "he's a bit of a liberal theologian." "Oh, I'm not a theologian, just one of Perpetua's followers." "And why have you come here?" "To spread the word about a revitalised relationship between God our Parent and all humanity." "I'm sorry that Father Mark isn't here," said Helen, "because I know he would be really interested, but he's having a couple of days off after Holy Week." "Yes, I understand. I have talked to some people in the social housing." "That's good," said Clement. "We find it so difficult to talk to them and so any progress that is to be made in establishing a relationship between them and God is really important. It isn't doctrine that counts, it's the personal relationship with the Godhead." "I don't suppose that everybody will be as open-minded as you." "No, but by coming here you have made a good start. Father Mark will naturally not want to throw away the whole of the Christian tradition—I know you don't—and he will find it hard to leave behind some of the custom and comfort that he has enjoyed from his kind of witness since he sat at his clergyman father's knee. I think it won't be doctrine that gets in your way, but simple, straightforward tradition, conservatism, fear of difference and the fear that a new way of looking at things will somehow endanger the insurance policy which is what Christianity is to many people." "Well, as I have said before, I am no theologian. I was brought up in Grunge Park—and after Perpetua you all know where that is—and did poorly at school. I would have been in Hypo all my life stacking shelves and things like that if it hadn't been for Perpetua. I often think of those fishermen with Jesus. I'm sure they had more skills than me with my shelf stacking, but it's the same thing. Since yesterday—and it's only yesterday—I'm not frightened and I seem to be doing all right."

When Meg came back with a report that Iris was fretting because of her failing sight and weakening limbs, they gave her a glass of white wine to comfort her, then the two left and Clement and Helen enjoyed a quiet evening with snails at eight o'clock, fish at half past, a pheasant with bacon at nine, and just a nibble of cheese and fruit after that. Helen had two glasses of white and Clement had a bottle of 2000 claret from his cellar rack of 200. Helen, as usual, went to bed just after ten and Clement lingered over his second cigar of the day, a nightcap of dark rum and his prayer book until just before eleven.

For most of the rest of the week Kylie stayed in Meg's house, praying (something she was getting better at) and reading Meg's Bible rather than her own because she liked all the helpful notes that Meg had written over the years. She also read through Perpetua's file, which Trina had given her. All the material seemed so much simpler than it had in the past, but she missed Perpetua's presence terribly and called constantly upon her Sister the Spirit to keep her strong.

On Tuesday morning the Prime Minister surveyed his press digest with amusement. Whether or not The Oak had been prescient or whether the newspapers were supremely adept at picking up the mood of the people, there was now general agreement that the communications malfunction had resulted from a clever piece of hacking. There was no point trying to explain, even to technical and media correspondents, that taking over the world's broadcasting networks was a totally different proposition from hacking into a bank or even the Pentagon's computer system. Let sleeping dogs lie. Gordon would have to sort it out.

John Dobson, the Bishop's Chaplain, leafed hurriedly through the mail, hoping that there would be nothing too pressing so that his over-worked Bishop could have a day off. There was only one letter to trouble him. For the first time ever, Lady Gowers had carried out her threat to write to the Bishop about Mark Price's sermon.:

> My Dear Bishop
>
> As you probably know, my husband was a close associate of your predecessor, Bishop Tony, and served for a time as his adviser on historic churches. I have continued to take a keen interest in the well being of our Church and am, may I say, the chief benefactor of Holy Trinity.
>
> I am writing in connection with our Rector, Mark Price, who has become increasingly ill-judged of late in his pronouncements from the pulpit. I have resisted the temptation to write until now but his Easter Day sermon was a blatant piece of heresy, giving credence to the outrageous claims of Perpetua. I believe, if I may say so, Bishop, that it is your duty to curb the intemperate outbursts of our Rector so that orthodoxy may be restored to our beloved church.
>
> Yours &c

Dobson hated this sort of letter written by people who felt entitled to go straight to the Bishop without starting at the bottom so that a complaint could work its way up where necessary. They felt entitled to direct contact because of their perceived rank and influence. Her husband had been a very faithful servant of the Church, but as far as Dobson knew, Lady Gowers had done nothing that had been remarked. She said she was Holy Trinity's chief benefactor, but he pondered the widow's mite. He photocopied the letter and put it into Aleford's pigeon hole, but before he could file the original Bishop James had come in to see what was going on and the letter caught his eye. Dobson explained what he had done. "Yes, John, quite right in theory, but I don't want to look discourteous." "I understand, Bishop, but if you begin to reply directly to people who pole vault the system, you will end up even busier than you are now and the system will collapse. Simon Taylor is trying to leave things in good order, but it is so difficult with so many layers unless we are strict." "Looking at what Marianne has to say, it seems to me that there is a teaching issue here." "But I've already copied the letter to Hilary," said Dobson, truthfully, but failing to mention that he could remove the copy from Aleford's pigeon-hole. "Heresy is a serious charge, John." "Yes, most often made by people who don't know what they're talking about; remember Jenkins of Durham and the empty tomb?" "I am not sure whether to write to her or to Father Mark." "If I were you I would do nothing but if you must, the obvious thing is to talk to Mark before putting anything on paper. For the time being at least, I would let Hilary deal with it." "I won't do anything for now, then. Thank you John." James soon drifted out of the office and Dobson got on with the Augean Stable.

On Wednesday Clement had lunch with the Religious Correspondent of Humanity. After civilities had been exchanged about friends and family that had been close when they were junior reporters together more than twenty years ago, Clement said: "I don't suppose you asked me to lunch because of our former associations, to recall old times, Ranjit?" "No, of course not, but we have to make a pretence of approaching our desires slowly." "Desires?" "A word you Christians don't like at all but how would you describe the things you really want?" "And how would you describe the particular thing you really want at this moment, to steer us away, for the time being, from your interesting, but rather open, question?" "Perpetua." "Ah, yes." "What's your take on it?" "Another huge open question, rather like: 'What's America like?' so you will have to come a bit narrower." "All right; what effect is Perpetua's life and death and, er, recent manifestation, going to have on Christianity?" "That is still a rather big question, so why ask me?" "I know you aren't asking me that in order to be flattered, but you always were a cool head when all around were shouting Marxist rhetoric. It is quite a feat to be an Aristotelian in this wickedly Platonic world." "Stop! I'll try. I don't need to tell you that what has happened is a chronologically telescoped isomorphism of the Jesus story from Maundy Thursday to Pentecost?" "No, you don't but it's a useful way of putting it." "So there are, taking this angle first, three options: a) God is deliberately repeating a pattern b) It's a coincidence c) It has nothing whatsoever to do with God. Looked at from the perspective of Judeo/

Christian literature, it is full of patterns attributed to divine intervention in history, whether you are thinking of God's Covenants or the way prophets talk; so divine intervention in human affairs is a strong possibility. As you know, I don't believe in coincidence, but the third possibility, that Perpetua was aware of divine patterns and deliberately set out to mimic them in order to proclaim herself divine, has to be considered. This last ball is much more in your court as a professional journalist." "Taking you up there, then, and allowing that it's the job of a Religious Correspondent to report what people of belief are saying and doing, rather than opining on whether what they hold is true or not, ..." "... Admirable, I wish your political colleagues were similarly principled, ..." "... I don't see how she could have planned her end. She lived in a certain way, she had premonitions of a violent death, she went into Grunge Park on that Friday night with open eyes, but I doubt she thought she was going to be killed. After all, from what I can tell—and we're still digging—the people who received her, if that's the word, surely didn't plan to kill her. Our evidence so far suggests that they wanted to humiliate her publicly, though the motives are somewhat knotty. So we have reached a point where we agree that it could readily be held by many Christians that Perpetua repeated a previous pattern. We might be even more specific by saying that she might have wanted to do to contemporary Christianity what Jesus did to Judaism." "I can see the pattern, but whereas Perpetua was quite specific about wanting Christianity to concentrate on small cell teaching and worship and on breaking down social divides, it is not clear to me that Jesus wanted to do anything to Judaism other than to take it back to its basics." "But surely Perpetua wanted to take Christianity back to its pre-Constantinian basics?" "Good point, Ranjit, definitely one to you." "So we have a pattern that includes wanting to reform Christianity, not in a radically 'forward' way, but in the way of all so-called reformers, wanting to take us back to a 'golden age'?" "I doubt she thought about it that specifically. She seems not to have been a Christian historian and her followers repeat her mantra that they are not theologians." "Fair enough, Clement, but you are one." "In a modest sort of way." "Well that's the sort I want. I don't exactly need Karl Barth nor even Karl Rahner at this point, nor even Hawthorne in his more recondite musings. How is Christianity likely to react?" "Come on Ranjit, it depends which bit." "All right, Rome?" "The interesting thing here is that Perpetua's theology is nearer to Rome than to any other piece of Western Christianity. There was more than a hint at Vatican II that the sacrifice of Jesus could be full without being final. This was just before the first moon landing. What would God have to 'say' to what he had created in other parts of the universe or in another universe? So, theoretically at least, Roman Catholicism should be able to pick up the idea theologically. It will have a terrible problem ecclesiologically because, in spite of Vatican II, it is sclerotic. Ever since Vatican I it has steadily become more centralist. This is not a matter of deliberate policy. Local diversity was tolerable before mass communications, but what was once quaintly permissible is now inconsistent. Pope Benedict is likely to continue the trend. Vatican II was very special but it will take another

50 years to work its way properly into the Catholic system. My guess is that Perpetua will have little or no effect on Western Catholicism. That said, given the even more theologically conservative Eastern Orthodox wing, it will have no effect there at all. We have to accept that a change in the composition of the Godhead from three to four 'persons' is a little bit radical, but not insurmountable;. What is likely to cause the real trouble is Perpetua's attack on the highly structured and building-based church. Behind every debate about theology you will find a power struggle about ecclesiology." "That's a bit harsh, isn't it?" "I don't think so. Men are like that. Churches of all denominations dominated by men have tended to become 'political.' Churches with a high percentage of women in positions of authority will adapt better to Perpetua—not because she is a woman, but because of themselves." "Which leads naturally to your beloved Church of England?" "Your irony does you credit. I left Rome because whereas I could accept the Pope's stamp, what he calls his 'infallibility', on Christian doctrine, I couldn't take his claim to have authority in matters of morals. What I could not have known then, as I had not thought about it carefully enough, is that the Church of England might be numerically tiny and it may look to outsiders to be institutionally weak, even rotten, but it could be argued that it is the power house of theological speculation now that Rome has clamped down on its finest. I suspect that what Hawthorne says about perpetua will turn out to be more important, in the long run, than what Benedict says." "Really?" "Yes." "And what will Hawthorne say?" "I have no idea what he will say, but I bet that he will give Perpetua a fair run against tremendous opposition from Torans who will turn this into ammunition. Their use of the Bible as a kind of textbook closes down most of their theological options. Ultimately it makes them militant and lazy." "That's all very interesting, Clement, fine background for my blog and all that, but it is hardly a story." "Look, Ranjit, I'm no longer a journalist, I'm one of over 450 on the Great Synod and nowhere near the centre of things." "There's a rumour that Tony Blair thinks Perpetuanism—if I can call it that—might break out in liberal Roman Catholic circles, but that it will have a slow burn in Anglicanism." "I'm not surprised at the first suggestion, it's possible but I do not deem it probable. I think he is wrong about Anglicanism. It was going to be homosexuality which was the Toran issue to take over the Church of England from the inside, like Militant in Foot and Kinnock's Labour Party. The Perpetua issue will more deeply divide Anglicanism into renewing liberals and literalist Torans and, because it is not an issue of the Evangelicals' choosing, they will be on the defensive." "More good stuff, but what about the story?"

Although he had been concentrating very hard to be as clear as possible for Ranjit, whom he really respected as a thorough professional, Clement had been thinking about Kylie. Should he mention her? He was so tempted because, i spite of his great modesty in many ways, he liked to make things happen which would redound to his credit. In the end, however, his well trained, and severely disciplined, belief that decisions should be taken by the people most affected by them won out and he said, "Perpetua's followers are on the road. Why not ask

Trina whether she has any ideas?" "She's difficult to get hold of, but I'll try again. Thank you for your help. It will be interesting to see if you are right."

Later that day Ranjit rang. "You do live in Walmbury, don't you?" "Yes." "And you didn't tell me one of Perpetua's people was already there, one of only less than a dozen in the whole country and you didn't say anything." "If you had come back to me saying Trina had turned you down I would have had a difficult decision to make, but even then it would not have been mine but Kylie's. I would have given her your number and she could have chosen to ring you or not. As it is, the decision has thankfully been taken from me. When are you coming down? You can stay with Helen and me to make up for what you see as my rather unhelpful attitude." "Clement to the last, fastidious and generous. But I can be fastidious in turn. If I stay with you and write a story that stirs things up in unpredictable ways, you will take some of the flak. Thanks. Pretend you don't know me." "How horrible." "But necessary." "All right."

Late that afternoon at Church House, Aleford saw the letter from Marianne Gowers and a scribbled note from Dobson. "She should have talked to Price but as it came to Bishop James I am passing it down the line so that you can deal with it or pass it down as you see fit—JD). Hilary had it copied for his records and put a copy into the Archdeacon's pigeon-hole. Brian Sedge, who was well known for his quiet diplomacy, picked up the copy as he left Church House a day later. He read Dobson's comment and then Hilary's curt, "Yours unless it gets critically pastoral—Hilary." Brian who, if anything, hated snobbery even more than Dobson, wished the letter had started with Mark. He was only briefly tempted to talk to Mark immediately, knowing that he could over-react when he felt cornered, so he merely confirmed with Jane that Mark would have an hour between early evening meetings and dinner and that, although Brian was anxious to talk to Mark personally, there was nothing to worry about. Mark came in briskly and alerted on his mobile that Brian was on his way, he showed no signs of worry. Although they came from very different traditions, Brian could not have been such a successful Archdeacon without his sense of fairness. When he arrived, they went into Mark's study. "I wanted to see you personally because something which is rather trivial might become an issue as the result of the way it has been broached. Lady Gowers—you know her of course—has accused you of ill judged remarks from the pulpit and has actually used the word 'heresy'. Now, don't react like that, just think for a moment so that we can get this into perspective. You see, I don't think it's a problem, but she did rather mess things up by writing straight to Bishop James. No. Just stay quiet for a moment. Now I've said my piece, things can only get better from hereonin." "And what, pray, ..." "Mark, I'm your friend. Don't adopt that tone of voice, it won't help us." "Sorry, Brian. What does she specifically say?" "She says that you have declared your support for Perpetua." "Fortunately, that is not the case." "I never thought it was, Mark." At this point some Archdeacons would have pressed home their point and left, but Brian judged it both fair and prudent to let Mark have his say. "I simply pointed out that Perpetua's death had messages for us in the way we judge people. It was, I know, a somewhat odd message for Easter Sunday but I did not think I could ignore the issue. My Parishioners tend to be well informed and they would expect me to say something. You know the way in which I was brought up and how difficult it would be for me to breathe a word of anything heterodox. Yes, I'm a liberal—and I have reason to thank you for your respect of that position although it differs greatly from your own. The Church could not survive without that kind of give and take by all of us—but when it comes to the Creed, the Sacraments, and so on, I cannot imagine myself breaking from the witness which I have faithfully supported and which has faithfully, with God's Grace, supported me." "Very good." "And when I preached on Easter Sunday morning I had no inkling of what was to happen later that day." "Would that have made any difference?" "I don't think so. I have had three days to think about it and I am a long way from coming to any conclusions. If in doubt, as usual, I trust to the leadership of our Archbishop." "Very proper. So what are we to do with Lady Gowers and the Bishop?" "I think ..." "... Sorry, Mark, that was rhetorical, not a real question to you. Let us break the problem into two pieces. The Bishop will insist on replying, so we need to persuade him to adopt a certain approach and you, I think, will need to talk to Lady Gowers?" "Yes, but only by virtue of her late husband's Knighthood. She's done nothing for it." "That is beside the point in her eyes, in spite of what you or I might think." "And she only comes to church at Christmas and Easter and on family Sacramental occasions." "That is the Church Established for you." "And I doubt she really would spot a heresy if she heard one. She would almost certainly confuse blasphemy and heresy." "A nice point, but we only have a limited time to agree on a course of action. I will talk to James, rather than writing—as one never wants written advice to be recorded and then ignored—suggesting that he says nothing. If he must say something by way of reply he should simply confirm that she should agree to meet with you." "I prefer the first to the second, but not because I am a coward." "I know you are not. I too prefer the first and will do my best. Meanwhile, let us pray for ourselves and each other."

Minutes after Brian left, Meg phoned. "I have been worrying about this all week, Father Mark, not knowing whether to tell you or not. When I asked her she said that I should have told you as soon as possible. She was surprised that I hadn't told you and she wants to put it right. So if I have done the wrong thing I'm very sorry." "Whatever it was and whoever she is, Meg, I'm sure you were trying to do the right thing. Let us start at the beginning, who is 'she' and what is 'it'?" "Kylie." "Not a name I know and I'm pretty good at names in the Parish after all these years." "A follower of Perpetua." "Yes, there was—is—a Kylie, a bit overweight, I seem to remember, rather flat, dull face." "Yes, I'm sorry to say that's somewhat accurate, but you'll have to be careful." "Why, Meg?" "She's staying in my cottage." Mark who, as Brian had noted, was bad at receiving big news or a dilemma over the telephone, broke out, "I will not have a person such as that in my Parish." "Mark." "I will not have ..." "... Mark, stop saying 'I will not have', it's so unlike the real you." "Sorry Meg, terribly sorry." "And," she continued while she had the upper hand, "you can't actually keep her out of the Parish, nor even out of our church, for that matter, which is what she wants to see you about." "See me?" "Yes, she has been worried about upsetting you and wants to see how far you can agree with each other. She would have done this sooner, but I wasn't sure, so it's my fault." "Never mind, Meg, I will be very happy indeed to see her." "I think she wants to propose something." "Well, if it's theology I will see her whenever she wants but if it involves the Parish I better have Helen." "That's a good idea. Clement's out." "Good. I love them both dearly but together they are rather overpowering even if they don't mean to be. I presume Kylie is at your cottage now. I'll ring you when I've talked to Helen."

In minutes Mark had moved from slight fear after the Gowers intervention, through anger with Meg and Kylie, to excitement at something new and challenging. Unlike Clement, who talked about the personal relationship with God but who frequently veered off into the systematic end of theology, Mark liked a very direct, almost fierce relationship with God. "Helen, I presume you know about Kylie?" "Yes, Meg brought her round the other night and I knew Kylie wanted to meet you." "Yes, Meg has explained. Kylie wants to make some sort of proposal and as it might involve the Parish rather than simply being a doctrinal discussion, I thought you better be present as the 'people' Churchwarden." "Come round here as it will be 'neutral' ground." "Thank you."

Meg brought Kylie to Helen's and Mark soon followed, so Meg tactfully withdrew to take care of Iris. Mark saw that Kylie was not skilled at small talk so he asked, "What do you want to propose?" "It's simple, really. I'm going to talk to the social housing people at their club tomorrow night and will propose that they start coming to your church and that, in the manner of Perpetua, we then form rich/poor house groups." "My church is open to all people, that is the under-stated genius of the Church of England. How many do you think you will bring?" "I don't know but I guess no more than twenty." "I will see that the sidespeople—Stewards, Kylie—are aware of what might happen so that they can see that all our unaccustomed visitors are looked after properly." "Very kind," said Kylie. "I think they will be a little frightened." "So far so good," said Mark. "Your objective is to bring people to Holy Trinity, but the second part of your proposition is more difficult for me. If these house groups are to involve my parishioners in departing from the doctrine of the Church of England I can't sanction them, although I can't stop people doing what they want. I would be sorry to lose my people without a great deal of thought on their part." "I can see that," said Kylie "but traditional Christians who listen to God's word through Perpetua are giving nothing away, they are simply being given extra help to establish their personal relationship with God Our Parent." "I understand the theology, but you are asking me to go rather faster than I reasonably can. Could I ask you not to press the house group idea until we've thought it through a little bit more?" "Yes you can, but it won't be me that sets the timetable, it will be the God we both worship." "I think," said Helen, "that that is a good place to leave it. The Gamaliel syndrome."

Mark wondered whether to mention The Crux to Kylie. This was, in Church of England jargon, the "Fresh Expression of Church", obliquely mentioned by Keith. It was intended to be a worshipping unit independent of the parish system and, although it claimed to be an organic out-growth of the Church of England, The Crux had very little Sacramental or, despite its claims, Scriptural, content. It favoured Saint Paul over Jesus and, as its name implied, the Crucifixion over the Resurrection. Unlike the majority of Parish Churches, it offered high quality coffee and doughnuts, a professional-level rock band, stimulating activities for children, moral stricture, a fierce fund raising drive, the cult of personality, and simple language. For these reasons, and because it had been unconstitutionally imposed on the Parish, Mark might have been expected to be hostile but, out of loyalty to Hilary—who liked this kind of novelty—and because liberalism was his identifying trait, he was extremely tolerant and even accepted some mentoring duties over its 'Pastor', Jim Crawley. Although the idea of 'Fresh Expressions' was to extend the reach of the Church, most of its strength depended on brand switching which is why Mark was so worried. Jim had ambitions on the social housing in Walmbury. Mark's dilemma was whether to warn Kylie of the hostility she would arouse from The Crux or whether to let matters take their course. Reminded by Helen of the Gamaliel Syndrome, he decided to let things be. As he left Mark said, almost as an aside, "Clement is preaching on Sunday, isn't he? I know you will let him know that there will be visitors." "Do you have any special instructions?" asked Helen. "No. He will know what to do."

From the moment when he had seen her image so clearly during his Easter Day Consecration, Mark knew that there would be a decision to make within the painful framework of his internal civil war. His spiritual and personal loyalty to Hilary and his love of precision and suspicion of change pulled him one way but his intellectual break with Saint Stay's College over the issue of women priests pulled him in the other so that his choice was not going to be simple. He set himself a Pentecost deadline to make up his mind, taking his lead from Hawthorne for whom he had a profound respect.

When Kylie arrived at the social club—Meg had gone to choir practice—it did not look promising. There were only a handful of people drinking at the bar. Kylie handed over some money to the Chairman and said she would buy a first drink for everybody. By half past eight, however, there were more than 40 people and the Chairman judged it a good time to begin. "Some of you will have heard about Perpetua who died in tragic circumstances last week. She was a quite remarkable woman who wanted to bring God to poor people which hasn't always been the obvious ambition of the established church. I'm not saying anything against our Vicar, Father Mark, because we know he genuinely cares but he's fighting against impossible odds from inside his own establishment. There's just too much drag in the Church of England. Anyway, this is to be a constructive evening. Keith met Kylie, a follower of Perpetua, earlier this week, and she asked to speak to us for a few minutes and I thought it would be a good idea to give her a hearing seeing that she came to us first. Kylie."

"Friends, like you, I knelt at the manger when I was in primary school, and later I learned about the death of Jesus on the Cross and how he rose from the dead. As I became a teenager I began to lose touch with what this meant and I drifted away from God as I am sure many of you have done. There will be some amongst you who don't really know what the Crucifixion means. Well, this is no time for complex theology, and I can't do it anyway. I only want to leave you a simple message. Because the Cross of Jesus became so distanced from our lives, God Our Parent decided to renew our resources to love that Godhead and each other by sending Perpetua, the Sacred Vessel. She preached the Kingdom of God as Jesus did. She died at the hands of humanity, as Jesus did. She came back to communicate with humanity after her death, as Jesus did. Her message, re-affirming the message of Jesus, was that we were created to choose to love God, because love given by choice is the only true love. So when people come to you and say that all that you have to do is to trust in God and everything will be all right, they are telling an untruth. Love requires choice, not sitting back and hop-ing that somebody else—anybody else, Jesus—will sort things out. That is why Perpetua was so concerned to carry God's message to poor people, to people like me who are not very educated, not theologians nor historians but simple people trying to survive in a complex world. Perpetua said that there was no com-munity on earth with no resources to enable it to make choices. Look around you now. I am sure there are people here with all kinds of skills and talents that they are nervous about showing. I want us to help each other to take control of our lives. Now I know this is not easy for us because we are so used to steering clear of the clever and the powerful; but we cannot live our lives to the full if we cut ourselves off from the other people. Often we argue that because others are more powerful and much cleverer than us it is for them to make the first move, but this is not a game in a school playground. I am here to help us to make a move towards gaining control of our lives. The people who go to Holy Trinity up the hill really do want to embrace the whole community but they don't know how. They are quite as frightened as us. I want to encourage Father Mark to establish groups where we can mix with people who go to his church so that we can help each other, through the mission of Perpetua, to understand God bet-ter and to establish that on-going personal relationship which we abandoned, through indifference, early in our teens. I have already talked to Father Mark and he will welcome us to his service on Sunday morning. Who is prepared to come with me and see what it is like?" There was an edgy silence and no move-ment. Then Keith slowly put up his hand and was followed by others until there were some twenty hands raised. "Great! Now let's enjoy ourselves," said Kylie as she was handed a glass of white wine.

Mrs Pugh was not one of those who raised her hand, for her life consisted not in building, but destroying. If a bad construction could be put on anything, Mrs Pugh would construct it. Although she did not have a good word to say for anybody or anything, she was never short of shop work because she knew everybody and had a phenomenal memory. On Saturdays she worked in Ellis's Quality Family Butcher and was ready for Father Mark when, as usual, he came in minutes after opening to buy his weekend meat. "So you're going to be invaded tomorrow?" "Pardon." "That Kylie, Perpetua's stooge, was talking to us at the social club last night and she will be bringing a load of people to Holy Trinity tomorrow to disrupt your service." "How many people?" "Perhaps 40." "Come, Mrs Pugh, I've heard there were only 40 people there last night and I doubt all of them agreed to come. Your absence, for instance, would make it 39." "Where did you hear that?" "As you can see, I've already bought my paper." "Oh yes." "And I've met Kylie and don't expect she wants to interfere with my service at all." "Wait and see, Father Mark. You can't trust people like Kylie. They look docile enough on the surface but they are cunning." There was nothing that Mark could do to tone down her baleful influence. He knew that she would spend the rest of the day bad-mouthing Kylie, but there was nothing he could do. Mrs Pugh was a highly skilled operator. She would not waste her time on people who could not further her ends, so she reserved her confidences for all the church goers who came to buy meat. The story was always the same. The people from the social housing, led by a Perpetua stooge called Kylie, were going to wreck tomorrow's Family Eucharist. Kylie was going to seize the sound system and denounce Father Mark from the pulpit. Good Christians should be ready to defend the traditions of the Church of England, a sentiment which more than once brought the tart response that Mrs Pugh had never been known to defend anything and that she had never been seen inside Holy Trinity for a Christian service or even a concert. She was particularly vitriolic when she warned Helen of what was going to happen. "As Churchwarden you should be particularly careful, Mrs Sutcliffe, because you will take the rap when tomorrow's Communion descends into chaos. Father Mark may be humiliated but the Bishop will come down on you for failing to keep good order. If I were you I would keep them out." "I have no intention of keeping anybody out. The Church of England is open to all, Mrs Pugh, even to people like you, as nobody is beyond God's love." Mrs Pugh did not appreciate Helen's rare employment of irony and resolved to get her own back at the first opportunity. "And I should say," Helen went on, "that if you continue to spread these unfounded and malicious rumours, you may well gain some satisfaction in the short term—though why you should enjoy the disruption of the worship of God I cannot possibly tell—but it will do you no good in the long term." Naturally, what started with Mrs Pugh soon spread throughout the village with a variety of embellishments. Nigel, enjoying a pint in The Oak before going to the last home match of the season, heard that the people from the social housing were going to demand Father Mark's expulsion from the Parish to be replaced by Kylie. Although he tried to ridicule this story he was worried for Mark.

Whether it had been part of her design or not, Mrs Pugh's acidic injections goaded many to church who would normally give it a miss on 'Low Sunday' and others who rarely came to church at all, but wanted to see what happened. The result was the largest congregation outside the three major festivals of Christmas, Easter and Harvest. As soon as he heard the side door latch click, Clement could feel the tension emitted by Mark even before he came into view. The Family Eucharist was the high point of Mark's week and it had to work spiritually and theatrically. It had to be perfectly as well as reverentially enacted, but today's special circumstances made Mark even more nervous. Meanwhile, at the back of the church, Helen was overseeing the distribution of books and the weekly sheets with Scriptural references and words of 'songs', as Mark called them, not included in the books. Seating visitors proved difficult because it was impossible simply to say, "sit where you like", as so many regulars had their own particular spots. Matching visitors with regulars prepared to lend a hand was also quite difficult, but Helen had given this considerable thought and managed to pair off most of the visitors. The operation was made more difficult by the attendance of people who had just come for the spectacle. Unlike the people from the social housing, they made no effort to integrate themselves into the proceedings. They weren't 'players' but merely spectators. As he passed Clement, Mark said, "This could be difficult but I thought your draft sermon was very good and I don't see any reason why you should change it except, perhaps, by simplifying some of the theology." "Thank you, Mark. I can feel the tension, even hostility, but we must overcome this. Many of our regulars are frightened." "Clem, we are all a little frightened," said Mark who touched Clement with this highly unusual use of his diminutive.

Mark began, "Christ is risen!" "He is risen indeed, Alleluia!" replied the choir, with very little support from the congregation. "Come on, you know that this is still, technically, Easter Sunday." They had heard it before and were not really impressed. Mark went through the Gathering and the Ministry of the Word without any variation of his usual practice, except for being very careful to give page numbers and to remind people when to sit and stand. When Clement climbed into the pulpit at the end of the Gospel, there was a sense of expectation. This was supposed to be the moment when Kylie would make her move, bidding to preach in Clement's place. Some were surprised that Clement was there at all as Mark should have been centre stage to repel the Perpetuan onslaught. But most of the regulars knew better. If anybody could stay cool under fire it was Clement. He had been a Parliamentary Candidate, he was a good debater and he never lost his cool. Mark was very wise to leave this in his hands as he had a short fuse.

"In the name of the one God, Creator, Redeemer and Sanctifier.

"Today's reading from Acts, which replaces our customary Old Testament Reading at this time of year, could hardly be more appropriate for our time. In Acts 5.27-32, Saint Peter is brought before the established church and told that he must not preach the new Gospel of Jesus but must stick to the old ways. Peter's reply is that he must obey God rather than human beings.

"Throughout our lives our purpose must always be to discern—to find out— what God's will is for us so that we may make a distinction between that will and the satisfaction of our own earthly desires. By that I do not mean we shouldn't have earthly desires. After all, God created the whole world with all its beauty and variety. What matters is why we choose what we choose. We should choose out of love for the Godhead and each other. In choosing love we will frequently, although not always, find ourselves in a state of enjoyment where we realise our most intense desires.

"But deciding—the Church's posh word is 'discerning'—what God wants is not always easy. When Peter appeared in front of the Jewish religious court he was making an outrageous claim. He said that the respectable authorities whose main purpose was to promote the worship of God had made a terrible mistake by murdering Jesus who had been sent by God. Any impartial observer at the time would have characterised—thought of—the authorities as wise and Peter as mad. It was that sacred madness, which we might call the Holy Spirit, which ensured that Peter and the other Apostles prevailed over conservative religious forces. Without the Holy Spirit, Christianity would have been crushed by the establishment.

"What, then, should our reaction be to recent events? When Perpetua's followers challenge the religious authorities of our day should we unconditionally side with them? Should we say that Peter, inspired by the Spirit, was brave and right at the time but that since then everything has been set in stone forever so that the Church can never evolve? Much of what we believe, that we will say in the Creed when I have finished, would have been incomprehensible to Peter and his contemporaries. Christian theology has been evolving since the day of Pentecost. Our problem is to discern—using that word again—which developments accord with God's purposes and which divert us from those purposes.

"Let us start at the beginning. God is love. We are to behave at all times out of love. We are not here to judge the motives of others, but we have been given brains by God to work out whether theological proposals—what we say about out God—seem to fit with God's intentions for us. Having considered everything on the record that Perpetua and her followers have said, it seems to me undeniable that she was acting out of love. On that basis, we ought to follow our Archbishop in approaching her mission, death and subsequent manifestations with an open mind.

"Secondly, we should not confuse the value of what she had to say with how that affects power structures within Christian communities. We must be careful when we hear church people saying that Perpetua's proclamation of her mission was heretical. More often than not the declaration of a heresy is a device to support the status quo, particularly the power status quo, keeping things as they are.

"Finally, remember that when we are discussing God in human language we are using figures of speech, metaphors and analogies, earthly images of things which are beyond us, and there is very little purpose in people fighting about the validity of metaphors. Doctrine exists to crystallise what humanity has taught itself, with God's help, about God. It is provisional and capable of radical improvement. It might just be that Perpetua was sent by God to bring about such a radical improvement. At this moment I do not know, but I do know that it is too early to dismiss Perpetua's claims, and that of her followers, out of hand. To dismiss her without proper consideration is to behave like the religious rulers who wanted to silence Peter. The Holy Spirit will decide. We should leave ourselves open to her power. I believe that by the time of Pentecost we will know what we are to do. In the meantime, we must pray.

"In the name of the one God, Creator, Redeemer and Sanctifier."

The congregation was so stunned that it could not reply with an "Amen."

The service went on as usual although there was a sense in which everybody was simply going through the motions. The choir sang a short anthem as befitted 'low Sunday' and then ran out of material because of the extra large congregation. Mark blessed the visitors from the social housing carefully and noted that there were many villagers who rarely, if ever, came to church who did not come to the altar at all. He read the Banns, again prompted by Helen, read the notices and introduced the last hymn with a voice which had lost all of its tension. Nothing had happened except for Clement's slightly outlandish sermon, but he and the congregation were used to that. The spectators left as soon as Scott began the voluntary. The people from the social housing stayed for coffee and the regulars did their best to engage them in polite conversation. Mark deliberately engaged Kylie in conversation to show that they would do their best to work together. Except for the arrival of visitors, this might have been just another Sunday, but just below the surface things were not so calm. Clement usually aroused respect, if not admiration, for his sermons. He was Mark's out-rider and people recognised that he often said things that Mark wished he could say, but on this occasion he had gone too far. There was no sympathy for Perpetua if that meant undermining what they were all used to. On Easter Sunday Mark had used Perpetua as an example of a principle, but Clement had gone further than he ought. The regulars were civil to their visitors, but when they were gathered together in knots they expressed hostility to Perpetua. Clement could feel the hostility and, as the coffee drinking came to an end, Mark was aware of it too. He wondered now if he should have been more circumspect when he read Clement's draft. If he thought that being open and tolerant was the better course, he was wrong.

3.

Just before the visitors were ready to go, it happened that the remaining congregation formed an almost complete circle around Iris's wheelchair. Because she had stayed in Meg's House, Kylie was being introduced to Iris. "How are you? Meg has told me a lot about you." "There isn't really much to tell." "As you know, I followed Perpetua when she was with us and now I am doing her work." "She cured people, didn't she?" "Now and again. Not for effect but out of compassion and to show the power of God among us." "I remember that Saint Peter cured people after Jesus had ascended into heaven. Can you do that?" "I've never cured anyone. I am just a simple follower." "I wish you could cure me. I'm not that ill, you understand, but at 92 I am almost blind and am wheelchair bound and I hate being a worry to Meg. I am ready to meet my maker when the time comes, but until then I want to fend for myself." "Well, you know what Perpetua said about controlling your destiny. Why don't you try to stand up and take those glasses off." Iris slowly put her feet to the ground, stood up, reached up to her head and removed her glasses; her stick clattered to the floor. "Meg, I can see you again!" she almost shouted, walking towards her daughter. The circle, like dancers, stepped back a pace, all in time. Ranjit, discreetly standing behind the circle, took a series of photographs as Iris approached Meg and then embraced her. The people were stunned. Mark, aware that he must say something, reverted to his years of discipline. He said, "Let us thank God for this marvelous work." Kylie, as astonished as everyone else, stepped back into the circle of spectators to be replaced by Mark who stood next to Iris and Meg. "We thank you, Lord, for your wondrous gift of life and health. Help us to be grateful for all you do and to worship rather than trying to understand. Amen."

Ranjit edged towards Iris and Meg while Mark tried to edge people towards the door. His pastoral reflexes had kept things under control but he felt uncertain of what to do next. He just wanted to get people away so that he could go home and pray for guidance.

Ranjit said to Meg, "I am the Religious Affairs Correspondent of Humanity, I wonder if I could ask you a few questions?" At that moment Mark became aware of what was going on and put on his 'I will not tolerate' face which Helen immediately de-coded. She somehow got between him and Ranjit and said, "Yes, I know it is a breach of good manners. He should have asked you but it doesn't help to antagonise journalists. I will tick him off. Just leave it." Mark calmed down immediately but, in any case, he had another situation to deal with as the 60 or so remaining people showed that they had had their minds changed by what had happened to Iris. They were chanting, "A miracle. In the name of Perpetua, a miracle." Mark raised his voice and shouted, "In the name of God, a miracle!" But he could not compete. In order to hide his frustration he began to help a couple of stalwarts, not distracted by what had happened, to clear up.

"What can you see?" asked Ranjit. "There's no point handing her the Bible as a reading test," said Meg. "She knows just about every line of it." "Praise the Lord!" Said Iris, fervently. "Here's yesterday's Humanity Mediatrix," said Ranjit. Iris began to read steadily. "What could you see before today?" "Just light and dark." "Who is your doctor?" "Webster. A very good man." "And how far could you walk earlier this morning?" "A few paces across a room with a stick, but not much further." "And how do you think this cure came about?" "The Lord, through the power of Kylie, Perpetua's Disciple," said Iris, schooled in the correct terminology. "And a comment from you, Meg?" "It's absolutely wonderful. I never minded looking after mother, but I am so pleased for her." "Could you all stand behind ..." Ranjit was saying to the chanters when Helen intervened. "No—it's Ranjit isn't it?—no, you can't do that. You're here to report the news, not choreograph it. You've got a good story, be satisfied. You've been very good so far not to acknowledge your long term acquaintance with Clement but he will be damaged if this story is distorted in any way. It's going to be difficult enough as it is, and that comment is definitely 'Off The Record'." As usual, Mark could only admire Helen's deftness. The crowd was beginning to drift away, slipping past Mark without the customary handshake. One of the last was Lady Gowers who would not even look him in the eye. He sensed more trouble and wondered whether to let her by without comment but he thought things were so bad that he could not make them worse. "I am sorry to hear, Lady Gowers, that you thought it fit to complain about me to the Bishop without first bringing your complaint to me, your mere Parish Priest, but I suppose I am not allowed to make any comments in my own defence." Helen looked over desperately but Mark deliberately avoided her glance and she saw that her intervention in front of Lady Gowers would humiliate him. "I had nothing to say to you after Easter Morning," she said, "but even less so now. Your offences are such that they could not possibly be a private matter between me and you. I might have written to Aleford, but he's soft, so I decided to go straight to James. As for that scoundrel Sutcliffe ..." She pushed past him rudely, almost knocking him against the door post as she went.

Meanwhile, Clement had taken Kylie into the vestry to calm her down as she was completely overwhelmed by what had happened. "I didn't know anything was going to happen," she said. "I was just trying to encourage her. My gran, well, prefers her wheelchair and her thick glasses. She's accepted that kind of almost still life. She prefers it to the effort. So I thought that I would just give Iris a bit of a push in case it would help her to make more effort and look what happened. I didn't even use Perpetua's name, did I?" "No. We will have to make that clear to the journalist." "Journalist! Oh dear! I suppose it's all right because he would not be here without Trina, but I am supposed to say nothing directly to journalists in answer to questions. I must simply let them hear what I have to say to everybody." "Very wise," said Clement. "There is no need to be worried. Stay there a moment." He slipped out of the vestry and approached Ranjit. "As Father Mark's Reader I would like to help him, as this is his church, by ensuring that one thing is clear." "What is that, Mr Blue scarf?" said Ranjit, playfully.

"That you are particularly clear on one point. That in spite of what everybody else says about the power behind Iris's cure, Kylie did not say or do anything in the name of Perpetua. She is a follower of Perpetua, so you can draw whatever inferences you like, but you can't attribute words to Kylie which she did not say." "Thank you, Mr blue pencil," said Ranjit, still good humouredly. "I think I have a good enough story, but I can't speak for my sub editors. Who can?" "Do I detect a slight note of resile?" asked Clement. "So cynical, when I thought your farthest limit was scepticism." Clement knew he had reached his limit, so he went back to Kylie, but he was followed by Ranjit. "Could I have a picture of you with Meg and Iris?" "You've already got some," said Helen, arriving. "Fair enough," said Ranjit, "but you won't be this lucky again. You won't be able to control the show once this gets out." The tone was cheerful but they all picked up the undertone. He then courteously but briskly thanked Mark and acknowledged with the warmest of smiles that he might have overstepped but they had all been taken by surprise; and then he continued to interview and photograph the more enthusiastic stragglers on the other side of the street with the church in the background.

There was a summit meeting in the vestry comprising Iris, Meg, Clement, Helen, Mark and Kylie. "My first concern," said Mark, "is Kylie. Of course you can talk to whoever you like and although it was somewhat unfortunate that you were caught in the act, so to speak, in my church, it would have happened in somebody's church sooner or later. As I have already been reported to the Bishop I might as well take all the flak for as long as I can. If you are to stay here, and that is your choice, you don't want to be in the house of the daughter of the person in whom a cure has been brought about—I'm sorry but I can't yet bring myself to connect you directly with the cure, forgive me—or you will be besieged. It will be bad enough for Iris and Meg as it is." "We will manage," said Meg. "What's happened to mum is so wonderful that it will give us the strength to put up with the media until they find something else." "In the circumstances," said Helen, "I suggest that if Kylie wants to stay here we should ask Marie to help. She's a lawyer, very discreet, particularly loyal to you, Mark, and very firm." They agreed and Helen phoned Marie. "Now," said Mark, "it's very important, Kylie, that you are clear in your own mind what has happened. I can't say, as I have just said, so I think you need advice from Dexter or ..." "... Trina," said Kylie. "Very good. You go with Marie and she will look after you, but please get in touch with your friends." After Kylie and Marie had gone at the same time as Iris and Meg, Helen and Clement were left with Mark. "Well, Clement, I suppose I should take the lead here, but what do you advise?" "Helen has told me about Lady Gowers' letter to Bishop James. As this is the first time she has been in church other than on a Festival, she no doubt came to make mischief and she now has plenty of material from my sermon. Although you sanctioned me to preach it, I am, naturally, happy to take total responsibility. She'll have even more from what happened to Iris in church. I happen to know Ranjit, though he was good enough not to let on. I met him last Wednesday at his request to give him some theological background, but I didn't tell him about Kylie. He got that from her press person, Trina. He will be as fair as a commercial medium can be, but he will lose control of the story inside Humanity and breakfast television will be full of it." "And I know that Doris Hall loves breakfast television," said Mark. "So the key, Mark, is where you stand because you have to have a place to stand with these people that is so robust that they can't pick away. Your first line might be that you will wait for Hawthorne's proposed Commission to report, but the response will be that that is all very well, but where do you stand as an individual. You could say that you're just a humble priest and don't know very much theology, but that's like a doctor saying he doesn't know very much medicine. If you become a laughing stock it will be all the more easy for Bishop James to be less than scrupulous—not that I am saying that he would be, but he will be under enormous pressure to act if it looks as if he is losing control of the Perpetua situation—so you need to work out where you are." "I can see that," said Mark, "but it's a lot to ask. We have been rather taken by surprise." "Well, I suggest that you turn the question back on Perpetua's people. As Kylie doesn't know how Iris's transformation took place, how should you know? You can't be asked whether you believe in something or not if the questioner can't define the belief in question. That will hold the line for a few days." "Thanks, Clement, very helpful. Now to my area of expertise. I need to tell you my strategy with Bishop James because I have no doubt you will be asked about it. First, I allowed a large group of unaccustomed people into my church, led by Kylie. That was a perfectly proper thing to do. Secondly, I know you keep the texts of your sermons and post them on your web site. In the circumstances, what you said was both reasonable and brave. Thirdly, there is no record of what I said on the morning of Easter Sunday in my sermon. I will paraphrase as fairly as possible. Fourthly, I had no idea what was going to happen between Kylie and Iris and Bishop James can't get to the bottom of that without asking Kylie, who is not responsible to him, otherwise he will be flouting natural justice and Church procedure." "Again," said Clement, "that will hold the line for a while, but it won't last." "No," said Helen, "but the whole Parish will be behind you." "No, it won't, Helen, though it's nice of you to say so. There are enough conservatives who have held their fire for want of an opportunity and a leader and as she is 'Lady Gowers' they will gather round her. Then there will be those who believe in Perpetua's power who will gather round Meg. Then there's Jim Crawley. He will be furious that Kylie has 'stolen' some of his prospective flock and he will go running to Hilary. I have no doubt he will say that I gave Kylie some encouragement. How we Christians betray our 'New Commandment' of love."

Lady Gowers thought that she would take a little run over to Alchester for Choral Evensong so after her modest lunch she wrote a hurried note and handed the envelope to a verger on the way in. "If you could see that this reaches the hand of Bishop James, Roberts." "Certainly My Lady. He does not often come to Evensong, as you know, with so many other Diocesan duties, but Doris is a regular attender."

Clement and Helen were sombre when they got home. Although they had been uplifted by what had happened, and although they were so pleased for Meg and Iris, they both knew that the first casualty of the new situation would be Clement. Mark had suggested that he should train as as a Reader, but halfway through the two-year course he had known that he had made the wrong choice, that he wanted something more, not a parish Reader, but a high powered teacher, He had been Licensed as a Reader and left it a year, during which he started his Systematic Theology MA, and then the issue of his calling to priesthood had surfaced again. He had been turned down flat. Since then he had tried to be a good and faithful Reader, keeping the promises he had made to his Bishop at the Licensing, but he knew his card would now be marked, even as a Reader, that Hilary could withdraw his Licence without giving a reason and without any appeals procedures. "The problem," said Clement, "is that if I am fired by Hilary and then 'defect' to the Perpetuans it will look like sour grapes, but I will have to live with that." "Might you really 'defect'?" "Yes, it will be difficult, but I have been moving that way for some time. I have no problem with the theology, it's just breaking away from all the things I have loved: the form of Eucharist; the choral services; but, above all, friends and bonds of fellowship." "I will support whatever you do and you never know, many may come with you. I am slower than you to resolve such issues, so be patient." "I would never force you either way. I will say nothing to you about yourself." Clement worked for the rest of the day on his creation project as there was no point just waiting for the axe to fall.

On Monday morning, Ranjit's coup was picked up by all the later editions of the papers and by all the major broadcasting networks. Smoother was jolted initially but soon regained his composure. He saw a way through at last. "Archbishop," he said, "I don't think you can delay any longer. You will have to form your promised Perpetua Commission immediately and give it a remit to report by Pentecost." "Theology does not work like that, Chris, we have to take our time to discern God's will." "Yes, Archbishop, but who said that the Spirit moved like the Civil Service? It didn't during the period described in Acts. We have to force the pace so that we are no longer on the defensive. Either we have to work with the times or choose our ground of resistance but if we do not act we will surely be overtaken by events. I doubt this will be the last 'miracle' performed by Perpetua's followers."

Bishop Hall was in his office early. He had already seen the breakfast coverage of the so-called miracle and he had Lady Gowers' note in front of him:

> My dear Bishop,
> Further to my note of last Sunday, I am writing to inform you of further outrages. Clement Sutcliffe, Holy Trinity Reader, preached a sermon yesterday, with the Rector's sanction, positively exhorting us to follow Perpetua. At the end of the Holy Communion Service, the Rector looked on as one of Perpetua's followers, a certain Kylie, performed a religious stunt in the name of her demonic mistress. I am resolved to withdraw my benefaction from Holy Trinity unless firm action is taken.

Yours &c.

"I see no problem with Sutcliffe," said James to Dobson, "but Mark is another matter." "Sutcliffe's sermon is on his web site, Bishop, and it does nothing but support Archbishop Hawthorne's position in terms of his general theology and it specifically backs his proposed Commission." "So it may, John, but I'm fed up of Sutcliffe." "So you may be, Bishop, but I advise caution." "This is no time for caution—in the sense that we need to take firm steps in this minor case, but of course there is the more general point that the Archbishop's position must be carefully assessed—and I am therefore minded to take this small step." "Sadly, I have to record my dissent, Bishop." "Yes, Yes, John. As for Father Mark, I will leave that to Hilary as it's his patch and as they are good friends. I just hope that Mark will see sense." "I would resolve the Father Mark issue before doing anything about Sutcliffe. A precipitate move in that matter might push Mark over the edge. He sanctioned Sutcliffe's sermon, after all." "No, John, the two things are quite separate."

Archbishop Hawthorne worked all day on setting up his Commission but neither the Petrans nor the Torans would join it. By the end of the day his plans were in ruins, but he resolved to give himself more time before making a public announcement when the time was right. It never was.

Clement duly received the withdrawal of his Licence on Tuesday morning and telephoned Ranjit. "I've been fired by Bishop Hall." "Why?" "As far as I can see, for backing Archbishop Hawthorne." "Have you any comment?" "No. I'll fax you a copy of the letter and you can do what you like."

Clement's much loved house group, Living Water, met on Tuesday evenings and he prepared with his usual thoroughness to deal with the first few Chapters of Hosea and Ezekiel Chapter 23 to discuss the metaphor of sexual unfaithfulness in the Jewish tradition of monotheism. He opened with a specially composed prayer and then the Lord's Prayer and began to work his way through the text, but he had hardly got past the first few verses when one of the group broke in. "Look, Clement, we're all really close to each other. You have helped us to build up trust, to grow together so that we can say anything in absolute confidence that we will be respected. There's a rumour going round that you have been fired as a Reader." "I am sorry to say it is true." "Why?" "For my sermon last Sunday which supported Archbishop Hawthorne's Perpetua Commission." "That is scandalous. What should we do?" "I have discussed this with Helen, and prayed as best I can, and I have concluded that I will follow Perpetua's guidance in the renewal of God's church on earth." There was a moment of deep silence and then someone said, "We are with you." More silence. Then a second said: "I think we are all with you." "I don't want a vote," said Clement. "Why don't we go on for this week as usual and next week I will know by who turns up whether any of you are really with me. You need to pray about it." "No we don't," said a third. "The Spirit is with us." They all assented. "Well in that case," said Clement, "the sad but joyful reality is that we will have to think about breaking ourselves up so that we can be the germs of new house groups which include the people from the social housing." They were all very sad, as they deeply valued Living Water as it was, but they assented in principle. In silence they drew lots to break into four sets of three. It was the Spirit; but they could not face it quite yet. "Don't do anything until I have told Father Mark," said Clement. "Let us meet again tomorrow evening." "I have to reserve my position," said Helen, "as I'm Churchwarden."

On Wednesday morning Ranjit's story did not make a big splash in all the papers, but it caused a disturbing ripple in church circles. Smoother was appalled by Hall's behaviour but, again, it helped his purpose. "Archbishop, you can see from the story about a certain Clement Sutcliffe that Alchester has already rubbished the Perpetua Commission, as have a number of other Bishops. I don't think headlines like 'Senior Bishop Defies Hawthorne' are very helpful. We must either announce a Commission or announce that the two extreme wings of the Church are hostile and that we will launch a discerning process based on your open principles rather than trying to forge some kind of lowest common denominator consensus." "Regrettably, Chris, I think you are right. We will have to abandon an official Commission. I think this is why I was moved by the Spirit to accept this terrible job. It is all fitting into place."

Clement went to see Mark just after nine. "I am so sorry, Clement, but I suppose we both knew it would happen. Just before you arrived, Hilary rang to report Bishop James's reaction and Hilary has offered me a Sabbatical so that I can go away and pray about my own position." "That is tricky. I don't want to mix up Helen's role as my wife with her role as your Churchwarden but I don't think she would very much like to manage a Sabbatical period resulting from Bishop James' precipitate action." "I will ask her." "I will step outside so as not to embarrass you. I promise she is not expecting your call."

"Helen, this is Mark. Bishop James has offered me a Sabbatical to consider my position." "Well, you will have to find two new Churchwardens to manage it. I would do anything out of loyalty to you, but my loyalty tells me to support you as our Priest or as a Perpetuan Priest. I haven't finally made up my own mind yet where I am, but if he has not already, Clement will tell you what happened last night." "I see, Helen. Thank you. It is very clear. We will talk later."

"What happened last night, Clement?" "Living Water all decided to become followers of the Perpetuan movement and, when we are brought by the Spirit— and can bring ourselves to do it—to split ourselves into four small units to start new house groups with the people from the social housing." "I see. That does not leave me very much room, with the core liberals moving away." "I am sorry, it was not meant like that. It just happened." "I know. The Sprit is with us. I suppose what is holding me back is rather mercenary. I have to live, you know." "I think we may be able to sort that out as long as you truly feel that your calling is to join Perpetua's followers." "I think that is where I am going pretty rapidly." "I spent some of yesterday talking to people, including Trina, Dexter's new CEO Max Silver, and a lawyer colleague of his, Adrian Brooks. I think we should ask them to come down this afternoon if they can. I also took the liberty of talking to Violet Smythe and Ronald Simpson." "Why?" "Because they are the Trustees of the Church Renewal Fund. They are sympathetic to Perpetua and Adrian Brooks suspects—though he will need to see the Deed of Trust—that 'Renewal' as such is not limited to the church re-ordering which we were planning and he is certain that the funds are not part of the property of the PCC." "Good Lord, literally, Good Lord."

Early on Wednesday evening Kylie, Max Silver, Adrian Brooks, Clement, Helen, Joel Ross, her Churchwarden colleague, Violet Smythe, and Ronald Simpson met at the Rectory. "This is a quite extraordinary occasion," said Mark, "and I am not quite sure how to begin so let us start with the Lord's Prayer."

"May I particularly welcome Max and Adrian who have come down to advise us. Here is the situation as far as I can see it: I have been asked to take a Sabbatical to consider my position, but I feel that I have come far enough to know where I am. It is really very difficult for me—I am not saying it is not for others but I need to express myself honestly—it is really difficult to leave all I have known and to move into a different kind of spiritual milieu. Now I know that I am giving nothing away, that what I am moving towards is Christianity Plus, but I know I will lose many of the, what people would call 'trappings' that I have been so used to. I don't mean the things we make jokes about like the fancy lace vestments, but I mean being able to go into church and find the Blessed Sacrament there." "I'm no theologian," said Kylie, "but we don't want to take any comfort away, Father Mark." "I know you don't, but it's been a long and difficult life for me as the champion of liberal causes from a catholic background and I would not have survived it without the comfort of the daily Eucharist and the presence of the Sacrament." Clement nodded. "Anyway, I am not sure whether to take the Sabbatical or just resign. There are a number of financial matters I would have to sort out which may sound mercenary but I do have a family and my retirement to think of. Clergymen are called upon to lead a holy life but not to render themselves destitute through imprudence." "Very true," said Max "which is why I am here." "Next," said Mark, "Clement has been fired, simply on my behalf, for supporting Archbishop Hawthorne." "Yes, Father, but I was moving somewhat rapidly towards the Perpetua position anyway." "What about the Churchwardens? Helen?" "We are not entirely in the position to 'side' with Perpetua. For us there is a community or social dimension as well as a theological dimension; but we are not prepared to deal with the consequences of the Bishop's imprudent action. If you take a sabbatical we will resign and if you resign we will resign. In that sense what you do is not very material." "And the PCC?" "We have taken soundings and most of the PCC are prepared to support you in whatever you do." "Perhaps, then, it's time to ask Max to say something." "The situation as I see it—and I have only been here for less than an hour—is as follows. If you, Father Mark, the Churchwardens, and the PCC all resign, the Bishop can hold none of you responsible for the upkeep of the Church, for its assets and liabilities, nor can the Diocese receive its Parish Contribution until there is a new Treasurer to forward the money. I suggest, therefore, Father, that if your conscience will allow you, you should resign rather than taking a Sabbatical, as long as the Churchwardens and enough of the PCC resigns to render it inquorate. Of course it can co-opt a couple of people to keep it going, but I doubt there will be much temptation. The PCC is a Registered Charity and if those who support Perpetuanism in some form transfer their financial commitments from the PCC to Perpetuanism then the PCC may not be a going concern unless those who stay radically increase their contributions. Now this is where Violet, if I may, and Ronald, come in. We have had a brief, but I think satisfactory discussion with Adrian about the situation of the Church Renewal Trust. Adrian, I may say, was one of my colleagues when I worked at my merchant bank before we were both fired in a merger coup. He was my right hand man and company lawyer. Adrian." "I don't know whether it was bad drafting or highly skilful drafting, ..." "... I think the former," said Violet. "... But the legal purposes of the Church Renewal Trust do not specifically, or exclusively, apply to the church re-ordering for which I think the Trust was established." "That is correct," said Violet. "We fully expected—perhaps assumed is a better word—that when we drew up the Deed of Trust we were providing a fund for the re-ordering of the Church, but instead of specifically using that word, the lawyer, perhaps out of caution, used the term 'renewal' and we did not query this." "It is very important at this stage, as you are the two senior Trustees of the Trust, that we are clear about your intentions." "I have been a regular churchgoer at Holy Trinity," said Violet, "since I was baptised here in 1929. Except for holidays I have not missed a Sunday or Festival worship. It has long been my wish to have the building of Holy Trinity re-ordered so that it can become the centre of the village's spiritual and cultural life, so that the Sunday School can flourish within the walls of the church and so that our meetings and other gatherings are under God's roof. To that end, Ronald and I, with faithful followers, have been raising funds for the Trust for over ten years now and we have amassed more than half a million Pounds." "But," said Ronald, "we now see it as God's will that we should devote that money not to the physical re-ordering of Holy Trinity. We thank God that the Holy Spirit moved us not to make the purposes of the Trust specific to the physical re-ordering and we accept what Adrian has said. We believe that it is in the best interests of the worship of God in this place that we make the funding from the Trust available to the cause of Perpetua's reformed worship in accordance with Father Mark's wishes, whatever they are."

As the implications dawned on him, Mark looked stunned but he bowed his head slightly and said nothing. Adrian looked at his notes: "What we are moving towards—and these are early days—is an ecclesiological model as follows:

1. Each group of current churches, what you would call a deanery, selects one church which it would like to keep as a regional centre of worship. It will be there for major festivals and for re-affirmations of all kinds, and be open seven days per week as a lively centre of spiritual and cultural life.

2. It will be presided over by a 'bishop' figure elected by all the faithful peo-

ple who ascribe to the basic tenets of Perpetuanism which we will shortly set out, but it will include the Old and New Testaments and her Revised Creed. We are also assembling a set of her sayings and writings from the god4u archive.

3. The bulk of worship and teaching will take place in socially mixed house groups and the 'bishop' will ordain those who are presented by the groups and preside at the Eucharist. Such people must be deeply aware of what they are doing, knowledgable in the tradition from which this sacred act arises and they must lead holy lives. The only ground for turning them down will be failure to meet these criteria.

4. Local leaders will not be paid, but the 'bishop' will have a full time salary. The model we are working on is Foundational Stipends, that is, each grouping of house groups will work towards amassing the funds to pay for its 'bishop' from the proceeds of investment instead of being condemned to a fund raising treadmill."

Mark looked uncomfortable. "However, the Trustees have agreed that the Church Renewal Trust should defray the costs of Father Mark's first year's salary at an amount to be agreed, to include a fair Housing Allowance on the understanding—and this is not legally enforceable—that the supporters of Perpetuanism raise more than the amount of expenditure for this purpose in the first year so that the amount in the Trust grows, and that this arrangement will then continue until the Trust has reached the full Foundational amount required to maintain its 'bishop'. From that point on, funding from the community will be for mission and for activities around the 'bishop's one and only church." "And which church will that be?" asked Joel. "I have already had an informal conversation with Simon Taylor, the retiring Diocesan Secretary, and suggested that, subject to various minimum conditions being met—so that we neither inherit a church which is ideal nor in need of massive expenditure—we will be prepared to accept any church in the current Deanery which has undergone the same vacation procedure as that which I propose for Holy Trinity. As this church is somewhere in the middle between ideal and a ruin, it might end up being the one, but I can't yet say. All this is informal and it will be a lawyer's paradise sorting it out. The Diocese will be shocked when it discovers the amount of liberal funding it has relied upon to survive. It has always assumed that the Petrans give least and the Torans most and it has not looked at the 'middle' component. By and large, sociologically, liberals tend to be slightly younger than the average churchgoer and considerably better off as more of them are still working. In parishes like this we estimate that the liberal contribution is nearly 75%. I therefore propose that we organise a co-ordinated set of resignations following the completion of terms between The Trust and Father Mark. I cannot say at this point that he will be elected a 'bishop', but if he is not, I am sure we can find some arrangement which keeps him properly employed until he is ready to retire." "What should we do next?" asked Mark, looking a little confused. "I think we need to ask Kylie, who is our leader here and who has been very quiet."

"I am moving on now, my friends. I think I have done my work here. I am most grateful for all the warmth I have received and all the help I have had and I thank God Our parent, Jesus and Perpetua, and Our Sister the Spirit, for all the acceptance of my message I have found here. I will go to London with Max and Adrian to seek further guidance from Dexter." "What should we do here?" asked Mark. "I advise you," said Max, "to delay the announcement of your position for as short a time as possible. Although I trust everybody here, the news will get out somehow." "I owe it to the Parish to tell people on Sunday. I will celebrate the customary, traditional, Eucharist for the last time, then tell the people, by which time my letter to Bishop Hall will be in the post."

While this meeting was going on, Nigel was holding court in The Oak. His status in that venerable institution largely depended on his knowledge of rugby as a player and referee but now he had the enviable asset of being the only person present who actually knew what they called "The Vicar". "There is a rumour," said one, "that the Vicar has been fired by the Bishop and he's going to be de-frocked." "It's a popular phrase which summons up a sub conscious vision of a priest in his underpants," said Nigel, "but it is not really like that." "But I have heard that he is to be publicly denounced by the Bishop for being a heretic." "Always supposing that our beloved Bishop could bring himself to define anything as heresy, he isn't the denouncing sort." "Well whatever you say, Nigel, the Church of England is falling to bits. Of course that's inevitable because it hasn't been prepared to stand up for proper moral standards." "Coming from you, Tom Smiley, that's a bit rich. A church isn't an abstract organisation which, as you put it, 'keeps up standards', it is a collection of human beings who observe a set of ideal standards from which they often, as imperfect human beings, fall short. If the Church as a whole changes its standards then that usually happens after a long period of soul searching. As for you, Tom, if you think that according human respect to gay people is a sign of a falling standard, you can always join a sect that agrees with you. There are plenty of them about. Alternatively, you could stay in the Church of England of which you are a nominal member and speak up for your point of view. As it turns out, you only went to church for weddings and funerals until you thought you needed to go to get your kids into the school and you've never shown any interest in a fixed standard of behaviour in anybody else or yourself." "That's a bit sharp, Nigel. But, anyway, it is true that the Church of England isn't in touch with real people." "I somehow think that 'falling standards' and 'being out of touch' are opposites but, anyway, I think you could say that that was true in some of our city areas but not, for example, in villages like this. The Rector is always up and down the High Street shopping, talking to people, making visits and the church is open all day every day and is the venue for many of our cultural activities and particularly our Walmbury Weeks." "But the Vicar and you lot do come over a bit superior to people like us." "Well, you can't precisely have it both ways. One minute we're behaving superior, the next we're not upholding these magic standards that tabloid readers are always calling for." "So what do you think is going to happen, then?" asked

Tom, anxious to change the subject from his own inconsistencies. "Not much. There's always a lot of fuss over short term things but in the long run not much changes. This Perpetua woman seems to have made a big impact on what we are doing but so did John Wesley and it all settled down. Her people might form some kind of sect but sooner or later it will re-merge with the mainstream, it always does." "Well it didn't after the Reformation." "True, you've got me there, David. But a lot of people in the Church of England are moving back towards Rome. However, you are right that the Evangelicals, the Protestants, what we call Torans today, did constitute a radical break with Medieval Catholicism, but this doesn't feel like that." "There was the miracle of Iris who had her legs restored." "No she didn't, she just found walking difficult and used a wheelchair." "And had her sight restored." "Yes, well, that can't be denied." "I don't remember Martin Luther or John Calvin performing any miracles," said David, getting into his historical stride. "Doesn't that mean that what Perpetua is offering has greater divine sanction than what Luther and Calvin were offering?" "It might mean that, but that does not mean that it will be a greater departure from the norm, does it?" "This is getting just a bit silly. We don't care so much about the departure from the norm but whether what she's offering has some kind of divine sanction." "I couldn't say, David. How would I know? Whether it is or not, Father Mark, our Rector, won't change radically. He's a bit of a liberal in some things but he's very conservative when it comes to ritual. I doubt he will want to give up his whole life's spiritual superstructure for some new fangled bit of doctrine. In the end, human beings are very conservative. They see the sense of doing something radical, but prefer not to do it. It takes a war or something like that to shake us out of our lethargy and conservatism."

At 6.30 p.m. Smoother took a call from Ranjit. "I've got this story which says that the Bishop of Alchester has sacked a Reader." "Not much of a story," said Smoother. "But wait, the significance is that this Reader, you'll know him as he's on the Great Synod, Clement Sutcliffe ..." "... Yes, a bit of a liberal ..." "... Well, he's been fired for preaching in favour of the Archbishop's proposed Perpetua Commission. So, in effect, Bishop Hall is rubbishing the Commission." "I see your point, Ranjit. Is that all?" "No. Alchester is also threatening to fire a Priest for supporting Hawthorne's approach. I just wondered whether you had a quote." "I'll ring back, I promise, within half an hour."

"Excuse me, Archbishop, I don't like to disturb you from your evening prayers but I fear I must. There is a story that Bishop Hall of Alchester has de facto denounced your proposed Perpetua Commission. Taken together with the fact that the Petrans and Torans have refused to co-operate, we need to do something now before the Alchester story breaks in tomorrow's Humanity." "Bishop James has always been a bit of a fudger, but he seems to have gone against the grain this time. It may well be that in taking a precipitate action to try to keep the Church of England together he has taken the minor—but decisive—step which will shatter it." "Which will give him the pretext to go to Rome which he has always been seeking." "yes. But that is not the central point here." "I agree," said

Smoother, beginning to see the grim, or glorious, depending on your point of view, implications of what was opening up, "and I think we will have to be honest and announce the failure to set up a Perpetua Commission which represents the various—forgive the word because I know you don't like it—churchmanship perspectives." "That failure will involve my resignation." "I can see that it might but let us go slowly." "I am not minded, Chris, to go slowly. I think as a theologian who wants to keep his spiritual life open and active, I have to listen to what the Holy Spirit is saying through Perpetua. I cannot ignore the reports of this apparently authentic miracle which one of her followers performed." "We still have to check that, as it happened in one of our churches." "I know, but the procedure isn't the point. I wish to pursue a theological enquiry into the implications of the life, death and post death manifestations of perpetua. My ideal position is to pursue this enquiry within the Church of England, within its tradition of a broad church, tolerant approach; but if I cannot do that there are only two alternatives: that I abandon the Anglican tradition and set up a narrow church enquiry of like-minded people, or that I pursue my enquiries privately." "If you tell the media you are considering your options you are already a 'dead duck'. To say you are considering resigning means you have resigned." "I need just a little more time, not because I'm prevaricating, but because I need to consider what is best for the Church. I am convinced that a majority of leaders within it do not want me to stay; the Petrans and Torans together are just under half of the Great Synod; the liberals, being less well organised, are less than a quarter; the rest might just back me if I appeal to their loyalty on a personal basis, but it's a risk I don't think I'm prepared to take. It's one thing for a king to sack or behead an Archbishop of Canterbury, quite another for him to receive a vote of no confidence from the Great Synod. For the time being, then, all we can say is that the Commission has been abandoned because there isn't a consensus on its composition. I will wait until Friday before making a final announcement, but you need not say that. Just stick with the failure to constitute the Commission." "What about Hall?" "Just say I'm sorry that he didn't seem unequivocally to support my stand, but I appreciate there may have been reasons why." "That's very generous of you, Archbishop, if not verging on the disingenuous." "Not that it will do me any good, but we aren't generous to do ourselves good, are we?"

"Ranjit, two things. Firstly, the Archbishop is sorry that Alchester appears, on the face of it, not to support him. Secondly, we are about to announce that we can't presently constitute a cross-churchmanship Perpetua Commission." "Put the two together and we have a serious story, don't we, that Alchester has taken the first step to destroying the Church of England?" "Hang on, Ranjit, that's a bit extreme. This story started with Perpetua who may have intended to reform rather than to destroy the Church of England. She certainly wanted less hierarchy and less building-based worship. I don't want you to portray her as a destroyer and neither do I want you to portray Alchester as a destroyer." "Take your pick, Chris. I have a destroyer story, but you can choose who is responsible for the deed." Smoother thought for only a moment: "All right, Ranjit, Alchester.

He will have to take what's coming on his way to the Vatican."

Clement and Living Water met for the first time other than on a Tuesday and the business was not instructional but strictly logistical. "I must tell you," said Clement, "in the strictest confidence—and I trust you all, but no doubt the news will get out somehow—that Father Mark is to resign from the Church of England to join the Perpetuans." "I'm not surprised. How will he live?" asked one. "He will be funded by the Church Renewal Trust on the understanding that its payments to him are made good by fund raising," said Helen. "We should recall the early Chapters of Acts," said another. "I have just got a lump sum with my pension settlement," said a third. "I can always get some out of my tax free savings scheme," said a fourth. By the time they had finished they had guaranteed £40k. "I suppose Father Mark won't be able to go in precisely the tidy way he would like," said Clement. "His 'discussions' with Bishop James will be in the Church press at least and might reach the daily papers."

He was not wrong. Ranjit made the best of his discussion with Smoother in Thursday's *Humanity*:

ALCHESTER CRACKDOWN BACKFIRES

The attempt by James Hall, Bishop of Alchester, to crack down on "Perpetuan dissidents" backfired dramatically last night as his actions were taken as an attack on Archbishop Hawthorne.

Hall's attempt to gag supporters of Hawthorne's Commission were said by Church sources to be a contributing factor to the ruin of the Archbishop's containing strategy. As Petrans and Torans snubbed the Primate's attempt at a consensus a spokesman confirmed that any formal procedure has been abandoned for the time being. "He is going to pray about it and I hope he prays for Alchester at the same time."

This was taken to be a rebuke to Hall for what was described as his "precipitate action."

The firing of a Lay Reader and pressure on his Rector to consider his position were Hall's first moves to maintain what he calls "orthodoxy" in the Diocese but they may be the straws that finally break the Church of England's back.

Last night the Church was in turmoil as Bishops began to consider their positions. "We are in for a vicious period of dogmatic cleansing," said an influential Toran. "The sooner we clear out the heretics, the better," countered a Petran stalwart.

Sources said the Archbishop was not yet ready to quit, but the suspension of the Perpetuan Commission proposal immediately sparked a rumour that the Archbishop will resign and lead liberals out of the Established Church. His spokesman refused to comment.

Bishop Hall was appalled by the *Humanity* story. Admittedly, he had perhaps been a little hasty over Sutcliffe, but Aleford's approach to Father Mark Price had been generous. He had been sure that the offer of a sabbatical would sort everything out. Instead his actions had coincided with extremist intransigence over the Commission and it seemed that he was going to have to take the rap. Although he was something of a prevaricator, he was not a coward. Without even consulting his Chaplain he rang Lambeth Palace and was immediately put through. "Archbishop, I am terribly sorry for putting you in such an awkward position." "Never mind, James, I think that my press spokesman was rather hard on you, in the circumstances. It was just bad luck that you were singled out." "Thank you, Archbishop but, nonetheless, I am prepared to tender my resignation if that helps—but of course that depends on what you might consider to be helpful in different ..." "... Quite, James. Without any disrespect to you as a senior bishop, I do not think it makes very much difference what you do in the circumstances. Even without your intervention the proposed Commission was already in doubt. I think the best thing for all of us is to stop speculating and manoeuvring and generally to try not to behave like secular politicians; and to pray and examine our consciences." "Yes, Archbishop." "God bless you, James, and don't be too hard on yourself. We are all being taught at this critical time of what little account we are in the scheme of things. This, I am convinced, is an extraordinary breaking into us of the Holy Spirit after a period when we have behaved very badly as a Church." "Yes, Archbishop." "I will pray for you, James, and please pray for me." "Yes, Archbishop."

"Mark, I fear I may have been somewhat precipitate." "Thank you, Bishop, but I do not think in the long run that I could have stayed where I am." "Well, Mark, I am sorry if I appeared to push you. I was only doing my best—and of course for each of us the word 'best' can mean so many different things but to me it meant trying to keep a certain degree of orthodoxy ..." "... Quite, Bishop, I really do understand, but I am moved by my conscience—I would not presume to invoke the Holy Spirit—to take Perpetua's life, death and re-manifestation seriously and I genuinely thought that it was my duty to support the Archbishop." "Yes, Mark, I understand. We should all support the Archbishop when we can but I have been extremely worried at his tendency to retain some of those liberal positions which he brought with him into his exalted office—well, of course, it depends what you mean by liberal, but I take it to mean a weakening of the traditional positions ..." "... Quite, Bishop." "So what are we going to do about you, Mark?" "You need not worry, at least for now, Bishop. I will write to you and Hilary confirming my resignation and, as a matter of courtesy, I will outline what I see as my future." "Thank you, Mark, and God Bless you. I am sorry if what I did in good faith has turned out differently from what I intended—though of course almost everything we do does turn out somewhat differently ..." "... Quite, Bishop. I would like to thank you for all your kindness to me while I have been a servant in the Diocese. I will keep you informed as my plans develop."

The shape of Father Mark Price's plans was being discussed by Adrian Brooks, one of the Prime Minister's friends when they were studying law together. "The situation is this, Tony, er, sorry, Prime Minister." "Tony's okay, you know, Adrian. Everybody calls me Tony except for Gordon who has reverted to the formal in the past few years." "Well, Tony, what we have is a splitting up, a fragmentation of the Church of England into its component parts. I suspect that Hawthorne will go but Archbishop Mwanga will stay. We who are of the Perpetuan persuasion are inclined to cut our losses, get out, and then seek to acquire and maintain a selected number of churches and cathedrals. This will leave the Established Church with far more buildings than it can maintain. It is already under great financial stress and the loss of substantial revenue from erstwhile liberals, now Perpetuans, will be a serious blow." "I have been very surprised over the past decade that the Church has not made more financial demands on an avowedly Christian Prime Minister but, then, it has had other concerns which most of us fail to understand, over the Ordination and Consecration of women and the propriety of gay clergy. I've had gay cabinet misters, you know." "Yes, Tony. I recognise we have put the Church into a difficult position but there's no help for it. What we must do is take possession, on fair terms, of the churches we need, thus reducing the burden of the Established Church." "I am sure Gordon would applaud your efforts." "Parliament will have to pass emergency legislation allowing us to do this as the Church's Great Synod is incapable of getting a measure through in under two years." "You'll have to ask Gordon about that, Adrian. I'm sorry but I'm about to go off to be a Catholic." "Yes, Tony. I was hoping, however, that you would have a word in the appropriate places without needing to involve Gordon." "I will do that, Adrian, if only to help poor Hawthorne who has had a wretched time since I recommended him to Her Majesty. The Church doesn't know its good fortune in having him. I am sure if you meet Sir Justin Peal who looks after the interests of the Church in the House of Commons you will be able to sort something out. Sir Justin is very solid and impartial. He will want to cut the Church's losses and won't hold it against you that the Perpetuans have caused a split. He always said the split was inevitable, it was just the issue—what they somewhat pretentiously call the 'presenting' issue—that was in doubt. Dominus vobiscum!" "Et cum Spiritu tuo, Tony."

At the request of Bishop Hilary, Brian Sedge agreed to talk to Mark in a final attempt to stay his resignation. "Look, Mark, forget the little bit of news that's been generated this week by what has happened in Walmbury. Just think, if you would, about three things. Firstly, your own position, what your conscience dictates you should do as an individual believer. Secondly, consider what your duties are as somebody who has made serious promises to your Bishop. Thirdly, think of the welfare of your Parish, not just the people who agree with you but all the people, particularly those who rarely come to church." "I have been through this over and over again, Brian, but, out of respect for you, I will, of course, go through it one more time. Firstly, I believe that as a Church we have gone profoundly wrong since the 1960s when we failed to grasp the extent of social change. I am not saying that a church should simply follow fashion but I have always believed that we should not oppose a fashion unless it goes against the grain, if you like, of God's will. Even then, we should always be careful not to be an institution which is simply identified with moralising. We are here to witness to God in Word and Sacrament not to pretend to know God's opinions on every passing issue whether that be contraception, alcohol, topless bathing, or blood transfusions. In insisting on moralising we have simply got it wrong. In spite of my very traditional upbringing and my time at Saint Stay's, I very early came to believe that it was God's will that women should be equally accepted as called by the Holy Spirit as clergy. I think the gay issue is pretty marginal but, for what it's worth, I can't see it as an obstacle. Almost all the Petran clergy in this Diocese are gay including, as we all know, Hilary himself. The things Perpetua has said have simply given shape to what I felt for a long time. I am not a theologian, I am ashamed to say, but I can't see any particular point at which God's intervention in history has to stop—who are we to say? So at a very fundamental level, I am comfortable where I am. Secondly, with respect to my promises to the Bishop, I took them more or less in good faith but, like many other Ordinands, I slid over the problems presented by the 39 Articles. I have tended to slide over some of the more nimble-footed, two-faced theology of Cranmer in the Book of Common Prayer, but I expected my Bishop to extend to me the traditional and common latitude of the Church of England, not seeking to impose any given hard line. His insistence on his own 'orthodoxy' has put those who genuinely disagree with him into a difficult position. It was he, Brian, who absolutely insisted when women were first ordained, that there should be a special provision for those who could not, in conscience, agree with the majority position. Now he refuses to recognise the need to allow for differences over a wide variety of issues! So the perpetua mission has simply brought the problem out into the open. The Bishop has broken his word to me and, therefore, I am no longer bound to him. Thirdly, most of those who advise the Bishop have deliberately misled him into thinking that we liberals are so weak that we are about to be crushed out of existence by a pincer movement of the Torans and Petrans. Perhaps you will not be surprised by this, Brian. As an experienced and fair-minded Archdeacon you cannot possibly have failed to notice the strength of liberal commitment. There are a great many professional social class B people in Alchester, who at least balance the conservatives and landed people who, in any case, are notoriously mean. Whatever I do will split the Parish. I can't, in the Bishop's words, be a focus of unity—just as he can't—as I can't side with the three different groups simultaneously."

"At least you could wait for a while." "I don't see what good that will do." "Nor do I, to be fair, but Hilary has asked you to exercise some restraint and give us a few more days to resolve the issue." "I don't think the issue will be 'resolved', as you put it, and it would be unfair to hold out any hope, but I always take what you say seriously, Brian. You know how deep my relationship is with Hilary." "Do you think it would help if you called him?" "I think it would be quite complicated. We are close personal friends but, as a Bishop, he has let me down badly, both in terms of his pastoral care and in terms of his imposition of The Crux without properly consulting me. I've not said a word in public against this competition in my Parish but, sadly, in this church we make the same mistake as politicians in interpreting restraint as weakness. Because I have not complained about The Crux in Church and State, Hilary has just continued to push." "I see what you are saying, Mark, so would you like me to do anything?" "I don't think anything would help at the moment, Brian. Let us leave it there. I'm making no promises to you or anybody, but I respect you for trying and I will think carefully about the three points that you put to me."

On Friday evening Helen arrived a quarter of an hour before choir practice to talk to Marie. "How did you get on with Kylie?" "Just fine. She kept herself to herself and I saw it as my job to keep herself to myself. Until I hear anything definite I propose to go on as normal. There is nothing else we can do. I heard rumours that Father Mark is going to resign, but until he says something official I continue to see him as my Rector and spiritual guide. I'm not very strongly in favour of, nor against, change. I will seek guidance from the people who brought me into the Church and I will pray about it. To be honest, my problem is that I love the music so much that it is almost as important as the religion." "I know. It isn't for anybody to say. Clement serves God through study, teaching and preaching. You serve God through music. I serve God through keeping everything going. Who is to say that one way is more important than another? So don't under-estimate the importance of your commitment to the music. What I wanted to say to you—I know I can absolutely trust you—is that this might be Mark's last Sunday as our priest. There are large overlaps between the PCC which has said it will support him whatever he decides to do, Clement's Living Water, which has pledged financial support for him if he needs it, and the choir, so we need to think of how we are going to approach it." "I think we should be matter of fact," said Marie. "I will simply tell the choir that we are in a time of uncertainty, but that our job is to give Mark our very best, particularly at this time of uncertainty." "That's the right thing," agreed Helen.

Choir practice superficially went on as usual. Marie, without even hinting that this might be the last traditional Eucharist with Mark, said that they should sing Ireland's Greater Love and the members of the choir who knew about what was going on through the PCC or Living Water said nothing. They polished the anthem, went through the hymns, responses and mass setting, and left later than usual for the pub. Conversation was restrained, almost stilted, as those in the know exercised caution and those who were curious tried to restrain themselves. "The essence of virtue", thought Clement, "is self-restraint. Civilisation is gratification deferred. I know it is also closely connected with the capacity for storage, for creating surpluses, for planning, but if you squander the surplus you don't have civilisation. It's storage plus restraint." Nonetheless, the group could not entirely ignore what was going on. They had all seen the items in Humanity and one or two of them had read Church and State which was covering the Perpetua story in depth. They were all really sorry for Clement whom they thought should have been on his way to ordination. They could not understand why he had not automatically been approved, and they had heard that Mark was considering his future. Those close to Mark were more settled because their commitment to the Church was centred in themselves, but there were choir members who were not all that bothered about doctrine, but who were very committed to the music and the ritual. They felt threatened because there were not all that many church choirs left to join. As with most people who know each other very well, but are not intimate friends, Meg's "brush with the divine", as Nigel put it, half ironically, was only briefly mentioned before they fell into their usual, comfortable counterpoint. Scott fretted about the state of the organ, Marie wondered if the top line were up to Sunday's anthem, and Nigel had had a much worse week than Clement. Even after such a remarkable week for their church, life went on. It was just another Friday. After his one attempt to say something about his misfortune to Nigel, Clement lapsed into gentle, customary silence. Helen, as usual, kept everything going, always finding the appropriate word of encouragement or knowing when to say nothing.

On Saturday evening, at five o'clock precisely, Mark entered his beloved church. This was the time every week when he ensured that everything was as perfect as it could be for the following day's eight o'clock and 9.45 a.m. services. He checked the sound system, the readings on the lectern, the frontals, his vestments, the alignment of his President's chair in the chancel, and the supply of wine, wafers and candles. He put everything in order as usual, and then prepared all his other vestments and the contents of his desk in the vestry to be carried away when he had finished saying his office. He had hardly begun when he began to feel a profound discomfort. As he proceeded, with great difficulty, Brian Sedge's questions kept coming back to him. By the time he had reached the Magnificat he was sweating. He could see the image of Perpetua alongside the image of Mary. Christians had been saying Luke's words for almost 2,000 years, in this church for almost 1,000. He had to stop saying the words so that he could calm his spirit. 2,000 years of Christian witness, almost 1,000 in this place. His own family's clerical tradition going back generations, his own life as bound up with the 'professional' witnessing of Christ as a peasant farmer was with his strip of land. It had never been any different. What was he being asked to do now? Surely not to throw all this over? He had tried to convince himself that to follow Perpetua was to give away nothing but was simply to add to the glory of the Godhead. As he looked up at the Blessed Sacrament, always there except on the blank time between the afternoon of Good Friday and the Easter Vigil, he knew he could not be without it. The occasional festive visit to a church and the plodding seriousness of house groups was not enough. He needed the continuity, he needed the ritual—all right, he needed the security—but most of all he needed the Eucharist as it was, now. He put all his vestments back in their customary places and re-checked everything for the last time. Nothing in life was clear cut. He could follow Perpetua and risk his spiritual cohesion, or he could stay within the Church and suffer the pains of a liberal. He would stay.

Jane shared Mark's division between traditional High Church practice and liberal principles, but her contradiction was not so multi-dimensional as it was in Mark. She knew he suffered because of this division within himself and the primary focus of her interest in the division was that it should give him the least possible pain. She had watched him agonise for the past two weeks, ever since

Good Friday evening when, passing his study door, she had seen him watching Perpetua die. When he told her what he had decided she checked her natural enthusiasm because that would make the real issue clearer than it was, but she hoped that fences could be mended with Hilary and even with Bishop James. "What should I do about Clement?" asked Mark. "Send him an email." "I ought to talk to him." "Not on Saturday evening." "What about Hilary?" "Leave him alone this evening. You know what he's like after a few glasses of red. Tell the parish first where you stand and then deal with the rest. Admittedly you sanctioned Clement's sermon, but he wrote it and gave it. He's no fool—he knew what he was doing."

The Family Eucharist for the Third Sunday of Easter went like clockwork— too much like clockwork and not enough like Godwork, Clement thought—until the very end. After the notices Mark said, "I have two important announcements to make, without embellishment or comment, in connection with events which some of you may have seen in the press. Firstly, Bishop James has withdrawn Clement Sutcliffe's Licence as a Reader. Secondly, I have no intention either of taking a sabbatical or of resigning my tenure as Rector of this Parish of the Church of England by Law Established. Scott was reassured, the good old C of E would continue to give him a warm feeling, particularly as he sat on the organ bench of a Sunday morning. Marie felt relieved that her musical activities would continue. Nigel felt justified in his confidence that the common sense status quo would prevail. Helen immediately felt for Clement and then steeled herself to be loyal to Mark. Clement felt somehow let down and isolated as he sat in his unaccustomed choir robes which he had only worn when not worshipping in his capacity as a Reader. Meg was completely shocked as she looked anxiously down the nave to where Iris was sitting. In the vestry Nigel said, "I told you so, Clement. I'm sorry about what's happened to you, but, like all professionals, they close ranks." "Why didn't you tell Clement?" asked Helen, as she cornered Mark at the back of church. "I sent you an email." "Enthusiastic and hard-working as we are, not even we open email after dinner on a Saturday evening. You don't think, for all his loyalty and friendship, he deserved a call?" "I suppose this means that you will resign?" "Certainly not. I'm an adult. I have promised to be loyal to you and I will be. I am also loyal to Clement in what he is trying to do, but the two things are separate. You each have to do what you have to do. You haven't actually talked to him about his lost Readership. The Perpetua situation has kept his mind off it this week but your decision will hit him hard. He has lost his place and he has lost face. Now that you have made your decision he will be out on a limb." "Sorry, Helen. As you know, I find talking to Clement difficult because he's so persuasive." "Don't have a discussion, Mark, just say you're sorry and that you'll pray for him, something comforting." Clement put his Reader robes carefully in a special carrier he had brought for the purpose and carried them to the back of church where he found Meg on the verge of tears. "I know," said Clement, "it cheapens what happened last Sunday, in a way. Have faith. If God was the cause of Iris's cures then it will not be long before God makes that clear. Meanwhile, thank God because whether the cause was clear or hidden, it is God that does everything for us and not we ourselves. We are his people and the sheep of his pasture. Without his grace we are nothing." "I know," said Meg, "but it puts us in a difficult position. Are we going to go on coming here to church or should we find a place where the Perpetuans worship?" "You're worshipping God either way. The only difference is that Perpetua gave us some guidance on how to worship more fully and gave us back an enlivened sense of God's presence in Eucharist and sacrifice. No matter what it costs me, I am determined to stay for the time being. Mark will need me at some point and I'm not about to go. I am tempted to seek out the Perpetuans because I am so in tune with what they are doing, but for the time being I will just shut up and get on with it." "If you can, Clement, so can we," said Meg, smiling weakly.

Lady Gowers, in church for a third consecutive Sunday for the first time since it was compulsory at her boarding school, took it for granted that her sharp words to the Bishop had done the trick. The tide of socialism—she tended to classify every possible evil under that broad heading—had been halted and turned. She would begin a campaign for Matins to alternate with Holy Communion. This 'Family Eucharist' had been given a quite unjustifiable monopoly. Having curbed Mark's socialism, she must now curb his Papism. Mark felt the pain but he could do nothing about it—he just had to live with it. He would talk to Clement and Meg in a few days, when things had settled down a little but, in the meantime, all he could do was behave as 'normally' as possible which meant that he behaved totally abnormally. Clement recognised his embarrassment and slipped away as soon as he could. Helen recognised it and saw to it that Mark's temper remained reasonably cool. It was as if Iris had never been cured.

Mark phoned Hilary. "Is this official or personal?" asked Aleford. "Don't be so stuffy, Hilary, it's both. They can't be separated." "I think they can, Mark. You are my very good, personal friend and I think you're a fabulous priest, but as your Bishop I find you very difficult to deal with because of your liberalism." "All right, Hilary, I know. Anyway, I have phoned to say that I won't be resigning or accepting a sabbatical so Bishop James will not be getting a letter from me with my future plans." "What happened, Mark?" "It's the old Saint Stay's pull, Hilary. I live in a permanent tension between my high church practice and my liberal principles, but it's the home and the heart not the brain and the book which ultimately anchor me in my relationship with God." "Admirably put, Mark. Can I tell Bishop James or would you like to do that yourself?" "No, Hilary, I don't want it to seem any bigger than it is. Last week was just a blip. You can tell him." "I will be seeing him tomorrow. It will be a nice surprise at the beginning of the Monday morning meeting."

Aleford, however, did not have the pleasure of breaking this good piece of news to Bishop James. Lady Gowers had established another adult record by attending Evensong at the Cathedral on two consecutive Sundays, leaving a note for the Bishop in the hands of Robertson.

4.

Although Bishop James Hall was, even by his own admission, given to over elaboration, he was never content with pursuing his goals sequentially. Indeed, part of his problem was that he always needed to be pursuing two or more objectives which were frequently partly or wholly mutually incompatible. After reading Lady Gowers' note he resolved to do two things which were logically compatible, but politically opposite. To crush the remaining liberals in the Diocese and to get rid of the Dean. The Bishop phoned Bruce and Hilary on Sunday evening to warn them of his twin resolves and such was the warmth of their welcome that all three anticipated their forthcoming meeting with unaccustomed pleasure. The Bishop was going for goal.

Being theologically trained, they were attracted by the logic, but innocent of the politics of what they planned. Yet they were not entirely naive. Castlegate and Aleford both realised that if they were to succeed in the Bishop's twin aims they would have to overlook their differences. As with the political extremists of the 'right' and 'left' in the middle of the twentieth century, much more united than divided them. Over the issue of women in the Church they had seen this, and for a time it had—as with the Hitler/Stalin pact—symbolised the relegation of all other considerations. They therefore resolved not to allude to their many differences. As this was Simon Taylor's last week as Secretary, they felt that they could dispense with his advice and John Dobson was conveniently on leave. This being so, they only had themselves to please.

"I'm thinking of issuing a Pastoral Letter to be read in all the churches of the Diocese next Sunday." Aleford and Castlegate eyed each other, not wanting to speak first. "I think it is important to set out in detail precisely what action I intend to take and why." It was both the profusion of detail and its lack of precision which frightened the Suffragans. "I wonder," said Aleford, cautiously, "whether such a broad brush approach is what we need." "Perhaps it would be better to pick them off—pardon me, take them aside individually to offer guidance— quietly, one at a time," said Castlegate. "The trouble is that there are too many for that approach. I estimate that about 20% of our clergy are unsound." Castlegate doubled the Bishop's tally of suspects but managed to hold his tongue. "Perhaps," Hilary went on, braver now that he recognised Castlegate's restraint, "if you tackle—offer guidance—to one or two leaders, the others will go back into their shells." "I am not sure whether that is where I want them to go—or should I say stay? It might just be better if they were all brought out of their shells to be seen for what they are." "The problem with that approach," said Castlegate, trying desperately hard not to sound bitter, "is that they were what they are when you agreed to send them for training and then ordained them." The Bishop winced and Aleford twitched. "I think I might have a better idea. As you know, Mark Price and I go back a very long way and although we have had our disagreements at a professional, theological level, we have stayed good personal friends.

Perhaps I should try to persuade him to talk to some of his erstwhile fellow travellers." "Or," said Castlegate, warming to the subject, "we might ask Brian Sedge and people like him from the 'middle ground, to use their influence." "I am well aware that I am often thought of as somewhat untidy in my dealings but on this occasion I think that a grand gesture, a clean sweep, will be much more effective than a piecemeal approach. Private compromises made on my behalf without a clear record of what has been said and agreed will make things worse," said the Bishop, on the verge of tipping from assertion into irritation. Castlegate and Aleford sourly contemplated the prospect of a three-page Pastoral Letter which would anger those who could de-code it and would mystify the rest. They had to keep the conversation going until one of them thought of a bright idea. "I don't suppose it can wait for the clergy get-together—In the Spirit—just after Pentecost?" asked Aleford, knowing perfectly well what the answer would be. "We could do something at Deanery level," said Castlegate, equally alive to the answer. They knew that if they did not get somewhere in the next few minutes they would be lost. Taylor and Dobson generally managed to tone down the worst excesses of the Bishop's pronouncements and without them this strategy was unthinkable. "I know," said Castlegate, suddenly coming to life, "why don't we get all the clergy to sign a declaration of commitment?" "Because," said Aleford, growing suspicious but trying to keep his self-control, "it would be impossible to agree on a text. In any case, they will all argue that they made a full declaration to James at Licensing and have not gone back on it." "Gentlemen," said the Bishop, "remember what we agreed." The two Suffragans subsided into gloomy silence. "Got it!" said the Bishop. "I won't send a Pastoral Letter, I will follow what we might call the 'Sutcliffe strategy'. I will recall the Licenses of all Readers and re-licence when I'm ready. I will do likewise with respect to all the clergy who do not have tenure—not enough in my opinion—and, most importantly, we will draw up a prioritised list of those in tenure whom we suspect and we will divide them up between the three of us, working our way down from the top until the remainder fall into line." "Or we could start at the bottom, with the low hanging fruit, and see how far up we have to get before the rot sets in," said Castlegate. "Clergy who want a move, clergy who want central heating, clergy who—how should I put it?—have records of, er ..." "... Careful!" snapped Aleford. "Pardon me," said Castlegate, "I should have said clergy who owe a particular loyalty to James." "That sounds a little ominous, Bruce, but these are trying times. I will, of course, be careful, Hilary, to see that the gratitude I am owed is not connected with, er, lifestyle issues." "Thank you, James." "So we need to choose between top-down and bottom-up" said the Bishop, "or, given the circumstances, should we not have a little of both." Whether it was prudence or cowardice, Aleford and Castlegate were agreed on starting with the weakest and working their way up. "Bottom-up," they said, almost together. "Very well. Now," said the Bishop, greatly relieved, "how does one get rid of a dean?"

Later that morning, Janet Smythe and Ronald Simpson called at the Rectory. "We are sorry to disturb you as we know how highly you value your Monday mornings at the computer," said Violet, "but we doubt that there is anything more important than what we have come to discuss." They walked past Mark into his study in the nearest thing to bad manners that either had ever shown. They brushed aside the offer of coffee and tea and Mark gave up any idea of easing them into a conversation. "I daresay you know why we have come," said Ronald. "I have a very good idea and I want to begin by saying that I will not tolerate ..." ".... With respect, please wait a moment," said Ronald, "as it might be a question of what we will tolerate." "As the Rector of this Parish, ..." "... Just a moment," said Violet with all the calm authority of her 40 years in teaching, "... this may prove to be very difficult, but it need not be unpleasant. We realise, Father, that you have your job to do and that it is not easy at the best of times; but you in turn need to realise that we, too, have a job to do. Occasionally the different jobs we do bring us into situations of incompatibility." "In which case, I beg to assert that my position as Rector over-rides your ..." "... Not necessarily," said Violet, firmly but without edge. "Forgive me, Father, but your duty as a Priest and our duties as Trustees cannot be ranked in a neat and tidy way. I think in the circumstances it would be better if you were to allow us to say clearly what we need to say. You may even find that it is not so terrible as you imagine."

Ronald looked at his notes. "I don't think we need to go into a long history. We all know how we got where we were on Wednesday of last week. We would like to say, on a personal level, and not as Trustees, that we were somewhat taken aback—and were very sorry—that you made the statement that you did yesterday ... please let me finish ... but we recognise how difficult that must have been for you, so difficult, indeed, that we think it best not to say any more about it, but simply to let you know that you have our sympathy and prayers. We realise, as I have said, that it is for you to decide not only on your own spiritual commitments and allegiances, but you are also responsible for determining and leading the worship of the Parish. Just as you cannot subject your parishioners to an orthodoxy test, neither can you be dictated to by anybody, even a majority. We therefore respect and, although it is technically not for us to accept or reject your decision, we accept it, knowing that you have acted in good faith. Nonetheless, Father, we need to be clear how we stand as Trustees. You will recall that we were advised by Adrian Brooks that the purpose of The Trust is not limited to the physical re-ordering of Holy Trinity and it was for that reason that we were able to make you the offer that we did. Needless to say, now that you have made your decision, you will continue under your current terms and conditions with the Diocese and our funding will no longer be needed." Mark was growing just a little impatient with the speed of the presentation as it seemed to be a series of statements of the obvious. "However," said Ronald (and Mark was aware of the importance of 'howevers') "we are resolved that we do not wish at this time to commit any funding from the Trust to the physical re-ordering of the church as long as there is a possibility that it can be used for spiritual renewal under the auspices of the Perpetuans." "You can't do that." "I am sorry, Father, if we have not been as clear as we should have been," said Violet, "but the point we are trying to make is precisely that we can do that." "But we have agreed all along that the purpose of The Trust was for church re-ordering." "Until the advent of Perpetua we were in complete agreement, it is true, but as Trustees we are obliged by law to spend the funding entrusted to us in the way best suited to meet our legal objectives and we judge at this time that funding a Perpetuan initiative would be closer to the purposes of The Trust than re-ordering a building. It may seem rather petty from your perspective—Rectors are so used to working on the basis of unwritten rules and conventions—but we have never made any formal verbal or written statement committing any of our funding to the church re-ordering."

"Even if I accept your interpretation ..." "... Forgive me, Adrian Brooks' interpretation,..." "... all right, even if I accept Brooks' interpretation, you are still bound to spend the funds of The Trust on the 'renewal of the Church.'" "Yes." "But Perpetuanism isn't 'The Church' it's a heretical sect." "We have considered that point most carefully and even put it to Mr Brooks. The way that our Deed of Trust is drafted is not clear on this point. Nowhere does it mention the Church of England, the Anglican Church or even Christianity. Mr Brooks says that there is enough case law to prevent us from interpreting the Church to mean, for example, the furtherance of Islam or Hinduism, but when we put the specific point to him about Perpetua he said that case law would allow us to make financial contributions to the Unitarians who are Christians, but hold a variant view of the Trinity. We are not, therefore, bound to contribute to an aspect of 'Church' which is Trinitarian. As Perpetuanism is not Trinitarian it therefore stands in the same category as Unitarianism." "But the people who gave you the funding all knew that it was going to be dedicated to the re-ordering of Holy Trinity, that's why they gave it to you." "We understand that. We are under a strong 'moral' and conventional obligation to spend the money in the way that our donors intended. We are the people who have worked for years to assemble this funding. We are not boastful," said Ronald, "but we are very proud of what we have done. But, as you know, the powers of Trustees in this area are enormous and difficult to overturn. Trusts were established initially not as charitable instruments, but as a means for disposing of probate where 'pushy' relatives might try to overturn the wishes of the deceased. We have therefore resolved that we will follow our consciences in this matter, ... please wait ... but we wish to seek your guidance on one point." "Guidance? After all that you have said." "We are trying to be fair. I will be finished in a moment. As I have explained, we are determined to follow our consciences, but we feel that those who have donated funds to The Trust are entitled to an explanation." "I should think so." "But the matter is not so simple as your reaction indicates. If we provide donors with an explanation it will involve setting out the case for Perpetuanism as we see it and, by implication at least, the presentation of an unfavourable comparison with the Church of England as is." "Not necessarily." "I am afraid, Father, that we must disagree. If we provide the explanation to donors to which you think they are entitled it will have to explain our decision and that, in turn, means showing why we think that Perpetuan regeneration is called for."

Being fundamentally fair, Mark saw the logic of what they said, but he neither wanted a public statement that the re-ordering plans were in financial ruins nor did he want people as influential as Violet and Ronald to issue a statement questioning the validity of his ministry. "Have you taken a formal decision on the expenditure?" "No, Father," said Violet. "We wanted to tell you before we formalised anything." "Well, in that case, given our long standing relationship, I would be grateful if you could delay formalising your decision for as long as possible so that I can think through the consequences with the Churchwardens before you issue your statement." "We do not see the need for any hurry, Father. We understand your unhappiness with our decision and we will do all we can to keep this to a minimum."

After they left, Mark yet again compared the glamour of forging a new Perpetuan path against the odds with pursuing his traditional ministry while staying true to his liberal principles, but he only had a few moments as the visit of Violet and Ronald had made him late for a meeting with Clement which he did not relish. Normally when he walked down the High Street he exuded self-confidence and dispensed a feeling of general well being to all who saw him or talked to him. Just as many who were not really frightened of crime wanted to see "bobbies on the beat", many who never went into a church liked to see "The Vicar" up and down the High Street, in the shops, in the school, and at important village functions. They might defraud the Inland Revenue, remove small amounts of office supplies from their places of work, smile and say nothing when they were under-billed in restaurants, and generally elbow their way through life, indifferent to those who suffered from their sharpness, but they expected to have an exemplary vicar who would teach their children the difference between right and wrong.

Clement's office was just past the shops in the High Street. It was, as he explained, a place designed specifically to encourage thinking. The cream and terra cotta walls were decorated with Mondrian, Gorky and Rothcoe prints, the furniture was a miscellany of second hand domestic items including a small dining table where Clement sat, the two metal filing cabinets were hidden and there was a small CD stack with the radio pre-sets on classical frequencies and a neat pile of CD boxes of mostly baroque music. Cheryl, Clement's PA, who particularly liked Mark even though she had no religious feeling, offered coffee which he could not refuse and then indicated that she would leave them alone if they wished.

"This is not easy," said Mark. "I know," said Clement "but spare us both the scenario of the boss firing the worker who says, 'This is hurting me more than it's hurting you' because, all things being equal, on the surface at least, that can't be true as the boss goes on drawing his pay and the worker doesn't. There must be circumstances in which that may be true but I can't readily think of them." "All right, Clement, point taken, but I am genuinely not sure what to say." "Perhaps it would be best not to think too much, but to say what immediately comes to mind." He was about to suggest that Mark might in some way show his sorrow for what had happened, but Clement hated the 'do you love me?' syndrome. If you had to ask somebody to say sorry then they were not genuinely sorry at all. This part of his temperamental composition explains why he was so attracted to Perpetua. He valued decisions which arose from the exercise of the free will and he valued love which came from the same source. "I am afraid that nothing comes very naturally to me, Clement, as you know. As a Priest I am somewhat tied up with the formalities, they keep me anchored, they make me comfortable, they stop my natural tendency towards over reaction getting out of hand. I am not good at spontaneity. This is often taken to mean that I am a stickler with no feelings, but of course all this stickling disguises my shyness." "Quite. I understand." He wanted to tell Mark how much he valued his good opinion of himself but, again, the 'do you love me?' antipathy kicked in. "I don't want you to think that I think I am entitled to an explanation of what you announced on Sunday." "I have no intention of giving you one." "Fine, Mark, but don't be quite so stiff. You're positively bristling in reaction to what I think was a generous gesture. Many people in my position might have felt entitled to an explanation. It says a lot both for the respect in which you are held, but even more so for the open-minded, liberal orientation of many in the Parish, that most of those who are sad at what you have done nonetheless do not feel entitled to an explanation." "True. I am sorry I snapped. Of course, technically, nobody is entitled to an explanation, but it is quite reasonable for people to want one. That isn't my way. The problem is that I'm liberally oriented, but hierarchically trained. I broke away from my Saint Stay's cohort to back women priests, but I still have an ingrained self-image of what it means to be a Priest. I could not stand the Roman dogmatism for a moment, but I am totally comfortable with the Roman view of what it is to be a Priest." "Quite. The liberal outlook is what drove me away from Rome, but I still maintain my Roman attitude to priests. That is why—this is becoming circular—I do not feel entitled to an explanation of what you have done. However, I do not think you came here primarily to discuss your course of action, not least because your starting point is that you are not prepared to explain, to me or anybody else, what you have done." At this point Clement knew that he should move the discussion to his own situation which was the purpose of the meeting but, again, he needed the initiative to come from Mark who momentarily recognised the situation. "I am in a difficult position, Clem." "Oh dear, the boss firing the worker again," Clement thought. "Because, technically, I gave the sermon you gave because you gave it from my pulpit with my sanction." "In secular politics," said Clement, drily, "people expect Ministers to resign when their subordinates make a serious mistake, but I am not pressing for that. I said what I said. I believed I was right to back Hawthorne and you believed that, too. You are entitled to change your mind just as I am entitled not to." "Yes, but I am in an awkward position because Hilary has told me that my decision to stay where I am may not entirely remove the possibility of further action against me for allowing sedition—his word, not mine, you understand—to be preached

from my pulpit." "Setting aside the absurdity of supporting the Archbishop being interpreted as sedition, if I were you I would leave things as they are, keep
a low profile, and say nothing. The text of my sermon is on my web site, as you
know. Let people deal with me. I won't lie by saying that I did not submit my
draft to you for approval, but I won't say that I did unless I am asked. There is
no point both of us suffering for the one act. I've already been fired. They can't
do anything else to me." Again, Clement wanted to go on and explain how hurt
he was, but could not because he needed to be asked. "I am temperamentally
attracted—and theology, being essentially a series of metaphors, is primarily a
matter of temperament—to Perpetuanism, but I will not allow that to obscure
my duty to you until such time as I remove myself from the Electoral Roll. I recognise that as an ordinary member of the congregation my loyalty is not of very
great value"—he longed for Mark to contradict him—"but it's there for what it's
worth." "Thank you," said Mark, just a little stiffly, as he rose to leave. "It's very
difficult trying to balance the need for stability in the Church and the need for
a liberal outlook. I had to decide where the balance lay. I'm sorry you disagree
with me about this, but, there we are." When he had left, Clement was only momentarily sad. He was resigned to the fact that most of the discussions he had
with most people, ostensibly to discuss some aspect of his life or outlook, ended
up being discussions about the other person, Helen being the only miraculous
exception. He had hoped that Mark would say something about the blow he had
suffered in having his role as a Reader terminated, but he had expected nothing. The irony was that when he had applied to be a Reader he had almost failed
to pass because, it had been observed by Hilary, that the interviewers found
it hard, "to discern (his) pastoral heart". Clement reflected that this said more
about their discernment than his heart. He was exacting with those in authority,
but gentle with those in need. As for his relationship with Mark, it had become
almost depressingly predictable. Mark talked, sharing his problems and even
asking for advice now and again, and Clement listened, tentatively giving advice when it was requested. Mark never recognised that the relationship was the
wrong way round and Clement never told him. He was still thinking about this
when the phone rang. "And another thing," said Mark, "which I forgot during
our meeting"—"I wish he would take notes instead of relying on his memory,"
thought Mark. "He's so proud"—"is that you will have to suspend Living Water.
I will not tolerate a heterodox study group." "I wish you had mentioned this
when you were here. I accept that some of our discussion will be heterodox but,
as you know, in a recent session we dismembered the Nicene Creed and decided
that a new one was needed. You can't grow theologically without speculation."
"True, but you are planning to spread heresy under the guise of a Parish house
group." "Mark, just a moment. Firstly, I am planning to continue to teach the ad-
vertised set of modules. Secondly—and I am reluctant to put this so bluntly but
I must—nobody, not even you, can stop me leading a study group. But thirdly,
before you explode, you can withdraw your support, stop advertising it in Parish publications, and take any other measures you think fit." "As Rector of this

Parish ...” “... Mark! Just stop for a moment. Think of what I have said and ring back if you need to.”

Clement briefly considered telling Helen what had happened so that she would be forewarned before Mark saw her, but he concluded that this would be a betrayal of their principle to separate their roles as husband and wife and (ex) Reader and Churchwarden. All that he said when he called her was, “Mark is naturally a little flurried by the consequences of trying to maintain a liberal stance while remaining faithful to his traditional view of church.” “I know,” said Helen “It can’t have been easy. What did he say about your position as Reader?” “We didn’t discuss it.” Helen was going to say, “But I thought that is why he came to see you”, but she stopped short, just in time. If Mark was going to say anything that Clement would value she would have to persuade him to do so, so that it would seem to come from Mark. She would not discuss this any further with Clement. “I know you will be gentle,” said Clement, glad to change the subject from Mark’s pastoral failure, “but be careful not to be totally taken in.” “I’m not a fool.” “You know I don’t think that, but he has shifted so rapidly from one position to another that he may swing too far against the people he was supporting this time last week.” “True. Thanks.”

Mark started off totally on the wrong foot. “First of all, as Rector of this Parish I will not tolerate ...” “... Mark, before you go any further, stop using that tone of voice and that phraseology immediately. Just stop it. I recognise that you are the Rector and I am only a Churchwarden but—even though there was no election—I am an elected official. We have been working together for more than five years; so just stop using that pompous tone and talk to me as the mature adult that I am.” “Sorry, Helen.” “Anyway, what is it that you are—to use that silly phrase—not prepared to tolerate?” “What I meant to say, Helen, is that there may be some problems having a Churchwarden whose husband is of, at the very least, a different churchmanship.” “Mark, that is not the best start to this discussion. First of all, you and I both know that Clement and I are very capable of separating our official roles from our marriage to each other. You know how much we love each other and how we discuss everything, but I have not tried to persuade Clement to moderate his interest in Perpetua and he has not made the slightest attempt to persuade me to follow her. There’s a difference between open dialogue and exerting pressure. Secondly, Clement will not, as you know, use the word ‘churchmanship’ as it is, in his view, anthropocentric.” “True, but I was trying to use the word generously when he might more accurately be described as a heretic.” “It’s a hard word. What did he say when you used it?” “I didn’t.” “That was kind. What did you say to him?” “I told him my position was difficult.” “No, Mark, what did you say to him about him? I’m not asking as his wife, but as Churchwarden. What did you say to a leading figure in our congregation who has been publicly humiliated by his Bishop and has been abandoned by his Priest?” “Putting your rather sharp language to one side, Helen, I said nothing to him.” “But, Mark, for years he has been your out-rider. He has said the things you wanted to say, but could not or would not. He has walked in front of you

and then walked behind you, according to what you wanted. We both know that
Clem should never have been a Reader. We know when you advised him to be
a Reader that you were wrong. He was made to be a theology teacher, but the
Diocese is so inflexible that once you embark on one course, you can't switch
tracks. He has never said a word about this misdirection to anybody but me,
and I am only telling you because in your heart you know it. You had nothing to
say to him?" "I am sorry. I was so bound up in what all this means to me that I
overlooked what it means to him. Will you tell him I am sorry." "No, Mark, I will
tell him nothing. If it comes from me he will think that I have said something
out of kindness on your behalf which you did not say. How often have I to tell
you that he values your good opinion more than anybody else's but mine?" "You
have said that before but you know how much I respect him. Just looking at him
reminds me of all the theology I'm not reading and I am just a little apprehen-
sive of his intellect." "I know, Mark, but no matter how great his intellect he still
needs to feel the love that is the core of your raison d'etre. We ought to assume
that we are loved, to know it simply in our hearts, but we are human and we like
to be told, even what we know we know. I love it when Clem tells me he loves
me. He would love it if you were to tell him you loved him, or at least to thank
him for what he has done, to say that you are sorry how things have worked out.
However, Mark, that is not why you came." "No. I came to ask what you think
we should do at the PCC." "Well, from your point of view, isn't it business as
usual? I mean, you may have been sympathetic to Perpetua—and you were certainly most gracious to Kylie—and you did hold those discussions with Max and
Adrian but they did not amount to anything formal. Bishop James made some
noises but, again, this did not amount to anything formal. I suppose you could
have got away with saying nothing last Sunday but you said what you said." "But
what I need to know is whether it will be hostile?" "What a strange question,
Mark. Ever since you came you have treated the PCC as if it were dynamite.
You hate discussion to a degree which is scandalous for somebody who calls
himself liberal. Nobody dares to suggest anything without knowing in advance
that you will approve of it, except Clement and me. The PCC is generally docile because it doesn't want a taste of your bad temper and because, at the same
time, it happens largely to agree with what you want. More often than not you
waste time arguing, defensively, for something it would let you have on the nod.
You make it unnecessarily difficult for yourself. However,"—Mark shifted in his
seat—"on this occasion there will be problems." "Why?" "Has it not crossed your
mind, Mark, that Ronald or Violet might have talked to me since they talked
to you?" "Well, honestly, I thought that conversation was private." "No, Mark.
Violet and Ronald were courteous enough to tell you first what they needed
to tell the Churchwardens and, in turn, the PCC. In wondering whether you
intended to withhold the burden of their message from Joel, me, and the PCC,
I will give you the benefit of the doubt. However,"—he shifted again—"there
are a number of members of the PCC who would be only too happy to resign.
Firstly, some think that the meetings are a complete waste of time because you

hate debate. Secondly, there are some who are genuine followers of the new Perpetuan movement who were galvanised by what happened to Iris. Thirdly, there are some who will follow Violet and Ronald because of the respect in which they are held. Finally, there are some who only joined the PCC to put through the re-ordering. When they see it isn't going to take place as soon as they had hoped, there will be nothing for them to do." "What is your estimate?" "I think that well over half will resign." "What about Clement?" "I have deliberately not asked him, but I suspect that he will attend this meeting simply to answer any questions put to him about his situation and to resign formally. He's only *ex officio* as a Member of the Great Synod but I suspect he will prefer not to turn up in future." "In which case I will have to use the spaces for co-optees to bring in Maurice Walmbury and Lady Gowers." "I don't see how either of us can possibly work with them." "Needs must." "Whose needs?" "The Parish will need new blood and, given the situation of the Trust, it will need the kind of money that only Maurice can command." "I wish us both luck of it, Mark." "You mean you will stay?" "Of course I will. I took an oath in the presence of the Archdeacon." "Thank you, Helen." "It's all right, Mark. As long as I can maintain my loyalty to Clement and to you without completely tearing myself apart, that is what I will do."

On Tuesday Clement went to London to see Max Silver. "I suppose you have heard that our Priest, Mark Price, has performed a somersault?" "Well, I've heard, but as he's ended up in precisely the opposite position from that in which we found him six days ago, it isn't a somersault, unless, of course, you take his starting position to be somewhere before the death of Perpetua. In that sense he has performed a somersault. ... Just joking, Clement. ... Yes, we have heard what has happened." "What is so funny?" "Nothing at all, really but, contrary to all the theory of Marx, the planning of Lenin, and the hyperbole of Mao Tse Tung, you can't organise, timetable, and regulate a revolution. They just don't work that way. If you had told Voltaire what Robespierre would end up doing, he would have been appalled. Likewise, if you had told Jesus what Constantine would do, he would have been appalled. It only took Luther a few years to get from the Theses on the door to the Peasants' Revolt. So, if I am laughing at all it is because at least I accept that what happens in the next few months will be unpredictable. Believe it or not, Our Sister the Spirit does not check in with me on an hourly basis. People will be moved to follow and then they will change their minds. There will be fanatics with us, fanatics against us, waverers, and pacifiers. Bishops will proclaim, bishops will obfuscate, priests will see visions and priests will see blackness. I could go on but you get the picture. I might give you the opening lines of Dickens' *A Tale of Two Cities*, but I am sure you know them. The first thing you learn about banking and God is that control is illusory. Have you ever noticed how you give up your hard earned money to men—it's mostly men—who decide what to do with it not on the basis of rational analysis, but on the basis of 'sentiment'? As a rational person yourself you should resent that. You should expect your money to be disposed of by people with better analytical skills than you have yourself, but the market is a place of bears and bulls, of greed and fear, of the macro and the micro, of the butterfly wing and the terrorist strike, of frost in brazil and a volcano in Indonesia. In other words, banking is an interesting meta-scenario for theology. Perhaps that's why I have come to like theology. It's all about confidence and metaphor. The substance is beyond our reach." "Very good," said Clement, impressed by the grandeur and the precision of the analogy. "But that does not help me to work out what to do in Walmbury." "Clement, you are an estimable theologian, so I am told by people who ought to know. Your Tutor at Prince's College where you studied, I gather, alongside Damian who works for Smoother, said that you demonstrated remarkable flexibility while maintaining a central core of postulates. Be that as it may, what I am saying is that in a sense that is central to both banking and theology there isn't much you can do other than behave like a rational, prudential person. Do what you think is wise, but do not expect this to determine events. They will, ultimately, determine you. That is the essence of understanding the relationship between God Our Parent and the created. If Our Sister the Spirit wants your Father Mark to be a follower of Perpetua she will sort it out, but God won't fix what he gave us the capacity to fix." "So is there nothing I can do?" "For a theologian and a philosopher you are remarkably restless. Do what you normally do. One, assume everything is to the good unless there is evidence to the contrary. Pessimism is as bad a planning error as optimism. Two, don't pretend to agree to anything you disagree with. Tree, don't confuse theology and earthly reality. A piece of granite is a piece of granite but the Holy Trinity is a metaphor. Four, don't pretend that you can plan your way into or out of what is happening—Our Sister the Spirit is mightily active at the moment. Five, consequently, don't be downhearted by apparent reverses. If we only gain untried converts it will be like the seed sown on stony ground. We are going to need some helpers who have suffered for their convictions. I daresay that neither you nor I really believe in the kind of spiritual realisations which cause thousands in stadiums to confess their shortcomings and to swear undying allegiance to a God who is more like an inexhaustible ATM. I don't think either of us holds with that kind of religious outlook." "I understand that, but is there anything I should be doing?" "Live normally. Follow the simple rules I have just set out. Most important of all, remember what Perpetua said about love. The mission of the liberal and the Perpetuan—which is why so many of the former are becoming adherents of the latter—is that you are there to create space for others, not credit for yourself. You might make life happier for a neighbour, but the important thing is that the neighbour feels liberated in the space you have made, not trapped because he is obliged to thank you for what you made for him." "I can see that," said Clement, "but I live in a real community of real people who will ask me what to do." "Tell them to pray and wait just as the Apostles prayed and waited between the Ascension of Jesus and the coming of Our Sister the Spirit. I have no hard evidence of what is to happen—how could I?—but Dexter believes that the key moment will occur at Pentecost. He is planning to launch Perpetuanism officially on that day. But, one more thing, Clement, banking and God are very difficult to get hold of, but everybody knows what they are all about. The central concept is confidence. Bankers call it that but theologians call it faith. Never mind. Live in faith. Go on doing the simple things. Be meticulous; good bankers and good theologians are meticulous; flamboyant bankers and theologians are dangerous." "What good is all that to Walmbury?" "Not a lot, but to you it is invaluable. This is the Perpetuan equivalent of the Gethsemane request to watch and pray."

The PCC was even more tense than usual. Mark asked if there was any other "urgent" business of which he should have been notified by noon that day. Nobody said anything and he was about to move on when Violet Smythe said, "As this is the slot for discussing the content of the Agenda, I am somewhat surprised that you have not revised it since it was first published last week. Obviously, it is not for me to choose the timing of any discussion of major changes of policy by the PCC. It is for you to decide, but I cannot sit here knowing what I know and pretend that I don't know." "Procedure," said Mark, stiff and limp at the same time. "I think this is a moment for being flexible," continued Violet. "If we can put AOB on the Agenda until noon on the day of the Meeting, so can you. You may be relying on tradition or your personal preference, but it isn't procedure. Well, Mark, if you won't, I will." "I would prefer to place an item on the Agenda in my name. I propose to add an item of business entitled 'Update'." Everyone agreed. Violet felt weary and under-valued. Mark must have known she would have to do something if he did not. As if nothing had happened, they ground through the routine business, listening to long reports and Mark's comments and saying next to nothing. Helen tried to lighten the atmosphere during her report by making some modest suggestions about children and church but Mark slapped her down brutally saying that that was nothing to do with the PCC. The Rector alone dealt with worship. Helen went on bravely and the Sunday School and Toddlers Group leaders both wondered why they bothered with the PCC. At last, at 9.43 p.m. they came to AOB which was introduced with the comment: "We don't have long for this as I like meetings to end at 10 p.m. precisely. I just want to say that the Church Renewal Trust has informally indicated to me that it is likely to withdraw its offer of funds for church re-ordering and, at my request, Miss Hurst and Mr Simpson have agreed that they will delay the announcement of that decision for as long as they possibly can. Any questions?" There was total, resentful silence and Mark was almost resolved to close the Meeting with the Grace when Clement said, "I am not sure how wide you intend your update to be. Your introduction simply mentioned the funding of the re-ordering. The PCC knows that I have lost my position as a Reader, but although I can stay on as *ex officio* I will not. It is only a matter of time before my presence makes it more difficult for Father Mark to do what he needs to do." "We will therefore put on record our thanks to Clement for all he has done," said Mark. "Do you mean that you are taking it lying down?" asked Clarence Ford, an old timer. He hated Mark and his Roman and liberal ways and, in consequence, he did not care for Clement's sermons, but he was a strong believer in Parish autonomy and didn't like "those people at Church House always taking our money and giving us nothing back but trouble." "As I understand it," said Mark, "Clement's withdrawal of Licence was simply a harbinger. They are all being withdrawn." "A purge," said Marie, who usually limited herself to choir items. "That, if I may say so, Marie, is disrespectful." "As a Member of this PCC I'm called upon to be faithful and truthful, not respectful." There was another awkward silence until Meg said, "In view of my commitment to what happened to Iris, I feel it is only right for me to resign." Mark was about to make his customary statement about recording appreciation when Violet said, "And you will not be surprised at my resignation." The two young women who ran the Sunday School and Toddler Group took the opportunity to resign after their snub, using Perpetua as an excuse. "In which case, you will have to resign your positions." "We were chosen by our groups," they said, "not by you." "I will have to look into that," said Mark. "We can't have heresy being taught to our little ones." "We will teach what we have always taught. We can always do the basics and leave parents to decide if their children need extra tuition in Perpetuanism. Anyway," said one, almost cockily, contemplating freedom from the Sunday morning grind of more than five years, "you try finding somebody else." While this was going on, Marie was balancing her loyalty to the Choir with her strengthening commitment to Perpetua following a couple of long evenings with Kylie. "I am resigning," she said, "because I know others in the Choir can represent it perfectly well." Mark was beginning to panic and he looked at Helen for support. "I am sorry that I did not warn any of you earlier," said Joel, "but the news from The Trust means that my role in the re-ordering is at an end. I will write a letter of resignation tomorrow." "I am staying," said Helen, "in spite of all the turbulence, I feel it is my duty to support Mark. We try not to mix our church and personal lives and I deeply appreciate Clement's commitment to support me as long as I stay. His loss of Licence was between the Bishop and him, and he does not see how Father Mark could have done anything to prevent it." This statement did not stop a couple more resignations. Mark then formally proposed the co-option of Lady Gowers and Maurice Walmbury; he would take advice on how to proceed to fill the other places and the vacant post of Churchwarden. By the time that he said the Grace at 10.37 p.m. he had one Churchwarden, a Treasurer, five PCC Members and the prospect of two co-options. When he went home in a very grim mood, Jane did not help. Although she loved him "to pieces" in her own phrase and would do anything to support him, she would never do anything in the short term that would make his long term suffering worse. "You have had a very tough night, Mark, I know, but you would have been better off losing the lot. I know Helen is a good soul, but the steady influence of Clement will turn her in the end. I know you think that the Treasurer is there just to do the books but Douglas is very much in cahoots with Ronald Simpson. There is bound to be trouble there." "Yes dear," said Mark, half wearily, half ironically, but he knew that the rump of the PCC, all hanging, flogging Prayer Book and Tory Party, would give him a difficult time unless he could find some liberals who were not inclined towards Perpetua. In other words, unless he could find people who shared his peculiar duality.

Brian Sedge could not be indifferent to the disturbances in Walmbury as it was one of only two churches in its Rural Deanery that paid more than its Parish Contribution, not quite balancing the Deanery's books, but rendering them acceptably close to the top of the Diocesan league. He had heard a rumour that South Whortling with Brig and Browncoombe was thinking of seceding to Perpetua but as it had an Electoral Roll of 42 and a loss which accounted for more than half of the Deanery's woes, he proposed to do very little about it. His main priority was to ensure that Walmbury survived as a financially and spiritually viable community, giving strength to the Deanery as a whole. It would have been nice if he had a Rural Dean to do the heavy lifting, but there was a vacancy nobody wanted to fill.

"I see," he said to Mark when they met on the Friday morning after the PCC, "that you have co-opted Lady Gowers and Maurice Walmbury. I doubt you will be as happy with that in a month as you are now. The problem is that you can't co-opt any more people, and if you have either a substantial byelection or a completely new election, those who have resigned, and their supporters, still being on the Electoral roll, will have the right to vote." "They might not bother." "I agree, but I don't think we can take any risks. I am going to ask Hilary to use his special powers to appoint a Churchwarden and the remainder of the PCC until the next due election in just under a year from now." "But, Brian, they will all be BCP stuffed shirts." "I am afraid, Mark, that that is one of the prices you have to pay for staying where you are. You will have a few days to draw up a list for Hilary to approve."

A week later the new PCC met under a special power of the Bishop. It could not have been more different from Mark's previous PCC. Where Clarence had been an almost lone voice stirring up trouble, made completely ineffective by the lack of support from other quarters, the new PCC almost completely comprised Clarences with hives of bees in their bonnets. Mark, Helen and even Clement had tried to find 'moderates' who could, in good conscience, join the PCC but the two universal rules of commitment applied. The more extreme, the more committed, the more committed, the more active. Whereas the Church of England in general was constituted of a theological spectrum from Petran at one end to Toran at the other, the flexibility of the human outlook and the ownership of cars meant that parishes were points on that spectrum rather than being microcosmic reproductions of it. In villages where there was no choice of Parish Church there might be some minor tensions over doctrine, but where there were differences these were largely represented by different attitudes to the worship on offer. People who might have been Torans, had they troubled themselves with theology, were pro BCP and against a Eucharistic monopoly. People who might have been Petrans, had they thought about it, were in favour of a Eucharistic monopoly and the Reservation of the Sacrament. The majority were not particularly bothered as long as neither faction gained a complete victory. Meanwhile, as the children's leaders frequently observed, this dispute about worship did not take into account the needs of the young. Their pleas for child friendly worship were invariably greeted with indulgence and indifference. Never mind that the Eucharist was solid food when they needed milk and that the BCP was totally incomprehensible, even to a teenager with an English GCSE, that was where the battle lines were drawn.

The first sign of change was that the Eucharist, which was an integral part of the meeting, was only attended by Helen and Douglas, but as soon as it was finished, bar the Blessing, the new members all came piling in, talking loudly and making jokes like the winners of a school sports day. Mark had hardly finished the formalities when Clarence began: "As this agenda, under the Bishop's Special Powers, allows us to discuss anything material to the good health of the worship of God in this Parish, I move that Sunday Matins be re-instated." Mark had anticipated that this would happen in due course but not at the first meeting. In spite of its monastic origin, he loathed Matins because it symbolised Protestantism and a breach of Eucharistic monopoly. "The motion is out of order," he snapped. "How so?" replied Clarence. "Because the form of worship is in the sole control of the Rector." "I understand that. I've been on this PCC long enough to know your attitude, Padre"—Mark squirmed at the terminology— "but your right to determine does not limit our right to propose." "Well, you can propose all you like, but I will not tolerate interference ..." "... I think we better get a complete picture of our respective, er, positions, before you decide what you can and cannot, will and will not, tolerate, Padre." "I second Clarence's motion," said Lady Gowers. "In due course," said Mark, trying to calm down, "but first we are called upon to recognise the Bishop's appointment of Maurice as Churchwarden with Helen until the next Annual Meeting." "Agreed!" they all shouted, anxious to get on with their own business. Helen had tried to dissuade Mark from the appointment, but without any success. Mark was that kind of socialist who had a profound respect for gentility in general and private education in particular. He therefore liked Maurice Walmbury and thought they would all get on very well. Helen, whose commitment to social justice was less confusedly dogmatic and more practical, thought that a Churchwarden from the big Tudor mansion at the edge of the village gave all the wrong signals and harked back to a previous age when the Walmburies thought they should be Churchwardens by right in perpetuity. She did not think that Maurice would be interested in the social housing but, then, she added out of fairness, none of us has been, not really. She had talked with Clement about how to act at the PCC and he had advised her to say as little as possible at the first meeting to see how the different individuals and groups would behave. She could not support Mark effectively until she knew where her allies were but, like Mark, they had not expected an immediate onslaught. "It's worse than the Tory Party in full cry," she thought, feeling sorry for Mark, feeling sorry for herself, and feeling sorry for Clement who had been at every PCC she had attended. "As we were saying," said Lady Gowers, once Mark had been rudely hurried through the formalities by a series of shouts of assent and even some table banging, "the motion before us is the reinstatement of weekly Matins. I take it that we are all of one mind on this issue?" "No," said Helen, followed by Douglas. "We are not entirely of one mind." "Well, in that case, we will have to vote," said Lady Gowers with that unique blend of tartness and sweetness otherwise known to cheap perfume and fake Chinese cuisine. Mark tried to take control but failed. "All those in favour?" asked Lady Gowers. "And against? Well, that is clear enough, only three against and one abstention. What's next on our list, Clarence?" "Following on from that vote, I move that any plans for re-ordering approved in the past three years be re-submitted to this Council for re-consideration." "But that is academic," said Mark, "because you know as well as I do that the Church Renewal Trust has withdrawn its support." "But that does not apply to the first phase, for which you have a Faculty and we have the money, to construct a permanent nave altar and to move the font to the front of the church." Mark almost groaned aloud. "We could go through a lot of formal nonsense," said Lady Gowers, "but the long and the short of it is that we don't want this new fangled arrangement, it's Popish and populist. We want the high altar for the Lord's Supper stipulated by Cranmer." "But he didn't stipulate what we've got now," said Mark. "The high altar was built by the Victorians whereas Cranmer wanted roughly the kind of table I want but I simply want it further forward." "We don't like having to stand to receive Communion," said Clarence. "It's irreverent." "But nobody is forcing you to stand under the new arrangement, you have the choice." Then Clarence uttered the death knell of Mark's hopes for a way of accommodating widely divergent views. "If it's irreverent, it's irreverent. It can't be irreverent for me and reverent for somebody else." Helen looked at Mark with deep sadness and pity. She could see that he had recognised the price he was having to pay. For more than three hours they ran the meeting almost regardless of him, with Helen being the only constant vote against their proposals. She spoke little. She saw no point in it. There was nothing to be said. They worked through their list of conservative measures and when Mark showed any sign of opposition they made it clear that if he stood in their way they would complain to the Bishop or resign, whichever he cared for least. When it came to major re-ordering, they confirmed their opposition but agreed to start a fund, under Maurice's patronage, to restore the ancient stained glass, Victorian pews, and Medieval font in particular, and in general to restore the Church to its Victorian glory under the impression, which was the only detail that gave Mark bitter pleasure, that they were fulfilling Cranmer's wishes.

The Family Eucharist for the Fifth Sunday of Easter apparently went like clockwork, but it was flat. The Matins party, promised satisfaction on the following Sunday, stayed away and the Eucharist-centred part of the Parish, being liberal rather than Petran, attended, but without enthusiasm. At the end of the service Mark announced the changes. "From next week, the beginning of May, we will be starting a new worship schedule: on First Sundays there will be a BCP Holy Communion at eight followed by our usual child-friendly Eucharist; on Second and Fourth Sundays there will be a Common Worship said Eucharist at eight followed by BCP sung Matins at 9.45 a.m.. On Third and Fifth Sundays there will be an eight o'clock BCP said Matins with a 9.45 sung Common Worship Eucharist. I have also been asked by the PCC to consider the role of Evensong." Mark could hardly believe what he was saying. He had abandoned Perpetua to preserve his Eucharist-centred personal spiritual life and his priestly ministry and he had ended up with this. Clement saw the irony of a greater potential role for a Reader now there was no Reader. Marie weighed up the musical balance but found the occasional Morning Canticles would not make up for the loss of Eucharistic music, but the institution of choral evensong would. Scott was slightly more comfortable with the days before Eucharistic monopoly. Nigel had seen it all before and had wondered whether he would live long enough to see it all again. Helen felt the different tensions in Mark and Clement and knew they needed each other precisely at the time when they were drifting apart. They had never been close in a conversational way although they spent official and social time in each other's company, but knowing they had each other had been vital to the well being of each. Helen could feel that quasi-telepathy breaking down.

Fissures began to appear in every aspect of Parish life. The Mothers' Union, a long-time, low key bastion of the Torans, apt to pay less attention than it should to the position and views of its Rector, had tolerated liberals on the basis that numbers were really what counted. After Mark's announcement of the new schedule, the MU leader, Martha Prate, told Veronica that those who were not happy with the new arrangements would not be welcome. "We have compromised for too long," Martha said, "but with the Church under threat from all kinds of liberals with their pagan ideas on drugs, sex and medicine, we need to take a firm line." A similar, but less dogmatic, rupture took place in the Over 60s Club where who sat next to whom was always a marker of fashion and falling out. There were hard words and frosty silences for the parents of those who were termed "traitors" although they had nothing to do with the views of their children. The Choir might have gone the same way but Scott's easy manner and Marie's stern discipline combined to keep it together. "Their job was to lead whatever worship the Rector determined", said Marie, with Scott looking on amiably. "We survived the ASB, the onslaught of happy clappy songs and the First Sunday crisis, and we will survive this. We have Morning Canticles to learn and there is the prospect of new Anthems that we will not have heard at the Eucharist to go with Readings, and maybe even Evening Canticles. There will be fewer sung Eucharists and so we will have to make them special occasions."

Brian Sedge, watching from his Archdiaconal lookout, saw Parishes disintegrating, with factions pulling away from each other. Even before the Bishop began the exercise he had discussed with his Suffragans, the disease of disunity was spreading. He was by no means a venal man, but he could not help seeing the financial disaster confronting his patch and the whole Diocese. He did not believe that the contributions of those who left would be matched by greater contributions from the triumphalists who stayed. His experience told him that the well off were rich because they were mean and that they invariably exaggerated their contributions because they thought these should be seen to accord with their status. People who were against taxation and criticised charities for spending too much on administration (while expecting a thank you letter for the smallest donation) also wanted their church on the cheap.

In the absence of a Diocesan Secretary, Brian phoned John Dobson. "It is bad enough now, John, without the special initiative to enforce what Bishop James calls 'orthodoxy'. Last year the Walmbury Rural Deanery more or less broke even, with a strong showing from liberal parishes supporting some small, traditional churches, but this year we are facing—I don't want to exaggerate— something close to meltdown. We will certainly be in deficit even if this current bout of trouble is brought to an end immediately." "I know, Brian, but Bishop James is set on his campaign, particularly as he has the support of Bruce and Hilary. I will try to talk with him again, but I fear that, after being in the 'centre of the park' for so long, he now has the goal in his sight. The only thing we can hope for—and it's a bleak hope in itself—is that he spends more time worrying about the Dean and leaves the Parishes to get on with handling the current situation as best they can."

Brian Sedge's analysis was borne out by the second emergency meeting of Mark's new PCC, which took place a week after the first. Mark had said Eucharist in church for Clement and himself before they parted, saying nothing by mutual consent. Learning from the previous week, Mark hurried through the formalities before handing over to Douglas who showed a graph of the rise in giving during the Lent Initiative and its fall since some commitments had been withdrawn completely. On his projections the Parish income from giving would be halved in the current financial year, leaving a deficit greater than the reserves deposited with the Diocesan Board of Finance. Without a very special effort to increase giving, the Parish would no longer be viable. The news was greeted with complete silence. Mark, looking round the table, recognised that these people might just make a donation to restore the stained glass if there was an accompanying board listing donors, but they would not commit themselves to anonymous, regular, high level giving. The Treasurer went on calmly to discuss aspects of liability as it related to charity law, and although the likelihood that they would be held responsible for what had gone wrong was highly improbable, even a distant threat was too unsettling for them to bear. Lady Gowers said that she would be forced to resign because she had not been informed of the true financial situation when she had agreed to serve. Clarence had no such excuse, but resigned anyway, to be followed by all the rest, including Maurice, leaving Douglas and Helen. Without any serious business being transacted, or previous decisions reversed, the meeting brought itself to a sudden end. Mark gave a sad Blessing and within a minute was left alone with Helen, Douglas hurriedly explaining that he would have to do some more work on the figures before reporting to the Rural Deanery Treasurers Group.

"Poor you," said Helen. "It's all unravelling. You have tried your best to keep yourself and everything together, but it just can't be kept, can it?" "I hardly know.

For years I have lived with this inner contradiction, but it has become horribly external. It's like watching the two parts of me fighting each other in a militaristic way. When it's inside me I can deal with it. I know the rhythms of the contest, the ebb and flow, the way I make peace with myself. But I have no control of this external battle. I should have known better. I thought perhaps that liberals would not behave like liberals, that they would offer some kind of counterbalance to the conservatives, but I should have known that liberals don't do that. They stand up for pluralism, they make space in which they are then massacred by conservatives. With so many good liberal friends fighting alongside me—if a liberal can be given a military metaphor—I forgot how ruthless conservatism is. I thought it would take them weeks to sort themselves out, but they are natural hunters, attacking the weak, avoiding the strong. They sorted me out before I knew what was going on." "But now they have gone, Mark, what are we to do?" "Well we must do the formal things like talking to the Archdeacon and Hilary— even James if he wants to say something—but as to the fundamental question, I don't really know. I would like you to talk to Clement about it." "No, Mark, no matter how difficult it is for the two of you, I am not going to carry messages. Without knowing it, I would put Clement's language into what you asked me to tell him and your language into what he asked me to tell you. I would be making the weather instead of reporting it. I'm incapable of carrying a straight message because I want you to reach an accommodation. I knew it would sometimes be difficult working with you, because you are such a strong character, but at the moment you are lurching between apparently strong forces. You have to settle your own position before you are properly fit to negotiate. I say the same thing to Clement. He is suffering from a very serious episode of near depression, a lack of self-confidence. He thinks—and I would not say this to anybody else— that you have failed him pastorally when he has been so faithful to you." "I have done my best, Helen, given the situation I am in. Aren't you in danger of carrying the messages you said you would not carry?" "That was a message about my beloved husband not about settling the current crisis in the Parish. Clement is your parishioner. I would carry a call for pastoral care from any of your parishioners. Don't confuse doctrinal disputes with people. You can be as hard as you choose over your precious theology, but when it comes to people you need to learn a little more gentleness."

She walked out of the room, both of them wondering whether she would be the next to resign, leaving Mark alone.

5.

After his licence had been withdrawn, Clement's desolation manifested itself in carefulness. Like a drunk who knows he is drunk, the worse he became, the more care he took but, unlike the drunk, this was not a piece of self-deception. It kept his outward surface calm so that only Helen knew how he was suffering. He would not lie about his state of mind but this presented no problem because he was never seriously asked. His close friends and even his most intimate friends had fallen into the habit of talking while he listened, the silent confessor who never said a harsh word or handed out a penance. He was less constructive than Helen, but more perceptive because he never read his own wishes into the situations of those to whom he listened. Although he sometimes slipped from a state of perfect, exterior calm, he never forgot the teaching of Jesus that those who fast should spruce themselves up and eschew the outward appearance of piety. His private witness was internal. He was dogged rather than heroic, pedestrian rather than extravagant, occasionally self-pitying, but never bad tempered. He did not work faster nor much harder than usual, but ensured that his waking time was carefully apportioned so that he could work fruitfully. His office was a godless bastion so that he was most comfortable there, working along customary lines and sharing the small triumphs and setbacks, humour and friction, of the working day. He had to be more careful at home where his time was split between a small portion of news programming and a large portion of Bible reading, theological study, and writing. It was during these periods that he was most prone to becoming desolate. Although he would hardly have mentioned his hardship if he had found a congenial person, the core of his trouble was that he had nobody to talk with other than Helen and he was always careful, in spite of their marriage vows, never to go deeper than was required by the necessity of letting her know that he was not indifferent to his situation. He imagined conversations with bishops, spiritual directors, priests, theologians, philosophers of religion, professors, and even historical figures, but these always ended with the ringing of the phone, the ping of an incoming email, the lurch of the dishwasher, or simply a slight shift in the balance of his internal and external consciousness. In spite of his awareness of internal debilitation, he still had a great deal of strength in reserve. Being an Aristotelian rather than a Platonist, an anomaly in his Cambridge days which he had enjoyed flaunting, he was less prone to introspection and disillusion than his contemporaries. When they had been lauding Marx and Mao, on the back of thinkers they hardly knew, leading back to Plato (Rousseau and Descartes in particular), he was immersed in the alternative tradition, as he saw it, of Aquinas, Kant and Maritain. During his studies he developed a deep attachment to the writing of John Rawls. He thought that thinking could solve problems and that the essence of creativity was that the whole was more than the sum of the parts. Consequently, he was not easily thrown into despair nor projected into elation. Meticulousness was more important than vision, which is why he now referred to himself—not really joking—as a "visionary bureaucrat". One example of his coping strategy was the way in which he tackled his weekly task of polishing the north choir stalls. From the outset, he had established an elaborate schedule of work which involved a complete application of polish every four weeks, with a rotation of applications in the other three, except for the book rests and the stall ends, but now he abandoned the rotation and performed the complete application every week, spending even more time than previously on Marie's area because of the respect he bore her as leader. It had often been put to him that his time would be better spent reading or writing but he said that he was not entitled to be a theologian or a teacher if he did not undertake some manual work. At the end of each session he polished a small book stand which stood beside the President's Chair, starting on its flat surface and finishing with its cross. He was especially careful with this because it was Mark's. It was the only thing he could do for him now. Except for common politeness, their words had ebbed away into their mutual and individual desolations, but it was so intrinsic to Clement's character that he should be particularly careful to give as much lustre to Mark's book stand as he could, that no amount of self-knowledge, with which he was greatly gifted, could help him to see that he was over-compensating. Sacrifice was private, careful and caring, for all the Protestant caricatures of Roman Catholic flamboyance, his upbringing had been in an environment of meticulousness, patience and humility. The Virgin might be processed through the streets and the fields on an occasion of joy, but she was nonetheless quietly revered in the Rosary and the Novena. Thus, Clement's habits of mind and worship, the combination of nature and nurture, temperament and cultivated sensibility, had prepared him for the course of action he must take. He had been schooled in penance and sacrifice. He knew that to be a true witness there must be suffering. The exercise of conscience not only was not, but should not be cost free. There was nothing of the hair shirt nor the martyr, and in spite of his occasional lapse into self-pity, the object of suffering was the glory of God and the practical commission of charitable and noble deeds. Again, this was so ingrained that he did not like people to find him at his polishing. God knew what he did and that he never shirked the nooks and crannies that humans could not see. Yet he knew as the days went by, that his efficiency was declining. His application never failed, but his output became stilted. He was not a Mozart whose life-affirming fluency never faltered during his periods of private grief. In his writing, Clement sadly surveyed the falling off of his fluency and the narrowing of his vocabulary, the constriction of his syntax and the loss of his easy, graceful style which was sometimes too elaborate, but which was never ponderous nor terse. Conversely, his reception of cultural fuel became more acute, particularly with respect to his twin mainstays of Bach—his wife, he had once joked—and Mahler—his mistress. Without apparently paying any greater attention, he was conscious of counterpoint he had overlooked, a harpsichord decoration, a distant cackling of woodwind. The pathos of structure was complemented by the pathos of detail so that he could no longer bear to continue his invariable adult habit of never working without music in the background. Now it was Bach and Mahler, or work, but never both. Before long this had an effect on his output which he tried to overcome by working for the same number of hours in addition to his listening, but that began to have a serious effect on his never very restful sleep. After less than a week he began to see how these trends would steepen a descent into exhaustion but he could not see how to avoid what he knew must happen. At the very heart of his dilemma was an inability to determine God's will for him. He had to be ultra careful not to react to his rejection for ordination by seceding too easily to Perpetuanism—it would be wrong to go to her on the rebound—but he thought he had felt a genuine call to service in this renewed—he hardly dared, even to himself, to use the term "post Christian"—context. His prayer was confused on the point of the Godhead. He sometimes prayed to the Trinity when reading from his prayer book and sometimes to the Four Persons when he was extemporising. This brought a disturbing degree of instability in spite of his years of training in the fundamentals of prayer. He knew that if he lost his prayer life, his personal relationship with God, that he was lost. He knew that to be a creature was to be in a relationship with the Creator. What mattered was not the consistency of the doctrine about God but the consistency of the dialogue with God. Inevitably, the dialogue grew thinner as he began to doubt the validity of his own experience. He began to think that there was a widening gulf between what he taught and what he did himself. He could speak eloquently of prayer, but as his eloquence increased, the richness of his prayer life diminished. One compensation was that he spent less time thinking about his coherence and more time thinking about his brokenness. He had always been aware of it as a fundamental theological tenet, but he had never felt it in himself. As the dialogue dwindled into doggedness, he increasingly felt more broken. It was not that his faith diminished, but that it grew more visceral, more absolute, more stark. Although his outer means seemed unimpaired, his inner means disintegrated. There was himself and God. His brokenness became powerlessness. He must wait for an intimation, a sign, a word, an opening.

Mark had never been in doubt of his brokenness which, like the colour of his eyes, was the product of nature, not nurture and, being so, it was the foundation of his temperament which nurture built upon. He knew from his early childhood that he was deeply flawed in ways which he could hardly define and that the response to this lay in prayer and penitence. Perhaps, too, he was more comfortable with this way of being because it was a reaction to his Rector father who was an easy-going, mildly academic, Christian positivist who had never shaken off the Christian Socialist optimism which had illumined his pleasant years at Oxford at a time when F.D. Maurice and Charles Gore still influenced some idealist secular thinkers as well as Christian students and ordinands. As a teenager he rebelled against that optimism which had been run into the ground in Auschwitz and the Gulags. Although as a student he enjoyed the self-indulgences of the late 1960s, he never saw them as anything but that. He did not believe that if you took all your clothes off and made love in public as well as in private that wars would cease. He did not even believe that the general explosion of benign platitude would make any difference. There was a lot to be said for the contraceptive pill, The Beatles, rising middle class incomes and more easily available higher education, but he did not believe these would alter the condition of mankind. He was confirmed in this during his theological studies by a deep attachment to the thesis of Donald Mackinnon—which was closely related to the views of his friend George Steiner—that the history of the Church was one of tragedy. This did not make him a pessimist, it simply drove him to be more aware of his imperfections and to be more penitentially attentive. As with most people, his psychological composition was a mixture of homage and reaction to his father such that his obsession with detail was as ingrained as his brokenness. That obsession, a very special kind of meticulousness, governed the whole of his life and outlook. In spite of his respect for Roman reform after Vatican II on the one hand and his Catholic dislike of the Book of Common Prayer on the other, he occupied a liturgical space which his congregation described as "bells but no smells" about which he was fastidious. The latest events had not only robbed him of his control of the composition of the liturgy, he felt in danger of losing his ability to render each act as a perfectly shaped offering to God. His whole life had been built on a fastidious control of his clerical life. Whatever emotional, spiritual, and intellectual currents altered the way he thought about God and the Church, the constant which made that change viable was his ability to frame a perfect liturgy to match the tenor of what he held to be true. Vatican II was theologically sound but liturgically sloppy whereas the BCP was theologically suspect but liturgically sound. Between these two extremes he managed to fuse a deeply liberal theology with a deeply Catholic liturgy. He did not enjoy theological controversy and so his views were largely private. His basic sentiment was that most things that were good enough for Hawthorne were good enough for him. As the days went by, after the Gowers coup, the lack of control resulted, as it always did, in an equally disturbing disruption of his routine. He found the scaffold of his clerical life shaking as he started to undertake tasks which he then realised were now redundant. He could not think about Lectionary choices as these were set in BCP stone. He could not think about the beautiful complexities of the Eucharist when the main service was to be Matins. He could not even think about the kind of sermon he might deliver because he had been clearly given to understand that although a sermon was desirable in most circumstances, it might be best to wait until "things settled down" before he went into the pulpit to say anything other than platitudinous about the set Readings. One area where he could not be 'closed down' and which accorded both with his brokenness and meticulousness was his love of the weak and the sick, reflected in the substantial—some people said inordinate—time he spent in home visits. During this period he increased their range and frequency and, in addition to any good he thought he might have done, he found great comfort in sitting with the sick and the dying. They both reminded him of the transience of life and our physical weakness. They consoled him with the thought that it does not take very much to give comfort to human beings who do not expect much in the first place. Often during his visits he listened to people who, only a few months before in their physical and financial prime, had been beyond content. In private houses he saw the victory of the Cross as clearly as he saw it as he stood at the altar. This care for people, the maintenance of a semblance of routine, and his lifelong attachment to the Roman Office, partially delayed the deep private reaction to his changed public condition which he knew must come. As the days went by, the feeling of brokenness increased and the critical point was reached when he thought that he was damaged so greatly that he was no longer capable of caring for people. Without liturgy and his parishioners he was empty. Thus, he steadily sank into the painful dichotomy of penitence and bad temper, the latter making the former ever more necessary. Each aspect of his dilemma in its way also inhibited any constructive thought about the future. He thought he was not worthy to make proposals, and every time he tentatively made a start he upset people. He was therefore driven ever more in on himself as the dreaded morning of 9.45 a.m. Matins approached. On the Saturday evening he had reached the point where he lost track of the beginning of his misery. He had forgotten how it had all begun, and for the first time since he was in his early twenties he thought of escaping the troubles of the world and entering a monastery where he could have Eucharist without politics. At that time he was deemed unsuitable because he would be deprived of control in this gently corporate but deeply obedient environment. As he pondered his helplessness he was again tempted by the trade-off. Better to live in an ordered rather than a disordered environment, no matter who had control. He turned to his Office and was thankful that the one gift that remained to him was his ability to focus and to pray. Like people who go to the gym every day, whether they feel like it or not, he had subjected himself, with thankfulness, to daily prayer and spiritual exercise since he had first thought of following his father. As he knelt in front of the Blessed Sacrament, he saw the broken bread and the broken body of Christ on the cross, and these and his own broken self came together into a picture of almost unimaginable hope and pathos. For him the bread and wood were not in opposition, but were integral, part of the same reality of the life of Jesus, brokenly reflected in his own. Now the image was more intense, almost unbearably real, as if it was about to break down all the controls he had put in place in order to survive. At root, all the control and the detail, the precision and obsession, were devices to dilute an almost toxically beautiful immanence which was always in danger of making his own woundedness the central focus of his introspection, a kind of idolatry that took the theological notion of the fusion of the human and divine, not only in Jesus but in all humanity, and personalised it. If being divine meant being broken like Jesus that was both appropriate and scandalous. He could not afford to go down that route, to serve required a degree of mundanity and for him that meant routine and detail. He was losing them and he could feel the toxicity level in him rising. He might find a way of living with it, but that would have to wait until he had passed his Matins ordeal.

Helen did not identify herself by reference to other people but, in spite of their various outreachings, she was much more porous to the emotions of those she met than were either Clement or Mark. As a counterbalance to their respective studiousness and holiness she affected a down-to-earth practicality which could, however, not have been effective without deep thought and holiness. She tempered Clement's somewhat distanced and Mark's somewhat mercurial compassion with a steady degree of empathy and an insatiable capacity for taking care of every last detail. Not—as in Mark's case—to meet her own needs but ,exclusively to meet the individual needs of others. Not surprisingly for someone who was so meticulous on behalf of others. She had her own obsessions which were ostensibly for the benefit of others, but which were psychological addictions. The longest running of these was text proof reading and layout, but she had more recently acquired an addiction to email which was consistent with her personality as it combined her love of detail with her need to be loved. She did not serve in order to be loved, but she felt pain when love was denied. Since the beginning of the crisis, she had tried to maintain her usual pattern of meticulous service, but she had found pieces of her life eroding. Rotas began to be unnecessary. She supposed people would want coffee after Matins as much as after Eucharist, but it did not seem quite appropriate. Eucharist, after all, was a celebration of fellowship but she could not see what Matins celebrated other than the glorious language of the BCP. The Chalice Assistants, Servers, Prayers of the Faithful, and Offertory rotas had been curtailed. The bell ringers, being a largely agnostic law unto themselves, would sort themselves out no doubt. Yet it was not the formalism of sorting the rotas that she was missing most but the sense of being at the centre of things, of being available for whatever was needed. She was not given to introspection, but the diminution of her duties gave her more time to wonder in what direction she was going. In a manner that reflected a long tradition of English religiosity, she did not think very greatly about whether she would obtain a reward in heaven for her generosity of spirit. She neither felt any obligation on God's part nor did she ever think she would not be worthy of her eternal place. She was, in that respect, serious without ever being presumptuous or sceptical. She occasionally felt that her lack of learning and patent lack of holiness put her at a disadvantage, but most of the time she was not prone to comparison and, without ever being explicit, even to herself, she knew that the Church depended on people like her to survive. Bishops might pontificate, priests might posture, theologians might speculate, but the life of Jesus, informed by the Spirit, largely consisted of practical love and service. As the days went by, she became more worried about Clement and Mark, but she also felt herself weakening. She was not a structure, nor a miasma, but a muscle, and so she realised that much of her strength was gained from her genuine wish to make the lives of those she loved as peaceful as possible. Now that she found that she could neither help Clement nor Mark the muscle was growing flabby for want of exercise. By temperament and inclination she was an intervention-ist, but this tendency was checked by her extreme fear of criticism which always hurt her very badly. As the email traffic dwindled, and she contemplated what she might do to turn matters around, she became more frightened of making the wrong decision or—not quite the same thing—being hurt. Unlike Mark, whose outlet was individual ministry, and Clement, whose outlet was study, her only effective milieu was the corporate enterprise which was disintegrating and, worse still, she was unable to use her most supreme power, that of making peace. From her childhood she had been the peace maker rather than the theorist. Her skills were of the diplomatic rather than the ideological sort because she saw that it was what people did that mattered. They argued that motive, why they did things, mattered even more, but she was inclined to think that too much was made of intellectual coherence and too many people claimed it when their real motivation was a muddle of half perceived desires and accidents. More than twenty years on the Bench and various criminal tribunals had taught her that much of what people said about their actions was post hoc justification. She was not thereby made cynical. In her understanding of people she was ultra liberal because she did not have an ideology of coherence that justified leaving people out or shutting them down. She would not make boundaries because there was no coherent justification for them. She was deeply suspicious of models, adopting—although she only vaguely knew it—Godel's proposition that the more perfect a theorem the less universally it applies. As a counterbalance to Clement's learning and Mark's compassion, she was the one who possessed the greatest wisdom because she had the least inclination to impose patterns, and certainly not her own patterns. Clement might be convincing when he said that the key factor in human development was pattern recognition, but that recognition accounted for division and war, for intolerance and cruelty, for a disregard of difference. The divisions which had occurred since Kylie's arrival were a good example of the failure to respect difference. She could not see why the Godhead should not be equally female as male and she agreed with Clement, without going into the matter in the same detail as him, that the possibility of the Godhead consisting of more than three 'persons' was worth considering. When it came to it, she would have been happy to serve in a worshipping community that simply acknowledged that the infinite Godhead might be made up of infinite attributes, an idea which she put to Clement and which fascinated him. She had seen Hindu piety and Buddhist piety, she had seen Christian and Islamic cruelty, and, ultimately, she was an archetypal Protestant who deeply suspected the institutional church, not least because of its ridiculous attitude to women. As she worked her way through her frustrations, feeling weaker and more helpless, she felt the strength of her marriage. It was not that Clement was more warm than usual, although she could tell that his attempt at calm self-control, partly for her sake, was costing him dearly, but that they had such a large common store of understanding that she could feel his patience calming her impatience. At the same time, she knew that he was absorbing her limitless softness for him which was balm for his intellectual and spiritual ache.

While they were living with their private desolations, partly out of reticence, partly to spare each other, the episcopal triumvirate began its work of rooting out clerical heterodoxy. By starting with the weakest of their opponents, however, they forced their stronger brethren to make a definitive choice between caving in or sticking to their liberal principles. Consequently, the prizes which they gained were trivial and the opposition coalesced ever more determinedly round its leadership. Male curates only just ordained might worry about the ladder ahead, perhaps ending with a Canonry, but their female peers had nothing to lose by refusing to cooperate with those who quite openly lacked respect for them. While some weak souls might tone down their language in exchange for a vicarage makeover, the sort of allies worth having were likely to greet such proposals with contempt. Thus, as the Fifth Sunday of Easter came and went, word travelled round the Diocese that, far from repressing the rebels, the episcopal campaign had badly misfired, leaving Bishop Hall in the awkward position of having to choose between exercising what disciplinary powers he possessed—which were nugatory—or climbing down. Nonetheless, in spite of the general futility of what was attempted, it caused a great deal of misery because of what it proposed. All over the Diocese priests and lay leaders who thought that they had been comfortably conforming Anglicans were forced to ask themselves where they stood on the issue. "What issue?" was a question that they needed to resolve but, like voters in a referendum who refuse to answer the question put to them because they have one which is much closer to their immediate concerns, more pertinent or personally relevant, they concluded that the question was not whether Perpetuanism should be taken seriously in the Church, but whether the Bishop had a right to impose a narrow doctrinal settlement, not on the Diocese in general, but on their particular parish. There were priests who were not sure about the Virgin Birth, the Resurrection of the body, the feeding of the 5,000, the orthodoxy of Paul, the wisdom of the Reformation, the Oxford Movement, praying for the dead, synodical government, and many other doctrinal niceties, who had been left to their own theological devices since a bishop had laid on hands. For their peace of mind, parochial quiet, and the good order of a broad church, that is how they thought it should stay. Most lay people, deeply suspicious of ideologically based theology, instinctively supported this position, with the added consideration that what they most wanted was routine, quiet, low octane religion which exemplified the good order which they valued in their secular lives. The tabloid press might write off humanity as greedy, anarchistic and cruel and, although their personal experience was almost entirely opposite from this caricature, it served to underline the value of self-discipline, restraint, and good order. From their point of view, the bishops and other senior churchmen—almost entirely men—had behaved irresponsibly, self-indulgently and selfishly. They were willing, as a demonstration of their commitment and expertise, to raise funds for a clerical establishment that thought that this was the only fit task in the Church for the laity, but they were not prepared to do this if the clergy behaved like politicians, and that resentment was increased by the knowledge that, whereas they could get rid of politicians, they could not turf out their bishops. Hall's initial diagnosis that there were very few liberals was profoundly incorrect because he was only thinking of ideologically coherent liberals when the majority of his flock simply took it for granted that they had no right to tell other people what to do and, by extension, nor did anybody else. They were consumers exercising choice and, in the case of the Church, they were paying handsomely for a service which gave them very little choice. If Catholics could flout *Humanae Vitae* and still be Catholics, then there was very little that their bishops could impose on Anglicans. Hall might argue that he was only imposing negatively—trying to keep something from adulterating doctrinal purity—but his argument was not heard. He had launched a crackdown on freedom of theological speech and was thereby left with the Petran and Toran core groups with a temporary truce over what such restrictions might mean. The rest of the Diocese showed every sign of marching away or, more likely, simply disappearing into the secular mist.

No sooner had an ideological determination been established to have done with the episcopal hierarchy, however, than the practical disadvantages began to make themselves clear. People might not like the bishops cracking down on dissent, but they could not imagine a world without bishops. There was a good deal to be said for freedom of speech, but somebody had to set limits. The Diocesan officials were generally obstructive in permitting church alterations, but somebody had to set standards. Thus, those who felt that the bishops had acted badly also felt trapped within the system that had mistreated them. There was a deepening sense of gloom that things were bad but that very little could be done to improve matters. The body ecclesiastical could not expel the bile and so it began to wreak internal havoc. Brian and the Rural Deans knew that they were heading for financial ruin. Toran generosity was well known, but it would never be enough to sustain the current structure and estate and the Petrans, who had been most vocal behind Hall, were notoriously mean.

Even before its wider implications became clear, the campaign began to have a serious effect on Walmbury. During Mark's brief flirtation with Perpetuanism some congregational and financial support had been withdrawn, some to support Perpetuanism, some as a protest, but when Mark changed his position the support was slower to return than it had been to depart. After Mark's reorganisation of worship a little more support was specifically withdrawn but, to his chagrin, not as much as he had expected. He had mistakenly thought that the parish's commitment to a Eucharistic monopoly of worship was as strong as his own. Nonetheless, the withdrawal tipped the balance against viability. In parallel, the effect of the crackdown was substantial and immediate. People in the Parish knew that the majority of their contributions went towards a Diocesan Contribution and it did not matter how often they were told that this was redistributed to pay for the Rector and other services, they did not see why they could not pay their own Rector and let the Church Commission pay for the Bishops and all the paper pushers at Church House. Although it would be difficult, Mark knew that he would have to discuss the situation with the Standing Committee. The sooner he got through this the better, he decided, so he took the unprecedented step of asking for a meeting on Saturday evening after dinner. Helen asked Clement if he would come. "Well, I'm not even a Reader now and I have no locus standi," he said, predictably. "I know that," she said, patiently, "but this will be a critical meeting for us all. Douglas will say nothing other than give us the financial picture—he has only stayed out of dogged, professional loyalty, but he has no imagination—and I can't deal with Mark on my own if he gets dogmatic. In fact, I don't know if I can go if you are not there." "But if I turn up that will start the meeting on the wrong footing and that could be a disaster." "It's worth the risk. If you're not there it will be a disaster. If you are, it might not be."

Helen's instinct was correct. When she walked into the Rectory with Clement, Mark did not comment, sensing that she needed him to be there and that making a fuss about protocol was not precisely what was wanted at that moment. For although he was worried about finance, he thought this was secondary to working out how the Parish could survive as a worshipping community and for that he would value Clement's advice, even at the cost of some tension. Clement, however, was determined that there should be no tension, not only to justify Helen's faith in him but also because he would continue to treat Mark as his priest until such time as he was not. Douglas went briefly through the figures showing that the parish was tipping into insolvency and then asked if he could leave to analyse the figures further. The three were therefore left to ponder the future.

At Helen's gentle prompting the discussion began at a practical level, following on from Douglas's figures. "As usual with people," she said, "building up is much more difficult and time consuming than knocking down. I am blaming nobody, so don't look at me like that. We simply have to face the fact that we are in danger of being non-viable. So what are the options? Firstly, we could go back to where we were before Perpetua ever made an appearance. This would mean putting our liturgy back where it was and temporarily upsetting the traditionalists who have recently gained some power. This is my favoured option because it actually says nothing about any current controversies. Except for Clarence, nobody openly objected to our liturgical pattern before Easter. It isn't associated with heterodoxy in general nor with Perpetua in particular, it's what we have done for years. When you pulled back, Mark, from supporting Perpetua, I don't think you needed to change any of the liturgy. I know you were under pressure, but it turned out to be very superficial pressure. Secondly, and in my view less acceptably, we could keep things as they are now, but as we keep finding out from our own parish and elsewhere, people like us are making a much larger financial contribution to the church than our opponents thought we were. Thirdly, you could re-consider the Perpetua option once the position becomes much more clear. There is considerable sympathy for this, particularly from Violet and Ronald. I know that this is the most radical of the options, but we might need to consider it. The fact that you actually did consider it means that what I am putting on the table as an option is not that outrageous." "I will not ..." "... Mark! But in the case of all three of these options, you already have." "Sorry, Helen, what I meant to say was that I will not go back on what I have decided about Perpetua, but I am open to thinking about the liturgical pattern. What do you think, Clement?" "First of all, I want to say, as I usually do, but it's important, that Helen and I have not discussed this. We have quite deliberately avoided trying to reach an agreement on the range of options, let alone which one or combination of parts we might choose." "I respect that," said Mark. "Our current troubles have not led me to question your integrity." "There is something extremely grounded about the Church of England because it was founded by politicians, not theologians. Yes, I know that Cranmer was a theologian of sorts but he was deeply influenced, almost to the end, by politics. I wonder whether his martyrdom would have gone ahead if he had thought there was any possible way out of it. Needless to say, none of us is pure theologian or politician. Because theology is written in language it can only say—metaphorically—what the language allows it to say; just as politics is bounded by the possible, so is theological language. They can both stretch as time goes by and it can be Lamarckian rather than Darwinian." They both stayed quiet, knowing that Clement might take his time, but he said nothing that was not to the purpose. "Because Anglicanism was founded by people with primarily political motives, it is a highly concrete edifice. This is why it is built on a prayer book and not a confession. What mattered in the sixteenth century was stopping people fighting over abstractions and the best way to ensure this was to see that they all went to church in the same place at the same time. The English became attached to the Prayer Book because it became part of a non-contested ritual pattern. So my first piece of advice is that if you want to restore stability and viability the best place to start is not with doctrine, but with liturgy. Had you been inclined to Perpetua, but kept the liturgy as it was, you would have been seen to be less radical than you were when you drew back from siding with Perpetua but changed the liturgy. Very few people are that bothered by doctrine but they are giving up valuable time to attend church and they expect you and the rest of us to be sensitive to how that time is spent." "So would you agree with Helen that we should go back to the pattern of the last ten years?" "Yes, because liturgy should be connected with doctrine, but it is not as co-terminal as it should be. But, secondly, the tactics of retreat are very complex if you accept the option which Helen and I recommend." "Let us, then, settle on that before you go on. It fits with my instincts, but my bearings have been rather shaken recently." "Secondly, then, we need to consider the tactics. Sadly, these are more complex than the decision on options. I said that the Church was practically founded but, next to pragmatic outcomes, the thing that interests politicians most is process because it is through this— and money, of course—that they achieve their objectives. Unlike Hawthorne, most people are not interested in process as an end in itself, as the successor in our culture to product as the marker of where we are. In our culture at least, retreat is very difficult because we are so definite about direction. We use terms like 'road map', 'flow chart', and 'end point'. We are not open to aleatoric processes at all. This means that we get ourselves into very narrow channels which make it difficult to turn round or even go sideways. Because of a habit of political rhetoric, based on Christianity, newspapers often say that people who make mistakes should apologise and be forgiven, but they are never forgiven. They are better off pretending that they never did anything wrong to start with. Equally, our culture is always calling for flexibility and humility. It calls our politicians arrogant and inflexible, but any change of mind is termed pejoratively a 'U-turn'. We therefore need to find a way to go forwards not backwards." "But how can you go forwards to precisely where you were before you began to make changes?" "There is a third factor, which is that people will accept reform as long as it is sold as going back to the golden age. So you have a paradox. The culture designs action to go inexorably forward but it likes reform to take us back to a former time." "So what do we do?" "I think this is where Helen's skill is greater than mine. I am fine at analysis, but I would be over elaborate in execution, whereas she is invariably simple." "I think you simply say that there was not enough support for your proposed 'experimental' changes. Some people will disagree, but as there is going to be no voting, people will have to take your word for it." "So I simply say at Matins that although I was pleased to propose the experiment, there isn't really enough support for it?" "Yes." "And what about money?" "This is more difficult because it will take us some time to recover." "Will Ronald and Violet help?" "I will ask them, if you like," said Clement. "But don't you support their stance on the money?" "Yes, in general terms, I prefer to spend money on people and actions rather than buildings. In particular I hope one day that they will use the funds to promote a much more outward looking church but, in spite of my private feelings, I am happy to explore help for us for now because I am not prepared to go any further in my support for Perpetua until I have heard what Hawthorne has to say, on his own behalf or through whatever instrument he determines. Which leads us to a point I think we need to explore. I know it's rather more pertinent to me than anyone else, but I did lose my job over my support for Hawthorne's position." Helen looked alarmed. "We've done well so far, do we really need to discuss this, Clement?" "I think we do, but so as not to get our wires crossed I think we should agree to the discussion's conclusions so far—including my proposal to talk to the Trustees—as a quite separate matter from any theological discussions. That means that if we disagree on Perpetua it won't undo what we've just done." "Very wise," said Mark, getting a clear sign of assent from Helen. "I think it is important," said Clement, "without making a meal of it, to establish where you stand, Mark, between my position in support of Hawthorne and Bishop James's apparent break with the Archbishop." "I think that, in spite of my many disagreements with James, he is my Bishop. I feel warmth towards Hawthorne, but James is my boss. That may be uncomfortable but that is where I am." "I am sorry to hear it." "I can understand that, too, but I see no way of changing, at least in the short term."

The decision over the worship pattern made the main service tolerable for Mark, even though he noted how small the congregations were both for the eight o'clock Eucharist and the Matins. Both services were largely attended by traditionalists. He had lost all the children, young families, and most 'middle of the road' worshippers. Helen was on duty and Clement, who needed the Eucharist, returned for Matins, even though the choir was not ready to sing the Service, out of loyalty to Mark. It was like being a rejected lover—you still tried to see as much of the beloved as you could, even if it caused pain. At the end of the service Mark announced that the experiment was over. It had met with very little support and he would revert to the usual pattern of worship. He could not have said this to a more hostile group of parishioners, but it was as if they had never really believed their luck and were being jolted back to reality. A few complained to him afterwards, but most did not wait for coffee and departed, sullen but unrebellious.

Word got round quickly to those who were not in attendance. At lunch time in The Oak, Nigel was glad to report that matters were as they were before this silly episode started. "But it's caused terrible damage to the Church", said Smiley. "I don't think so", said Nigel. "Everybody says that kind of thing and a day later it's all blown over. They sell papers and advertising by blowing everything out of proportion. Besides, one minute you say that the Church doesn't matter and you aren't interested in it and the next you say that press coverage is going to damage its credibility." He took much the same line that evening at a dinner of "The Six". Nigel, who had always had a soft spot for Matins and Evensong from his time at secondary school when he had done the "full set" every Sunday as a chorister, was nonetheless happy that things were back to normal. Scott agreed with Nigel, but had a slightly stronger preference for the occasional Evensong. Marie was a little put out at the wasted work on a Stanford *Te Deum* but thought it could be used on a special occasion. Meg was getting used to the pleasure of her mother's independence without the superstructure of supernatural intervention and the controversy it had caused. Helen was glad that things had settled down, at least on the surface, although she was sure that there would be more heartache before things got back to normal. She particularly felt Clement's pain. When things 'got back to normal' Clement would no longer be a Reader. People would commiserate for a while and then forget his pain. They had all "loved" his sermons, but would easily learn to live without them. Clement was pleased with the changes that brought his beloved Eucharist back into its proper position but he was distanced from the process. Every time he took part in the fellowship of the Eucharist it was now incomplete. The comfort it had brought him throughout his life was diminished. He concentrated as hard as ever, never thinking that comfort consisted of sitting back, but he heard Perpetua knocking at his spiritual door and, such was the insistence and the coherence of the call, that he knew it could not long be denied. Naturally he did not say any of this. These were his guests and his friends and he did not wish to cause them pain. Neither did he want to draw attention to his pain to exact sympathy. The only care that counted was that which was volunteered and that was now confined to Helen. Although he continued to be kind and concerned about others, he was almost completely isolated.

True to his word to Mark, Clement went to see Violet and Ronald the following morning. "This is not easy, as you can imagine," he said, "not least because you know the position I find myself in, but I promised Mark, and Helen as Churchwarden, that I would talk to you about the situation, to see if there is any way in which you can help without betraying your principles. As you know, the liturgical pattern has reverted to where it was. Mark wants to reconstitute the PCC in the way it was before the aberration. However, as you also know, we have suffered a temporary cash flow crisis. I hesitate to ask whether you are prepared to help with this, but I promised that I would." "There is no doubt," said Violet, "that we could indulge in some 'creative accounting'. Many people do that and manage to persuade themselves that they are doing no such thing. The only way we could help is if we were prepared to meet the situation head on, convinced that any donation would contribute to the renewal of the Church. There may not be a Church to renew if we do not help. We are satisfied that the funding must be spent in this region or for the benefit of this area, but what persuades us most strongly is that Perpetua's mission is based on working with existing church communities to forge new and wider communities. We are, therefore, prepared, without any hedging, to meet Mark's costs for six months while we see what happens. We are not prepared to meet the costs of any building related expenditure and, as it's Spring and we won't need the heating, that is reasonable. We will review the situation in September." "Could you possibly tell Mark?" asked Clement, suddenly tired, as if the adrenalin had drained out of him after his final effort.

For it was his final effort. He had helped to restore the situation that existed during Holy Week. He had come to the end of his usefulness. How short were individual and public memories. Except for Iris's recovery—which would soon be elided into normality—nothing would be seen to have happened in a few months time. This was the way that humanity protected itself from disasters, but it was also the way it protected itself from inconvenient truth. Just as a family could slowly recover from a terrible disaster such as the criminal behaviour of a child, so a believing community could smooth over incidents of discredit or inconvenience to itself. Mark could forget the social housing as it was intractable; Lady Gowers could forget how her hypocrisy had been exposed. All the rest of the divided—but superficially coherent—community could forget its compromises to the point where it had not made any. Only Clement remembered, and only Helen knew that he did and what it cost him.

Surveying the Diocesan scene on the day before Ascension, the three bishops were content. They had "picked off"—no, rather, offered guidance to—waverers. Many who had seemed to be drifting away were firmly within the fold. The "usual suspects"—those resisting orthodoxy—had hardened in their attitudes, but at least they were "flushed out"—identified as requiring further guidance—

and although the financial situation was "extremely grave"—requiring further work—it provided an opportunity to reassess pastoral provision on a rational basis. There was no hurry. "I suppose we will have to set up a Commission to look into recent events and see what lessons we can learn," said Bishop Hall. "That depends on whether you want to learn anything or simply to have a fall-back position if we are asked what we are doing," said Aleford. "I would have thought that the lessons are very clear," said Castlegate. "That's the problem, Bruce," said the Bishop, "you always think that everything is very clear and simple when nothing ever is. No matter which way you look at it, being a profession whose governing documents, so to speak, are Scripture rather than a set of laws or a shelf of textbooks, makes life difficult. At one level we can invoke the Holy Spirit when we want to do something which suits us but we all know that it is, to say the least, a little fraudulent." "All we need is a little more Toran direct-ness." "Or Petran solidity." "Thank you, gentlemen. Neither of you can afford to renounce the truce quite yet. We still have the Dean and matters in the Diocese are untidy but, then, contrary to your views, Bruce, I fear they always will be. I am thinking of a Commission neither to learn nor to delay, but simply because I can't think of anything better to do. We must be seen to be doing something. For us it might all be a little professional difficulty, but there must be people in genuine spiritual turmoil who are suffering from this instability." "And do you think a Commission will calm their turmoil.?" "No, but as I said, I honestly can't think of anything better to do." "Well, at least after the Commission we can all get back to normal." "If normal means your usual sniping at each other, Hilary, I suppose that is what we will get back to, but we still have a fundamental problem to face," said the Bishop, settling down. "What is that?" asked Bruce. "My con-tinuing concern that the Church of England should find a way to be an acknowl-edged part of the Holy Catholic Church." "But it should be Protestant," protested Castlegate. "I agree with James," said Aleford. "The Elizabethan settlement," said the Bishop, warming to one of his favourite subjects, "didn't give us any way of 'doing doctrine' by the method, recommended by Newman, of organic devel-opment. The problem for you, Bruce, is you have to draw time lines. Was the Christian Church the Christian Church before the New Testament was written? Was the Medieval Christian Church the Church? Does theological development and Scriptural exegesis stop with Martin Luther, Calvin, Henry VIII? Choose your person." "Or," said Castlegate, nettled, "does your kind of Catholicity mean that the Pope of Rome has a veto on Anglican theology? We got away from Papal diktat and now you want the Pope to have a veto on what we do. That does not make sense. What's worse—although I will never agree to women priests and bishops—there isn't any point in your saying that women bishops will put back the cause of Catholicity when Rome doesn't even think that you're a priest, let alone a bishop. It's a game of smoke and mirrors. You have your Ecumenical dialogues, to which I know you are personally committed, but Rome simply has to sit on its hands for centuries, asserting that you aren't, in its terms, a 'serious' player." Hall looked uncomfortable. "Well, we can't go into that now." "No," said

Hilary, irritated but also more puzzled than he cared to admit. "Let's leave that until after the Commission."

On the Tuesday evening before Ascension, Living Water's topic had been suffering. Clement had prepared the ground with his usual care and the group had responded with its usual confidence. Clement proposed that suffering was an inevitable reality in a God-created world where humanity's purpose as created beings was to choose to love. Without suffering there would be no real choice, only a flat, Utopian existence with no moral significance. To suffer was to accept our creaturely condition and, in choosing to suffer for the sake of our Christian witness, we were making a free offering to God. The necessary precondition for that offering was humility. We had to accept that although we were created to choose freely, we were operating within God's created framework. We were not to suffer out of a sense of nobility, we were not to be proud of our fortitude, we were not to accord glory to ourselves because we chose to suffer. We might choose to suffer for the best of motives, but this should not be considered as a "down payment" for salvation. We could not set a price on suffering, it was not a commodity that could be traded for a stake in everlasting life. Following Perpetua without quoting her, he said that we should care for the suffering child because it suffered so that we might choose. That is why the Christian should, above all, love the suffering and that was why Jesus was always with the suffering. Indeed, he was suffering alongside the human sufferers as his tribute to the choice that the Father had created for all humanity.

When they all left, quiet and grateful for his leadership, Clement resolved to face his own suffering in this way, but during a sleepless night it became ever more difficult to see the situation in the way that he had portrayed it. As he moved restlessly between his Bible, prayer book and attempts at silent prayer, his condition kept breaking in on his devotions so that he watched his broken life assemble before him, piling desolation upon desolation. He had been a prodigy, but his precociousness had increasingly backfired as he grew older, characterised as arrogance by a world that was increasingly suspicious of straight talking. The paradox of individuality and consensus—the former was rhetorically prized, but routinely punished—had progressively throttled his prospects of prospering through directness of speech and decisiveness of action. Time and again he had proposed ethical ways of cutting pragmatic Gordian knots and time and again his solutions had been rejected as impossible, eccentric or, worst of all, idealistic. The paradox of expression resembled, he thought, the paradox of fashion. Everyone was free to be as heterodox as they liked as long as the heterodoxy was uniform. There was a time when wearing blue jeans to a formal works meeting was a sign of rebellion, but the only sign of rebellion allowed was the wearing of blue jeans. In the same way, individualism of outlook and expression were sanctioned as long as they conformed to a template of individualism. At every interview he had attended, he had been asked how he could square his "outspoken" views with the need for consensus. His reply, that it was impossible to reach robust consensus without the different parties putting their cards on the table, was greeted with bewildered scepticism. His insistence that he would only say what he had to say once—that saying it twice would not make it twice as valid—and would accept collective responsibility for decisions, determined collectively, was never accepted. Consensus was not the outcome of negotiation, but the starting point for it. There was no room for views which did not fit inside the orthodox template. When he produced evidence-based propositions—there was a fashion for an evidence-based approach—these were at best dismissed as "refreshing" but, much worse, they were often characterised as "thought pro-voking" and, worst of all, "provocative". Under the influence of George Steiner, he had come to characterise himself as an "intellectual", but there was no room for that kind of self-identification and the thoughts that flowed from it. There were no golden stars for reading Dante in Italian or quoting Hegel. There was nothing to learn from Proust or Dostoyevsky. He watched as the optimistic, idealistic edifice of his Cambridge days disintegrated under the pressure of what he could not properly characterise, but which he thought of under the inad-equate heading of intellectual thinning, best exemplified by the gradual impov-erishment of the language. His strings of closely woven syntax were regarded as obscurantist, his insistence on the correct ordering of clauses and words was regarded as pedantic, and as sentences became shorter, with paragraphs los-ing any sense of complexity, simply attempting simplistic, sequential thought, they suffered from the kind of ambiguity which was thought to be a peril of his kind of writing. Whereas his complexity was lucid, common simplicity was ob-scure. This lexicographic and syntactic disability—not in the sense that he was disabled in himself, but in the sense that his facility disabled him in the social context—forced him to the margin. He would not give way, in a sense that he never defined in case it made him self-satisfied—a danger of which he was never unaware—he knew that he was defined by the way he read and wrote. Think-ing that this was a characteristic of a venal world, he had expected more from his venture into theology, but he was equally frustrated by reactions to him and more wounded because of his greater expectations. In spite of his care with the metaphors of God and God's purposes, which he reverently and humbly forged, he was still regarded as an oddity. His crisis with the Church reached its climax when his ordination disernment process stalled. It had been like playing black at chess without a rule book. The Diocese would advance a pawn and he would react directly in the hope that he was doing the right thing. If he accepted the refusal of officials to reply to emails, return calls, or make appointments, this might be interpreted as a lack of enthusiasm. If he pressed, this might be inter-preted as a lack of humility and an assertion of his sense of priority, of his pride. As it turned out, the latter was the case. He had pressed too hard, volunteered information that had not been requested, been honest to the point of pain about what he thought were his strengths and weaknesses, and he had been dismissed as "driven" without any recommendations being made as to how he might 'cor-rect' the situation. As night turned into dawn, he saw his life, his secular and ecclesiastical careers, in ruins.

When morning came, he had composed himself to spare Helen but she knew him too well to be spared. Behind his cheerful greeting as he brought tea, she saw the pain not so much in as behind his eyes. "What are we to do?" she asked. "I don't think there is anything for us to do. I feel as if I am completely abandoned, left alone, desolate, except for you. I do not think that that should have any influence on what you do. Solidarity does not lie in imitation but in living difference in mutual respect. I respect what you are doing for Mark and I know you respect my disposition towards Perpetua. There is no solidarity in my abandoning Perpetua to fit more comfortably with you and Mark and no solidarity in you leaving him and becoming a follower of Perpetua." "That is logical, of course, but I need to align my sympathy with your pain. For me solidarity does not lie in pursuing a parallel course to yours as an expression of my own integrity, it lies in being with you, feeling your pain rather than simply knowing that it is there. I think I should resign as Churchwarden and be at your side, emotionally as well as physically." "Please do not do that. It would be a terrible blow to Mark and to your own sense of being needed. I grant that there is a certain element of self-satisfaction in being needed, but we all have our need to be needed. Who am I to say that your need to be at the centre of things is unworthy? I like to be at the centre of my own intellectual and spiritual life in spite of my intellect telling me that God has to be at the centre. We are both human. We need to have a realised place on the earth." "It doesn't matter what you say. My understanding of our marriage vows—and for me they come before anything else—is that I must be with you in every way." "I don't want to get pompous and say you must not do this. The force of the argument will not increase with my vehemence, but think again." "All right, I will think about what you say and make my decision before I see Mark on Friday."

As the hours went by—he had unwisely taken some days off work to think through his position, when he knew he would have been better off maintaining a balance between work and introspection—he began to find consolation in his own suffering. He had been consistent, he had been brave, he had made sacrifices for his principles, he had given everything up—or, rather, he had lost everything because he would not abandon his integrity—for Jesus. As the day went by, he found it easier to read his Bible and his prayer book and the times of silent prayer were almost surreally calm. He was aware that this was not a sequence of genuine experience, that he should be deeply suspicious of a spiritual ecology that was almost bland. Still, he went on through the day, alternating reading and contemplation; and, as time passed by, he slipped almost imperceptibly into pride in his suffering and the integrity that had brought it about. Instead of being the fuel of his incarnate spiritual life, his spiritual concerns became an escape from it. He was no longer praying to God for assistance in a complex world, he was praying because it gave him incomparable comfort. He was committing the 'sin' he feared most, the abandonment of Christian humility, for spiritual hubris. For although he had trained himself out of his youthful impulsiveness to comment on the shortcomings of others, he had not yet stopped himself commenting to himself. No matter how hard he tried to subdue his opinions, he could not help inwardly castigating those who had wavered and been 'found wanting'. He tried to exclude Mark from this category but, privately, he could not. He had reached that most dangerous of all points, that where he was the only one who was completely right. Even as he denied the idea that anybody could be completely right, he admired his own coherence in a self-satisfied way which he must always deny as a creature and as a creator. There was no piece of thought, music, poetry, narrative, art, or sculpture that could not be improved in some way, but he was exempting his own mental landscape from a standard he would, almost without thinking, apply to everything else.

At last, after weeks of frenetic activity, Mark had lost his way. His adrenalin had drained and he even found no consolation in his computer for it brought news of good people crushed. His own decision to revert to his pre-Perpetuan stance had not blunted his sympathy for those who had decided to follow her. In the internal warfare which he underwent between traditional Catholicism and liberalism, the former usually prevailed in liturgical and ecclesiological matters, but the latter always prevailed in his attitude to people. He had abandoned many of his Saint Stay's College friends to support women priests and bishops, and now he saw many of those he had worked alongside being 'turned' or subdued. There was a small part of him that wanted the Perpetuan hard core led, he gathered, by the Dean, to emerge as a new force. He was no lover of uniformity and was not frightened by diversity, as long as he was left as the big fish in the pond of his own devising. He could not see how the Church could ever abandon Trinitarianism, but the upheavals might, in spite of what was happening now, see the liberals making some headway. Every time he looked at his emails there were more casualties and when he checked his favourite web sites there was silence. On Wednesday afternoon he decided to turn off his computer. He needed to pray. As a Rector he knew he spent too much time doing things and not enough time praying. Today he would put that right in a small way. As Jane was due to be out all evening, he settled down in his study and tried to leave himself open to the Holy Spirit. Not surprisingly, given his spiritual temperament and history, he came to focus ever more sharply on his brokenness. He sometimes worried that resort to this self-image too easily excused his faults, seeing them as an inevitable consequence of his condition, but today he saw the extent of his fractured form, more radically broken than any explanation of his human frailties. He saw Jesus on the cross, broken for him, the bread broken for him, and himself broken for Jesus. He turned to Luke's short account of the Ascension, the completion of the healing of Christ's own brokenness. He prayed for healing, leaving himself entirely in God's hands. In his emptiness he was fulfilled.

Helen had consolation neither in Clement's spiritual hubris nor in Mark's sense of brokenness. She was desolate simply because she was diminished by the lack of a role. She felt suddenly old. She still had her paid work which was very important to her, but what she prized much more highly was her position in the community. She would retain her role in the Walmbury Weeks, but to lose her position as Churchwarden was a terrible sacrifice and she had no conception of the blessing of sacrifice. She always supported Clement and when he sometimes said that he had a fatal flaw, that his integrity too often metamorphosed into gratuitous tactlessness or, worse still, pride, she never agreed with him, as that would have devastated him, but part of her calm, constructive, tactful, modest self-recognised the analysis to which she dared not even accord internal, secret consent. Living with Clement was wonderful because of the love they had cultivated together, but she knew that from now on there would be a greater plangency in their lives which must inevitably reflect the human condition of schadenfreude. She naturally longed for this not to be so. She wanted the rest of her life to be joyful. It was not a bargain she wished to strike, but a gift she prayed to receive. Her caring was unconditional and she prayed for the strength to bear whatever she was asked to bear. She still hoped that she would not have to bear too much or, rather, this was an indirect plea because what she wanted most of all was for Clement to be spared, for there to be a way out which would preserve his integrity but, above all, give him comfort.

As night fell, each in their different ways attained a sense of tranquility in their desolation. They had reached, in their different ways, the nadir of their spiritual trajectories and, in doing so, they naturally reverted to their strengths. Clement's hubris gave way to doggedness, Mark's brokenness generated a new sense of obligation to his parishioners, and Helen's feeling of redundancy gave birth to new plans. But in each case they were under no illusions that a 'new dawn' would come soon. It was simply that, as they could not imagine how their situations, individually and collectively, might get worse, they naturally, even without thinking about it, began to anticipate that things would, inevitably, get better.

6.

Meanwhile, London was preoccupied with its own issues.

The primary art of news editing, as Sneer knew, is to appeal to the Darwinian delusion, to the imagined sense of superiority, which results from the innate competitiveness of the species: the disasters of the poor, the misfortunes of the rich, the triumph of the 'ordinary bloke', and the complaisance of the tart. No matter how powerful the politician or beautiful the celebrity, the craven reader must never be barred from the thought, no matter how distant or fantastic, that he could do better than the politician and could seduce the celebrity. This psychology of a spurious superiority was behind the mechanics of raising and lowering people brought into the public eye, for without being raised high they could not be laid low. The cynically bogus notion that Prime Minister Blair could walk on water was a sure harbinger of political havoc.

The secondary art of news editing, as Sneer also knew, was to forge a credible link between the ordinary and the fantastic, so that each could be enhanced by the other: a meat pie with the face of the Virgin Mary, a dog that responded to more than a dozen commands, a wheelchair user who had saved a baby from drowning, a fashion show at the summit of Everest, or a nymphomaniac priest. Each provided the alluring symbiosis.

The tertiary art, which Sneer had reason to know best, was the perpetration of speculative innuendo always, for legal reasons, suffixed with a question mark. Was a leading politician having an affair? Would a starlet admit to rumours of an orgy? Was that bank as solid as its directors swore? And would the taciturn Italian become the next manager of London United?

Of course, these arts were only part of Sneer's equipment for filling his newspaper. It did not matter how much nor how little 'real' news there was, that is to say news that was of public interest with implications for the way in which the world and its peoples lived and chose but, rather, information of interest to the public, which must be just credible enough to allow them to believe that it was news, as opposed to fiction. Sometimes the boundary became impossible to discern when the news was of events in a soap opera or in a 'reality' television programme, but that was only an extreme example of the common desire on the part of editors and readers to blur the distinction. Only intellectuals and nostalgic pedants—not the contradiction it appears to be—looked back to a golden age when news was news and comment was comment, when you could believe everything you read in The Times, when it was "impartial". Sneer, who had left school at sixteen without any conspicuous talent, even in English, was not the least bit interested in these philosophical complexities. He was much better schooled in how people are than how they ought to be, for his one peculiar intellectual pursuit was the politics and the society of eighteenth century London, inspired by the immediacy of Hogarth, the vulgarity of Gay and Fielding and the venality of Walpole. Had he had greater inclination to pursue his thesis of the immutability of human frailty and folly, he might have chosen almost any period of recorded history other than, perhaps, the zenith of Pericles, the Roman Republic before Pompey, the early eleventh century in Western Europe and Britain between the end of the First World War and Suez. It was this last period of common sacrifice and increasing equality, depression and war, triumph and hope, when deference and public power were in such a balance that crime seemed to be confined almost entirely to a known class of people called criminals whose opposite, Sneer, knew was the backdrop to contemporary discontent and moral panic. He would never attempt—not just because of his own limitations but because of the damage he vaguely knew such an exercise might do to his circulation—to consider the 'down' side of this apparent mid-century stability, the acceptance of child abuse and domestic violence, the petty tyrannies which could wreck the life chances of 'small' people without any appeal, the disproportionate sacrifice and suffering of the poor, and the general exploitation of the weak, which never received any criminal classification.

Sneer sat at his desk on the third Wednesday in May, unaware that it was the eve of the Ascension, with a thin portfolio of stories: the running untidiness of the Prime Ministerial hand-over, a minor train crash which, unfortunately, had not yet produced a scapegoat; a minor royal, photographed in a Nazi uniform, subjecting a figure in an Arab head-dress to a mock beating, which was still with the lawyers; a politician so junior that his "midnight romp" was hardly worth reporting; yet another mad bishop linking the current bad weather with divine retribution; evidence of a financial down-turn which was too boring to explain; and, naturally—or unnaturally—more melting glaciers. There were foreign stories, of course, of dictators and massacres large and small, of bombs and outrages from beirut to Helmand Province, of famines and floods more or less man made, of children with seven fingers, of hands blown off by land mines, of grand excesses in Bombay and Los Angeles, and a sprinkling of the curious and the improbable, but these were always second best to domestic disasters and curiosities. It would be a grim day and the only consolation in the cut-throat, declining tabloid market was that it would be no better for anybody else.

Almost without thinking about it, he watched the ticker running at the foot of the 24 hour news channel and physically twitched when he saw "Philomena Macmillan, 3, disappears from Spanish resort." Had he prayed, this would have been the answer to his prayers. Thank God it was a girl, because nobody was really interested in missing little boys. They did not evoke the same superficial sympathy nor the unacknowledged, prurient, middle aged male response, the vicarious enjoyment of sex abuse and the wish to share in it. It was a spicy change from the normal run of celebrities and models. They were, thought Sneer, necessary sexual fast food, but a bit of spice always went down well. Neither did boys evoke the fear that it could be one's own child, nor the unacknowledged fantasy of sex with one's own daughter. The sagas of missing girls offered all kinds of subliminal opportunities for hidden pleasures under the sympathetic guise, which nobody dared challenge, of worrying for lost innocents while imagining lost innocence. If the story ran for a few days there would be the opportunity to sympathise with the grieving parents and then to castigate them for carelessness and even imply their complicity. The pendulum of sympathy and condemnation might swing right through the boring necessity of covering the political hand-over. It might wipe Brown off the front pages.

It was also fortunate that, although the incident had taken place in that forbidding territory called "abroad", it was near enough to reader experience to cause no problems and it provided just a touch of exoticism. A missing girl in Spain was perhaps worse than a missing girl in Hertfordshire but it was better than a missing girl in Slovenia.

Sneer hoped that she would be blonde and that her parents would be reasonably articulate. Flat-faced, flat-vowelled families in the North sold some papers on the basis of sheer gloominess and hopelessness, but readers became bored with 'sink' estates, particularly when they reminded them of their own circumstances. The accounts of broken lives, broken windows, bad drugs, and bad faith were not news. What counted in these circumstances was a story that would garner some more 'Social Class E' readers but would also hook middle class people who thought they were above taking an interest in—as opposed to caring for—a missing girl.

Sneer hoped that she would not be found for some days. Not only did he want the pendulum of sympathy and accusation to swing, he also needed to get a return on the necessary investment. If she was missing for more than a few days, the tabloids would have to consider the usual problem of the reward. None of them wanted to spend the money, but neither did any of them wish to be caught out by one of the others. Likewise, it was easy to spend a large amount of money on family photographs, interviews with relatives, under-cover investigators to out-do the police, and informers within the police. The longer the story ran, the more return there was on the investment. The worst possible scenario was a three-day story where all the money had been laid out just before the girl was found, alive or dead. If the latter, the story would run a few days longer, but there would still never be a full return on the investment.

The office suddenly became electric. The television had gone live to Madrid, and as there was nobody on the spot, the internet began to fill with conspiracy theories. The newsroom was already calling for archive material on previous missing children, and stringers in Southern Spain were being contacted—an easy place because of the extensive network of English language publishers and radio broadcasters. Then news came that the family were from Devises, a much better option than a Northern town or city suburb: nice market town, good backdrops, concerned vicar, a not too stroppy police force. A Star TV contact at the airport retrieved Philomena's picture from the security database, together with that of the two parents and her older brother. She was blonde! Bingo!

Thus began a saga which wiped almost all other news off the pages of the tabloid press and even saturated the more self-regarding 'Berliners'. It dominated television news and made a considerable impact on radio, even though its primary appeal was pictorial. Before long the pendulum which Sneer had not only wished for but forecast was in full swing. The Macmillans were heroes and villains by turn. Either way, sympathy for "Little Phil Mac" could be maintained. The foreign press and the foreign police were in turn praised and pilloried for, it was implied, the British police would never have made so many blunders, nor would the British press have simply swallowed what it was told by prevaricating officials. The Foreign Office was naturally exempt from such British virtue for it was wondered why its officials had not 'single-handedly', so to speak, found the child.

Sneer had been hours late in winning the race to offer a reward. The corporate executives had not quite finalised their calculations when the first edition of The Mercury splashed its benevolence. Executives then had to decide whether to go into an auction, how likely it was that a reward would be claimed and what difference the Mercury initiative would make to relative sales. Sneer advised that the best form of defence was attack. In spite of the TT's plans to offer a reward, and its long history of such offers, it should attack the offer of a reward in this case which might, he said, induce foreigners to volunteer bogus information. Rewards were all very well in their place—their place being England (for he had a proper suspicion of the 'Celtic fringe')—but The Mercury had clearly lost its senses, if it had ever had any.

In a way which he could not have anticipated, Sneer was correct. No sooner was the reward offered than scores of photographs of blonde three-year-olds in the custody of people with much darker complexions were being sent to the press as proof of "Little Phil's" 'discovery' which all turned out to be of no long-term use, although many were published with enquiring captions, the source of the confusion being that nobody in a London news office seemed ever to have heard of Berbers many of whom, in spite of living in the North African desert, were 'angelically' blonde.

With the exception of the reward, Sneer was in pole position throughout the months that the story ran because he never had any sympathy at all for the parents or the child. To him they were just objects which were of use to his paper. Whether and in what condition the child was found or if it was not found were all variables of which he would need to take advantage. There was an optimal point, when he had gained a handsome return on the paper's investment, and when the readership fell below its pre-Phil level, when it might be best for her to be found and, if so, it was marginally better for her to be found dead in terms of the inquest and the grisly aftermath, but he had no control over this, so if she were not found, he could always run a speculative story about her or her parents on a bad news day.

Sneer was correct in his assessment of the "Little Phil" story on political coverage. The Prime Minster had arranged an elaborate Swan Song—a wit in the TLS referred to it as a Swann Song, but not even its own readers got the joke—not simply for the purpose of trying to give his legacy a more rounded and tidy conclusion, but also to pass his remaining time out of the orbit of Gordon.

Nonetheless, Tony would have liked just a little coverage of his fond farewells to Party workers who could not wait to see the back of him, to business leaders who had taken what they needed in exchange for nugatory political contributions, to trade unionists who thought he had just about been worth the money but who, quite misguidedly, considering his public pronouncements, thought that Gordon would bring the revolution nearer, and to many 'ordinary' people who would not realise how nice he was until he had been gone for some months. The political coverage that appeared down the agenda for broadcasters and writers was neither subtle nor even concrete. The only sentiment that prevailed was the need for a change. Not only had Blair been there too long for the good of the country and for the good of his party—although none of them cared for either—he had simply become boring. The political columnists and sketch writers wanted a new face, a new voice, a new dimension to the inexorable business of government and opposition.

Political coverage did not suffer simply because of "Little Phil", but also because, for all the superficial differences, everybody knew that Gordon was hardly different at all from Tony. It was still New Labour, it was still centrist, it was still managerial, it was still a massive under-use of Parliamentary and fiscal power, it was still hospitals and schools, it was still keeping the Conservatives out of power by out-flanking them to the 'right' on enough key issues. A few thought that they could see a fatal weakness in Gordon, that his unbending humourlessness, regardless of his policies, would undo him, but nobody would say such a thing as long as there was even a scintilla of a possibility that Tony would acknowledge this danger and change his mind.

The brew of unstated prurience and change for its own sake was an ideal combination which gave people what they thought they wanted while giving the impression that those who peddled this fare were both caring and responsible. As long as there was such a high profile missing child, nobody need cover the circumstances of hundreds of missing and murdered children who had never known a stranger. The man in the bushes was always more feared (and loved) than the man in his slippers. Likewise, the sheer volume of coverage of the process of change spared anyone the responsibility of reporting how that change might affect the life chances of voters. Had anybody thought about these matters for a moment, they might have wondered why they were so interested in "Little Phil", as opposed to millions of children who had been starved to death by oppression or corruption or who had 'gone missing' because of unimaginable social disruption. Clement kept thinking about thousands of children in the Sudan, any of whose stories were likely to be quite as bad as Philomena's but one could not say such a thing without causing deep offence. Likewise, he wondered whether the advent of Mr Brown would make any difference to the millions of UK citizens who had to count every penny, who feared violence from their own people, and whose escape through drugs and alcohol was so short-lived and inadequate. Yet, again, politics were rarely discussed in terms of how choices might affect those who needed social solidarity most. The nature of the political landscape meant that Mr Brown as Chancellor had been forced to do good by stealth, never able to admit—for it would be a grave political error—that he had determined to and had partly succeeded in helping the worst off at home, although there was the strange phenomenon of sympathy for the Millennium Development Goals.

What was clear to everyone, however, in spite of what failures they might anticipate in Gordon Brown, was that Tony Blair had been a dreadful Prime Minister, the worst since any name they might pick at random, excepting Winston Churchill, who was accorded the status of inviolable sanctity, and Mrs Thatcher who, it was held, had been a great Prime Minister because of her inflexibility and length of service. It never crossed the collective 'political mind' that when she had said that economic hardship was a "price worth paying" that she and her sort had not volunteered to pay it. It was therefore clear that Blair was the worst since Major, Callaghan, Heath, Wilson, Home, Macmillan or Eden, depending upon how far back your memory (not, of course, your knowledge) went, or according to how bad you wanted to make the comparison. If, for example, in some dim corner of your mind, you could remember Roseberry, you could therefore say that Blair was the worst Prime Minister since Roseberry more than a century ago, thereby making the comparison terrible indeed while displaying your historical gifts. Comparisons could be bogus in proportion to the low esteem in which readers were held or in proportion to their known laziness. So Blair was a failure, not least among those who had called for the war against Iraq, before he had finally determined on that course of action himself. He was, after all, for all his attempts to accommodate 'middle England', one of the enemy. As he made his valedictory progress, however, he smiled at the falsely high level of disappointment that was attributed to him. He had not come into politics for the thanks he would receive, and he expected none. The charge made most often and heavily against him was that he had gone to war against Iraq when he should have held back. It was a difficult charge to contest because it would never stay in focus. If he was wrong to go to war without the Second United Nations Resolution, would he have been right to go if he had gained it? And if such a resolution, in addition to all the others, were really necessary, why had a similar procedure not been thought necessary for the war in the Balkans? Why did people on 'the left' always respect the Security Council vetoes of corrupt dictatorships? Did they really think that Russia or China, a handful of near Fascist Arab states, and a miscellany of basket cases South of the Sahara should be allowed to thwart the will of democratically elected governments? This was a quite separate question from that of whether there was justification on the basis of the intelligence to which the answer was definitely positive, but it was in the nature of intelligence that he could not reveal it all and he reflected, almost ruefully, that the media always covered events as if they knew everything when they almost always knew less than he did, even when they bothered to read 'small print' in the public domain. The charge that he was acting simply out of deference to President Bush was correct to the extent that the consequences of not allying with Bush would have been much graver for Britain, with its obligations and ambitions, than it would be for Germany and even France. He had sent troops to the Iraqi border to boost the leverage of Hans Blixt, a move which most of his later critics supported without being able to say at precisely what point they would have withdrawn them. As with most situations involving a multitude of ever changing factors, he had had to react to events as they were, not as they were seen retrospectively (the curse of good analysis) and, just like his critics, he had never been able to identify the appropriate time to withdraw. From the moment he took the decision to fight alongside the Americans he knew that his premiership, from the perspective of contemporary critics and voters, would be characterised as "blighted", but he had no choice. He had to say that he thought the invasion was "right" but the more accurate word would have been "inevitable", which was one he was not allowed to use. He had known before he entered politics that almost all wars began in a burst of enthusiasm and ended in disillusion. As Jim Callaghan had said when the Catholics had pleaded with him to send British forces into Ulster, "It will be easier to get them in than to get them out." The persistence of this tendency was not only evident in the controversy over the war in Iraq, for it was now conflated with the United Nations sanctioned invasion of Afghanistan. It was, however, impossible to conduct even an ordered, let alone a rational, discussion on these issues because the media were so febrile and venal.

As he surveyed his legacy—much less diligently and much more detachedly than was generally supposed—he was less troubled by Iraq than by his failures to tackle poverty head on because of the necessary stealth required by selfish voters and his failure to meet the pensions crisis head on because he could not persuade anybody to take an interest in it. He dimly suspected that his greatest failure might be doing nothing about stratospheric asset prices, but Gordon had insisted that the Government's plans depended on buoyancy and the only economic reality people seemed to care about was the price of houses where the usual double standard operated: people wanted to retain their massive windfall profits which arose largely because house owners opposed the building of new houses, but they blamed the Government for the plight of first time buyers who would be helped by both a rise in the number of houses and a fall in their price.

Behind this emerging crisis there lay, he knew, a deeper problem of debt and imprudence but, even if he could get to the bottom of it, there was very little he could do about it. He was forever being caught by the populist paradox: people who generally supported the free market and voted Conservative—and papers like the TT—were always calling for the Government to "do something about it". Before long they would be howling about the financial sector and asking why the Government had not stepped in to save it from its own greed and folly. His treatment from the beginning had been unfairly adulatory and, later, unfairly condemnatory but he resented neither—he had known from the beginning what it would be like. Before he went into politics he had seen all the dangers and disappointments in general terms without being able to give them proper names, so he had gone in with his eyes wide open. He was not the cleverest man in his Cabinet but he was more astute, rational and honest, and less dogmatic, impulsive and cynical than most of his colleagues or critics. His major fault, as he saw it, was a failure to tell the truth he knew, but to tell the truth in politics is to renounce any chance of doing good. Sadly for the country, Gordon would be a disaster, but it had been impossible for him to prevent the inevitable—he could only delay it and, what was ironic in the extreme, was that Gordon's problems would inevitably be in the area of his economic expertise and some of them would, partially at least, have been of his own making. There was no such thing as succession planning in politics. You just had to do the job until you were forced out and then leave without regret. Like the profoundly under-estimated Wilson, his mild consolation—for he cared very little about it—was that he would look better in retrospect than he did in retirement.

Of the underlying issues in society which worried him most, the failure of personal responsibility was the greatest. Having abandoned any sense of religious commitment, most people had come to assume that their fate was in their own hands and had then very rapidly transposed this onerous view of their obligations into thinking that their fate was in somebody else's—anybody else's—hands. Society had descended into a state of incessant, competitive victimhood. Here was yet another paradox, that of the exercise of total independence with the demand for a comprehensive safety net funded and maintained by somebody else, anybody else. What annoyed him most was the complete vacuousness of discussions about personal responsibility. Every time somebody was stabbed or shot to death he was asked what the Government was going to do about it, to which the answer he was never allowed to give was that it had not been the Government wielding the knife or the gun. The people responsible for crimes were criminals, not the Government. Neither could he say that his proposed solution to reducing crime—as its incidence corresponded precisely to income levels—was to increase the income of the poorest. He could not say that it was not drug and alcohol consumption that were dangerous in themselves, but that the reason for using them was the key issue, as he would then have been regarded either as snobbish or unscientific. Gordon had done the best he could with poverty, but it was little enough. Yet there was no moral force—not even the churches—that could bring the debate back to a proper understanding of personal responsibility. He had never imagined when he was in opposition that the moral corruption of his generation would become so complete that they would blame their children for their own selfishness. If there were feral children—and from what he could tell there were very few—it was their parents who must take responsibility for the way they had turned out. It was a terrible generation that could both heap all its own corruption on its children and destroy their futures by wrecking the environment. Of course there were large, unchartable, cultural forces at work but he could not help thinking that Margaret Thatcher—whom he admired much less than was supposed—had been responsible for at least articulating the amorphous trend by transforming greed from one of the Seven Deadly Sins into a civic virtue, a stance which was widely applauded by the rich and the powerful under the guise of a liberal principle that would ultimately benefit everybody through the 'trickle down' process. He supposed that there had never been an age when greed had not been the most prominent political driver, but the scope for it and the damage it was doing were now so great that, even if the macro threat of climate change was somehow averted or mitigated, there would be an almighty moral crash unless Perpetuanism, or something similar, came to the rescue.

For what he saw in Perpetua which he instinctively warmed to was her insistence on personal responsibility. He had asked for her speeches to be included in his press briefings and he particularly applauded her call for the abandonment of the victimhood paradigm, even amongst those who might justly think of themselves as victims. Like her, he knew that the only real answer to victimhood was God's strength to persevere. No amount of ideological coherence nor campaigning would ever be enough. The Scandinavian laboratory was not replicable, even in twenty-first century Scandinavia.

The Police Commissioner and Lady Broadparks were enjoying a late night drink before retiring to their respective clubs. "I am most grateful for your tact in the Perpetua affair." "There are some interesting loose ends there." "Yes, funny that there are no records of the CEC programme." "Much worse from our point of view, many people claim that they saw a murder and not only has the programme gone, but there's no body." "What about the television appearances on Easter Sunday?" "Not a criminal matter, although I don't envy Edwards at DIM. He's lucky that the Government's about to change, but I will have no such luck, people expect the police to be all purpose social servants." "What do you expect?" "Well, for a start, I would expect your Church to do better. At the moment crime is falling—although it will inevitably rise when the recession comes—but nobody seems able to stem the fear of crime and to stem the hysteria about sentencing." "Well, there are liberals in the Church who would agree with you, but I'm not one of them." "True, you're not a liberal, but neither am I. What we need is responsible agencies like the Church to be rational about risk. For example, the people who fear crime most live where it occurs least, in sleepy villages, and we need them to be honest with themselves, admitting that most of the crime against people actually takes place in families, whether you're talking about murder or child abuse and most of that is in socially deprived areas. Although I know you won't like to hear this, why can't the Church make people so happy, or hopeful, or whatever the word is, that they don't need drugs or alcohol? You people are supposed to be specialists in the fundamentals and yet you just put out bland reports." "Well, Commissioner, if they were less bland they would be less unanimous. You know the game." "Yes, but people being killed and people ruining their own lives isn't a game." "Sorry, I meant the report game." "But reports, perhaps not individually, but cumulatively, have an influence on perceptions of reality. I am faced with a set of problems, associated primarily with poverty and alienation, that nobody wants to fix. You are supposed to be specialists in social justice and fixing alienation. If you don't fix this problem with your highly principled friends, then the call for stupidly punitive sentences will continue, which won't do any good for society or the individuals." "One rarely hears that from a policeman." "I hear it all the time from most policemen but, like people in the military, what we have to do is confused with what we think we should do. There's a limit to what we are allowed to say. That is why we need others to say it for us. Now Perpetua at least used to say that people should take more personal responsibility and not 'buy in' to the liberal agenda of victimhood and society being to blame, even though I have just admitted, to some extent, that it is." "Well, I fear your faith in her was ill founded. She's off the front pages, even off the inside pages of the church press." "Well, that is my point, really. The papers are stoking up enormous fear because one little girl has gone missing, implying that it could be any little girl at any time—which, in theory, it could—but we can't go on with this exploiting of the possible at the expense of the probable; it will ruin us. However, what I really wanted to say was that I don't suppose Jesus spent much time on the metaphorical front pages. Strange, I have more faith than you."

As he looked yet again at a chart of the receding glaciers of the Andes, Will Dignot remembered what Perpetua had said at their first meeting. He had laughed then at the thought that she could run a successful campaign against consumerism, but he was not sure now. As usual with politics, it was all about timing. How late would politicians leave it before they took draconian action to save the planet? They knew that the longer they waited the more draconian would be the action, but as long as it could be pushed away, until the next month, year or election, that was for the best. Will wondered whether the planet would respect this prevarication or whether the action, no matter how draconian, would come too late. He wondered whether the current passion for genealogy, allied with the long-standing obsession with heritage, were all part of a selfish mind-set that could not handle the future except in terms of the next gratification. It was as if people had gone back to being animals, only worried about the contemporary equivalents of the next meal and the next mate. He wondered, too, whether this accounted for what amounted to a hatred—with some exceptions, of course—of children. This was not the deep, directional hatred of two, usually related, enemies, but a general malaise of affection. Because children were commodities and not individual creatures made in the image of their creator, as Christians described it, they were loved as long as they performed their supposed function, but, like broken televisions or faulty washing machines, they were condemned and then discarded. He saw it in Grunge Park as he tried to make sense of the social dynamics. Young children were dressed and lavished with gifts as if every day were a wedding day, yet as soon as they began to speak for themselves, the lavishness declined into indifference and then renunciation. Will wondered whether it was the lavishness which caused the teenage fracturing of self-awareness, but he doubted it because he found it hard to explain why treating people well would 'spoil' them. There was an argument that gratifying a person's every wish robbed them of fortitude, but it was an argument almost exclusively advanced by people who would not deny themselves anything on the basis, he supposed, that they had the fortitude to withstand the spoiling. More likely the root of disenchantment was the recognition that the clothes and goods, no matter how frequently given, would not make any difference in the long-run. They were being used as badges of esteem which, it was hoped, would, for as long as possible, hide the lack of self-esteem. It was this that led to drug abuse and it was that which led to crime.

He smiled wryly when he had to cover interminable stories about new initiatives to control knife and gun crime. The debate was always conducted in abstract terms. There was a 'problem', which was 'caused' by a 'breakdown of community', which needed to be 'solved' by a 'crackdown' by 'the Government'. He could not accept that any of the terms in this surreal equation were real. Even as a rather indifferent journalist with no drive to dig deep, he could see two propositions which seemed as near eternal as he could imagine. First, that human degradation was the result of human wickedness, and that human wickedness was part of the human condition, which might only be mitigated by a higher purpose—which Perpetua had called God—than an ethical code, no matter how altruistic. This second proposition seemed coherent not because Will was particularly prejudiced in favour of religion—although he had thought much more about it since his contact with Perpetua before and since her death—but because he had learned, as a postmodernist, to suspect the self-referential, the only validation worth having was external.

He looked at the chart again. In spite of the way in which people took global communication for granted, watching World Cup football on television, sending digital photographs to relatives on the other side of the world, taking weekend breaks as far away as Bangkok, there was no sense of ownership of the environmental crisis. He remembered an American businessman in Peru, confronted with the evidence of receding glaciers, finding it hard to square this with his belief that global warming was a 'plot', although he was not clear who had hatched it. One theory was that the energy producers were using scare tactics to increase the price of oil and gas and it was these industries which were most in denial about the phenomenon. Another theory was that it was 'anti-liberals' interfering with the free market, but only people on the way up believed in free trade, whereas incumbents always wanted regulation in favour of incumbents. The American could not disentangle the supposed outline of the plots, but neither could he disentangle himself from his prejudices. Not for the first time, Will wondered how businesses made money when they seemed to be driven by prejudice and, to cite a stock market truism, 'sentiment'. He could only repeat that it was all natural, the meteorological cycle would turn. We had, after all, survived the ice ages.

It was easy to castigate the Americans, but Will saw a rising tide of resentment—he could not help thinking in the cliches of his trade—against the rising price of petrol. Instead of accepting that price was the only lever that would ultimately cap and then reduce consumption, people expected the tax on consumption to be reduced without saying what other tax they proposed that the Chancellor should raise. What they were proposing was an increased subsidy on petrol and a decreased public sector budget, but nobody ever seemed to put it that way.

His Channel was prevented from raising these vital issues because it was in deep financial trouble and the notion that investing in cutting edge journalism and raising difficult issues would improve the viewing figures was bogus. Intellectuals, particularly of the liberal and 'left' tendencies, were very fond of saying that unpleasantness, apart from being culturally valuable, was economically viable, but they were totally innocent of commercial logic. People might want a certain kind of unpleasantness because it gave them an adrenalin rush—crime movies, real murders—and they did not mind exposees as long as they placed the blame squarely on 'other people' in general and politicians in particular, but they were not prepared to use their leisure time, let alone pay, to watch a programme which told them how irresponsible they were.

Will, believing that it was not intrinsically bad, could not find a convincing argument that people should reduce their consumption for some notional planetary gain. He recognised Perpetua's argument that consumption should be reduced because that was good in itself, that as 'stewards' of the planet we should exercise restraint, but he could not see why non-believers should do anything which negatively affected their life style without any evidence that it would do any good. On the other hand, morally literate people did not decide whether to lie or tell the truth on the basis of what good or harm it might do. Giving ethics an actuarial, utilitarian bias was dangerous, Will thought, not because of any intrinsic fault but, again, because all such calculations were mutually reinforcing, internally consistent and self-validating and, ultimately, circular.

Will's partner, Annie Price, in her role as a manager of a Hypo superstore, was in more direct contact with the realities of climate change and global warming. She knew that all the major retailers were competitive athletes in never-ending regulatory flight: if the Dutch imposed conditions on the kind of fertiliser that could be used in the cultivation of flowers, they sourced their supplies in Hungary; when the EU made a new regulation they sourced in Kenya; when Kenya was leaned upon to impose regulation with grants from the EU, they went to Bolivia; and when a competing economic imperative generated a level of pollution which rendered horticulture uneconomic in Bolivia, they would have to look elsewhere. Annie knew all about 'clapped out' soil, the expansion of deserts, the deforestation of jungles, the de-vegetation of deltas, the salination of wet lands, the evaporation of lakes and, most obvious of emblems—icons, or even sacraments—the recession of glaciers. Under Perpetua's influence she had seen the folly of selfishness, not the self-indulgence of a glass of wine or a spliff, but the use of foul language in public which polluted in a manner similar to cigarette smoke. She saw that actions which damaged other people, particularly the less powerful, had a moral 'down side', but she equally saw that consumption, in spite of wrinkles in the market, benefited producers. She understood how Perpetua could discuss limiting consumption without understanding its effect on producers, but she did not have equal sympathy for green lobbyists who seemed to overlook the underlying trend, which showed no signs of weakening, of rising consumption of everything which would, with supply rising more slowly than demand, make net producers richer, but net consumers poorer. The era when consumers were able to impose unjustly meagre margins on producers was over for the time being. The producers were about to enjoy their period of dominance, but she pictured to herself the unproductive urban slums of Latin America, Africa and Asia and did not see any measure that could help their starving and hobbled people. Whether it was Corporate Centre at

Hypo or 'talking heads' on late night television, they were obsessed by models of desired, required or forecast behaviour where the greatest virtue was assumed to be consistency, whereas her job required her to recognise patterns in actual behaviour. There was no point in insisting that people "should" be buying fruit because of the forecasts of a marketing campaign when they persisted in buying ice cream. The superstore provided fascinating information about human behaviour, which demonstrated the heroic and persistent altruism of the 'fair traders' as well as the susceptibility of part of the customer base to every form of advertising. Like Will, she concluded that a change of attitude to global warming and its consequences would only happen when the crisis was imminent by which time action, no matter how drastic, would be redundant.

She thought about Perpetua's death and the way she had re-appeared on Easter Sunday and she recalled how the followers of Jesus had been obsessed, after his Resurrection, with the idea of foreshortened eschatological time and wondered why this generation, so close to disaster, was not similarly obsessed. It seemed less worried than any previous generation by the idea that its behaviour had consequences. Perhaps it was this freedom from retribution that had cut people free from their moorings and, if that were true, society was handling its new found freedom reasonably well. Society could function without the limitations placed upon individual and collective selfishness by the fear of divine retribution, but she wondered whether we were not reaching a critical limit. It was not the Grunge Park symptoms of substance abuse, vandalism and violence that worried her, but the complete failure of intellectual and moral leadership by the governing class, with its self-conscious cleverness, its postmodern refusal to take responsibility for anything, its loss of any notion of truth and, during the past decade, its loss of the ability to conduct dialogue.

Damian, still working for Smoother as a volunteer, but looking for a paid job, was thinking of the forthcoming conflict, or "death throes", as he put it to himself, with deep pessimism. During recent weeks he had received a series of setbacks in job applications and interviews. He was, by nature, a very straightforward person who answered the questions asked as directly as possible. He found, however, that the more straightforward he was in completing application forms, the less likely he was to be asked to an interview, and the better and more originally he performed at an interview, the less likely he was to be offered a job. On one occasion he had carefully studied all the answers which he would be expected to give at an interview, had followed the correct brief without deviation and had been so disgusted, on that basis, to be offered the job, that he had turned it down.

When he put forward his strong, evidence based views on a topic he was invariably asked if he held such strong views how he would be able to work alongside colleagues to reach a consensus. He vainly pointed out that there was a vast difference between all parties agreeing in advance of a discussion and agreeing to a consensus after a discussion in which a variety of standpoints were put forward. New Labour's reaction to Thatcherite assertion and to multi-culturalism was to try to marginalise all disagreement by proposing a bland, jargon-ridden form of lowest common denominator decision-making which, it mistakenly thought, offended no-one, but as all major agencies were now governed and administered by people wish sensible shoes and a safe pair of hands, with power so dispersed that it was impossible to locate where the buck stopped, public services would ultimately absorb the same or more funding without any long term improvements. The culture no longer wanted passion or richness.

This supposed need for unanimity also had the effect of 'thinning language' and turning what should have been vigourous and challenging proposals into the platitudes of communiques, a trend which had now crept into Church affairs, replacing both robust and strongly argued and humble and questioning theology. It might be too pessimistic to call this the "death of discourse" but he felt that it was deeply damaging. The Church had lost the ability to conduct its own dialogue and, like a great many secular agencies, it needed external facilitation. The common ground of rationally employed and received language was breaking up and he had noticed in a number of recent political biographies that some politicians had stated that they had refused in office to say things which needed to be said because they knew that they would be deliberately and maliciously misinterpreted by commentators who would claim that the language had been so ambiguous that a variety of readings were possible. This posed a danger even greater in the context of theological writing and the current bitterness.

He linked this deterioration of dialogue with what he thought of as the decline of seriousness, although he admitted that much of what had been thought serious in the past was only superficially so, being more often merely ponderous and redundantly complex. On this point he was no snob, accepting that a DVD today was the equivalent of a novel 150 years ago. He did not expect people to read Dickens when they could watch films by Mike Leigh and he thought the latter likely to do adults more good than reading the interminable volumes of Harry Potter. Diligent seriousness had been replaced in the mind of 'Middle England' by a sloppy adherence to heritage in the mistaken belief that age conferred worth. Likewise, he thought that much contemporary rock music had more value than the obscurantist musings of John Cage and he deplored the use of classical snippets as mood music. Associated with this, his tolerance did not extend to the easy acceptance of rampant individualism whose most unpleasant symptom was the loss of a proper distinction between the individual and the person and between private and public space. He did not much mind people using obscene language in their own houses, but hated its use in public places. He disliked noise pollution even more than air pollution, and he was deeply embarrassed by the kind of material which he heard at his end of mobile phone conversations. The three words which echoed through public life were "Me" "Want" and "now" and he knew that if this narcissism persisted civilisation, built on respect for the other and delayed gratification, could not last. In the face of these clear dangers, Damian wondered how the Church had stumbled its way into cultural incoherence by concentrating on such a narrow area of ethical controversy that most people did not understand. For him the gay issue was simply part of a failure to understand the meaning of love which, as it was the core of Christianity's raison d'etre, was a serious shortcoming. Unlike liberals who thought that "love" gave them a dispensation to do anything in its name, Damian believed that an understanding of love involved both the experience of living without it and being willing to sacrifice it. Just as Petran dissenters should not be allowed to enjoy obeying their consciences over the exclusion of women from clerical life without having to make some kind of sacrifice, so liberals should not be allowed to be sentimental and hedonistic about love.

Down the corridor, Chris Smoother was dejectedly turning over the batch of documents for the next meeting of the Grand Synod: mental health, inner city crime, the environment, the conservation of ancient churches, rules on marriage in church, rules for missionary activity, rules for governing the Anglican Communion—and then, of course, rules about sexual intercourse, rules about gay people, and rules about women priests and women bishops. He wondered whether any of these debates would take place or whether a proposed emergency meeting of the Synod would finally signal the split which would probably have been inevitable, even without the advent of Perpetua.

The joy which he took in contemplating the glory of God, the wonder of Jesus, the power of the Spirit, had all been ground out of him by his full time post with the Church. Obviously, to be fair, every institution of a certain size required governance, but if you looked at the Church dispassionately it would be difficult to see why it existed. He had heard the argument that after Catholic emancipation it no longer had a purpose, that it should have been disestablished—and that, at least, would have saved it from having to replicate all the bureaucratic and legal complexities of a Parliament—but he valued the way in which, for centuries, it had managed, in its very English way, to embrace almost all shades of Christian thought and opinion, reflecting the view of one of its founders, Elizabeth I, that she did not want "a window into other men's souls". What depressed him now was not so much the legislative and social turgidity of what lay before him, but the knowledge that the discussions would lack that Anglican spirit which he so much loved and valued. Synodical governance had replaced careful and tolerant discernment with party politics; the curse of the dichotomies of conservative and liberal, catholic and evangelical, had seemingly robbed good men—and they were mostly good and mostly men—of their ability both to imagine the position of the other and to grant it space in spite of their own disagreements with it. He could not understand how the Church had got itself into a position of sanctioning discrimination that even a secular, prevaricating, mean spirited state would not sanction. He could not understand how the sexual obsession, so understandable in a male, hierarchical organisation, frightened of the 'secret' powers of women, had survived the contraceptive pill and the bikini by half a century; he could not find any reason for the ferocity of the anti-gay campaign although he could explain it—which was quite a different thing—in terms of its unimaginable otherness, as distant from the feelings of most people as is the equally strange phenomenon of people with no feelings at all. What was worse was the constancy of the focus on sexuality which, in spite of repeated calls by the Church leadership for a shift to world poverty and injustice, had merely resulted in those same leaders returning like the Biblical dogs to their vomit. Even the media had grown tired of the two topics that still obsessed his colleagues. If you could not sell sex to the tabloids you were more or less finished as an organisation.

Yet, worst of all, he felt that God had left the Church. He could discern the sacred presence in the person and thought of Hawthorne and some other individuals but, as an institution, it was spiritually dead. Having abandoned the Holy Spirit for majoritarian democracy, it had made the Ordination and Consecration of women, and other improvements, inevitable but, at the same time, democratic governance with all its bitterness and compromise had marginalised the theological. It was said, as a neat formula more nice than true, that the Church of England was Episcopally led and Synodically governed but it was now Episcopally governed and not lead at all. The bishops were concerned not with leadership, but with managing the more difficult issues that came before the Grand Synod to such an extent that they would frequently amend motions not by adding an extra clause or deleting a word from a motion but by deleting the whole motion from "This Synod" and inserting a massive compromising but constitutionally wrecking amendment. He had no sympathy for those against Synodical government whose opposition arose from their prejudice against women or their hankering for the Holy See, but neither could he side with the liberals who seemed not to understand that their social gains were being outweighed by a massive spiritual loss.

No wonder there was so much frustrated, unfocused, individualistically obsessive, spirituality—it had nowhere to go. The Vatican had inevitably reacted to globalisation with centralisation—the steamship and then the aeroplane had brought local anomaly to an end—and although its claims were frequently exaggerated by opponents, they were outrageous enough both to alienate most reasonable people and to to command little respect from those who stayed faithful. Evangelical sects, on the other hand, seemed even less in touch with the concept of love than a mean spirited, media frenzied Papacy. This did not mean that Smoother advocated anarchy. He thought that an institutional, corporate church was a necessary precondition for Christian faithfulness, not just because Jesus had founded it, but because, reflecting in his different way the intellectual preference of Will Dignot, he thought that everybody needed external validation. Talking to yourself led to bad decisions in general and to bad religion in particular. It was not just Prime Ministers who ultimately seemed to lose touch with reality, religious leaders such as James Jones of Guyana had gone off the rails because they were surrounded by uncritical people of like prejudice. At least the Church was in no danger of this, being at the other extreme, self-dedicated to controversy, and that was better than the terrible delusions of self-absorption, but it was still a lost cause. What was a Church for if it had abandoned God or if, as some people put it, it had been abandoned by God?

He conceded that this worry was, to a certain extent, a selfish concern as it so directly affected not only his spiritual and mental landscape, but also his means of employment. Non-believers were apt to under estimate the importance of religion which went wider than the self-interest or self-absorption of adherents. Secular society was 'free loading' on a Christian tradition even if the Church was 'running on empty'. The founders of small businesses who routinely over charged their customers cheated a way for their children into church schools—even pretending to be Christians as well as simply church attendees—so that they could be taught that it was wrong to steal pencils. The people who still believed in ethical behaviour, not because of a theory of utilitarian collective security nor because of some vague hope of reciprocity, were still most trusted to teach ethics. If God was thought to be dead, ethics would soon follow 'him' to the grave. The atheist jibe that religion was more responsible for war than any other phenomenon was a clear case of prejudicial grandstanding. If a balance could be drawn up—and it was more difficult than the Church's opponents granted—religion had done much more good than harm and the most compelling argument for this calculation was to imagine a world without it or, as an approximation, to look at the collective behaviour of Hitler's Germany, Stalin's Russia, and contemporary China where it had been subverted and marginalised. Religion had been no more responsible for the troubles in Northern Ireland than it had been for the bloodshed in the Balkans after the death of Tito. Granted, there had been a religious impetus behind the Crusades, but you could not tell Muslims that they were launched in response to the seizure of Jerusalem by invading Muslims. It was one of the shortcomings of intellectual life that people who said they were opposed to something excused themselves from the need to understand it both before their irrational conclusion and after it.

He put the booklets to one side and tried to concentrate on Hawthorne's address to the Grand Synod and to his own future which was bound up with it. Hawthorne had successively made and broken deadlines for his own decision—now everything rested on this. Having spent all his life in journalism and public relations he was no hero worshipper, but he recognised genuine holiness in Hawthorne and, in spite of the prevarications, he did not think he could have a better guide to follow. Hawthorne, after all, was one of the few bishops who took theology seriously and who talked about God with an easy if complex familiarity. You always felt when Hawthorne said that the Church was a perpetual question which would never be answered that he was not dismayed by the prospect of a lifelong quest that would yield no answer, and when he said that "fact" not "uncertainty" was the opposite of "faith", this was not a clever reversal of conventional wisdom but a careful response both to the glib and the struggling. Yet this made his job of Archbishop very difficult because people expected answers and not questions.

It was this very holiness which made him wonder whether it was worth drafting a Presidential Address for the meeting scheduled for early July. By then,

Hawthorne might have led many liberal followers out of the Church in pursuit of Perpetua. Yet, as he recalled the media coverage of the past week, it seemed more likely that, having been reluctant to take the post in the first place, Hawthorne would rather retire than either stay or break away. Archbishop Mwanga would probably resign out of loyalty and a number of other bishops would follow. This would leave the Petrans and Torans in control which, in turn, would lead them to abandon their marriage of convenience and declare all-out war which, because of their near parity in money and fire power, neither could win.

Archbishop Hawthorne was as near to despair as a committed Christian can be. He had not wanted his job in the first place, but had thought God was calling him; he had not wanted to abandon his liberal principles, but he thought that the unity of the Anglican Communion was more important than his personal convictions, for reasons which were becoming ever harder to explain, let alone justify. He profoundly disliked the alliance of bigotry between parts of the North American Church and sub-Saharan Africa and the language in which the current conflict was being conducted caused him terrible pain.

As he wondered what to do, his eye was caught by a picture of the missing girl who had become the nation's icon of hope, helplessness and prurience, a successor figure to Princess Diana, and he saw in her story a reflection of the Church, lurching between adrenalin-inducing crises. He saw his graceful —in both senses of the word—theology roughly handled as marginal ammunition. Where he thought about the institutional church in terms of questions, the combatants traded crude answers.

For a few hours at the end of Easter Sunday, he had seen some hope in Perpetua, not because he felt instantly committed to everything she had said, but because it offered an opportunity for a fundamental theological discussion which might ultimately subsume the 'presenting' issues. Any theological process which concentrated on essentials was better than the current dispute. If the Anglican Communion was to split, then let it split over something worth the pain. He could see why Trinitarians could never accept an idea of God with more than three 'persons' or 'attributes', but he could see how he might and, this being so, he could see how a split might occur although historically the Church of England had been better at living with theological difference than with much less important differences over liturgy.

Over the past four weeks, as the effects of Perpetua's post murder manifestation inevitably wore off, he still hoped that he could return to fundamental questions, but his time was running out. He was deeply tempted to leave his office and pray, but he recognised that prayer could be an escape. He would definitely decide before Pentecost whether to continue in his post or to become an 'ordinary' follower of Perpetuanism, if that were still possible. Otherwise he would go back to being a Priest. He had done what he could, but the Church needed a different kind of leader, someone who would make a move decisively in one direction or the other, to define an on-going institution and a breakaway group. So deeply did his temperament run against institutional religion, which made his acceptance of the job so difficult, that he hoped that the Torans would be strong enough to stay and that the Perpetuans and other liberals would have to leave. He walked to Smoother's office and said, "In confidence, Chris, you need not trouble to write a speech for the July Meeting of the Grand Synod. If it takes place, I will not be there, and I have decided to stake everything on the Emergency one-day meeting on the Saturday after Ascension. There will be one item of business, namely, the Perpetua Commission, and I will write my own speech for that." "I can see the logic, Archbishop, but why cause a split over Perpetuanism when it might not exist in a month from now?" "Because theological discussion of any sort is preferable to our current moralising. I have spent the past five years trying to hold the Anglican Communion and the Church of England together as a matter of principle. I now want the split as a matter of principle. Trying to find new metaphors for the wonder of God is far more important than rows about sex and gender. My own part in this is not important, although I will have to make a speech. What matters is that the Church discharges its theological duty and, in doing so, if it dies, the Holy Spirit will have to sort things out. She has been doing that since Peter and Paul had a row, and she may well just have to do it again." "Do you mean that you are certain that you will lose the Emergency Motion?" "Yes. That is why I know I will not be present if there is a Grand Synod in July, but the only reason I am not prepared to announce my intentions at the moment is that I should not be seen to forecast what I think will happen and I do not want to weaken those with whom I agree. They have a right to leave in good order and not to lose heart before the meeting."

Sneer saw the announcement of the special meeting and ignored it. There was no circulation in turgid discussions about theology. If you could not generate any interest in women bishops—even supposing you could get your hands on a surreptitiously taken photograph of one of them going topless—or even gay vicars, a row about a Perpetuan Commission was of no interest. Besides, tomorrow was the day when he would switch from sympathising with the parents to attacking them for allowing the child to be taken through their neglect. If the story ran for much longer he would have to work out when to switch back. He had got all the mileage he could out of attacking the Spanish media, the legal system, the police, the hotel security, so the parents would have to be next. It was a dangerous game, particularly if they turned up other evidence on the day he switched sides, but the risk was worth it. The nation was addicted in equal parts to fear and self-loathing and this story nicely met both requirements. Some people thought, Sneer vaguely recalled, that Jesus was supposed by some nutters to stand alongside the suffering, but he knew better. God was dead.

From the attendance at the annual Church & State reception, the behaviour and facial expressions of the drinkers, and the general air of comfortable occupancy, the casual observer would not have thought that the Church was dead and, consequently, would have assumed God to be very much alive. As part of their duty to a civilised society, bishops and priests, officials and 'leading' members of the laity, thought it proper to attend gatherings such as this whether or not they could manage the vin de table and they thought it equally proper to maintain superficially cordial relations with everyone that came into their orbit. There was still a deep feeling of mutual affection and solidarity which, some thought, might yet save the Church from itself. Nonetheless, faced with the underlying tensions, Hawthorne found it very difficult to concentrate on a discussion of contemporary church architecture with a specialist and, in spite of all his experience, found it hard to be civil to Sneer who had turned up to try to get Hawthorne onto the Phil Mac bandwagon. Will was also finding the evening difficult, but that was because he was known to be a television journalist and chat show host which made him the centre of attraction for a persistent knot of bishops, deans, and archdeacons who, he was surprised to note, wanted to talk about everything and anything, except the 'presenting issues' which might shed new light on the concerns of the Church. When it was gathered together, in more or less loose congregations and consistories, it seemed to be concerned with a multitude of ordinary matters which gave rise to trivial, if persistent, disagreements, but when it was gathered together formally, in committees and Synods, it seemed to be unable to shake off its obsessions. Will could have filled his programmes indefinitely with items about church towers, modern hymns, the levying of water rates, the theft of lead, Scripture for toddlers, organ restoration, cathedral admission charges, post offices in churches, and the state and status of religious education. As Will thought that he could not get an audience for any of these topics, he wondered whether the media was actually distorting the Church agenda by concentrating on issues which did produce an audience but, as the evening wore on, he began to see past the ordinary civilities and cares of the Church. When he asked Varnish why everybody was managing to be so cheerful, given the gloomy news, the Archdeacon said, "One of the problems with the media is that you can only really think of one big thing at a time. It is as if you thought that during the War nobody did anything that was not connected with it, as if all artistic, cultural, family, and obsessive life stopped so that everybody could devote themselves all day and every day to the War. It is like that now with the Church. No matter what controversies, what dangers of schism or complete disintegration there may be, as long as there is a church to run we have to run it, just as politicians who know they are going to lose an election go on campaigning because that is their job, just as civil servants in occupied countries try to go on doing their job, as with gardeners in a storm or entertainers in the rain, the show must go on." "And how much longer can it go on?" "Not much longer. The Petrans are already booking their passages to Rome and the only real issue is whether the Torans will hold the bridge and force the liberals and Perpetuans out or vice versa. It's my belief that Hawthorne would sooner be out and take people with him, leaving the Torans in charge. This would make financial sense because they have the money to maintain the historic fabric of the Church but I can't imagine why they have ever wanted to be inside the Church of England as they say they don't care for the buildings, don't like the liturgy, don't like bishops, and don't like many of the other varieties of Anglicans." Hawthorne came by as part of his wish to greet everyone. "I am sorry, Archdeacon, that I have not paid so much attention to your letter about the restoration of Saint Stolid's as I ought, but I fear I shall be remembered as the man who presided over the disintegration of the whole of the Church of England, as opposed to one of its buildings of modest worth." Will introduced himself, as anxious as he could be to get a story. "Is the disintegration next week or some time in the middle distance?" Hawthorne thought, "in the middle of next week", but professional loyalty to Smoother prevented him from being totally frank. "I think Perpetua has challenged us and we cannot wait any longer to meet that challenge. By the end of next week we will know the mind of the Church and each of us will then act accordingly." "Does that mean that you will resign?" "I think it more likely that the Church will resign from me."

7.

Back in Alchester, Bishop Hall was thinking about the Dean. Had he been in office two generations before, when ideologues of both 'right' and 'left' had an approximate idea about the theory of revolution and the practice of industrial relations, the theory of international law and the practice of street demonstrations, Dean Prior would have been labelled "The Red Dean". Not only did he exercise the powers of his office and utilise the facilities of his cathedral (and, given his complete difference of outlook from the Bishop, the one instance of his appealing to his independence and rank was the use of the term "My" in connection with the cathedral) in the cause of the outcast and the under-dog. He revelled in the outlandish and rejoiced in the rich untidiness of diversity, so that the august, but not so architecturally distinguished as York nor so venerable as Hereford, Church of St George teemed with objects and people that, under his care, seemed to complement rather than clash: posters for the release of the Durham Seven, Malawian dancers, slide projections of melting glaciers, breakaway Sikhs, the Realist School of contemporary Laotian painting, finalists in a Dance for Christ competition, canned food for the poor, a bean bag retreat, save the sea shells, a Cuban guitar quartet, Trident Missile petitions, an immigrant and asylum advice point, Stations of the Cross, engineers against natural disaster, Biblical face painting and as wide a variety of worship styles as the whole contemporary Church had variously proposed, were all grist to his eclectic pastoral mill, but his motives were not, as many supposed, political. He was a liberal by temperament, upbringing, and experience, and because he was convinced of the fundamental goodness of everything and everyone created, his enthusiasm for incarnational celebration led him to the simple conclusion that unless somebody was able to show him the bad in something or somebody he would assume that everything that God made was good.

Both his eclecticism and his independence irritated the Bishop although neither had initially caused much friction. James thought that the Church of England should follow the Medieval pattern and combine the offices of Bishop and Dean into one, integrated entity, one which he would have loved to have filled, but he recognised that this was not possible under the rules of the Church Established and, given the choice, he had taken the episcopal route for although he was a scholar he would not have classified himself as an intellectual, and although he was a shepherd he was shy. The friction had arisen when the Dean, as the Bishop saw it, had begun to use the cathedral as a rival centre of power—or, should he say "Pastoral care"?—which gave voice from the pulpit and in countless other groups, events and displays to opinions that he found distasteful, and since the latter days of Perpetua there had been a dangerously heterodox series of sermons preached by Cathedral Officers and the Dean which were brazenly published on the cathedral web site.

Yet there were two principal reasons, from opposite ends of the 'political' spectrum, why the Dean was almost beyond criticism. The first, which was far beyond the Bishop's imagination, even though it should have been one of the foremost pieces of intelligence in helping him to understand the socio-cultural composition of his flock, was that what looked 'liberal' to Petrans and Torans inside the Church hierarchy and laity involved in active campaigning looked decidedly ordinary, or even indifferent, to most 'ordinary' Church members. They might look upon gay people with a mild distaste, moderated increasingly by first hand experience of them among their acquaintance, but this did not extend to imposing discriminatory rules, particularly as the theological case was narrow and obscurantist. The great benefit of following Jesus was that while his demand for love was unrealistically exacting it was simple and clear. Secondly, in contrast with his extremely broad minded view of ethics, ecclesiology and liturgy, he carefully maintained the traditional worship of the cathedral at unaltered times, while supporting alternative services which had to fit inside the traditional framework. An arch-traditionalist might enter the cathedral by its side door, reach the choir and retrace his steps as he had done for the past 50 years without any change in the words, only incremental changes in the music as new composers 'tipped' over that imperceptible boundary from *enfants terribles* to knights of the realm, totally oblivious of the riot of colour, movement, sound and political ferment which constituted the ecology of the main body of the church. Such people were prepared to stomach the outlandish and even subversive language of the Dean, as long as it was confined to occasions which they were not forced to attend and not introduced into their own Matins and Evensongs, and as long as nothing that they really valued was changed. There was a point of friction, because although the Dean understood these unwritten rules, he felt that he could not observe them in his Sunday Eucharist sermons, the high point of his missionary week, but the traditionalists had ultimately recognised that this inconvenience was a price worth paying for large and relatively cheap draughts of spiritual comfort and cultural ennoblement. For while they were not unethical nor theologically indifferent, being largely conservative and acquisitive, they necessarily split their religious practice from their moral behaviour, seeing the former as largely aesthetic and therapeutic and the latter as intrinsically competitive.

Yet there was one further major factor in the Dean's favour and that was his way of speaking and arguing. Although he held his views passionately, he argued for them lucidly and although his indignation at injustice blazed within him, his speech was warm and quiet. He was courteous no matter what situation he found himself in, as the victim of abuse or as the clear winner in a debate, because he offered his sufferings to, and accepted that his gifts were all from, God which meant that he was not disliked for his lucidity or passion, for they were part of his holiness. Conversely, the Bishop's indecision and imprecision, which might have been accepted as an integral part of his holiness—the ecclesiastical equivalent of the mad professor—came across as Jesuitical, if not 'clever', in the worst senses of those words. Consequently, the Bishop, although he was sure he had the majority of his flock on his side, was weaker in general than he thought, and extremely weak in cathedral circles. As if this were not bad enough, he found that his ambitions to rid himself of the turbulent Dean would almost certainly be thwarted by the legal arrangements which separated (and protected) them from each other.

It did not help that the key civil servants in the Prime Minister's Office had already got wind of proposals by the in-coming Prime Minister to change the appointments procedure because, by extension, dismissal was its reversal and there was, as is always the case in the professional classes, an underlying reluctance to get rid of anyone. In addition the Appointments Secretary still bore the scars inflicted by two over exuberant deans who had quarrelled with and survived the retirement of, their respective bishops, and so the somewhat tentative call of Bishop Hall to explore the possibilities was greeted with a response as near to raillery as a civil servant dares to venture. "For a start, Bishop, I have to warn you that it would be for the best if this were a completely informal discussion. One cannot keep anything secret these days (even if one wants to) and the notion that any email marked confidential is guaranteed to be given that status by the recipient is wishful thinking. However, I think I can honestly say that our system for monitoring telephone communication is such that we can talk with relative freedom and, at this point, we will be so informal that I feel a minute would be superfluous." "Oh, don't be so stiff, Theo. We've known each other how many years? How do I get rid of my Dean?" "Well, Bishop, as you know, he strictly isn't 'your' Dean, so to speak, at all. I need hardly remark on the peculiarity of the Church of England which so radically separates and allocates parallel responsibilities to bishops and deans, but it worked perfectly well until the two—how shall I say, professions, cardres, disciplines, ranks, offices, jurisdictions, whatever?—began to be interested in religion. Until then there was no *casus belli*. However, now that the Church has become so radically disestablished, in fact if not in law, that it presumes to involve itself in religious matters—I know you might argue that the Grand Synod legitimises what the Church does but I have my doubts about the whole proceeding—we have noticed a trend towards friction between deans and bishops which is deeply to be regretted in office holders who may have doctrinal differences, but who are, under our settlement, primarily administrators. It would never do to allow personal differences to poison smooth working relationships." "I understand your point of view, but what can I do about the Dean?" "In general terms I fear, very little, but you need to be aware, on a strictly informal basis, that the in-coming Prime Minister is likely to make changes to the system so that it would be untimely to continue to operate under the existing procedures, pending the new arrangements." "Changes?" "Yes. It seems that Mr Brown is not over fond of becoming involved in the high level appointments of a Church of which he is not a member and with which, I venture to say, he is not in sympathy. He therefore proposes to relinquish his powers under the Royal Prerogative to the Church itself." "What? Give us responsibility for appointing our own bishops?" "Would that not be logical?" "Indeed not. It is only the Office of the Prime Minister and his excellent advisers that prevents the Church from being completely over-run by liberals." "Indeed. Yet was it not also the current system that produced 'your' Dean?" "Yes it was, and I daresay if my Diocese had had its choice of Dean we would have got somebody much more to my taste but, on balance, looking at the issues in the round, bishops really don't want to be held accountable to transparent Diocesan bodies. We are much better where we are, responsible to Her Majesty who will ensure that we all retire or die, whichever is the sooner, without undue embarrassment." "On that basis, however, you would be in a position to remove the Dean if power of recommendation for office and for the termination of office were in local hands." "Yes, but can nothing be done in the meantime?" "I very much doubt it in general terms, but you might want to forward any particular grounds for your disquiet to me because, whereas the general principles and the reasons for delay because of their revision are matters which I will happily discuss, if there are any peculiar factors pertinent to a particular dean I would welcome the information even if I did not feel that I could immediately act on it." "Yes, I am sure you would, but I do not feel inclined to give you that patently one-sided pleasure." Irritated, the Bishop terminated the conversation after some face saving pleasantries.

Having been so emphatically warned off by Number 10, the Bishop was reluctant to act unilaterally, feeling the need of support from at least one of his Assistants and as Aleford was, as usual, somewhere in the Diocese with his mobile phone and his Chaplain's mobile phone both switched off for days together, he somewhat reluctantly contacted Castlegate. "Bruce, I'm having a problem working out how to shift the Dean." "I thought you might. He will be well protected by his fellow pagans, masquerading as good Christians, in the Cabinet and in other strategic positions. I sometimes think that the only people in power who understand principles are the Roman Catholics. At least they vote against relaxing abortion laws, gay adoption, Civil Partnerships, Frankenstein embryos, and the like." "I hate to disagree with you, Bruce, particularly as I need your help, but I am inclined to believe that the Roman Catholics have a much firmer grasp of obedience than principles. Be that as it may, there is no immediate possibility of ridding ourselves—finding a mutually satisfactory accommodation—of the Dean through strictly formal channels." "Perhaps what you are suggesting is the use of the Network for Truth?" "I was not thinking of anything so concrete but, now that you mention it, we might consider, er, working alongside ...". "... I am sorry, Bishop, in spite of the language of sharing and solidarity in Christ, you must resign yourself to the fact that the Network for Truth retains control of all its operations to guarantee a consistency of approach concomitant with the clear teaching of Holy Scripture. You propose an end and we either agree it or disagree, and if we agree, we will be responsible for the means. We do not like our clear-sighted strategy to be mired in good intentions." "Hilary would be appalled." "It's the Network for Truth and the end of the Dean or it's neither." "Sometimes, Bruce, you are so brutal." "I didn't ask to be an Anglican or a Bishop. God called me to sojourn for a while in this rotten church as the prophets sojourned in the corrupt courts of Israel and Judah." "Thank you, Bruce. If you go on much further in that vein I will have to consider the procedure for firing—dispensing with the services of—suffragans as well as deans." "If you do that, James I promise you, you are finished. You have only been kept here, because Blair will only appoint liberals, until Gordon floods the Church with Evangelicals." "I will ignore the crude insult, Bruce, and confine myself to the observation that Mr Brown is being accorded a wide variety of attributes which he does not possess. Just as 'left' wing people think he will follow their agenda in spite of his—to his credit—repeated denials, similarly, whatever you say—and he may appoint Evangelicals for all kinds of reasons—he is a 'progressive' 'son of the Manse' who will not want to side with the Petrans on human reproduction nor with Torans on gender issues. In any case, I gather that Gordon wants to wash his hands of Ecclesiastical Appointments as quickly as he can." "In which case we will soon be in control. The Petrans are transfixed—excuse the slight humour—and the liberals, always inclined to go their own way, are now placing their faith in Perpetua, a woman ..." "... Not now, Bruce, I just wish you could stay focused on the business in hand rather than blazing away in all directions, unnecessarily insulting—if there is any such thing as necessarily insulting—people you need, at least for the time being. By all means enjoy your triumph—if that is what it turns out to be—when the Church gains control of its own episcopal appointments but, in the meantime, we are supposed to be working together—although so far I think I have done all the work—to arrange for the departure of the Dean for our mutual benefit, "mutual" meaning that it's to your benefit as well as mine." "Sorry, James." "As you may have guessed, we have made no progress through the official channels." "Professional solidarity." "Quite. So we need another approach." "What about using the Populist Alliance Network for Theology and Society." "I don't like the acronym." "What, I never noticed it!" "Never mind. What is it?" "It's a loose alliance ..." "... Loose," mused the Bishop, "... between Evangelicals and journalists—mostly from the tabloids—to combat media immorality." "By which, I presume you mean the display of naked women." "Exactly." "With very little regard for their other much more serious vices such as greed, cruelty, lying and, worst of all I thought you would think, idolatry. In a way that many people might find it difficult to understand, I am more worried about the hypocrisy of condemning teenage sex in an article alongside a near naked teenage girl than I am about the picture of the girl herself." "I was only trying to help." "Sorry, Bruce, I'm forgetting. I'm doing what I accused you of doing. What does this Network do." "It tries to place morality friendly items in the media and tries to exclude items which are unfriendly." "Evangelical censorship." "A bit harsh, James. The point is that not all journalists are corrupt and we work with allies inside newspapers and broadcasting." "How does that affect the Dean?" "I am not sure whether we can help; it was simply a suggestion."

Castlegate reported into the Network. Two days later a story appeared in the TT under the headline:

GAY DEAN OUTED

It was met with total indifference from those not interested in the Church and near total ridicule from those who were, as the whole life of the Dean— from his university indiscretions to the tragic early death of his wife and his subsequent avowal, against numerous advances from always beautiful and often rich women, of lifelong celibacy as a tribute to their love which no other earthly love could equal—was well known to the establishment and Church activists alike. The following day he was accused of giving moral support to illegal immigrants and the day after his cathedral was described as a "Disorderly House", which he rather liked. The coupe de grace—if as such it may be described—was a tale, obliviously a contradiction of a previous story—for if there had been a charge to be laid of bisexuality it surely would have been—of the Dean and a model under the headline:

DIRTY DEAN IN SEX ROMP

All of which made Bishop Hall extremely uncomfortable as he could not fail to connect the series of 'stories' with Castlegate's Network. Its effect, however, was much worse on Doris Hall who was one of those beautiful and rich women who had proposed marriage to the Dean and been refused, but who still loved him with a not altogether platonic intensity, with a persistence which was indifferent to his friendly but firmly stoical outlook.

Their coincidence within the same close had been one of those accidents which neither was able to avoid. The Dean had settled happily into his cathedral work before James was nominated for Alchester after the Prime Minister had turned down two sets of two names for the Diocese because he deemed all four nominees "theologically shallow". James, who might have been similarly described, had been appointed as the last ditch option and, as she knew he would never have another chance of such an appointment, Doris accepted her inevitable suffering. She was a wise and worldly woman who was well able to estimate the limited impact of tabloid fiction on the Dean or his reputation but, still, the coverage hurt her because of its intent. She had no doubt that Castlegate was behind it and she therefore intensified her intermittent campaign to persuade her husband to force his resignation. "I know you say you need him at the moment to preserve the Petran/Toran alliance against women bishops," she said, on a point where she was wise enough not to remind him of their difference over the issue, "but these kinds of dirty tricks will not only land him in trouble, James, they could quite easily destroy you." "I could deny I had anything to do with the Network." "Shame, James! I did not mean that these activities will destroy your ecclesiastical career—although, of course, they might—but that it would destroy your moral integrity."

Their pained discussion was interrupted by the arrival of Castlegate whose triumph was plain. "The Dean's a busted flush, James. Today's papers will ruin him." "There is no need to be so loud, Bruce, nor so blatantly crude." "But you wanted him ruined, don't be so hypocritical." "You are over-stepping, Bruce." "You wanted to get rid of the Dean—there's no point pretending otherwise. And I told you about the Network and you you knew that it would have to resort to unpleasantness although we were both tactful enough not to mention it." "So that is your idea of ethical journalism, is it?" "It was the lesser of two evils. The journalism is always unethical, but you can replace an unethical dean with an ethical dean you have gained." "I don't know what kind of ethics you call that, but I doubt it would pass at a Selection Conference for Readers." "Are you threatening me?" "Just stop it!" said Doris. "There are only two things to say. Firstly, the Dean is not, in your clumsy phrase, 'a busted flush' because neither his reputation nor his self-possession will in any way be affected by this vile tabloid coverage. It's a mistake of the insecure—and the proud—to think that what other people say is important. Secondly, in spite of the complete failure of this dirty little campaign, I never want to see you again in this house." "But, Doris, you can't ..." "... Listen, James. I did not forbid your Suffragan entrance, I simply stated my preference which you are at liberty to honour or ignore." "That's unfair." "Not so unfair as your Suffragan has been to the Dean. In any case, you should count yourself lucky that your own reputation has not been sullied so far by these underhand—and possibly illegal—dealings." "Now we see your true colours," said Castlegate. "I have always wondered about those stories." "What stories?" asked the bishop. "The husband is always the last to hear," said Castlegate. "There have been rumours for years that your wife and the Dean have been closer than they ought." "For all our sakes," said Doris, leaving, "I will say absolutely nothing. Remember, James, I leave you to decide whether you will admit the Suffragan into this house. I now leave you with the additional task of deciding how to deal with what he has just said."

The bishop, who was not a bad man, but whose muddled progress often took him where it was better not to go, knew the true story of Doris and the Dean and, after a long and painful discussion about it during their courtship, they had agreed, by the mutual exercise of tact, never to allude to it respectively when she was tempted to compare the quality of the two men and when he was tempted to blame her love of the Dean for her lack of love for him. "I think I might say, Bruce, that our alliance of convenience has come to an end, that we should confine our dealings to the formal and orderly conduct of our ecclesiastical duties,and that until matters have settled down, your presence in the Palace is confined to its official offices." "That's the thanks I get for my trouble," said Bruce, who bowed slightly to the Bishop and left.

Hearing a garbled account of these proceedings, Aleford, who was growing tired of his alliance with Castlegate for all its apparent mutual benefit— the Dean's faction certainly appeared to be weakening—hurried to comfort the Bishop. "I am sorry to hear that Bruce has been sniping." "Don't worry about it, Hilary, I am used to his behaviour and accept that he is a burden I have to bear, but I do so because we have all agreed what use he might be in our common cause." "So how are we getting on with shifting the Dean? The newspapers have been rather unkind lately, although I find the use of the term "gay" as an insult somewhat irritating." "A point on which our very 'straight' Dean would support you. In spite of all our differences, I think you owe the Dean thanks for supporting gay priests—and even bishops—like yourself." "I haven't been involved in this campaign as much as I should, James, as I have been so busy providing pastoral care to the wavering clergy, and so I came to catch up on the situation with the Dean." "I can only say that I think the newspaper coverage will make no difference, except that it might just rouse the Dean. The essence of my policy has always been to secure a modus vivendi with a quiet Dean but I fear that we may soon see a very noisy Dean indeed."

Although he might have given way to over-reaction in his youth, the habit of suffering had tempered the Dean's volatility so that when he climbed into the pulpit of his cathedral to preach a sermon on Ascension Day, he gazed with satisfaction upon a congregation almost as large as that on Christmas morning. His methodical use of the local and regional media, as well as helpful paragraphs in the major 'Berliner' national papers and an off-the-record briefing to the BBC's Editor for Belief had brought a large number of media people and strange worshippers to hear him preach.

"Today we celebrate the Feast of the Ascension of Our Lord and Saviour, Jesus Christ into Heaven. The story of the life of Jesus which began, in the worldly sense, with the Incarnation of God as a helpless child, celebrated by so many in the Feast of Christmas, ends today with an equally mysterious fusion of the human and the divine in the departure of the Risen Christ from the Earth he graced and which repaid him with a cruel death.

"I am often asked how I can explain what happened at the Resurrection and Ascension of Jesus. What form did his alleged person take after he 'left' the tomb? What precisely happened when he 'disappeared' at Emmaus? How did his person become absorbed in the heavens when his feet left earth? I always have to reply that these are mysteries, but that they are no more mysterious than the initial incarnational arrival of Jesus. The mystery lies not in the individual events of the appearance and departure of God made human, but in the actuality of the gift of God to us in the person of Jesus. When theologians begin asking how something occurs they are likely to fall out—as they have over Penal Substitution and transubstantiation—because they are beginning to forget that language about God is metaphor. They would be much better off sticking to their vocation which is to help us to give shape to the substantive, to the 'what' question of theology, which will enable us to form and sustain our relationship with God. Theology, the very Church, is simply a perpetual question, a search for better language to help us relate to the God who created us out of pure, impartial love.

"Given that even love, as attributed to God, is a metaphor, we must proceed with some caution when discussing the subject. Love is a word which is apt to be tossed about to mean a great many different things from 'I love chocolate' to 'I love that boy or girl'. The trouble with these two kinds of love is that they respectively suggest consuming and imposing. In the consumption model, a person desires something, or more usually someone, and, if successful, in some way comes into a state of possession. In the imposing model, a person or thing is identified and directed. We can easily characterise these two kinds of love by identifying them with two partners in a sexual act. One person chooses to receive or absorb part of the other who equally wishes to impose, thus there is the complementarity of penetration and reception. In using these words I do not mean that such acts are not beautiful, graceful and full of grace, I am merely saying that these acts are quintessentially human.

"What I want us to think about, however, is a love which more nearly corresponds to the statement, "God is love" which opens the marriage rite. The essential, defining love which we attribute to the Creator is modelled in Jesus whose love, recounted in the Gospels, is not of that human, mutual kind that I have mentioned. It is neither consuming nor imposing. It is, rather, a love which simply creates the space in which the other can operate freely. Moreover, it is not confined simply to the "beloved other" but to all others. Love is not about choosing nor about judging, it is simply about being for all others.

"It is that idea of love, of its unconditionality, lived and taught by Jesus, which we have seen again in the life of Perpetua. She lived as Jesus lived, taught as he taught, and died as he died and. In a way which we do not yet understand, she has been with us since she was killed by us. Except for their time, place and gender, there is nothing which separates them except for our ecclesiological and doctrinal structures, which brings me back to my earlier remarks about the purpose of doctrine. The two major factors which obscure our clear understanding of the life and teaching of Perpetua are the doctrine of the Trinity and the structure of our Church. The doctrine, which Perpetua discussed herself, says that God has three 'persons' or attributes, but it goes on to say that that state of three-ness is timeless. It accepts that Jesus was a timeless aspect of the Godhead which took human, historical form, but it also says—with no evidence from Scripture—that the Godhead has chosen, is only capable—here the phrases are very difficult—of taking an historic form only once for all times and places. So if there are creatures in another solar system who were made by God out of pure, impartial love, so that they might choose to love freely, hard luck, you will have to put up with the almost impossible task (so heroically undertaken by the Jews) of trying to form personal relationships with a God who is essentially abstract. Perpetua said that God could have as many 'persons' or attributes as might be required to revitalise the dialogue between the Creator and the created, to load the dice in favour of love, to give a boost, in our particular case, to a culture that has turned away from God."

Only a few, a very few, began to grow restless. The Dean sailed very close to the wind in his sermons, but he usually got back to port safely enough, having made his hearers think on the voyage, but this was the most provocative he had ever been. The rehabilitated Poppy Smoother nervously checked the meter on her field recorder while her father carefully checked the advanced text, hidden inside a hymn folder, against what was being said. Max Silver, listening to the public address system in a side chapel, feverishly texted contacts while Kylie sat in a distant corner to help her concentration. The Cathedral's staff and clergy saw a break coming, and Doris Hall's energy was divided between the enjoyment of the words and the need to conceal it.

"The second obstacle to our clear understanding of Perpetua's message is so obvious that it should be much more easily overcome—it is the Church itself. Perpetua pointed out that we are too inward looking, that we are not taking the Word of God to the majority who are ignorant of it. We are not trying to bring people back to God. We live in an age which is identical to that in which the Apostles lived. We have to convert pagans to the worship of the one, true and living God. Now, the observant among you will have noticed that I did not say that we had to convert pagans to Christianity. That was not an accident."

Everyone became very still and tense.

"It is my firm belief that Christianity has itself become an obstacle—as rigid legalism was to Judaism during the time of Jesus—to the establishment of our individual and corporate relationships with God, rather than being a blessed conduit. Yet, before you protest, let me remind ourselves that the Apostles did not deny the validity of their Jewish tradition—Paul was worshipping in the Temple when he was arrested at what was the end of his public mission—and I am not denying the essence of Christianity, but simply the way in which it has become deformed.

"I believe that it has become deformed in three ways. Firstly, as I have mentioned, its doctrine has become a static end in itself, not a means to help us in our relationship with God. Secondly, as I have also explained, the institutional church is so enfeebled that it cannot help itself which is, presumably, remembering our caveat about metaphor, why the Godhead thought it was time for another divine shot in the arm, in the form of Perpetua. But, thirdly—and although I do not want to dwell on this, it must be mentioned for completeness—the inward looking Church is more interested in excluding than embracing. It has replaced love with judgment, and it mimics secular politics and secular jurisprudence.

"Because of my support for the inclusion in God's church—not our church, God's Church—of gay and female clergy, I have been accused of not being a Christian. Well, if supporting the calling of all people to serve God is not Christian, then I am afraid I will have to count myself as not being Christian in the sense that it is defined by those who disagree with me.

"I therefore declare before you all, that I shall ask Dexter to receive me at Pentecost as a follower of Perpetua and that, insofar as I am able, I will dedicate the facilities of this cathedral to advance God's purposes on earth so that the Kingdom may be realised here and now, in each of us. I shall continue, as a follower of Perpetua, to be a Christian, just as the Apostles of Jesus continued to be practising Jews. No doubt there will be legal difficulties as this supposed Church of God uses its energy to establish its right to buildings and money. I will work for a reasonable settlement between those who wish to stay as they are and those who wish to travel with Perpetua, even though those who have disagreed with me within the Church of England have shown no sign of granting any such consideration to me.

"As we consider the Ascension of Jesus into heaven it is now given a new aspect. Until Perpetua, it was thought of as the close of the single chapter of God's entry into history. We have now seen another chapter completed. If the new way is to replicate the old, we shall soon be inflamed by another Pentecost."

Nobody had been so angry that they left the cathedral during the sermon but a few pushed their way out at its conclusion and even more left under the cover of the Peace. Smoother underlined a few phrases and smiled. Poppy checked her field recorder and smiled. Doris smiled.

Just before going to church for the Ascension Eucharist, Mark flicked through his favourite web sites for gossip on the latest developments in Church affairs. He was just about to check the cathedral site to see if it contained an advance text of the Dean's sermon when the screen went blank. Then Perpetua looked straight at him. "Mark! Mark! My mission has no part in church politics. End the war within you and follow me. Do not worry. My Sister the Spirit will tell you what to say."

Thank God Jane had already gone over to church. He gave himself a minute to recover and then walked the short distance. The choir only just out-numbered the congregation and he thought with regret of his indecision. He had inherited a healthy Ascension congregation, but had told the choir he did not want a sung Mass, five hymns and an anthem. Members had drifted away to other churches where they could give of their best and, accordingly, the congregation had gradually thinned. When he changed his mind and reinstated the original liturgy, it was a struggle to win back the choir's commitment and the congregation. Yet what he felt, as he looked at them, was love for their loyalty. He had treated them carelessly and so many were still there. Through all the recent traumas, the core of the choir and congregation were still there. Jane looked at him, slightly turning from her conversation as he went past. She saw that he had changed, but he hurried on to avoid any discussion. She knew better than to follow him into the reserved territory of his vestry.

The Eucharist followed its usual pattern without variation. He wondered when the Spirit would intervene. As usual, he gave his short address—designed to keep the whole service down to forty minutes—standing between the two facing banks of choir stalls: "In the name of the one God, Creator, redeemer and Sanctifier." He thought of inserting Perpetua but there was no inner compulsion. "Today we celebrate the day when Our Saviour returned to the Godhead and promised the return of Our Sister the Spirit."

Clement, sensitive to the significance of every word, tensed.

"We have grown accustomed to think of these days as the closing episode of the life of Jesus which began with the mysterious and miraculous incarnation of Our Lord, but we must never close our minds to the possibility that the Godhead might intervene again. In these times of materialism and cynicism many have given up hope; in these times of intrigue and bitterness in our Church, many have said that we are lost, that we have thrown away our Christian heritage."

Clement, without wanting to distract Mark, looked straight at him.

"But we must never give up hope. Perhaps this day was simply the beginning of the end of one chapter of the Godhead's graciousness towards humanity. Some of us have wondered lately whether the mission of Perpetua, which I discussed on Easter Sunday, was a new chapter. It is so difficult to see God's work among us when we are so busy with our own concerns which we prosecute in the name of God."

Jane looked puzzled. Marie stopped thinking of whether the altos would find their D in the anthem. Scott was bewildered. Helen concentrated.

"I have been so bound up in Church affairs that I led myself to believe that Perpetua was simply another element in the tussle between Torans, Petrans and liberals like me, but I have now come to believe, absolutely, that in celebrating the close of the Chapter of Jesus, who brought new hope to his Chosen People and the world, that we are called to celebrate the more recent renewal of hope in Perpetua, built on the eternal foundation of the mission of Jesus."

Clement almost lost touch with what was going on. Jane, accustomed to Mark's sudden shifts, resolved to be with him. Helen looked at Clement and then Mark and saw unalloyed radiance in their faces.

"Christ is risen and ascended. Perpetua is risen and ascended. Christ sent Our Sister the Spirit and that sending is renewed with us today. In the name of the one God, Creator, Redeemer, Sanctifier and Perpetua the Sustainer. Amen.

"We will say the Creed, each of us seeking the guidance of the Spirit as to what it means to us today."

There was silence as expectantly profound as that which awaited the lighting of the Easter fire. Veronica led the Prayers of the Faithful faultlessly inserting, in spite of her usual hesitation, references to the new dawn of hope made real by Perpetua. At the Peace, Mark came straight to Clement and, instead of the usual comment on the shortcomings of the just completed prayers or an instruction about the Sanctus bell during the Consecration, accompanied by a terse offer of a tense hand, allowed Clement to intersperse his soft, straight hands between his equally pliant hands. Helen came across the chancel to Clement. Violet and Ronald left their places, in spite of their difficulties with walking, and greeted Mark and Clement. Mark was oblivious to the time it took and did not hurry to the altar.

Clement anticipated the Consecration with new hope and deep longing.

"On the night before our Lord and Saviour was betrayed, he took bread, broke it and gave it to his followers, saying, 'This is my body, given for you.' then he took the cup and said, 'This is my blood, given for you.' Likewise, Perpetua, on the night before she offered herself for us in her bodily death, took food and said, 'This food, brought from God, bears the divine presence within us in all the unity and diversity of God Our parent, Jesus My Brother, My Sister the Spirit and my own self, the Sacred Vessel of God; receive us all in one.' She then took wine, blessed it, and gave it to them, saying, 'This is the wine of life, the wine of light, the strength of solidarity, the risk of dispersion, the strength of passion, the risk of excess. This is the wine of the free choice to love which earth has made and which is offered to us from God as a symbol of all the good we might do and all the risk there will be in doing it. This is the wine of pleasure and pain. It is the wine that sums up in itself all the love of God Our parent, the Brotherhood of Jesus, the Sisterhood of the Spirit and the renewed commitment I bring as God's Sacred Vessel; this wine is God in us."

Clement, not knowing when to ring the bell, had waited, but now rang it with unrestrained affirmation. When Mark finished the Great Prayer, the choir and congregation, without being bidden, formed a circle round the table. Helen brought a chair for Ronald and, as if this were a 'house' Communion, they gave each other the bread and wine, each improvising a blessing as it was given. Mark, no longer tense, trusting in the Spirit, gave the blessing in the name of the Fourfold Godhead and, instead of departing, sat on his Presidential chair, surrounded by his loyal people. Marie did not even mind that the anthem had somehow not been sung.

After a while, the need for spiritual celebration was complemented by the need for a more earthly celebration, so they made their way to the Rectory to drink wine and eat the food which Jane, taking all she had before the weekend shop, turned into a serviceable meal. Sensing that he could not have been alone, that he was not worthy to have received such unique blessing, Mark wanted to take Clement into his study to look at the internet, but somebody turned on the television and shouted, "It's her!"

"On the day that Jesus My Brother was folded back into the mystery of the Godhead's love, promising that that love would be made alive on earth in My

Sister the Spirit, I want you to re-live that triumph now in the new salvation of my mission. As Jesus came to bring new hope, I bring new hope now. Never forget what Christianity gave to the world but never return to its rigid and exclusive ways. Take the message of God's love to the whole world, to the world among you, to those who are poor and depressed, who struggle in ignorance of the good that surrounds them, whose ears are deaf to God's unceasing power to communicate with them. Pray and praise, see and serve."

The screen went blank before the BBC logo replaced god4u. After a nervous pause, the continuity announcer said, "We are suspending our regular programmes to stage a special discussion on the Perpetua phenomenon."

There was the Dean, outside Alchester Cathedral, surrounded by friends and journalists. At first everybody was excited to see their Dean on national television but they soon became bored. The interviewer only pretended to be interested in what the Dean had said by asking a token first question and then interrupting the Dean's reply—he was only really interested in speculating on what Bishop Hall might say and what Archbishop Hawthorne might do. The Dean refused to speculate on either point, returning again and again to the importance of Perpetua for the renewal of the Godly life in the world. He was asked about his own future, but he said that would depend upon Dexter and his colleagues. As always, the interviewer wanted his subject to talk about other people but not himself. This rather flat exchange, which would have been considered poor quality on regional television, was followed by a panel discussion comprising a leading Petran, a leading Toran, Max Silver, and Hawkins, the notorious atheist. All but Max were ill tempered and the arguments were circular. The Toran said that Perpetua was unbiblical, the Petran said that she was heretical, Hawkins said that she was just another example of fantasy and Max said that Perpetua was the incarnation for the Third Millennium. The Toran said that, like the other liberal gimmicks, she would make no difference to the true church. The Petran said that she would never be accepted by the Holy, Catholic and Apostolic Church. Hawkins said that it did not matter. Max, following the agreed line, said that the Ascension Day breakthrough needed to be assessed, but that there would be a special event on Pentecost Sunday. Asked why none of Perpetua's original followers were prepared to appear on television, he said that as long as Perpetua was still making herself present, they felt that they and the rest of the world should listen to what she said. The other three were nervous when her recent appearance was raised and changed the subject, as did the chairman who knew that his BBC bosses were deeply puzzled and embarrassed. When the theology and bickering became less nuanced, Mark and his parishioners became more exultant as the impact of the evening's events became clearer to them; they knew they had reached a turning point and when Max mentioned a "breakthrough" they finally succumbed to the internet and saw the extent of the change in the landscape of English Christianity.

Next morning, Mark rang the Palace to arrange an interview with the Bishop. He had thought of breaking the news to Brian or even Hilary, but he thought

it was important enough to resort to his Diocesan. He was told, when he finally got through, that more than 20% of the Diocesan clergy wanted to see the
Bishop but that he was currently in a meeting with the Dean. It was an easier
meeting than either man could have anticipated—the Bishop had no expectations of the Dean and was therefore not disappointed and the Dean felt so sure
of what he was doing that his usual self-confidence was reinforced. "Although,
technically, I need have said nothing to you, James, I feel that I owe you an apology. I would have liked to have given you some advance warning of what I was
going to say yesterday evening but, I have to confess, I allowed the enjoyment of
the surprise to over-ride courtesy." "That is good of you, Dean. I must confess
that while I was not surprised by what you said, I was surprised by the way in
which you acted. We have always had our differences, which is why the courtesy
we have both exercised has been so important." "Again, I can only apologise,
James. However, the reason, as you probably surmise, why I came was to say
that, insofar as the crowded schedule of the Cathedral can accommodate your
wishes, it will. I do not believe that opening our hearts to Perpetua renounces
the saving work of Jesus. Of course, there will be some who will be tempted to
offer conditional access, to say that a traditionalist can only officiate if he or
she invokes Perpetua, and some people might in turn retaliate by refusing to
officiate unless any reference to her is dropped. I know that neither of us is like
that. For all our differences, I believe that you have always been more open to
difference than your office allows you, yet now that the Church as we know it
is beginning to change its shape under this new influence, I hope you will feel
that you need not be so bound." "I appreciate your generosity, Dean, but I doubt
I will be able to enter the cathedral in the current situation. Strictly speaking,
you and your fellow enthusiasts have given way to a massive doctrinal altera-
tion which renders Christianity redundant, without any reference to any other
part of the Church Catholic." "James, let us not have that discussion yet again. I
have too much respect for you and for the Holy Spirit to think that I can argue
you into changing your position and you know that, having followed my liberal
course steadily over the years, you will not be able to alter mine." "No, Dean, but
you might just tell me, in your own way, what Perpetua has to offer, to say how
Jesus has failed." "The last remark, James, was atypically unfair. Jesus has not
failed, just as YHWH did not fail. We have. The creator created us to love freely
but we lose heart, we lose fibre, we lose muscularity. So Jesus was incarnate to
build a bridge between the Creator and humanity, but after two millennia the effect has worn off. You might argue that that is a calumny against the Holy Spirit
but the essence of Christianity, of reformed Christianity, is that it is concrete
and organic. That is its great mystery." "Yes, Dean, I know we have failed." "We
have all failed. There comes a point when what they call 'bug fixing' is never going to be enough. At some point there needs to be a wholesale re-appraisal, but
instead of a Council of the Church, or even the humble Grand Synod, we were
given Perpetua to help us." "But how can you turn your back on the Trinity?"
"I see how important this question is, but how did we arrive at the Trinity?" "I

think we are in danger of doing what we said we would not do." "I agree, James. I apologise. Let me just repeat that as long as I am Dean—and who knows how the authorities will react—you are welcome to continue to do what you have always done in the cathedral." "Thank you, Dean, once again."

On his way out, he saw Castlegate and Aleford talking together. They paused for a split second, ostentatiously ignoring him, before continuing what, to the Dean, seemed like a somewhat fractious conversation, Castlegate looking even paler, and Aleford even more flushed, than usual. Having curbed himself for so long, the Dean could not resist remarking, "Dividing the spoils, I suppose. Now that we are leaving, there will be no need for the 'unholy' alliance of Petrans and Torans. You can resume your deadly battle while we unite behind our liberation agenda." "It's unbiblical," said Castlegate. "Well, if you are right, Bruce, you won't be tainted by us any more although, having said that, I have often wondered why you want to hang on to huge churches when you propose Spartan liturgy. I also wonder why you are so exercised about women as bishops when you're only just in favour of bishops or, rather, cannot quite bring yourselves to be honest in your rejection of them. As for you, Hilary, I am sorry, but I think you will have cause to regret our departure. How will the huge number of gay, Petran clergy fare under Toran domination? I know you can claim that the Holy Spirit made you choose your allies, but I think it is fraudulent to cite her as a supporter of every mad, misogynistic, homophobic outburst." "Even if you are right, your movement is schismatic and heretical." "I seem to recall that that was precisely what the Saducees—too often confused with the Pharisees with whom Jesus had so much in common—said about Jesus. Anyway, I must be off to our new church. I wish you joy of each other." And, with an almost malicious gesture, the Dean left the Palace.

"Good riddance", said Castlegate, but Aleford was not quite so sure. Boosted by the prospect of a new global Anglican 'pillar' to counterbalance Hawthorne, Castlegate felt confident that his cause was in the ascendant but, with his jibe about the loss of allies, the Dean had scored a clean hit. It was only with the prospect of their departure that Aleford recognised the extent to which he had been screened by the liberals. Castlegate and his allies would show no mercy. The Petran rump would dwindle as the Diocese became ever more swamped by a new wave of Toran ordinands. Faced with this unpalatable prospect, the Bishop would either go over to Rome or go through the motions until retirement. It might suit James, but the prospects of his going to Rome were hardly appealing. Too many Roman Catholics conflated homosexuality with paedophilia, and the once relaxed attitude to gay clergy had now given way to ever tighter regulation. As Aleford's face became gloomy, Castlegate had no thought of magnanimity. "Well, it isn't precisely how we envisaged the departure of the Dean, but he's gone now. Next on the agenda is the large number of 'unbiblical' clergy." "Oh, you're back to that, are you?" "I am indeed. As long as God's Word was in danger from secularists it was important that all believers should stick together but now that we have forced them out, we will have to look much more carefully at what it means to be a believer." "That process will simply force more and more people out of the Church." "God chooses who is in the Church, not us. The Elect will, necessarily, be a small number." "In which I gather I am not included." "It is not for me to say, Hilary; but it would appear that you are making it very difficult for God to receive you." "And you tell me that you think that the Pope is a dictator. Perhaps the fatal flaw in Protestantism is that it exchanged Papal for personal, contested, dictatorship." Their voices were now so loud that it brought the Bishop out of his office. "I thought so. Now that the Dean and his people have gone we will realise what a force for moderation they were, keeping the more extreme factions quiet. It appears that I will be left to preside over the final, bloody battle between your forces." "I do not think you need worry," said Castlegate, not even trying to conceal his triumphalism. "He who is not with us is against us and we have only reached this sorry state because of weak leadership. Hilary and his friends hardly served as useful allies over the key issues. They were never worried about the principle of women clergy so much as about their own hierarchical and financial positions. I need hardly say how compromised they were on the gay issue." "If we must discuss this," said the Bishop, "I hardly think this is the right time or place. May I advise a little prayer, a little thought and a great deal of silence. We have a crisis to deal with which affects hundreds of thousands of ordinary churchgoing people who quite properly think we have been too immersed in our own affairs. Having failed them during the past two decades, it is perhaps a little late to try to mend what we have broken, but we must repent and do our best."

Mark proposed to write a letter and, unusually, asked Helen for advice. "I have to leave the theology to you, Mark, but the legal and administrative situations are likely to be very complex for the time being. So, please, be careful. I have to remind you about your pension, the use of the Rectory and Jane's interests. If I recall correctly, your marriage vow comes before your Ordination promises. If I were you I would do nothing until you have talked to Ronald and Violet, and I would not write any kind of letter until you have to. Wait until the Bishop asks you to explain your position and, even then, use the processes that are open to you. I have no doubt that the Dean, who is now the de facto head of the Perpetuans in Alchester, pending further guidance from Dexter, will give you good advice."

The advice Mark needed, however, did not come from the Dean but from Max Silver who was the Chief Executive of the Perpetuan movement until such time as major issues could be settled. Dexter had made it clear from the outset that he did not want to be an administrator and that his task would be to form the spiritual leadership of the Perpetuan movement. Meanwhile, Max was asked to deal with the financial, legal and structural issues which would take some time to resolve. "I know that Perpetua wanted a new kind of church," said Dexter, "but there are so many people who will need special care because of the pain of divided hearts. Many will recognise the call of Perpetua, but will naturally be reluctant to leave old friends and old ways of doing things. We must show

our commitment to Perpetua through how we liberate people, putting their relationship with God above all other considerations." "I know," said Max, "but
care includes salaries and at least a lightweight structure until people are used to
being out in the open. You can't move people overnight from being institutional
to being free spirits. We must not make the mistake of facilitating a massive
importation of people from an institutional setting, deluding ourselves that they
are free spirits, only to find that they have brought all their baggage with them.
Saint Paul was lucky, he saw Jesus, but many of the old Jewish school who came
into Christianity soon ensured that its open spaces, made by Jesus, were neatly
fenced in."

On the day after Ascension, Max put a letter on the god4u web site and sent
it to all the contacts on his list.

> Dear Brothers and Sisters,
>
> After the overpowering presence of Perpetua on the first day of Easter,
> many people thought that her mission had flared and died, but yesterday
> there was a remarkable injection of energy from her which showed us the
> extent of God's will for all people.
>
> In view of Perpetua's continued presence with us, which parallels
> the presence of Jesus between his Resurrection and Ascension, we have
> thought it right to leave her to guide our actions and, while her followers
> have travelled throughout the country carrying her word, there has been
> no systematic attempt to proselytise. Nonetheless, as there was a massive
> surge of commitment to Perpetua's mission yesterday, we thought it right
> to provide some information and guidance:
>
> 5. We expect that a number of leading figures, including bishops, will
>   make their position clear after the special meeting of the Grand
>   Synod.
> 6. Some Deans and Rectors of large parish churches have indicated
>   their support for Perpetua's mission.
> 7. While we re-affirm our commitment to base our mission in the spir-
>   it of Perpetua, on the formation of multi-class, diversity-affirming
>   house groups, we will require the use of major places of worship for
>   core regional activities and festive worship. We therefore call upon
>   the Prime Minister to facilitate a rational dialogue to settle church
>   property in such a way that it will not be held by those who do not
>   need it and cannot support it but be put into the hands of those who
>   make a realistic commitment to it.
> 8. Our core facilities will be relatively few compared with our numbers
>   and so we will be able to support them. The bulk of our resources
>   will be dedicated to full-time co-ordinators (or Guides) at these
>   core facilities who will be supported by foundation finance, freeing
>   future revenues for mission.
>
> Dexter will host a major celebration of the Sacraments of Union and
> Affirmation on the day of Pentecost at which followers of Perpetua will be
> welcomed and commissioned.

For the first time since the Perpetuan crisis began, Helen felt a deep hope and excitement. She saw a future in which Mark would finally be freed from his internal civil war and, even more importantly, she saw a future for Clement, serving God as he had always wanted, in Word and Sacrament.

Meanwhile, Ronald and Violet had spared Mark embarrassment by requesting a meeting with him. They renewed their offer of support which Mark happily accepted. They had conducted a lightning survey of the Deanery and concluded that Walmbury was the best place for a core facility. They pledged the balance of their funds to the necessary re-ordering, subject to Max and his colleagues confirming its position and, necessarily, subject to legal matters being resolved.

The resolution of legal matters was beginning to concern senior officials in Church and State. The Dean, who was on friendly terms with the Prime Minister, even though the media had drawn the opposite conclusion because it wrongly assumed that the Prime Minister had resented the Dean's attack on his Iraq policy whereas he thought that it was the Dean's job to speak for Christian values and to point out how they were in perpetual conflict with pragmatic politics. What he actually resented was the Dean's private observation that his sincerity was not in doubt because, like all Prime Ministers, he had massive self-belief which allowed him sincerely to persuade himself of anything. "Tony, I suppose you have heard what i've done." "Not only heard, but I have read your Ascension sermon." "You are very kind." "It's more than that, Dean. Once I have 'gone to Rome' as people so clumsily put it, I will need to advise His Holiness on how the liberal mind works." "Always supposing that you know." "Unkind, Dean, but I will forgive you because we both know that liberalism, unlike faith, is bound to fail." "True enough." "But even though you're a Dean I presume you did not telephone in the hope of an enjoyable theological discussion." "No. I rang because I think it is important for us to work out what the realigned church should do about property." "I thought that might be so. In the first instance, possession is nine tenths of the law. I would stay where you are until you see what can be worked out. Personally, I am split between my admiration for Perpetua's sense of renewal and personal responsibility and my need for a more traditional form of religion but, either way, this is going to be just one of Gordon's many problems. There is a rough justice here, Dean—or would you invoke the Holy Spirit?—because ever since I became Prime Minister Gordon and his friends have wanted to get rid of me and now that I am ready to go (needless to say I have been much less concerned about their sniping than the press supposes me to be), all kinds of financial chickens are coming home to roost: food prices, oil shortages, tax gimmicks, absurd asset price inflation, and now this. The trouble with an issue like Church property is that if it is solved elegantly nobody will notice, but if it is messed up it will be just one more black mark against the Government." "What is Gordon likely to do?" "Well, I wouldn't answer that question for most people but I ought to be able to trust a Churchman like you. He will do two things: first, arrive at a crude solution and try to brow beat everyone into accepting it; then, when that has failed, he will do nothing. He has the precise temperament of a bully whose aggression is fuelled by an over-estimate of his strength and then subsides in the face of opposition." "What would you advise?" "Get Max Silver to work out the finances. If the numbers stack up, Gordon will give way in the end. He doesn't really believe in heritage. He thinks it's senti-mental rubbish, but he will be so beset by troubles by the time you have worked out your figures that he will be anxious for any help. Incidentally, he doesn't like Torans because they remind him of himself." "What about Petrans?" "Come on, Dean, he's a Scot." "So what about us?" "His head likes you but his heart doesn't." "Who does he like?" "Nobody much." "Any further advice?" "No. Just get the figures right." "I hope we will meet once you have left office." "So do I. I think the debate between Perpetuans and other Christians will be quite fascinating. The outcome depends on vision, a narrative and, er, the Holy Spirit." "Nice of you to mention her, Prime Minister."

The Dean reported this conversation to Max who was encouraged. "We don't want to be unfair. We need the cathedrals and churches which coincide with our demographic although, of course, that will change and so we need to do things organically. We need to be able to give watertight undertakings." "What about money?" "Liberal, and now Perpetuan, resources, have always been un-der-estimated because in so many places liberals have been reluctant to commit to an equivocal church. The same, incidentally, is true for Torans. This realign-ment will produce large quantities of new money at least from these groups. It is not clear how Petrans will fare because they have always taken the existence of the Church for granted. They have a simple rule: the only role for the laity is fund raising and repairs." "That," said the Dean, "is why we needed Perpetua so badly." "I think you will find," said Max, "that you can hardly imagine yet how much we have needed her. We have just over a week to organise the leading out,but when it comes, it will be like Pentecost. I just know it."

Doris's admiration for the Dean's sermon was tempered by her duty of love to the Bishop. After he had down-loaded the text, James had kept out of her way, making it clear that he wanted to be alone, and had stayed up much later than usual so that she would be sleeping—which she pretended to be, for his sake—when he came to bed. Next morning, she had gone out early to let him breakfast alone but they both knew that this evasion could not last. When he came home for lunch, he showed his customarily concealed courage by saying, "I suppose you are much more sympathetic to the Dean than you are to me." "Theologically speaking, yes." "I have always felt that your preference went further than theol-ogy." "We both know the history of my relationship with the Dean." "I did not mean, as you must know, to cast any doubt on your virtue because you have al-ways put your faithfulness to me above your personal preference for the Dean." "We cannot pretend, James, that we have been a pattern of romantic love, but in the sense in which Perpetua defines love, of making space for each other, we have been true to our vows." "What should we do now, Doris?" "Whatever you do, I will support you. You know my position, but I regard it as part of my prom-ise to you that I should not press my view. I will warn you when I see trouble and hope that you can avoid it, but your conscience is as sacred as mine and I know that it is well tuned." "Thank you, but I really do need some advice. I can see the skirmishes between Bruce and Hilary turning into all-out war."

"James, any institution that uses God-given human language to try to bridge the gap between the transcendent and the human is, necessarily, bound to fail. We will always need a mutual exploration of metaphors as ways of 'understanding' God. The only difference between us is that you have, as a matter of upbringing and temperament, sympathised with the exploration of known space whereas I, on the same basis, have sympathised with open-ended, transformative possibilities. You like jazz, I like the inventiveness of rule-breaking, acknowledging that you can't break rules unless there are rules. Superficially, because you are a professional bishop, some people might think that you are hanging on to traditional beliefs because it is in your personal interest, but I know you better. If you 'go to Rome', I will come with you. If you stay where you are, I will stay with you. If you try to find a new way with Perpetua, I will travel with you. My love was crushed by the Dean's grief, but called out by your humility. I am not fooled by your indifferent attempts to play church politics. Whereas many—including the Dean—enjoy politics, I recognise that you regard them as a necessary evil." "Where shall I go, then?" "Be still. Whatever our differences, the Holy Spirit will help us to be still in our proper place."

8.

After the triumph of Easter Day, Dexter went North to Stumpy Knoll. It was not that he needed a break—recent events had increased his always large store of nervous energy—but he did need to get away from the scene of Perpetua's death and re-manifestation. The euphoria of Sunday had allowed him only a temporarily escape from his deep feeling of guilt at his desertion. It did not matter how often he was reassured, even by Perpetua, he knew that this failure would live with him for the rest of his life, and yet he also knew that without that failure he might have begun to approach his mission in the wrong way. He had always been 'full on' in everything he did and without his recent crisis he might have launched Perpetua's mission too triumphally, too sure of himself and even, in a strange way, too sure of her. When he thought back over all the things she said, there was always an openness in her language, no hint of authoritarianism, trying to shut people down. Having once been something of a thug, he knew he was apt to see morality in too stark a way and he was prone to moralising; but after he had left her when she needed him most, when he actually saw her in pain and distress, under the control of a gang of which he had once been leader, he knew that moralising would be impossible and, at the same time, he was also aware that there was the opposite danger of being paralysed by his own guilt. He saw now that getting himself back into equilibrium was the most important task before him until such time as it became clear what Perpetua wanted. On the Monday of Easter they had agreed to fan out across the country to undertake some quiet, exploratory mission work, leaving Trina in London to work with Max. Nothing very public would be undertaken until Perpetua's wishes were clear. Thinking of the Gospels, which Perpetua's life had so closely parallelled, Dexter believed that there would be a deliberate break, a final Perpetuan departure, and then a huge injection of energy.

In the meantime, testing the message quietly would be enough.

He chose Stumpy Knoll because he knew people there and did not want to be alone when he was not spreading the word. He knew how near he might come to despair and addiction and that addiction would lead to violence and wreck his mission. When he looked at the Apostles of Jesus he wondered how close they had been to committing a fatal act—getting drunk at a celebrity wedding, beating up a Sadducee, being found in flagranti with the daughter of a Levite—which would have ruled them out forever—yes, Jesus never ruled you out forever, but society did—and what difference that would have made. He looked at them through their rose tinted Gospels and knew it was messier than that or, at least, he hoped it was, if what he and his followers had to do was to resemble what they had done. He was under no illusions about his own weaknesses. He would never be far from despair, addiction and violence nor from the need to lash out, fight back, use a harsh word, issue a stark judgment. He had never managed to establish adult relationships with women—oscillating between adoration and contempt—and his culture had taught him a violent homophobia which experience did not justify, hating gay people in the way that white people in areas where there are no blacks have the strongest racial prejudice.

At the Monday Meeting they had discussed whether they needed more Apostles—like Matthias—but decided on a more modern model. They would stay as they were, but bring Max in as a sort of Chief Executive. This would allow them to leave London and mount low key operations, leaving them plenty of time to think and pray. That was another thing Dexter was worried about. He had no idea how to pray. He could say prayers, but he wondered why Perpetua had chosen him to be the *de facto* leader when he was not in the least holy. As he sat on the train, looking out at a milky sky, he thought of Trina and Miles happy together both in their love and in their praying. He knew that Miles prayed regularly and that Trina had tried meditation and contemplation. With them it was a 'live' issue whereas with him it was an abstract idea. When he had talked to Perpetua about it she had simply said, "There are all different kinds of prayer. Yours will be in action and in regret, in strength and in sacrifice. You will need to live your spiritual life in corporate prayer. Try to talk to God as often as you can, but be prepared for your apparent failure. Often it will just not feel right, but try because there will be a time when you will be alone and will need to handle being alone. There is a kind of prayer which puts you on God's wavelength and enables you to act in God's name. There is another kind, like going to the gym, that builds up your strength for when you might need it, like a battery charger. Do not worry about the prayer of others as they can only talk about it in metaphors and will generally veer from euphoria to melancholy. It is difficult to be balanced in a self-assessment of prayer. It is like sex—full of good intentions, bad execution, and exaggeration of achievement." He could hear her now, as he tried to shut out the noise of the train, to say a few words, and in doing so he found a simple pleasure because this might, for the time being, be the limit of what he could do, but at least he could find some words.

They were not quite words of thanks. He tried to work out where he was and how he had got there but answers to neither question came easily. He knew that he was the leader of Perpetua's followers until it was clear that a change was needed. He knew that he would be a sporadically good and bad leader, but he had never wanted to ask her why she wanted him because that would have been to fall into the "do you love me?" trap. Her love was only worth having if it was volunteered, and it had been, although that was before his cowardice. Had that changed his mind or hers? It seemed not. He had been moved to address the crowd, to officiate yesterday evening, to sit at the centre of the group without thinking about it. And they had been equally clear—Trina had more brains, Miles had more theology, Wayne had a way with words, Andy with figures— that he was in charge. Throughout his life he had been used to being in charge but that had involved brutality and violence. Now leadership had been handed to him as a gift in exchange for his treachery. He did not know how long it would last nor how well he would do, but he was going to say the simple words that came to him and teach himself to say some regular prayers when he was alone,and that was as far ahead as he could see.

When he got off the train, he was met by Steve, the new leader of the Hypo shelf stackers who had not been around when Perpetua had visited, but who had recently shot to prominence out of nowhere. Dexter hardly needed the few minutes as they walked into town to become deeply worried. It soon became clear that Steve was a passionate believer in Perpetua's divinity which he said had been confirmed by her technological power. He was clearly obsessed with controlling behaviour through the use of the internet and had been thinking of leaving Hypo to dedicate himself full-time to the study of technomancy. "You are missing the point, Dexter. People like you describe us as 'geeks' and 'anoraks', but we are the people holding the real power. We can shut down the global economy, and what Perpetua offers is a divine sanction for our exercise of control on a global scale. We can use information systems to ensure that Perpetua's writ runs throughout the world." "I think you have missed the point, Steve. Perpetua stood for self-determination, for affirmation, for the ability of people to lift themselves up towards the Godhead. She never wanted people to be compelled to follow her." "But we could do so much good." "Steve, you have hit the nail on the head. You are not talking of the good that the Godhead might do, you're talking about us, about what we might do." "But we are Perpetua's workers. She can't operate without us." "True, but we have to let her operate through us. In her own words, we are glass through which divine light passes and turns into every combination of human colours. I think you need to spend some time with your brothers and sisters thinking about the meaning of Godhead and, incidentally, while of course I thank you for your greeting and hospitality, you cannot lead the group here until you have straightened yourself out." Steve became very sullen and, once he had handed Dexter over to his erstwhile friends, he went home to plan an internet attack on Perpetuanism.

Dexter was therefore thrown back on the generosity of Pastor Drone who had once, somewhat reluctantly, allowed Perpetua to preach in his church. He was less certain of repeating the offer because, although he was not that way himself, he knew that his congregation generally associated blacks with fecklessness and violence. He understood that there were flourishing black churches where they sang and even danced and he was vaguely aware of Martin Luther King but, on the whole, he did not think that black people could be counted on to preach a reliable sermon. Dexter confirmed these doubts by saying that he did not propose to preach, as words were not his "thing", but he would like to conduct a healing service. Pastor Drone felt immensely comforted by this because he knew how popular such services were, in spite of their poor results. People went to them in droves the way they watched Stumpy Knoll Athletic, week in, week out, in spite of runs of atrocious form. Drone, whose gift was preaching lengthy sermons, could never bring himself to try healing services. His idea of the perfect religion was that it should be uniform and challengingly dull, and healing services smacked of Popery and enthusiasm. Nonetheless, as long as other people were prepared to take the risk and attract the crowd, he was happy to sit in the corner until he said the prayers at the end. One more healing service with no results would do no harm and there was the hope that some of the crowd of strange faces would return to hear him preach on a less excitable occasion.

The church was pleasingly full, with Stella and Lucia sitting in the front row, wearing lilac crop tops and mini skirts. He shuddered, caught between horror and desire. They immediately fastened on to Dexter because he was the visiting celebritym but also because his virility was irresistible. "You were with that Perpetua girl, weren't you? She was nice to us and I think if she had stayed around she would have made us better. That's why we're here, to see if you can go on where she left off." "That's the idea." "So can you heal us?" "I don't know. I've never done it before. It will depend on the pleading of Perpetua and on the response of Our Sister the Spirit."

Dexter gathered volunteers in the unused vestry and, house group style, got them to brainstorm the key words for prayers and discussion. The service began with an untidy hymn, then some prayers from the book, leading into a discussion of the different meanings of healing, then extempore prayers from the volunteers. Dexter stood up and said, "We have called upon God Our Parent, Jesus Our Brother, Perpetua the Sustainer and Our Sister the Spirit to heal our hearts of their pain and anxiety and, if it is right for us, to heal our physical and mental pain. If you want to make a declaration of your illness or worry, or the sufferings of another, speak out. If you want to keep silent, keep silent. We are all friends, but friendship does not have to mean talking."

Each member of the congregation came forward to kneel in front of Dexter so that he could place his hand on each head and make a small mark on the forehead, a cross within a circle. When he had finished, there was a strange and beautiful silence, wrecked by a final, untidy hymn. Pastor Drone was about to lead the closing prayers when strange things began to happen. A young man, who had shattered his legs in a motor cycle accident, pushed the rug off his knees and, as if it were the most natural thing in the world, got out of his wheelchair and walked carefully down the aisle. A man who could only just tell the difference between light and dark, turned casually to a neighbour and complimented her on the colours of her outfit. The verger stopped twitching. Stella felt all the aches and pains of her body disappear, and Lucia knew that she had been cured of her heroin addiction. Drone shut his prayer book. "As Perpetua said," Dexter told Lucia, "any cure is just to allow you a new start. Use it well. And, by the way, go and find yourselves nice boy friends instead of looking at me and allowing yourselves to be looked at in that way by Pastor Drone." "But can we follow you?" asked Stella, only half playfully. "Not now. We need you as witnesses to the power of God called upon in Perpetua's name. The local leader is dangerous and will no doubt try to wreck our mission here and so we need brave leaders like you." "What about you, Pastor, will you follow Perpetua?" "I am sorry, Dexter, but I don't think I can, really. I am too worn in my ways. Come back for a healing service whenever you want but, between times, we need the quietness of our weekly time together to ponder the weighty responsibility which God places upon us." "What about the joy of creation, Pastor?" "Looking at the wicked world, I think the idea is a piece of over optimistic humbug. We are all terrible sinners." "All sinners, yes, in that we fall short, but surely not that terrible?" "I have to confess," said Drone very quietly, making sure that nobody else was in earshot, "that I feel impure thoughts when I see those two shameless women." "Who wouldn't, Pastor? The great trick is to resist the temptation and to see Jesus in them instead of seeing your own desire." "But the Gospel says that you only have to lust after a woman and you have committed adultery." "Yes, Pastor, but I think that might be different from a little involuntary spasm."

The young man said he would tell the local paper what had happened. "Forget it," said Dexter. "Live your life as an example of God in you. That will influence far more people than being one-day wonder in a local newspaper." The young man looked disappointed. "Look, half an hour ago you were in a wheelchair and all you could think about was your shattered legs, your shattered relationships, and your shattered career. Now you are restless because you want to be a local celebrity. It's the best and worst of humanity." The verger hardly noticed the absence of his twitch and the blind man forgot to say thank you even though many people, who seemed to have no particular reason for offering thanks, formed a queue to talk to Dexter. In some cases it took days or even weeks before people realised the good that had been done to them or those for whom they had prayed. Not one went unhelped.

As the days went by, and nothing seemed to happen, Dexter did not lose heart. Perhaps if he had been more theological, more intellectually restless, he would have wanted something to happen. In an earlier phase he would have wanted to make something happen, but he had absolute trust in the Spirit. He had made one, massive error and he would not repeat it. His trust must be simple and uncontaminated by speculation or rashness. He occasionally received messages about the successes and failures of his colleagues, but Trina protected him from most of the passing 'news' so that he could concentrate on building his inner resources by strengthening his communication with God. She was performing a particularly valuable service because most of the news was bad. The occasional successes and special signs went largely unreported, but there was a steady stream of hostile material in the 'serious' newspapers and in the church press. Only three weeks after Easter Sunday, the remarkable manifestation of Perpetua on world television had been erased from the collective memory and the commentaries were full of lugubrious speculation. First there was the phase of forecasting a split—or, much more dramatic, a schism—in the Christian church, but as the Perpetuan movement waned, this gave way to a second phase of speculation about the time and manner of its collapse. It was a time for standing firm and not giving way to depression. Max was working steadily at organisation and finance and Trina did her best with the media, but what kept them going was the news from Miles who was working in Grunge Park in the middle of a new bout of gang warfare.

Miles had been a severe Evangelical critic of 'liberal' tendencies. He had believed strongly in retribution and in rigid, predictable punishments. He thought that the essence of justice was knowing in advance what would happen to you if you performed a certain act such as stabbing somebody. He had been obsessed with outcome and indifferent to motive. He had been attracted to the notion of nature, the idea of original sin, and "The Elect", and had been deeply suspicious of nurture, of social arguments to explain "evil". He had hated working in Grunge Park, but had persevered because he thought that it was his duty or, as more 'churchy' people would have put it, his calling. Perpetua had loved him because he had stuck at his task in spite of his loathing of it. This was a true measure of his capacity to rank loving over liking. The day after Easter he had volunteered to stay in Grunge Park. They had all been opposed, particularly Dexter, but Miles insisted. Given immense energy by falling in love with Trina, and convinced that he would die for Perpetua very soon, he was fired with the Spirit. Dexter saw that Miles needed precisely the opposite of what he needed himself. Miles was on a wavelength whereas he would have to struggle to tune in.

What transformed Miles was a mixture of Perpetua's sayings and his ability to see things anew, putting his observation before his prejudice. So, at a time when the media were beginning to panic over the increasing number of stabbings and shootings by teenagers, he persuaded Will to invite him onto Fang and, as an experiment, Will decided to conduct a lengthy, straight interview instead of pitting a number of guests against each other. Thirty years ago Will would have been a liberal, perhaps even mildly Marxist, a police baiter, and an anarchist. Oscillating between the scruffy asceticism of the squat and the sit-in and the sybaritic sensualism of dropping out and loving in but the twenty-something of the twenty-first century was at once much less ideological and internally consistent about his politics and much more cynical and sophisticated about the source and value of his pleasures. Will did not hold 'liberal' or 'moral' views about street violence. In essence, he held no views at all, not because he thought that an investigative journalist should try to avoid having views on subjects, thus stiffening his impartiality but, rather, because, like many of his post Thatcher generation, he held a profoundly ambivalent view of society. On the one hand, as an intense individualist, he wanted to maximise his freedom of choice, to maintain that there was—in the words of Mrs Thatcher—"no such thing as society" but, at the same time, he slavishly aped the central paradox of the TT. Enjoyment of unfettered liberty required "them", the state, somebody else, anybody else, to fix everything that went wrong so that, for example, Will thought that the 'nanny state' was guilty of imposing all kinds of unnecessary 'red tape' on school outings—children needed to be inculcated with a spirit of adventure and self-reliance—but it was also guilty if a child slipped on a ledge and was swept downstream to his death while the teacher was round a bend in the river trying to find the entry in his leader's manual on the correct procedure for the provision of sanitary arrangements for a multi-religious, multi-ethnic class. Beyond content, Will reserved the right to complain, but do nothing about anything. The consequence was that although his interviews could sometimes appear to be rather bland and lacking in fire, his guests frequently 'hanged themselves' on the unlimited supply of rope he allowed them.

Conventional wisdom, reviewing Miles on Fang, almost unanimously agreed that he had hanged himself. Miles' position was as follows: the root of all our longing is the longing to be in communication with God, both to hear and to speak. This underpins self-esteem and self-respect which, in turn, is a necessary precondition for esteeming and respecting others which enables collaboration both for self-interest and for mutual interest, leading to a recognition of the idea of society. When this began to bore Will, he pushed Miles on. Increases in the number of the police, harsher legislation, longer prison sentences, even the restoration of the death penalty, would not significantly affect the level of violent crime. Thatcher's "price worth paying" had been paid by the poor for the sake of the rich. It always was. If there was a credit squeeze, as seemed likely, the rich would bleat about the fall in the value of houses—to some extent cutting their huge capital windfalls—but it would be the poor who would be thrown out of work and back onto the scrap heap. Perpetua had insisted, however, that through all the terror and the turmoil, the insecurity and insanity of life on desolate housing estates, the important thing was to begin to make decisions, even the tiniest decisions, to affirm self-determination. People needed love and if society could not go that far, they at least needed respect. They needed education and the ability to manage their emotions. Finally, he said, when he allowed himself to be pushed even further by Will, nobody had a right to ask for anything from these poor, benighted people, unless they were prepared to take personal responsibility for their plight. The poor might be addicted to alcohol, heroin and cocaine but the rich were addicted to hypocrisy, complacency, and callousness. "If I could choose to spend my time on a desert island with a Grunge Park Gang or a sophistication of Sloane Rangers I would choose the Grunge Park people because, after indulging in a bout of victimhood and self-pity, they would learn the truth of their weakness and their strength, but the Sloane Square people are so full of self-delusion that it is almost impossible to teach them to understand that they have social responsibility. This is the clue to the saying of Jesus about the eye of the needle and it's the clue to Perpetua's concern that the church should involve inter class rather than international twinning.

Of course, Miles was slated for what he had said, as naive and soft. It was useless for him to protest that he had been working for three years in Grunge Park and that he was spending every day there now, in constant danger of being injured or killed, while those few of his critics who had visited the most deprived and depraved slums in the country had barely been out of their vehicles.

Smoother watched placidly as the media continued to delude itself and its viewers and readers. He agreed with Miles but it would do no good at present to say so because what concerned him much more was the contempt in which the Perpetuan movement was generally held. As far as he could see, she had not harmed any of the journalists who were so negative about her. They might have argued that, on behalf of their readers, they were defending the traditions of the Christian church except that this kind of defence was highly selective. Whether they were promoting sales through publishing soft porn or attacking Archbishop Hawthorne, discovering schisms or 'outing' gay vicars, they generally demonstrated a high degree of opposition to a church which, had it been more brave, would have attacked their cynicism more effectively. His concern was not the customary sort which focuses on the insult to his colleagues and the organisation, but to see that the media was beaten at its own game until he was ready to drop Hawthorne's bombshell. His opportunity came on the day before the Grand Synod when, with the permission of the Dean of Alchester, he 'let it be known' that the fellow was "out on a limb" and that he was "getting somewhat over-excited by a little local success in a largely inhospitable diocese". The Grand Synod would not be inclined—a statement which was literally true, but deliberately misleading—to take what the Dean said seriously. Thus, without being forced to misrepresent Hawthorne in any way, he had given the impression that the Church was staging a rapid recovery from a slight loss of nerve over Perpetua. A couple of more principled and well trained journalists reminded Smoother that the main issue was Hawthorne's proposal to give Perpetuan theology Christian house room. "I am not sure that that is as big an issue as you make out, but in view of the spectacular events over Easter we thought it right to clear the air. An organisation dedicated to theology as a tool in mission must take it seriously." Did this mean that Hawthorne was still in favour of a Commission and, if so, would this lead to a schism? Yes he was, but the use of the term "schism" was extremely unhelpful because, when it came down to it, most people did not actually know what it meant. The veterans were not quite satisfied with these answers and wrote judicious pieces about the future of the Christian church being in balance, but most of the coverage on the morning of the Synod talked about the Church's new confidence. There were no stories about splits or schisms.

At last it was his day. He could delay no longer. He had repeatedly delayed any public statement, but now there was no going back. Smoother was the last person Hawthorne saw before he climbed onto the platform of the Grand Synod. "God Bless you, Archbishop," he said, self-consciously, aware that the greeting was customarily the other way round. "Well, Chris, life in the Spirit is a tortuous journey but I know I will not turn round now." In his place in the gallery, Smoother carefully compared Hawthorne's opening statement with the text in his hand. He had begged him not to extemporise, not to add extra clauses, enriching the subtlety—but also the complexity and the opacity—of his position.

> The motion before this Special Session of the Grand Synod is that a Commission of eminent theologians be established to investigate the life, work, and teaching of Perpetua and whether they have any particular relevance for the mission of the Church. As you know, the House of Bishops was split on this issue, with only a handful agreeing with this proposition, which is why I am moving this motion on my own behalf. It seems to me that, just as we undertake serious discussions with other Christian denominations and indeed with other faiths, we should make every effort to understand the witness of this remarkable woman. Take away the Ecclesiology and she might be seen as a contemporary replica of Jesus in her acts and her teaching. Even in denying the claims she made of herself, we might find something valuable in what she had to offer.
>
> Now the chief objection to this proceeding is that we are a Trinitarian Church and her claim overturns that settlement, but we need to ask how far the Trinity is fundamental to Christianity and how far it represents a historical development so significant in what it said and solved that there has been an understandable reluctance ever since to re-open the discussion on the kind of formulations we might use to describe God. We are familiar with the Creator—why is there something rather than nothing?—and we are bound up in our lives with the affirming life of the Redeemer—the incarnational bridge perpetuated in Eucharist—and anyone who dedicates their life to the Church will have been extremely unfortunate not to have felt the presence of the Spirit. So far, so good. But space travel, indeed

our wholly wider view of astronomy in the twentieth century, might lead us to ask what we might know about God if we consider the prospect of the creation of other creatures for the purpose of giving God pleasure in an identical way to that in which we were created to give such pleasure. Further, we need to question how justified we are, particularly in view of Johannine theology, in asserting that the Creator has eternally set an ordinance of self-denial that rules out any further incarnational or other intervention in the earth's affairs, to say nothing of what might have happened in prehistoric times.

Finally—and I recognise that this argument will hold less force with many of you—even if Perpetua's influence is thought to have been slight, we are closer to our purpose in considering it than in being involved in any more hand-to-hand fighting over gender and sexual issues where our grasp of the science seems to be peculiarly weak. We have been too concerned with power whereas Perpetua warns us to be mindful of the powerless. The Church is a question, not an answer, and Perpetua has put the question in an intriguing new way.

Even the ultra liberals found this speech difficult to absorb. The motion was furiously attacked from both wings of the Church. Predictably, the Torans denounced it as a denial of the Bible and the Petrans denounced it as a denial of traditional doctrine. An impartial observer might have said that there was no sense of the failure of the Church's mission, but, then, no-one was an impartial observer. Even those who were agnostics, atheists, Epicureans, sceptics, and cynics were deeply conditioned by ideas of what the Church ought to be or not to be and what it was succeeding in being or failing to be. So far had the idea taken root that it is a moralising rather than a spiritualising force, anthropocentric rather than god-centred, hierarchical rather than a 'Royal Priesthood', that what Hawthorne said was simply dismissed as his usual sort of 'woolliness'. Those on the floor of the Grand Synod characterised him as wooly for much the same reason as the external critics because they had given up the idea of theology long ago, and his idea that Christianity was a question rather than a set of answers was characterised as empty cleverness.

Conscientious as he was, Hawthorne found it difficult to follow the debate with any interest. It was like being forced to play endless hands of contract bridge without the excitement of the bidding. There were slight tactical errors and infelicities, a trick missed and a trick surprisingly gained but, for the most part, the debate was distant from his conception of what such a debate should be. He knew not to expect theology, but he hoped to find just a little doubt. Occasionally notes were passed to him asking for advice. He courteously replied that he had to separate his private and public views. People had heard what he had said. Most of the 'usual suspects' spoke predictably, but Clement was not called.

Just before the summing up, Smoother sent some text messages when it would be too late for anyone to change the outcome. Likewise, Max had managed to fill the visitors' gallery.

Hawthorne rose to reply to the debate. "I wish simply formally to acknowledge the debate and to request the Chair to allow me to make a statement after the vote."

This was a somewhat irregular proceeding but the Chair agreed. The vote went decisively against Hawthorne: 8 Bishops in favour, 33 against; Clergy 62 for, 133 against; Laity 67 for 156 against. More than two-thirds in each House had voted against the establishment of the Commission.

Hawthorne was then asked to speak.

> I did not attempt in my opening statement nor did I want in my closing statement to say precisely where I stand personally in case this might have been construed as an attempt to turn this debate into a kind of confidence motion or loyalty test, for I know and appreciate your affection for me in spite of our many differences. One of the problems with referenda and critical votes of this sort is that they cannot force people to vote in answer to the question they have been posed. I did not want the vote on the Commission to be a vote on whether or not you want to keep me as Archbishop. I did not want to be thought in any way to be introducing an element of what some people might call moral blackmail into the discussion. From that you will quite correctly infer that I am strongly of the view that we as a Church should form a Commission. I say this in as gentle a tone as I can muster as your shepherd. It is impossible for people to go on forever separating their conduct, the exercise of their preferences, from the consequences of doing so. In our secular life, many people vote for parties which support selfishness and attack social capital, but then bemoan the state of society. They never seem to connect their vote with the outcome. Likewise, in this connection, it will be dishonest of the more than two-thirds of you who have voted against the Commission to say that you did not foresee what would happen. I have frequently been accused of being equivocal and prolix, but on this issue I could not have spoken more directly and unambiguously. If many of you who voted against the Commission think that you can nonetheless keep me as the devil you know, you are incorrect. I cannot continue to serve in a Church that has turned its back on theology in favour of moralising. I could just bear the persecution of gay people and the marginalisation of women in the name of the Bible—and, worse, in the name of Jesus Christ Our Lord—as long as I thought that there was a chance that I might turn the Church back to its central purpose of bringing people closer to God. Contrary to popular opinion—and even some opinion in this Synod—the business of the Church is not to moralise nor to manipulate. It is not to exercise power even if it thinks this is for the good. The Church exists to enable all God's people to draw ever closer to God; and its purpose is therefore to concentrate on the means, no matter how fragile and uncertain, metaphorical, and malleable, through which this individual desire, shaped corporately, can be realised. Our central business as a Church, then, is theology. It is our purpose to understand the mystery of God insofar as it is given to us; and to convey the truth of what we apprehend to the whole world.

We have turned our back on our mission. Perhaps I have been partly to blame—it would be arrogant to say that I bear no responsibility at all— but

I have tried my utmost to keep us focused on the purpose of our existence and I have failed. I am therefore confirming in front of you the terms of a letter I sent earlier today to Her Majesty and to the Prime Minister resigning my position as Archbishop as of 5pm today, less than five minutes from now.

After a few moments of stunned silence, there was a ragged series of exclamations. "Further, at the moment when I no longer hold office as your Archbishop, I will submit myself to Dexter as an ordinary follower of Perpetua, as a priest with no special claim upon his attention. I bless you as Archbishop for the final time and hope that those who repent of their decision—not because of what it has forced me to do, but because of its intrinsic defects—and, indeed, those who stay where they are, will find a way to become ever closer to God."

As the Chairman formally closed the proceedings, Smoother and Max stood by. Hawthorne turned and they helped him to hurry off the platform before his erstwhile fellow bishops could reach him. He got through the narrow corridor unimpeded as the crush of followers slowed each other's progress. A car was waiting at a side door and moved off without incident. All the media was crowded at the the steps to the main entrance.

Hawthorne was driven to a quiet house near the canal where he could take a light dinner and pray. As soon as he arrived he called the Prime Minister. "I am sorry if news of my resignation has reached you before my call." "It has, but I can see why. You don't have to say it. You didn't want a leak. The trouble with systems designed for partial leak is that you can never totally control them. You would not want the news of your resignation to precede your speech because that would have changed the way the vote went on the principle. I know that your intention to resign would have swung the debate in your favour but, you would say, for the wrong reason." "All that you say coincides precisely with my judgment of the case. I ought to warn you that I expect at least six diocesans to resign in the next two days, some of them in the more ancient and prestigious dioceses." "I suspected as much. I have been talking to my old friend, the Dean of Alchester." "Yes. I owe him an apology. I allowed myself to be persuaded to imply that his break-out was a damp squib." "Congratulations, Archbishop! I would ask you to come and work for me but I am leaving in three weeks' time. What will you do now?" "I will submit myself to Dexter and see what he wants." "I admire your humility. I'm looking for a nice, plump portfolio." "I want to be of service. I think that Perpetua has a lot to offer a flagging Church." "I hope you are right. The Church, in spite of your best efforts, has been punching below its weigh. You can tell that from the press coverage. Whenever an institution receives increased coverage you can assume that that is because it is performing, or more likely perceived to be performing, poorly. The public relations industry is a fraud. All the best institutions are ignored by the media and do not suffer but, rather, the opposite, because of them. However, if you have to be noticed, doing something on a Saturday is by far the best because the fabrications of the Sunday Berliners are much more ingenious than their daily cousins. They have more time to think about them and, by and large, better brains doing the thinking. The tabloids, on the other hand, have more time to think up fantastic stories. By the way, do you want to remain in the House of Lords in your own right? This is an unprecedented situation as far as I can tell, but I am sure you would be valued there." "I am most grateful, but no thank you. I presume that in due course Mr Brown will consider how to achieve faith representation in the Upper House." "Yes; but he will take his time. I wish you a rich spiritual life in your new calling, and I am most grateful for the care you have shown for me. I, too, as you know, am taking a new direction." "Dominus Vobiscum, Prime Minister." "Et cum Spiritu tuo, Archbishop."

As might have been predicted, Hawthorne, like a person who has just died, was better appreciated once he had gone than when he had been centre stage. Writers suddenly found all the virtues they had somehow overlooked and overlooked all the supposed vices they had felt themselves bound to expose. The Archbishop whose indecision had ruined the Church was now the Archbishop whose departure had ruined it. What had previously been described as indecisiveness became healing; what had previously been described as dithering became inclusive. Suddenly, now that it suited their purpose, journalists turned up the Easter Sunday statement proposing a Commission. They forgot that they had forgotten it for six weeks. Hawthorne, mildly amused, was greeted by such headlines as:

BROKEN PRIMATE BREAKS OUT

HAWTHORNE SCRATCHES FOES

The more serious analysts were split as to whether his departure, together with some "leading"—they always Are "leading", "senior", or "influential"—diocesans would be a death blow to the Church. There was much talk of the "Militant Tendency" in the Labour Party, the breakaway of the SDP, and the final fusion back into New Labour. The consensus was that there would be a temporary split and that, as a result, the idea of Perpetua would become so powerful in the mainstream Church that the breakaway group, like the SDP, would wither away. Hawthorne thought, "The seed must die to germinate." He was not concerned with the immediate prospects. He simply wanted to be of service in a minor way and to pursue the studies he had sacrificed to the call of the Spirit. He had a clear conscience. He had led the Church which did not want leading. He had been even-handed with a Church that did not want even-handedness. He had been gentle with a Church that did not want gentleness. He had been subtle with a Church that did not want subtlety. As a keen observer of human behaviour, he apprehended that some would appreciate him now that he had gone, but he was neither inclined to rejoice in that nor to use it as the basis for a comeback.

Those who had immense respect and affection for the Archbishop, but had nonetheless voted against the Commission, were calling for a new opportunity. They were torn between begging Hawthorne to come back and blaming him for tricking them into a false position. If only he had told them plainly what he had wanted, they would have foregone their individual preferences for what he saw as the good of the Church. They did not want his blood on their hands—they did not want the Church's blood on their hands. They saw at last that they had gone too far and pushed him too far. Instead of being faithful to their calling they had played a political game and pushed him as far as they could in the hope of getting ever more concessions. They were more sorry about the tactical error of pushing too hard than about the more fundamental error of behaving like politicians and not like members of the Body of Christ, but they were very sorry nonetheless, not least because the choice of a successor would lie in the hands of the new Prime Minister who was an unknown quantity in Church affairs. No matter how much they loved Hawthorne, they could not help, like politicians, leaning forward to the next contest even though the better part of their natures knew that the immediate problem was how they would cope with a substantial exodus.

After he had attended a quiet Eucharist on Sunday morning, Hawthorne asked if he might see Dexter who, he understood, had just returned to London from the North, to discuss the exodus—he was not presumptuous enough to use the term "transfer"—and how it might serve Perpetua.

Dexter came to see Hawthorne, accompanied by Trina and Max. He was very nervous. "I don't know how to deal with people like him," he told Trina. "You don't have to know how. Just rely on the Spirit and say what you need to say. He's a friend—look what he has sacrificed for Perpetua. He will not mind if you and he have different approaches. He wants to serve Perpetua, that's all you need to bear in mind." "What should I do, Max?" "What the Spirit tells you. I'm no theologian. I'll help implement your strategy, but the Spirit must design it through you."

When he came into Hawthorne's room, Dexter simply sank to his knees and said, "Let us pray. Grant to us, God our Parent, the grace to listen to our Sister the Spirit in Jesus and Perpetua." There was then a long silence before the erstwhile Archbishop, seeing his discomfort, opened the discussion. "Dexter, I have been longing to meet you to listen to stories about Perpetua. I read so much in the newspapers and saw her on television but, apart from shaking her hand at a semi-official gathering, I never got to meet her." "She was wonderful, Archbishop. Sorry, what do I call you?" "Hugh will do." "Well, Hugh, she was truly wonderful. She changed our lives." "And now, in a way I could not have imagined, she—or should I be thinking of the Spirit?—has changed my life. I want to put myself at your service, not in any big or special way but as a minister." "I am so glad, Hugh. I want us to have a much simpler and more trusting structure—forgive me—than the official Church. I think we need bishop-like people—I think we may call them Guides—based at our permanent places of worship, providing guidance to perhaps twelve house group leaders responsible for leading worship and exercising pastoral care. I believe that we should accept all the orders of all who come to us from Christian churches and that we should rely on existing Guides to find new Guides and to oversee the recruitment of other house group leaders. We might need some kind of national forum, in addition to the internet, for mutual support, but this must not be another layer of hierarchy. I want Perpetuanism to be based on collaboration at the local level between a group of small villages and towns, or across a whole medium or large town. Max will ensure that those who are ministers will not have to undertake administration, which will be a different, volunteer-led function.

"I would like you, Hugh, to say where you would like to minister. On the day of Pentecost—when I have no doubt that Perpetua will come among us to say her farewell—we will hold a Sacrament of Affirmation, not ordination or consecration." "I understand. Perpetua has made possible what I could never make possible, the simplification of the Church, the sweeping away of the weight of precedent and legality. A fresh start." "I gather we may be joined by other bishops." "We may be joined, but I cannot guarantee that those who leave the Church will necessarily want to join us, and, of course, I cannot assume that you will automatically want all the people who come to you." "As long as people agree to our basic principles we will accept them. It seems to me from what I have heard that the Church approaches people as if they were somehow unfit and forces them to prove their fitness. We will assume that people are genuinely bringing their spiritual gifts until such time as the evidence shows they are not, but as our model of Eucharistic Presidency—that's the word you use, I think—depends upon house group election, and as Guides will be locally elected, we will have to develop remedies for the people who fall short." "It all sounds so wonderfully simple, but forgive me if I prefer not to to become deeply involved. At the moment I simply want to serve you in a simple capacity."

Naturally, once the initial shock and adulation wore off, those who were left to pick up the pieces from Hawthorne's resignation became increasingly resentful. Officials in Downing Street were excited rather than irked, as it became clear that there would be six or seven Dioceses in addition to Canterbury. The only doubt now was over York, as Archbishop Mwanga struggled with his conscience. Filling one bishopric was never easy, but there was so much more room if a number could be considered simultaneously. A nice balance could be struck, always supposing the quality of the shortlists were adequate. On this occasion there might be a lack of good liberals, but rumour had it that Mr Brown was much more inclined to the Evangelical and the Catholic, as both stressed the importance of rigid ethical codes. Indeed, some said that although he had vowed to renounce his power of patronage over bishops, he might very well become accustomed to exercising it and go back on his promise. Whatever the long term outcome, the short term effect was that officials could do what they liked doing most, exercising their power of putting people into positions. Like all of the activities of high mandarins, it required a good deal of elegance in the design and subtlety in the execution, but making such nominations had the added spice of exercising power.

At a lower level, however, matters were less comfortable. As is frequently the case, those who had won the debate which led to Hawthorne's resignation began to blame him for not sending them clearer warnings. Within days, their plight was his fault. They were left to face the inevitability, which Bishop Hall had pointed out, of new hostilities between Torans and Petrans who had enjoyed a temporary truce in order to attack Hawthorne. In the days Before pentecost an ugly campaign was launched, characterising Hawthorne as a traitor and a coward, saying that he had abandoned the Church for the sake of his private theological whims. They said he had not valued the Church, by which they meant that he did not value the Church as they wanted it to be. He certainly continued to value the notion of church as question and as process, but they were annoyed that he had refused to work as their cart horse, pulling along the lumbering wagon of ecclesiological baggage. But what annoyed the remainder most was that they had under-estimated the damage to the Church of England of a liberal departure. The Church had been built on a model of mutual support. All four kinds of members put in their money, knowing that all four kinds would benefit, and, as happens with most structures, the money had more or less balanced with the needs. But now the Torans, Petrans and Medians were left with a traumatically down-sized Church, its buildings and debts, its contracts and obligations. As Max had foreseen, there might be a good deal of posturing over the distribution of assets, but as the Perpetuans wanted approximately 20% of the buildings, and would guarantee their maintenance, they were in a buyers' market in spite of the posturing of the traditionalists. Whatever the Archbishops' Council might say, think or do, the matter would be fixed, sparing the Government as much embarrassment as possible. Ranjit had written a perceptive piece in Humanity's weekend supplement showing that, without a substantial infusion of Toran money, Petrans, Torans, and BCP traditionalists combined could not guarantee the funding necessary to maintain a Church structure and revenue after the departure of liberal Perpetuans. An enormous number of people who were counted—or who had counted themselves—among the great and the good were now shown to have greatly exaggerated their contributions to the Church, hiding behind the generosity of poorer and more liberal folk. Similarly, the Torans had exaggerated their hand by threatening to withdraw their funding from the Church of England umbrella and they now found that they needed to be selective in the buildings and infrastructures they chose to support. Thus, the fragmentation exposed the underlying financial weaknesses of the Church and put the future of stipendiary clergy in general, and an over supply of bishops in particular, at great risk.

When he thought about it, Hawthorne knew that the core failing of the Church had been its obsession with philosophy at the expense of theology. This had started as an open project in the eighteenth century, but had slowly found its way into the very life blood of the Church as a debilitating virus so that many of its clergy and people were philosophers of religion, arguing about the existence of God instead of believing, arguing about morality instead of being, arguing about prayer instead of praying, arguing about metaphors instead of loving, clinging to history instead of creating it and, in his own words, in attempting to take hold of the future instead of waiting on God, they were imprisoning themselves in the past. That is why, perhaps, he had become known to Christians and non-Christians alike as a remarkable man. The way they described his personality—to his acute embarrassment—was "holy", but what he thought they meant was that he kept focused on the existence and meaning of the Godhead for and in itself. He saw his task as articulating the mystery in as precise a question as he could and to ensure that the process of questioning was secured. His critics had been able to see the difference without understanding its nature. Sometimes it led to admiration, at others to frustration, but at this point it took the form of denial. What had seemed to be a substantive difference between the Archbishop and his Grand Synod was now characterised as something tiny, not worth the upheaval. He knew better than his critics how wrong they were about the magnitude of the issue. He knew that what mattered was not internal doctrinal or moral consistency, but a searching for language that mutually connected the Creator and the created. What held people together was the common quest to come to terms with the mystery of Christ, what separated them was thinking that there was no mystery. So important did they think God was as a philosophical core to their lives that they would go to any lengths to explain how Jesus had effected our salvation or left us with his body and blood in Eucharist, not seeing that the mystery of what had come to them as gift was much more important.

Once Hawthorne had visited a small country church where bad organisation had meant that very few people turned up for a Eucharist and reception. The organisers were mortified, but he enjoyed the 'normal' atmosphere once the nerves of the organisers had been calmed. He enjoyed even more the opportunity to talk to people afterwards about their faith. "I know you are a great theologian," said one, "and I don't want to sentimentalise God in my life, but I am a simple man, and I can do no better than thanking God for the baby Jesus and what he gave for us. Whether he succeeded or proceeded is of no importance to me. All I care about is that he is with me always, and in a special way in the Sacrament, for he said he would be, and that is enough. I am not saying that it isn't your job to think and talk about these things, but I sometimes wonder whether bishops aren't an obstacle rather than a channel to God."

In a rather unfocused way, people agreed with Hawthorne's simple man that his resignation was bad for the Church no matter how good it might be for Perpetua. Just as the authorities had easily persuaded themselves that Perpetua was a passing fancy, most people had forgotten anything distinctive about her as she merged with other personalities and pretty nineteen-year-olds. People were not very worried about the Church of England, but they recognised the need for spirituality to be channelled in some way although, like must heterogeneous groups, they could always find a majority against any proposal but never a majority in favour of one. If Dexter did not take care, the Perpetuan movement would be as middle class as the Church she had come to reform.

Ultimately, what tipped the balance was a theology in action that no phi-losophy could match. In spite of all his attempts to stay out of the public gaze while he prepared for Pentecost, Dexter's presence kept triggering remarkable events which were attributed to him. He had been shaken by his impact on the congregation at Stumpy Knoll and, although he knew he must put himself as an agent in the hands of God, he prayed that he would be spared. The 'tough' part of him wanted to win people for God by commitment and persuasion. Miracles seemed too easy, and yet he also realised that in a culture dominated by the mass media, miracles might be the only effective way of spreading the word. Still, he tried his best to avoid public gatherings. The local newspaper coverage of the church healings was overshadowed by a murder, but his visit to a London hospital caused a sensation. He had promised a young girl from Grunge Park who had been hit in the stomach by a stray bullet that he would visit her and he could not go back on his word in spite of his fears. He spent an hour in the children's ward, talking to Rags and her friends and joking with the nurses. He said goodbye and breathed a sigh of relief—nothing had happened. Then, as he walked down the corridor, he became aware of people following him, and when he looked round he was amazed to see the entire ward, flanked by its nurses, walking behind him in total silence, as if in a trance. He stopped before the dou-ble security doors to the lifts and turned round. The children who had been seri-ously incapacitated were standing in front of him, each on their own two feet. He had to stop himself shaking. Perpetua had got away with it because her great signs had been performed outside London, except for that final Sunday, but he could see the tower of Metropolitan Independent News through the third floor window. The children stood between him and their ward and their evacuation had triggered an automatic security alert which temporarily blocked the use of security passes to the lift area. He was trapped. The Head of Security naturally had an arrangement with MIN which involved an unethical exchange of data on both sides and so it was only a matter of minutes, as Dexter prayed with and over the children, before a camera crew arrived.

He boarded a train going North which went through a red light at 70 mph, but somehow stopped in half its specified distance, sparing a school bus on a level crossing. Nothing would have happened had the driver not told the guard who recognised Dexter and used his mobile phone to alert the Northern Fron-tier which was able to interview the shaken, but relieved driver of the school bus before Dexter was met on arrival by one of its reporters. The early afternoon sto-ry was perfect for the evening paper and the early evening bulletins but, again, matters might have calmed down had he not happened to walk with the reporter past Glitty City, an entertainment complex attached to the station, comprising hundreds of gaming machines, a casino, an 'Adult' movie theatre, and a barely disguised brothel which imposed no entry restriction on children or drug deal-ers, defending its conduct with an arcane regulation governing private clubs. As Dexter passed, the whole of the building's operations seized up. The tills and gaming machines jammed, mobile phone coverage disappeared, screens went blank, movies stopped, and all but the emergency lighting went out. Frightened people rushed out of the building, triggering another story for the newspaper. He rang Max, desperate to disengage, but all he said was, "Dexter, I sympathise but the Lord rules. Usually agents have some choice but, for the time being, you don't seem to. Come back down and we will see what happens."

He had been recognised on his Southward train and Max warned him not to come all the way into Central London as the station was swarming with journalists wanting to talk to him—as usual, short of language with any resonance—about the "triple whammy". He took a suburban train around the edge of London and met Max at the station nearest to Bleak Villas. "I don't know whether I can face staying there after what happened," said Dexter. "Apart from the terrible moment when she was dying, this is the last place I saw her." "Well, if she wants to protect you from further manifestations, I think this is the place. Pray to her and think."

For three days he stayed in the protection of the borrowed apartment where they had spent their last evening together, but on the Thursday before Pentecost he could not stand the solitude any longer. He had prayed all he could pray and contemplated all he could contemplate. He needed movement and action. He walked through the streets, deserted except for the homeless and the seriously dysfunctional, remembering how he had gone searching for them on Perpetua's Christmas Eve and, as he passed each sleeping wretch or said a word of encouragement to those who wished for sleep but could not find it, his power went through each, restoring life and hope.

This was the quiet use of gifts, but all around him a storm was raging because the media, robbed of its Labour leadership contest, was thrashing around for something both spectacular and long-running, and latched onto Perpetuanism as impetuously as it had dropped it a few weeks before. Suddenly there were background pieces on the life of Perpetua, bogus biographies of Dexter and his followers, speculation about the future of the Christian churches, surveys of religious feminism and endless blogs, emails, and phone-ins. Following the "miracles", as they were called, there was a build-up to Pentecost worthy of a cup final, with leading chains taking bets on whether Perpetua would again dominate the air waves. Never since the beginning of newspapers, had such religious excitement been generated, but as the only event planned for Pentecost was a Service with the Sacraments of Union and of Affirmation, led by Dexter for his new followers, there was nothing that Trina could or wanted to say. Inevitably, the lack of hard news only drove the media to ever more outrageous claims, and when editors were confronted with charges of exaggeration, their automatic response was that if only the Perpetuans could bring themselves to tell the truth and to stop being secretive, everything would be all right. It was pointless responding that no lies had been told, even by omission, and that nothing was being hidden. The god4u Channel and web site carried every last detail of the progress of Perpetuanism. There was nothing else.

The media interest, however, engendered the wish for privacy which it in turn interpreted as secretiveness. Dexter wanted his followers to pass the days before Pentecost in quiet reflection and prayer for, in spite of his own difficulties, he recognised their necessity. Perhaps because it was so far away from their usual haunts, Bleak Villas had remained undiscovered and so, with all its mixed associations, that is where they prepared. By agreement, the separation of their spiritual life and the organisation of the movement was maintained. Max said that he would make everything ready and that all Dexter needed to do was to be briefed early on the Sunday morning. Nobody could be certain of anything but, as the day approached, the Perpetuans became ever more convinced that it would be the make or break moment. They had to have faith that it would have a positive outcome. If you had asked them how their expectations had come to focus on this one day they could not have told you precisely. There was nothing in what Perpetua had said to give any indication that she would 'return' and so, if anything, it was the influence of the Acts of the Apostles which brought them to their conclusion. And so, with that precursor in mind, they "watched and prayed", uncertain but excited.

9.

Nigel Bourne counted his sheep as they munched the late Spring grass. He was deeply troubled. He disliked the uncertain in general, prizing the differing cyclical routines that governed his life—the Church's year, the rugby season, choral events, the holidays of his grandchildren—and although he was by no means a conservative, and certainly not a Toran nor a Petran, having been brought up in the public school tradition of the Church of England he particularly disliked liturgical uncertainty, not knowing what would happen in the course of a service. He had found the breach of the BCP monopoly troubling, and although he received the bread and wine with deep reverence, he prized the service of the Eucharist less highly than the chorally enhanced Offices of Matins and Evensong. Like many who go to church regularly, his reverence and awe were much more a part of him than any need for theological clarity. It would not have mattered very much to him if the Church of England had come out in favour of Unitarianism, except that it would deprive him of the joy of numerous doxologies which needed "A bit of welly" at the end of the Evening Canticles and, to the same degree, he was not all that concerned about the Church's interest in Perpetua, from a theological standpoint, although, again, he saw the potential threat to his doxologies. He feared that there would be an extended period of liturgical disruption and the casting aside of huge swathes of sacred music which he had grown up with and continued to love. For it stood to reason that a new casting of the old faith would require new words and new music.

The prospect was less daunting to Marie who had come into the Church in her late 1930s and therefore lacked Nigel's deeply emotional attachment to any particular music. She saw it from a more practical perspective. The choir would probably lose a good deal of its repertoire but, as she had learned from her studies, church music often survived theological change and was even itself occasionally heretical, and so Holy Trinity would probably retain a good deal, particularly relating to the Eucharist which, she gathered, would survive the forthcoming changes. On the other hand, she hoped for new music and new challenges for, unlike most of the congregation which was only aware of, and hostile to, new music written by Graham Kendrick and his contemporaries, her holidays spent at choral seminars and festivals had introduced her to a wide variety of new compositions ranging from Tavener to Gabriel Jackson and Francis Pott to such an extent that she was beginning to think of Jonathan Harvey as somewhat dated. Her main concern was that Mark's tendency to improvise and only communicate at the last minute would be exacerbated by the volatile theological and liturgical situation, making her scheduling even more difficult.

Scott was similar in many ways to Nigel, having been brought up with public school daily worship, but he was less emotionally attached to this music because, unlike Nigel whose interest in music was confined to sacred choral, Scott's musical tastes were very broad and, in some areas such as nineteenth century continental opera and twentieth century English music up until the death of Vaughan Williams, very deep. Paradoxically, then, his requirement for church music was that it should make a good impression. He had watched the "steady decline" of the sacred choral tradition both in the public school and the parish church with the sadness of the man whose life coincides with the decline of the golden age. The situation had reached such a state that he was grateful if Marie scheduled a "decent" anthem once every two or three weeks. Like her, he knew that there would be good, new music written with the impetus of religious reform, but he doubted much of it would reach either the College or parish church at Walmbury.

Meg, like Nigel, was worried by changes of routine, but in her case the root cause was the fear of getting something wrong. She had learned to undertake tasks in church far beyond anything she had achieved outside it. Whereas her church life was relatively tidy and took her on a steadily upward trajectory, both as a chorister and an assistant to Mark in various guises, her life outside was chaotic and desperately improvised. Her finances, family, employment, and emotions were all simultaneously and symbiotically in a state of flux, and so her theological commitment and her need for one area of calm and achievement coincided in the church. She might, therefore, have worried greatly about impending change except that her most salient characteristic, in spite of the chaos of her life, was thankfulness for what it brought. As Perpetuanism had brought her an added lease of life for her mother which had, in turn, freed her to try to organise her own life and finances better, she was grateful beyond telling for, like the really good person that she was, her gratitude far outweighed her concern for her own prospects.

Clement, who pursued his theological interests—he sometimes thought that he was unfaithful to his calling by veering away from lived theology to the philosophy of religion—more regularly and methodically than anyone else in the parish, was content to let the liturgical consequences of the Reformation for the Third Millennium take their course. Like Nigel, he enjoyed singing Choral evensongs, not least because of the doxologies that needed so much "welly" but, in the grand scale of things, he could give them up, just as he had, over the years, spent less time listening to test match cricket and more time reading the Bible and writing sermons. There was a time when it was inconceivable that he would miss a ball of a Test Match Saturday, but now, particularly if the opposition was batting, he could go a whole day without checking the score. Unlike most people he knew, his life had steadily evolved over the period of his middle age instead of becoming ever more static. He had spent successive periods concentrating on party politics, the Parish Council, amateur dramatics, the foundation of the village arts festival, and, most recently, his religious vocation, just as he had successively written a large number of secular poems, hymns, and sermons. More significantly, he had steadily narrowed his musical interests from buying an annual Proms season ticket to collecting cycles of Bach Cantatas and Mahler symphonies. Although his love of routine and ritual deepened with age, the activities which were fitted into these frameworks evolved such that he thought of himself as a process conservative, but a product radical.

Helen's two concerns were, naturally, totally unselfish. She wanted Clement and Mark to be happy. Valuing human relationships much more highly than abstractions, she did not care what theology they followed as long as it gave strength to the holy life lived out in generous relationships. She was sure that Clement had found his natural home in the generosity of Perpetuanism, having been frustrated ever since she had known him by the innate, and somewhat paradoxical, stiffness and lethargy of the Church of England. Ever since his escape from the at once imprisoning and exalting Church of Rome, he had been looking for a combination of exaltation and generous evangelism which he had found not only in Perpetua's teaching, but also in her revival of Sacramentality.

All these shades of concern and optimism had been shared at the regular dinner of "Les Six" after the Friday choir practice, with the usual mutual goodwill and failure to engage. Conversation had soon shifted to the likely shape of the new Prime Minister's Cabinet. Only Clement, who knew more about what was likely to happen precisely because he actually did not believe what was in the newspapers, as opposed to saying that he did not believe them when he did, was saddened by the turn of the conversation. "It is strange", he thought, "how people give inversely proportionate attention to issues according to their importance and/or their power to affect the outcome. Thus, while people are to a considerable degree in control of their spiritual life, they have very little influence indeed on the formation of the Cabinet." Because he was conscientious in his pastoral care he stayed silent rather than chiding. They would not, in any case, have paid any attention to his well informed prognostications. It was not for him to make people think as he thought or believe as he believed, or even know what he knew, but he must simply listen and help people reach their full potential.

For Mark, matters were more acute than for his faithful, not simply because he was their priest with a professional concern for theology and liturgy, but because the settlement of his inner war in favour of Perpetuanism did not mean that hostilities were at a complete end. In recognising his own brokenness, his own provisionality, he could never escape from inner turmoil, he could never be sure that he had made any right decision. His humility and vulnerability, protected by the aggressive defensiveness of the porcupine, was no less deep for being unrecognised by most of those for whom he cared more deeply than they could imagine. Jane and Helen both knew what he was going through and were able to comfort him in their opposite ways for, whereas Jane exercised great moral power, in spite of her apparent agreement with every change in his outlook. "Apparent" because she was always prepared to overlook his temporary fluctuations as long he came to the sensible conclusion in the long run. Helen offered near unconditional service, only near because she drew lines which they both knew he must not cross, particularly in respect of his tendency towards impetuous authoritarianism and verbal violence. Mark himself, having settled on the basic theological liberalism which his head demanded, set out to adorn it with a degree of liturgical conservatism which his heart required. Nigel, Marie, and Scott, therefore, need not have been so concerned as they were. The historical Trinity, which was now being modified, stood in the theological succession with as much relevance and coherence as had the Old Testament stood in the first two millennia of Christianity. Just as he had always sung hymns about Abraham and Jacob, he would continue to value the Trinitarian economy as a way of looking at the Godhead for an even longer time than the span of the Old Testament. He would introduce the minimum change necessary, primarily in the Eucharistic Prayer, to accord with the new theology of the Godhead and the revitalisation of the Eucharist, but he would not refer to it as the Sacrament of Union and he did not see any need for wider change. In due course, the 'powers that be' for which, in spite of his being a political radical, he had inordinate and irrational respect, would issue instructions and offer new prayers. Some of these would stick, but most would quickly disappear. The words of the Creed would doubtless change, but it would be no more deeply loved nor respected in its new form than it had been since its Nicean birth. Like a professional who has struggled with change but come to see its inevitability, it was his job to see that it was implemented with the least possible disruption and pain, even with the least possible notice taken of it. Thus he had spent the previous day—as usual, at the last minute—going through the liturgy in minute detail before producing his Pentecost Mass Booklet, giving thanks for the heavy emphasis that Perpetua had always placed on Her Sister the Spirit. As he worked, he occasionally looked at the news flashes which popped up on the screen, and so he was aware of the almost hysterical build-up to Dexter's Service of Unity and Affirmation, but his job was to look after his own people. Like many professionals, he was more attracted by gossip than actual events, so that he spent more time reading the almost hourly postings on polemical web sites than it would have taken him to attend the events on which the tittle tattle was very loosely based.

Just as there is no smoke without fire, so there is no tittle tattle without a source of anxiety or pain. The Bishop of Alchester, gloomily leafing through print-outs of internet downloads—he disliked the ephemeral 'feel' of the digital information inundation—asked himself whether the tide of events represented divine judgment and tried honestly to work out where he had gone wrong, for his honesty consisted primarily in an examination of his own motives and actions rather than in trying to marshall a series of facts which gave the appearance of objective development. True, he did have deep ecclesiological doubts about his position, but these were always subordinate to his own self-judgment. He understood the necessity of the establishment of the Church of England and respected the role it had played in national life until the early nineteenth century, but he thought that religious emancipation had seriously weakened the justification for a national church. In spite of the merits of the Tudor settlement, the Church of England, like all reformed churches, had a serious problem locating where authority lay. He had been pushed, admittedly in tune with his temperament, but against his better judgment, in favour of believing that the only real ecclesiastical authority was the Pope. This accounted for his problem both with women priests in particular and with Synodical decision-making in general, and while it was illogical to think that the Pope had a veto over the theological and ecclesiological decisions of the Church of England, he could see no other way. Nonetheless, these considerations weighed very little compared with his worry that he had somehow failed his own clergy and people. He had been too ready to look at the situation from his own perspective—like many people in power, he thought, he had been cut off from reality—failing to judge the extent and the depth of 'liberal' feeling but, most of all, he thought that he had failed to fulfill one of his major roles, to act as a theologian. It was not enough simply to say that the Perpetuan challenge was outrageous, outlandish or obviously heretical. Hawthorne had asked for a debate and he had refused it, and now he saw more than 25% of his clergy and, greatly to his surprise, an ever larger number of his flock, moving towards another pasture. He saw the administrative turmoil ahead, but he did not fear it as the Church of England lived in a state of permanent administrative flux, combined with idiosyncratic intricacy, and neither did he resent the loss of authority and a contraction in his sphere of influence but, as always in such realignments, he worried that many valued friendships would be impaired. Like most successful Church of England bishops, he had been chosen because of his capacity for deep relationships with people with whom he theologically disagreed, seeing beyond the abstractions to the priest.

These thoughts having encroached upon his morning prayers, he concentrated, hoping to recapture some sense of the immanence of the Holy Spirit. He was interrupted by Doris who apologised but said that his two Suffragans were outside and seemed in need of his pastoral care. With a heavy heart he made the Sign of the Cross and opened his door. He was in no mood for near mindedness and factionalism and said nothing, waiting for one of them to begin. "We're sorry," said Aleford. "We believe that we have been partly responsible at least for the catastrophe in which we now find ourselves. We allowed our prejudices to cloud our judgment and, therefore, to screen you from the broader truth." "The narrowness of our disputes," said Castlegate, "blinded us to the broader picture. We were so obsessed with the issues of gay and women clergy that we did not look wider, to see that many of those who disagree with us are not fighting on single issues, but have a broad, theological approach which differs from our own. We should never have said that they were not Biblical." "We should never have said that they were not doctrinally orthodox." "We should never have questioned their motives." "We should never have questioned their sincerity." "Hilary, Bruce, there is much about which we all need to be penitent, but we must not over-react. We all allow our theories and our emotions to run away with us, but nothing is ever as bad as it seems, and guilt is a poor response to error. We must collectively articulate our penitence and our sorrow and we must not use our energy to try to pull people back towards us who want to go away. Tomorrow is Pentecost. It is the day of the Holy Spirit. We must be with our flock, listen to what people are saying, teach as clearly as we can, and pray. Earlier I was tempted to write a Pastoral Letter, but I think that this is a time to revert to the proper role of bishop as teacher and comforter. For some it will be too late. Tomorrow is the first day on which we will know how many have left us. Many of our most beloved priests have hired halls where Perpetuans will gather to receive the Holy Spirit. We must not see what lies ahead as some kind of 're-covery' operation to regain people and churches, but as an exercise in humility under the power of the Spirit. Sometimes there are events over which we have no control, in the face of which we must stay silent, and I think that this—like the Reformation—is one of them." "I understand that in general terms, James, but what must we do?" asked Bruce who, in spite of being at the opposite end of the theological spectrum from the bishop, was deeply aware of how James had defended him. Aleford equally knew how, in spite of his revulsion, he had defended him from personal attacks. In spite of their ceaseless private bickering, in public they were both deeply loyal because they could see that, unlike themselves, James had held those differences as of no importance when exercising his episcopal role. "I can't be particular about what you should do. As I have said, perhaps a little floridly, I think this is a time not to 'do', but to pray and listen. We have been doing too much doing lately. Indeed, for as long as I have been a bishop, ever since the Grand Synod came into its own, we have had nothing but doing. People always resent political activity and say that politicians, and Synod Members, should refrain from legislation in general, but they always have just one particular piece of legislation which is an exception to the generality. We must get out of the mind set of always having to do things. Jesus walked and taught and healed and listened, but he does not come across as an administrator. He collected some followers and sent them out, but he does not come across as a church bureaucrat. If he had wanted a church of administrators he would have turned to the Pharisees, not against them if, indeed, he actually did turn against them. That is why I won't write the letter. That is why I will go to tomorrow's confirmation at Grangebury with great joy." "What about the Dean?" asked Bruce, with an unfortunate tinge of his former resentment breaking through his newly acquired humility. "I fear that perhaps my greatest oversight of oversight has been in respect of the Dean who had the right to expect more of me. Instead of being his bishop, I was his sparring partner. He never chided me for not be-having properly as a bishop. He never would, knowing in his wisdom that I am, like most people, my sternest critic, rendering external criticism a cruel redun-dancy. See, Bruce, how easy it is to slip back into former patterns of behaviour." "I am sorry, James." "We must be vigilant and leave ourselves open to the power of the Spirit."

The Bishop knew that he must see the Dean, no mater how uncomfortable that might turn out to be. He was not frightened of discomfort—for what ap-peared to be indecisiveness and even pusillanimity was simply over scrupulous-ness not cowardice—but he liked it no more than anyone else. Being brave did not make him immune to the pain which his bravery would inevitably bring about, not least because it would be, in the real sense, self-inflicted because the Dean, who would never criticise him, would simply by being who he was, make it even more clear to the Bishop how he had failed.

Before he could say anything to the Dean, who was looking intently at a stained glass window of the parable of the Prodigal Son, he turned, sensing the Bishop's approach, and said, "Sometimes in our sophistication we forget the simple. I look at this window more than at any other to remind me that I, too, am a prodigal, always needing to return after mis-spent time. It is so easy to be lured into intellectual pride, reduced to eating spiritual husks before gaining the courage—or is it desperation?—to return home. I am sorry, James for, although I genuinely believe that I am doing the right thing, I am deeply conscious that I have been a fortress of intellectual hubris and that I have not come to you, and through you to God, as I should. In the heat, or perhaps the cool, of intellectual difference, I have forgotten that you are my Bishop in spite of the absurdities of ecclesiastical jurisdiction." "I, too, came to say sorry for dismissing your genuine feeling and only seeing the intellectual argument, which gives me hope. First of all, and I suppose it should be least in the order of things, I hope that we will not lose each other. I have been so worried about losing friends and have feared that our differences have pulled us apart when we are both capable of friendship above difference. Secondly, if we are both sincere in what we believe, there is hope that the different routes we take will not diverge so far that we cannot reach mutual sympathy, if not agreement, before all paths meet at the end. Thirdly, as I have just said to Castlegate and Aleford, we must not fall into competition for people or property. There must be a better way. Finally, I need to hear from you, if you have a moment, what was the critical factor in your change?"

"I thank you for everything you have said, James. I could not disagree with a word of its analysis or promise. How could I have befriended so many people in this building and overlooked you? I shall always regret it and never forget it. What changed me was my perception that theology, the metaphors we need to come to grips, in no matter how illusive a way, with God, needs to reach out from the core of God instead of trying to close down possibility. I know how tradition has enshrined the Trinity and read it into so much of the New Testament and made it our core doctrine, but even as a student I felt that there was something wrong with narrowing God to three 'persons' or phenomena, or sets of attributes—whatever you like to call them—because once you conceded that our idea of God, our theology is about personal relationship and did not aggregate all God-ness into a nameless, characteristicless deity, it was irrational and unhelpful to 'close down' the options to three. I thought about how the culture of God has changed from power and might to lowliness, vulnerability and pain, God alongside the broken, in the form of Jesus, or the parent, or the Paraclete, and I asked whether there would be more powerfulness in a contemporary manifestation of God living beside us in our brokenness. I thought that many years ago when I could never picture Jesus in Auschewitz. My mind, therefore, has always been open to a less Greek, less geometric, idea of God, not that it has ever been amorphous, it has always had form because I believe that form is the characteristic that gives meaning. I know you have always known that the accusation of my critics, that I am little different from new age spiritualists, is a caricature. Perhaps, However, I over reacted to what I was taught in theological college, because I kept hearing arguments about closing down and shutting out. It was as if theology were analogous to a critic who goes to a concert and only reports the bad things, in the way, in fact, that the word "criticism" has become pejorative. I respect your attempts to be open, James, but we both know that there are many in the Diocese, Petran and Toran, who want to narrow the doors. When I visit Greece I am always moved by the sight of babes in arms receiving the Host."

"Thank you, Dean. I will think about what you have said. In the meantime, is there anything practical that we need to do?" "In theory, James, there are almost countless things we need to do, but I am not anxious to be precipitate. We do not know what the authorities will want to do but, more importantly, we must wait on the Holy Spirit. I could worry about the way that we talk about and portray a Godhead of more than three persons, one that includes, for the time being, the new element of Perpetua, but I think that this will require mature reflection and, for the time being, nothing will change here except for—and I grant these are big issues in themselves—the form of the Creed and the Eucharistic Prayer. No doubt in time the Perpetuans will issue guidance. I only hope that we do not become burdened with prescription and proscription. That has been our trouble all along, but you only have to look at history to be worried that, in spite of everything, it might happen again. We start out with so much hope, James, and look where we end up if we don't trust in God." "What about those who cannot in conscience accept the changes?" "As I said, theology is about opening up, not closing down. The new forms of service will, for the time being, not replace the regular schedule. They will be fitted in around it. In wishing to do otherwise some days ago I was over-stepping the mark, trying to impose, betraying myself and God. I personally believe that the old words and ways are not so helpful as the new words and ways but that does not invalidate them. However, as I will probably need to lead the modified worship in the absence of like minded people, I expect that others will lead most of the traditional worship. For me this is pragmatic, not ideological. We have been fighting for too long over our metaphors. If the Church cannot bring people to God it is worth nothing. I will try to combat my worst failing, my intellectualism, and hope that you will always bring me to penitence which I surely need more often than I admit. It is one of the illusions of today that people who are broad minded are somehow more virtuous and that, conversely, people of more fixed views are somehow closed minded and prejudiced. There are sins peculiar to liberalism such as being illiberal to those who are illiberal, adopting an attitude of moral superiority, and taking pride in one's tolerance. So, James, we will, with a few additions, go on much as we have been for the time being, in the liturgical sense although we should make a new start in our relationship which cannot wait some ecclesiological outcome. Whatever happens to us, we must not allow a dispute about metaphors to spoil our relationship." The Bishop put his hand on the Dean's shoulder and then left him, again contemplating the parable.

Brian Sedge could not find a parable for the inconsolable ruin that confronted him in its various forms as he conducted what would be a valedictory tour of his patch, not only in terms of his own career, but also in the sense that in five years time the Church of England would be changed, not beyond recognition, but beyond resuscitation. In parallel with his civic contemporaries in the Foreign and Commonwealth Office, his career had almost entirely consisted of managing decline without the partial salvation of an emergent European Union. Its nearest ecclesiastical equivalent, the Covenant with the Methodists, worked well in some places at a local level, but was dead at the institutional level. For every new church that had been built in a new suburb or housing estate, three had been closed, and the ratio was set to rise. New building-free church gatherings would be substituted for new buildings, and many churches which were now only just hanging on would soon have to close. The repair bills, which always looked impossibly frightening, were less of a problem than raising money for stipends, and an enlivening flow of volunteer priests (particularly women) would not come quickly enough to save the substantial number of tiny, Medieval churches, that would have to shut down.

From his operating level, theology was not a key issue. The slight majority of his estate consisted of tiny country churches which had hardly been touched by the cross currents of twentieth century controversy and 'progress'. Their regular diet of BCP Matins and Evensong, with an occasional BCP Eucharist, kept them well away from theological controversy, fulfilling the Book's intention, as did the majority of sermons. Theirs was a gentle, if somewhat melancholy, sedate, and possibly shallow, spiritual observance which gave them great comfort, although Brian wondered how deep this might go in a crisis. It was certainly unwise to measure their commitment by their financial contributions as the Alchester gentlefolk were much meaner than poorer, Northern working folk. The exception was the extraordinary lengths to which parishes as a whole would go to preserve their buildings while taking offence when they were asked to support their vicars. One church with a congregation of 30 was self-confidently mounting an appeal for £250k for its endangered spire, but only paid 40% of its annual costs and expected the Diocese (parishes of poorer but more generous people) to subsidise it, much in the way that it expected, without much thinking about it, its grandchildren's university education to be subsidised by families who could not even imagine such an aspiration. Some of these beautiful, dying churches would be picked up by the secular heritage industry, but most would be lost. As their congregations shrank through death, there would be ever fewer replacements and their end would be sad and quiet. Yet, reflected Brian, if people could drive twenty miles to the hairdresser why did they expect their churches to be within walking distance? What was wrong with the Christian generosity of giving lifts? His distress at this part of his estate's plight was, therefore, to a certain extent, simply nostalgic. Whatever the physical problems of 'middle of the road', Tudor settlement Anglicanism, it had no real spiritual core. It had been constructed to keep the peace and was no longer needed. At the two extreme wings of the parishes were the decaying Petrans and the thriving Torans. Brian might have been nostalgic about his country churches, but Petran parishes were monuments to it. Many worshipped in a style pre-dating Vatican II (except for using English), were more Marian than contemporary English Roman Catholics and still prayed for the "Conversion of England". There were more marked differences between them and contemporary Roman Catholics. They were much more accustomed to, proficient at, and theatrical in, ritual (one church lowered the host to the chancel in a golden monstrance). Many of their priests were gay and some lived in stable partnerships with other priests. Above all, they showed no interest in raising money or attracting new adherents. It was as if their nostalgia was so intense that they were not prepared to share it or prolong it. For all their quirks, Brian loved these parishes because their priests were dedicated and, with the exception of an exotic, gin drinking orchidity, they were indifferent to material well being, working and half starving themselves to death. These were the people that the Church would lose, through natural wastage or early departure, as the tide of opinion flowed ever swifter and stronger in favour of women bishops. It would be a terrible loss because the liberal church, no matter how catholic, would never have that reverence and depth which meticulous, timeless liturgy and intense prayer provided.

At the other end of the spectrum, the Torans were doing well, even in their ancient buildings, but they were doing even better through their 'fresh expressions'. They would continue to thrive because, Brian thought, somewhat ungenerously, their kind of Christianity did not depend upon deep thought, love or sacrifice. They were rather like the new golf clubs springing up all over the countryside, all needing a large number of new members, all full of enthusiasm for what they were doing, all promising fulfillment with the minimum of effort. There would be some who would want to play every day, but the ideal model was to have a massive membership that did not overtax the facilities. They might be under the Anglican umbrella, but that was to save the faces of bishops frantic about falling head counts and the requirements of elegant administration. They would flourish in or outside the Church of England. One day their "male headship" dogma would come home to roost, but that was for the future.

The parishes which concerned Brian most were the large, mixed, vaguely liberal parishes in large villages and small towns, with binary congregations of families with primary school children and people over 45. People always worried about the absence of worshipers between 15 and 25 and 35 and 45 but affirming churches were always going to have problems with teenage children and parents at critical points in their careers. Many of the people in their mid-50s who were the financial backbone of these parishes were liberal and would be Perpetuan. In Alchester they had had an unfair deal from a hierarchy that had tried to squeeze out their ecclesiastical leadership (the Dean being its greatest failure) and it had, with a duplicity which only people who are self-referentially 'holy' can manage without feeling guilt, taken their money without even bothering to listen to what they said. From Brian's perspective, although he could not count himself among them because he was an 'open' Evangelical with strong BCP leanings, these were the only people that really accorded with all of the Anglican core values. The Torans only bothered with Scripture, the Petrans only bothered with tradition, and the Medians clung to the BCP and thought they were preserving tradition but it was of a very narrow sort and tended to be cultural and nostalgic. But the catholic and evangelical liberals cared about Scripture, tradition and, crucially, reason and experience. If these people went, there would be very little left other than two different brands of nostalgia and a Toran faction that hardly needed the church within which it lodged for reasons Brian could not understand.

As he inspected broken panes of stained glass, the dilapidation of churchyards, the acres of precariously tiled, slated and leaded roof, the miles of inhospitable and inflexible pew, he wondered what he was trying to represent. The Church was alive with plans for re-ordering buildings, introducing activity into old buildings seven days per week, restoring the Medieval purpose of churches when they were built. Everything that could be put in the way of this constructive development was put in the way, not least by the Diocese whose interests it was his job to represent. Worst of all, however, was the extent to which people who had nothing to do with the central mission of the Church could stop it doing its work. Heritage bodies which had no financial obligation nor any Christian missionary purpose could erect massive obstacles to change and force small congregations to spend huge quantities of money and effort on purposes central to the heritage remit but irrelevant, or even counter productive, to mission. It was as if the Society for the Preservation of Victorian Medicine were allowed not only to stop hospital building improvements, but also to forbid any modification invented since 1900 in surgical techniques, diagnosis, and drug treatment. If such interference was not allowed in the physical well being of people, why was there so much tolerance, or indifference, when it came to spiritual well being?

Yet in spite of the gloomy round of his days, which became ever gloomier as the Perpetuan phenomenon began to take hold, Brian Sedge was full of hope. He did not expect the Holy Spirit to behave like a 'super bishop'. All that he expected—and seemed to be observing, which confirmed his optimism—was the unexpected. Being an Archdeacon rather than a parish priest, his favourite book of the Bible was Acts, the book about the spreading outwards of the Word of God, the book which is infused with Jesus, but blazes with the Holy Spirit. He had taken naturally to being an archdeacon because he was both meticulous and open-minded, with no claim to be particularly wise or theologically deep. Perhaps more than anybody else in Alchester, he had seen the power of the Holy Spirit in thousands of people and places and it would not fail. It would never fail.

Walmbury was one of those parishes which Brian most admired for, in spite of Mark's occasional administrative lapses, some accidental, most deliberate, the community was lively. He proposed to have dinner with Helen and Clement on the eve of Pentecost, not only to check up on what was going on, but also to enjoy their company. As a widower and lover of good food and wine he had a select list of places he liked to go and, in addition to the table, Helen and Clement always opened interesting lines of conversation. He asked Mark if he minded, as the dinner was semi-official, and he said he was happy as—he need not say this to Brian—he had come to trust the couple in spite of his natural reluctance to delegate.

"How are we managing the new situation?" "It's not too difficult," said Helen. "We started with the most bereft, in our case the cultural traditionalists and Petrans, and made sure they had neighbouring homes to go to. There are plenty of little BCP churches round here, as you know, and so it was only a question of car pooling. We also found a pre-Vatican II Petran church for those who don't want to have anything to do with Perpetuanism or women priests. We used to have a few Torans, but they left us when The Crux was founded. Equally, Perpetuans from neighbouring churches will come to us. Our current problem in the Deanery, as you will know, is that we have a larger proportion of Perpetuans than the Diocesan norm." "You would be surprised how many there are," said Clement. "I think that the bishops were genuinely shocked." "And this means," said Helen, "that we have some difficult financial decisions to make which directly affect you, so I thought you would like to know, because our model is for fewer paid clergy and many fewer buildings." "I will do what I can to help," said

Brian. "But it is us who are going away," said Helen. "We are so apt in this po-liticised Church of ours to use land-transport metaphors about staying and leaving when we might better think of entities, once lashed together, that have gently floated away from each other. I don't think that there has been a radical move by any group to tear itself away in the almost forty years that I have been watching. The Petran adhesion to their vision of pre-John XXIII Rome, the slow evolution of Toran Biblical simplicity and, also from America, the influence of flower power on theology, have all been absorbed. John Lennon might have been wrong when he said that he was more famous than Jesus, but he never knew how much influence he was to have on the way we see Jesus and the Church he founded. I would not blame anybody. Where I have my doubts—and you know I would only say this to you—is in Bishop James thinking that it can all be settled by some kind of formula. There isn't one. Theology isn't reaching closure so that all the ground is mapped out, it is exploring vast territories with primitive maps containing enigmatic markings like Chalcedon and Nicea. I have always most valued the practical theology of our priests but, Clement, there is a need for more speculative ventures." "I fear that they have led us into frighteningly unfamiliar territory, the most unfamiliar, apart from the Reforma-tion, since those Councils you mentioned." "I would be worried if you were not frightened." "I am, now that the adrenalin has subsided a little. I remember how difficult it was deciding to leave the Labour Party for the SDP in 1981. Compared with today that was relatively easy." "Always bear in mind, Clement, that most people are not so deeply worried about theology as you are. They need a tran-scendent dimension to their lives to give it full meaning, a point not grasped—and how could it be?—by atheists, but the metaphors, as you would call them, of doctrine, are not very important to them. In many ways our current Christians are not very different from the Medieval worshippers whom the Reformation sought to purify. People really believe that their own goodness will speed them to heaven, goodness that includes charitable giving. They largely pray for things, particularly the healing of the sick, rather than pursuing an adult relationship with God. They also have a deep sense of the cultural, worrying about hymn tunes much more than catechisms. What must matter, if the disruption is to be justified, is the revitalisation of our culture's ability to understand the need for a personal relationship with the Creator. I know that Helen understands my posi-tion because you are, as a Churchwarden, much nearer to the priest than the theologian, looking for practical outcomes." "Yes, I don't understand prayer and that worries me." "There are all kinds of relationships with God and you should try not to rank them." "Clement is always telling me that." "Well, he isn't auto-matically wrong, you know! On this point I agree with him." "The problem, Brian, for Helen and me, is that the Church is so clericalised that we don't feel valued by our clergy. Mark tries but, although his head knows that we are his co-workers, his heart says that we are in a different class." "I recognise the prob-lem, and do you think it will be different with Perpetuanism?" "At first it will," said Clement. "There will be a huge levelling down so that we are 'hierarchically flat' but it won't last. History shows you that hierarchy meets two fundamental needs: the need of the powerful to exercise power, and the need of the feeble to be excused responsibility. Between those two extremes there are people who live in a 'mixed economy' of seeking power and seeking exemptions from exercising responsibility, campaigning sporadically, doing something occasionally, but mostly grumbling without ever formally complaining." "That is a little cynical, Clement." "No, I think not, Brian. Iit is just that you have a disposition to be generous to everyone which is the necessary gift of the pastoralist, but a philosopher cannot survive simply by saying that every point of view has its merits. Sooner or later he has to analyse and even rank. That is why we are in a terrible muddle today about respect for people. We must adopt your pastoral stance in respect of their persons but not necessarily in respect of what they stand for or propose as general rules. For example, to say that all Muslims living in this country have an automatic entitlement to equal concern and respect is not to grant that their philosophy with respect to the treatment of women is as good as either the Christian or secular liberal traditions. For that matter, to say that all Christians have a right to expect impartial pastoral care from you does not mean that the attitudes of all Christians to women are equally proper. The sooner we pull these two clusters away from each other, the better. I have been barred from the Priesthood because, in the exercise of my theological function, I have been deemed unpastoral simply because I reach conclusions after ranking propositions. The assumption that I therefore rank people according to whether they agree with me, according to their intellectual abilities, or according to the coincidence of their temperaments with mine, is a travesty." Brian was reminded of Clement's pain. "So how will this play in your Perpetuan role?" "I don't know. I am going up to the Union and Affirmation early tomorrow morning and will not precisely submit to what I am told, but I will give Dexter the benefit of the doubt." "If I were you, Clement, I would be guided by the Dean. I know you know and like him, but he has had to spread himself so thinly that you probably don't know how deep his foundations are." "Thank you Brian." "As for you, Helen, there will be a new challenge." "Yes, bringing people together will be interesting but my one fear is that Perpetuanism will yet further exacerbate the tendency among Christians to worship with the kind of people they agree with, sparing them the exercise of loving, as opposed to liking, which is supposed to be the reason for our existence." "Yes, but you will find that what divides people is not really what they believe. Admittedly, liberals will group together as will Torans, but you will find that believers in anything are closer to each other than any of them are to people who believe nothing. Amongst any group, differences of temperament will soon emerge. Even among liberals there will be those who want hierarchy and want to be part of it and those who are against hierarchy and can tolerate a high degree of intellectual and organisational untidiness. Then there are the people, unlike you, Helen who, in spite of their liberalism, find it impossible to suppress unkindness of heart." "Thank you, but what about our ability to mix with people who are different?" "It is much more difficult than the liberal theory which proposes it. Identity based on competition, difference and the external threat are deeply ingrained. If the liberals have one over-riding fault it is the inability to distinguish between the theory and the practice but, then, reflecting on where we are, we might say the same about the Torans on the Bible and the Petrans on tradition." "Very wise. I know I frequently confuse the ought and the is," said Clement. "All the same," said Helen, "I just wish we had managed to sort out our long standing difficulties before this new development. It seems shameful in a church that preaches peace and reconciliation that we might even have thought of external mediation." "I fear that we have been beyond that for some time," said Brian. "One of our problems is that we are not prepared to be honest about the issues, and unless you are honest it does not matter how skilled the facilitation, internal or external. Let me give you a couple of small examples. If you are a Toran and you accept the Old Testament's dated chronology, it is impossible, if Moses wrote Deuteronomy, that the people could have known about iron. Much more obviously, there are two precisely opposite accounts of the death of Saul. Now the Toran will say, and there is no arguing him out of it, that God can have put the idea of iron into the mind of Moses, and he can say that he does not know why there are two conflicting accounts of the death of Saul, but God does. There is no way of persuading him that the Word of God can stand if he relaxes his grip on the chronology or simply admits that different authors wrote the two accounts of the death of Saul. Similarly, no matter how hard you press the case, you cannot persuade a liberal that Paul means what he says about homosexuality or that Jesus meant all his followers to be male. They will tell you that Paul was simply citing Old Testament nostrums or that the kind of homosexuality which occurred at that time was different from the sort practised by two vicars in a loving partnership. That the mores of the time meant that Jesus could not choose female official followers when he had already broken so many more important articles of conventional codes. If you ask why Jesus flouted convention on so many points, but not on this one, you get no answer. Worst of all, however, for the facilitator, is the problem of getting the Torans to rank." "True, Brian," said Clement, "but as a liberal I find it hard to anchor myself as I should. I tend to dismiss Toran literalism, but I also read into the New Testament particular things that might not be there. If Jesus was human, had emptied out his divinity kenotically, then he did believe in slavery and there was no harm in it, but we want to say that he didn't." "Yes, Clement, keeping you anchored is not easy but you have this on your side, that the age tends to be intellectually slippery—forgive me, I don't mean to use that word as an insult—or, shall I say, subtle and shifting. Whatever the right word, there is no longer the rigidity which sees statements as absolute for all time and all people. As a Church we have simply not kept up with the way of understanding the culture and have seen it as somehow dishonest when it is, in many ways, deeply pastoral if a little superficial. As an Archdeacon, asked to choose between the dogmatic and the pastoral, I would always choose the pastoral. Jesus, after all, was no theologian." "What are you going to do in the new situation?" asked

Helen. "As you know, I am about to retire and so the coincidence of the structural and the personal has worked out well for me. One thing that does worry me is the pension provision which a 'down sized' church will be able to provide, but I trust in God, the Church Commissioners, public opinion, civil service decency and political expediency to see me through. It's a winning combination! Quite often in these controversies people forget that priests have lives to live and bills to pay, children to please and wives to cherish. I know that you have been working to ensure that everybody is safe and one of the reasons I came was to thank you for your efforts, putting pastoral care above any doctrinal consideration. It was kind of you to take the trouble." "It is no trouble," said Clement. "We would not want to change our relationship with our friends by oppressing them. I suspect that when the dust settles the geometry, or did I mean choreography, will be different but the total aggregate participation will be little different. Except that we believe that Perpetuanism will give love of the Godhead a huge boost." "I hope you are right. I enjoyed what Perpetua said about people themselves and about God, but forgive me if I am not supple enough—and I think in many ways it is a matter of suppleness—to move to new formulations. Perhaps some—although I know not you—will think that I am simply lazy, reciting formulae that have no real depth, but I have never claimed depth, merely breadth."

After dinner, Mark had not been able to sit in his study to contemplate the next morning's worship. He usually jotted down some notes for his BCP eight o'clock and his 9.45 a.m. Family Eucharist sermons, but frequently forgot to carry them with him. On this occasion he felt he needed to be in church and so he walked across and let himself in. His dilemma was how far he should be explicit. He had taken the decision to alter the essential prayers as little as possible, but, still, changing the Creed and the Eucharistic Prayer were quite radical moves. He looked again at his Pentecost Mass Booklet. He had changed the Creed in line with the god4u site but, as was his custom, he had not printed the Eucharistic Prayer. He would have to preach on the Creed or there would be utter confusion. People were so used to saying it without thinking that they would all fall over each other. It was as much a matter of aesthetics, of elegant worship, as of doctrine for Mark. He could not bear the thought of a mess. He read:

"We believe in the mysteries: that God who is love created everything out of love and created humanity as imperfect so that we might freely love God in a personal relationship and love each other. That, in love, God Our Parent sent a Son, Jesus Christ, as God to share our humanity, and by such sharing He brought new hope, but His perfection was too much for humanity to bear and so we killed Him. That He absorbed all humanity's wrong choices and gave it new resources to love through our consciousness of our Sister the Spirit which attunes us more closely to God's communication in love. That, by His resurrection, Jesus confirmed that, because no wrong choice, including killing Jesus, will limit God's limitless love, all humanity will be enfolded back into the Godhead from which we came. We affirm the mysteries of our earthly purpose of living a

Sacramental life of physical encounter with the divine through the Church and accept the privileged responsibility inherent in that encounter to bring the news to all humanity that it will be re-united in God."

Just as we often do not see errors in a text that we have written, but require an external proof reader, so Mark had not seen the key omission in this text. It was Perpetuan—taken from a Creed workshop she had conducted—but there was no mention of Perpetua's Membership of the Godhead. From his traditional, Christian perspective, it was a much better Creed than Nicea, but it could have been said by many Christians. He noted in particular its Petran/Liberal tone and the omission of any reference to Scripture. The question was whether it was worth the trouble as it was not so radical as he had assumed. The answer, as so often, did not come down to principle but to practicalities. The booklet was printed. He could take the congregation part of the way this Sunday and see whether Dexter and his followers would develop matters further to incorporate Perpetua.

Kylie was visiting Meg. She intended to go with her to church next morning before getting back to London in time for the service of Union and Affirmation. They were eating bean salad dressed with herbs from Meg's small garden. "What happened when you reminded them of Perpetua?" "I knew it was going to be unpleasant because I've worked in shops and I know what pressure there is on village shops in particular. Ever since the 'double whammy' of mass private car ownership and big supermarkets, village shopkeepers have lived in a permanent state of fear so dreadful that when you ask them how they are, they tell you, fear so gripping and sapping that they are in perpetual need of somebody or something else to blame. It's never them. They are permanent victims who forget that they are shopkeepers out of choice. They are even worse than out of work actors who at least have the grace to admit—except for a very few—that society doesn't actually owe them a living. Anyway, I was watching the god4u Channel earlier in the week and that weird television man, the one from Fang ...". "... You mean Will Dignot?" "Yes, him. He was talking about the first time he saw and then met Perpetua. He said it doesn't seem so odd now, but it seemed very strange then that she was campaigning in favour of lower consumption. That we should only buy what we really needed—and this was before the beginning of the scare about food and energy prices. This was when we were still talking about spending our way out of crisis instead of saving our way out of it—and that we should not do this because it was good for our figure, or lifestyle, but as a duty to the world and the poor people in it. So I thought, 'If that is the starting point of her mission we should not allow ourselves to forget it,' so when I went shopping this morning I thought I would try it out. I went into the butcher's and said I would like two rashers of bacon. You would have thought that I had asked for credit. I got a blank stare and then the boy said, 'You mean you don't want your usual packet of eight rashers?' 'No,' I said, 'I only ever eat four in a week and find myself throwing away the other four and as I might not want four in the week I'll just take two for tomorrow morning.' And he said, 'but you know we only do bacon in packets of eight rashers.' 'Yes, but remember, I used to work here and I know you make the packets up in the back with the vacuum pack machine, so you can just cut me two rashers.' He had to go into the back to ask the boss who came out and looked at me as if I had been hauled in for shop lifting. 'I know you were a little eccentric when you worked here, Meg, but if everybody behaved like you we would all go out of business.' 'But,' I said, 'that's precisely what I want. Not for you to go out of business, but for everybody to behave like I'm behaving. We're too greedy and it has to stop somewhere. Now seems a good time and place for it to stop.' 'But what about small businesses like this?' 'I'm not an economist,' I said, 'but it isn't just small businesses that will have to alter. Everybody will have to alter. We'll all have to scale down.' 'Well,' he said, very rudely, 'if that's the kind of stuff that you are picking up at church I will have to think about stopping my contribution. If we're all going to get poorer, your precious, moral church will have to be poorer by my annual contribution.' Well, I know I should not have said it, but I said, 'If it's like your contributions to everything else, it will be too small to be missed', and then I walked out." "But did you get your two rashers?" "Yes. In all the disputing I almost forgot about it and so did they, so it was going to be bread and marmalade for Pentecost,—which might be taking Perpetua further than I intended, but perhaps that's no bad thing—but as I was going out of the door he said that selling two rashers was better than nothing." "Did you go anywhere else?" "Yes, I went to the deli and did much the same thing. They were a bit nicer, but still very puzzled. The problem is that most people, including many church people, have stopped linking religion with the things that they do. It's also true of politics. I remember Clement standing for the Lib Dems many years ago in the local elections. He lost by seven and the next day a woman came up to him and asked him what the village was to do about the only bank branch closing. 'Did you vote for me yesterday?' he asked. She blushed and said, 'No. I always vote Conservative.' and Clement said, 'Lady, you voted for the market, you've got the market.' People think they can vote Conservative and get Labour or Liberal policies without having to pay for them. They want reduced taxes and better services, and they are always talking about eliminating waste. So, when I start a personal campaign to eliminate waste by cutting down on what I buy, but then throw away, you would think that people would instinctively understand, but they don't. As I said, it's like people in our church who drive the mile in sunny weather in their huge gas guzzlers, not thinking it bears any relationship to what they hear about climate change when they get inside the doors." "Well, in spite of Perpetua, I don't suppose it will be any different in whatever our new kind of church is," said Kylie, looking sad. "The old tendencies always creep back, but what this makes me alive to is that if we go on like this we will make an enemy of shopkeepers and business." "Well, yes, I had not thought of it quite like that, but it's inevitable." "I'm not a theologian, just somebody who was called out early by Perpetua and I was always touched by the way she dealt with people and practical situations. Perhaps it's no coincidence that she started talking about frugality. Perhaps that is the

next great moral need." "It will take such a culture change, but Iris and I are going to try very hard. I mean, we don't have all that much money so we should
find it easier than most to cut down, and it has to start somewhere. It isn't the
lifestyle thing that really matters, is it? I mean it's the way it changes your attitude to yourself that matters, the way you learn to value life rather than just
enjoying consumption." "True. It will be strange coming to grips with this as we
all came from Hypo which was devoted to getting people to buy more." "Which
reminds me that the most difficult place to deal with in my morning's shopping
was Lakshmi Local. I went in and asked for a small tin of beans. They said they
only had big tins and four-packs of small tins. Well, I didn't want to make too
much trouble as it's a chain and the shop workers aren't in control of what they
sell in the way that the butcher is, or the deli. I bought a four-pack, paid for it
and then, before going out, took the cardboard sleeve off the four small cans and
left it on the counter. You would have thought I'd planted a bomb or a dog turd.
They called the Manager who told me to take my litter outside. I asked the woman behind me in the queue if she would mind taking the polythene wrapper off
her newspaper and leaving behind all the bits she didn't want, like the sports
section. While she was doing that, as a bit of a laugh, I think, the man behind got
into the action by taking the polythene wrapper off his loo rolls. While the Manager was getting more and more angry a pile of wrapping began to mount up on
the counters in front of the tills. People thought it was really funny but, of course,
it will get serious on both sides before long." "Perpetua would have liked that as
long as you were all cheerful." "We were, and in the end even the Manager had
to smile. Instead of telling us all to carry our wrapping outside to put it in the bin
he had the brilliant idea of bringing the bin in. He said he would report our
protest to Head Office, but didn't indicate whether he supported or opposed it.
Well, that was a lot of excitement for one day. "There's a time for being calm, as
Perpetua would always tell us, but it's nice to become calm with a smile on our
face. It doesn't happen often enough."

Bill Midway was smiling. He was listening to Jim playing the flute as he went
through his notes for tomorrow. This would be the first time since Easter that
he working well, and he had also spent a couple of Sundays with the followers of
Perpetua who had not moved away from the South. He sat on the front steps and
lit his pipe so that, in his fancy, the music of the flute coming out of the church
door mixed with the aromatic smoke. He was facing right into the sunset which
he was enjoying for the first time since a crumbling tower block opposite had
been demolished during the Winter. This was his chance to enjoy the music and
the smoke and the sunset as a preparation for his all night vigil. He knew that
tomorrow would be the key day for Perpetuanism. He did not know what would
happen. Nobody seemed to know. Everybody was living in a state of trustful-
ness which would have provoked nervous breakdowns, even in the Church of
England. He had phoned Dexter to find out how he was. "Fine, Bill, thank you
for calling. I don't know what's going to happen, but I am sure that Our Sister the
Spirit, in league with Perpetua and in the brotherhood of Jesus and in obedience

to God Our Parent will make sure that it all sorts out. No doubt we will degener-
ate in time into a bureaucratic and ecclesiological—that's the word, isn't it? I'm
learning fast—into an ecclesiological paralysis, but if you can't be loose before
your launch, you're never going to be loose, are you?" Bill supposed that Dexter
would sometimes veer away from this purity, longing for a bit of structure, but
he sounded fine or perhaps it was just that Bill was naturally a person of the moment, savouring everything in its turn, not downgrading the present because
of some vague aspiration or desire for something in the future. That was why
he was so pastorally gifted. He would give all his attention to the person he was
listening to and only when a greater need, a real need, meant that he had to ad-
journ the session, would he say something like, "I can't keep them all waiting for
Communion, but I'll see you straight afterwards." Neither did he, on the other
hand, allow his time to be monopolised by the self-indulgent. He would listen
and then say, "Don't ask me. The matter is really in your own control. You have
to make that decision." He sometimes wondered whether his Perpetuanism was
simply temperamental. He had come into the Church of England at a time when
it had almost disappeared from public gaze and even from itself. He had not
liked the 'trendy vicar' movement, but neither was it so egregiously off line that
he thought he needed to say anything about it. His theological education had
been largely pastoral rather than doctrinal and he had only ever wanted to work
in a poor parish to see how he could help. He was not sentimental. He knew
more about vice and personal danger than he had imagined possible as he sat
in his chilly study at theological college, but he had also learned about goodness
and fulfillment to an extent equally out of his student imaginative reach. He
believed in the power of God and the mirage—or was it the chimera?—of liberalism. If he had made sacrifices he had hardly noticed them. And then he had
inherited Jim whom he had grown to love because of his utter simplicity. He had
begun to wonder whether Jesus might have had some kind of syndrome that
had made him utterly simple, but he recognised the heresy. Somehow Jesus had
been utterly simple, but utterly lucid. He was not some kind of freak or jester.
He knew this now through seeing Jim who had been so wonderfully nurtured
by Perpetua. He remembered their long talks about God and humanity, not in
words, but in feelings. He had known then that what mattered was following
what she said without trying to turn it into a set of propositions which had to be
connected and consistent. As it was, she was extremely clear for somebody who,
he knew, had never received more than rudimentary secondary education, but
he needed to carry away the love not the message. Sometimes he wished that he
had been one of her followers, in the way that Dexter, Kylie and the rest were
followers, but there needed to be a Nicodemus, he thought. Nobody knew what
happened to Nicodemus after the burial of Jesus, but perhaps he was still in the
Sanhedrin when Peter came before it. And had he blocked his ears and thrown
stones at Stephen? She had asked him to look after her young followers because
their raw energy would need some channelling.

The music stopped. He tapped his pipe out on the bottom step and watched

the sun's final few seconds before it slipped below the horizon. "Thank you Jim."
"Bill, do you remember what I told you about the light in the church when She
was dancing with the Cross, and the light when She was taken from where we
laid her?" "Yes." "And do you remember she told me and you at the last that I
had this special gift?" "Yes Jim." "Well, there's going to be this huge light tonight
and it will last into the day." Bill knew better than to ask for any more detail but
he had no doubt of Jim's strange wisdom.

Dexter, in spite of genuinely believing what he had said to Bill, was trying
to pray and suffering from a terrible blank. He could not pray. He could not
imagine tomorrow. He could not imagine success. He kept thinking of failure
without being able to give it any concrete sense. It was an irrational but overpowering feeling of pessimism.

The text prompt on his phone jingled:

c u 50cOST—P

10.

Bishop James liked to drive himself, particularly when the journey took him
to small churches down narrow country lanes. In a way that he found satisfying, he always seemed to end up in the smallest places on the greatest occasions
thus, he thought, demonstrating to all, including himself, the proper place of a
bishop amid his flock, no matter how small the gathering, no matter how distant
the church. It also gave him the opportunity to listen to Faith without being distracted. It was a somewhat worthy offering, he thought, but it was more acceptable than the Music Programme which only played little pieces or extracts from
big pieces. The best you could hope for was a Bach Cantata now and again, but
he had begun to stow a few favourite CDs now that he had bought a smaller car
with a CD player.

"The church of England, and perhaps the Christian Church as a whole, will
never be the same again," said the anchor, introducing the programme who then
almost contradicted himself by continuing, "So in today's programme we will be
asking what difference the Perpetuan movement will make to traditional Christianity". James was seriously annoyed by this kind of contentious rubbish which
made a sententious statement before staging a shallow debate to test it. "Besides," he thought, "whenever has it ever been the same?" He tried to remember
what he knew about the birth and growth of Unitarianism which had been the
last major doctrinal challenge to Christianity. Names like the Wedgwoods, the
Darwins, and the Fieldens came to mind and he vaguely recalled some Victorian

gothic architecture in Todmorden, but nothing else had stuck, so that can't have been a very big upheaval. I wonder if the Times thundered that, "The Church of England, and perhaps the Christian Church as a whole, will never be the same again", after the first Unitarian tract reached the news desk. He thought back to all those "change and continuity" essays he had written about the Constantinian conversion, eleventh century reform, the 'rediscovery' of Aristotle, the Reformation, Wesleyanism, and the Oxford Movement. Even given the slower communications before motorised travel, each of these developments had taken its time and been organic, with salient incidents speeding up the inevitable. The Christianisation of the army and the Battle of the Milvian Bridge, the decline of Barbarism and the rise of the Cistertians, the Moorish intellectual stimulus to the Renaissance and the brilliance of Aquinas, the decadence of the Papacy and the peculiar personality of Luther, the rise of industry and the genius of Wesley, and the decay of the Church of England and the conjunction of Keeble and Newman. In each case the wider movement would have worked its way through the church, reaching a zenith before declining. All that people did was alter the timing and speed. We usually knew those who had speeded things up, but there were also those who had managed to slow things down. Somewhere deep in his analytical heart, James had held onto the core of Hegelian methodology. The real answer, he knew, had to include the Holy Spirit, but you couldn't write an essay on continuity and change giving the credit to the Holy Spirit! It might be theologically necessary or even a matter of personal faith, but the philosophy of religion had infiltrated theology to such a degree that such a simple, Christian explanation would never have been accepted by the examiners. Continuity and change was much in the news with the imminent departure of Prime Minister Blair and the arrival of Prime Minister Brown. James was not ducking the politics when he said to those who asked him about it that the external forces would dictate most policy. The person would simply give it a slightly different emphasis, slow something down, speed up something; as with the Church, so with the polity, the only difference being the attribution to the Holy Spirit. Nobody supposed that Mr Blair's arrival or departure were a matter for the Third Person, although James did wonder why the Church should assume that the activities of the Spirit were largely confined to itself.

Max Silver was 'in conversation' with a Petran and a Toran theologian. The Toran said that Perpetuanism was unbiblical, a heresy which was bound to fail, just as the liberal project as a whole—with its condoning of gross immorality—would fail. The Petran said that Perpetuanism would fail because it was heretical and particularly because it did violence to the Sacrament of the Eucharist. Max said he was no theologian, but that he would trust in His Sister the Spirit. The two gentlemen were right, if it was an inauthentic way of establishing personal relationships between the Creator and the created it would wither away. On the other hand, if that process was so inevitable, why were his fellow guests so combative? As for Sacramentality, he gathered that the form of the Eucharist, which Perpetua had slightly altered, had been altered many times over the centuries, particularly in the first 400 years. The Toran said that Perpetuanism was misleading because it wrongly convinced people that it provided a route to God. The Petran said that it was misleading because there was only one sure route to God. Max said that Perpetua had been listening to and working with people who had either left the Christian church or who had never been reached by it. We would have to see whether it was an authentic route to God, but it was better to experiment than do nothing. He did not want to be aggressive, but the established churches did not, on any criteria he could think of, appear to have been very successful in the past 200 years, in the West at least. The Toran said that there was a genuine revival in Biblical Christianity. The Petran said that numbers did not count. Max said that if Petrans claimed a monopoly channel to God, numbers must count, and although he granted there might be a numerical advance in the strength of various Evangelical movements, it was his judgment that they did not do justice to the depth and complexity of the Christian Gospel. For his part, he believed that there were many honest routes to God and that Perpetua had proposed a way which built on Christianity just as Jesus had built on Judaism. The Toran said that Jesus was the last word. The Petran said that Jesus was the only Word. Max said that he would accept the first proposition if he was advised at precisely what point theological development had been arrested in the name of orthodoxy. The second point had been largely disowned by Vatican II. James' mind wandered as he looked across the fields to a distant range of hills. Granted, radio had to fill its space whatever the issues on the agenda, but surely it did not have to present the same few views so repetitively. If you stayed in any profession long enough, the greatest risk to your sanity was boredom. For the past ten years he had been embroiled in endless discussions about homosexuality, women bishops, and, latterly, the strident claims of Toran and Petran 'fundamentalists' who had managed to get past the 'presenting issues'. James wanted to talk about global warming, family breakdown, stem cells, and a tangle of medical issues now well over the horizon, and the need to substitute beauty for sentimentality in the Church, but he was never allowed to get round to it.

He drew up outside the tiny church of Saint Swithin at Grangebury which he had reached by an unmade road, passing through the gates of the Old Manor into what had been its grounds with its own private church. He had wanted to close it, but the locals, atypically of their class, had offered him a guarantee of a full diocesan contribution for the next five years. In exchange they stipulated a weekly morning service, alternating Eucharist and Matins, a monthly Evensong and, as they insisted on their moneysworth, a Curate who could sing and preach. His Chaplain was waiting by the door alongside the Churchwardens and the Team Rector and the Curate. "The Church of England will never be the same again," he thought, as he shook hands with the welcoming party. This BCP Church had probably not changed much in its worship since the introduction of Victorian hymns. Neither the ASB nor Common Worship had darkened its doors and, he suspected, contemporary hymns were only used at weddings where the young couples chose what they had learned at school in the late 1980s.

He walked down the aisle, looking at the old box pews and past them to the memorials on the walls. The Binghams, who had lived at the Grange until the Second World War, were well represented, notably in a tablet which listed their First World War dead. Now there was a different dimension of continuity and change. If there had been a Bad Morning on the day after that fateful assassination of Archduke Franz Ferdinand in June 1914, would it have said, "England, and indeed Europe, will never be the same again. In today's programme we will ask whether the assassination will have any effect on the currently delicate state of international relations." Every church but the most modern, every village green, was disfigured by First World War memorials, and what had the Church done about that war? He could see why the Church should have—pace George Bell—gone along with the war against Hitler although the prosecution of it appeared at times to be excessive—although it was impossible to quantify the counter factorial, such as how long the war would have gone on without carpet bombing—but the refusal to intervene in the First World War was surely one of the greatest failures in Christian history.

When he entered the vestry to give his 'pep talk' to five early teenage and two adult Confirmation candidates, one of whom was being baptised, he could not help asking, "Can any of you tell me about Princip?" The Rector and Church-wardens looked at him oddly. "It's Latin," said one of the young girls without seeming to notice the oddity of the question. "It's something to do with maths," said the only boy. "Very good, but I am actually thinking about a man. He shot the Archduke Franz Ferdinand, which is why you have that tablet out in the church, honouring all the Binghams, and the rest, who died." Everybody waited, wondering what this had to do with Confirmation, but aware of the deference owing to bishops who were entitled, like judges, to be eccentric if they liked. Now that bishops spent more time in schools than churches, the five teenagers were familiar with their ways, or at least with the open friendliness of Hilary Kernow of Aleford, and a surprising number of them knew a surprising amount about the ways of judges. "On the way here I was thinking about change and when I came into Saint Swithin's I could not help thinking of the massive change brought about by the First World War and how little the Church did to put a stop to it." The Churchwardens, seeing that the talk had got well under way, slipped out. "Old James has a strange way of going about it." "Yes, but he usually gets there in the end."

"So, coming to the end of this talk, if you see something that you know is against the teaching of Jesus you are to say it out loud. Confirmation turns you from a private Christian into a public Christian." He was then invited to robe in a specially reserved little room, but he opted to stay where he was, amused by the blend of collaboration and competition as the girls, for want of a mirror, checked each other's appearance.

Processing down the aisle, the Bishop once again looked at the Bingham tablet. Something had changed with Princip. It was not simply nostalgia that gave a special significance to that sunny August of 1914. It was the end of aristocratic war games and the recognition, doubtless unloooked for by campaigners, that the democracy of politics and slaughter had to keep roughly in step. A framework of social stratification that had been maintained and modified for almost a thousand years was shattered in the trenches. For good or ill, it was a genuinely radical change. One could, he thought, looking at the Cross carried in front of him, not conclude otherwise than that the introduction of a fourth 'person' to the Godhead would be the most fundamental theological change to Christianity since the initial formulations of John and Paul. Given the marginalisation of the theological—as opposed to the socially caring—church, this might not have the same impact on the lives of people as the First World War, but in terms of its significance to institutional Christianity it would be massive. How he hoped, in spite of the superficial attractions of Perpetua, the enthusiasm of the Dean and the new perspectives which fundamental questions always raised, that the Perpetuan phenomenon would fade and die, hopefully leaving behind it a precious deposit of new perspectives which the Church could absorb.

Having focused, he went through the first part of the service deliberately trying to give it freshness through the way he spoke. For him it was one of so many such services but for the candidates it was their unique day. What was true for the liturgy was even more true for the sermon. As parish priests have core wedding and funeral sermons which they adapt slightly according to the personalities involved, so the Bishop had a core Confirmation sermon, but he always tried to introduce at least one radically new element so that it would colour the whole of his familiar text. He climbed into the pulpit, looked at the Bingham tablet and was about to raise his hand to make the introductory sign of the Cross when a mobile phone rang. The Churchwardens glared and the woman concerned dived embarrassedly into her handbag, convinced that she had turned it off before entering church. She had only just begun rummaging when another phone rang, and then another, and then another. Within twenty seconds, every phone in the church was ringing, including those of the Churchwardens and that of the Bishop. "This is highly unusual," said the Bishop, knowing that he was expected to take the lead, instinctively taking refuge in the obvious. "I suggest that we look at our messages and I will then continue." He took out his phone and checked his incoming messages. There was one:

4 G IS 4 IN 1

He signalled to the Churchwardens who came to the foot of the pulpit steps. "And what does yours say?" he asked. "Mine says 'PERPETUA ASCENDIT', Bishop." "Mine says 'SPIRITU PERPETUAE DESCENDIT', Bishop." "Very symmetrical. Could you ask some of the congregation to read out their messages?" They included:

MY LAST MSG—P

DEXTER 2 LEAD

CONFIRM IN MY NAME 2

All the candidates had identical messages:

MY SISTER THE SPIRIT CONFIRMS U

The level of hubbub which had reached its peak when all the phones began to ring steadily subsided through the exchange of messages into complete silence. everybody was waiting for the Bishop, but they knew he could not possibly hurry. He was, however, for him, remarkably swift in coming to his conclusion. "Let us pray," he said, and began.

"Loving God our heavenly parent, look down on all your children here present as we seek to do your will. Help us to understand your goodness in sending your Son, our Saviour Jesus Christ and your Daughter, Perpetua who has, in our own age, renewed your incarnational commitment to us as the Sustainer and Your Sacred Vessel. We make this prayer to you through Jesus and Perpetua and in the power of Our Sister the Spirit."

He then climbed back into the pulpit to preach.

> There is no point in ignoring what has happened. The message has been brought to us differently from that which was brought to the Apostles on the day of Pentecost, but the message is fundamentally the same. They had a "mighty, rushing wind" and we have text messages. What they are saying to us is that we are to see Perpetua's life, death, and later manifestations as conforming with the pattern of Jesus in every way. In teaching, in sacrifice, in Resurrection, ascension, and in the sending of the Spirit.
>
> For a long time I have resisted this new Covenant. The Church is properly careful of new developments, and although people with new questions—and even new answers—often complain that they are being under-rated, the Church has a duty to discern carefully over a period of time before changing its practice. We are a Church of Scripture, tradition, reason, and experience. If this has been true for amendment of ethical perspectives—slavery, the role of women, the nature of gender, the requirements of social justice—it must be even more true for such a radical departure as the overturning of the doctrine of the Blessed Trinity. Yet I see no alternative and I am bold enough to surmise that this is not the only church to which such messages have been sent. This is an especially blessed day for our Candidates, one that we and they will never forget, the re-launching, in effect, of God's enterprise on earth. This will require additional theological reflection and instruction, but I want to baptise and confirm now in the sure knowledge of the love of God and with the confidence that the Spirit will be with us as we learn to adjust, as those who listened to the Apostles on the first Christian Pentecost had to adjust. The Acts of the Apostles tells us what a wonderful time it was as the Spirit was almost visceral in the new Christian community. We have been told that this is about to happen again.
>
> I must, however, ask each Candidate for permission to proceed on this new basis.

The Bishop was not wrong. As Castlegate climbed into the pulpit of Saint Chad's in Coombeside, he was greeted by a cacophony of telephone ringing. He felt his own phone vibrate and brusquely turned it off. "Some sort of electrical storm!" he said. "Just turn them all off and settle down and we will start again."

He sat down on the tiny bench at the back of the pulpit, out of sight of the congregation, and prayed that the rest of the service would go peacefully. He rose, consulted his notes, opened his Bible to Acts 2 and was about to begin when his phone rang. There was complete silence. He took it out and saw that there was a new MMS. He felt like sitting down to deal with it, but somehow he could not bring himself to move. He opened the message and saw Perpetua smiling. She said, "Don't be afraid. God our Parent has brought new life to the world through me. My mission is accomplished."

Even though it was a new church, Saint Chad's had a bright acoustic. Everyone heard the message. Bruce stood for a moment looking at the screen and then he played the video clip again.

"Just as Scripture records the way in which the first Apostles of Jesus tried to change the minds of the Jewish people and the religious establishment, so we must now, on this New Pentecost, seek to change the views of traditional Christians so that they are in accord with the New Covenant."

Mark received a message as he was about to climb into his pulpit, but somehow it did not surprise him and instead of referring to his uniquely, carefully crafted sermon, he simply told the congregation what he had just seen on his screen and proclaimed the day of Pentecost of 2007 as uniquely special. For the first time since his initial confrontation with the issue of the role of minorities in the Church of the early 1970s, he felt liberated. He felt that he could at last serve God in a way he had hoped when he was ordained. He spoke to his beloved people, looking to each in turn about this unprecedented day. He could feel Clement's concentration and joy. He could feel Helen's support. Whatever administrative chaos lay ahead, they could all face it now. She had said:

U R BLEST OF 4FOLD G—P

By lunch time the picture was becoming clear as reports were received by local radio stations and collated by news agencies. Every Christian church had received a message. In some places there was mass communication, in others a few or only one person was contacted, but all the messages were similar. Perpetua proclaimed her Godhead in the pattern of Jesus. The only question now was whether she had finally appeared in the morning in so many places or whether she would make a spectacular appearance at the Service of Union and Affirmation.

The Christian press had been in general agreement about the Grand Synod of the previous week, reported in almost identical headlines. The Fortress said:

DOWN BUT NOT OUT

The Church of England, reeling after the shock resignation of Archbishop Hawthorne and other senior bishops, showed signs of recovery when the remaining 32 pledged to uphold the traditional position of the Church.

Speaking on behalf of the Bishops, Archbishop Mwanga said that he regretted the departure of his good friend Archbishop Hawthorne, but it was his job to hold things together until vacancies were filled. "The Church

of England is down but certainly not out," he said. "As long as we stick together in obedience to Scripture the Spirit will be with us."

A Fortress readers' poll shows that 96% support the bishops who have
stayed; 62% said that the Church was "better off" without the departing
Bishops.

Church & State said:

CALM AFTER STORM

Archbishop Mwanga has called for "a period of calm" after the recent
storm caused by the resignation of Archbishop Hawthorne and a number
of diocesans. "There is no need for us to do anything in a hurry," he said.
"We will give the Church a new lease of life with an unprecedented new
wave of enthusiastic bishops."

Church House sources said that the remaining 32 Bishops who met
together earlier this week were "relatively relaxed" about developments.
While regretting the departure of the Archbishop and other valued colleagues, they believed that the Perpetuan storm would soon pass. It was
simply the latest symptom of liberal febrility.

Meanwhile, there is speculation that Archbishop Mwanga will be translated to Canterbury once Mr Brown is settled in Downing Street.

A Readers' Poll in C&S shows voters evenly split on the effect of the resignations on the Church.

As The Stylus made clear, Petrans naturally viewed the Perpetuan phenomenon as the sole concern of the Church of England:

POPE REGRETS C OF E SCHISM

A spokesman for the Pope has urged the Church of England as the
leading body in the Anglican Communion to pull back from schism and
combat heresy. He warned Lambeth Palace that any concessions to Perpetuanism would further impair the ecumenical process. Our reader poll
shows that over 90% think that what Anglicans do is irrelevant to the
Church.

The general view among the correspondents and columnists was that Perpetuanism had run its course and that Hawthorne's 'belated' adherence was the
result of poor judgment. Church & State, in an editorial more trenchant than
usual, said that Hawthorne had:

... Impetuously resigned over a relatively trivial issue. In spite of the
pretensions of Perpetuanism to present a new theology. It was unwise of
the Archbishop to take the bait. The history of the Church is littered with
theological red herrings and the lesson is that these should be put aside.
There have been great upheavals in the Christian church at approximately
500 year intervals and so no doubt one is due in the twenty-first century,
but it would be absurd even to consider the possibility that a young girl

with an untrained mind, no matter how well intentioned, could be the starting point for such an upheaval. Incidents connected with her life, death and their aftermath leave certain loose ends but these, in themselves, are not enough to justify her outrageous claims to Godhead."

As the week drew to its close, the daily newspapers and news broadcasters were split between the anticipation of a spectacular event and the underlying culture of pessimism, but the latter steadily gained ground so that Ranjit, in spite of his unrivalled connections with the Perpetuan movement, was not unrepresentative when he wrote:

EXIT PERPETUA?

Sources close to Perpetua said late last night that the response to invitations to the Service of Union and Affirmation have been "disappointing". Although no figures have been published it is understood that London's Great Hall will be only two-thirds full for the key Perpetuan launch event tomorrow.

Speaking for Dexter, a senior source said that nobody had ever expected the hall to be sold out, but he could not hide his disappointment when he said that organisers had hoped for stronger support.

One key figure said that if Pentecost turned out to be a flop the whole Perpetuan movement was in danger of imploding. "We should know from Perpetua and the Spirit one way or the other," he said.

The Sunday papers were no less gloomy, heaping further blame on Hawthorne for behaving like "a rat deserting a righted ship". There was a vicious profile piece on Dexter in the Sunday Examiner colour supplement and Sunday Money ran a highly speculative account of the fall and rise of Max Silver.

Contrary to the reports, the meeting of the 32 Bishops had been fraught and fractious because it concentrated almost exclusively on timing and tactics rather than on the fundamental theological issues. Some of the bishops were moved by the novelty of Perpetuanism, but wanted to wait and see. Others saw it as a threat and wanted an immediate offensive. The first group wanted any definite statement to wait until after the Service of Union and Affirmation. "The one thing we do know," said the Archbishop, "is that we must stick together through this crisis. We cannot behave now in the way that we have behaved in recent years. Even if you do not agree with me, I am afraid I am going to have to ask you for your loyalty. I am not the Pope, as you know, and you know that I have no pretensions to be a leader, but I do know that we are going to have to forget our differences about tactics. I need to say that things are going well, to give us some time. If Perpetuanism triumphs it will make no difference what I have said. If it fails, we need to have a strong Church to open its arms to returning exiles. It will be hard for those who return—we must make it as easy as we can. These people will need us, but we will also need them, for our stability, for our credibility, for our mission. We are still, uniquely, the Church which exists to serve its non-members. Our failure of late has been to expect too much of people, to put obstacles in their way. I have to say to the Torans here, this has not worked, and it will certainly not work if there are Perpetuan exiles. We will have to put hospitality above exclusivity, or conformity, whatever we want to call it. Likewise, the Petrans among us will have to be more generous, less grudging in our understanding of what it means to explore the concept of Godhead. Heaven knows, I am no liberal, but I do see that we all have to be hospitable if Perpetu-anism fails. If these people are going to have a home fit for their return we must ensure that we remain loyal to each other in these next days.

"I am therefore, unusually I know, asking you to suspend your private prefer-ences and allow me to speak on behalf of us all, so that I can tell the world that we are confident of being able to ride out the storm, that the ship is righted, that we are on our way back."

In spite of reservations, the Archbishop was given unanimous support.

All the negative news was kept from Dexter who was struggling with himself and his speech. At almost hourly intervals Max came in and helped him to sim-plify what he was trying to say. "Look Dexter, you're no orator. We both know that. So try not to write these long and complex sentences. Keep your statements short and punchy and put back those nice lists you had instead of stringing all the items into long, rambling sentences. I'm not sure you would not be better off speaking spontaneously—in the Spirit—but if you can't bear to do that, think of what you are writing as notes. Let the Spirit move you. You are a leader, so when the time comes, lead!"

As far as the English media were concerned, Perpetua had done her stuff. The Sunday lunch time news broadcasts were full of reports of the 'manifestations' which had taken place throughout the country. Bewilderment was greatest among the Roman Catholic hierarchy, which until this point had been watching from the sidelines. At least three Roman Catholic bishops had received 'mes-sages' from Perpetua and there was an as yet unconfirmed rumour that the Pope himself had received some form of communication. As there was no Football broadcasting scheduled, the major channels announced that they would be cov-ering the Service of Union and Affirmation which had been put back to four o'clock to allow more people, at their urgent request, to travel to London.

By two o'clock the Great Hall was filled to capacity and stewards had to make hurried arrangements with the broadcasters to provide coverage in the Great Square. The police put out messages discouraging any more people from com-ing to London but the crowds grew rapidly until it was estimated that there were more than a million gathered round the Hall.

Dexter and his followers walked towards the Hall, collecting new adherents as they came. It could not be called a procession. There was no visible organisa-tion and no special clothes. The only way that people could tell that they were at the centre of an important event was the presence of the police helping the leading party to get through the crowds. There were more than 1,000 walking in groups behind Dexter and the initial followers of Perpetua, mostly clergy who had decided to affirm their new commitment. Television commentators passed the time identifying erstwhile celebrities, with Hawthorne receiving the most coverage as he walked along, more than half way back.

As he waited for the broadcast, Nigel felt slightly irritated. Why would it not stay still? Why did it always have to change just when you were getting used to something? It had been all right until the 1960s and nothing had stood still since then. He would get used to it, but as you get older it takes longer. He hoped this would be the last change. It was certainly the most difficult, but there was not much point in singing "God moves in mysterious ways" and then expecting him—he still thought of God as "him"—not to. Claire was looking forward to the challenge of the new music which would not replace the best of the old. Helen was pleased that things had sorted themselves out so smoothly. It would not have been possible without Ronald and Violet. She felt that Clement was comfortable and that Mark was settled. Even so, she had reluctantly, but willingly given up the immense satisfaction of going with Clement to the big event. She felt that Mark might just need her. She was not going to take the risk. She knew their love would not be diminished by her absence. To an extent which she never fully quantified, if it could be, Clement had a spiritual life which was exclusive to himself. Perhaps he would not talk about it out of a kind of modesty but she suspected that it could not be talked about. He had said that he would offer himself as a servant of Perpetua's organisation and take it from there. She could not imagine whether this meant a kind of Ordination, the thing he had most desired for many years, but she imagined there would be some occasion to which she would go other than the general Affirmation which was about to take place.

Clement was much more than 'comfortable'. He felt that he had been waiting for this all his life, even before he had first articulated within himself the idea that he wanted to be ordained. As he made his way into the Great Hall alongside Kylie, among those who had offered their service, he was only perturbed by the thought that it seemed not to be a sacrifice, that it seemed to be the easy, almost the pleasant, option. There was the joy of pastoral care, the prospect of presiding at the Sacrament of Union, the challenge of the new theology. He counted himself blessed that he was living now and, in the short walk from the start of the ragged procession to the Hall, he thought how all the rest of his troubles had faded to nothing. God was good.

Mark's mind had already moved on from the grand event, even before it happened, to the professional tittle-tattle of the new arrangements. He looked eagerly at the loose procession, spotting many of his old friends and acquaintances. He ticked off the bishops, the deans and the archdeacons and even recognised a couple of Roman Catholic priests. He had offered himself and had been accepted, but he excused himself from attendance as he had so much catching up to do.

Bishop James Hall held his wife's hand as he scanned the advancing leaders. As the Dean came into the picture he felt her react involuntarily, just a tiny flicker. He prayed that he would be helped through this crisis. He was so poor at changing. His theological training, so rooted in the Fathers, made it difficult for him to move very rapidly. In spite of his reaction in the morning, he would, without being able to say this to people even though they knew it anyway, wait and see what Rome decided to do. Castlegate and Aleford had agreed to meet after their Confirmations to pray together. After what they had experienced, they needed to. The overpowering feeling of Spiritual energy had driven them past truce into deep bewilderment and penitence. They felt the need of their Bishop, but respected his need for a little peace and quiet. They prayed for him and themselves, denying themselves the thrill of watching the build-up.

Sneer was intrigued by the mobile phone stories. He was not a spiritual man, but he had reluctantly accepted that there was something special about Perpetua after she had exercised some mysterious power over his technology and then singled out his offices for serious damage when she was dying. Looking back, he also recognised that she must have been behind the strange 'interference' with the copy that had gone into the paper about her and her followers. There was nothing much doing. The Phil Mac story had gone quiet. He was not sure he could get much change out of yet another mysterious appearance by Perpetua. She could hardly top her Easter performance, but Monday papers were always full of regurgitated rubbish.

Will and Annie were only interested because they had been personally touched by what happened on Easter Sunday when Perpetua seemed to have appeared to them while they were enjoying their first 'romantic weekend' in Spain. Annie had picked up the vein of anti consumerism in Perpetuanism which was now being heavily trailed by Trina. She was worried, but having nothing better to do, they watched. Marta, with Lucy on her lap, could hardly wait to see Max.

Tony Blair picked up his private phone. "Hello Gwyn. Dominus Vobiscum." "Oh, not you again!" "Now then, Gwyn, I am still the Prime Minister and one day very soon you will wish I still was." "Et Cum Spiritu Tuo, Prime Minister." "That's better. Now, about these strange phone calls which seem to be directed exclusively at people attending church." "I don't know. I don't know. I don't know about what happened last Christmas Night. I don't know what happened with the Perpetuagate tapes. I don't know what happened on Easter morning, and I don't know what happened today." "Well, if you are to provide a realistic report to Gordon, somebody is going to need to know." "Not quite, Prime Minister. We are an evidence based regulator, but it doesn't stop politicians bending our remit." "Heaven forbid." "And most official reports are not worth anything except for providing politicians with the time to re-write history while the punters forget the sharp detail. Journalists are almost incapable of reading a sentence of more than 30 words without complaining that it's 'impenetrable' and so you can write just about anything you want. All that counts is the Executive Summary and the press release." "And you call politicians, cynical! You might be right, but what matters is that you produce something that Gordon can accept and defend. What you have to remember—sorry, I know you were at Number 10 and know this, but I like saying it—is that we have to defend the crap that we are given by officials. You would think that we are still presiding over the Palmerston Ministry, the way they call for us to know everything and resign the moment somebody mis-counts the used paper clips. If an MP rigged his expenses the way, just picking somebody at random, Sneer rigs his, he would not stand a chance." "I know, Tony, but you don't need to go on about it." "Anyway, I didn't ring just to have a bit of fun—although I never mind fun—but to make a helpful suggestion." "Well?" "You don't sound very keen." "I've been on the wrong end of too many of your helpful suggestions." "Sorry, Gwyn, but you try getting elected." "All right." "I suggest that you cut out all the nonsense and technical jargon and the 'on the one hand' this and 'on the other hand' that and keep it simple." "Yes." "Just say that the behaviour of communications systems was subject to the power of God." "What!" "The power of God." "You can't put God in an official report." "Why not? You don't have a logical or a scientific explanation and all the evidence points to the supernatural." "We would make ourselves into a laughing stock!" "Calm down, Gwyn, and listen for a moment. There's a good reason why I'm a politician and you're a king pin quangocrat." "Thanks." "If you come up with a naff explanation you will be pilloried for a couple of days, then it will all die down. If you blame it on God you will be pilloried, but in a less forensic way. People will think that you have 'gone religious', but the real point is that they will be forced to find the explanation you have failed to find. You will be able to say, quite simply, 'Well, what do you think, then?' and they will have nothing to say." "I don't know how you think them up, Tony." "It comes naturally. Apart from Major, who came out of nowhere because of a string of accidents, most Prime Ministers are naturals. The ones who try to force it don't make it because you can't turn yourself into one. I mean, look at Gordon. He's forced himself, he's political rhubarb, whereas I was always an apple, just grew in reasonable rain and sun. Not too sour, not too sweet, jolly, wholesome, and English." "Give over." "All right, Gwyn. Sorry. Anyway, think about it. If it was God there isn't much point denying it. Come to dinner after Gordon kisses hands. Dominus Vobiscum." "Et Cum Spiritu Tuo. Amen."

Dexter and his followers filed in to music from Jim who was being supported by Father Bill who had played guitar in a rock group at his theological college. The Great Hall had been chosen because spectators looked down to the focus of action rather than looking up. The vast, flat space at the bottom of the raking was filled with those committed to Affirmation.

Max introduced the 'Service'. "I welcome you all here today, and those hundreds of thousands physically present, surrounding us with their love, and the countless millions watching on television, listening on the radio, and following us on the internet. We do not know how many you are, but the number is growing by millions every minute.

"The purpose of this Service of Union and Affirmation is to give the opportunity for our followers to profess their commitment in public so that those who seek them as leaders will have seen what they have said. Just as Judaism needed to develop with Jesus, so Christianity needs to develop as the result of the life and witness of Perpetua. I am simply the organiser of today, the person who makes it possible for things to happen. I want to thank everybody who has helped me, and now, over to the Leader chosen by Perpetua, our leader and brother, Dexter."

Max told me to keep my sentences short. I intend to follow his advice. My job is to talk about next steps. Now I know that this is boring for those of you who are expecting a miraculous appearance from Perpetua, and it's right that you should prefer listening to Her more than me, but I have no more idea than you if she's going to say anything. She was fairly lively this morning by all accounts, but we are just going to press on with what we have to do here.

What is the entity going to look like? We have—the original followers, Father Bill and Max—we have decided not to call it a formal church at all. For the time being we will be called the Perpetuan movement, with a small m. We will keep the small nucleus of people who walked with Perpetua—I suppose you might call us Elders, although we're mostly young—just to manage the essential things like sorting out funding and making agreements about the use of churches. We realise that some Christians will have a problem with the inclusion of Perpetua in the Godhead, but anybody can come to us to receive the Sacraments we will offer and we will not ask questions about personal behaviour or religious belief. This is a bit unconventional, but we are an organisation built on trust. If people are fooling themselves, the damage is done to themselves. There will be proper checks on people to see that they are fit for the job they have offered to do, particularly as they are in positions where many will call on them for help, but we will not question their actual calling. If somebody says she has been called by the Spirit, who are we to say that she has not? There will be some rough edges, but it is our intention to live fully in the Spirit.

Apart from the nucleus there will then be only two kinds of people. We didn't want to split people up at all, but, realistically, there are two kinds of people. On principle I don't like splitting people on the basis of whether they are paid or unpaid but, realistically, most of the people who act as our Guides will be paid. At least they will all be offered a proper salary so that there is no financial bar, but perhaps there will be some full-time Guides who are not paid. We thought of calling them shepherds, but in a world which is so urban we thought this was a bit sentimental. The Guides will preside at major festivals, administer the Sacraments, in groups of three or more select and provide guidance for those who administer the Sacraments on their behalf and for house group leaders and all those who offer service to God and neighbour, and look after an activity centre which is the focus for celebratory worship, but which must also be a resource for the whole community. As you know, our Sacrament of Affirmation is offered for all those who serve, abolishing the traditional distinction between once-only Confirmation, once-only Marriage, and three-fold Ordination. People will want to affirm new service or receive the Spirit at critical turning points in their lives. We want the Spirit to be as present to people in Sacrament as Jesus and Perpetua are in our Sacrament of Union. I also want to remind us that Perpetua has brought us the gift of the Sacrament of Response so that all people can give their lives in Sacrament. The problem with the old ways of Christianity is that Sacramentality has become a clerical monopoly. Anyway, we are going to make a new start.

We have already received offers from more than 1,000 people to be Guides. It's a comforting sort of number in our culture but it wasn't a target. We don't know yet how many Guides we will need.

Now I know that it's right that we should all count ourselves equal in service to God, that there's no distinction in value or quality, only a distinction in role, between what people do. However, it would be a failure of politeness and an exaggeration of the general principle of equality if I didn't ask us to remember in particular the role played by the former Archbishop Hawthorne in opening his heart to Perpetua and in resigning from such a venerable and distinguished office. He told me earlier that he didn't want the job in the first place, but as he took it in humility and anguish, I have no doubt that he left it in much the same condition of mind, that he suffered yet more anguish, but gave himself up to the will of God in humility. He has kindly agreed to work with us to formulate our Creed, based on the work that Perpetua started. Theology is like that, it's always incomplete. He will work to provide us with as open a stance to the Godhead as human thought and fervent prayer can devise. We asked him to become a member of our core group, but he said that he did not feel that this was the right thing to do as he had not been a follower of Perpetua and had only met her a couple of times very briefly. I know he won't really like this, but I think it is important that we recognise his service, so please could you stand, Dr. Hawthorne.

He rose reluctantly and was greeted by warm and sustained applause which went on long after he had sat down again.

There is not much more for me to say before we move to the Affirmation itself. You will have gathered from what I have said that I am not an orator. It's like Moses. I don't know why Perpetua chose me. I'm waiting for my Aaron. I want to say that I can understand the pain of Christians who see what we are doing. I am sorry they are pained. We want to value Christianity in precisely the same way in which Jesus valued his Judaism, but we have to move on so that more people can get in touch with the Godhead. Whatever the structural arrangements we are forced to make—and I pray that these will be minimal—what matters most, what matters exclusively, I should say, is the relationship between God Our Parent, our Creator and we who have been created, who are creatures. That is the one thing I want you to take away.

Many of those watching the television became bored as the file of Guides passed Dexter, each being touched gently on the head, as Jim and Father Bill played. Sneer did not see a story. The Prime Minister wondered whether it would be such a great upheaval after all for Gordon to deal with. Gordon tried to reduce the problem to a series of managerial steps, yet one more piece to be fitted into his strategy framework and announcements timetable. Gwyn re-tuned to golf. Will and Annie went to bed. Marta wondered if Max would appear again as she set the sleeping Lucy on the tatty sofa. Nigel, Scott, Meg, Marie, Helen and Mark all looked out for Clement and said a prayer when Dexter placed his hand on his head. Those who offered service as workers, but not Guides were collectively blessed. Then Dexter and Hawthorne concelebrated the Sacrament of Union, using for elements the contents of the Hypo Snackbox handed to everyone on the way in.

There had been a problem with the ending. Nobody had a very clear idea how to finish. "It's not a performance," said Dexter. "I know," said Trina, "but we want people to leave with some sense of occasion. This is a new start, we want to inspire people." "Well, I can't do that," said Dexter. "We will have to leave it to the Holy Spirit." Trina was torn between her faith and her worry that the Holy Spirit would not produce, that it would end with a sense of anti climax. It had been agreed that Dexter would give a blessing and that the Guides would then process out and then strike out towards the four corners of London, symbolising the world. Dexter raised his hand. Then, suddenly, the whole room was filled with the most glorious golden light which shone and did not hurt but, rather, caressed the eye. For an instant everybody in the Great Hall could only see the light. People outside stood in silence watching the screens as those inside were absolutely still and silent. Then the gold faded and Perpetua's smiling face filled the massive white screen behind Dexter.

> I wondered whether—to use human language—I should speak to you today or whether I should simply communicate through Dexter, and it is no slight to him that I have chosen to speak. I am aware that anything short of my personal presence would have been regarded as a terrible setback and I do not wish to endanger the movement of all children back to God Our Parent for want of a little manifestation. I am aware that the powerful and the possessive would want to characterise anything that comes from me as fraudulent. That is how the Gospel of John portrays those who were privileged enough to hear the words of Jesus My Brother. And so, just to confirm my presence before you today, here is a picture of the cloud formation which will be seen from the front of this building at 18.00 hours today. I have provided this image so that the evening news and tomorrow's newspapers will be able to match the two pictures and affirm that I am who I say that I am.
>
> Today I want to talk to you about my death and what has happened since, so that I can give true hope to those who have agreed to follow me. You are so used to me addressing you as 'we' but in my altered state I have to change. I am sorry in a way, because it was so comfortable. I am sorry particularly as I have some hard things to say, but they must be said.
>
> I never quite brought myself to say this while I was among you because I thought that I would be misunderstood, but now that I have suffered the death of my human body at the hands of human beings, I feel that I can say what I must with less fear of being completely misunderstood. Naturally, I

will be deliberately misunderstood, my meaning will be twisted, but we all need a clear starting point for our relationship with God Our Parent, and the incarnation first of Jesus and recently of me are starting points.

One of the questions which has been asked most frequently since my death is what happened to all the filmed records of it. I swept them away. I did not want the film of my death to be a kind of pornography, enabling people to wallow in the terrible degradation I suffered at your hands. We only have to look at Christianity to understand that the pornography of the Cross has completely overwhelmed the affirmation of self-determination in hope, by which I mean that the central message of the death of Jesus My Brother is that it does not matter what you do, you cannot do anything, even murdering God, so to speak, that will stop God loving you. It is not possible for you to do anything about God's love. The only thing over which you have control is your use of the capacity to love. The death of Jesus My Brother was only important insofar as it tells you something about you. But all the time you think that it tells you something about God. It does not tell you anything that you do not know, it does not tell you anything that you would know if there had been no Passion and death of Jesus. You know that God is love. That is the only reality that matters. The Cross will only tell you that you can change but that God will not change. To think that it has freed you from the responsibility to forge your relationship with God, directly and through all of humanity, is to misunderstand. I call the Cross 'pornographic' because you use it as a substitute for the real thing, the love of Jesus and me in God for you and your nature as creatures made to love God.

And so, if the symbol of the Cross has exercised such a powerful religious and cultural influence that it has almost destroyed the central meaning of the incarnation of Jesus, what effect do you think that a whole movie of my death would have?

Recognise the Cross for what it is. It is the symbol of the love of Jesus My Brother for the whole of humanity in spite of what you have done to us. I hope, on that basis, that you never find such a symbol of my incarnation and death. I do not want one. I want you to remember what I said and did, not giving yourself some theologically self-indulgent shorthand.

At the centre of love lies personal responsibility. You cannot love by proxy. You cannot ask other people to love for you. That wish to transfer your human purpose to other people is the root of the problems you face. When you turn to drugs, you are saying you have lost the capacity to choose and must escape. When you say that teachers must give children what they need, you have given up your responsibility as parents. When you think that paying taxes and a little extra to charity is enough, you have given up service. When you give yourself another ice cream and say there is nothing you can do for the poor, you have given up sacrifice.

The terrible danger of religion is that you heap onto God the things you were made to do yourself. God is not a 'fixer'. You have the capacity to fix. God is divine love and will not sort out human love for you. You have access to unlimited divine love and the resources to offer human love, not in return, but as a free gift to God of what you have been given. Giving human love is difficult, but that is your condition. You have the resources, but must struggle. That is not cruelty, it is your condition. You could be no different. You, the recipients of unlimited divine love, are responsible for human love, each one of you is responsible. There is no one with no resources. People have different resources because that, too, is part of your condition, and that means that each love will be different. Instead of trying to relate your human love to the human love of others, try to relate it to the love of God because your love is unique. You can imitate language and appearance, you can approximate, but each one of you is unique.

I therefore call on you to use my life among you as a resource to take up more fully the personal relationship offered to every child by God Our Parent. That relationship is the necessary source for the fullest expression of your human love. Try to wipe clean the slate. Forget the aspect of Christianity which has down-graded the human love you were made to express. Forget the dependence that the churches have encouraged, dependence on the Cross and dependence on churches. You do not go to heaven, as we might call it, because of the Crucifixion or because of your choice to undertake good works, works of love and sacrifice, you go to 'heaven' because you were made to be enfolded back into the Creator. You are not 'good', as you call it, either to earn eternal life or to make you feel good, but because it is human to be good. That is why you were made. To choose not to be good is to deny your nature.

You may deny your nature and you may deny the nature of others but God Our Parent will not deny your nature. The world's suffering arises in part from the condition of humanity as people made to choose, but the source of wickedness, as opposed to suffering, is your denial of your own nature and the nature of others. The use of power to deny nature is the greatest wickedness that you practice. It is bad enough to deny your own nature but much worse to deny the nature of others.

Even when you think you are doing good by denying the nature of others, you are doing harm. When I was among you, I lived in Grunge Park, a very deprived area, and often policy makers used to visit the area and say that the drug dealers needed to be rooted out. I repeated time and again that you will never control the supply of drugs because there will always be people who want to exercise power for their own financial gain, even if it ruins others, and that what you must do is reduce the demand for drugs by allowing people to live in their nature, to live naturally, to learn how to develop a relationship with God and to translate its fruits into human love. The greatest delusion is consumption. Many of you base your lives on consumption. Many of you even judge the success of your lives according to your consumption. But consumption is a desperate attempt to escape from your nature. Yes, your nature is to eat and to have children, but these are only the means of allowing you to live your full lives in love. There are very good reasons why you should reduce your consumption, in order to save the planet from catastrophe, but the fundamental reason is that it is distracting you from your true purpose.

Yet the real problem that faces you is the exercise of power. The prospect that hovers before the eyes of the powerful is closure and limitation, the power to make rules, to include and exclude, to narrow and oppress. I say to you that this is precisely the opposite of what you were made to do.

You were made to open, to free, to enable, to give. You have heard me say that love is the creation of space in which the other can love freely. I cannot say it often enough. You will reply that human beings are so wicked that we need laws and oppressions to maintain social stability, and I say, try, every one of you, to love and sacrifice to your limit and see how much restraint you will then need to control others. The idea that you 'fell' in some way is an excuse, it allows you to think that wickedness is intrinsic to the human condition and that you are freed from responsibility, but it is choice that is intrinsic to the human condition. What you do with it is entirely your own responsibility.

These are hard words, but I have summed them up here so that they will be alive in your memory. Just as Jesus My Brother gave humanity a new start with his incarnation, God Our Parent has given you a renewed start through me. No doubt you will, as humanity always does, look for patterns which you call 'theology'. That is part of your nature, but it is not so important as all that. It is much more important to think of your personal relationship with God Our Parent and your nature as loving creatures.

The language of God has changed from the time of Jesus and the institutions founded to witness to God's love have lost their energy. I bring you new hope. I bring you new language. I bring you new life, but the central message is the same.

As Jesus said: "Love one another as I have loved you." Reach out.

I shall not talk to you again. My Sister the Spirit is with you. Reach out.

The hall was again filled with a wonderful golden light and when it faded the screen was blank. She had gone, never to return.

So ended the earthly mission of Perpetua, the Sustainer and sacred Vessel of the Godhead.

They left the Hall, praising God for the wonderful gifts received by humanity, vowing to make a new start.

Outside the actual phenomenon of the appearance, there was no real story. The newspapers duly photographed the cloud formation and, while some printed it alongside Perpetua's picture, the superimposition of the two pictures was more telling. Sneer printed the superimposition for its novelty value above a very short story of the day, but although he was not interested in what had happened, he was sure that, following Perpetua's mission, the world would be a different place.

II. METROPOLITAN

11.

This is the story of how the word of Perptua reahed into high places.

There was no pie of any consequence, large or small, in the whole world, in which Sir Pluto Millman did not have a finger. To take just a generous handful at random: Cardamon, Guarneris, Appalachian Aggregates, the Gymcana Club of Buenos Aeres, weapons grade plutonium, Antiguan pineapples, Venus & Adonis Swim Wear, Napoleonic medals, the Nice Trocadero, the Grunge Park Partnership, green peppercorns, South Korean Automotive, the Arctic Claimants Consortium, colonial stamps, greengages, Lunar Futures, Grandma's Home Cookies, hairy nosed wombats, wheat futures, the Folio Society, orchids, pancreatic research, the Davos Directory, Plane Saling, Carmenere, the String Quartet Forum, Emirates Oil, skittles, Starburst Software, the West Highlands Light Railway, Boutique Inks, truffles, the New York Mercury, Malaccan Fisheries, pottery marbles, Lithuanian Cement, Wine'n'dine, crystalised tropical fruits, Istanbul Tobacco, Tudor seals, the Seattle Seafront Plaza, forest mushrooms, Japanese/Brazilian painting, the Wallop Inn, opals, Alpine Cable Transport, Grangebury Cricket Club, sheep cheese, Armenian chess sets, Peruvian potatoes, vintage motor cars, Constantine Brancusi, Felt, the Bilberry Bank, What The Dickens, tripe, Sarawak Long Houses, Font Fiesta, drill bits, Niagra Nubile, mock tartans, Secret Recipes, Kenya Cut Flowers, the Todmorden Morris Men, field recorders, the Rice Revolution, Christingle Charities, the Forced Rhubarb Federation, the Fellowship of Marzipan Confectioners, all required and duly received his attention. Although he had minions of every kind, from personal servants to corporate executives, nobody knew when he would require a service of them or demand a file in order to take direct control. His passion, which accounted for so many of his varied interests, was Hypo. Thus, in spite of their heterogeneity, his interests were neither frivolous nor quixotic. Sir Pluto had made his way inexorably to the top because he had clear sightedly acquired assets and then judged to a nicety how much of his intervention was required to realise them. Some enterprises, such as BigBerger, were acquired simply to make easy money. Others, such as the Artichoke Research Centre, were acquired to stop competitors getting hold of them. Others again, such as the Tuscan Marble Collective, were acquired to provide the challenge of turning an ailing enterprise into a going concern and there were a tiny number of interests, such as Raff First Editions, which were pure self-indulgence. Sir Pluto never allowed himself to confuse these broad classifications. Neither could he be counted among those who were moved by over-reaction in the financial markets. The secret of his success was as simple as it was, to most of his competitors, elusive, for he had mastered the science—or was it an art, or even an instinct?—of buying cheap and selling dear.

With the exception of his name, he had always been considered by his parents and their peers and his own peers to be a very ordinary boy, but his father's small business, which involved infinite patience and unceasing labour—except for indulging his taste (Sir Pluto never knew whether it was a matter of affection or affectation) for big-boned, programmatic orchestral music which accounted for the choice of Pluto as Holst's missing planet (an omission, in his view, not put right by Colin Matthews)—exercised a profound influence on his outlook. Whereas he was anxious to match his father's application, he was determined to exceed his achievement.

On the Monday after Pentecost—Sir Pluto was aware of the ecclesiastical date in the way in which he was effortlessly aware of almost infinite detail—he surveyed the press brief which sat, in splendid isolation, on the polished surface of his work table. One of his researchers had marked a passage from Perpetua's 'manifestation' dealing with the need for reduced consumption. The researcher was indeed—to use a cliche—sharp-eyed for the evening news and the morning newspapers had been almost exclusively concerned with the phenomenon of Perpetua's manifestation rather than with the content of her speech. Only the Financial Mail had picked up the point:

PERPETUANS TO CAP CONSUMPTION

Sir Pluto had always held the Church in benign regard, although it must be said that he cared more for restoring church roofs than for worshipping beneath them, as long as it contributed to the sum total of human happiness without affecting his interests. He was all for the rich giving to the poor as long as the beneficiaries bought his goods and services. By and large, the niggardly charitable donations of the rich converted their marginal expenditure on fripperies into meeting the solid and urgent needs of the poor. The rise of the 'Fair Trade' initiative had caused some temporary friction until he realised that it presented a win/win situation such that he chaired the Fair Trade Alliance and made a substantial profit on its products. The headline did not immediately worry him, for he never came to premature conclusions. He walked to his office door and asked his Private Assistant, Laura Moy, to locate the Editor of Church & State who was only too pleased to talk with him.

"Have you seen the piece in the FM?" "Yes." "Is there anything in it?" "If you had asked me a week ago, I would have said 'no'. I thought that Perpetuanism had passed its short-lived zenith, but yesterday's strength of representation and Perpetua's remarkable appearance both lead me to believe that it has every chance of establishing itself as a major religious force." He called his Head of Research. "What effect would there be on the labour market if domestic consumption fell by 1%?" "80-100,000." "What if it were 2%, would it double, more or less than double?" "Slightly more." "Send me the detailed brief by lunch time, please." Sir Pluto considered his options for contacting the Government. He did not want to go so high that he appeared to magnify an issue which was perhaps not so important as it seemed on Perpetua's 'morning after' and he did not want to go so low that he was not properly estimated by Ministers. Accordingly, he called Horace Strider, the Junior Minister at the Department for Productivity &

Enterprise. "Horace." "Yes, Pluto." "What do you make of the impact of Perpetu-anism on the economy?" "You do make the strangest connections, but then you always did." "Lateral thinking. That's why I'm so successful," he thought but nev-er would have dreamed of saying it. "Of course I have seen the FM piece, but I must admit that Ministers have much more immediate concerns." "Like wheth-er they will be Ministers by the end of the month." As soon as he had said it, Sir Pluto wished he had desisted but, in spite of his exercise of extreme self-control, he could not resist an occasional sarcastic flourish. Strider, who had known him since they were at Cambridge together knew that Sir Pluto enjoyed his little joke. "There is the matter of the WTO Dohar round, you know." "I certainly do." "And then there's the beginning of what we think will be a severe spike in the oil price and then—and you will be more aware of this than me—there is the sub-stantial rise in the price of basic commodities and food which shows no sign of slowing down. Of course there will be temporary respites in the rise of oil and commodities, but we see no similar reliefs—always supposing that you think rising prices are a bad thing, which is a not altogether wise assumption—with respect to food. The world's middle class has expanded, is expanding and will not imminently diminish." "Very nice, Horace, ever the student of the Pitts. What about the prospect of a severe recession because of inflated asset prices and irrational credit?" "Well, there is the occasional doom-monger but nobody takes this seriously." "I am one of the doom-mongers, as you call them, but let us leave that there for now. All this having been said, however—and I would be pleased to assist in any assessment of the impact of the rising price of food on the UK economy—we need to understand whether the Perpetuan movement will act as a restraint on consumption." "I wish it were as simple as that. As you know, we are publicly committed to a variety of measures to restrain consump-tion, notably in the energy sector, but we also recognise that such restraint may have an adverse effect on growth, profitability, employment and the 'tax take'. It is a devil of a job to balance current political exigencies with the long term health of the planet, not least because it is not clear whether the kind of meas-ures we might take will have any real effect on the global trends. There is no point making short term sacrifices if their results are nugatory. There are no rewards for virtue, as you well know, in the international arena." Sir Pluto con-sidered the implications of this ostensibly Delphic advice and concluded, cor-rectly, that public pronouncements concerning the restraint on consumption were cant to placate 'soft' greens. People quite naturally wanted to know that they were doing their bit as long as there was no sacrifice involved and although they resented higher prices, particularly for filling their motor cars, they would never countenance restraints on their private consumption. A country that had so stubbornly insisted on private medicine and education would hardly tolerate being told it would have to abridge its pleasures and, collaterally, reduce its debt. On that basis, sir Pluto was reasonably sure that Perpetuanism went against the grain of the British temperament. He was not so sure less than a minute later when, having agreed to meet Horace for a quiet drink, he was told that the markets were tumbling. This in itself was no bad thing, unless one intended to sell, but it was another symptom of the degree of volatility which might exceed the changes of sentiment which made buying and selling profitable. The market was over-reacting—it always did—but the computer generated selling was approaching 1987 proportions. The same caution which feared exaggeration as much as non-intervention caused him to pause before calling Sneer. "Have you seen the piece in FM about Perpetua?" "Wasn't our own good enough?" "There's no need to get prickly, we just have different interests." As he listened, Sneer riffled furiously through the 'opposition'. "I thought we did a good job." "There. You've devalued the praise by inviting it." "What?" "Never mind. Anyway, the FM piece?" "Says that she's threatening to wreak economic havoc." "That's more like it. I don't own the TT for it to behave like the FM, do I?" "No. But I insist on my absolute independence as Editor." "Of course. It need not be said. In fact, as I've already noted, it's more certain for not being said." In this they were both indulging—if Sir Pluto could ever be said, strictly speaking, to indulge—in a 'necessary' fiction. Sir Pluto knew that Sneer would do as he was told, but that, for that very reason, he should never be told. Sneer knew that he would always do as he was told unless he was told what to do. In this case, Sir Pluto calculated that he could do as much damage to Perpetuanism as Sneer could manage without it affecting the markets, giving him time to assess his position. He toyed with the idea of promising some research material, but thought that would simply cloud the Editor's judgment. "Wreak havoc, you say?" "Yes," said Sneer, absolutely certain in his own mind that he could take this line in a state of complete independence. Having done all he could, Sir Pluto did not linger or fret, but dipped his fingers into a wide variety of pies, great and small—Peking Porcelain, bite sized nectarines, The Bhutan Prospectus and, of course, Hypo—until lunch time, keeping an eye on the markets which steadied and then began to make modest headway. His instinct to do nothing had been right. How could a bunch of religious fanatics have an effect on world markets? He looked across the river at Saint Paul's, not so much enjoying the view as the right he had earned to enjoy it, as his table was covered with a heavy Indian silk under cloth and a Sardinian lace table cloth. He liked fine napery, eccentric glass, square china and plain, heavy cutlery and he always ate well if sparingly, but he did not believe in flaunting his position and what it brought. No doubt very few people in the World Commerce Centre (Pluto's Palace as it was almost inevitably called) would have objected to a Director's private dining room, but there might come a time—and his working life consisted of a myriad of tiny adjustments to improve performance and stave off setbacks—when such a facility would be seen as the waving of a white linen napkin at a sullen bull. He despised celebrity chefs and their celebrity-packed restaurants. When notice of the arrival of his guest reached the outer office, the drinks, in matching venetian glass carafes, were set on the table; the wine was excellent but, as might be surmised from the foregoing description of him, he preferred not to display his excellent if eccentric taste. His guest might care to guess the provenance and the vintage, but he would say nothing unless he was directly asked, which he knew he would not be by this guest at least, for the former Archbishop Hawthorne was not only tactful in the extreme, he also knew his wine better than his host. They greeted each other warmly, hugging briefly before sitting down opposite each other, Sir Pluto with his back to the picture window so that his guest would have the pleasure of the view. "We live in changed times. I little thought when we made this appointment that you would be a former Archbishop, and it says much for our long and happy relationship that you have kindly agreed to keep the appointment in spite of the change. The last ten days must have been very tiring for you." "I have to admit that it was not so tiring as you might expect. I went through the real stress on Easter Day. I must confess that by the time I came back from North America I had more or less made up my mind that the Perpetuan dimension needed to be considered seriously by theologians." "And how did you feel yesterday?" "I felt as if I was finally coming home. I never wanted to be a Bishop, let alone an Archbishop, but—without wishing to make too much of it and saying something to you that I would not say in public—I felt that it would be unfaithful of me to refuse the appointments when they came. I thought I was better fitted to continue as an academic, but who was I to argue with the Holy Spirit? Nonetheless, I am relieved to be out of office although I did not give it up—as I am sure you know—because of my personal preference. I genuinely believe that Christianity must adjust to Perpetuanism in the way that Judaism was called upon to adjust by Jesus." "What will you do now?" "I am sure that I will be able to return either to Oxford or Cambridge, depending on where I can undertake the duties of a Perpetuan Guide, and I have, as you know, been asked to assist in the formulation of Perpetuanism's core theology." "I noticed that. So you will have quite enough to do." "More than enough, and I fear that the theological task will be difficult, and perhaps even unpleasant. As I know to my cost from the assaults I have undergone simultaneously from Petrans and Torans, people are cruel in defending the things they care for most. That explains family feud and civil war." "But the Perpetuans appear to be so—how should I say?—ordinary." "True, but as soon as they acquire a taste for doctrine they will grow harsh. Even though we are only dealing with metaphors, they are shapes, forms of feeling and thinking, which inform the way people live and die. It would be strange if people were not passionate about doctrine, but it is sad that such commitment finds it difficult to embrace pluralism, the metaphors of others." "I have heard you say such things before and I am sorry if you are about to enter another period of controversy." He poured himself half a glass of white and helped his friend to a refill of red. "I really don't know how you find such good wine from the Becar Valley when it is so subject to turbulence, but then no detail is too small for your attention." "I had no doubt that you would—excuse the use of the word—discern its origin. Let me, if I may, ask you some questions about Perpetuanism, not wishing, as we are such long-standing friends, to mislead you into thinking that they are not unconnected with my business interests." "By all means. We have long agreed between us that you must be the judge of the extent to which your conduct is ethical, regardless of external appearances. We could not keep our lines of communication open if I plagued you with shallow criticism although, hardly surprisingly, some aspects of the behaviour of some of your enterprises, such as the Toxic Times, naturally gives rise to questions." "It would be strange if such a diverse collection of undertakings did not manifest the occasional flaw, and while I do not wish to appear to be self-satisfied, I think that I have managed to maintain a balance between a huge variety of what people rather pretentiously refer to as stakeholders. As you know, I have always found that treating people well is pragmatically as well as morally justified. However, on the matter of Perpetuanism, will it succeed?" "You don't want a long theological presentation from me, so I will only say that I believe that it will change Christianity as profoundly as Jesus wished to change Judaism. Whether it will split off from Christianity or subsume it is a more challenging question. We have to remember that this should not be seen entirely from an English, nor even an Anglican, perspective. The key factor, I believe, will be the attitude of the two great religious conservative forces, the Vatican and the American Baptists. Liberal Christians will readily warm to Perpetuanism because it liberates that spirit within them that has been trying to break out since the Papacy resiled from the letter and the Spirit of the Vatican II Decrees." "Interesting, but what about the Perpetuan attitude to economics?" "Ah! At last. I wondered how long it would be before we reached that point. I believe that you have an extremely vital decision before you, vital not only for your own wide variety of interests but—and I do not think I am exaggerating—for the whole world. Where you stick, others will stick. Where you lead, others will follow. There is no doubt—and you know it yourself—that the current global pattern of resource consumption cannot continue. I daresay you know better than me that there will be new developments, currently unimaginable, that will maintain a high level of consumption—after all, the development of steam, electricity, medication, computing, and fertiliser have all brought massive, unanticipated increases in consumption—but I fear that we are approaching a crisis." "Thus far, I agree. The central question is how we handle the necessary change. You know me. I believe that all that we can do—begging your pardon on the sacred dimension—is to slow down or speed up inevitable trends. I believe that we will have to generate more food, goods, and services, but that there will be an inevitable per capita decline in consumption. The challenge will be, given the rising per capita distribution costs, to maintain profits as this new consumption pattern develops. I am therefore anxious that we take our time. Perpetua's announcement alarmed me because it might precipitate a per capita decline in consumption that would more than outweigh the increased number of consumers." "But does that not mean that you wish to maintain the same absolute level of consumption, even if it is distributed more widely?" "I cannot say whether that is possible, but I have found it to be mistaken of people to believe that they can forecast much past five years. We are told that oil is running out, that the climate is changing beyond recognition, that the deserts are expanding, that new crop technologies are a threat, that entry level tractors in India are so expensive that farmers are reverting to the camel, but I still need to be convinced that the progression of the human—if not the spiritual—condition from as far back as archeology can take us, is about to come to an end. In my view, irrational pessimism is as misguided as irrational optimism. I equally deplore under expenditure as over expenditure in my enterprises. What might this mean for your public position?" "I am anxious, as you know, to go with the grain of the material world as far as I can. Religious leaders are too apt to make foolish generalisations and to seek, or at least get into the habit of, conflict where it is unnecessary, even an indulgence." "I fear that if you are correct about the impact of Perpetuanism, that it might behave in the way that early Christianity behaved, giving rise to immense spiritual fervour." "I hope it will do that. We need the Holy Spirit's active presence with us." "I can see why you say that. I know that you deplore the rather milk-and-water sort of religion that suits me and most English people very nicely, but my major concern must be to see that change is managed, that we are not overwhelmed with enthusiasm. Imagine, if you will, a fall of 5% in food consumption in the country. You and I both know that people could absorb a cut more than twice as deep as this simply by not buying food that they throw away. We would have to lay off staff at Hypo, generating unemployment among a class of people least well equipped to find another job. We would have to re-write our contracts with suppliers, here and overseas, causing hardship to farmers all over the world, and we would have to re-consider our pension plans. All these developments, replicated by our competitors, would have a profound effect on individual people, business health and government spending, here and in poorer countries." "As usual, Sir Pluto, you make a powerful case and leave me with a dilemma. I am naturally inclined to oppose excess consumption and I am properly worried about the prospect of climate change, hardship and starvation, but I see change in terms of individual lives, not statistics, so the alternatives we are faced with are almost certain harm if we go on as we are and potential harm if we change our behaviour." "It is extraordinarily fair minded of you to see that." "Nonetheless, I am as certain as I can be of anything that Perpetuans will address the issue of over consumption with determination born of lively religious fervour." "In which case they will find me to be a determined and rational critic of their campaign for pragmatic, as well as for sound business, reasons. Is there no prospect that a religious movement can behave rationally rather than self-indulgently? Forgive my language, but the lives of people must be considered carefully. I am sure you would agree that people should not allow their feelings—no matter how elevated—to govern their behaviour, particularly if that behaviour unwittingly damages others." "I am glad we have had such a frank discussion and I wish that leaders of religion and commerce could enjoy such dialogues. I will try my best to generate a theology of rational concern. I agree with you that it is not morally acceptable for people not to consider carefully the consequences of their actions, no matter how apparently worthy. For too long—we only have to think of the current debate about homosexuality—many church leaders have felt themselves, by virtue of their 'direct line' to God, to be exempt from human reasoning which is a gift of God."

Sir Pluto sat for a few moments in silent concentration. He could see now that thoughts long in play were coming to a head. A critical tipping point had been reached where the balance of the mix between a pragmatic and a moral approach to rising consumption had shifted critically towards the moral. Nevertheless, the only way to win the moral argument was through rational means. He therefore resolved to reverse his morning's work, even if that meant a mild loss of face. Having concluded this topic which Hawthorne had anticipated would be central to his friend's concerns, they discussed a variety of philanthropic causes with which they were associated. Their lunch, consisting of some of Hawthorne's favourites, carpaccio of alpacca with Peruvian black potatoes and miniature spherical courgettes, followed by Galician smoked cheese with artichoke chutney, concluded with Jamaican coffee. There were no labels but Hawthorne knew that, out of consideration for him, all the ingredients were from ethical enterprises. "Let me know when you are settled. I know your wants are modest and that they will no doubt be met by a university salary, but your reluctance to accept my offers of help in no way blunts my enthusiastic offer of it." "If there is some way in which your generosity can be used to fund theological enquiry without compromising you or it, then that would be helpful." "I take your point. I will consider the matter. If I were seen to be funding a forum on the theology of consumption—as you might call it—it would be more counter productive than drug companies funding research on general practitioner prescribing. I will think about it and come and see you when you have decided where to settle."

As soon as Hawthorne left, Sir Pluto telephoned Strider. "Having considered the subject, I believe that we should seriously consider, as a matter of public policy, the implications of a managed fall in per capita middle class, as opposed to overall, consumption." "Anything you say must be taken extremely seriously. After our helpful conversation earlier today, I have given some thought to the topic, and believe I can persuade ministerial colleagues to take some modest steps to meet your concerns." They were both so intimately acquainted with the meaning of "modest steps" that they had no further need of discussion. Horace would convene one of his special task forces and Sir Pluto would be invited to chair it to the mutual satisfaction of both. He would have to move rapidly in view of the looming re-shuffle where, in theory at least, anything might happen, although he had received as firm an assurance as any in-coming Prime Minister could give, that his unprincipled loyalty would be rewarded with promotion in his favoured economic sphere.

Sneer was beginning to get his fangs into the Perpetua story when he took Sir Pluto's call. "Do-gooders need to be cautious. Of course they do. Rash behaviour can wreak havoc." "I would not put it that strongly. I would rather say that nothing should be done without due thought. The concerns of Perpetuans are entitled to sober consideration." "Sober consideration," said Sneer, putting down the telephone and mourning the demise of havoc.

Sir Pluto needed to gain information without setting off any alarm. Instead of using his corporate mobile phone, whose use was quite properly monitored, he took his personal phone and called Annie Price. "It's Sir Pluto." He waited. She waited. "Yes." "Is that all you have to say?" "Yes." "Can you confirm that you are Annie Price?" "Yes." "Are you in a position to talk in extreme confidence?" "Yes." "Can you say anything other than yes?" "Yes." "Annie, I'm the CEO of this company." "Yes." "Are you making fun of me or are you frightened?" "Neither. I'm simply waiting for you to say what you want. I have received a message from you once before." "Yes, when something went wrong with the stock and payments systems in your store." "Do you remember everything?" "More or less." "That's amazing, with all your interests, but you did not call to listen to me." "It would be a poor chief executive who did not listen." "Which is only one reason—I don't mean to flatter you—why you are a good one." "I want you to do a little work for me. I note that you are the most improved Store Manager in the Hypo family and that you have recently acquired an external degree in consumer economics. I want to know what the impact would be on your store of a cut of 1%, 2% and 5% in average monthly turnover." "Are you anticipating a recession as serious as that?" "No. It is precisely because I trust you not to panic that I am talking to you rather than going through the usual channels. I am anticipating a call by Perpetuans for a cut in consumption and I need to know what its impact would be." "How strange. I believe I saw her make her first public pitch for decreased consumption right here in our car park, the day the systems went wrong and you left me the message." "I suppose you did not take it seriously." "No," she faltered, wondering if she had left herself open to criticism. "Perhaps her visit and the systems failure were linked!" "Don't worry. You could not have known it would catch on. You must tell me about it when you bring your report." "When?" "How long do you need?" "I can ask my deputy to take over." "Without causing any alarm?" "It's my practice—somewhat male, I think—when appropriate to tell people what I intend to do but not to explain why." "Very wise. Let us say, then, that you can report on Wednesday. I recall that we walked round Grunge Park together, so when you come on Wednesday, you are doing so in your capacity as a member of the Grunge Park Partnership, nothing to do with Hypo." "Very good, Sir Pluto."

"I think," said Sir Pluto to the Editor of Church & State, "that I can safely say, on the record, that one would hope that the Perpetuans adopt a rational attitude to consumption." "How do you mean?" "I think that going into detail at present might lead to unnecessary complexity. You have my simple message."

The markets were suffering from a new attack of the jitters. On the basis of a wildly exaggerated estimate of Perpetuan influence, Wall Street had opened almost 2% down and was continuing to slide. Sir Pluto called the New York Mercury. "Good morning Randall," he said, careful adjusting his greeting to the local time. "I see that the markets are misbehaving." "Excuse me Pluto" (he could never bring himself to say "Sir" and his proprietor did not insist on such niceties) "but you Limeys do produce the most outlandish creatures. Who is this Perpetua?" "I know we are a populist publication, but I expect you to know just a little about the world outside New York. I don't mean to chide, just my little joke." "Well, you will have your joke, Pluto." "To save your—er researchers— too much trouble, Perpetua was a—how should we say?—revivalist religious leader whose followers, inter alia—amongst other things—believe that excess consumption is bad for you?" "A belief that has never afflicted the most devout Evangelicals in America." "But it would be easy—as the markets have amply demonstrated today—to over-estimate the importance of what Perpetuans say. The movement is new and fragile. It might get nowhere, but if it does it will be our job to ensure that it is gracefully woven into our social fabric." "Gracefully woven?" "Yes. I recognise it is not precisely the phrase you might want for your headline, but I thought, as a Yale man, you might nonetheless appreciate it." "Gracefully woven, Pluto." They did not need to discuss the line. Unlike British newspapers which pretend to a broad view of society, leading them to believe that they can choose between capitalism and any alternative that presents itself, American newspapers do not have to think about their line, on economics at least, because business success is in their DNA.

In spite of what restraint Sir Pluto could organise throughout his widely dispersed domains, the global reaction to Perpetua's call was predictably hysterical but short lived. Sneer's headline ran:

PERPETUANS! HANDS OFF ECONOMY

This was only exceeded in mildness by the Financial Mail, which had so innocuously broken the story, which reported:

MARKET JITTERS AT PERPETUAN CALL

The remainder of the media, valiantly led into irrationality by the BBC, obsessed with the possible rather than the probable, indifferent to real lives, forecast a world depression which, to a certain extent, would result from their forecasts. Much of the world was puzzled by the 'London Lurch', but temporarily lacked the courage to buck the trend. By Thursday, however, the markets had regained most of their losses. Sir Pluto, by no means convinced that the Perpetuan phenomenon had been laid to rest, was nonetheless relieved. The most valuable asset in the face of a major crisis was time.

Hawthorne had carefully reported that part of their conversation which he deemed of public interest, to Max Silver. "I know that neither of us will fail to do our duty, even if this makes us enemies of capitalism, but there is a genuine issue here. We must not allow our feelings to run away with us." "I recognise the line. It's very like Sir Pluto, never an intellectual or emotional hair out of place. What do you advise?" "It is important to be clear what I do not advise. I think we both accept that trying to manipulate the media or the economy, is impossible. I therefore advise that we consider the issue, and that we put this ahead of the work which I was commissioned to do. The new Creed can wait—Christianity did without one for its first 300 years or so—but the lives of poor people may be affected by our decisions. Love requires care as well as emotion." "I have no reason to think that Dexter will object to your proposal. Indeed, I think he trusts me to do the right thing." "If my previous existence is anything to go by, Max, we will upset some of our most ardent leaders and followers." "No doubt, but we must start by doing the right thing."

On Wednesday afternoon Annie Price had reported to Pluto's Palace, wearing a Grunge Park Partnership T-shirt. "Very fetching," said Sir Pluto. "Not 'alf. Anyway, it spared me having to explain myself." "What have you found?" "Here are the figures. You will see that a 5% reduction will be disastrous. It will not simply represent a return to how we were when we were that size, it will unleash a mass of consequential dislocations. People can handle debt when prices and sales are rising, but not when they are falling. If we take the 2% position it will be difficult to handle, but we will probably manage, a bit of a cut in costs here, a bit of a cut in the dividend there. As for 1%, that is sustainable with very little short term worry, but only as a one-off. If you are asking me what a 1% per annual slide will do, that is quite a different issue. Naturally, we would prefer any drop over an extended period rather than suddenly—we will make more wrong decisions if we are hurried—but it will make little difference in the end. The global economy is structured to handle indefinite growth. It is so used to it that it will convulse if there is a recession. If you thought that 1990-91 was bad, you ain't seen nothing yet." "Yes, but we need to get back to the main point. As you know, I have many interests, but let us start with Hypo. What contingency plans should we make?" "Firstly, and perhaps counter intuitively, we should raise our payments to all our Fair Trade producers, giving us edge over our short-sighted competitors and slightly raising our own margin at the same time. Secondly, we should identify some products which are high bulk, low margin, such as ready-made furniture. Even under your vigilant eye, some things just 'happen' because a manager wants a larger empire. Furniture takes up space and although the margin looks good that is not judged in terms of the space it occupies. Profit per cubic foot is much better on almost anything than furniture. You might also announce that we have abandoned selling furniture whose wood is not guaranteed to come from a renewable project. Thirdly, exchange middle management fleet cars for a straight salary rise. This will cut energy consumption and cut our costs slightly, but over the whole fleet significantly. This will give you enough saving to ride a 1% drop in turnover in a quarter, but we can't go on doing this quarter after quarter. If you know where you can get it, buy some objective research." "The think tanks are too opinionated, always looking for a headline that will get them the next job. I have always thought it to be a sham sector. Academics are just too slow, wanting to answer their own questions, not the ones that you pay them to answer. Hawthorne warned me against publicly 'buying' research which will automatically be discounted as biased, and there is no such thing as private research. It does not matter how much you pay for privacy, the temptation to be part of the media circus is so great. Government research has the combined disadvantages of being slow, politically manipulated and discounted. In the most complex society ever developed, we are in the ridiculous situation of being almost completely unable to commission reliable research." "In which case, why don't we start by doing something simple and asking Max Silver what he thinks. I know he's partisan, but he won't want to make any terrible policy errors that damage the poor."

Max was engulfed by the surge in public reaction to the launch. Threats, letters of protest, messages of support, offers of help, calls for action, calls for reflection, people wanting quick settlements, people wanting moratoria on settlements, the digital and human traffic poured into the small god4u office. Annie was able to have a brief word with Trina. "If I can write down what I am asking for in a single paragraph, will you see that Max gets it?" "Yes. You were very good to us at the beginning and we are sensible enough to know that we should not accidentally or thoughtlessly alienate people. We will not be faced down by the powerful, but neither will we assume that they are hostile. I will call you as soon as I have a response." On Wednesday evening Trina called Annie. "As our office is in the Grunge Park Estate, Max can slip out for half an hour to walk round part of the estate with us tomorrow morning."

Sir Pluto was recognised all over the world by people of influence, but his face was remarkably unfamiliar to the general public. He therefore found it easy to park his second-hand Ford Fiesta down a side street and slip into the god4u office where Max was preparing a submission to the Church Commissioners, the Office of the Voluntary Sector and the Prime Minister's Policy Unit. Nonetheless, he greeted Sir Pluto warmly and gave him his full attention. "Let us walk around," said Sir Pluto, "as it would interest me to see the results of the Partnership, and it will also allow us to talk without the distractions of your pressing business. I promise it will take us no more than half an hour." They walked towards The Hollow. "What I want to say, Max, is this. I am not being penitent when I say that I accept the need for steadily reduced consumption. I don't want to mislead you. I simply observe the inevitability and recognise that, although we may come at the problem from different directions, we have a mutuality of interest. What we cannot afford, as many people will be damaged, is a fall which is too sudden and too steep." "As an economist I recognise the sanity of what you say, but the wisdom of the Holy Spirit is beyond the wisdom of humanity." "I recognise the sentiment, it's the kind of category analysis I studied in philosophy,but how could you argue that the Spirit might urge people to undertake a policy that will do harm? Are you discussing a theological issue or a tactical problem caused by some of your extremists?" "I often wondered, many years ago when I met bishops at the bank, how they could be so worldly, but I find myself following the same course. I have no doubt that there will be some extreme anti consumptionists who will advocate proportionately extreme action. Every movement attracts such people. Instead of Marx or, in my generation, Trotsky, they will no doubt call on Our Sister the Spirit as the inspiration for their campaign, and we must do our best to resist them." "Without seem-

ing to be doing so on my behalf. My involvement will compromise your position." "I am pleased that we both recognise this." "As a founder member of the
Grunge Park Partnership and one of Perpetua's earliest friends, Annie can act
quite naturally as a channel of communication. What we lack at the moment
is a means of securing objective research to understand the impact of falling
per capita consumption on the UK and then the world economy. I can find the
money, but not the means. I am almost certain that you should not take my
money." "I agree. I can also secure money for research and we will then take
responsibility for it." "I am sure Annie can help." "We would be grateful for that.
I think we should start by looking at the matter locally, at the level of a single
hypermarket or a small group, and then go wider. We want quick, reliable results and means to protect the poorest who might be the collateral damage of
headlong idealism." "Salutary caution for such a young movement." "Revolution
has always disproportionately damaged the poor. We should never be misled
by ducal heads in Madame La Guillotine's basket or the ducal bones hurriedly
buried on the Russian steppes. The larger and the more rapid the change, the
greater the damage. I would like to think that Perpetuanism will avoid the excesses of fanaticism. We, after all, are a rather strange movement, for we are
affirming but liberal; we are passionately committed to openness, which is why
we need Our Sister the Spirit, as humans find being passionate about generosity
rather difficult compared, say, with being passionate about defining difference
as a precondition for exclusion." "You, along with our friend Hawthorne, have
almost convinced me to be a Perpetuan." "I was not speaking in order to bring
you to that conclusion by subtle means. You will no doubt make up your own
mind—if I may use a deliberate 'category error'—in due course with the good
offices of the Spirit." Sir Pluto, remembering that Paris was worth a Mass, was
wondering whether he would be better in or out of Perpetuanism, regardless of
the promptings or otherwise of the Spirit.

It was then that he made his mistake, abandoning his usual care in too rapid
a pursuit of his object. Catching sight of Dexter as they finished their walk, he
asked if he could have a brief word with him. "I'm sure you don't know me, but
I own Hypo where, I'm told, I once worked." "Yes." "I'm very anxious to be
of assistance by undertaking some research on how you can achieve your ends
without causing social disruption." "Of course we don't want social disruption,
as you call it, but we are living in the power of the Spirit." "I would also like to
live and work in that power." "I don't want to be unkind, Sir, but you can't buy
Our Sister the Spirit." "I have no intention of trying, I simply wanted to help
you." Max, who had got the drift of the discussion, gently inserted himself into
it. "I think that it is vital that we continue to live in the power of Our Sister the
Spirit, but that should not be seen as inimical to considering our ethical issues
carefully. I grant that there is much in our doctrinal search for which we will
need the special gifts of the Spirit; and Dexter will lead us in our new forms of
worship and Sacrament. There is a wide area where we need to use the gifts of
human wisdom that God has given us."

Sir Pluto sighed a deep sigh of relief. Max had saved him from being seriously misunderstood as a rich man trying to buy the opinion of the Perpetuans. He had never intended this but even such a careful man as he sometimes forgets how easy it is to exercise power, as he does it so naturally and habitually.

At the end of the week, Dexter gathered his followers together at the god4u (now frequently known as the 4ingod) headquarters. "We all know that we will have to leave here. In spite of our idealistic wish to remain in the place where we started, to stay among our people, there simply is not enough room. Max and I have looked at other buildings round here, but there is nothing suitable. The only two that are big enough were seriously damaged by the riot which our beloved Perpetua quelled.

"There are, however, other more important issues which we need to resolve. The most immediate is our attitude towards the economy. It is a bit of a surprise topic, but after what has happened this week it's on our plate and we need to sort it because our credibility is at stake. Now we know that Perpetua said that we were all consuming too much, that we were self-indulgent, that this was harming the earth, but it has now been pointed out to us that if we stop this consumption too rapidly there will be a recession which will damage the poor. I would like Max to lead off on this. Even though he isn't one of the group he is, along with Father Bill, our trusted adviser." "It looks simple, decreasing what we consume, saving the money, but even though everybody thinks saving is a good thing and borrowing is a bad thing (well, credit card borrowing is bad, but mortgages are good!), changing things round always causes problems. For instance, if we consume less, but we put the money into the bank, it might help investment in new business, but it will reduce what we buy and therefore will reduce the need for goods and services. I know this is all a bit boring, but it's important.. So what we really need is a gradual decrease in what we consume, transferring the savings to poor people so that the economy can adjust to new expenditure patterns." "But if we consume less and even poorer people than us consume more, the world is a no better place," said Andy. "That is true in terms of the globe, but at least it is better for the poor." "That isn't enough." "Well, if we really do want to reduce our consumption, but do not want to give our surplus money that we don't spend to the poor and opt, for example, for lower wages, it is giving it back to the rich." "Look!" shouted Andy. "Keep cool," said Dexter, "and let us not start fighting before we've hardly begun." "Sorry. It seems as if it is quite difficult giving money to the poor and saving the planet at the same time." "One idea," said Kylie, "would be to reduce what we buy, which would cause some unemployment, but we could use the money we saved to employ them doing things with hands and feet that we do with machines." "But one of the real marks of progress," said Bob, "has been the machine. People don't have to walk, they can drive, and soon they won't have to go down coal mines. We don't really want to turn our unemployed people into manual workers, do we?" They looked puzzled. "Obviously, Dexter," said Max, careful to defer, "we need to think about this carefully." "So what we say," said Trina, "is that we've going to do just that. We will be made to look stupid if we jump to wild conclusions so we have to be serious and credible. What we probably need is to cut consumption steadily over a number of years, funnel some of that to the poor to level things up and put some of it into projects to reduce energy consumption and try to hold back climate change." "I am sorry to say that if we do that I will have to leave," said Andy, "as I am fully signed up to what Perpetua wanted rather than making compromises." "I'm with him," said Bob. "There has got to be a better way than making the weakest and poorest among us do the hard work." "I didn't mean that, precisely," said Kylie. People were becoming heated.

Dexter said, "we have to learn from what has gone before. Taking hard positions, as if Perpetua was writing some text book for the future, won't work. Just look at the Torans. Likewise, you can't take something she said and turn it into an iron rule, just look at the Petrans. We have to stay calm and learn from each other, and to pay attention to the best brains that God has given us." In spite of Dexter's attempt to calm his followers, Andy and Bob left which triggered a crisis of confidence. "I don't think I am fit for this work," said Dexter. "Instead of providing a bit of extended family leadership, I am being asked to behave like an economics professor. I am already out of my depth." "You did very well today," said Max. "You understood precisely how Pluto went too far, and you put the simple case for being careful." "Perpetua asked you to lead," said Bill, "and I see it is my job to help you to do that." "I feel like Moses." "Trina can be your Aaron." "I am encouraged. I will try, for just a bit longer. I can't imagine more than a month ahead."

Trina came in with a statement.

> Perpetuans today confirmed their determination to press for a concerted global effort to reduce the consumption of food, goods, energy and all non-renewables, and services. We realise that economies will need to adjust to falling rather than rising consumption and we will campaign to protect the poor and fund energy saving projects with savings from reduced consumption.
>
> We are trying to locate the best minds that the world can offer to help us to solve this vital problem which Perpetua identified as one of the most important before us.

"Simple enough that I can understand it," said Dexter, "but they will probably make fun of us."

They did.

PERPETUANS COMMIT TO SACRIFICE BUT DON'T KNOW HOW

PERPETUAN DO GOODERS RISK SLAMMING POOR

BAD OUT OF GOOD   PIOUS FOOLS

PERPETUAN DUCK!

These were just some of the headlines at the top of stories which all more or less told the religious community in general and Perpetuans in particular to stay out of politics and economics. A little Fair Trade here and there was all right, and the Jubilee Development Goals were admirable, but that was quite different from meddling with macro economic decisions. The week's events had been a warning that pious do-gooders could end up doing enormous harm.

The headlines pained Sir Pluto strangely. He had recognised the naïveté and the generosity of the Perpetuans and did not think that they deserved ridicule. On the other hand, he had put himself in the wrong with Dexter, although he was certain that Dexter would not count that against him. Normally he would have been inclined to give himself time, but his mistake of acting too quick-ly needed to be countered quickly. He telephoned Max. "I realise that I was somewhat precipitate in offering help to Dexter, even perhaps a little clumsy." "It doesn't matter." "I thought I might make a statement next week." "Coming from you, that would be helpful provided, as I assume it will, that it says helpful things." "Tending towards the helpful, I think. I am due to address the Davos Register on Monday evening. I will leave an invitation for you at the door of the Royal Institute." "Thank you."

"I am sorry for phoning you at home, Horace, but I thought I had better warn you that I am going to make a statement on Monday evening at the Royal In-stitute about the need to re-calibrate our economy from exponential growth to planned decline." "Damn! Excuse me, Sir Pluto, but you do surprise me. I secured the Minister's agreement for your Chairmanship of our committee, together with the Terms of Reference, earlier today—I was just waiting for the written confirmation—so this puts me into a bit of a tight corner." "In what way?" "Well, I gave the Minister to understand that we needed proper mechanisms to deal with economic and climatic turbulence, you know, to keep things on an even keel." "Given what is going on in the world economy, even an even keel is going to cause climate change." "But the fact is, Pluto, that there is no political appe-tite for that kind of thing. People are already frightened to death of a supposed recession, an oil spike and associated energy price rises, blighting the arrival of our new Prime Minister. There are very disturbing rumours about Southern Gem." "I am sympathetic to Gordon's position, Horace, as you know—I like the country to succeed—and I thought that calming the economic weather might just be enough, aiming for a very gentle decline in the consumption of the better off, with a very gradual fall in differentials." "Well, in theory the Government is deeply committed to a fair society but, as you have often pointed out, it is easier said than done. For more than a decade now we have been redistributing to the poor, but the gap is still getting wider." "I understand, but now I believe that we may very well have to go further by looking not only at a transfer from the rich to the poor, but also a parallel transfer from rich economies to emerging econo-mies. In other words, we might have to do the two things simultaneously, and quite soon." "There again, we have been enthusiastic about the Jubilee process ever since the Edinburgh Summit, but this cannot be sustained if you want to give money to China, India, and Brazil to clean up their acts and not cut down their trees. This is asking a great deal." "I am not only asking, but I am aware that the gestures of one man, even as rich as me, will make no difference. People call for role models and good examples, but it is subsequently barely followed. For all the good example I generate, I might as well do nothing." "We must always try to move forward, Pluto." "I know. I just had a cynical moment. Anyway, if the committee's TOR simply talk about a modest shift to the poor, it won't address the problem. See what the Minister says on Tuesday. I will send you and her a ticket if you think you can use them." "I had intended to come along on behalf of the Minister, but the prospect of a Pluto bomb might just tempt her. It will take her out of herself while she waits for the re-shuffle." "What is the latest?" "Well, I do not think I would be giving away much—and you are one of the very few people who can be entirely trusted ..." "…. I have nobody to tell, Horace. ..." "… not giving away much if I were to say that Mr Brown and I have always enjoyed more than cordial relations." "Yes, I seem to recall that you were behind the 'dump Blair' move last September," said Sir Pluto, and immediately regretted it. No matter how hard he tried, he could not resist showing off his inside knowledge and digging the pompous in the ribs. "I have heard that some people have alleged such a thing," said Strider, momentarily cold, but recovering himself almost without an intonal flicker, "and those cordial relations are highly likely to take me into pastures new." "By which," said Sir Pluto, in an attempt to mend fences which Strider recognised and appreciated, "we do not mean that you will be put out to grass." "I think not. As for the Minister, Gordon is said to be keen on the clever, but frightened of the beautiful, and as our Minister is remarkable in both respects, one will have to wait and see. In the meantime, it is our duty to talk up the economy and talk down the depression, if only because this is in direct contradiction of the media."

Sir Pluto spent the weekend in his externally nondescript but internally elegant house on the canal just East of Camden Lock, enjoying some gentle and discriminating food shopping, cooking, and the occasional pint of real ale. He would have had no problems finding women to keep him company at his board or in his bed, but he had fallen out of the habit and was, he thought, happier in his own company. This lack of companionship, however, did not drive him to work. During weekends he usually read the heavier economic papers and journals and contemporary 'serious' fiction, or watched a 'serious' DVD, but his major pastime was trying to reduce the backlog of recordings of documentaries which dealt with his enthusiasms and interests. During this weekend, however, he worked hard on his speech for the Institute. It would affect his standing and influence, and might be a small contribution to a better world. Word soon got round that he was going to enter the Perpetua ecology and economics debate, but even the most pugnacious journalist knew that there was no point trying to get him to drop any hint of what he would say and that, with such a barren prospect, there was no point in annoying him unnecessarily. He worked from early Sunday morning on writing the text and then went to watch Grangebury playing Moorholm. Everybody in the ground knew who he was, but nobody alluded to anything connected with him, confining themselves to cricket talk. The President repeated his routine invitation to Sir Pluto to join him for dinner, but knew that he would drink one and a half pints of County Ale after the game and then be driven home. He knew better than to discuss the club's finances as one of Sir Pluto's juniors acted as Treasurer and Sir Pluto made sure that he maintained a proper balance between his generosity and the need for others to make an effort, and feel that their effort was necessary, significant, and valued.

Not a man to under-estimate his influence, Sir Pluto was nonetheless astounded when he arrived at the Royal Institute to find that arrangements had been made to install large screens in an overspill hall and the restaurant to deal with hundreds of influential people who did not have a ticket for the main hall, but who had assumed that their position would allow them easy entry. There was not the usual press pack, but he did notice Keith Knight of the FM and Bill Frobisher of BBC Money in the audience, trying not to be noticed. Sir Marcus Gowder introduced him without giving any hint of forthcoming controversy, as if he were introducing a lecture on flower arranging.

Sir Pluto sketched the economic history of the United Kingdom since the late 1980s and elegantly introduced the rising consciousness of ecology. He then made a gracious reference to Max Silver, "who will always be known and admired as a wise counsellor" and he then tied together the points he had made in an elegant Perpetuan bow. "Whether we think that religion answers the ultimate questions or whether we think that man made God, nevertheless, the person who therefore thinks that religion has nothing to say of any relevance to society is making a grave error. At its most vital, religion has always posed challenging economic questions. I venture to say, for example, that it would have taken enlightenment atheists much longer to abolish slavery than it took committed Christians like Wilberforce and Clarkson, and in spite of what we might think about missionary activity in what was the British Empire, I doubt that we would today enjoy such a consensus on Third World debt were it not for the indefatigable promptings of our major faith communities."

All this was heard in a very peculiar kind of silence, as nobody had ever heard Sir Pluto discussing such topics before. He was known as a bit of a 'dry fellow' who generally stuck pretty close to his economic brief, and had never made what might be called a 'memorable' speech. That was not why he was wanted. Yet there were those in the audience who had heard him talk intelligently and sometimes almost movingly about some aspect of collecting or the arts, usually at small, private gatherings.

He came to his first major point. "And now we have been confronted with a direct question by the Perpetuans which we have, as a society, been toying with for more than a generation. How long can we afford to wait before we begin to plan declining consumption? Or, to put the question in a slightly different way, would we prefer the gradual decline to begin immediately or are we prepared to risk a crash?"

There was an almost audible gasp. Sir Pluto had used the word "crash!" Knight and Frobisher were seriously torn between getting the story out immediately and waiting to see what happened next. Each texted, "PLUTO CRASH WARNING".

"I have no doubt that my words will be interpreted as the warning of an inevitable crash," he said, looking keenly at Knight and Frobisher as he saw their thumbs working, "but I must emphasise that catastrophe is not inevitable and the Western economic system at least has many sophisticated tools at its disposal. What I wish to emphasise is the choice we have. One of the most valuable contributions which Perpetua made to our society when she was with us—and one of which all libertarians should be aware whether they come from the 'right' or the 'left' (and it is a mistake to think that one side has exclusive ownership of all the many different aspects of liberty—is that she believed in choice and self-determination and deplored victimhood, passing the buck, freeloading, expecting others to make tough decisions. I will never forget her almost harsh, certainly tough, messages to drug addicts about beginning to learn again to choose. What she said to drug addicts—people for whom we have no respect—I am saying to you. We are addicted to all kinds of nostrums, ways of life, lazinesses and quick fixes, but now we are being asked to choose between a managed change in our domestic and in the world economy and a series of economic and social disasters that will initially wipe out much of the progress we have made in the last 50 years. It is too early to say what will happen thereafter—as you know, I am deeply sceptical of most forecasting because it is incapable of predicting surprises—but if our economies are thrown into rapid and uncontrolled reverse, it is hardly likely that they will somehow come to a gentle stop and then move forward over the broken ground that their plunge has created.

"I therefore call upon the in-coming Government—there is a conventional, although rather silly, argument that nothing can be done during this hiatus—to make plans for an initial decline in the expenditure of the rich and a transfer of modestly increasing resources in real terms to the poor, followed by an overall decline in national consumption. This should take place no matter what the temporary economic conditions, such as an energy price spike or a credit shortage. What is more, these policies should be implemented in parallel with measures to help the polluting world to right itself. The Millennium Development Goals are out of date.

"Finally, I want to say that these proposals have not been worked out. We face a crisis in impartial research and I am looking for solutions. I also want to make it clear that my thoughts are parallel with, not subject to, the pronouncements of Perpetuan leaders. I am not a Perpetuan and have no right to speak on behalf of people whose motives are much more principled, but not necessarily any less pragmatic, than mine. I urge you all to study Perpetua's life and teaching as a matter of public duty and private well-being, and those who know me well will know that I will not be taking the plunge yet a while, but, as I hinted earlier, I do not think this massive and difficult realignment can be attempted, let alone completed, without a vital religious impetus of sacrifice behind it, and we must pray—if you will excuse an old sceptic like me for saying it—we must pray that Perpetuanism succeeds."

Sir Mark was of the opinion that this was one of the most historic pronouncements ever given at the Institute, and such was its weight and clarity that he thought questions might only leave the audience with a sense of anti climax and with a falling off of coherence which often happened when a grand peroration was followed by a scatter gun of more or less trivial enquiries. The media, other than the FM, thought otherwise, with headlines such as:

AGE OF 7OZ STEAK

11 EGGS, PLEASE

19/20 OF A PINT, BARMAID

Sir Pluto, who had been ridiculed throughout his progress, particularly when, at that same Institute, he had first articulated the retail policy: "Pile them high and sell them cheap", was not in the least bit perturbed by the headlines in respect of how people might see him. He was worried about the overall cause—with or without the Perpetuans—and was finding it ever more difficult to assess whether his support would be a help or a hindrance, for when the media becomes perverse, no argument will persuade it. Just as it had taken against the EU—largely on behalf of its proprietors and, therefore, even more insistent on its independence—illustrating the absurdity of Brussels by citing trade rules signed up to, if not supported by, 'Sovereign' UK ministers—the straight banana being the most celebrated case—it now looked likely that it would mount a campaign against thrift as virulent as its recent campaign against re-cycling. The Perpetuan campaign had hardly begun, but it had already roused the anger of the media. Yet, as Dexter noted, this had not been the anticipated issue. Before Pentecost, Max had concentrated on the funding and buildings the new organisation would require, and the way a settlement might be agreed with the Established Church. Regardless of its more long-term and idealistic objectives, Max's first priority was to give the new organisation a core of assets and committed people that would sustain its goals. He prayed that the opposition from the establishment would be less virulent and undiscriminating than that meted out by the media. The coming week would·be critical.

12.

Archdeacon Varnish had hardly imagined and certainly not hoped, that he would be a Bishop, let alone the Archbishop of Canterbury. Not quite with the utilitarian cynicism which had graced the Church with the second sons of the minor aristocracy and the gentry in the eighteenth century, but still with a degree of pragmatism which was beginning to be anachronistic by the second half of the twentieth century when the Church had been infected with renewed religious vitality, he had taken orders out of a much greater love and concern for church buildings than for those who worshipped in them and that Church, no matter how religiously enthusiastic, had found him useful in taking care of those matters, at once sentimental, but tedious, which were required by the state to be dealt with in respect of the nation's heritage. In spite of the upsurge in religious feeling within the Church in the late 1960s excited by Bishop John Robinson the theological curriculum had not kept pace, and so Varnish had found that his classical foundation from The Old Merchant Tailors, a love of history, and a certain kind of 'dry' theology rooted in scholasticism, had been almost enough. At Barnard House, a 'middle of the road', slightly fusty establishment, the curriculum was not intellectually nor spiritually exacting, but he found himself a niche as a person of impeccable architectural refinement and an advocate of sumptuous non-Eucharistic liturgy centred around the Offices. At the retreat before Ordination, its Leader, the recently retired Bishop of Chalkbury, had sent the Ordinands to the Bishop with a warning (hardly ringing in their ears) to eschew impure thoughts if necessary, as a last resort, by taking a wife, no matter how plain, who might assure them of their conjugal rights and guarantee safety from accusations, not only of a "glad eye", but also of that darkest of errors, the sin of sodomy, which had recently climbed the Church's Agenda—much faster than the birth control pill—because of the good offices of Home Secretary Roy Jenkins. Thus fortified with a variety of sharp, if marginal, implements for his purpose, Varnish had served an indifferent, but passable curacy, made tolerable on both sides by a Rector who wished to maintain his spiritual monopoly both in ecclesiastical and pastoral affairs. As Rector, he Presided at the Eucharist, composed homilies full of feeling, ministered to the sick, and kept a firm grip on the PCC and the wayward tendencies of an independent-minded Leader of the Mothers Union, leaving his Curate to lead the Offices and consort with the Fabric Churchwarden for the improvement of the building. Having served his Title, he was fortunate enough to be given a Parish with an over-sized and crumbling church and an under-sized and crumbling congregation, both of which had a much closer relationship with the Book of Common Prayer than with any subsequent developments in architecture, worship, theological development, or spiritual fashion. His bishop, having given up on the congregation, was impressed by the improved fortunes of the building, which was fully restored within six years through Varnish's persistent and ingenious fund raising and Faculty handling. Nothing so grand, the bishop knew, could be accomplished without a close relationship with the Department of Culture and Heritage. Consequently, he was drafted into Church House as a 'gamekeeper' after the bishop had mistakenly appointed an archdeacon on a 'buggins turn' basis who was totally incapable of doing the job and who would have been better suited to a monastery, leaving a massive backlog of business. The bishop, trusting that he could take on the spiritual dimensions of the archdeaconery, was glad to hand over the tedium to Varnish, in spite of the ripples he knew it would cause because three supposedly more eligible—but actually more long-serving—senior clerics were passed over and because Varnish had made a number of enemies in his attempts to goad his predecessor into making key decisions. For almost twenty years he had happily worked as Archdeacon of Patchminster which, as a Diocese comprising a large swathe of Southern London and a generous tranche of countryside, offered a wide variety of architectural challenges, including three churches of Saxon origin, seven Normans, five late Gothics, two Wrens, three Hawksmores, and a huge variety of churches built during the Victorian revival which he loved as much as its musical counterpart for what more astringent critics might call bombast. Consequently, he had more eroding sandstone, broken slate, ladder proof guttering, dessicated organ bellows, quirky clocks, tilting towers, lurid stained glass, improvised fastenings, uncommodious pews, venerable aumbries, warped frames, overwrought iron, distressed paint, peeling plaster, stranded fonts, crazed flooring, tattered tapestries, unaccountable keys, rusty railings, monstrous monstrances, disfigured grilles, frayed ropes, tarnished pewter, worn steps, chipped cruets, tottering pulpits, redundant high altars, odd candlesticks, moth eaten frontals, overgrown churchyards, unregarded memorial plaques, unreachable light fittings, grubby surplices, battered Bibles, cracked bells, unserviceable chests, outdated prayer books, jerry carved choir stalls, irascible boilers, fake old masters, faded kneelers, crumbling plasterwork, battered baroque chalices, faulty wiring, protected bats, bequeathed vulgarities and musty registers than any man could wish for. The wonder of it was that that was precisely, for want of a similar position of guardianship at the Church of the Holy Sepulchre, what he wished, as if the essence of beauty consisted primarily in the tarnished glories of a tasteless bygone age. For him the faculties, wills, contracts, bylaws, regulations, decrees, promulgations, episcopal pronouncements, grants in aid and local traditions, and obfuscations of every kind were not a tissue of inconvenience, but a cohort of allies against change, giving him more time to fight wet rot, dry rot, rising damp, vermin, woodworm, leaks, ants, pollution, pigeon droppings, mildew, fungus, lichen and every meteorological manifestation, as if they were Satan's warriors. The devil incarnate was the mania for church 're-ordering' which its proponents claimed was necessary to invigorate worship and bring people back into what they characterised as "forbidding fortresses" claiming that quite ordinary, sane people were somehow put off going to church because their doors were heavy and shut, their altars at the East end instead of at the foot of the chancel steps and their baptismal fonts hidden away in dark corners. Additionally they claimed that contemporary worship required movable chairs and that this would have the added advantage of churches being suitable for yoga, aerobics, sales of work, concerts, Post Office counters, and dances. Finally, they said that if churches could be fitted out with kitchens and toilets, they could be 'true' community centres. Over this issue Varnish and his bishop could not agree and, as a result, all the complex legal and procedural manoeuvring at Church House was brought to nothing by sweeping edicts from the Palace by a bishop who was determined as he was impetuous, and although many in the Church deeply deplored the Perpetuan secession, Varnish and many others saw it as the end of the re-ordering threat, restoring that peculiarly English chasm between mediocre religiosity and the vibrancy of life. Thus it was, in the week after Pentecost, that a powerful, although not overwhelmingly enthusiastic, traditionalist caucus, comprising BCP adherents and Medians, gathered around him as "The right man for the job", "A special man for a special time", and "someone with a safe pair of hands". Anxious to avoid upheaval and expense, they forced the remainder of the establishment, made up of Torans and Petrans, to maintain their uneasy alliance over women bishops under the banner of "Spirituality". It is a measure of the regard in which the Church of England is held by its guardians that heritage should have conquered eecclesiology so easily, extending a tradition that has reduced the Authorised Version of the Bible to a work of literature and the Book of Common Prayer to a weapon against worship. Given a greater degree of ambition in that direction and a slightly better than average run of luck, a Varnish might have become the leading churchman at almost any time between the Glorious Revolution and the Great Depression, yet his position would not have been so advantageous had it not been for the peculiar civil political circumstances which ran in parallel with and now intertwined with the ecclesiastical situation, for Prime Minister Blair had given the date for his resignation and Gordon Brown was certain to be granted an audience of Her Majesty to kiss hands.

The two men had agreed, after much in-fighting that, in the month or so between Blair's announcement and Brown's 'coronation', in all matters excepting the gravest of crises in which case Blair would postpone his resignation, he would consult Brown and only over-rule him in extremis. Blair, accordingly, sided with the Spiritualists and advised Brown to translate Archbishop Mwanga of York to Canterbury, but Brown, although he had already publicly stated that he would renounce Prime Ministerial ecclesiastical patronage once he became Prime Minster, hung onto it now, whether because he had no choice or to thwart Blair for perhaps the final time, and was minded to refuse the advice for four reasons, in ascending order of importance. Firstly, in spite of what was said of his religious background, he was deeply suspicious of the Spiritualists. Secondly, translating Mwanga would leave York vacant and present only a slightly less complex problem. Thirdly, the people of York had come to hold Mwanga in great affection and the Diocese contained a significant number of marginal seats. Finally, Brown was much more concerned with the solid issue of Church finance than the nebulous issue of spirituality. Brown therefore cast about him for a Traditionalist among the Bench, but found no-one to his taste. More than two-thirds of the remainder were Spiritualists and of the possible candidates from the Traditionalist faction, Spellman of Wessex was widely believed to be in an openly gay relationship, Brewer of Anglia was in the middle of messy divorce proceedings, and Hall of Alchester would not come off the fence. Furthermore, although the Spiritualist alliance was firm enough in the matter of principles, it was divided over questions of office holding. Thus, Brown, surveying the list of candidates from the Prime Minister's Appointments Secretary, could not find a way through. On the Friday after Pentecost, the Ecclesiastical Appointments Committee held an extraordinary session under an Order In Council to make good the gaping cavities of the Ecclesiastical Bench. With the liberals having seceded to the Perpetuans, the field was left open to the two opposing factions who, although they were able to divide the spoils of eight dioceses evenly, were hopelessly split over Canterbury. After adjourning in the early evening to 'pray', which involved the copious use of mobile phones, they gathered for yet another affray which was summarily cut short by the Secretary who reported that the Prime Minister Designate was only prepared to forward the name of Varnish in first place to Her Majesty with an obvious 'also ran' as his second choice. Blair had not been pleased with the situation in which he found himself, but was not prepared to affront Brown for no apparent gain. Brown said that the Commission was welcome to do what it liked with diocesan appointment, where individual bishops could pursue their traditional or spiritual leanings to their hearts' content, but he needed a solution of the Church property problem which only a pliant, but appropriately skilled Archbishop of Canterbury could expedite. Moreover, the Church Commissioners, worried about the state of the markets, wanted to off-load as many real estate liabilities as could be managed consistent with their duty to ensure that worship facilities were available to all those, within reason, who wanted them. Sir Felix Crimp-Walker, speaking on their behalf, fully supported by their trusty in the House of Commons, Sir Justin Peal, said that there would be a constitutional crisis if the in-coming First Lord of the Treasury were not to have his way. Thus was Varnish caterpaulted from being Archdeacon of Patchminster to Archbishop of Canterbury without the intervening step of being a diocesan, or even a Suffragan. There were those who found fault with the proceedings, but they were generally characterised as bureaucrats, insiders, and nit-pickers who could not see the necessity of acting quickly and firmly. The Church of England, after all, was ultimately subject to Parliament, whatever the Grand Synod might say, and any defence it might have mounted in the name of high principle had been rendered ineffective by its civil war going back over a decade when most voters—and whatever else they might be, Mr Brown only ever saw them as such—could not understand why women should not be bishops and why gay people presented an issue of principle. Accordingly, on Saturday morning, well in time for the Sunday Papers and 'politics shows' 10 Downing Street announced that Mr Brown had taken "decisive action to save the Church of England from an impending crisis", further stating that "although the position was somewhat anomalous, by Order in Council, the Archbishop Designate would have powers to act de facto and that any decisions he made would become de jure at his Consecration which would be expedited insofar as that was possible without compromising the dignity of the occasion." Mr Blair, having followed the agreement with Mr Brown to the letter, then thought it his duty to offer further, more general advice. "As far as I am concerned, Gordon, you have made an unfortunate choice, but the delicate position which the Church of England finds itself in is that I am on my way to being received by Cardinal Podric into the bosom of Rome and you are a son of the Manse. I hope that you are genuine in your wish to renounce Church patronage and I wish now that I had done so. Nonetheless, a Church that thinks its buildings are more important than what happens inside them is almost certain to fail. For all his internal agonisings, I would have trusted Hall to come up with the right solution, even though some say he is determined to follow me to Podric. I think he can always be counted upon to come to his own personal conclusions on an issue, but then to subject these to the needs of the Church to which he promised to stay faithful. For all his superficial bonhomie and his apparent accord with the feelings of the core of those who remain in the Church of England, I would advise you to take care when dealing with Varnish, and I certainly would not advise you to ask him to pray for you." "Look, Tony, I've taken almost as much as I can of this pious drivel." "Sure, Gordon, but although you are free to act you are bound to listen." "This is just one more crisis that you have dumped in my in-tray." "Gordon, as I have said before, and am now saying for the last time, victimhood does not go down well in a Prime Minister. The people hate it. You might be right. The Prime Minister has to take what comes, and if he claims credit for the accidents which make him look competent, he will also have to take the blame for things, no matter how far beyond his control, that go wrong." "Thanks, Tony." "Dominus Vobsicum, Gordon."

Sir Felix, as was his wont, took matters in hand by making a flurry of phone calls to all the key players and was confident of an early success. The aims of the Prime Minister Designate and Archbishop Designate were clear. Archbishop Mwanga was prepared to leave such "sordid" matters in Varnish's hands as long as certain minimum demands were met with regard to 'key churches'. Max Silver, as the petitioner, was accommodating almost to the point of docility. By the Monday after Trinity he had drawn up a list of requirements. Varnish wanted the churches of most historical significance plus the vast majority of Victorian buildings. Mwanga wanted large, solid churches for the Torans and some neo-Papal monstrosities for the Petrans. Max wanted large churches, mostly in the major towns. There were very few overlaps and the issues surrounding them were soon resolved. The established Church would keep everything it wanted and Max seemed satisfied with buildings that it—and Sir Felix as Commissioner—would gladly give up. From the business standpoint, the Perpetuan secession was a 'godsend', ridding him of commitments he could not possibly have renounced in normal circumstances. There were sticking points such as the status of Alchester Cathedral, where the Dean and Bishop Hall were anxious each to defer to the other, and London Minster, which the Government wished to retain for great occasions, but which he and Max wished to include in the Perpetuan package and, oddly, the Parish Church of Stumpy Knoll, which was the subject of dispute between Varnish and Max, the one claiming its historical significance, the other claiming that it was already part of the Perpetuan heritage. By Tuesday night the negotiations were complete. Max had given up London Minster in exchange for Stumpy Knoll and the Dean and Bishop Hall had agreed to work out their own arrangements for co-governance. The deal was about to be ratified when Sir Justin intervened to say that there was a growing feeling in the House that the settlement would not do. Members alleged that the established Church had been left with the most financially exacting buildings whereas Max had scored a substantial victory by acquiring a corpus of solid churches in good repair. Further, as most of what he had gained was property on inner city land, it was alleged that he would somehow—nobody was very specific on this point—realise the assets.

On Wednesday morning the press were damning the deal as a "betrayal". Downing Street was alarmed, Varnish was nervous, and Mwanga pulled back. Sir Felix proposed a levy on the Perpetuans to be paid to the Commission for the benefit of the most distressed churches in its care, and Max was on the verge of rejecting this as an impossible imposition, when Dexter intervened to support the levy. "If God wants us to thrive, we will thrive," he said. "Our Sister the Spirit is with us. We will go on." Number 10 sighed with relief; Varnish drew up grandiose restoration plans, and Mwanga grudgingly assented.

If Max thought that the twin troubles of the anti-anti-consumption backlash and the churches levy were as bad as things could get, he was wrong. No sooner had the churches deal been signed than Horace Strider made his move. Rumours had reached him that the Prime Minister Designate was not so certain to promote him as he had hitherto supposed. There were debts to be settled and, as usual, the troublesome rather than the loyal were to be rewarded, and so his only recourse was to make trouble. Fully cognisant of the damage it would do to his long-standing relationship with Sir Pluto, but calculating that this was less of a loss than high office and that, in any case, if the high office were achieved Sir Pluto would have to come round to maintain his gallimaufric interests, he texted Sir Pluto to say that he had been reluctantly forced to give the Chairmanship of the Consumption Committee to Sir Mittal Joffree, an insult compounded in Sir Pluto's eyes by the fact that his replacement was the owner of Lakshmi. Sir Pluto refused the sinecure Deputy Chairmanship and quietly withdrew not making any public statement nor any calls to his editors, confirming Strider's calculation that he would not spend his capital on a lost cause when neither of them knew when they would need each other. Politics was not a matter of principle, but of playing multi-dimensional chess. Sir Pluto had lost a pawn and he was not therefore disposed to risk his queen. Strider had taken a pawn in order to strengthen his own position, but he would not make any further moves which might risk a sacrifice. Strider was determined to use the new Committee to ensure that the Perpetuan initiative was strangled at birth, buoyed by the knowledge that Mr Brown, like the Leader of the Opposition, was only a 'paper green'. There were more headlines about.

THE SHORT SAUSAGE

THE FLATTENED SCOOP

THE MIDGET FOOTBALL

Suddenly the supermarkets were no longer a pestilential cartel charging exorbitant prices, using the global food and climate change crises to rook harassed customers, but the thin check-out line standing between the Bulldog British and an international conspiracy to promote short measures without proportionately reducing prices. Sir Justin, seeing which way the wind blew, suddenly found it impossible to confirm that the churches deal would find favour in the House. Within a week of its signing, it was dead. Max was spared the levy but he was at a standstill over finding Centres where Guides could be based. He began to receive hate mail and the lurid headlines in the newspapers were replicated in even more scurrilous graffiti against the Perpetuans.

Dexter called his followers together. "Some of you have advised me to call on Perpetua to appear again to help us out, but She was emphatic that Our Sister the Spirit would be with us. I accept that. Some of you have advised that we should launch a major campaign against our opponents, but Trina rightly points out that we do not want to be seen as 'anti' anything. Our proposals on consumption were positive not negative, but if we go into battle against the media we will lose. This is a time to gather together and to pray, to make new adherents quietly and in hope, and to look to each other and the Spirit to sustain us until the time is right to move. Max is rightly worried about gathering places but we will concentrate on the house groups until we are led into a new and wider way. Bill has kindly agreed to lead us in a retreat for three days so that we can focus on what we need to do."

Eight days after Trinity, an Early Day Motion was tabled in the House, proposed by Sir Rufus Tartan, an Ulster Loyalist, and seconded by Sir Justin, "That the Perpetuan sect is inimical to the Trinitarian Christianity which is the glory of the realm of our Sovereign Lady, Queen Elizabeth, Defender of the Faith." With the Prime Minster preparing to depart and his successor engaged in more earthly matters, support for the Motion steadily gained strength. It could not be argued that Perpetuanism was not different from Trinitarianism, but Unitarians, Jews, and Muslims were not seen as any threat to the Church Established. By Thursday the Member for Patchminster North, in which Grunge Park was situated, took advantage of Parliamentary Privilege to assert that the Perpetuans in general and its leaders, such as Dexter, in particular, were part of an international conspiracy, tied up with the drugs trade, to subvert the morals of the nation. His remarks were greeted with a mixture of heckling and horror but, to use a cliche—and Honourable Members are never far from that eventuality—many thought that there was no smoke without fire. There was, too, an element of incipient racism because although the Government, and more recently the opposition, had steeled themselves to political correctness, the exercise of such self-discipline was as difficult as a working Class Northerner trying to maintain a Home Counties accent. As long as matters go smoothly and as long as he can keep himself sober, the pretence is remarkably convincing, but if he loses his temper or gets drunk, the facade crumbles within minutes. So it was that the easy-going and sober House was almost instantly turned into an assembly not far removed from that presided over by Robespierre. Blair, in his last known act of political bravery, urged his Cabinet to keep its nerve and take no steps to appease the high feeling in Parliament, but Brown refused to back him, sitting in sullen silence, mentally noting those who insisted on backing Blair even in his final hour and, for the seventeenth time, re-drawing his Cabinet. Blair's supporters leaked in order to exonerate their leader but the tactic, as it often had before, backfired to fuel the anti-Perpetuan campaign which was automatically assumed—as the result of the habit of confrontational dichotomy—to be backed by the silent Brown.

Besieged by the madding crowd, Varnish naturally found himself at a loss. A life of studied dessication found him wanting and a prey to his factious advisers. Smoother, wise in the ways of the media, advised vigilant inaction, whereas Crozier, the Chair of his Council, wise in the ways of the Lord, advised robust steadfastness. Caught between the two, Varnish did the worst thing possible by doing both by fits and starts. Had he followed Smoother, he might have secured a period of calm, even if that risked allowing the gathering storm to gain strength unopposed, and had he followed Crozier, he might have carved out a recognisable position, even if that risked aggravating his opponents, but the bricolage of his policy, muddled, shapeless and untidy, alienated his allies more than any firm policy, and encouraged Sir Rufus and his followers to greater excess. Where he was fastidious they were brash, where he was cautious they were bold, where he was reasonable they were emotional, and where he was mild they were vituperative. A nation that customarily called for its Archbishop to take the moral lead without ever intending to follow it, now regretted that it had shouted "fire!" too often, for the louder it called, the further Varnish retreated into his legalistic shell. His repeated protestations that people ought to behave better was countered by the cry that they were behaving in a principled, if somewhat lively, fashion while he was not behaving at all. In vain did he protest that to do nothing is a decision in itself and that to be moral might mean serving rather than leading. The calmer he was in public the more turbulent became his detractors. Matters might have been tolerable for such an industrious administrator and indefatigable fixer had it not been for the growing realisation, in spite of his former staid career, or perhaps because of it, that he desperately wanted to be Archbishop of

Canterbury, for he was like a peasant farmer who had suddenly struck buried treasure that he was legally obliged to declare and could only claim after a period of waiting. As the days crawled by, rumours began to circulate that he would not survive to the date of his consecration—what Downing Street had made it could easily unmake in spite of supposedly hallowed conventions—and this led him, without consulting his advisers whose disagreements he found irksome, to take a step which was to sow the seeds of further disruption by promoting an alliance with other religious minorities which felt threatened by Sir Rufus. This was a not altogether unattractive course of action as it put the Church of England at the centre of affairs, loyal to its tradition of seeking to protect the interests of all the people, and it seemed to find favour with the other major religious leaders. The Chief Rabbi, the wisest religious leader now that Hawthorne had departed, ever mindful of the suffering that his people had undergone at the hands of easily incited Christians, had made a series of speeches—one of which was broadcast on national Television as the Steiner Lecture—calling for a constructive alliance between all religions which stood for the worship of the one God and, in doing so, for the maintenance of human dignity. Cardinal Podric, ever mindful of chauvinist anti-Catholicism embodied in Sir Rufus, had preached a powerful sermon which altogether broke with the Ultramontanist stance of his superiors. A group of leading Muslim scholars, mindful of the opprobrium in which they were held because of a handful of incendiaries spawned in the rankest filth of Pakistan, held a seminar on the Islamic tradition of religious tolerance. The Congress of Sikh Elders, mindful of the tendency of most Caucasians to make no distinction between themselves and the Muslims with whom, ironically, they advocated unity, reaffirmed their belief in a unified, global religion, in spite of their exclusion from the Abramic trio. Varnish, being no theologian, saw this tactical alliance as a way of bolstering his position. If all "people of goodwill", as the phrase has it, could unite against the forces of intolerance, all would be well and all manner of thing would be well but, as Smoother at least could have predicted, the formation of the alliance caused a terrible reaction which gave yet more strength to Sir Rufus.

ANGLICAN PACT WITH INFIDELS

MULTICULTURAL MANIA

PAPIST PACT   JILTED JESUS

CHRIST DIED FOR NOTHING

These were typical of the reaction. What had started as a campaign against the Perpetuans lurched into a campaign against religion in the name of religion, an outcome made even more curious by Varnish's unaccustomed failed attention to detail. In his haste he had overlooked the central purpose that any alliance might have served, which was to protect the Perpetuans who had been the object of the original assault by Sir Rufus. Thus, instead of approaching them from a position of strength, he was now forced into trying to reach an agreement with them when it was clear that he had overlooked them. Not that it made any difference, for Dexter and his followers, pressed though they were with threats of violence, were not prepared to join any formal religious alliance, for while they had great sympathy, for example, with the Jewish model of the home and the Synagogue, they were deeply suspicious of the kind of organised religion from which Perpetua had led them, and so Varnish had put his Church in the firing line for nothing.

For the first time in 200 years outside the Celtic fringe, there was a call for the restoration of the spirit of the Glorious Revolution. Leaders were written upon it; callers to phone-ins spoke incoherently of it, historians were pushed in front of microphones and told to get a move on because of the up-coming weather forecast, hurried documentaries were patched together, and there was an epidemic of car stickers, lapel badges, printed t-shirts and carrier bags with the logo:

1688 AND ALL THAT!

Like many of his kind, Sir Rufus was a blustering bully who defined himself not by what he favoured, but by what he was against—which included the European Union, long hair, modern art, comprehensive schools, gay people, blue jeans, cats, pacifists, frisbies, animal welfare, foreigners, modern architecture, regulations, fast food, liberals and lefties, and mobile phones—found that from being a marginal figure in an Ulster that had come to enjoy an uneasy peace, whose only contribution to British life was his popularity among amateur impressionists, now became a figure of national importance. Reared on slogans, he now set about learning his religious history and theology with determination. In a remarkably short time the Pope was transformed from a bonfire effigy into a set of doctrines. William and Mary came off his tea caddy to enjoy lives of complexity, service, and sorrow. The politics of Europe, from the Treaty of Westphalia to the War of the Spanish Succession, slowly disintegrated from its symmetrical superficiality into a tangle resembling the wiring which lay behind his television, DVD player, and CD stack. Naturally, his lack of in-depth information had not dissuaded Sir Rufus from talking—and, as circumstances required, shouting—in slogans, but he now felt more secure when confronted by clever Oxbridge interviewers whose task it was not to expose his views, but their incoherence. As a performer he was both 'tough' and 'nice guy' by turns, with an instinct even more ready than his interviewers, for diagnosing a weakness in his opponent. He bullied the reasonable, charmed the surly, demoticised the arch, and lauded it over the amateur. He found to his surprise that the British were not so different from the people of Ulster as he had supposed. Having spent most of his time in England in hurried visits to the House of Commons and its environs, he had come to stereotype their under-statement, weary cynicism, trivial passions and ephemeral commitments, as opposed to the hy-

perbole, enthusiasm, overwrought passion, and ancient rancour which characterised his own people, Protestant and Catholic. He found, as he travelled the
three countries, that with very little effort he could transform the former into
the latter. Whether the enlivened emotions of his hearers were synthetic, self-
interested or a revival of spirit, he did not know but it did not matter as long as
he could secure his aim which was to impose his brand of Presbyterianism on a
morally ailing United Kingdom. In this respect he was much closer in his ends
to Perpetua than he supposed because, without wishing to use words with an
impolitic overtone, he was an advocate of a "New Puritanism", but their means
could hardly have been more different, for whereas she had stood for a moral
outlook based on independence of choice, his utopia was based on subjection.
In spite of the Unionist necessity of keeping Catholicism at bay, his clan had
always considered the English to be an effete and decadent necessity. At last, the
tables were about to be turned.

The circumstances could hardly have been more auspicious. Mr Blair was
within days of making his final, bravura performance at the despatch box. Mr
Brown was re-composing his cabinet for the twenty-third time. The Archbishop
of Canterbury designate, weakened by the very Perpetuans who were the prime
target, had pushed himself into a corner with terrorists, blacks, Jews, and Catholics. The people were bored with their lives and their pastimes. Little Phil Mac
was still missing, the football season was over, and the weather was unseasonably wet.

Tartan's first task—and as a man who believed that the means justified the
ends this presented no moral problem, although he was not conscious that he
was following the classic Nazi procedure—was, as neither could singly maintain
a campaign for any length of time, to ally high principle with low feeling. True
religion, about which just about nobody cared, provided his high principle, and
persecuting the novel and the different was the surest way of appealing to the
lowest of feelings. The trick was, as he knew, to push all his opponents into a
spineless, unprincipled, liberal camp even though many of them were far from
being any of these, while his erstwhile supporters were often all of them. The
first step was to call all his opponents "liberal" and "politically correct", but to
turn these into terms of abuse, as in, "these liberals think they can do anything
in the name of freedom", "they hide behind political correctness to permit fecklessness", and "their liberal habits have led to drugs and knife crime among their
children". The second step was to effect a separation. "They don't fit in", "they
have betrayed British values", and "they want to put their religions on a par with
orthodox Christianity". The third step was to make the separated inferior. "They
are not fit to share our public facilities", "their habits are inhuman", and "their
conduct has placed them outside society." Now it might be thought that in such
circumstances in which, regardless of the moral content of these accusations,
they were so inconsistent, attempting to find some commonality of anti-social
practice between fundamentalist Mullahs, contraceptive using Catholics, sexu-
ally-promiscuous Afro Caribbeans, and social liberals who thought it essential

to find space to allow all three groups to follow their traditions or preferences, or attempting to identify some kind of political commonality between New Labour voting Catholics, Conservative voting Bengali small businessmen, Liberal Democrat voting baby boomers, and the vast majority of the poor and alienated who did not bother to vote, that Sir Rufus would be open to ridicule from the media. However, he had rightly judged that bourgeois Britain was fed up with being nice to people who were so obviously alien to its traditions. For too long the liberal establishment had failed to 'crack down' on the worst excesses of Pakistan-based Islam. For too long it had refused to make the link which was obvious to anyone, that the vast majority of knife and gun crime was committed by Afro-Caribbean youths. For too long people of all races, Creeds, and persuasions had been 'infiltrated' into positions of influence in society under rules which disadvantaged white males. Those in power, in pursuit of the high ideal of offices being open to all, had made it almost impossible for a properly qualified white man in the South East of England to hold a public appointment, and it was such shutting out that tilted the balance of the well-off middle class in favour of Sir Rufus. They were "fighting for fairness and equality". They did not see why they should be "told what to do" by people who had abused British hospitality by running the place. It was as if they had invited a black couple to dinner out of kindness and had ended up doing the washing up while their guests helped themselves to liqueurs and chocolate before claiming the master bedroom and inviting them to sleep in the box room. Such resentments had been checked to a large extent by a steady rise in the standard of living but, as the economy slowed down and the prospect of a recession grew—and, worst of all, as the value of their houses began to fall, their resentment grew. The country was too crowded and there were too many concessions to immigrants. They invariably conflated legal and illegal immigrants, UK citizens of foreign origin, EU citizens and asylum seekers into one. Blair's New Labour had been "too soft". In advance of a political election which might be another two years away, they were ready for more than a little steam venting and, if pushed, a little vicarious blood letting. Thus a process which had taken years, even under the fanatical rule of Hitler, took place in a matter of days, fuelled by a mass media which thought only of short term passions and shorter term sales.

By the middle of June, Sir Rufus was ready to begin the second phase of his operations. This involved turning populist hysteria into political capital. It might be thought that after more than a decade of New Labour success, tugging the opposition behind it into the centre ground, that the task would be almost impossible, but Mr Blair's socially enlightened gains were shallow. Firstly, the very success of New Labour had depended upon a characterisation of the least advantaged in society as requiring a considerable degree of social engineering in the form of a tax credits system, special initiatives, action zones, and task forces. Secondly, it soon followed from this set of initiatives that those who did not work were to be blamed—based on the fallacy that, given enough support, anybody could be trained to do anything—for their own 'idleness'. Thirdly, politicians were deeply aware that the poor rarely registered to vote and, if they did, they were tempted by soap opera to stay in at 'knocking up' time. Finally, the 'new enlightenment' of the opposition which had renounced 'nastiness' was superficial, for it had been out of power for so long that it would reject its tactic of tolerance if nastiness would bring it the power which that same vice had lost it. Just as skirts rise and fall with the fashion, so do ethical stances which alternately bring compassion and toughness into vogue. Mr Blair's skill was to propose that the two could be promoted simultaneously but, after ten years of trying, he had been proved wrong, although whether this was because of a failure of policy or totally independent of it. Illiteracy rates were stubbornly high, knife crime appeared to be growing, and above all, people had formed the habit of divorcing their private and public experience so that no matter how safe their village or wonderful their hospital and school, they claimed that crime was rising and that the health and education services were in ruins. New Labour, having achieved the removal of Mr Blair—and, possibly "New" from their party title—was determined to be loyal, for the time being, to Mr Brown, but as it was not clear what loyalty would entail, many of its back benchers were prepared to give cautious support to Sir Rufus and the official Opposition with the silently implicit support of the Prime Minister who refused to comment while knowing for sure that half of his MPs were 'signed up', which produced the unusual situation of a majority in the House supporting an initiative on a bipartisan basis without any explicit leadership from the Prime Minister or the Leader of Her Majesty's Loyal Opposition. Sir Rufus had not so much banked on this failure of leadership as moulded it, remembering from his days as a July street fighter that a little ruthlessness goes a long way, provided that the opposition insists on being reasonable or, better, cowardly. All he had to do, before Mr Brown took office, was to bring the situation to such a head that it could not be reversed by the new administration. Accordingly, he designated the third Saturday in June as "Britain Day" and called on the people to meet for peaceful demonstrations in every city, town and village, followed—and this was the coup de grace—by communal banquets. He urged such demonstrations to be organised on a community basis rather than in city centres so that absentees could be more easily recognised. Note would be taken of MPs, Councillors, and other worthies who did not take part, with data collated by a network of local correspondents using video cameras feeding back to a co-ordination centre. The new technology meant that the actions of every leading figure in the country could be tracked according to their presence or absence. The device was piloted on the Isle of Wight to show to all who needed to be informed that it worked to perfection. There was no hiding place and anyone of note who was absent from a demonstration would be deemed to be on the side of the "traitors"—this was how far the language had become inflamed—and against true "British Liberty and Orthodoxy".

The one fly in the ointment was the BBC. The commercial broadcasters had all agreed to cover Britain Day as it promised windfall revenue for Saturday Summer day-time viewing, but the BBC refused to mount any coverage. The management had been anxious to compete with its commercial rivals, but it was the most multi-cultural large organisation in the country and middle management warned that there would be problems. Commercial channels might have the occasional high profile black news reader, but the BBC had pursued an equal opportunities policy at all levels. Furthermore, Sir Joe Florid, the newly appointed Chair of the newly constituted BBC Foundation—created to represent viewers and to exercise independent control over management—had presided over a number of decisions which had laid him open to the charge of being a "pussy cat" and he therefore resolved to assert a policy of independence over which he had no choice, because the BBC Staff Association privately insisted on it. Sir Rufus appealed to DIM which said that it had no editorial control over the BBC, but that it would, as a matter of public interest, refer the issue to its Fairness Board which reached almost immediate deadlock. One side said that the BBC, as the recipient of a 'flat tax', was obliged to cover all matters of national interest. The other said that, no matter what that might mean in principle, its independence outweighed any single wrong decision that it might make and that, in addition, using its resources to collude with Sir Rufus' surveillance network was a misuse of public money. The Board was therefore powerless even to make a gesture and the BBC was left free to broadcast a variety of minor sports while its rivals mounted nationwide coverage.

The only fear which Tartan harboured was that his movement would be infiltrated by his opponents who would act as agents provocateurs and discredit what was a peaceful campaign. Local stewards had been appointed for every community event, but the preparations had been so hurried that their bona fides could not be thoroughly checked and so the vast majority of volunteers were checked against a variety of faulty criminal records databases. Some were fair-minded citizens who thought that the right to demonstrate, whatever the cause, should be upheld. Some were passionate adherents of the cause, and some thought they would gain political or social advantage. Sadly for Sir Rufus, there was no database of political agitators.

Like all such major occasions, it started—to repeat a cliche heard on all channels—in a "carnival atmosphere" with thousands of sturdy citizens gathering at three o'clock, dressed in or waving Union Jacks which had been supplied with remarkable efficiency by a retail sector which operated on a "just in time" rather than a "just in case" basis. With eight days' notice the factories and freight airlines of the world had worked flat out to produce items such as underwear and swim wear, flags and banners, bags and rucksacks, car stickers and lapel badges, confetti and streamers, ties and scarves, all eagerly sold by the major retailers.

The one exception was Hypo as Sir Pluto could not abide chauvinism nor vulgar display. Every screen was filled with red, white and blue, giving every appearance of being a festive day out such as that enjoyed at Her Majesty's Silver Jubilee or the 50th Anniversary of VE Day, but the Queen had left London unseasonably for Balmoral, the Cabinet seemed to have disappeared into thin air, and the only sign of the establishment was a coterie of Sir Rufus' upper crust supporters. There was only a token police presence as its representatives had warned the Home Secretary that the events were so numerous and dispersed that, even with all leave cancelled, they would be hard put to deal with any serious trouble. Besides, morale in the force—to repeat yet another cliche—was "at rock bottom". Many officers, while maintaining their impartiality, were more than a little sympathetic. Sir Rufus had been wise to state that all the manifestations would be more or less static, with minimum movement from the demonstrations to the impromptu banquets, and that there would be no marching, but the ghettos of the poor and the ethnic minorities, and even the well-to-do Jewish enclaves of North London, were lightly barricaded, in a gesture that was more symbolic than defensive. Those within their confines feared the worst.

At four o'clock, well in time for the evening news and the Sunday papers, Tartan, at a small and homely demonstration deep in the heart of Norfolk, addressed the nation, viewed throughout the land on screens large and small, set up in parks or protruding from pub casements.

> I address you all today with very mixed feelings. I am happy that so many of you have turned out to celebrate our Britishness, but I am sad that it has come to this. If our leaders had shown more wisdom and more patriotism we would not have had to take such trouble to remind them of our duty, but at least we can enjoy ourselves while making a serious point.
>
> You all know that this crisis of British confidence was brought to a head by the alien forces of Perpetuanism. Those of you who read your newspapers carefully will have noticed that its leaders are a disreputable gang of thugs and perverts who have crawled from their slime and now claim to have been transformed into brightly coloured butterflies. Under the guise of making a new start, they propose that the religion which this land has cherished for over 400 years should be overturned in favour of a hydra-like monster. We are at one with our Holy Trinity, but they were not satisfied and have added Perpetua, herself a half-caste, unemployed, almost illiterate teenage girl, as a fourth "member of the Godhead". I do not doubt that they are planning to add more. Do you think that you want to place that drug dealer and former gang leader, Dexter, alongside Jesus Christ? Do you want the kind of religions like that which primitive Indians observe, where there are a multiplicity of strange, deformed deities?

At this point television executives wondered whether they would have lawyers on their backs and the commentators noted that the crowds were becoming "bored and restless with the theology."

> Well, strange as those deities might be, as strange as those of Greece and Rome, they are nothing to the strangeness which Perpetuanism proposes. Now its leaders say that they are not in an alliance with the other major groups who sneer at Britishness—ethnic minorities, political activists, liberals, and even the leaders of the Church of England—but we know better. The Perpetuans are simply being clever, keeping their powder dry, but their cover has been blown, they are exposed, they have failed to hide

behind all those elements of society which have infiltrated into positions of
power under the benign and careless gaze of a 'leftist' government whose
so-called 'newness' has been a fraud.

The cameras at this point sought and found a large number of New Labour worthies looking embarrassed, but unable to escape from their respective
throngs.

Look at our major institutions, the House of Lords, the House of Commons, the Orders of Chivalry, our so-called great institutions such as the
BBC and numerous QUANGOS, the Bench of Bishops, the Trade Unions,
the town halls, the civic associations, even our Parish Councils. Nothing is
too great nor too small for the insidious attention of these people who have
infiltrated society at every level.

Well, now it is time to strike back. I have four major proposals.

Firstly, I propose a contemporary Oath of Allegiance to the Queen
and to Britain. It will be framed in such a way that any reasonable person
will be able to swear to it. It will be taken by all of those in public office,
whether working for the Government or any organisation Funded by the
Government. It will also be taken by all those seeking state assistance and
those seeking state documents such as a driving licence or a passport. In
the first instance it will specify adherence to Orthodox Religion, but we
will consider modifications for other religions on the basis of how well
their adherents behave.

Secondly, we will do away with all the nonsense of the so-called 'anti
discrimination' legislation. It is part of the liberty of every British man—er,
British person—to choose to employ or associate with whoever he likes.
There is nothing in natural justice or British law that says that people
should be forced to employ people because they are black or Catholic or
Bengali or Perpetuan. We British people should be free to choose who we
want. These other people are here for a large variety of reasons, mostly the
result of betrayals by our ruling classes, and we need to reverse this. And
we need to reverse these betrayals!

Thirdly, we are going to take immigration seriously. We have been
swamped with all kinds of people we don't want. We will institute a programme to send as many home as we think fit. Now there are those who
say, "'but although my grandparents were born in Pakistan I was born
here'', but that just won't do. We will make all our foreign assistance and
military assistance—most of which is wasted on corrupt governments—
conditional on them taking back their people." (Enthusiastic applause)

Finally, we are going to pull out of the European Union.

In addition to all the treacheries of our own government, the biggest
has been handing over our liberties to foreigners. We will use the savings
on this wasteful bureaucracy to institute citizenship classes so that those
who genuinely want to become Britons will have the chance.

I am therefore calling for a grand coalition to put through these laws
as a matter of urgency. I know that Mr Brown sympathises with much
of what I have said, but he needs courage. I know that the Leader of the

Opposition supports these measures, but he needs decisiveness. The rest really don't matter. In an ideal world we should fight a General Election on my proposals, but I doubt that Mr Brown will want to give up the power he has fought for against his own leader for the past decade. I do call upon all Liberal Democrats and their wishy-washy friends to resign and fight byelections against us, and then we will see what true Britons stand for.

Each of the four proposals solicited increasingly enthusiastic applause. The reactions of embarrassed New Labour and uncertain Conservative MPs were shown as their party leaders had words put into their mouths.

On Monday I will be moving a motion of No Confidence in the Government, calling on all those who support my proposals to vote for the motion and against the Government. We are on our way.

The immediate reaction to the speech from the pundits was shock at its audacity. In the normal way of these things, the channels had found ardent, uncritical supporters of the proposals, but they had greater problems finding out-and-out opponents. There was much talk about practicalities, of how pulling out of the EU, although very popular, would be difficult and, one commentator pointed out timidly, it might cause a down-turn in the economy and a loss of jobs. The Tartans said that this threat about lost jobs was simply bogus economics. It might mean a few jobs lost at the EU Commission for bureaucrat insiders, feathering their own nests at the taxpayer's expense, but this would be made up for by the prospect of much more open trade with our friends.

The one issue which was not discussed at all was racism: nobody stood up for any of the minorities. Some Liberal Democrats had proposed to appear but their leader had said they should wait to see what happened. He was already worried that he was about to be toppled and until he knew the Party's mind, he counselled neutrality. This only led to charges of cowardice. Where were all these people who had until quite recently backed the equality legislation, Membership of the EU, disability rights, immigration, and all the other disastrous laws of recent years? Where were all those who had spoken so bravely against the Blessed Trinity and Orthodox Religion? They seemed to have disappeared altogether. Were they hiding or did they know that they had been defrauding the British people? They would not be able to hide for long.

Mr Blair seriously began to consider postponing his resignation. It was clear that things could not be allowed to go on as they were. He needed to get control of the liberal media and Parliament to hold the line. If he was brave—and he had nothing to lose—he could save the situation and crown his liberal legacy. He called Mr Brown. "Gordon, what do you make of today's events?" "I think they are very serious. I think it would help if you could resign on Monday morning and leave me in charge of the future. If you had gone earlier, this would never have happened." "And if I do that, Gordon, what will you do?" "I can't say. Nobody could have foreseen this. We will have to hold emergency talks with

Tartan." "Talks!" "I see no alternative." "No alternative! Gordon, I don't like to put it this way but there was a time, although most people have forgotten this, when we forged New Labour together, but you seem to have reached a state of arrested analysis. There has to be an alternative. If you can't come up with one very quickly I will delay my resignation because I am sure I can come up with an honourable alternative." "You can't!" "I will. I will call you in an hour."

For the final time in his Prime Ministerial career, one of his aides leaked the conversation in order to strengthen his leader's hand against Brown and, for the final time, the move backfired, although one immediate consequence which proved favourable to the Government was that Tartan's speech was second on the news agenda. Whether or not Mr Brown took over on Monday or a few days later instantly became a "Constitutional crisis" and there is nothing that the media likes more, even though such high (or low) politics leave its audiences indifferent. For all their shallowness on many issues, most people can distinguish between a crisis and a put-up job, although that does not necessarily mean that they will not pretend to believe in the latter if it suits their purposes, but a faked constitutional crisis is not one of the put-up jobs they are prepared to put up with. Nonetheless, the 24 hour news services were incandescent.

Brown called Blair. "I see that your people have made a complete mess of it as usual." "I have to admit, not for the first time, that that might be true, but, as I have more important things to do at the moment, and as I can't immediately find out who did the damage, I have been concentrating on the matter in hand. For once, unbend, be reasonable, give us both a chance. I know you don't like my aides—and now I'm about to leave I can admit that I don't like most of them either, clever, little, self-regarding climbers—but now isn't the time to go over that again as we both know that yours are just as bad and just as incompetent. What I propose is that we move a motion of Confidence in the Government's policies on citizenship. We will get almost all of our own people and can rely on most of the Lib Dems, and then we will see what the official Opposition is made of. We will simply ignore the EU issue and stick to the things that you and I absolutely agree upon." "And your resignation?" "I do wish you would stick to the important matter in hand, instead of simply thinking about your own political position. What's a few days after all this time?" "I've never trusted you since ..." "... Look, Gordon, you will never make a decent Prime Minister if you put your own reputation—or what you see as your reputation—above clear policy. Now, let's get back to the point. If the motion goes through substantially, the crisis will be over; and I will resign as planned. It is in your interest, as well as mine, as out-going Prime Minister but, above all, in the country's interest, that it goes through with a large majority. I suggest that you open and I wind up." "No. I should wind up." "But you, as Chancellor, have been accustomed to making set piece speeches, whereas I can improvise, even though I haven't always been a roaring success at PMQs." "Well ..." "... Let's just put a stop to this unless you have a better idea." Silence. "Do I take it that we are in agreement?" Silence. "Gordon, you've got one last chance to settle this or I'll think again. Even though you are the PM Designate, that has no constitutional significance, but Chancellors don't usually open or wind up Confidence motions and so, if I need to, having determined on this course of action, I can go elsewhere." "No, Prime Minister. It's a deal. I'll open." "Thank you, Gordon."

While the two leading politicians of the country were gently—and in their terms it was gentle—wrangling over Parliamentary procedure, Sir Rufus and his 'kitchen cabinet' were in a state of near euphoria. The day had gone better than they had hoped. The major speech had been greeted with a great deal of enthusiasm and there had been little negative reaction. The Government (as far as they knew at that moment) was in a state of disarray, and through their network of webcams and some extended television coverage, they could see the British people enjoying themselves. Meanwhile, a group of experts was making a tally of leading figures who had been seen and not seen so that a 'black list' could be drawn up of those who would be discredited once the vote of No Confidence went through. As the real picture began to emerge, however, there was a note of despondency in the camp. The television shot selection had been misleading and only 29 Labour MPs had been photographed in the crowds and one known maverick Lib Dem. Even the Conservative Party had only produced some seventy. The first editions of the Sunday Berliners were much less friendly than the commercial television channels, not fearing to accuse Tartan.

RACIST BIGOT THREATENS CHAOS

ENOCH LIVES!   DYSTOPIA THREAT

I HAVE A NIGHTMARE

These were just some of the headlines. Sir Rufus was caught between two sets of accusations—that what he proposed was both nasty and impractical. Even his allies were bound to point out, for the sake of their credibility, that what he was attempting was immensely ambitious and likely to fail. He had over-stepped the mark and allowed himself to be carried away. He was moving dangerously close to British National Party territory, while he could combine banqueting and bigotry on one day, on the following day only the bigotry would remain. By the time the later editions came out they featured the Government's intention to move a vote of Confidence in its citizenship policies and even the most right wing commentators agreed that they would have no problem getting their vote. The Britishness bubble seemed as if it was about to burst, and then, as it seemed from nowhere, in committing its worst act of violence, in making concrete what Sir Rufus had said in a political speech, in killing innocent British citizens, it killed itself. As Tartan rapidly lowered the estimate of where he stood, the first report came in of freelance marching. The party was over.

13.

Not even such a master as Proust can fully account for the immense variety and complexity of elements which coalesce to bring a person to a conclusion which in turn generates an action. There are some factors, such as upbringing and habit, which will direct an individual towards what later seems inevitable but, then, at any point along the way in which the tendency is directing, a chance factor might occur to nudge the trajectory a fraction clockwise or anticlockwise leading, ultimately, to a different conclusion than that which would have been reached had the direction been consistent. Thus, a variance of one degree in the direction of travel will, over a long distance, lead to a final point far away from that which was initially planned and, in the course of pursuing the new course, yet another variant may intervene either to bring the travel back to its initial course or take it further away, always supposing that the traveller has a course in mind and is merely subject to insignificant variations in it. In addition to which there is always the more radical element of chance in which, to cite a well known instance, one lapse of concentration or error of judgment might change the course of a life forever as it did in the case of Sherman McCoy's wrong turn in The Bonfire of The Vanities or, to think of something slightly more commonplace, a life might be changed by a car being arrested, or narrowly passing through, a set of traffic lights either to find itself in the middle of mayhem or spared it or, more picturesquely, there is the case of the man who sees a woman through the window of an underground train and either boards it and makes direct eye contact with her or just fails to board it and never sees her again. Alterntaively there is the case of a sudden jolt or even temporary arrest in a life through sudden illness or unexpected loss when everything looks completely different to the viewer, even though nothing external has changed. Why people do or fail to do certain things, either forecast for them or desired by themselves, is therefore such a complex matter that an author, in choosing to describe a period in a life, necessarily simplifies to maintain some coherence and strength in the narrative line, even when he and the reader both know that this necessarily entails a sacrifice of reality for structure and forward movement. There are, inevitably, exceptions. It is one of the most remarkable features of our literary corpus that two works, Homer's and Joyce's Ulysses, should have been concerned with such widely different time spans and that other works which deal with short time spans may yet have powerful forward momentum, but in general there is a graceful proportionality between simplicity and forward projection whereby the author and reader enter into a pact in which the author says, "I know you know that there are many more complex reasons why my hero takes his course of action, you may imagine for yourself what these are", and the reader replies, in the act of reading, "Let me consider what the other complicating, contributing factors might be which the author has chosen not to specify." Thus, in the case of Will Dignot, there were no doubt an unlimited number of reasons, connected and disparate, acting upon or independent of each other, which might have brought him to change his way of life—the blossoming of early promise stunted for a time by cynicism, or a realistic assessment that effort would not be proportionately rewarded; a change in the terms of trade in favour of his kind of creativity which he perceived almost without thinking about it; the gradual triumph of his ego over his enjoyment of idleness; a casual remark by a friend about the potential he was dissipating; a half heard remark on the radio as he drove to work, about the connection between vigorous intellectual activity and longevity; the quality of light as he looked across a landscape, rendering the familiar radically changed, calling him to understand better those forces which make for new ways of seeing the world—but the two principal reasons which he recognised were widely different. The first was the enjoyment of his relationship with Annie Price which, though not entirely predictable, was probable from the moment when he realised, on their short Easter holiday in Spain, that he loved her so much that he would do almost anything she wanted. The second, which could not have been predicted so easily, and which followed actions taken as a result of the first, was his growing fascination with Miles Wycliffe. On their last day in Spain, Annie had told Will that it was impossible for her to have a sustainable relationship with anyone who did not have a personal, developing self-narrative, and that for most people this meant their work. Whatever her qualities and enjoyments, she said, Hypo provided her with a continual narrative of usefulness, change and growth, whereas his time at CEC was apparently spent in as great a degree of idleness as he could manage, consistent with his drawing a salary. She therefore urged him to look about for something more stimulating and, as luck would have it—another instance of an extraneous factor having a strong influence on a course of action—an old friend at the BBC had just been appointed to look after the creation and maintenance of community archives, where people told their own stories instead of being the subject of the highly artificial sneerings of upper middle class, white, well paid journalists and film makers. Only the BBC, with its huge financial clout, could undertake such a massive project which was by no means certain to result in an adequate return of material fit to broadcast, but agreement had been reached to launch four major pilots and, perhaps because of Perpetua, the choice was made by a lady whose hairdresser lived there, or because it fulfilled some demographic requirement laid down by the commissioners, or because it was handy for central London and, therefore, cheap to service, Grunge Park was one of the areas chosen and Will was appointed head of the pilot. It might have been objected that he was hardly of the community and therefore might be accused of being one of those very intermediaries the project was supposed to bypass. It might have been objected that he knew nothing about community history and archiving, or it might have been said that there was no purpose in collecting gigabytes of tedious and unbroadcastable material, but he had been lucky and the urgings of his new love and the promise that he would have a free hand worked together—although, if he had been a person who liked close supervision they would have worked against each other—to lead him to accept the assignment with as much enthusiasm as he had ever shown for anything.

Not unnaturally, his arrival was greeted with deep scepticism. Not only were the criminal elements suspicious that he was trying to document their drug dealing and related activities, but those who might in ordinary circumstances have been inclined to support him, such as community leaders, parents at their wits end to find ways of diverting their teenage boys and girls respectively from drugs and pregnancy, and the supposed beneficiaries themselves who, in their better moments, recognised that their way of life would lead to the same misery into which their parents—or those of them which could be identified—were rapidly descending, were deeply sceptical of the concept of telling their own stories. They were far distant from the hazy ideal of third-rate university undergraduate ethnographers who wrote derivative essays with an unacknowledged debt to form critics about the "integrity of the oral tradition as an engine of community cohesion" and "the unique contribution of Afro-Caribbean tradition to an emerging British narrative tone". Having been brought up entirely as media consumers, many of them were anxious to imitate the celebrities they saw on television or on their computer screens, trapped in endless gyrations of fashion, football, rap, and pornography. Even if they had been inclined to upgrade their media skills from consumption to production—a shift which public policy, obsessed with information consumption and processing, and averse to any creativity outside the CV and the spread sheet—they did not believe that their own way of life would ever be a fit subject for production. Just as even the most gifted of writers balks at an autobiography which only tells him—although hopefully in a more refined and accurate way—what he knows already, the youth of Grunge Park did not wish to dwell on what they knew further than they must, which is why they were so keen on every kind of escape. The proper course of action in these circumstances would have been a programme of community acclimatisation to the project, winning people over, allowing them to waste time and steal equipment until, at last, one key 'stakeholder' would be attached to become a champion, followed by others and by their sub-groups or cohorts. As with many such 'pilots' where the documenting of the process should be as important as the outcome in order both to test its efficacy and enable replication, this was not a pilot at all but the first small wave of a national roll-out where the key indicators of success were rapid and, if possible, spectacular, results.

There was, however, a further factor which made Will's task more difficult than it might have been. Following the death of Perpetua, a terrible lethargy had overcome those at the community's centre which had momentarily experienced hope. Having briefly seen what might be, their lapse therefore did not take them down to where they had been, but deeper than they had ever known. The god4u office still functioned but, for all the efforts of Dexter and his followers to maintain their closeness, people felt—without any real evidence—that Dexter was more interested in the nation as a whole. Having seen such wonderful events and their disintegration, they were not inclined readily to try again, even to tell their own stories to a stranger when it was not clear how they would benefit. Naturally, they told Will they would say anything he liked for money, but he said the whole point of not offering money was that it would not influence what they said, and that, in any case, this was their project, their way of talking to the country and the world. To them it seemed to be just one more example of the poor doing something for nothing from which the rich might benefit, whereas the process would never be reversed by the rich. "What sort of story can we tell except that we are poor and want more money? They know that already and just ignore us. It won't make very interesting television. Anyway, I wouldn't watch it." Will was more inclined to accept what they said than to resent it because he had watched the minor gyrations of social policy over more than two decades with deep scepticism. He was inclined to divide politicians into two sorts: those who were in favour of giving money to the poor, and those who were in favour of giving them everything but money. At CEC he had added together the costs of all the special initiatives and divided them by the number of beneficiaries to see what it might do to their annual income, for at one time in 2005 Grunge Park was the focus of nine special initiatives dealing with pregnancy, the first year of life, under fives, primary education, drugs education, responsible sex, crime control, mental health, and small business development. The last of which, as Will and the recipients noted, provided very comfortable jobs for 26 people in the field and numerous others in offices where the programmes were designed, advocated, adopted, financed, monitored, evaluated, documented, and either replicated as 'examples of good practice' or revised 'in the light of benchmarking'. The total direct annual employee cost for the year was £1,600,000, with indirect costs, overheads and a proportion of head office costs, of well over £300,000. Rounding down his figures he reckoned that the nine special initiatives cost, on average, £200,000 per year, or nearly £17,000 per month, benefiting approximately 200 people which, divided between them, would have yielded an addition to their monthly income of some £75. This, he decided, was not so significant that it would make a difference. To be fair, he thought, the initiatives would not make enough difference, but neither would the cash. Something more fundamental was needed than liberal social policy. Thinking about it with Annie just after the visit to Spain, he was convinced that life required a spiritual dimension which social policy could not supply—people needed to be able to contribute to their own lives and to make sacrifices for their own good, and that of their families and friends. The idea that everybody could be made happy without some kind of self-determination and sacrifice was a utilitarian illusion. He also suspected, without being able to be specific, that the goal of social policy was to keep the lid on problem communities rather than helping them to flourish in their own, perhaps unorthodox, ways. For these reasons—and others which he could not diagnose—he had problems with Sir Rufus Tartan's notion of "Britishness", which he saw not as some outlandish growth, but simply as a more extreme version of a general tendency to think of it as unifying, even uniform, rather than as encompassing and enabling. To him, the essence of Britishness was the ability to support the opposition country in a Test Match without inviting comment, to regret our shortcomings without taking them too seriously, to indulge in irony and vulgarity without cruelty, and to refuse to define Britishness by any binding common characteristics. So when he considered the position of his potential project partners, he understood why they were reluctant. Neither social services nor redistribution had significantly helped them, they had no real stake in Britain, and the ideas of Britishness which were being promoted by an alien establishment sought to capture rather than free them.

This was the dilemma which Will faced two weeks after Easter, needing to liberate creativity, but understanding why this was so difficult, when he met Miles or, rather, saw Miles, standing on a shaky, improvised platform at The Hollow, proclaiming Perpetua's good news. "She gave you back your dignity; now look at you! She told you that you could do anything because you were in charge of your lives; now look at you! She told you that if you were constructive and looked after each other, you would never fail; now look at you!" "Hello!" "She told you ... Who are you?" "I'm the Community Media Pilot Leader." "Oh yes ... She told you ..." "... Just stop for a minute, won't you, and get down from that—er, silly—platform. If you want to talk to people you can find far better places than ranting in the middle of this mud patch. You can see that all the doors and windows are shut. You are spoiling their day-time telly." "That's the point, I have to get them back to how they were when She was here. They're slipping." "Come for a drink." "I don't drink." "Come for a walk. Let's just talk to each other." They ended up in the Down & Out. "I haven't been here since Perpetua," said Miles. "She persuaded me to consume a small alcoholic drink and I was a little tipsy". "Were you now? Don't worry, I'm not recording, I'm not reporting. I remember quite a lot about you, though, Miles. I remember that you stuck at trying to make this a better place when other youth leaders wouldn't come in. I remember your telling me, though you've probably forgotten, that you came every week even though you hated it. I remember being impressed with that, and I remember Perpetua being impressed with that, even though you weren't peddling her sort of spirituality." "No, I was very dogmatic in those days, not at all constructive—goodness me! Don't look but Wayne is over there with Father O'Helly. They look like a couple! Corruption—sorry, Will, I just can't help it—and they've slipped back." "Miles, it's for a reporter to report not instruct, you know, but haven't you slipped back, too? What would she have said about Wayne and O'Helly? One of the things I will never forget about Perpetua—there are many, but this is small and big at the same time—is that when she was with us, she always said 'we' and not 'you'. While you were out their shouting you were telling people off and implying that you were fine and they were not, you were somehow better and separate." "Oh God! Trina is always reminding me, and I am so ashamed of myself. She is so good and I can't even live up to her, let alone Perpetua. It's terrible." "Cheer up, Miles, there is bound to be a reaction against Perpetua's death. People are naturally low." "I know, but with Trina as the wonderful love in my life, I should be doing better." "Sometimes it's difficult to get your private love into the way you do your public life. I'm finding that. I have a new love, too, but it isn't making my job any easier. So why don't we try to do some work together? As I see it, you want to revive the hope of people here and I want to hear their stories. Without a revival of hope they won't talk. So why don't we set up a project to document the life of Perpetua, told through the stories of people here? That will get me the material I need and it will help you to revive hope by being among the people instead of standing on your—pardon me—silly box and shouting at them. It's also work that might interest Trina, and my Annie, as part of the Grunge Park Partnership, will certainly lend a hand." When they were getting ready to leave, Will said, "Go and say hello to your friends and pretend you're Perpetua." "Hello Wayne, hello Father Joe, you look very happy together." "We are, except that I have to go up North for Perpetua and Joe doesn't want to come. It's not really unhappiness, but I will miss him." "Live your love to the full, in togetherness and in mission," said Miles as he smiled and turned away. Wayne looked shocked. "Not bad," said Will.

The process of bringing people out of themselves was painful, both artistically and emotionally. From an artistic perspective, the difficulty was persuading people to be authentic, to be who they were. On the first days of filming the young people larked about, making faces and showing off, while their parents, dressed in their best clothes, spoke as formally as they could remember how, which produced a series of stilted pieces of bad acting as the kids could not really do any showing off worth the name and their parents had forgotten the timbre of the history they were trying to act. From an emotional perspective, even the younger people were reluctant to go back to the Perpetua story. She had not only been greatly loved, she had been, just for a moment, a national star, and then she had been killed right in the middle of their community and they had done nothing about it. For the older ones, the hope she had brought of better times had so quickly faded and died. They saw no end to the 'spiral'—as analysts described it without really knowing what they meant—of decline for which they knew, in a way they could not crystalise which, in a sense made it worse, they were partly responsible. It was true enough that they were given little chance in the economic mayhem of the early 1980s when 'featherbedding' was ruthlessly eliminated—so that the money saved was later transferred to the prisons budget—but they also knew that they should have done better, that people 'back home' on lower incomes were doing better, that their descent into a materialist cave of shining goods, flashing lights with dark corners and demons, where the light was an illusion and the darkness a reality, had been a catastrophe from which there had seemed to be no exit until she came. Then, like their children, they had let her be killed. What changed the atmosphere completely was Kish's mother talking about Perpetua saving her injured son's life and asking her to say nothing. At last there was a real story to tell. Then an old lady told a story about how the Council had thought of making political capital out of Perpetua's birth because of some crazy temporary housing scheme. A strange young boy called Kelvin told a story about Perpetua giving him a chance to study Caribbean birds. A prison officer told an outrageous story about a Christmas lunch miracle. Before very long, Will was collecting fascinating material about Grunge Park, its people, and their beloved Perpetua, and Miles began to see a revival of hope.

Will and Miles worked steadily, helping people see how their very different stories might fit together, using the material they gathered to restore some coherence in the views people held of themselves. As the external environment grew grimmer, their immediate reaction was to continue to build hope through the project, hoping in a way that they could not clearly define, that some good would come of their efforts, not just in terms of the material they were gathering but in the way that it would somehow stave off the worst. In all such situations there is a tipping point where the external pressure is so great that it begins to damage the fragile structures of self-belief, when a kind of self-sustaining optimism is no longer sustainable, when heroism begins to appear to be illusory. Such a point was reached in Grunge Park, ironically, on the day when Perpetua made her last appearance, for although it had a massive impact as a spectacle, it did nothing for morale. Her very distance, the distinction she made between now and then, made them lose heart. In the days that followed, the Project began to lose impetus. People began to recidivise to their bad acting, to dwell on their victimhood, to blame everyone and everything outside Grunge Park for what was going on inside it. In spite of their private bliss, enjoyed separately from their working environment, Trina and Annie volunteered to overnight in Grunge Park with Miles and Will, encouraged in their efforts by Dexter who went round the community tirelessly as the prospect grew ever worse, and by Father Bill whose presence was enough to bring a smile if not real hope, but as Britain Day drew closer, a siege mentality set in. Instead of telling stories about the past, people feared for the future. A few of the young people began to adopt militant language, threatening to fight back, and in spite of all that the Perpetuan nucleus could do, they resolved to build barricades against the world outside. Yet their brave talk and their threats carried little weight. Since Easter Day, the gang leadership had disintegrated as many leading figures became Perpetuans. In the face of the oncoming hostility, they could neither find enough belief in their Perpetuan future nor restore their criminal past. They were suspended, waiting for something to happen, but not knowing properly how to prepare. They had been brought up in the knowledge of the effectiveness of violence to impose a pattern of behaviour, but they had never learned to organise. They could always find a crude word to brow-beat an opponent, but they had learned no rhetoric. Above all, they could not convert their reactionary tactics into a prospectus. Although their friendship strengthened throughout this period, Will and Miles reacted in completely opposite ways to the threat, for although Will did not relish the prospect of what was being forecast by the media, at least he could see this as an opportunity to document the stories of people under threat, whereas Miles saw the power of Perpetuanism crumbling under its first great challenge. What was the point of such high feeling if it could not sustain people in a crisis? Where had the Spirit gone? Why had She left them? Trina and Dexter encouraged him by saying that the Spirit would be with them, that it was not for them to question the time and the place.

On the evening before Britain Day, Dexter used all his moral force to gather the Grunge Park community together for the Sacrament of Response. "Look, dear people, at how far we have fallen back into our old ways, being fearful of what is happening outside; waiting for events to heap their misfortunes upon us; and what have we done? What have we offered? What have we resolved to give God Our Parent? I ask you now to come forward with something that you have so that we can offer ourselves to God; and when I have blessed the offerings, each will take something from the store so that we all go away with something. Do not stint; now is the time to pledge yourselves again to God and to each other." Weeping, people came forward with treasured possessions or with symbols, as they remembered from Perpetua, of their own brokenness. Bullets, ear rings, Dinky Toys, a Little Red Book, marbles, sea shells, a bundle of love letters, African carvings, half a Delft tile, an alleged piece of the Berlin Wall, pictures of a lost girl friend, Owari seeds, a tarnished hand mirror, a set of cricketer cards, a pewter rum tot, a ball of lemon wool, an orphaned Toby Jug, three 'bun' pennies, eight soft toys, a flute—the variety was endless . As each stood at the makeshift altar, Dexter blessed them and, as he put his hand upon each head, the Spirit passed from him into each heart. When the second procession formed, to collect a blessed gift, there were faces filled with hope. They began to sing "It's The Sign That Counts" and, later, they began to dance, forming a long line, moving round the perimeter of Grunge Park, taking down the barricades and posting placards reading "THIS PLACE IS SACRED TO THE NAME OF PERPETUA, OUR SISTER". Will, Miles, Trina, and Annie, each with a camera, fed the pictures back to the god4u Channel and they were broadcast as they were edited together. Perpetuans and other minorities might be under fire but, In Grunge Park at least, the Spirit was with them. When they had finished their procession and re-assembled, Dexter spoke to them again.

"Whatever happens tomorrow, you must trust in the Spirit and in Perpetua. I know in my heart, I can feel it through my whole body, that Our Sister the Spirit is with us now. On behalf of the beloved Perpetua, the Sustainer, who called me and to whom I have dedicated my life, I promise you that She will remain with us. Tomorrow, if the enemies of God come to assault us, we must, above all else, not resort to violence. Whatever happens tomorrow, we must stay true to Perpetua and the Spirit that has been sent. I am saddened in my heart that I feel now that there will be some here who are about to give their lives for the cause of affirmation—I do not know who, perhaps that is as well—but I know that this will broaden our road. Much as I want to preach the Word of God to all of you and to the whole world for many years to come, I also wish to be one of those who are taken up to God Our Parent, to die for what I believe. I do not wish this so that it might give me glory on earth. I wish it because I long to be where Perpetua is now, but I will take what comes, as we all must, trusting that all will be well. Sisters and Brothers, let us sing our song one more time, and then pray through the night for the goal of universal peace and love, for the affirmation of our gifts, given to us that we might raise ourselves up above the things of earth while we are still here, that we might come to know God's liberty here in our hearts. I bless you in the name of God Our Parent, in the name of Jesus Christ the Son, Perpetua the Sacred Vessel and in the name of Our Sister the Spirit." They sang "It's The Sign That Counts" once more and then went quietly home.

Since their mild Easter Day rapprochement respectively with father and uncle, Rory Varnish and Oliver O'Helly had begun to travel back, downhill, past where they had been, to greater depths of cynicism, cruelty, profiteering, callousness, and depravity. They had grown tired of their pornography business—and even of a small racket in immigrant virgins—and grew in their addiction to violence even more than in their addiction to easy money. The memory of Perpetua's death haunted them not with regret, but with the prospect of yet unrealised pleasure in acts of cruelty. They had only briefly envisaged limiting their operations to Excelsior Gardens, not just because the sphere of action was rather limited but because it received more than its fair share of police attention, and so they resolved, in view of the power vacuum in Grunge Park, that they would establish their headquarters there, where the police had no real interests. As long as gangsters killed each other and as long as the drug dealing, prostitution, and racketeering were kept within its bounds, the police did not so much turn a blind eye as persuade themselves that—contrary to everything they knew from their training and text books which showed that crime bred crime and that there was no 'floor' to depravity—crime in a restricted area was rather like an economic microcosm. The market would take care of it, and when matters had reached a certain level, the phenomenon would burn itself out. They actually got wind of the planned move, but persuaded themselves that coherent gang leadership might be better than a vacuum and they also—again, against their training and textbooks—somehow thought that white crime would be less unacceptable than black crime. For Rory and Olly there was the added advantage of a dramatic backdrop for their dealings, exchanging the blandness of Excelsior Gardens for the altogether seedier territory of The Hollow where they had 'enjoyed' their first real taste of violence. Their only problem was how to make an effective entry, and they decided to use the occasion of Britain Day to 'invade' the territory of a demoralised and divided community.

At 9.45 p.m., as the Prime Minister was completing his wrangling with his successor, and as Sir Rufus was surveying the threadbare celebrity list of his supporters, Rory and Olly detached themselves, together with a few drunken associates, from an impromptu street banquet at the edge of Excelsior Gardens, which had consisted almost entirely of alcohol and potato crisps, and made their way towards Grunge Park. Fired up by export (foreign) lager, patriotism and the anticipation of a 'good fight', some three dozen 'protesters', clad in Union Jack garments, made their way to the entrance of the quiet estate. When they saw no barricades, but only two placards saying "THIS PLACE IS SACRED TO

THE NAME OF PERPETUA, OUR SISTER" flanking the crumbling concrete entrance, they stopped, bewildered, as if robbed of their pleasure. Meanwhile, Dexter and his followers were gathered at The Hollow. "Now is the time," he said, "to show who we are. Let there be no flinching and no fighting. The Spirit will work through us in whatever way She thinks fit. We are not to move forward nor back, not to shout insults nor cower. We are to proclaim God's liberty among and within us." Will, filming at a discreet distance, was frightened. He zoomed in on Annie and, in an almost self-conscious gesture, took a close up of her, at the same time thinking it slightly absurd and self-indulgent. In his mind's eye he saw her radiant with light and then dead on the ground. Yet the skills, which he had always possessed, but which he had allowed to rot in his idleness, came to him now without the need to think. Carefully, he took as many pictures of faces as he could, to identify the people who were there, in case they might be needed. As his 'footage' was going out live on god4u there was no question of there being any confidential sources. There was complete silence. Then, in the distance, he heard the sound of breaking glass and, a moment later, cautiously peering round the corner and looking towards the direction of the noise, he saw flames. Fortunately, they were approaching from the West and the transmission point was to the East of The Hollow. There was some incoherent shouting and then, focusing as far in the distance as possible, he made out dark figures with pieces of lighted wood in their hands, moving erratically down the street, haphazardly plunging their torches into windows. When they were just a block away from The Hollow they suddenly became aware of the crowd of people all standing in silence, facing away from them with Dexter at the front, facing towards them, his arms outstretched as if in crucifixion. As if setting people alight was even too extreme for their tastes, the front marchers hurled their torches into a side alley and all their followers did the same. They formed a tight knot and came slowly down the final stretch of road, and then through the parting crowd, until they were only yards from Dexter's motionless figure. As if he were some strange emissary, looking more like a grotesque jester in his Union Jack shorts and black singlet, Rory Varnish stepped forward to within four feet of the silent man.

"In the name of Great Britain," he said, with the carefulness of a drunk, "we reclaim this shit hole for Britain so that we may cleanse it and make it fit for our kind."

Silence.

"In the name of the Trinity, we claim this place for the God of our fathers."

Silence.

"In the name of good, honest, citizens, we reclaim our land from foreign scum."

Silence.

Will moved stealthily to a position midway between the two groups which meant that he was seeing nobody face on, then to a position over Dexter's right shoulder so he could take as many pictures of faces as possible, more than twenty before Olly said, "Aren't you going to do, anything then? Are you such cowards?"

Silence.

Will moved in a gentle anti-clockwise arc until he was over Rory's left shoulder, taking pictures of Dexter in profile.

"Come on then?"

Silence.

The people behind the two leaders were becoming restless, wanting something to do. They pushed from behind.

"Hold on, let's just see if we can get a confession out of this little traitor. We made short work of Perpetua and we can do the same with him, but it would be sweet to get some sort of apology for all the evil he and his shitty, black friends have brought on our country and our religion."

Silence.

Exasperated, Rory struck Dexter full in the mouth. Will flinched, but went on filming. He struck him again, then Olly kicked him. The crowd behind Dexter stiffened, as if to resist, but Dexter rose to his feet and turned back to face them, holding up his hand in blessing. Will moved incautiously quickly to capture the pose of Dexter in the half light, blessing his people.

Then a shot rang out and he fell to the ground.

Will, losing all caution, but still obeying professional reflexes, scanned the mob for a gun, but could not find it. Miles quietly, without making a theatrical gesture or saying a word, moved forward and stood with the back of his legs touching his fallen leader. Rory and Olly, shocked by the bullet, but not wishing to turn, moved back slightly and stared at him.

"A piece of white shit!"

Silence.

"A real traitor."

Then, not knowing the source of the bullet, Olly ventured, "Do you want to go the way your precious Dexter has just gone?"

Miles, knowing that his time had come, but not wishing to replicate the dying posture of his master, knelt on the ground and bowed his head.

Silence.

Another shot, and Miles died in front of Dexter.

Still the crowd did not break as Trina moved to fold his head in her arms. She wept but, determined not to give in, she did not say a word. With her dead lover's head in her lap as she sat in the mud, she faced the two mob leaders. They flinched. They were losing control—it was not supposed to be like this. They did not know who held the gun. Would it be for them next? Then someone behind them shouted, "Camera!" As everybody scanned the perimeter to locate it, a shot rang out. Will fell dead and his camera rolled down a gentle slope of mud and scruffy grass, almost to Rory's feet. "Fuck!" he said. "Well at least we can get the memory card before it does any damage. Fuck! No card! Fuck!"

Annie rushed over to where Will was lying and, with some help, carried him to set alongside the other two bodies. Rory, Olly and the rest ran away as fast as they could.

Then there was silence.

Without hurry, without any kind of gesture, Father Bill came from the crowd and knelt between Trina and Annie. "We commend our brothers, Dexter, Miles, and Will to God Our Parent, confident that they have been enfolded back into the infinite love which made them. We make this prayer in the name of God Our Parent, Jesus Our Brother, Perpetua Our Sister, and Our Sister the Spirit." As if released, the whole gathering began to cry, kneeling on the muddy ground, filled with the terror of death and the power of the Spirit. "The Spirit is with us," said Bill. "Let us drink in the power of the Spirit." They stayed for more than a minute in silence, but then the outside world began to reach them, for although many people might be murdered in cold blood in a run-down estate in London, that must never include a journalist employed by the BBC who was rumoured to be the third victim of a multiple shooting. The god4u pictures had been syndicated free to any television channel which wanted them. Max, taking control in the crisis, sent Wayne to take over from Will so that there was only a short break in service while the drama unfolded. "Our way of loving God is to do our work as professionally as we can," he said, and although there were tears in the production suite, people went on copying, editing and distributing.

At 10.10 p.m., Tony Blair heard the news that the third victim was indeed a BBC journalist and he called Sir Joe Florid. "Joe, I am terribly sorry, particularly as your policy has to some extent stopped the headlong rush into demagoguery. This is a terrible reward for your steadfastness and a terrible warning to us all. I know I'm not supposed to contact you like this but I plead an exception. I'll make a public statement later."

Blair then made his final call to his successor. "This news is terrible but at least it is clear to me that it will end the crisis. I will go to the Palace as I promised. You have a unique legacy brought about by the 'martyrdom' of three good people. Sir Rufus Tartan is finished and you can unify the nation behind a tolerant policy which gives equal concern and respect to all citizens, but you must grasp that opportunity in your very first appearance as Prime Minister. There will be no room for dithering. People have short memories, you never know what unseen events may occur, so my very last word to you, my very last word, is give a human face to your deeply and intricately intellectual version of equality and justice. You will be called upon to act. I will say that you are precisely the man to do that. I feel that you, as the new man, will have a better chance of uniting the nation. Look, I will even run myself down, by implication at least, to give you the best possible chance. You can move the Vote of Confidence as soon as I have resigned, on your own terms." "Thanks, Tony." But he never did.

It was one thing for BBC journalists—the detail of freelance hire was soon elided—to be shot in a far distant land or a place where terrorism or war was the subject of their work, but quite another for such a thing to happen within miles of Parliament. Rarely can newspaper headlines, pictures and editorial comment, have so exposed the self-inflicted wounds of a hubristic press. The one exception might have been the TT, which had a last edition later than all the others, but when Sneer saw the first unconfirmed report of trouble he had, not wishing to spoil the elegant celebration and outrage of his paper, ordered to presses to run a few minutes earlier than usual, citing the extra copies of what would be a souvenir issue. Tabloid headlines which would be regretted, but bring no shame, included:

RULE BRITONIA

POLITICAL CORRECTNESS DEAD

BRITISH TIDE SWAMPS CHATTERING CLASSES

TARTAN TRIUMPHS AS GOVERNMENT TOTTERS

The editorials were topped by Sneer's finest:

As Tartan's armies, great and small, all over Britain, tucked into their well deserved banquets after being fed a wholesome diet of patriotic oratory, the politically correct Cabinet and its mealy-mouthed Prime Minister faced the prospect of eating the largest slices of humble pie ever consumed by a treacherous Government.

Millions of good, honest citizens, decent people with jobs and law abiding families, turned out to cheer the end of a failed policy of multiculturalism and scrounging. As the washed out Church leadership of Hawthorne cowered in the shadows, a new, vigourous brand of orthodox religion was declared with a mighty fanfare of joy as half a century of dithering and appeasement were swept away.

As Tweedle-Blair and Tweedle-Brown fought over the squalid remains of their failed party, unscrupulously thronged with immigrants, liberals, and bogus intellectuals, a picture of a new, stronger, more united Britain emerged, proclaiming the end of mix-and-match politics and a return to good, solid, British common sense.

When Sir Rufus moves his vote of No Confidence in the Government's inclusive policies, we will be right behind him and behind all people of goodwill.

Only Ranjit stood out against the pack, earning, even by the standard of what he expected, a vicious, concerted, and racist blogger onslaught which implied that he was incapable of being an objective reporter on "Christian and related matters" because he was of Indian origin. But, as happens so often, the pictures and headlines looked lurid and sour as they sat unattended on breakfast tables while the nation watched the unfolding of the story of murder and martyrdom. A senior Cabinet Minister said that she had had her differences with the BBC— and that was as it should be—but its refusal to jump on the Tartan bandwagon had been a sign of its true independence and she sent her condolences to the family and friends of Will Dignot who had died doing his duty, defending that independence in the face of wicked and cowardly aggression. A senior opposition figure said that the Conservative Party would always stand against right wing extremism, while the Liberals said they had been right all along to give Sir Rufus a wide berth, accusing the major parties of following in his wake instead of standing against him. Sir Rufus, who had taken the first Shuttle of the morning, besieged in his Picardy farm house, said it was not a crime to take a short holiday after such a strenuous week, and denied that he had constructed a surveillance network to entrap leading political and civic figures, it was simply a way of keeping in touch with events on the ground. In view of the alleged outrage at Grunge Park—as far as he knew no arrests had been made—he was reviewing his position and there might need to be a "temporary" moratorium before he moved his Motion of No Confidence. The Police, whose action in attending the speeches and banquets on Britain Day, leaving vulnerable citizens defenceless, without inviting any adverse comment, now found themselves under sustained and hostile attack to which their only effective response was to arrest the murderer. They picked up Olly and Rory without difficulty but in spite of their fervent wish to find enough evidence to charge them, it soon became clear that they could only be held for a short time. Frightened of worse, they gave the names of all those who had accompanied them to Grunge Park, and these were soon rounded up, but there were no clues and no weapon was found. The three bullets showed the gun to be of Eastern European origin, but there were no easy matches. Varnish was indisposed.

It was mid-afternoon before the focus shifted from the decline of Sir Rufus, the stabilising of domestic politics, and the apparent failure of the police to make early, dramatic arrests, to the "Martyrs" and so they began to play extended extracts from Will's final minutes of reporting. Perhaps it really was his heroism, more likely a severe reaction against the racism that had killed him, that produced the beginnings of the hero worship of Dexter as a "Martyr". The heroism of Miles was noted with praise and Will's role began to be seen as that of a defender of British democracy and an independent media. Max had ensured that every last second of Will's coverage was syndicated, gave an interview to a BBC reporter, and then closed the god4u office and studio. He said, among other things:

> It is not appropriate to comment on the events of yesterday evening. The depiction of the events in Will's filming speaks for itself. Nobody could speak more eloquently than Dexter of what Perpetuans stand for, and as we Perpetuans have stayed silent in the face of aggression, we will stay silent now. ... We forgive whoever killed our three friends, and although we are not hostile to the criminal justice process, it has many flaws, but this is not a proper time to open such a discussion except to say that Perpetuans, while recognising that certain acts are wrong, do not presume to determine the degree of wrong in any individual act. Only God knows the balance of tasks and resources allocated to each individual. It is therefore meaningless to condemn individual people for individual acts. The only

possible good it can do is to make the condemning person feel good. That is the major weakness of Christian moralising. ... The Perpetuan informal leadership wishes the whole country to concentrate on Dexter's message and to leave the politicians and the police to do their job.

Had the Perpetuans been willing to tell their stories, there would not have been much to say, and so the Sunday evening bulletins were full of generalised parables about a man of humble origins who had lost his way and then found it again through Perpetua. He had shown courage beyond anything anybody could imagine and he had died for his religious beliefs. He was Britain's "First Martyr" for almost half a millennium. Thus he was claimed by those whose selfishness, foolishness, or indifference had brought about the death they now celebrated. The newspapers were thwarted, but remained respectful. Their job was to perform a collective volt face as rapidly and thoroughly as possible, making no reference to their conduct of 24 hours ago.

MARTYRS FOR FREEDOM   INTEGRITY RESTORED

TATTERED TARTAN FLEES TO FRANCE

FREEDOM MARTYRS TRUE BRITS

GOVERNMENT MOVES TO STRENGTHEN EQUALITY AGENDA

These were typical of the headlines, and only Sneer's Editorial need be quoted to sum up the changed situation.

> In an act of passive heroism not seen since the Second World War, three True Brits died horrible deaths for the sake of their freedom of conscience. Confronted and then gunned down by Fascist Thugs, the Perpetuan community of Grunge Park refused to hit back, showing deep faith in its leader and her principles.
>
> The behaviour of the Grunge Park community demonstrates, yet again, the massive success of British multiculturalism in developing a framework in which people from different backgrounds can be British in their own way, preserving the values defended by Drake, Nelson, and Churchill.
>
> Although we are no friend of this Government, when the new Prime Minister moves a motion to strengthen British equality legislation, we will be right behind him; it is no less than the Perpetuan martyrs deserve.

Ranjit wrote:

> It is one of the more depressing aspects of established religions that they seem almost incapable of evolving except in the sense that they adjust to external secular circumstances. Christianity, for example, went through a Reformation largely resulting from the invention of the printing press, but it could be argued that its theology regressed from an open and ra-

tional tone in the Middle Ages to a closed and blinkered system by the time the "Enlightenment" began to dawn. Development, in the theological sense, ought to be characterised by an expansion of possibilities, by new understandings of the way that God is "understood" by "his" followers. The recent upsurge in chauvinistic and dogmatic theologising which began with the surreal Creationism of American Evangelism and which reached a nasty—and let us hope temporary and not to be repeated—pinnacle in the Campaign of Sir Rufus Tartan, should be a warning that theological development should spend more energy trying to understand God instead of anthropomorphising the supernatural. I claim no credit for standing out against the general tendency as my viewpoint might have been supported by a varied group of thinkers in all the major religions, but the truth is that most people—and that includes journalists responsible for reporting religious affairs—tend to think of religion as another branch of secular politics which does not require specialist knowledge or, heaven help us, religious faith. If we are to benefit from the dreadful deaths of three decent people, we should stop treating religion dismissively and disrespectfully and take Perpetuanism seriously, not necessarily with a view to adopting it ourselves as a new faith, nor as a replacement for what we already have, but because it deserves to be taken seriously. Taking it seriously for a journalist means, as I have done, reporting its effects on the ground and not just in seminar rooms and drinking haunts.

As the first wave of enthusiasm for "The Martyrs" ebbed, and as it became clear on the accession of Mr Brown that there would be no major Parliamentary occasion to strengthen the equality agenda, the position of the three murder victims subtly altered, for whereas the figure of Dexter had been the most immediately iconic, the ranking increasingly reflected the material available to keep the story alive and so, accordingly, as most was known about Will and least about Dexter, Will went to the top of the rankings ahead of Miles, with Dexter at the bottom although there might have been something racist in this which was never acknowledged. It is also the case that over time the importance of the BBC proved higher than Perpetuanism, the one being a national institution, the other a sect. During the following week, when the Miles/Trina "Love match" was discovered through a casual comment made by a Grunge Park resident during an interview for a background piece on the Partnership, Miles went to the top of the ranking and, the following week, when Kish gave an interview about his relationship with Dexter, how he had been cured by Perpetua and pacified by Dexter on Easter Sunday, Dexter went back to the top. By mid-July it had all been forgotten. Perpetuanism was a sect which had demonstrated a curious degree of pacifism, Tartanism had faded, the BBC began to receive its usual level of criticism, and terrorism and flooding topped the news agenda.

The Perpetuans themselves, suspicious of ranking and hierarchy, held the three murder victims equally high in their regard, although they were realistic enough to differentiate between the heroism of their leaders and the journalist recording their deaths, and although they were not immediately faced with the problem of official martyrdom, they needed some way of setting apart their leaders for special commemoration. The informal leadership of the remaining original followers, Bryan (the Chief Technician at god4u), Kylie (usually on the road in the south of England), Wayne (usually on the road in the North of England), Trina, and Jim, supplemented by Father Bill and Max, recognised that they would soon have to face up to the degree of structure and form their movement would need to carry Perpetua's message effectively. They agreed that they would wait until September before making any firm decisions. Their immediate task was to consider the way the funerals should be handled.

Trina's wish to remember Miles quietly and her ambitions for Perpetuanism were in direct conflict, but she saw that the worst solution would be compromise, that the funeral of her beloved should either be quiet and dignified or large and somewhat vulgar. She asked what Miles would have wanted and immediately knew that he would want to proclaim, that he had lived proclaiming and died proclaiming, that he had burned with massive, if sometimes misdirected, passion for what was good in the world, that he had discovered late that love was more important than judgment, but that, having learned this, he was faithful to it in his heart, even if he occasionally reverted to his previous type, when he suffered greatly for his lapses. He would want his death to proclaim not himself ,but his belief. Annie, whose relationship with Will had been much less intense than that between Trina and Miles, wanted a public funeral for him because she thought that, on balance, he had earned it. He had gone on filming when many other people would have crawled away. If she had been pushed—and by the Perpetuans she was not—she would have said that Will had behaved atypically in his final hour, but that was all the more reason why he should be celebrated. Bill, on behalf of Dexter, thought that he, too, should be marked as the first leader of the Perpetuans, designated by Perpetua. It was therefore agreed that all three funerals should be public and Annie, not knowing what Will's wishes might be in terms of liturgy, as she had never heard him mention church, said that he should have the same rites as the others as long as Trina and Bill agreed. As to the place, Varnish, in spite of his remorse at the conduct of his son, was determined to keep them out of London's great Christian buildings, but they were rescued by the Dean of Alchester whose agreement with Bishop Hall had led to a highly unusual arrangement in the way the cathedral was used. As was his new practice, the Dean consulted Bishop James on whether he might use the cathedral for the funeral services of the three and the Bishop duly agreed, on the basis that neither he nor the Dean would refuse the other without grave reason. Although James had slipped, rather than stepped, back from what might be described as his Pentecost 'conversion', this did not mean that he would go back on his word to the Dean. The Dean, Father Bill, and Hawthorne held a short teleconference to determine the form of the Service.

1. It would be a Requiem Sacrament of Union
2. The whole Church of England liturgy would stand except that
   a) There would be readings from the Old Testament, New Testament and

Perpetua

b) The Prayer of Consecration would be Perpetuan

c) The Funeral Rite would be joyful and not use "Ashes to ashes, dust to dust".

The Dean would deliver the sermon.

The First Reading, 1 Samuel 2.1-10, was read by Annie, the Second Reading, Luke 1.46-55, was read by Father Bill, and the Third Reading, read by Trina, was a note of part of an early discussion between Perpetua and her followers.

> Recognise dependency on God and each other; see God in everyone; respect and do not exploit God's creation; celebrate difference; imagine the impact before talking and acting; love and do not judge; put compassion before logic; cry in public; find common ground; stand up for principles firmly but gently; give more than we can afford and take what we are offered; never turn our back; never!

The music was to be eclectic, with contributions from the Cathedral Organist and Choir, The BBC Orpheans, a mixed race Gospel choir which Perpetua had once directed during her mission, and Jim.

The cathedral was full more than an hour before the ceremony. Bishop James had decided not to attend, but Doris was there. More than 250 Guides, including Mark, showed the growing strength of the movement. Hawthorne was given a discreet stall in the choir, and there were more than 1,800 people from the new house groups, including Helen, Clement and Violet from Walmbury, and a contingent brought by Wayne from Stumpy Knoll. Downing Street and the Palace had discussed representation but, on balance, agreed that it was not appropriate. The major political parties sent senior figures, but agreed that their Leaders should not attend. Other religious leaders were invited and the Chief Rabbi, a leading Imam and a Sikh priest were present but Varnish demurred. Rory and Olly asked if they could be present, and this was agreed without hesitation by Father Bill. They were worried about undue media attention, but the Dean, the BBC and god4u had reached a mutual agreement on "respectful" coverage.

After the Readings, the Dean said:

> The Christian tradition, from which Perpetuanism springs, in the way that Christianity springs from Judaism, makes me suspicious of the idea of martyrdom. The media have characterised the three friends we have come to celebrate today as 'martyrs', but I wonder. After the deaths of Peter and Paul, about which we know nothing, the Christian tradition has tended to focus not on what the Martyrs died for but how they died. We are presented with drama and heroism, we are encouraged to think about a kind of love which is active. At the Reformation there were 'martyrs', but they tended, in spite of their deep faith in God, a faith whose depth we can only infer from their dying, to suffer for a man-made view of God, a doctrine, a theological metaphor. I do not wish to doubt their worthiness but I suspect that their commitment sprang from a tendency to want others to do

as they did, just in the way that many Christians, exemplified in the recent demonstrations which concluded with the death of our friends, want others to do as they do. Such people think it is proper for them to condemn those who, on the surface, behave less well than they do.

Essentially, Perpetuanism is a pure religious form of civic liberalism. It stands for the creation of space in which others can operate unconditionally. It says "as children of God Our Parent we have a duty to extend to you the freedom to choose". So what happens when people overstep a recognised mark and commit wrongs? First of all, we need to be careful about the word "recognised". All kinds of deeds have been recognised as evil which we now count as good and vice versa. I need not quote examples as you will all have many such in mind. Secondly, even if we can agree on what is wrong—and the exercise is vastly over-rated—what role do we have in putting it right when surely our role is to live and portray love in what we do rather than find shortcomings in others? Thirdly, this is not to deny civic justice, but rather to say that it is inferior to love and that we must not confuse the two.

Dexter, Miles, and Will may have died for God, but it is, I think, more helpful to understand their deaths as living the openness of love which they urged others to pursue. They asked for nothing, they said nothing, they did nothing; they simply left it open to those who confronted them to choose to love. The fact that they chose the opposite should not be our cue to condemn them, but to marvel at the ability of human beings, the children of God Our Parent, to allow such choice. In a sense, to talk about saying nothing is a deeply troubling paradox when language is all we have, and so, having done my best, I leave you with one question which they were too Perpetuan to ask: are we all ready to do what they did?

During the Consecration—concelebrated by all Perpetua's remaining original followers, Father Bill and the Dean—just before Jim raised his glass chalice of sparkling wine, he was aware of the light. Without allowing his hand to shake, he said to Bill, standing next to him, "It's her light, I can see it coming!" They all raised their chalices high in the air as they were bathed in celestial, golden light, bright beyond belief, but not damaging to the eye. The whole congregation wondered at the sight and praised God. The person who had brought this event about, who had fired the three bullets, anonymous in the packed cathedral, saw the light.

After the Sacrament of Union and the funeral prayers the three bodies were to be taken in a modest procession to be buried in a corner of The Hollow acquired by Max from the Partnership as a focus for unity. Max had been reluctant to spend any money on the funeral or to buy the plot of land, as he was trying to build up funds for the Foundation that would pay for his full time people, but he received a large, anonymous donation "for the purposes of the rites and burial of Dexter, Miles, and Will". He suspected Sir Pluto, whom he knew had held a number of private conversations in recent days with Hawthorne, but he had no way of proving this and preferred to let well alone. There were some people lining the streets as the white coffins arrived and left but most people respected the wish of the bereaved that they should participate at home in the rites rather than seeing them as a spectator event.

14.

Trina reviewed all she had learned during her literature studies about the nature of love. It is commonly—but wrongly—supposed today that love is the experience of a combination of emotions rather than commitments or that, at the very least, the former should generate the latter. The idea of commitment is obvious in the case of partnership relationships established to secure the economic well being of parents and children—and albeit female partners and children are often treated worse than males—largely, although not exclusively, associated with 'primitive' economies where the idea of relationship based on emotion can only be a collateral benefit, a situation which has obtained in most places since the dawn of humanity and which still persists among the poor and, perhaps perversely, among the very rich. For such as these, romantic love was and still is a fantasy, a form of escapism or a reality only open to the brave or foolhardy. This is not to say that there are not romantic relationships, born of deep emotion, that develop into mutual commitment nor, on the other hand, is it to say that there are not relationships which are undertaken for the most mundane of reasons which blossom into great romances, but the tendency in Western Europe has been for the 'romantic' to overtake the utilitarian to such an extent that the latter element is often at least consciously ranked lower than the former, notwithstanding our increased consciousness of the subconscious, of the perception that the way we choose partners may depend upon a 'chemistry' which finely calculates the prospects of the birth of children and their survival in the choice of a partner or a double bluff in which we really know, but pretend not to know that two can live cheaper than one. Descending from the unrealistic purity of Dante, what was permitted to the rich on occasion in the Renaissance, if the interests of hereditary estates could be overcome, further 'descended' from the regal and outlandish in Shakespeare to the bourgeois and the brooding in Austen and George Eliot, and on and 'down' into the overwrought speculations of Proust until, at last, 'Romantic' love was buried in the cynical commercialism of Cartland and, finally, subverted in the selfishness of 'soft' pornography. The final 'twist' in the twentieth century 'West' was the possibility of separating sexual pleasure from the risk of pregnancy and, therefore, its separation from any kind of relationship, utilitarian or romantic. Nonetheless, the latter ideal persists in spite of—or is it because of?—the apparent chasm between the expected and actual pleasure derived from monogamous sexual intercourse. No matter how overwrought our escape—extreme in Wagner, mild in Tolkien, and childish in Rowling—we are all, sooner or later, if we are inclined to leave ourselves vulnerable to a partner (usually, although not exclusively, in a heterosexual relationship, with some physical and emotional content) bound either to face or to refuse to face the question of why we are so engaged. No confusion is more fatal to our understanding when we come to face this question than that between emotion and commitment, because the relationship based on emotion expects that the emotion of the lover will be accepted and that the emotion of the beloved will be acceptable, that there will be an 'ideal' reciprocity, the mental and verbal equivalent of the holy grail of the never-ending, simultaneous sexual orgasm, whereas the relationship based on commitment survives on the basis of the steady fulfillment of a promise not based on reciprocity, but rather its reverse, the promise to behave in a certain way in spite of, independent of, the behaviour of the beloved. The emotional paradigm is not only ill founded in its reciprocity, it is fantastic in its expectations, for just as a work of art relies upon the contrast between emotions and perspectives—intensity and relaxation, light and dark, loudness and softness, coldness and warmth, speed and serenity, even cruelty and kindness—so a relationship which hopes to endure cannot do so at a constant level of expectation and fulfillment. Although there are love songs which represent a frame of mind which says, at the breakdown of a relationship, "I am sorry I promised too much or expected too much", the vast majority are condemnatory, accusing the beloved of expecting too much or falling short in satisfying the needs of the lover. For this combination of reasons, what we suppose to be the 'breakdown of love' is no such thing, for there was none to start with. There was, instead, a contractual arrangement to provide mutual pleasure on a compatible and reciprocal basis subject to almost instant termination through a failure of mutuality because of divergent tendencies, a failure of compatibility because the partners began to see past the airy promises or self-deceptions, and a failure of reciprocity because of perceived 'freeloading', or, even more likely, a one-sided intensity, predominantly male, in the need to obtain gratification or 'give' to the other. This is not to say that all such contractual commitments are doomed to fail, but that their emotional basis is necessarily fragile, and they are also intellectually suspect because they regard love as a process in which people give their emotional build-up to the other, whereas true love involves steady giving, regardless of individual preference or the external environment but, paradoxically, it involves, above all—as Perpetua never tired of saying—the constant giving through taking, the creation of space by the lover for the beloved so that love is not the lover's self-expression but the enablement of the beloved's self-expression. There was a strong sense in which Trina felt that romantic love and pornography are almost identical, even though popular culture places them far apart.

Annie's 'love' for Will was of the first sort. She had first met him when he was somewhat lackadaisically compiling his first—indeed the first—Perpetua story in the course of which she was able to cast a professional eye over his shopping trolley and found in its predictable naïveté—bright labels, bogus special offers, exotic ready meals and a modest degree of impulse buying—a degree of charm which excited what is commonly termed her 'maternal instinct', but which might better be thought of as both a wish to 'better' him, first in this particular matter of shopping, but later in other ways, and in doing so to acquire a temporary partner who appeared, on the surface at least, to be malleable. Her own caution and his lack of initiative resulted in a sporadic 'walking out' which only reached intimacy when they agreed to spend a short Easter holiday together in Spain. For his part, Will gradually saw that there might be more joy and less effort in entering a relationship in which both provided the joy of sexual gratification and an escape from the chores of bachelordom than in staying as he was. As is not uncommon in the formation of an intimate relationship merely preceded by occasional visits to restaurants, both found that they had miscalculated. Annie discovered that accommodating the wishes of another and seeking to establish a degree of conformance was more difficult than she had imagined, and Will equally discovered that the pleasure he found in her was not adequately compensated for by the effort required of him. Initially they both found mutual satisfaction in their tentative, makeshift, and hurried sexual encounters, but as her inclination waned, his proportionately waxed, so that the widening difference became a source of friction, and might have resulted in conflict had not their growing joint involvement in the community project not given them a common purpose such that what united them was a mutual commitment rather than an alignment of emotional and physical need. Trina's love for Miles, she thought, on the other hand, was of the second sort. Their first encounters had been mutually suspicious, even hostile, because of their different religious standpoints, each seeing the other as a threat to what they held dear but, as they began to see the virtue in their apparently opposed positions—Trina's lively and Miles' dogged commitment to working unselfishly for a better and fuller physical and spiritual life for others whose concreteness steadily eroded 'doctrinal' positions—they grew reluctantly closer, until the death of Perpetua and her Easter manifestation joined them not only in a shared belief but in a deeply passionate physical relationship which grew out of it. Expecting nothing, wanting nothing but to accommodate the free expression of the other, their emotional and physical drives were enabling rather than projected, such that their satisfaction was not in their own fulfillment, but in that of the other, their encounters being a means to the other's ends rather than ends in themselves. This is not to say that they did not experience differences of approach, of tone, of timbre, but that they had taught themselves to respect and honour these rather than to try to reach a position of uniformity. Their passion was also deepened and quickened by their shared knowledge that their love would almost certainly be short-lived because of Miles' inability to moderate the drivenness of his mission which Trina would not attempt to moderate for the prolongation of their private bliss, for what they had only survived because it resulted from their pact not to inhibit the other which thus, paradoxically in terms of 'common wisdom', resulted in a higher degree of fulfillment than Annie and Will's self-consciously directed efforts at gratification were able to achieve.

The death of the two men did not excite reactions in proportion to the intensity of their relationships. Annie was taken completely by surprise, not only by the event itself, but by the manner of Will's death, for she had seriously under-estimated his commitment to what he was doing, whereas Trina, expecting Miles' unflinching commitment, felt as if it was a culmination rather than a cutting short of his mission. Annie's loss was more intense in itself and also created a sudden and terrible gap in her world, whereas Trina's loss, though intense, was blessed with a sense of a life well lived and nobly ended. The Perpetuans were, if anything, even more solicitous of Annie because of the simple fact of her otherness, they were naturally able to provide Trina with the kind of support which was more easily accommodating to her needs. As the days went by, the situation reversed, partly as a result of the needs of each to come to terms with their personal loneliness, but also partly because of the external perceptions of the roles of their beloveds, for Annie could only bear her loss by building Will's death into an act of heroism in defence of freedom, whereas Trina began to miss Miles' otherness and, as the coverage of the deaths took its course, the initial admiration for Miles' silent witness was eclipsed by a more readily understandable public respect for a defender of media freedom. For a time it did not matter how hard Annie tried to understand Miles's death and how hard Trina tried to value Will's professional heroism. Nor did it matter how hard they tried to ignore the public and their private inclinations to rank the two deaths. It was all beyond them until they came to see that freedom is indivisible, that Miles' belief was unsustainable without Will's concrete commitment and that Will's commitment was unsustainable without Miles' articulation of it, that God's will can only be wrought in the Kingdom through the agents created freely to choose to fulfill it and, in this recognition which eschewed ranking and saw the two deaths as integral, the two women were united in their different commitments to sustain what their loved ones had sustained. This commitment was made stronger by their shared and deepening sadness at the 'relegation' of Dexter from the first 'Martyr' for Perpetuanism to a footnote in a heated 'beauty contest' between Miles, the traditional, English champion of free-spirited religion—albeit in the rather unorthodox form of Perpetuanism—heir to his namesakes (Wycliffe and Coverdale), Tyndale, Cranmer, Parker, Hooker, Jewell, and Andrewes, and Will who stood in the rather more eclectic line of Caxton, Foxe, Smollett, Cobbett, Hazlitt, Dickens, H.L. Mencken, C.P. Scott, Ed Murrow, and the publishers of Oz. There may have been a strong racial element in this downgrading, but there was also a strong imperative on the media in the middle of summer to keep the story going with extensive background pieces, acting as a relieved counterpoint to terrorism and flooding. Consequently, the two women found themselves increasingly turning from their own deceased to a spirited defence of Dexter's primacy as an icon of Perpetuanism. The issue for Trina was somewhat complicated by the fact that, almost as soon as Dexter was buried, pressure began to build for a new leader to be chosen.

Max had been firm from the beginning that he was simply a Chief Executive, a servant of the leadership. Bill regarded himself as a close adviser, appointed by Perpetua to keep a watchful eye on the movement, but not to be an integral part of its leadership. Wayne felt that he had been called to work in the North, away from London, in spite of the difficulties this presented in his relationship with Father Joe. Kylie felt called to work in the countryside of the South and West, but did not feel equipped to lead. Brian was running the vital media operation and thought he was best used in that. Jim was regarded with special reverence because of his ability to see visions and to play music, but he did not feel called to lead. Trina kept reminding them that it was really not a matter of personal preference. They were all committed and the Spirit would call the right person, but it was not difficult to see that almost everyone thought that she was called to lead. The remaining followers met two weeks after the funerals and discussed three initial issues: whether they should expand the leadership, whether they needed a single figure as a leader, and whether the leader should be from the leadership or might come from outside. On the first issue, they immediately accepted the positions of Max and Bill who felt that they were doing the right thing. In principle they were not against expanding the leadership. They had no set number (no twelve Tribes of Israel), but they did feel that a core group of five was not enough. After they had discussed the issue, they prayed, and then unanimously appointed Cara after a long discussion about the effect Perpetua's cure of her disability would have on the way she was perceived. On the one hand, she was a living witness of Perpetua's power to heal, but on the other people might therefore think that she would "say anything". "It's a mistake which politicians make but we must not," said Trina, "to choose what you say not on the basis of what you need to say but on the basis of how it might be misinterpreted. That tendency has almost completely shut down honest political discussion in our country. Politicians can't say anything complex, anything even with a subordinate clause, without being wilfully misinterpreted. We accept that Cara will say what she needs to say because she needs to say it. We will all, including Cara, have to put up with being deliberately and maliciously traduced. Cara has been an inspirational house group leader and that is where we need to put our strength. On the second issue they were deeply divided along gender lines. Bryan and Wayne thought that there should be a single leader ,whereas Cara, Kylie, and Trina thought that they could operate a collective leadership. Jim said he would accept what the others decided. Behind the division there lay fundamental issues which they had begun to face in an unsystematic way. Should there be specific identifiers of Perpetuanism? And, if so, what should they be? Who should decide? They knew that the former Archbishop was working on these issues, but they were anxious to talk through the matters themselves. Wary of recent Christian experience where too much detail had caused division, but too little detail had made it difficult to recognise corporate identity, Bill noted that the system for governing the Roman Catholic Church had, effectively, broken down because the global access to railways and steam ships which eroded localism had coincided with the incomplete work of the First Vatican council, with the result that the Papacy had seized central power beyond that which the Council had intended, and had used it to obliterate localism and impose a standard ethical code, regardless of culture, which had resulted in a flight from faith. Congregationalist groups, however, seemed to do well. There had been a minor, and at the time much exaggerated, corrective in the Second Vatican Council, but that itself had been corrected. "The Papacy of John Paul II, about to be made a Saint, was a disaster. He may have been good for the world and he certainly travelled enough, but he was less good for inter-faith dialogue where little progress was made, less good still for ecumenism, and least good for his own Church where child abuse induced cover-up before heart searching. Rome is killing itself by ranking clerical discipline—the marriage of clergy, the admission of women to ordained Ministry—as more important than access to the life nourishment of the Eucharist. So we have to guard against over-regulation. On the other hand," Bill went on, "the situation where there is hardly any definition makes it difficult for people to relate to an organisation. If you look at Anglicanism you have the Evangelical equivalent of Papal fine tuning at one end of the spectrum over an issue like homosexuality and, at the other end, there are people who would prefer there to be no definition of Anglicanism at all, just to use it as a convenient umbrella, as ordinary people do when they fill in their hospital form, or as godparents make promises at Baptism they do not understand and have no means of keeping. Perpetuanism must not be miasmic spiritualism, it must cultivate the relationship between each one of us and God Our Parent, and people who are not interested in trying to do that should not be counted among us. There is no sense in the English dismissive aphorism, 'I don't need to go to church to be a Christian'. Yes, if you're a a Christian, you do, and you have to work at your relationship with God, individually and collectively, to be a Perpetuan." Warned by this, they came to the following broad conclusions which they agreed to submit to the whole Perpetuan body.

1. Doctrine is a means to relationship. The purpose of Perpetuanism is to enable every human to establish and maintain, broaden and deepen his or her personal relationship with God Our Parent, through the Grace proclaimed by Jesus and Perpetua, and in the power of the Spirit.
2. Identifiers should be few and vital. Perpetuanism's emphasis on the personal nonetheless requires a corporate core of identifiers, but these should be kept to an absolute minimum, to the nature of Godhead and Sacramental communication.
3. Text is a means to relationship. A list of texts in which the Godhead had spoken, initially from the Jewish, Christian, and Perpetuan traditions, but not necessarily indefinitely confined to that corpus, should be drawn up.

4. Welcome does not assume commitment. Anybody can take part in Perpetuan house groups or sacramental worship without any person asking any questions of them but, this would not make them Perpetuans per se, for which they would need to affirm a basic set of beliefs concerning Godhead and Sacramentality.

5. General principles and individual behaviour are not to be related. Under no circumstances would Perpetuanism confuse the establishment of wise, general ethical principles with individual behaviour. The Perpetuan ethic is to enable not to impose. Personal behaviour is entirely a matter between the individual and the Godhead although, naturally, there is a parallel, but 'inferior', civic justice process which Perpetuans will respect.

6. The Spirit will inform consensus. Whichever group or body emerges to make further decisions, it should be consensual. Under no circumstances should there be any voting.

7. Membership is a guarantee of equal involvement. Until such time as the movement makes this unmanageable, all major decisions shall be taken by all those registered with a Perpetuan house group.

Having reached these conclusions with very little friction, they returned to the leadership question. Max said, "It seems to me that we have a central issue to face. In the history of religion, there has been some argument about doctrine—Nicea, Chalcedon, that sort of thing—but because theology—metaphors about God—is so difficult, religions have tended to have their major, passionate, even bloody arguments, about power and discipline, not because human beings are wicked, but because this is one way they have of trying to get to grips with the big issues. They can't write a Creed, but they can write a rule book about liturgy or governance. We must try to avoid this mistake and give all our effort to struggling with the God metaphors. On that basis, leadership should be less important to us than it is to others." "So should we choose a leader at all and, if we should, then should it be us or the whole house group membership?" asked Bryan. "You have to distinguish between two kinds of leader," said Max. "I think we are choosing a leader to lead us in what we do on a day-to-day basis, like a Chairman of the Board. We're not choosing somebody like the President of the United States. It's an important distinction. If you want a President-type figure, then it should be the whole membership, but I don't think Perpetuanism wants that kind of leadership. We want the groups to function as the key entities, looking to their Guides for co-ordination. I think we just want somebody to help the core group function effectively." This discussion naturally led into the third area, whether the leader should be from among them or come from outside. "I think," said Max, "this relates to what I've just said. If you wanted a Presidential figure it might come from anybody in the Membership, but to hold us together I think we need one of us, not counting Bill and me." Bill said, "I think that it should be one of you. For as long as there is one who worked alongside Perpetua, who is a witness who can testify, such a person should lead us." Everyone looked at Trina, who said, "But I would not want to do the job because I'm the widow of our first martyr. I am not worthy in my own right." Jim said: "There's a light round Trina."

Nobody spoke. They prayed in silence. Then the four who had walked with Perpetua—Bryan, Jim, Kylie, and Wayne—laid their hands on her head. They then laid hands on Cara.

In spite of the changing media and public perceptions of the 'martyrdoms', the trend of adherence to Perpetuanism rose in such a steep curve that within two weeks of Trina's acceptance of leadership, the movement was facing a new theological crisis. Was it a movement or was it a church? The initial intention had been that anybody could participate, but only those who adhered to certain basic principles could call themselves Perpetuans. On the basis of their accepted practice, Perpetuans would simply take the acceptance of others on trust, but it became clear that this 'pure' form of trust was not going to work. A broad movement of people in support of a cause, such as the Green Alliance, did not need any kind of creed or organisation—as long as people were all moving in roughly the same direction, that was fine—but a movement that needed to design helpful metaphors for the Godhead, teach these, provide Sacramental focus, define Scripture, and organise mutual learning, support, and worship, could not pretend to be merely a movement. It passed the church test: it looked like a church and it did what a church does, so it must be a church. Again, the division on this topic ran along gender lines, the men favouring the idea of a church and the women favouring the idea of a movement. Jim settled the argument by saying, "I want to be in a family not a coalition. I can't live without a family. Perpetuanism is a family. It meets in small bits in houses and it meets in bigger bits in what were churches to celebrate. I can come to grips with that. I don't want us to use words that are semi-secret, that keep other people out—I hated it when they used Latin and Greek in church when I was at primary school—but you need a sense of being safe, of sharing communication. This movement means that anybody can say they belong." "And you can't build organisations simply to prevent the excesses of others," said Kylie. "You can," said Max. "It isn't defensive to choose something that is like a church rather than a movement. It calls for commitments beyond slogans. Movements are full of slogans, churches should be full of commitments. Movements always want somebody else to do it. Churches promise to do it themselves." "I think you have convinced me," said Kylie, "but this is where we need to go to our rapidly expanding family of house groups, so we will draw up what we have said and see how they respond. If the decision is evenly or near evenly split, we will call everyone together, but if there is a broad consensus, we will live with that." This was only the first of many discussions of this sort. The leaders did not, first of all, want to be leaders, and they certainly did not want to spend most of their time on organisation and doctrine because of their fundamental commitment to developing relationship—there was a hard 'Protestant' kernel at the centre of their 'Catholic' Sacramentality—but they felt forced to give some shape to their mission.

As time went by, it became ever more difficult to resist humanity's need for shape, pattern recognition, solid objects to make faith concrete, hierarchy and a degree of leadership, but there was also the less admirable wish of some to absorb the benefits of Perpetuanism without making any effort. The leadership's response was to lay even greater emphasis on the autonomy of the house groups where, it hoped, there would be less concern with the devotional and 'political' trappings of religion and more concern with its pure expression. Even here, things began to go wrong, for the people, so full with hope after Dexter's silent death, hoped that something would come of it of benefit to themselves. They began to pray, not only to Perpetua and the other 'persons' of the Godhead, but also to Dexter whose death, unlike Perpetua's, they had seen on DVD time and again. Posters of Dexter began to appear in Grunge Park and, as was the custom of the times since the death of Princess Diana, they began to bring flowers, hand-made cards, children's drawings, teddy bears, football scarves, and other objects which were all, with the exception of the flowers, strangely childish, to where he had fallen. There was a modest counter movement to celebrate Miles, but he had never been 'truly' one of them, always an outsider, always a little forbidding, always ready to point out their faults. Dexter had grown up with them, he was one of their own. In vain did Cara, Father Bill, and other group leaders appeal to them to remember the higher purpose to which Perpetua had called them. They were poor, alienated and, perhaps because of, rather than in spite of, Dexter's death, they felt that 'society' was against them. The need for special people—saints and martyrs—to act as intermediaries was soon followed by a craving for solid objects so that, in a strange echo of St Helena, they petitioned the Home Office for the bullet which had killed Dexter. The final leg of this devotional stool was the growing tendency for all prayer to become intercessory so that what had begun as open prayer-times, where God was thanked and praised and was offered penitence, rapidly deteriorated into a monopoly and a monotony of lists of grievances and illnesses. Within the remarkably short time of twelve weeks, Perpetuanism showed every sign of developing a popular devotional stance which it had taken Christianity 1,200 years to realise. Father Bill passed from house group to house group trying to damp down what he thought was not terribly harmful in itself, but was, in its emptiness, bound to fail to deliver any results while, in the meantime, people were failing to develop true communication with the Godhead. He said, "You can understand why people find an abstract idea of God difficult to deal with, which is why people have always built altars or founded shrines. People, being both spiritual and physical, want their spiritual entities to be bound up in the physical. That is why Christianity was so unique in having Jesus who was both God and Man. The Jews and the Muslims have to struggle with the abstract which is so difficult for them, but look how brave they are. Without a figure like Jesus, they have steered clear of hierarchies, a plurality of holy places, intermediaries we call saints and the massive cultural and emotional baggage which Christianity now carries. In spite of Jesus, Christians adopted Pagan holy places so that many now claim that although God is everywhere, the sacred presence is stronger in this place or that—in a church, at a shrine—and then there are the saints and the statues and the candles. So Christianity 'sold out' in many ways to the pagans when it should have centred on the Godhead in human form in Jesus. Even the birth of Jesus was pasted over a pagan festival and it has now become the most horrible pagan festival there is. Now that was all bad enough, but the Godhead 'realising' what was happening, that after almost 2,000 years we were finding it more and more difficult to live Jesus in our psyches—after all, it is difficult for us to imagine ourselves into first century Palestine, the Judaism, the culture, the Romans, the agricultural practises—sent Perpetua to us as the Sustainer. You know me, you know I've always been mild mannered and tolerant, thinking it best to listen and leave people to learn their own lessons on the basis that most people are their own strictest task masters—well, in the long run—but I have to tell you how disappointed I am that so soon after the death of Perpetua, sent to revive your relationship with the Godhead, you are plunging back into the kind of idolatry and selfishness which her life came to deny."

Fidel had been animated by Cara's new position in Perpetuanism, but his enthusiasm was mixed with a jealousy so deep that he hardly recognised it in himself. Shortly after she had become one of the leaders, he said that he had had a vision in the night in which Perpetua had told him to launch a massive healing campaign, to put right the wrongs of Her people. This sounded inauthentic to Cara and her sisters and brothers because Perpetua had always advocated people being helped to make their own free choices—she had only healed intermittently and for very specific reasons—but they found it difficult to make any outright statement against Fidel, trusting that the Spirit would resolve the issue. Meanwhile, Fidel began to plan a major campaign, convinced that he had the power to change the world. He recruited Rick to write and execute his business plan so that he was soon selling all kinds of merchandise both to finance and promote "The Perpetual Cure", not only the usual car stickers, t-shirts, lapel badges, bags, note pads, and hats with images of Dexter, but also statues of Perpetua with luminous paint or internal lights and silver plated replicas of the Dexter bullet. As his personality became more extrovert and individual, Max began to worry that he was not only obscuring but actually subverting the Perpetuan vision. There was no way of exercising any influence over him. Cara and the others saw the danger of what he was doing and tried to persuade him to slow down at least, but nobody claimed any authority over him. He was exercising choice—that is what he was here to do.

With an energy born of the fortunate combination of the love of an occasion and the prospect that it will advance a person and a benevolent objective, the organisation of Perpetual Cure expanded beyond any kind of structural control so that all over the country people claimed to have seen visions and to be the disciples of Fidel who had, in turn, been specially chosen by Perpetua to carry on her healing work. Little notice was taken of the Perpetuan response that this was both theologically contrary to her wishes but also that there was no evidence for the assertion that Fidel had been in any way specially chosen: he had been cured of blindness by Perpetua and had, with her encouragement, founded a social club in Grunge Park which had slowly metamorphosed into a Perpetuan House Group. They would not condemn him but they could point out the weaknesses in his case. His strongest follower was Steve in Stumpy Knoll who claimed that he too had healing powers which would be realised on the great day of Perpetual Cure. They were joined by a bewildering variety of spiritualists and mystics who registered to take part in the national simultaneous Perpetual Cure. Not surprisingly, the extravagant claims of Fidel, Steve, and their self-appointed colleagues, attracted great attention but very little scrutiny, for whereas Perpetua had always performed her special acts without warning, leaving the media to find out about them often weeks after they had taken place, and whereas she had on many occasions arranged matters so that what she had done was not traceable, Fidel was offering advanced billing and the opportunity for a great build-up. At the same time, competition operated in favour of exaggeration and against investigation where the reverse would have been the case if the story was only covered by one or two outlets. What might have objectively been thought an unlikely, if not preposterous, collection of instant healers, was treated with adulation. Nor was the concept of instant healing greeted with customary scepticism, if not cynicism; it was a repetition of the familiar phenomenon of the degree to which it is possible to forget individual and collective history. Followers such as the psychic twins and the snake charmer were particularly popular among photographers, but the whole troupe were uncritically proclaimed as if Dexter had never existed, let alone been killed in silent defence of his mission. At the same time, the weather was appalling, causing terrible floods, the threat of terrorism hung heavy, the Prime Minister did not know how to smile, and it looked as if England might not qualify for the European Cup finals and so a little cheer was needed, if only to make the darkness darker. Sneer, beyond challenge now that Will was dead, claimed to have had a special relationship with Perpetua in which she had "exclusively" revealed to him—again the unlikelihood seemed to strike nobody—that her vision would be realised in mass healing and the peaceful establishment by her followers of universal social justice. As the day approached, Fidel found himself pressed ever harder to solidify his promises. He had first said that he would cure many people, but, as he was pressed harder, this became thousands, and when he was finally asked whether he would cure some people and not others he said, "All will be cured". This promise led to an extraordinary outpouring of optimism and wherever Fidel's followers proclaimed themselves, plans were made for the great day of Perpetual Cure.

Without wishing to cast any doubts on Fidel's claims—the Spirit, after all, might be with him and they might somehow have misunderstood Perpetua— the task of Trina and her colleagues was to seek to distance Perpetuanism from the frenzy. "If Fidel and his people are genuine and they perform mass healing and find some way of achieving violence free, universal social justice, we will have to examine what Perpetuanism means in the light of these developments, but I am convinced that she was against all such activities as they propose. What we must do is see that people are helped when their hopes are dashed, and if we are to be credible helpers we must ensure that we are separated from them. I am therefore forced to the conclusion that while we do not condemn them, we will have to be very firm that we are not part of this and that, indeed, our theology is contrary to what Fidel and his people say." They made very difficult headway although there was a strand of media coverage which could make use of a certain degree of de-bunking amid the hysteria.

Trina managed to establish some form of differentiation in the minds of most of the major media groups and was particularly grateful to Ranjit who, as usual, gave due weight to what she said without committing himself to any side. "It must be admitted that in spite of the interesting use of 'Perpetual' for 'Perpetuan' and the use of the word 'cure' in a purely medical, as opposed to a spiritual, sense, the prospect of a massive medical and social 'fix' seems very distant from the Perpetuan emphasis on the freedom of choice and the centrality of self-affirmation."

The financial expertise of Rick and the technological expertise of Steve ensured that there was national television coverage of the great day, with Fidel's mass rally in London's Royal Park and Steve's mass rally in Grimsdike Park being shown on split screens. The two events proceeded with the slightly chaotic inevitability of major rock concerts. They began late, the introductions were too long, the technology did not work as smoothly as it should, and the music was too loud, but the vast crowds were enthusiastic. In spite of their better judgments, hundreds of thousands of loved ones and carers had come with sick relatives and friends in the hope of a cure, and many longed to hear how a world of justice might be brought about. Both Fidel and Steve said that the bigger justice movement would come once they had shown that they had powers which could not be ignored. What they did in the short term would have a massive effect on long-term social policy. Perpetua said—and in this they were correct, according to the strict letter—you could not ask others to do anything if you were not prepared to start the process yourself.

At 3 p.m. on that showery Saturday afternoon in early August 2007, there was complete silence at a series of mass rallies involving more than one and a half million people. Fidel said, "In the name of the Godhead who sent Perpetua to be among us as God's Sacred Vessel, the Sustainer, and in whose name I am acting now, in the name of the Godhead, I pronounce all those here who are ill in mind or body to be cured."

Silence.

Then there was a spluttering of applause; and silence.

From out of the London crowd a terrible cry pierced the silence. "Mum! nothing's happened!" Just beginning to worry, Fidel said, "Wait a moment, the impact will not be instant", but a seed of doubt had been sown. The cameras began to home in on those more obviously in search of a cure, particularly children in wheelchairs. Almost a minute passed and a cry broke the silence in Grimsdike: "It's not working!"

Steve, who was perhaps less secure than Fidel in the depth of his vision, or perhaps more alive to the dangers of failure, turned his back as if he was looking for something and, before anybody had caught on, he had disappeared behind the platform and made off taking, it turned out later, the substantial but un-recorded remainder of the campaign funds. Fidel, who had either persuaded himself to believe his vision, or who did not have the presence of mind of Steve, stood rooted to the spot, waiting for something to happen. It did. People began to throw things at him and in less than half a minute the expectant calm of Royal Park had turned into mass rage. The last thing Max wanted was to be seen with Fidel but, equally, the outcome he had been planning was to ensure that Fidel would not become another 'martyr', clouding issues yet further. Accordingly, he had hired four highly skilled security men who had once worked at his bank to ensure that Fidel came to no serious harm. As soon as people began throwing things, the four men moved purposefully onto the stage and, in one co-ordinated move, lifted him and carried him away. The assault on the empty space went on for a short time, but people soon began to disperse, angry and disappointed.

As he sat watching the disintegration of the Perpetual Cure, Varnish saw day-light for the first time. Since his nomination, he had been in a state of profound unhappiness from the twin causes of his son's foolish and irresponsible—some of his clerical friends would have said 'sinful'—behaviour and the refusal of the new Prime Minister to forward his name to Her Majesty. This was unfair be-cause he could not be held responsible for the behaviour of his adult son, but the two issues had become entwined because Mr Brown did not want to be seen endorsing the installation in Canterbury of a man whose son had narrowly es-caped a charge of murdering an inspirational religious leader. The issues might have seemed separate to Varnish, but in an environment of such suspicion that "conflict of interest" had become an issue in public life almost matching "risk" and "health and safety", the father and son were deeply suspect. Varnish was appalled and angry that one newspaper went so far as to imply that his son had been acting on his behalf, but as he watched the split screen he knew, although he was much more of a legalist tactician than a political strategist, that he had a chance of survival. If, as seemed likely, the Perpetuans were tarred with the same brush as the Perpetuals, then he could hope to see out the crisis.

"I don't like the idea of 'right'," said Trina late that night, "but to be, let us say, consistent and maintain integrity is not enough in this world of mass communi-cations. If we want to win people for God we must at the very least get our own message through while—and this is the difficult part—trying not to be drawn into comments on the beliefs and behaviour of other specific groups and people. Of course we must talk about justice, but be careful to separate the idea from those we are asked to condemn as unjust." "You have said all that before," said Max, looking worried, "but being 'right'—forgive me—about this does not make it any easier for us to succeed. I know, too, that we are to trust in the Spirit, but that does not mean passivity. We are to use the brains we have been given and, as long as we preserve integrity, we should do our best. After all, using the media is just a different kind of preaching." Cara came in. "How is Fidel?" asked Trina. "Suicidal. I hardly dare leave him, but Father Bill is with him at the moment. I have come to resign from any leadership position." "There are three reasons why I do not think you should do that, Cara," said Trina. "Firstly, you were chosen by us all and we have faith in your integrity. Secondly, whatever Fidel's mistake, it is not your mistake and we must break this damaging assumption that we are somehow responsible for the decisions of adults close to us when we are only responsible for listening and giving the best advice we can on matters of principle. We cannot tell people what they must do and, although you might have told Fidel that what he said did not align with Perpetua's mission, you could not know whether he really did have a vision that was driving him. Thirdly, it would help us—and I put it no more emphatically than that—if we could separate the activities of individuals like Fidel from the forward progress of the movement. However—before you speak—our primary concern is with Fidel himself, not with all these quasi-political ramifications. I grow so weary that we have to be so political. I suppose the Apostles were 'political' after the Ascension, it's just that they never use the word specifically." "I accept what you say. I have to because I was chosen by you all." "I think that you should make sure, with Max's help, that the campaign is closed down in good order, and that the money matters are sorted. Then perhaps you might want to go away with Fidel on a retreat. Whatever happens, the relationship you have with him is more important than the complications that might cause in the public perception of the relationship between Perpetuanism and Perpetualism."

The leadership decided on the simple device, used so often in secular crises, of settling on a simple message and delivering it politely but firmly. They would not be drawn on individual cases, and if they were misled before interviews they would persist with their line. If they were accordingly accused of being dishonest they would be entitled to quote the terms on which they were invited to speak. The line was: "Perpetuans believe in individual and collective choice grounded in solidarity and not competition. Perpetua occasionally performed signs, not to change the world, but to demonstrate the power of God in Her." This did not go down at all well on an individual basis, but it made its way into the collective consciousness and the combination of consistency—being 'on message'—and a general febrility which induced boredom, soon caused the Perpetualist memory to fade.

There was, however, one relic which could not be so readily dismissed, and that was the relic itself. The Dexter Silver Bullet had caught on, as had, to a lesser extent, the Perpetua luminous statue. Long after the falsehood of the Perpetual claims was exposed, people still wanted a physical memento to look at or carry. The 'purist' message of Perpetua, which her own presence had sought to purify, had already, to a very minor degree, been adulterated, suggesting that creatures created to choose cannot survive in the ecology of purity which, in essence, denies choice. As Max had already put it, there was nothing wrong with human beings behaving like human beings, they would always reach for the supernatural, but their means would often be analogous, metaphorical or verging on the idolatrous.

As the nights began to draw in, the house groups settled down on the run-in towards Christmas. Cara returned from a short retreat with Fidel to lead the movement and Fidel and Rick joined Max to help with finance as they all recognised that Fidel should have a back office role and be protected from himself and his detractors. Steve disappeared, and the other 'healers' faded back into their communities, footnotes in the Perpetuan drama. The key task was to build up a knowledge of what Perpetua had said and done and to separate this from the already exploding mish-mash of material on the internet, emphasising the centrality of choice and moving people away from Utopian politics or magic bullets. Progress was enormously helped by Father Joe, who had finally wrested himself into superiority over his previously unquestioned traditions, and who was readily accepted as a Guide. His Pastoral skills and clear theological training were wonderfully helpful at untangling knots, and there were some substantial knots to be untangled as the established Church launched an offensive to try to recapture some ground from its latest rival, for Varnish's position had finally been confirmed by the Prime Minister.

Varnish, as has already been noted, was no theologian, but he was a highly skilled tactician. He had no over-arching vision of how the Church of England or the Anglican Communion should be—indeed, he would have found it very difficult to formulate the problem, let alone respond to it—but he was acutely aware that the advantage was with him. He therefore held a meeting with Cardinal Podric during which they agreed to launch a joint offensive against Perpetuanism, claiming that it was a licence for licence: that the notion of humanity being created solely for the purpose of exercising the choice to love was a travesty of the true human condition; that imperfection was not a necessary precondition for choice but the reality of human weakness and sinfulness; that Jesus had not been "casual" about what happened after his Ascension but had been highly specific about the foundation of a structured church (although at this point discussion tailed off in embarrassment about the nature of that church and the source of its authority; and, finally, that only the (undefined) church could assent to developments in the theological understanding of God. The two men might disagree how the authority should be split between them but they were united in believing that they somehow jointly held the duopoly. Varnish was a little mystified by this, as he was vaguely aware of other claims, but he thought it best to keep matters simple. After all, the Greek Orthodox Church was not being forced to deal with Perpetuanism. Their greatest miscalculation, however, was not ecclesiological but anachronistic, for they failed to estimate highly enough the power of love and the power of choice bound up in the concept of the freedom to love, understanding this expression not at its face value but, rather, only seeing its corollary, that Perpetuans were accepting evil by saying that it was an inevitable consequence of choice. It was therefore not long before "FREE TO

HATE" was featured on web and graffiti sites. Driven by the potential damage this would do to alienated communities, and risking being understood only to care about Perpetuanism as a movement, Trina made contact with Cardinal Podric, rightly assessing that no matter how hostile he might be, he would at least understand what she was saying more fully than Varnish. They met in an externally nondescript, but internally luxurious little house near the canal, arranged by Max, but later, it turned out, courtesy of Sir Pluto. As their discussions broke down, there was no joint statement, but The Stylus account and Trina's notes agree on all the major points with Cardinal Podric's, sent to the Vatican.

Trina opened by saying that even if the Roman Catholic Church was hostile in the extreme to the Perpetuan movement, it should not cynically—she was sorry to have to use the word—and falsely accuse the Perpetuans of tolerating, or even promoting, hate. The freedom to love, which was supposedly integral to the Roman Catholic understanding of the notion of the exercise of the 'informed conscience', implied the capacity of human beings to choose not to love. The Catholic mechanism for dealing with this was penitence. Perpetuans believed in all of the aspects of Roman Catholicism mentioned so far but differed only in this, that although the relationship between the Godhead and humanity should be mediated through a corporate institution, this should not be a self-perpetuating, male hierarchy but, in fact, no hierarchy at all. As usual, the Roman Catholic Church was picking a quarrel over authority and discipline under the guise of theology. Podric replied that Perpetuans had misunderstood Catholicism and, by virtue of that, had misunderstood the nature of the Godhead. Christians did not have the "freedom to love" but, rather, had been given the grace to love and, although they were exercising their conscience in making choices, they were always likely to abuse their freedom and must on that account be checked by a Church which had the power to bind and loose. Trina gently interposed at this point that "The Church" might or might not have such answers, but in any case the Church was not the same thing as the male hierarchy of the Roman Catholic Church. Properly understood, the Church was all God's people. Podric, who gave way gracefully to this intervention without commenting on it, continued by saying that the Perpetuan paradigm was one-sided, all freedom to love and no checks on licence, thus it was no exaggeration to say that it was advocating the freedom to hate. Trina replied that even if he was right in everything he had said, the Cardinal should be careful of saying that Perpetuans advocated the freedom to hate because many would quote his authority in prosecuting hate campaigns. Did she look as if she advocated hate? The Cardinal replied courteously that of course it did not look like that, but that was the human problem. All kinds of apparently nice people committed all kinds of wickedness. Individually, Trina and her followers might mean the best, but their model of the holy life was inviting abuse. Trina again pleaded that whatever their theological differences, they needed to be able to unite in promoting community and individual calm, and that this was more important than theology. Podric relied that there were many issues which might be thought more important than theology, but theology was the Church's core business than which nothing was more important, and that, consequently, it could not compromise. Whatever the virtues of Perpetuan socio-economic policies—and the Roman Church was committed to the promotion of the Common Good in spite of crude Marxist criticisms— this was absolutely subservient to theological orthodoxy and that, therefore, in any case of conflict, it was the orthodoxy which must prevail. He was sorry if the Church's clear stance might be taken to mean that it supported the "freedom to hate", but it was clear that it supported precisely the opposite. Trina said that she understood what the Cardinal and his colleagues supported—she would not be partisan and crude enough to accuse them of supporting any act of hatred—but accusing her and her followers of somehow supporting hate would lead to some people then citing Perpetuanism as an authority for hatred. This was dangerous, particularly in alienated and highly charged communities. The Cardinal said this was an exceedingly tortuous piece of logic and he preferred to leave matters as they were.

As it turned out, the Perpetuans were not cast in the unlikely role of supporting hatred, but the dialogue warned them that it did not matter how simple their message, it would be misunderstood. They were trapped in the familiar 'no win' situation that they were accused of either over-simplifying or over-complicating. They could never get it right and, with her experience, Trina was not going to waste much effort trying.

In spite of her involvement in a wide variety of issues which had never engaged her deeply—she occasionally wondered how fishermen managed the Council of Jerusalem, even with the Holy Spirit—including getting used to herself as the subject of media attention, what occupied her most intensely was her reaction to Miles' death and caring for Annie. As the weeks went by, she slowly became accustomed to the emptiness of her bed—after all, for most of her life it had been like that—and even to the emptiness in her heart, but these spaces were steadily filled with a deep resentment that the death of Miles had been overlooked, that because of Dexter's leadership on the one hand and Will's journalism on the other, they had alternated in popularity while poor Miles, who had died as bravely—perhaps even more bravely as he had deliberately stepped, so to speak, into Dexter's dead shoes—and as completely as they had, had almost been forgotten. She was not jealous of Dexter or Will and she found it easy to listen to Annie talking about him, even when she was idealising, because she firmly believed that this was not a zero-sum game. She did not want the other two men recognised less, she just wanted Miles to be recognised more. Her resentment had to be ruthlessly controlled because her primary outlets were her close followers and the media. In the case of the former, she was still trying to dampen down the idolatrous streak that had so rapidly worked its way into the movement and she therefore dared not mention Miles in case this was misinterpreted as her recognition of the cult of the martyr. In the case of the latter she did not wish to alienate through resentment or use up her small store of credits by pursuing her own agenda, but when, quite unexpectedly, Miles was attacked, she hit back spontaneously and devastatingly which, she realised later, did her and her cause immense good. Self-restraint was not always the answer.

It started out as a simple enough interview on Bad Morning with Craig Knocker. As it was Saturday, the pressure was off. Craig asked her in his gentle, persuasive way, so much more effective than Owen Grumpy's hectoring, how the movement was getting on. "Some people are saying that you have not done as well as you expected." "First of all, who are these people? And, even if you can name them, how competent are they to say anything? Or are you using the phrase 'some people' simply to give some kind of credibility to your own abstract argument? Secondly, as I have said nothing, how can anybody know whether what has happened is better or worse than what I expected, as they don't know what I expected or even, indeed, if I expected anything. If I did expect something, they can hardly know whether my expectations were couched in quantitative terms—the number of followers—or qualitative terms—the depth of belief and/or commitment of the followers—or whether there was no measurement at all, but simply a feeling of expectation." "Goodness gracious, for the representative of an organisation based on love, that was a bit harsh." "If I love people it does not mean that I must admire their sloppy thinking. I presume the argument you wished to put to me on the public's behalf was something like, 'You should be doing better'." "Yes, something like that." "Always supposing, as I have said, that anybody can define 'better'. This is not game playing, it becomes important when so-called 'experts' forecast sudden surges which do not take place and then forecast sudden collapses, it plays with the emotions of people who need to understand the world they live in instead of being constantly frightened by it." "Turning away from the philosophical arguments for a moment, you surely have to admit that things could be going better for you." "You are beginning to make us sound like a political party suffering in the opinion polls or a retailer having a down turn in sales. In a sense which is ultimately meaningless because it is so general, we could all be doing better at all manner of things. What you want me to imply—and if I don't you will—is that we are failing in some way, that we are not reaching expectations set by you, your colleagues or even by me. The problem with this way of looking at things is that it is all 'front loaded' with journalists making predictions which are almost certain to end in disappointment, so that they can declare something a failure. Next, you only focus on what goes wrong, so that people form a false picture of the world. Thirdly, you only report during what you think of as a crisis, so that we are all full of unfinished stories. It is like book marking all the world's novels about two-thirds of the way through at their deepest crises and never finishing any of them." "Is the problem that your leadership team just isn't talented enough? I mean, you are the only graduate." "Now the classic, but somewhat silly reply to that question, is that none of Jesus' disciples were graduates, but they all seemed to do pretty well. There is also the argument that anti-intellectual Britons like to say that some people who have not gone to university have done very well, but the real answer to your question is that it does not matter in the least. Perpetua chose shelf stackers from Hypo of which I was one, and although we will do our best to talk clearly and simply, we rely, ultimately, on the Spirit." "I am somewhat reluctant to go there; but I do want to ask what you think now about the apparently pointless death of your then partner, Miles Wycliffe?" "How shameful. 'Apparently' is a fig leaf, and I have not had any partners since nor, for that matter, did I have any before Miles. You agreed, at my request, that we would not discuss him, but you have gone back on your word. So let me tell you about Miles in simple words which I hope are beyond cynical twisting. No, you have had your say, over and over. Every day you take words and do violence to them, using them as weapons instead of as tools for understanding. I will speak ... Miles worked in Grunge Park when nobody cared, and he went on working without recognition when the place was teeming with New Labour initiatives. He went on working when all the quick fixes and short-term funding faded away, and he went on working even though he hated being there. He didn't like the people very much, and he was frightened of them, but he loved them. That first took the form of trying to improve their behaviour, the kind of approach often adopted by anxious parents, but under the influence of Perpetua, he just knew he had to love them and make a proper distinction between what we generally accept as good behaviour on the one hand and individual behaviour on the other. That leads me to your sententious suggestion that Miles' death was, to use your own word, 'pointless'. How would you know? How, even, would I know? I am generally an admirer of passive resistance to violence because I am a general admirer, as I have just said in different words, of non-intervention with individual acts, but my general admiration for the behaviour Miles adopted does not lead me to conclude that his behaviour was more or less admirable or had more or less of a point to it than that of others. You tend to generalise on outcome, put less emphasis on motive and, because it is impossible for you, you have to dispense with any notion of seeing any individual act in its life context, which means that all your judgments are seriously flawed. You should know this from the periodic release of archived documents." "Well, that is taking us down a completely different avenue, so let me come back to the main point. Any objective person would have to conclude that Perpetuanism is finished. It has had a brief and glorious period of recognition, but it is on the wane." "I think if you could define what constitutes 'objective' your question might have more validity, but in a way that language cannot deal with easily, the only person who has all the data, who can be really objective, is God Our Parent. The earthly 'objective' view on Good Friday would surely have been that the Jesus movement was dead. Two thousand years later we can see that that was incorrect. Now, within months of the death and re-manifestation of Perpetua, we will work as God's agents and trust in the Spirit." "And are you thinking of making Miles, Dexter, and Will into saints?" "How old fashioned! Miles wasn't a saint, and isn't a saint in the earthly sense, but I am sure he has been enfolded back into the perfect love of the Creator. He doesn't need our labels. We will remember him with affection, and remember his example with awe, but as all of humanity returns into the being of

God, it would be inaccurate to imply that some people who die enjoy that state and others do not." "Are you saying that even mass murderers go to heaven?" "I am saying—and in a strange way this is a variant on extreme Protestantism, but one which its adherents would oppose—that we were created to choose to love and that that involves imperfection—you have heard this often enough before but it seems to need repeating—and that God would create nothing which was not destined, after fulfilling its offering of freely returned love—no matter how feeble its external appearance—to be enfolded back into that perfect love. This has nothing to do with behaviour, but with the struggle to choose to love. I think that Christianity's fundamental error, its departure from Jesus, was to think that love means behaving well or even sacrificially. These are admirable ethical qualities without which society cannot function, but love imposes an additional demand to these virtues, that we enable regardless of outcome because we are not God's law makers." "On that remarkable note, we will have to leave it there."

15.

Being a Cambridge history graduate, Horace Strider knew all about historiographical landscapes and had determined that there were, in essence, only two kinds of history: the macrocosmic, grand and blurred; and the microcosmic, mundane and clear. Although the latter provided some essential detail and, over time, some necessary correctives to the former, it should never be allowed to overwhelm it, rendering it incapable of providing the broad sweeps necessary for collective survival. The re-writing of history was a necessary social function which allowed cultures—and at this particular moment in history—nations to survive in spite of their own folly, the folly of others, and the arbitrary mishaps of nature. He also recognised that this collective necessity was reflected in family and personal histories. His father had changed his name from Streiter to Strider when he was brought to England in 1938, and his own Christening in an Anglican church as Horace was a deliberate calculation, a radical departure from the family line of Cologne Jewish antique dealers, but not so strikingly English as Horatio. Horace was more aware of his family history than most of his contemporary peers descended from German and other Continental Jewish families, but his disposition to detachment had led him to understand and then accept that of all places it was Germany which most needed to re-write its history, to heal its self-inflicted wounds. For his own part, no amount of self-reproach could induce him to feel a genuine anger at the way his parents had been murdered. He had been to the camp, he had signed the book, he had made his donation, but it all seemed so far apart from his life experience that it was a somewhat skeletal gesture, for although all the bones were in the right places there was no flesh nor blood, no warmth nor animation. Although this was, he thought, primarily a matter of temperament, he recognised that it was no accident that the British (or, he thought that he really thought that he meant "English") were such great lovers of history, for in it they had found the ultimate mechanism of self-justification. Whatever the microcosmic, forensic investigators had produced until well after his own studies were completed, it could be effortlessly incorporated into the English story of its own identity. He looked up at the picture of his most eminent predecessor who had risen to be the most dissolute, but possibly the most effective, Prime Minister in British history. For all his talent he would not have stood a chance of entering Parliament in the latter half of the twentieth century and certainly would not have survived, again for all his talent, because of his serial womanising and nightly drinking and gambling. People were able to see the essential features of his usefulness and that seemed to be enough but, Horace thought, even if that age had come to an end with the dawn of a prurient moralising, more vicious at the end of the twentieth century than the nineteenth, worse was to come. He wondered how individuals and social units would function once they were no longer capable of re-writing their history because of the intensive record keeping, starting with domestic letter writing and photography, escalating into family email archives and DVD. He wondered how he would have fared if there had been detailed video evidence of the suffering and death of his parents. Would he simply have suffered from recurring nightmares or would he have broken down altogether? Likewise, he wondered how long society could bear to be reminded incessantly of its own cumulative shortcomings. It was bad enough knowing what you were doing wrong or badly today without being loaded with all your yesterdays. His life, on the cusp of ubiquitous archiving, had witnessed a series of political accommodations which he absorbed, like his mildly Conservative (Butskellite) peers, without effort, beginning with the Second World War story which had dominated his early childhood and ending with the final overwhelming of the macrocosmic by the microcosmic. This was partly the result of rapidly expanded higher education and partly of globalisation, which coincided with his rise to prominence in public life, which had made the grand national story increasingly difficult to control and relate. The Prime Ministerial tableaux had succeeded one another with a smoothness and imprecision which was impressive. Churchill was the hero and England stood alone while America was the reluctant ally which stole the prize, Macmillan transformed benevolent colonialism with colonial independence as a reward for faithfulness, Wilson was a puppet of Moscow, Heath saw Europe as an escape from managed decline, Thatcher was a monetarist, and Blair was shallow. These were parallelled by a separate set of ethical assumptions which succeeded each other with equal smoothness but, because they were personal and could be acted upon, they enjoyed a much greater degree of clarity. Class is dead, women are equal, homosexuality is natural, sex is consequence free, pleasure is an entitlement, and consumption is a right. There were, naturally, a wide variety of shifting perceptions which were subconsciously absorbed. Dress is personal, punctuation is optional, nothing is obvious, seriousness is tedious, all statements are equal, the canon is bogus, games are serious, religion is private, authority is groundless, all space is public, peer review is superfluous, politics are boring, and childhood is anachronistic. Well before Mr Blair swept to power, Strider was effortlessly, almost thoughtlessly, able to enter and rise through the ranks of New Labour where Oxbridge, Anglican, free market, postmodern, Wagnerian technocrats were welcome not because of the particular merits of any or all of these attributes, but whereas a post-War Tory could have instinctively recognised a Jew, Blair's people were cheerfully myopic. Before that point, Strider's career had been conventional. He had been President of the Union when it still mattered, a BBC trainee journalist when it had a near monopoly, a travel writer before the glut, a think tank guru when they still thought, an enterprise consultant without a clear remit, and an opposition policy adviser before the major parties were only divided by management process issues. Yet in spite of the apparently cheerful openness within the Blair camp, there were deep factional under-currents which could not be accounted for by any rational process, which made it impossible for Strider, for all his powers of accommodation, to know which 'side' to take, and so he opted for the pragmatic. By this time the factions in the Party were easier to understand as they barely involved any policy issues and largely related to personal ambition. Strider found himself caught between loyalty that would keep him where he was and a change of allegiance which might produce better results in the future. He opted for a modest degree of risk and was just far enough in from its fringes to be counted in the "dump Blair" camp, while continuing to insist that his loyalty was to the cause rather than *ad hominem*. He was convinced that the stance he took would count for less than his competence which would be valued in a rapidly degrading Ministry facing a financial crisis of fatally unknown, but frighteningly vast, proportions of which the failure of Southern Gem was a mild harbinger, and that no amount of loyalty or risk would raise him to the rank of Departmental Minister. His suppositions were correct as it was his undramatic execution of complex business which saved him from demotion when the New Prime Minister, who could judge his equivocation to a nicety, came in. Thus it was that he was occupied during August 2007, when he was not involved in the fall-out from Southern Gem, the imminent collapse of world trade talks, and a puerile spat in Brussels over the regulation of the manufacture of fireworks, in weighing up whether the Government had always been in favour of decreased consumption, increased taxation, tighter regulation, or carbon trading, as part of a market solution to combat climate change. If you had accused him of being cynical, even unscrupulous, in putting the question this way, he would have been bewildered by the accusation. As an historian, he saw all manner of continuities and discontinuities in complex events, and it was his task to forge a cogent narrative, a grand picture, which the microcosmists might later dismantle, but by then he would be a footnote in the remaindered memoirs of his Departmental Minister.

The caution of Sir Pluto in refraining from reacting to his rejection had stood him in good stead, for as the rainy days of the last Bank Holiday weekend of the Summer dragged by, there was an increasingly pressing need for the Government to adopt at least an outline position on the mounting Perpetuan campaign to reduce overall UK consumption. It was, as he and Horace Strider both realised, a classic case of the conflict of two desirable objectives, to assist in the moderation of climate change and to maintain economic stability, particularly for the poorest sector of the population. They were faced with resolving an issue on behalf of the electorate which it would determinedly ignore, for it stubbornly held to the view that all major issues could be dealt with separately and sequentially, each case producing a favourable outcome, and so there was no reason in its mind why the Government should not both protect the poor and mitigate climate change. It would have responded angrily had it been told that these two objectives were indeed compatible, but only if there was a substantial shift in income and wealth from the rich to the poor, an observation which all senior politicians and their civil servants were far too wise to make. Strider and Sir Pluto both knew that there would be no overall rise in taxation and that, therefore, their options were limited. "How is the new Minister?" "Doing rather well, actually. Only clever, uncharismatic people are sent here as it is low profile and rarely a step on the ladder, but more usually the height of a middling minister's career." "With the exception of his predecessor." "Yes, she was clever and charismatic for which I fear she has been punished. Had she either brains or beauty the PM would have known what to do with her, but as she has both it presented him with a problem which, as you know, he might have handled better." "Botched." "Well, at least from her point of view. She might produce a brilliant Olympics, but five years is a long time." "And what of Sir Joffree?" "I put it to the Minister that we might make a new start on the Consumption Committee." "Very kind," said Sir Pluto who, apparently unknown to Strider, had shared a set of rooms with Granville Brompton at Cambridge. It was not the time to tell Strider that it was not he but Pluto who was responsible for replacing Sir Joffree with himself and there might never come such a time. "The Minister is looking for a 'quick win' and some 'low hanging fruit'—what Minister isn't?—but I have persuaded him that something a little higher up the tree might be called for. I fear, however, that whatever stance we take will be marginal. When the price of oil passes 100 Dollars, interest rates and inflation are greater than 5%, unemployment is on its way to two million and, most probable but least imaginable, the venture capital system collapses, dragging some clearers with it and replacing inflation with depression, saving the planet will, by comparison, appear to be something of a side show. Nonetheless, we do need to do some spade work. I have to see that the Department does its job as well as meeting the objectives of the Political Cabinet." "But you are a Party man, aren't you, Horace?" "Well yes, but—and I don't want to sound boastful about this—I'm a Department man first because that's the thing I understand. I can see options, but I can't readily see why one politician—all things being equal, and they never are— will opt for this and another for that." "Let us, then, try to sum up the situation and see how we might move forward when the Committee meets. If you want a living laboratory for the relationship between consumption and poverty, the next recession, starting next year, will tell you all that you need to know. Firstly, 'negative growth'—a silly term—will throw some bankers out of work, but for every banker there will be ten lowlier workers unemployed. Secondly, a rise in unemployment will hold back any real increase in welfare payments. Thirdly, falling markets damage pensions, and many millions of quite poor people were forced in a breathtakingly irresponsible diktat by Margaret Thatcher—and whatever little good she might have done cannot conceal the fact that she was the author of most of our present ills—to put their money through intermediaries into the stock market instead of Government bonds or National Insurance, and that ugly crow will soon come home—forgive me if I am mixing my ornithological metaphors—to roost. Fourthly, rising unemployment will push down wages in the lowest paid jobs. Finally, many in the Labour Movement—if there still really is such a thing but, anyway, quite a few MPs—think that climate change is another fad while improving the lot of the poor is fundamental. However, for a committee to ruminate about the medium term is much more common than for politicians and the work needs to be done. On the other hand, it's the right thing to do, although that rarely commands much support in practice, whatever people say. If we are careful we can target cuts in consumption on imports, and hopefully there will be a rise in savings." "I can't fault the logic except on your final two points. If we cut imports it will hurt poor farmers in developing countries, and the way to mitigate that is to cut consumption on luxuries with high margins. If the poor are to be helped by fiscal transfers that will not boost savings. I will draw up a short paper and we can start almost immediately, after the Party conferences." "And we need some research. I take your point about a recession, but managing a decline in consumption requires some preparation, some modelling. The problem is that there are two kinds of research, justifying a reasonable conclusion or exploring the unknown, but both of these have been swamped by companies and lobbyists producing their own bogus research. It's difficult to know where to find an impartial source. The best you can hope for is two biased, diametrically opposed conclusions, but that will not help us." "I will ask the National Audit Directorate. Their stuff is a bit dry, but it's the best we can do."

Strider hated the prospect of the Party Conference. He had not grown up in the Party and had no feeling for it, and had been parachuted into a fairly safe Tory seat, without any Party organisation to speak of, which had fallen as part of the 1997 landslide, so he owed nobody anything. Commitments made outside the processes of Government made him nervous, and the tendency of everyone—activists, politicians and journalists—to exaggerate its importance, justifying the few days away from London, irritated him. A junior minister, still hoping to rise in spite of the current plateau, must be seen at a handful of fringe meetings, taking the chair at one of them, and must be seen at the more important receptions and take part in the leader's standing ovation. This one would be even worse because the Prime Minister had, foolishly in his view, allowed election hysteria to take hold, and that would further rob the event of any sense of reality. He was thankful for the new technology which allowed him to work unobtrusively as the predictable speeches of the ambitious, the self-important, and the dutiful ground on. Then he hit upon the idea of holding a fringe meeting on his consumption problem.

Some Perpetuans were uncomfortable with the anti consumption message because the issue of its impact on the poor had not been worked out but Max was determined. "I know we don't know the answer yet, but when Jesus told people they should love their neighbour, people didn't object that this would put policemen out of work. What matters is that we do what is right and when that produces a 'down side' we put that right, too. We have to be firm about personal responsibility. When stock brokers and bankers are greedy, producing disorderly markets and crashes, people generally call for more or better regulation, but we should call for self-restraint. When people see crime rising and call for more policemen, we should call for more responsible individual behaviour. So when we are consuming resources so rapidly and causing so much pollution and rubbish that we are destroying our planet, the answer has to be personal, too. 'They' are not going to fix it, we are." Another worry was that this campaign was obscuring the central Perpetuan message about what was beginning to be called 'pure love', the enabling of the freedom of choice of others, but Max said, "We can, morally speaking, walk and chew gum at the same time. The two things fit together." But a third objection was more difficult to deal with as it charged that 'pure love' required the abolition of government altogether, because it was standing in the way of personal autonomy. Max could see that there were two dangers in this. It would push Perpetuans into an alignment with the Conservative Party's traditionalists, but, more importantly, it was yet another variant of the tendency to confuse the religious imperative with civic necessity. In reply to a right-wing journalist, Max commented briefly, "I can see why you say that we are backing off from civic government, but our view on autonomy is an ideal we are pursuing, and precisely because we will fail, because we are imperfect, we unfortunately need civic institutions to try to make good our faults."

The campaign grew as the movement grew, but progress was slow. They were working steadily, but could not help hoping for a major breakthrough which, when it came, surprised them all. Everybody, not least Bryan, was aware that their god4u channel was available on a number of foreign services, and the web site was popular worldwide, but they were taken by surprise in August when they began to receive thousands of enquiries about joining and financing the movement, and some requests for Perpetuans to visit, make speeches and lead worship. The immediate reaction was to ask Max if he would make a tour to some of the places from which they had received requests. He was used to travelling; he spoke French and a little of some other European Languages, and everyone had full confidence in him, but the problem was that he was holding them together. "This isn't a business," he said. "Until now I have felt that my calling was to stay with you and hold things together but, really, the Holy Spirit will hold us together, and I feel it is right for me to go." They held a special service of worship with the first-ever fully worked out Sacrament of Affirmation, during which the leaders laid their hands on his head and prayed. They were sorry to see him go, but elated that he had been called.

Before he made the final decisions, Max went on a short retreat. If it had not been so overwhelmingly positive, the last few days would have been "a bit much". He had been working late in the office, allocating foundational finance so that the first Guides were evenly spread over the whole of England (Perpetuanism had made little impact in Scotland, Wales, and Ulster) when he suddenly felt that this was the completion of his final administrative task. He did not hurry, but went on, concentrating on not rushing, deliberately checking every detail one more time than was necessary, a kind of conscientious self-restraint, a delaying of gratification. He put the papers together, dated and signed an adhesive paper and affixed it to the two covers of the folder. There was one more pile of papers on his desk. The top sheet was an analysis of traffic from Bryan. He looked at the figures for foreign requests for membership, financial contributions, and requests for a mission. "That's it," he said, quietly, wonderingly. "That's what I have been waiting for." He wanted to phone Marta, but he waited. He went into the chapel at the top of the building and sat quietly, looking at the Crucifix and the picture of Perpetua, the one that had been (mysteriously) taken from her final broadcast, the nearest thing ever to a picture of heaven. He was not praying for discernment, and he was certainly not praying for strength, as he felt the power of the Spirit, but he prayed for modesty and humility, for the restraint to be careful, to refrain from thinking that he was anything other than God's creature. After more than half an hour, he locked the office. His whim to phone Marta was selfish, it was because he had news he wanted to enjoy telling her, but the right thing to do was to tell her in person. He was so late that he had missed Perpetua's bed time. He looked with overflowing affection at the white pram in the corner which her namesake, risen from the dead, had given to them with her own, blessed hands. He wanted to call, but he waited. Marta, who had heard him, came in with a glass of white wine in each hand. "I know! I know! You gave it up, but the strong man can have one drink to celebrate without going back to where you were." "They say that nobody can." "They say that, I say this. We must celebrate." "What?" "Your new job." "How do you know?" "She told me." "Who? Perpetua?" "Yes, not little Perpetwa but our Sacred Lady." "Told you?" "Not a vision, nothing like that, but she still told me. I know you have new job. So, we celebrate." "But it will mean leaving you, going away." "Going, yes. Leaving, no. Babies can travel. Nothing here worth having; nothing here without you." "O Marta!" "So we get married." "I suppose they will bless me before I go, and we can get married then." "Good. Where do we go?" "I don't know, but I think America as that is where we have received most requests and—it can't be overlooked—that is the greatest source of funding after England even though we have asked for nothing." Max drank the wine without fear and told Marta what had happened. "Holy Spirit, Perpetua, same thing." "Yes. I still have not solved the four-in-one idea. I suppose if Jesus were alive now his movement would be called god3u which would lack the double meaning, but every time I see god4u I have to look twice. Perpetua, or the Spirit. I suppose in Acts it was Jesus or the Spirit, so that makes sense."

At the American Embassy his case was handled by Gregg, but the name badge did not indicate whether this was his first or his surname. "Business or holiday?" "Well, I suppose preaching and helping to sustain a religious movement is business." "I don't know about here. I haven't been in England long enough, but in America it sure is business, one of the biggest. What religion?" "Perpetuanism." Gregg seemed to flinch slightly which Max took as an expression of mild antipathy. "I've heard of it, but I don't think it will go down all that well. Where are you going?" "Boston first." "Well, it might go down there, they've got everything in Boston, like San Francisco only more genteel and buttoned up, but they have an almost endless capacity in Boston for religious pluralism." "I might also go to New York and Washington DC." "Well, as long as you stay away from the Bible Belt you should be all right. And the lady?" "We will be married next week." "That's all right then, but you will have to come back with the paperwork. We don't mind if you're married or not from the moral or religious point of view, but the lady's status is unclear in England and, although I am sure we would not mind entertaining her, we like to know that people are stabilised." He stamped Max's passport and, as he turned away at the other side of the glass, Max thought he recognised him from somewhere. It was something about the shape of his left shoulder and the hinder half of his left profile. It was something he must have seen in a film.

Now, looking across a stretch of completely empty Moorland, Max experienced a strange sensation of silence and wondered whether he had made a mistake. From his earliest memories until now he had always lived in a city and, when he was well off enough, he had always spent his holidays in cities at the beginning or end of a conference or business trip, wandering through the streets of Paris, Rome or Buenos Aires, relishing the tang of the working class areas as much as the luxurious avenues. As far as he could remember, he had never even spent a day in a national park, but now, here he was, in silence. He wondered whether his suggestion that he should go on retreat was simply mimicking Perpetua and her followers or whether, instead, he should have just got on with it. In asking himself the question he saw the sense of what he was doing. The silence would force him to face himself, to stop the running away from himself which had started well before he was fired from the bank. In retrospect, he now recognised, if he had not become an alcoholic as the result of his sudden fall from power he would almost certainly have become one because of his rapid rise to power. What he had to face was whether he was a fundamentally flawed person running away, or whether his life story had influenced what had happened to him. In other words, he needed to find out how much control he had over himself, how much autonomy he possessed. It would make no difference to how hard he tried to follow Perpetua, but he saw immediately that his external success would depend on his temperament and disposition, and this helped him to understand how cruel it was to be judged on external appearances. He had started his banking career in the straitened Seventies, the decade when the optimism of the Beatles and Flower Power had run into the realities of oil price rises and family responsibility and then, as he gained steady promotion, the windows were suddenly opened onto a new world of unlimited wealth and 'success'. Looking back, it amazed him how quickly clever people adjusted to the new system. History was so dead that the Wall Street crash might never have happened. The state regulation, which had maintained stability since the Second World War, was completely dismantled and deregulation was the fashion. The sense of solidarity which was also the result, he thought, of the War but also of the endeavours of Christian Liberals and Socialists, had gone up in the smoke of the regulatory bonfire—there really was no such thing as society—and greed became a civic virtue instead of one of the Seven Deadly Sins. The ultimate triumph of capitalism was encapsulated in the fall of the Berlin Wall, and it did not matter that the two great leaders of the 1980s free-for-all did not survive their triumph, Reagan and Thatcher had freed the genie from the bottle and Clinton and Blair could not put it back. Max had steadily extended the range of his risk, only slightly checked by the occasional blip, until the deals he did were so complex that he could only just understand them himself. It was this very danger, the feeling of risk and insecurity, which began to alert him to the fragility of the system, yet he could not stop. He had since persuaded himself that he had begun to drink heavily when he lost his job in the shotgun merger, but he knew now that he had started long before that, just after the fall of the wall in fact, when he saw that what he was doing could not be justified, that at some point it would end in a massive crash, that bad debt could only be pushed away by clever devices for a limited time, and that the more elaborate the device and the more intense the push, the greater the crash would ultimately be. He also knew that what he was doing was fundamentally unjust. Poor people were being persuaded to take risks they should not take by rich people who knew better, and when the crash came, it would be the tax payers, never given any leeway when they defaulted, who would have to bail out the banks and insurance companies that had robbed them. The cavaliers of unfettered capitalism would ultimately have to be saved by massive acts of state socialism, but when the dust cleared the rich would still be rich, but the poor, with eroded savings and pensions, would be poorer, and governments would then have to tax the poor to save the system but the rich would fight any attempt to increase their taxation. Looking back at himself, he saw that the drinking was a kind of recognition of his guilt, that it was almost a moral impulse. Although he recognised the evils of escapism, he also recognised himself to be a moral man who had found it increasingly difficult to be immoral without paying the price. It was not some moralist impulse that had helped him to stop drinking, but his increasing comfort with himself. Marta was right when she said that he could drink the occasional glass of wine because his alcoholism was a symptom of his social criminality—and, looking back, he thought that was not too severe a term—and that he was now capable of transmitting that comfort he felt in himself to so many others who needed it. If he could be 'saved' he thought, most people could at least live happier lives. The secret, which Perpetua had articulated, was living within yourself. Perhaps that was why he had always loved the sacred music of Bach, particularly the Cantatas, but had found symphonic music from Beethoven to Mahler oppressive. We need, he thought, to live within the true limits of creatureliness and forget the Promethian lie. Yet he could not foresee when society would mirror what had happened to him as an individual. The masters of the universe were still bestriding the world markets, making pygmies of governments, maintaining that globalisation could not even be controlled, let alone stopped. He would come face to face with this effortless arrogance even more in America than in London where there was at least always a slight sense of irony and self-deprecation which saved it from being totally insufferable. He prayed for the restraint to listen and the strength to comfort. He was not looking forward to his trip, but he still knew that it was the right thing to do.

Looking out over the moor at sunset he saw an earlier picture of himself or, rather, of how his family must have been before they uprooted themselves from Poland, frightened of the Soviet/Nazi pincer. They had been heath land people and, although he did not wish to romanticise them with a virtue they did not possess, he had never heard any stories of their pretensions to wealth other than his grandmother's fondness for lace. He wondered whether the realisation of the terrible propensity for greediness had only been checked in most people by circumstance. The ingrained solidarity, whose denial had led him so far astray, asserted itself to such an extent, as he looked out over the moor, that he momentarily wondered how he could be a genuine Perpetuan 'neutral facilitator'. Then he remembered that to love your neighbour by kindness or self-denial is second only to creating space: "They are not in contradiction," he thought. "Perhaps the way to think about it is that generosity in action is a necessary precondition for the ultimate generosity of creating space, just as most of us need a tangible way of reaching out towards the ineffable, so we need a tangible version of love, of loving, which enables us to reach towards the impossible ideal: virtue as a necessary precondition for love. I can think this to myself but wonder whether I can communicate it outside the small circle of people who are disposed to accept it. We will see."

On that same afternoon, Horace Strider had reluctantly come to the conclusion that Southern Gem—or what was left of it—would have to be nationalised, that any organisation stupid enough to buy it would be incapable of running it, and that to think that the failures of capitalism would be put right by capitalism was wishful thinking. He had felt the barometer tip from greed to fear. He knew in his bones what was coming, but he did not know how long it would take to arrive. He called his Minister. "I have been over all the arguments and I cannot find an alternative, Minister. We will have to take Southern Gem into public ownership one way or another." "I suppose you are right, but we don't want to use the dreaded word 'nationalisation'." "Typical," thought Strider. "He is only bothered about the naming of the phenomenon, the presentation, not the substance." "I suppose we will be accused of wasting taxpayers' money as if the poor employees and savers with the Gem are not tax payers. I get so fed up of selfish, sneering, middle class journalists who have seen the prices of their houses double in the past seven years, without any effort on their part, but think they have a right to go on getting richer without effort, and resent being asked to help out the poor. After all, the failure of the Gem was caused by the sort of mistake any organisation might make, given the current fashion. It borrowed too much at too high a price on the basis that the value of its mortgage book would go on up forever, or at least for long enough. Where will it end, Horace?" "I think the more relevant question is when it might end, Minister. I don't give it much more than a year. A crash during the 2008 Party Conference would be something to ..." He almost said "relish" but rapidly corrected himself "... experience." "Yes, Horace, I know what you think about the Conference, but the question is, how do we present this conclusion to the Prime Minister, and then the country." "I doubt anything we say will surprise the PM. I know that there has been some intensive work in the past week. All I am doing is presenting the detailed rationale, not the political imperative. I suspect that our problem is the novelty of the proceeding. When the crash comes, the right wing press will be shrieking for us to 'take action' and save capitalism from its folly with public money." "I know, Granville but, as you say, our problem is now, and I don't think it matters what words you use, people are alive to what is going on, so I think we should be frank." Thus it was that the first major nail in the coffin of free market capitalism was forged.

Max emerged from his retreat with a sense of wonder. He had never been with himself for so long in near or complete silence and he had found the daily monastic routine of worship, work, and silent communion first challenging and then stimulating. Parts of his mind that he did not know he had began to switch themselves on and he discovered that his self-characterisation as somebody who could only contribute by "doing" was not entirely accurate. Not having news was another strange novelty which caused withdrawal symptoms at first, but it was not long before the world and its cares went into deep background at which point he was better able to see the world and its problems in perspective. Instead of thinking about the latest crisis and his own reaction to it, he began to think more clearly about the human condition and its relationship to creation. He would not have said that he had become a theologian but he would have said that he had become adequately theologically aware and that this, as distinct from competence in the philosophy of religion, meant feeling that there was a possibility of becoming in tune with the Godhead. The monks had not tried to persuade him to be a Christian nor to abandon Perpetuanism. His Guest Master simply ensured that he knew the basic rules, had access to spiritual direction, was fed, kept comfortable, and had access to the snug, heterogenous theological library which would have surprised critics and might have caused the Pope some unease.

At the airport, his customary equanimity almost abandoned him when he and the family were subjected to the most uncivil, dispiriting and superfluous security checks. There was no reason for the officials to be so grim and unpleasant, it was irrational for them to be so suspicious of everyone they saw, and, in any case, the security industry was yet another manifestation of corporate greed and a waste of public resources. As he removed the baby's shoes, he thought grimly of a terrorist leader smiling in his tent or, more likely, his secluded mansion, cursing Western capitalism as he texted orders on his mobile phone. The amount spent on security would surely have assuaged many a radical if it had been used to improve the conditions of the poor.

A man in the queue told him some hair raising stories about security. He had carried his two cigarette lighters on an Easterly trip round the world onto nine different flights, but they had been confiscated at JFK when he took his homeward flight. He had travelled all over Peru with cigarette lighters, but that they had been arbitrarily confiscated at one tiny airport where there was a bin full of lighters waiting to be taken to the local market. In India some airports insisted on batteries being installed in electronic devices to show they were working, and in others batteries were confiscated to disable devices. While he could not take a plastic water bottle from the check-in desk to the security area, he could have bought a glass bottle in the duty free area, smashed it, and commited an assault. Max, who had had problems packing all that he, Marta, and Perpetua needed, could not work out why he was not allowed to carry more than one bag from the check-in desk to security, but was obliged to put one piece inside the other before reversing the process at security. He could not take nice English presents to Boston, but had to buy global brands in the air-side shops. This was a far call from the days when he had travelled for the bank when, throughout an extended period of airline hi-jaks, the impact on his personal convenience was marginal. He wondered whether the deterioration of trust and civility was the result of the democratisation of flying. Were these people being disagreeable because they were forced to serve the not so rich and even the quite poor? The magnificent climax of this tedious and ill-mannered imposition was that his bag was searched by a security man whose name badge declared him to be, at least nominally, Muslim. Max recalled the aphorism of a sacked Middle Eastern newspaper editor that while not all Muslims were terrorists, just about all terrorists were Muslims, so the bag searcher had a much higher statistical chance of being a terrorist than its owner. He met the same incivility on landing at Logan International Airport. In spite of the fact that his post nuptial paperwork was all in order, all three were hauled away and separated for questioning.

All the irritations of the journey were more than compensated for by their warm reception at a large, formerly liberal Episcopal church which had, even before his arrival, affirmed its commitment to Perpetuanism and was now in the early stages of litigation in respect of the building and property. Unlike the English Perpetuans who were largely working class with a middle class putative leadership, the Perpetuans of Boston were all more than prosperous. They took him to a luxurious out-sized sea food restaurant with an out-sized menu and, when they came, out-sized portions, but, by contrast, their demeanour was self-effacing, conscious that they were receiving a visit from a person who had known Perpetua personally. Their leader, Father/Guide Thomas, invited him to preach on the following morning, but he asked to be given a little time to accustom himself to his new surroundings. He had only been recently called and he had never preached before. He was glad of the respite, as the service which he attended on the next day was a work of beauty. The liturgy of the Eucharist had been maintained, with some slight variations acknowledging Perpetua as the Fourth Person of the Godhead, the sermon was a ferocious attack on the Vice President, Dick Cheyney, most un-Perpetuan, but very fine, and Bach's Cantata 82 was sung with a degree of under statement almost guaranteed to elicit the strongest emotions. A full programme of visits and talks had been arranged for him and, contrary to his fears, he was simply asked to tell his own story and what he had seen and heard of Perpetua. They had already mastered all the publicly available resources, but wanted to hear the real thing. The same went for the local television channels which were hungry for novelty and personal details, so that by the time he came to deliver his sermon on the morning he was to leave for New York, he felt totally comfortable. The build up had been steady all week. The great church was packed with the faithful and hundreds of non-believers. As he climbed into the pulpit, he felt a tremendous surge of energy which took the wobble out of his knees. He knew that it was the Spirit come to support him, and he instantly knew that he would not need any of the detailed notes he had made for his talk. Instead of the elaborate theological argument he had constructed, he told his story simply and well. He had been a banker, and had allowed himself to forget his humble origins and how lucky he was simply to be alive. He had fallen from power and taken to alcohol, and then been present at the death of Perpetua, which had changed his life forever:

"It was not a profound new theology that changed me—or, rather, it was, but I did not think of it as such—all that I knew was that my power to love and serve, to affirm, was in my own hands. I had pitied myself, thought I was a victim of the system, but in fact I was a humble architect of the system. I could love my neighbour but, even more importantly, I could trust my neighbour to love me. Perpetua brought hope to me, and she brings it to all of us now. We feel frightened of the looming credit crisis, but do not give in, do not lose hope. Love really does conquer all, but it is not only the active love but the love of acceptance. I call upon everyone here to bring the whole of their lives, their suffering, their acceptance, to lay at the feet of Perpetua who was God's messenger, sent so lately to us. She is now at one with the Godhead and Jesus her Brother, but wonder at

God's presence so near to us in this sad generation, so overwhelmed by power and pleasure. Give yourselves, and allow the whole world to give."

During the Consecration, which he concelebrated, he was sure that if Jim had been there he would have seen a miraculous light over the altar, and when he greeted the congregation afterwards they said that they had been deeply and strangely moved at that moment. They felt the presence of the Spirit. Hundreds of new believers committed themselves to Perpetua, and there was great rejoicing.

Word had travelled down the East Coast to New York where his reception was much more animated. As he stood at Ground Zero, he gave a message of hope. Although in his heart he could not quite take the final step to complete pacifism, the pragmatist as well as the believer saw that reacting to terrorism with violence was useless. The expression of activism, of refusing to be a victim, did not lie in a violent reaction, but in principled and steady acceptance, the determination not to lose control of personal integrity by handing the responsibility for personal commitment to soldiers in a dangerous and distant land. His message was greeted with bewildered hostility. How could any city simply "lie down and take it"? His answer was that it must stand up and take it, that evil and misfortune left people with personal choices and the choice must be to affirm ourselves, each and every one, as children of God Our Parent. Was he saying that pacifism was the proper response to violence? Being honest, he said that he could not envisage a case, although there might be one, where it was not. As he had said, commissioning others to go and fight was hardly an assertion of personal responsibility and commitment. It was hard for some New Yorkers to take, but many at the Church of St Thomas heard the Word of Perpetua and committed themselves to her. He had brought out latent divisions and now, at least, those who advocated moderation had an anchor, something to hang onto, something more powerful than the simplistic militarism of their detractors. His most difficult moment was when an interviewer reminded him that millions of "good Americans" were in favour of the war in Afghanistan. They were strongly committed Christians, so was he saying that they were wrong? One of the problems with Christianity, he said, was that it had abandoned the idea of the personal commitment to and relationship with the Godhead. Many who had come from the Protestant tradition were committed to a personal relationship with God and many, on that account, had denied the role of organised religion but over the centuries that very personal commitment had gradually been diluted by buildings, hierarchy and an all too prevalent belief that they had the right, even the obligation, to judge other people who saw their personal relationship with God differently. "Or not at all," said the interviewer. "Who knows?" he replied. "Many people appear to be unfaithful but we cannot tell. It is not for us to say. It is difficult for each of us to stay faithful without spending time and energy trying to impose our kind of faithfulness on others."

As he addressed a small crowd in Washington Square, a shot rang out and many feared that it was a repetition of what had happened to Dexter, Miles and

Will, but the bullet only grazed his arm and, after a visit to a casualty department, he was allowed to return to his hotel. The bullet was recovered and pronounced to be of Eastern European origin. Sadly, the incident received far more coverage than his message, but he did not allow himself to be diverted, helped by the fact that Marta remained calm. They gave thanks to God and rejoiced that Max had been preserved to be a servant of God. On the following day, he refused to condemn the act. He was opposed to violence, but would not comment on an individual case. Only God knew what was in the mind of the assassin.

His television appearances and the attempted murder combined to give even greater coverage to his visit to Washington DC. It happened that he arrived on the day of the preparatory meetings for the World Bank and International Monetary Fund and, as he was waiting to check in to his hotel, he saw Granville Brompton and Horace Strider walking through the lobby. He recognised Brompton from the newspapers, but he needed no such prompting to recognise Strider whom he had known since they were six. He still remembered Strider telling everybody that he was leaving to go to an English private school. He could still remember the strange mixture of envy and contempt which he felt, the betrayal of their Jewish heritage, and his own wish to escape. Almost sub-consciously, he had matched Strider's progress against his own as he struggled to come to terms with the tedium and mess of his East End school, while Strider used to return for the holidays, ever more polished and self-assured, but he gradually came to realise that Strider's departure was the best thing that had happened to him as he struggled in his wake. The more Strider progressed, the more Max was determined to keep up, and he wondered whether in the later days he had taken some risks which he should not in order to stay in touch as Strider seemed to move effortlessly up the economic and social ladder, while he had to get his hands dirty. He realised now, Strider's hands had probably been dirty, too, but he gave every appearance of knowing how to wash them, whereas he seemed to be sucked ever deeper into the shady and shifty compromises of international banking. When they were nine, Strider had moved away and they had hardly met since, except for exchanging pleasantries at Bah Mitzphas at the Liberal Synagogue, and he thought that he would pretend not to have seen him, but he felt himself drawn to his childhood friend and, without calculation, he left his bags with a bell hop and hurried after the two men as they ambled towards the exit. "Horace!" The man looked at him over his shoulder without stopping as if he was trying to solve a crossword clue. You could see him mentally arranging the letters and blanks. "Max, isn't it?" And then the polish and the politician took over. "How nice to see you. How have you been? What are you doing here? We must find time to have a drink. Oh yes, I know. Didn't I see you on television last night? Some ghastly story about a shooting. Are you all right?" "Yes, thank you, Horace. I am all right." "Granville, er Minister, this is an old friend of mine, Max ..." "... Silver." "Max Silver." He was feverishly trying to work out what to say while concealing his intense effort. "Max and I are childhood friends." "Nice to meet you Max," said Granville, clearly preoccupied with his business and looking anxious to get on, but aware, as all politicians are, that every encounter's value must be prudentially weighed. "Shot eh?" "It was nothing, just somebody who was disgruntled. It probably had nothing to do with me, but, in any case, I am all right." "What brings you here?" asked Strider who had noted his superior's willingness to allow a minute's grace from their inexorable dialogue in the world's financial soap opera. "Perpetua." "Oh yes, Perpetua," said Horace. "You will remember, Minister, that we discussed the idea of a planned reduction in consumption." "Yes Horace," said the Minister, slightly irritated by a topic he would have preferred to ignore as signs of a depression increased. "Joffree and Sir Pluto," said Sir Granville for, like most politicians, he was better at names, faces, and patronage than ideas. "That's it," said Horace, finally filling all the blanks, "you are spreading the word." He said this as if Max was distributing leaflets for double glazing. "And how are you getting on?" he asked, lapsing into a tone which was almost like a distant aunt asking a bored child during the school holidays about its classroom progress. "We are doing well," said Max, refusing to draw any conclusions from the tone of voice in which the observations and questions were inflected, and the accompanying body language, caught between flattery and impatience. "I would like to say that it is the integrity of the message that people find attractive, but part of the success is down to worry about the credit crisis. I daresay your Party will soon experience this in the revival of socialist rhetoric." "Oh I doubt it," said Granville whose contempt was more obvious than his certainty. "Well, we must be going, but I hope the two of you find time to enjoy old times." Horace gave Max his card with a mobile telephone number hand written on the back. "Phone me in a couple of hours when I should be free of the Brazilians who are proving very difficult to shift. After all, it's their forest." Strider wondered during the lengthy periods when the Brazilians—he did not know whether out of a habit of loquacity or in a deliberate attempt to stall—went off the subject—and their interpreters plunged into mind numbing incoherence—whether Max might be of some use. He did not want to open up the issue of consumption, but Max might well fly a kite for tighter regulation of financial institutions. When they met later that evening for a quick drink, however, Strider saw that Max was not capable of being manipulated. Instead of the calculation of the banker which he would have expected, he was confronted with a simplicity he could hardly fathom. "I had thought you might want to float your consumption idea while you are over here." "No. It is not worked out yet. I can talk about a one line principle, but to do that without any more idea how it will work out is asking for trouble. It is like saying, as Jesus did, that we must give all that we have to the poor without working out what that might mean. Jesus had the luxury of working without the mass media. If everybody gave all they had to the poor, the chances are that unemployment would shoot up to astronomical proportions, and it would not be long before the poor would get through their temporary windfalls and be poor again. When what Jesus was asking for was simply a redistribution of temporary wealth before mass storage, that was different from today's complexities. The same goes for the idea of reducing consumption. We are going to have to work out how this happens and, as my suspicion is that it can't happen without a substantial income and wealth transfer from the rich to the poor, we have to be sure of our ground. Not because we will be misinterpreted, which we surely will, but because we are taking something from people, lowering their reasonable expectations, so we have to be sure and we have to be clear." "So what are you going to do?" "I will join the march of those about to lose their homes in the credit crisis, and I will visit some of the worst slums here, to be with the outcast and the desperate. What will you be doing?" "Just one more day of preparation, ironing out the final details." "Of what?" "A deal to stave off an international financial crisis." "I don't like the thought of simply staving it off, but I suppose that is the best you can do." "Yes. Nobody wants to face up to the inevitability of a massive contraction when the bad debts come out of the woodwork. Our superiors just hope that it will happen once they have gone. It's all got mixed up with negotiations on climate change.." "I don't envy you, Horace, but do you really want to continue to be a collaborator in this process? You're not a victim, you could take a different course." "I know that's your new way. I looked up Perpetua during a rather tedious part of the meeting, but I am so tied in, it would be like trying to be a member of a new family if I gave this up." "Well, sometimes we just do have to become members of a new family, and that is quite difficult. After all, if we concentrate too much on the family we are in, we are so generous to it that we overlook those who are not in the family. Take, for example, the parents who buy a new car for their teenage child instead of sending that money to the poor of Africa. We don't think twice about it, we put our blood family above the human family. I can see how hard it would be for you to leave your current political and administrative family, but if you don't, Horace, how can you expect other people to behave better?" "But I don't expect them to behave better." "I suspect—without knowing your own disposition in detail—that a huge amount of establishment unfairness is built upon the cynical expectation that the less fortunate will behave well. It worked with nurses for decades when politicians refused them just wages because they knew that nurses would never go on strike and let down their patients who, in fact, were really the patients of the politicians, not the nurses who were simply acting as their professional agents. Likewise, when the crash comes—and we both know it will—you will not scruple to use public money to bail out high finance while those who pay taxes to bring this about will be suffering a fall in the value of their pensions. Yet your calculation will be that they will not turn angry." "That's harsh, Max." "I am sorry. I keep lapsing into my old ways. I am not being harsh with you, but simply describing the system. I have to separate the two, but it's a new habit of mind."

As if to confirm Max's analysis of the poor, the march of the potentially homeless, the people who had not been able to afford a mortgage but, to their surprise and relief, had been granted one, only to find that, after the euphoria died down, they could not keep up with the payments, was remarkably peaceful, almost good humoured. He was asked if he wanted to say anything and he said that he would like to say a few words, but he did not want to appear to be a European telling America what to do. "All I want to say to you," he said, "is that I know times are going to be tough for you. I urge the whole world, of whatever religion, to pray for you, and I bring just one message from Perpetua. Never lose control of your lives, even when you are faced with terrible reverses and adversity. Hold on to every decision that you can. Never be a victim, never be manipulated, never be sorry for yourself. How can you be sorry as children of God?" Many people found this message startling because their experience of religion was that its sole purpose was to make them feel sorry as children of God.

On the flight to Boston he had met an eighteen-year-old girl who was returning from the Ukraine to her home in Kansas. "What were you doing in Kiev?" "Bringing Christ to the people." "But, forgive me, don't they have an Orthodox Christian tradition in the Ukraine?" "Yes, but our job was to persuade them to abandon their primitive, heretical, superstitious ways and turn to Christ for his forgiveness." "So, before you went to Kiev, did you study the Orthodox Christian religion?" "Course not, we simply learned of the love of God for all people who are sorry." "Sorry for being Orthodox?" "Course." "So instead of trying to bring millions of American unchurched people to Christ, you are trying to bring Ukrainian Orthodox people to Christ?" "Yes." "It's crazy," he said, under his breath. "Well, I think that when you get home you should think carefully about this. There are many people who need the comfort of Christ who have nothing; perhaps it is better to bring them something than to spend your energies getting people to switch their Christian brand." "I don't get you. These people had gone astray." "Look, Stacey—I'm sorry, I shouldn't be so aggressive—there is a difference when somebody is sick between getting them to a doctor for the appropriate medicine and spending your efforts persuading somebody taking medicine to change prescription." "I don't see it. There is only one way to God, and that is to be sorry for our wickedness." "But you don't have a monopoly on bringing people to God in penitence?" "But there is only one way and that is through penitence, and we will not relax until everyone turns to God." He gave up, but he met the same attitude when he was introduced to scores of influential people in Washington. He had grown used to the quirky liberalism of Boston and the defiant liberalism of New York, but in Washington DC he met people who thought that wealth was the best indicator of righteousness, and that people were poor because they were sinful. On the local television channels, it was put to him repeatedly that individual self-determination was the American way and the Perpetuan way. "Yes," he replied, "but without solidarity it does not work." "But the poor are the people who have thrown their chances away." "'Good religion' is about worship, love and justice, but we too often forget the justice." Almost everyone he met was deeply suspicious of solidarity. They defined community narrowly and, even though the Berlin Wall had fallen almost two decades before, they were still worried about communism. He was deeply shocked by the almost universal correlation between wealth and salvation which was given life when he went to a Georgetown relief programme at which the moralising was as hot as the soup. The most pathetic and worn-down people, most of whom were alcohol and drug abusers, were constantly harangued as they queued for their ration. It was an exploitation of weakness which he thought was the opposite of moral. The benevolence of the soup kitchen came at a price which was the exercise of power by the rich over the poor, the 'moral' over the 'immoral', the saved over the damned, the pastoral over the weak. He waited until the soup detail and the repentance detail had departed for the next station. "You don't know who I am and you probably don't know who Perpetua is ..." "... The black sister and saviour," said a homeless man. "That's right. Well, I have come on her behalf to be with you." "What d'you bring?" "Just her message." "People who come here have nothing but messages," said another. "Wait!" said the first. "She was different, like an English, female Martin Luther King Jr, only even more specially blessed." "All right, get on with it." "The message I bring has nothing to do with the other messages. I am not asking you to do anything. I am simply asking you to take control of your own lives inasmuch as you can." As midnight approached, he was so appalled by the shallow optimism of his own message that he hardly knew what to do. Remembering Miles, he decided to stay. "I feel I have hardly got a right to speak at all," he said to a man preparing for a restless and hazardous night by arranging all his possessions below half of his blanket so that he could lie on them. "Well, you could perform a miracle," said the man. "What kind of miracle would that be?" asked Max, almost companionably. "You could free me from my drug dependence and give me a couple of thousand bucks to make a new start." "I could probably do the second more readily than the first," said Max. "Shit!" said the man. "You've done it. My craving has gone." "If that is true," said Max, cautiously, "try to make the best of it. Perpetua didn't perform mighty acts to over-ride self-determination, but to give it a new chance. Her whole life was dedicated to giving people a new chance. That is why she was sent." "A miracle!" shouted the man, and immediately figures appeared out of the shadows in every direction. Max was frightened, not of those who approached him, but of his own, apparent power. As long as he put his hands on people and they said they felt soothed, he could manage, but when three of them brought him a woman who was unconscious and, they said, near to death, he was startled when he put his hands on her head, saying "In the name of Perpetua, may you become the owner of your life" and she sprang up, vital and vocal, praising God. It was not long before the news spread and as more broken people came to him, he was aware of a feeling of hostility from community leaders. When there was a lull in the stream of people, he said to those standing nearby: "I know you are not cynical enough to object because you might lose your jobs—there will always be poor, needy, desperate people—but you seem troubled about something else." "You are performing some kind of magic in the name of a woman called Perpetua." "I don't know what you would call it. I have never done anything like this before, but I am sure that I am acting in the name of God." "Not our God." "Your God? Do you have one of your own." "Don't be foolish, we all have the same God." "In which case it can't matter what the outward appearances might mislead you to believe, I am soothing people in the name of the same God that you worship." "But you are not working in the name of our God." "This is becoming just a little circular," said Max. "I thought we had established that this God whom you worship cannot be yours in the sense of being a possession that you can dispense or deny." "But we are of the true religion, and in calling upon a mere woman—Perpetua—you are acting blasphemously." "You know, in the sense that you mean it, I probably am," said Max, "but I never was very good at the God/human interface. But you are religious people. If I am saying words in the name of Perpetua and people are being cured, surely I am doing some kind of good, and you can't do good in the name of evil." "But you are a blasphemer for claiming to cure people in the name of Perpetua." "But that's what Peter claimed when he healed in the name of Jesus." "Blasphemy!" they shouted. "Look," said Max, "why should it matter to you? Everybody here says it's a free country, so leave me free to minister to people, and if you or somebody else thinks I am doing something miraculous, it's up to you." "You don't understand, you can't go round curing people in the name of Perpetua." "Just go away. Please!" Max wondered later whether he might have made a more coherent argument, but he was journeying in new territory. He was shocked at the way people had reacted to his ministry. He was curing people insofar as he could tell. He was grateful that the news had reached local pastors, but not the local news networks. He went to ground to approximate some kind of prayer, some kind of grounding. He felt drunk without drink, with the kind of feeling he could remember from a sleepless night and a substantial time change on an inter continental flight, like living in a fish tank, everything blurred and slightly distant. What kept him grounded were Marta and Perpetua, real and needing him, Marta bewildered by the kindness of their hosts and the opulence with which they were entertained while he did his work, and Perpetua by the violations to her routine.

As he performed the grim rituals at the airport, he was buoyed with the sense of having achieved something. There were faithful leaders in all three major East coast cities, and the Spirit was with them. He had given his message, feeling the Spirit, and he had not failed. He had laid hands on those who had come forward, and they had gone out to form house groups and the rich and poor. He had almost been killed, but he was meant to live. At check-in they were upgraded because of his celebrity status and he found himself sitting next to a man he thought he recognised. "Gregg, isn't it?" He was momentarily puzzled. "Yes, Gregg." "You processed my US Immigration papers." "Yes, did I?" "In London." "Yes, I was temporarily assigned to immigration because of new procedures coinciding with a staff shortage." "But I seem to have seen you somewhere before that," said Max, standing behind him, looking over Gregg's left shoulder as he lowered his arms from the overhead luggage bin. "I don't think that is possible," said Gregg, "unless you have been in some of the less pleasant parts of the Caucasus." "No." Max sat down. Gregg showed no disposition to talk, ostentatiously occupied with the contents of his brief case until the stewardess brought newspapers. Gregg took a Washington Post and started when he saw the front page, for there was a picture of Max next to the headline:

PERPETUANISM BRINGS NEW HOPE

Gregg looked nervous. He began to pick at a thumb nail, and his hands began to sweat. "Is there something wrong?" asked Max. "No. Thank you. I am just embarrassed because I should have known you." "Don't be worried, most people on the planet don't know me." "But I should have remembered. I must be losing my memory." "It's nothing. What is more important is that you are able to feel new hope." "I'm not very religious." "Never mind, just find new hope." There was no thread to the conversation and so it lapsed again, both men sparing themselves further awkwardness by reading. Max fell asleep. Gregg studied his face as if his life depended upon it which, perhaps, it did.

They were greeted warmly in London where their mission had been followed closely. Max volunteered to pick up his old administrative tasks, but his offer was politely but firmly refused. "You don't need to go on a retreat to know," said Trina, "that there is more great work for you to do. You relieved so much pain when you were there. We could see it in the pictures of the public rally and your less public events. When I am speaking I am so bound up in what i am saying that I rarely see the faces, except to focus on one now and again to give some emphasis to a point, but watching the faces on television was a revelation. Will you accept now that you are part of our leadership?" "Yes. I think it would be perverse to deny that I have been called. Where there is despair, we will bring hope. There will be much to do in the next year."

As they disembarked ahead of Max from their first class cabin, Brompton and Strider thought much the same thing—they needed to bring hope. Without even knowing it, they were already part of the re-writing of history. Instead of being the triumphant ideology, the free market was beginning to slip into history as yet another good idea that had been disfigured into a dogma. There was a continuity of rhetoric from the 'old left' which would soon re-surface to call for state intervention. The Government had never rejected either of these strands of thought, but would not go to one extreme or the other. There had to be a balance between competition and regulation, but, above all, people needed hope. "Not at this Conference," said Sir Granville, half to himself. "They won't want to hear anything until the crisis has broken. They just want to celebrate the new leader. I wish them luck of it. If they really understood politics, rather than seeing it as yet another form of sport, a self-indulgence which gives them leave to opine on the basis of scant information, they would be able to see that it will not matter who is Prime Minister or American President." Without knowing it, his volume was rising. "When the ailing chickens come home to roost, the panic will make Stalin look like a prophet of free market capitalism." "You are a little harsh, Granville. How do you suppose you and I could have been elected without these people whose annual compensation is little more than a conference rant?" "Point taken, Horace. I would not be in this if I didn't care for people, but

I only wish we could all agree how limited is our scope. If you look at this rationally, the only solution is to seek the consolation of the Holy Spirit." "Do you mean that economic down-turns are good for religion?" "Good for the numbers who join religious organisations. There's nothing like a bit of misery to promote godliness, but the true heart is that which loves God because of who we are, not how the world is." "You have been listening to Perpetuanism, Granville." "Yes. I fear it will wax perhaps too strongly for its own good as the economic storm clouds gather. The question is how it will survive in the good times."

16.

Sir Pluto looked at his wall-sized map which he meticulously updated, not because he needed reminding of any of his interests, for he cared for them all equally, excepting Hypo, otherwise he would not have agreed to acquire them, nor because he wanted to display the breadth of his interest and power, for he needed the approbation of no-one, nor because he enjoyed gloating because, quite simply, his acquisitions were primarily intellectual and administrative challenges and not miserly hoards, but because he enjoyed the physicality of maps and the process of affixing dots to them. However clever and well qualified were those who worked with him, they seemed to lack knowledge of the more arcane geographical locations, having a problem with the Southern fringe of the Soviet Union and such generally 'insignificant' countries as Bhutan, Paraguay, Guinea Conacree, Tuvalu, and even Lichtenstein. Indeed, Sir Pluto often said, as a modest attempt at humourous perspicacity, that the greatest factor in the improvement of geographical studies in recent years was the growing internationalisation of football. This had, to some extent, improved the basic knowledge of obscure locations—which depended upon the arbitrary nature of the European and World Cup draws—but soccer did not assist his staff in associating products with locations and so, although he enjoyed affixing red dots to the locations of his interests, the more useful indicators were the numbered patches of green shading which showed where green peppercorns or greengages were grown. He had a separate UK map for the branches of Hypo and the location of the various voluntary organisations he supported, and a third which showed a projection of climate change by 2015 including land loss, rainfall, fish stock depletion, bird migration, hurricane damage, glacial retraction, and epidemiological migration. He would have liked to map the changes in the economic status of populations as they relate to climate change, but the data was inadequate, with predictions relying predominantly upon 'green' and development assistance lobbyists, with no countervaling data from the free marketeers who had lost the courage to defend their dogma in the arena of global warming. Simply saying that nature was going through a little climatic tremor, and that we could go on without changing anything, sounded facile. Recently, he had spent more time studying the third map than the other two, but he soon found himself making connections between its projected problems, the contemporary map showing the location of his projects, and the impact of these changes on the products offered by Hypo. The loss of caviar was regrettable, but hardly critical, the loss of the anchovy would be more serious, particularly for those cultures where it was a staple, and the loss of cod had had a serious impact on the fishing industry and on fish consumption so that, at the very time when pundits were calling for a decrease in meat consumption (because of the grain/beef ratio and the production of methane), the fish alternative was rising in price as availability declined. He had already commissioned research on the decline and obliteration of tuna stocks. He was not a coward. He would not run away from a problem because it was difficult, and he would not be misled by bogus data, but he was beginning to feel that he would never again enjoy Hypo in the way that he had before the establishment of reliable data on excess consumption. Retail had lost its rather untidy innocence, and he wondered how long he could centre his life round the management of decline. It might be better to be a promoter of the decline than one of its principal victims. Being an acutely self-conscious person, he had to ask himself whether his slow move—more than a drift, less than a structured commitment—towards Perpetuanism was a matter of principle or a pragmatic strategy for coming to terms with his changing world. He only had to look at his maps to see that the 'game' was over, but why should that lead him to Perpetuanism just because it happened to share his analysis? Religion, after all, should be more than socio-economic perspicacity, but he realised that he was being somewhat unfair. The Perpetuans were saying three things that particularly moved him. Firstly, action was needed now. Secondly, it involved personal commitment; and, thirdly, it offered hope. It was this last prospect which tipped the balance away from giving up Hypo and in favour of using it as a laboratory for hope. He would be ridiculed by competitors and the media. He would face falling profits, a falling share price and shareholder anger, but he thought that, on balance, he could hang on long enough to test the change he thought was needed. He did not care about the competition, he was not all that concerned with falling profits as long as there were profits (and that was one of the key points in his experiments), and shareholders were free to buy and sell at their own risk. He was not sure who to call. Annie Price was on extended compassionate leave, Hawthorne had disappeared to conclude his doctrinal work, and Max had just returned from America. Then he remembered the Dean of Alchester and invited him to lunch, this time confining himself to English bread, cheeses, apples, and micro brewery beer. "Mr Dean—or, as we are meeting on an informal basis, how are you, Simon? It is very good to see you, particularly as I am reminded of you every time I see your cousin." "Yes. Granville is making a name for himself, isn't he? I only hope that he does not overdo it and find himself hounded out. There was a time when it was a minister a week, but it seems slightly more settled now. Nonetheless, to parody whoever it was, the only thing worse than a weak minister is a strong minister. Best to be boring and middling and keep your head down, but Granville's not that sort." "Quite. In fact, I get the impression that he's a bit of a—we used to say 'Crusader', but we can't now—a bit of a—how awkward it is when the culture steals words—a bit of a—damn!—he's prepared to stick his neck out." "Yes, it's odd that he's ended up in international trade because he's always been a campaigner for the MDG and he's now becoming pretty keen on the planned decline in consumption." "I thought he might be, so how does that chime in with Strider, whose special responsibility it is?" "You'd have to ask Strider—and, of course, you could do that better than me, I know—but I suspect there will be some friction. Horace is always careful—one of those middling ministers—and he won't want to get pulled too far in any direction. Anyway, Pluto, you didn't ask me to come here to give you an insider briefing on trade politics." "No. I need your help to get myself properly—oriented—to Perpetuanism. I never do anything without ensuring that it's going to produce the right results, and I hate unintended consequences, collateral damage, or things turning out differently from that which I intended. So if I put my weight behind Perpetuanism I don't want that to exercise an influence on it such that it will change from what it is." "Well, perhaps I'm not the right person to ask, as I've already developed my own somewhat distinctive brand. It seems to me, if you will allow me a few words of explanation, that the Perpetuan core principle of creating space in which others can operate freely, 'choosing to love' would be the simplest way of putting it, necessarily points towards a theology which allows all other religions to operate within its open embrace. In other words, although Perpetua saw many shortcomings in contemporary Christianity and proclaimed that she had come to help put them right, that did not mean that she wanted to overthrow it. There is this Perpetuan dualism which says that you can condemn something in general—greed or Christianity for that matter—but you do not point your finger at individual people because you cannot know about their individual relationship with the Godhead. Perpetuans will both embrace and disagree with Christianity. It might therefore follow from that that Perpetuanism embraces all kinds of non-Christian believers, not in what I would call its 'line of heritage' and, in the meantime, I have taken this seriously in my own bailywick by arranging for Perpetuan worship and Christian worship to take place in the Cathedral." "Admirable. The aspect of Perpetuanism that concerns me, however, is not the 'high theological' but the rather 'lower' economic." "You are right to call this 'lower' because it's a part of the Perpetuan ethic which is, necessarily, 'lower' than its theology. Ethics always are and any religion is in severe danger when it puts its ethics above its theology. Anyhow, Perpetua thought that personal and collective greed was a bad thing—and she's not alone in that—but her criticism was that contemporary Christianity had not really come to terms with this, but that, in view of the importance of self-restraint and, pragmatically, in view of accelerating climate change, it was right that people should make sacrifices in order to help protect the poorest in the world and, not insignificantly, in order to preserve the world for their own grandchildren. Essentially, then, Pluto, it depends how you come at it, and Perpetuanism might well provide you with an economic project, but that would be a much less satisfactory—in my view—outcome than your considering the broader theology and seeing what you do within that. I wonder, though, how you will manage the creation of space as an enabler when you have spent so much of your life directing people and resources." "Strange you should ask that question, Simon, because I think that many people—and I would not include you—almost totally misunderstand people like me—no, I'm not asking for sympathy, as you know—because I can slow down certain developments and speed up others, but there is not much I can do in the grand scheme of things. I could permit or forbid 'soft porn' in my stores, adopt 'Fair Trade' coffee, raise or lower petrol prices slightly ahead of my competitors, introduce a range of herbs from Brazil, alter the packaging specifications for products, ease standardisation on vegetables and fruit, use pricing to encourage and discourage certain products but, in the end, those things would make very little difference. On the other hand, in the smaller enterprises where I have an interest, I can exercise a greater influence, but the organisations are proportionately less influential. It is not quite so simple as an inverse ratio, but it is approximately so. People, whose immediate need is for scapegoats when something 'goes wrong', attribute far too much direct control to people like me. I'm the captain on the bridge, but I can't control the sea and so, you see, it will not be such a break as you might think for me to adopt a Perpetuan way of looking at things. Why I really asked you to come here was to explain to me whether you think that the Perpetuanism is a more helpful guide to living than Christianity." "In a way, that is the wrong question because any 'guide to living', in the sense that I think you mean it, is a 'down stream' consequence of the relationship to which you aspire with the Godhead." "What is the difference between Perpetuanism and Christianity on that point?" "In essence, Christianity thinks that God's only remaining intervention with history will be through the invisible, though discernible, power of the Spirit, whereas Perpetuans believe that Perpetua was as much a part of the Godhead as Jesus, and that God might continue to intervene in history, not only here but on other planets. That is a major technical and theological difference, but not much of a practical difference, except that people can relate to Perpetua and use her as an intermediary to the Parent Creator in a way that Christians have always 'used' Jesus. Perpetua is more immediate than Jesus. Their teaching is almost identical, and one of Perpetua's roles was to reaffirm the teaching of Jesus against all the dirigiste inclinations of Christianity. To sum up, then, I am following Perpetua because I think she has made it easier for people to follow the principles which she shares with Jesus—there is nothing implicitly virtuous in difficulty—and it is my hope that this new energy, injected by her from God, will somewhat mitigate the terrible individual and collective greed and callousness of our society. There is something pragmatic in this. If we go on the way we are, there is the danger of a terrible crash—you would know more about that than me—and that is the issue which is really engaging Granville. It is the pleasing complementarity of doing what is right and what is prudent that attracts him." "I understand what you are saying, and I will gradually dispense with my more commercial interests—not that I think there is anything wrong with commerce in itself—to make some funding available to Max, but also because I want to spend more time on causes which work with the grain of Perpetuanism, but I do not want any fuss." "There will be no fuss, Pluto. We're not like the Catholics who make a big fuss when they 'receive into Mother Church', as has recently happened with Cardinal Podric and some high profile politicians. Everybody in Perpetuanism is encouraged to make commitments to God which can be revised as time goes by. Those commitments are all equal in God's sight, so there's no ranking like the Christian Confirmation, Ordination, Matrimony, and simply resolving to pray every day. They are all as one." "I am grateful, and I will also let Granville know, which might encourage him. Together we might plot a sensible course for the Government. But tell me," he asked, as they were coming to the end of their tasty but sparing meal, "how are you getting on in Alchester?" "Much better than I had anticipated. There was a time when it appeared—I use the word literally—that Bishop James and I were at loggerheads, but we never were. I understood his position and, although I did not agree with it, I did not think it was my place to say anything, as it was difficult enough for such a meticulously conscientious man. He, for his part, could not empathise with my position, but he never doubted my sincerity. To a considerable extent—or, rather, to a greater extent than controversialists will ever grant—we agreed on almost everything, and, strangely, once Perpetuanism came along, we were able to lower the temperature because liberals like me could be put into a nice new container that did not 'contaminate' Anglicanism which, as a Communion, is much better at ecumenism than internal dialogue, so it can talk to Perpetuanism better than to, or about, itself. After his brief 'wobble' towards Perpetuanism at Pentecost, James and I now live in an easy enough relationship. He never much liked the Cathedral, preferring more intimate occasions in parish churches, but he can use it almost any time he likes. He makes less use of it than he could and he has stopped worrying about me." "I don't suppose it is like that everywhere?" "No indeed, Varnish is beginning to get the hang of being an Archbishop. He might have gone into the position thinking that the less he did the better—that is the stance adopted by most conservatives going into power—but he has discovered that doing things and trying to change things is much more 'fun' than letting other people do things to him and the Church. He is beginning to 'enjoy' making decisions. Intellectuals are inclined to make fun of people like Varnish and George Bush because they say such people do not have the intelligence to make good decisions, but ultimately—as you explained so eloquently a moment ago—most people in power only have very narrow bounds to their decision-making although when they have two diametrically opposed options people will be deeply divided about which should be taken. This is an exception even though the media try to make every decision into such an extreme dichotomy. For my part, I think that Varnish has taken precisely the wrong decision—although I would— over the future course of Anglicanism. Left with the Torans and Petrans, he was probably more or less forced to do what he has done, and so there are huge mitigating circumstances, but his 'policy'—and we have to put that word into single quotes—of insisting upon what he calls 'Affirming Orthodoxy', will be disastrous for his own cause, driving millions of middle-of-the-road Anglicans out of 'his' church and, if only nominally, towards Perpetuanism. The tragedy of this is that it will ruin his life's work of maintaining our wonderful heritage of sacred architecture and music." "A stark example of how moving people out of their competence zone can prove disastrous." "Quite; but he naturally does not see it that way. Varnish has convinced himself—as you might suppose he would—that there is a strong symbiosis between architectural heritage and—I am reluctant to use the term, but can find no easy equivalent—structured theology and discipline. Did you see his Enthronement sermon on theology as the spire?" "Thankfully, no. I find that structure—or, rather, pattern recognition—is a very good way of making sense of masses of apparently heterogenous data, but the use of structure to marshall three or four thoughts is, I think, to impose unhelpful constraint." "How very Perpetuan in a Godel-like way!" "I often think that the use of structure conceals the paucity of breadth of outlook, it is as if tidiness conceals emptiness. I often notice how academics impose very rigid structures on their presentations and spend thousands of words saying what could be said in hundreds, but the structure supposedly lends weight and authority to what they are saying. They do not need insight, but simply a plodding and internally consistent methodology." "We are a long way outside my territory, but I do take your point in the homeliest of senses, that Jesus and Perpetua both baulked at the notion that they were primarily theologians. Actually, so would Varnish, but he is getting a taste for it."

Indeed he was. Varnish, who had started out so cautiously, had soon acquired a taste for decision-making; in contrast with his position as an archdeacon who had sparred with the bishop, as Archbishop he had a handful of advisers who, regardless of their private views, made it their business to brief him on all his options, emphasising that whatever he chose to do, upon hearing their advice, they would continue loyally to support him. This was a novel experience for him, as it would be for most of us who accord loyalty but rarely receive it, for it is one of the great ironies of power that those who possess it command a much greater degree of loyalty than those who do not and, therefore, need it more. Quite distinct from the obligations of contract or the obedience of the powerless, the weak accord immense loyalty to the strong, and this was Varnish's strange but gratifying experience. He might have been worried about the shrinking sphere of his influence, but he was not because attitudes to power adjust to the cycle of advance and decline so that, whereas a ruler who expands his boundaries is primarily interested in the breadth of his power, a ruler presiding over a diminishing area of power is much more concerned with its depth, which is why rulers whose empires are on the wane are much more prone to cruelty than those who are enjoying expansion. Thus Varnish, who was not foolish enough to delude himself into thinking that his Church would soon recover from its current decline, was anxious to impose a high degree of uniformity and loyalty over what remained of his shrinking jurisdiction. Predictably, the very strictures of the imposition accelerated the haemorage so sharply that his advisers having caved in, against their better judgment, to his 'policy' of 'Affirming Orthodoxy', urged him to trim before it was too late, not just out of religious conviction but because a point of decline had been reached which required reductions in the paid ranks at every level in the Church from bishops to vergers. Having made so much effort to formulate his religious stance, and having so much enjoyed the novelty of theology after a life of architecture, Varnish was deeply reluctant to amend the formulations which he hoped—never mentally far from architecture—would stand as his monument, and allied with this was the stubbornness of someone who was not entirely in control of the process. He was therefore incapable of subtlety for, only understanding the broadest of outlines, he could only contemplate making major concessions or none at all.

It was at this point that Smoother begged for an urgent meeting. "I do not wish to presume, Archbishop, but I do not easily see how we can make anything positive out of this story." "Surely we need to be truthful and direct, and the rest will take care of itself." "I fear not. One might hope that Christians would be faithful to their Church regardless of circumstances, but people of faith are liable to brand switching. Like politicians, people of different faiths have more in common than they have with those who lack faith and, also like politicians, people of faith, particularly those who take it seriously, are much less prone to the idea that any religion or denomination has a monopoly. The people who think Christianity, or a certain brand of Christianity, has a monopoly are taking themselves, but not religion, seriously. Anyway—I am sorry to have gone off the point slightly—the way I see it is that if the message which goes out from us is totally negative, it will exacerbate decline even further. People can see that we are waning while the Perpetuans are waxing." "Religion is not a numbers game," said Varnish, becoming very stiff. "No," said Smoother, keeping as calm as he could under the circumstances, "but we must be careful of not throwing away our broad church heritage." "It has failed. That has been our core problem, the liberals always undermining orthodoxy." "With respect, I think it would be fairer to say that the Church of England—unlike most of the Anglican Communion— consists of many overlapping ways of witnessing to God. Forgive me, it is not my job to advise you on your doctrinal position, but only on the effect it will have." "Thank you, but I think I can dispense with that sort of spin doctoring. Doctrine will speak for itself. We must rediscover the spirit of the Reformation." Smoother was about to ask, "Which Reformation?" but he curbed himself and looked sadly at Varnish, a man who had resorted to caricatures, the very kind of man that needed help to smooth some of the, almost certainly, unintended sharp edges. Given more time he would have become used to the ways of the quirky and wonderful Church, but there was no time. Smoother could not stop himself wondering whether he wanted to leave because he was disillusioned or because he was now, as a liberal, more in sympathy with Perpetuanism. He hated the thought of jumping, but he hated the thought of being pushed. He waited. "If you are not comfortable with Affirming Orthodoxy, I think you had better leave." Smoother was about to leave when they were interrupted by Bishop Hall. "I am sorry," he said, "but I have come on behalf of more than half of the bishops, and was told that I might come in." "That's my fault," said Smoother, "I came in the private way and forgot to tell the secretary." "Well, James, you're here now," said Varnish, a trifle irritably. "Do you want me to leave, Archbishop?" "I think that would be for the best." "You both looked a little grim when I came in, Archbishop." "He was overstepping the mark. People these days think the media are more important than substance. Well, James, you always were a bit of a prevaricator, what's the latest?" Ignoring a rebuke which verged on rudeness in the way it was delivered, Alchester said, "I have a letter here from half of the bishops who, while affirming their adherence to Affirming Orthodoxy, counsel you against making the Church of England into a narrow sect for that exclusive form of churchmanship." "Which shows how much you value orthodoxy. If it is that important, how could you tolerate unorthodox people in our midst?" "Before we get there, Archbishop, you might want to consider how we will shape Affirming Orthodoxy to encompass Petrans like me and Torans like my Suffragan Castlegate. It is all very well for us to say that we agree on fundamentals, but we don't. We simply agree on some things in the liberal agenda which we oppose. It is for this reason that bishops from both strands of orthodoxy have supported the call in this letter for a moratorium on any further doctrinal narrowing until we have had time to consider our position." "But with Perpetuanism raging at our walls, we must stand firm and fashion a much clearer identity." "Well, to be honest, Archbishop, they are not raging and they are not at our walls, they are walking away from them." "That kind of facetiousness will just not do, Hall." "I am sorry, Archbishop, I was simply representing the situation as it is." "Are you threatening to resign if I do not cave in to your demands?" "If you look at the letter you will see that it is couched in terms of advice from a majority of the House of Bishops and that we are all resolved to work with you within the structures of the Church to resolve this issue." "Well, if you are all so willing to stay, I can't see any reason why I should resile from my position. Then you can settle on a principled decision, one way or the other." "I am so sorry, Archbishop, that is just not the way we do things in the Church of England." "In such a crisis as this, this is precisely the way in which we are going to do things. The House of Bishops is a flimsy advisory body which has no *locus standi*, as well you know. I have decided to cancel its forthcoming meeting and direct the Church of England as I think fit, subject to the reserve powers of Parliament. The Grand Synod has been so decimated by recent events that we will have to hold a completely new set of elections, so that takes care of that." "If I might suggest, Archbishop,

..." "... I think not, James, I think not. I must say how much I have respected your steadfastness to the Petran cause over the years, and now that you are getting a little Petran medicine within the bounds of the Church of England you seem not to like it. I suppose it's always an admirable quality when it is administered elsewhere to others." "So what am I to tell your fellow Bishops?" "That our simple task is to iron out any minor differences between us over the meaning of Affirming Orthodoxy." "But am I not correct in saying that you have just cancelled the very meeting of the House of Bishops which might do that thereby, in effect, granting the signatories to this letter the very moratorium they have requested?" Varnish was stunned. If he reinstated the meeting he would look weak and foolish, but if he did not he would be caving in to the Bishops. "Look James," he said, trying to smile, "let us relax just a little. Sit down instead of drawing yourself up like a Guardsman." Alchester reluctantly perched himself on the edge of a chair. Varnish decided that the risk of Alchester spilling the beans was less than a public acceptance of any kind of moratorium. "Look, James, perhaps I was a little hasty—and of course I would naturally be grateful if the details of our frank conversation were kept between us—and I will reply to the letter you have brought. It might in fact be best to bring the meeting of the House of Bishops forward so that we can resolve any outstanding little doctrinal details. After that we can consider those who do not sign up to our position as a somewhat secondary matter." "But they are souls in need of care." "The Church is not a theological dust bin, James—but we seem to be becoming formal again—and I think you would prefer us to meet sooner rather than allow the House of Bishops to wither and die." Alchester was stunned by these highly irregular suggestions, and the brutality of the language in which they were expressed. "The point is not our position, but tolerance for those who do not share it. In Alchester we have reached a very comfortable arrangement with the Dean who is, as you know, Perpetuan in his leanings." "I daresay you have, James, I daresay you have. I would have expected nothing different—comfortable, you say?—but we have reached the time for a decision. Either you agree to a meeting of the House of Bishops simply to discuss the definition of Affirming Orthodoxy, with no discussion about those who do not agree to its terms, or I will simply not summon the House." "I cannot accept either of those alternatives, Archbishop, and I think I am safe in saying that almost all the signatories to this letter will agree with what I have just said." "Your adherence to Affirming Orthodoxy is such, then, that you will abandon me and it at the first difficulty." "I believe that we will think that being loyal to God's will is more important than being loyal to an overly narrow doctrine or to you as its chief proponent." Alchester was beginning to feel angry—a difficult emotion for him as it was so unfamiliar—and he had to prevent himself from reminding Varnish of the relative difference in their theological education. He also felt himself in a most exposed position, as he had never before been the leader of a faction or a group of 'rebels'. He had been outspoken in the Petran cause, and had occasionally exercised patronage and made decisions which were in its interest, but he had never been involved in the strategy or the tactics and, while he had signed a number of letters, he had never put himself at the head of a campaign or movement. The thought of walking out of the room in a state of open disobedience to his Primate—even though he was only a *primus inter pares*—frightened him in the way that an unhappy man or woman contemplates divorce after many years of marriage during which only the last few have deteriorated from tedium into hostility and near violence. It was not just the doctrine—in spite of his own somewhat rigid position, Alchester had sat on enough international ecumenical commissions to become a master of the nuance—but also the buildings, hierarchies, trappings and, above all, the friendships of his whole career. Varnish saw none of this. He had been engaged for so long in disputes about buildings that he had never considered the effect of 'winning' and 'losing' on the lives of those with whom he was in dispute. Yet when Varnish, with another tactical flourish, invited him to "sleep on it", Alchester was uncharacteristically sharp. "If there is room for Castlegate and me in the Church, there is room for millions of others with less restricted doctrinal positions within the Church of England. If there is not, it is not, and if it is not, there is no place for me and many fellow bishops in it." "But you have always hankered after a red hat from Rome, James!" "Whether or not I have thought that I would be more doctrinally 'comfortable' in the Roman Catholic Church, I have remained a Petran in the Church of England precisely because of its uncritical hospitality. It has been difficult for me, often painful, sometimes messy—but that is what homes are like—and I prefer that to the obsessive tidiness of Rome. However, that is not to the point now. Any observation you might make about my inclinations can only be a matter of speculation. Let me repeat, that the Church of England is, above all, an enabling vehicle for the Christian faithful of England, not a sect. Unless you consider an alternative to the two you have proposed, I will be forced ..." "... to consider your position." "No. I am neither a blackmailer nor a coward. Unless you offer a third option, right now, I will tender my resignation." "I have nothing more to say, James. Good day." Alchester rose slowly from his chair, looked at the picture of Hawthorne which had not yet been replaced by his successor, looked somewhat sadly and bewilderedly at Varnish, and walked out, closing the door quietly behind him. As he passed Smoother's neighbouring room he noticed two cardboard cartons just inside the door and the empty desk. Smoother was sorting cables, careful to take only what was his. "Are you leaving too?" "Why, are you leaving?" "I have just told the Archbishop that I am, and I believe that more than half of the House of Bishops will come with me." "It would have been an interesting story to handle." "You could come and work with us." "Sorry, James, it's over. I suppose it's 'affirming Orthodoxy' that's finally pushed you to the limit, but you were one of the first to use the word Orthodox inside the Church of England. I'm sorry, I don't wish to be unkind, or even personal. I simply wish to show that orthodoxy is fine when you're winning, and pretty horrible when you're losing. The terms of trade can change so rapidly. I'm sorry, James. I know you meant well. We all did, and look at us." "I have made the biggest mistake of my life, Chris. I should have been a quiet Toran and a public liberal instead of being a public Toran and a quiet liberal. They never were incompatible, but I allowed myself to be pushed by the campaigners for women and gays, and look where it has led. Never mind me, however, you are only in your early 1940s, how are you going to live?" "Well, I could write the book, but I doubt that many people will be interested in the death throes of the Henrican settlement. I will see if the Perpetuans want me, both as a professional and as an adherent. I have never been the same since Easter Sunday when I saw her on television. And what will you do, James?" "I will go on being a Bishop—I only resigned verbally—trying even harder to work with the Dean. What the Archbishop chooses to do is up to him, although I think he will find it somewhat difficult to do anything."

The followers of Perpetua travelled throughout the land, and brought many people back to God, and many more to God who had been indifferent, hostile or ignorant. They performed great wonders in the name of God, bringing great joy to the sorrowful, peace of mind to the afflicted, curing people of their illnesses and addictions. Everywhere they went, and every time they performed such wonders, they said that they were working in the name of the Godhead and that, as Perpetua had taught, such acts were not magic tricks to attract attention, but were signs of the love of God. Each act was performed so that each person might be given a new start in dedicating life to the love of God through the love of humanity, through taking control of life, exercising freedom, but, most of all, honouring the autonomy of others. There were those who said that this was the beginning of licence, that it went beyond the proper bounds of liberty, but they preached a doctrine of self-restraint and responsibility for the self, proclaiming that regulation and external discipline were a distraction from the real issue, that crime was not the responsibility of the Government but of criminals, that greed was the fault of bankers not regulators, that there was no "they" who should be doing anything because we must lead a life of the "I" of affirmation, and the Spirit moved throughout the land, and there was great joy, and the people praised God for their new sense of freedom.

Annie Price thought she needed an extended period of compassionate leave, but she soon found out that she was wrong. After two weeks of breaking her days up into bite sized pieces, performing ever more trivial and unnecessary tasks, going for walks she did not enjoy, and finding herself thinking of Will so much that the bad spots began to show through the gloss, she could not bear another day. Besides, the very few friends who came to visit her immediately after Will's funeral had all abandoned her, thinking that they had fulfilled their office of friendship with one or two duty calls. She had never formed close, personal, tell it all, relationships, and she loved her work at Hypo because, even when she was alone in her office, she had the sense of hundreds of people within a few metres, of staff working to their routines and customers passing through the store. She loved the aggregate predictability of it and the tiny variations in behaviour which statistically cancelled each other out, but which constituted the richness of life. With the keenness of a novelist imagining her buying a wedding ring, she watched a woman buying peaches. As keenly as a novelist imagining a captain standing on the bridge looking towards stormy weather, she studied the face of the man reading Fair Trade literature. As keenly as a novelist imagining a girl at her first dance, she watched a teenage girl alternately scowling (when her mother was looking) and smiling (when she was not) at a row of trainers. Now and again there was enough aggregate behaviour indicating a tremor which might coalesce with other similar tremors into a trend. There might be huge stickers in her front windows screaming "Prices slashed!!" but she knew that the essence of serious, long-term, reliable retailing was attention to detail. A few pennies more for chocolate, a Pound more per bottle for Australian red wine, a new biscuit buying routine, a switch from air and sugar breakfast cereal to Mousli, an adventure with bottled water or courgettes. When she thought about it, she knew that while the retailing was an intellectual challenge which she enjoyed, the people were the fuel which kept her alive. Perhaps she would never form a really close relationship—as she looked back she realised how little she and Will had actually learned about each other—but she recognised in this seemingly unending period of isolation that she needed people. At the end of her third week she phoned Sir Pluto. "I am so grateful for the personal note you sent me, and for the granting of what is, in terms of our Staff Manual, excessive compassionate leave, but I have not taken to it at all well. In fact I think that being at home alone is much less good for me than being at the store. Some people hurl themselves into their work after a personal setback as a way of hiding from it, but I do not think that this is so in my case. Perhaps my partnership with Will would have developed into something really wonderful—I think in my life my relationships will always develop steadily rather than reaching my heart like cupid's arrows—but, to be honest, I cannot pretend that we were deeply in love and, although I missed him and honoured him after his death, I am beginning not to miss him and to see him in a more balanced perspective. I don't know why I am telling you this except that I feel I need to articulate it, but I am beginning to think that Will died in the way that a well trained soldier dies. He was not particularly brave, it was just part of his training. I doubt he calculated the odds and took a definite decision to go on filming after the first two shots. My guess is that he never gave the odds a second thought. I am not going to pretend I am worse than I am to extend my leave, not least because I have come to dislike my leave. There is too much time which has to be consciously filled—I don't suppose you have ever seen day-time television? It's terrible!—and I have not yet found the skill to choose books that suit me. I can only take a couple of hours of music before I get fed up with it. I'm a bit shallow, I suppose, I love small things, but they are not enough to fill a home life." "That is by far the longest speech I have ever heard you make." "I am sorry." "Not at all, I wish more people made more speeches like that." "It's because I've been on my own so much." "Don't apologise. In my experience the people who have something interesting to say don't talk enough and the ones who have nothing interesting to say talk too much. I am very glad to hear you talk, not least because I have been thinking of a plan which will involve you and which will involve you spending less time behind your desk and more time interacting with people." "I don't want to lose my store. I love it." "You will not, although I think you are capable of managing a much bigger unit or a number of units, but, instead, the store you love is going to be a laboratory for social change and I want you to understand, believe in and promote that change. It will involve you in a complete reversal of everything you have ever learned about retail. Our job is to persuade people to buy everything they need, but not to buy frivolously or wastefully. The second stage is to persuade them—and we have to be realistic here—to donate part of what they save to helping the poor because, as you know, declining consumption always hurts the poor first." Annie's well regulated mind performed the reverse move just to see what it might be like: buy half a bottle of red, delay buying new trainers for two or three more weeks, buy a smaller Chinese ready meal, drink tap water, make your own salad dressing, continue to use chipped bowls at least in private, reintroduce eccentric vegetables and fruit, cut packaging, promote best value. "I know you will be able to meet this challenge, not least because you have something of a Perpetuan background, but we need to be clear about what we are doing, the risks we are taking, the hostility we will encounter and, perhaps most difficult of all, we will need to work out how any donations can best be used to serve the poor. Before beginning, I must ask you whether you would like to think about this for a few days." "No. I don't need time. I see the sense of it. It will be an interesting challenge, and I will learn even more about people. It's simply a matter of remembering what I have done and doing the opposite." "I hope we have not been quite so unscrupulously exploitive as you imply." "I'm sorry ..." "No. No. It's my kind of humour. I am somewhat suspicious of grand phrases, and am thinking of using the Grunge Park store as a laboratory for change." "I will do my best." "Come and see me as soon as you can and, if he's available, we will be joined by Max."

Being a man of much greater self-knowledge than Horace Strider, Granville Brompton knew that they were on a collision course weeks before Horace, and so he was able to devise a strategy which would make the breach between them as painless as possible for Horace who, he knew, did not enjoy the great consolations of Jesus, Handel, Dostoyevsky, Brancusi, and Margeau, but lived only for politics and judged his drink according to its quantity. During their time in Washington he had watched Horace balancing the twin, fundamentally incompatible imperatives—barring the prospect of founding growth on the manufacture of energy saving technologies—of growth and greenness, almost imperceptibly shaving commitments to the latter and adding every possible mite to the former. Granville knew all about reading the signs. He knew that although the public saw politicians making flamboyant statements and falling from the sky like spent comets, the essence of their trade was executing thousands of tiny moves for or against core propositions. He had learned to assess positioning on big issues on the basis of positioning on apparently small ones. Politics was not about 'left' and 'right', where you stood, but which way you faced, and a change of direction by one degree would—the Proust perspective—lead to a massive divergence over time from a previous position. Horace, elegantly executing his minute manoeuvres, was not conscious, as they were 'on the same side', of Granville's differences. He thought that all they really differed on was rhetoric and not substance so that, when they emerged from an extended session on carbon trading, Horace had said, "It is unusual for a committee like that to become so carried away by its own rhetoric. I hope we did not say more than we meant." "I tried to say exactly what we meant." "I hope we have not gone further than the agreed position, it sometimes sounded as if we had." "I will take full responsibility. I quite deliberately took our position slightly further than the agreed position, but that was because I want to end up with the agreed position, not at some place half way between it and the opposition. The art of negotiation, Horace, does not consist in making compromises, but in appearing to make them. As a moralist, I wish that we could start with our genuine positions and work from there, but I am afraid that we must resort to a certain degree of dissimulation." "Yes, Minister," said Strider, slightly ironically, "but are you actually saying that our agreed position was not your starting point, but your intended finishing point?" "That is precisely what I am saying," Granville said, looking directly at Horace who could not, characteristically, comfortably handle his gaze, and at that point he knew two things, as clearly as he could know anything, that would not occur for another two weeks. They would disagree about trade policy in such a fundamental way that they would not both be able to remain in the same Department. Even though he was senior to Horace, he would resign because the Prime Minister would be against him. When he returned to London his first objective was easily achieved: he asked his Permanent Secretary to ascertain from Number 10 where Horace's stock stood, and was told that his edging towards growth. His mild scepticism over some green proposals had left him in a much improved position, and that he was as safe at Trade as he could be anywhere. If he had an error free party conference—which was likely, as he only had a minor speech to make and was known to detest fringe meetings—unless he drank too much, which was always a possibility, he could look forward to another year in harness. His second objective was to ensure that the cause of the breach, when it came, could be attributed entirely to himself. Horace needed to emerge with credit, while he would not mind the two or three days of mild derision which would greet his departure. He therefore took the agreed position on growth and green issues, and carefully re-drafted it with such a radical shift towards the green that Strider would have to register his dissent. The alternative, of letting things drift, would be messy and painful and might not turn out well for Horace. There were ways of handling the inevitable and, as he read his re-draft, his mind turned to a substantial shelf of unplayed—and barely known—Handel operas.

No two Party Conferences are the same, and this one possessed the twin features of a Prime Minister triumphant after a decade-long campaign to unseat his predecessor and the prospect of a 'snap' General Election. Granville thought this could only mean that there was no confidence in the medium-term. There was a third feature, which went almost unremarked by the media, but which struck him forcibly, and this was a deep sense of wasted opportunity and time. It reminded him of the mid-1970s when flower power had given way to power cuts and the oil crisis. Somehow they had failed to ride the wave and knew that it would soon break. If Brown did not "go" immediately, many thought, there would not be another chance and, as part of that sombre under-current, there was a marked turning towards Perpetuanism. People on the 'left' were struggling with the tension between the desirable ends for which she stood and the deeply suspect means. They had been brought up to do good, to redistribute and to regulate, to inspect and monitor, to propose and report and, above all, to imprint their vision of social and economic justice, no matter how imperfectly, on a deeply damaged land. They applauded the idea of giving particular attention to the poor, but could not grasp the idea of its being achieved through the more assertive exercise of autonomy, a concept they viewed, in spite of—or perhaps because of—New Labour, with deep suspicion as a fundamentally Tory precept. Granville, knowing that his hour was not far off, but also determined to play his part so that his departure would be as quiet as possible, met his quota of fringe meetings and receptions, but concentrated not on his trade brief but on the more philosophical and even theological fare on offer. This included a Perpetuan stand, run by Wayne, who was cheerfully distributing educational materials while god4u played in the background. "I remember you," said Granville. "No, it's not just the cliche about politicians never forgetting a face. I remember how badly you were treated by the media because you're gay and how Perpetua stood up for you." "Unto death," said Wayne. "I still miss her terribly in spite of her promise, which she has faithfully kept, that the Spirit would be with us." He was about to pass on to the next stand when he was tapped on the shoulder by one of the Prime Minister's aides. "There's a rumour that you and Horace Strider are at loggerheads. Well, actually, it's more than that. He had rather a lot to drink at a lunch-time reception and complained in a rather loud voice that you are undermining his work on a growth strategy to keep us out of recession." Granville, more cautious in his habits than the young man who addressed him, walked, without haste, across the exhibition hall, and stepped outside. "Am I supposed to be having this conversation with you or the Prime Minister?" "I'm only telling you as a favour." "Nobody in your position ever onlies anything, and you never do any favours." "All right, I'll come clean." "Apart from being a horrible cliche, you won't." "How can I talk to you when you are so scratchy?" "You didn't come here to talk to me, did you?" "Not really. I just came to say that the PM is very angry." "With whom?" "With both of you." "He's angry with me because Horace got drunk?" "Don't be silly, he just doesn't like the in-fighting." "Coming from him that is Himalayan," said Granville, aware that he was beginning to enjoy himself too much. "What do you want me to do?" "Patch it up publicly with Horace." "Look, sorry, I never did ask your name ..." "... Geoff Brooks." "Look, Geoff, in the first instance, nobody would believe me, because they would not want to, even if I was telling the truth. Secondly, Horace and I fundamentally disagree about the balance to be struck between two diametrically opposed pieces of Government policy. So if the PM wants to solve this, he needs to get at the substance, not a symptom." "Well, I've told you." "Yes, you have." Granville dated his letter and went to the Prime Minister's suite where the silly hysteria of speech writing was well under way. Granville knew that they would argue for the next 24 hours about every line, but that whatever he said the effect would be minimal because of his disastrous delivery and body language which accounted for approximately 90% of the effectiveness of a speech. He asked to see the Prime Minister for a few minutes and was, routinely, told that he was not seeing people because he was preparing his speech. "I'm a Cabinet Minister and I don't ask to see the Prime Minister unless I need to. The obvious course for a Cabinet Minister, as you will learn—Geoff, isn't it?—is to keep away from the Prime Minister for as long as possible. Contact either means censure or interference." Geoff gave way. "I won't stay more than a minute," said Granville, on entering. "Horace Strider and I fundamentally disagree about policy. I am in favour of managing a fall in consumption, he is in favour of growth. You are in favour of him, he needs his job more than I need mine, and in spite of what those idiots who guard your door are saying, your choice to call an election or not will make my resignation a footnote. I've got my letter here." "I'm sorry on a personal level, as you are one of the straightest people we've got, but there is going to be a recession and we will need all Horace's ingenuity. Green politics were all right in the golden days that Tony enjoyed, but we have to be more realistic." "Look, Gordon, there is no point wasting our time rehearsing this. I'm ready to go at a moment of your choosing." "It's the speech." "I know it is," said Granville, only just concealing his scepticism. "We'll do it next week when I've had all the coverage I can get," said the Prime Minister. But Geoff, who was over-anxious to become a 'key player', and who was susceptible to flattery and sparkling wine, spilled what he supposed to be the beans to a junior reporter who, anxious to make a name for himself, filed a stronger story than Geoff's hints justified, and his editor, who hated the Government, printed a stronger story than his reporter had filed, as the result of which the Prime Minister's hopes for a good speech build-up and assessment were not ruined by his own clumsiness, disloyal MPs or even by a hostile media, but by those who claimed to care most for his interests. As he ruefully surveyed the "Split" headlines, Granville knew that he could do no good and might do some harm by staying. He helped Wayne load the tiny remainder of his materials into a van and drove off with him.

"Another little ministerial mess," thought Sneer, as he looked a little crossly at the short list of potential front page leads on his screen. The Labour Party Conference had been excruciatingly boring, except for the flurry of speculation over an election, but readers soon got tired with that kind of thing. The Ministerial resignation from Trade was hardly earth-shattering, just not prominent enough to count. The "Little Phil Mac" story was still dead, defying the massive emotional and financial investment in it. The economics of climate change were far too complicated to explain, and although sex always sold papers he was beginning to run out of the means to exploit it. He stared a little more closely. He must have nodded off for a few seconds, as he had seen Perpetua on his screen. Impossible. There was the menu with the shared documents log. Flicker. There she was again, for a split second. Flicker. Menu.

Sneer was not given to self-searching, not because he was not self-aware but precisely because he was. He knew that he could not bear too much self-examination. There was no justification for someone as well educated and gifted as he knew himself to be to be passing his days in the office of a mean spirited tabloid newspaper which survived on the misfortunes of humanity and specialised in a uniquely crude form of hypocrisy by promoting that which it claimed to decry: the glorification of sexual promiscuity, the delicious allurements of naked teenage girls, the status accorded to celebrities (particularly those who had done nothing to earn it), the glamour of narcotics, and the sensationalism of politics. He knew that he lived in a state of permanent denial, of low-level, chronic, intellectual, and moral pain which could not be assuaged by increasing his intake of red wine any further, as it had already reached a point where it threatened to derail his career. As he looked at the menu of potential leads, he came close to saying a prayer. Flicker. He saw her. Flicker. Menu. He phoned Poppy who was approaching the status of a girl friend. "Do you know where your dad is? I've tried his office and they say he isn't answering." "I think he's with the Dean of Alchester. He texted me to say we could meet later to compare notes." "How is he getting on?" "All right, though it's none of your business ..." "... Oh, go easy!" "He's a bit preoccupied. I think he's catching the Perpetua bug." "What makes you think so?" "He's been rather dreamy since Easter, and he no longer tells me what happens between himself and that old bore, Varnish." Sneer's news nose didn't even quiver. "I'll call you later to see if we can meet"

"Chris, it's Sneer, could you come round when you've finished your meeting?" "For the sake of my lovely daughter who, unaccountably, seems to have a soft spot for you, of course I will." As Chris came in, he looked around with his usual mixture of admiration for the technology and contempt for the content it handled. "I don't get it," he said. "Don't your readers ever get bored with girls in bikini pants?" "Apparently not, but, look, I didn't ask you round for yet another of your pious critiques of our slick and salacious publication. Spare me! I know what you are going to say, but in a way that you never grasp, Chris, the real decay lies not in the suppliers, but the consumers. We wouldn't supply it if they didn't consume it, I promise you." "But they couldn't consume it if you didn't supply it." "Of course they could, and do. Hardly a week goes by without a vicar, policeman, or school teacher being nicked for downloading thousands of frames of child pornography." "All right, but I didn't come here either to hear your crit." "Fair enough," said Sneer, turning towards his screen. "I just want to tell you a story. Earlier today I was looking at my Editorial Conference Shared Docs page when I thought I saw Perpetua. I thought that I must have nodded off because when I woke up the screen was there again, but it happened three times." "The Holy Spirit," said Chris, without thinking about it. "What?" "You heard. I really believe in the reality of the Holy Spirit." "Normally I would laugh, but this is getting too serious. Remind me." "When your paper tried to slag off Perpetua, the stories got changed between the final clearance of the pages and what came out of the presses. The film of Perpetua's death, which Poppy took, all disappeared, every last trace of every last copy of it. Perpetua has twice completely controlled global television networks, at Christmas last year and Easter this year. She even manifested herself at Pentecost. Now I know this is very difficult for atheists to handle, but nobody has a scientific theory for what happened. The trouble with our supposed culture is that if it can't find a 'scientific' solution, it claims there is no solution. Go back to being the investigative journalist and sharp thinker you were when you began, before you got sucked into this shallow, iterative world." "All right! I admit that the 'evidence', the 'facts', or whatever you might call them; there isn't a word ..." "... Try 'phenomena', then." "These phenomena send a compelling message which I can't ignore; but what is she saying?" "I don't know, but neither do I believe in coincidence. I have just parted company with Varnish, not on the friendliest of terms, and I am about to go and offer myself to the Perpetuans as a follower and, if they will have me, as a media helper. Why don't you come with me?" "It's a big leap." "I know, but you know that there's nothing to be done in this wicked world without sacrifice. Poppy's settled enough and, if she'll have you, I'm sure the two of you will get by." "Yes, I know about sacrifice, but I don't want her to suffer. This is a lot to give up." "If she loves you—and she seems to—You don't even need to ask her what she thinks about sacrifice. Don't look back, just empty your top drawer and walk." Which is precisely what Sneer did, moved by Perpetua, the Holy Spirit, boredom, guilt, or remorse. He was not sure, but he never did look back. He walked straight through the news room and was so anxious to be gone that he did not wait for the lift, but walked down the four sets of dusty stairs. He put his pass card into an envelope, took a business card, and wrote on its back, "Resigned —Sneer", and followed Chris across the glass and marble atrium and out of the front door, for good. For good. But his bravery deserted him when he walked into the god4u office which had recently been set up near London Minster. They were civil enough to Chris but looked at him as if he were a ghost or, much worse, the devil. Chris asked for Max, but was pleased and surprised to be greeted by Trina who smiled at him, and then retained her smile as she extended her hand to Sneer. "Surprised?" he asked. "Nothing surprises me about the Spirit," she said. "Let us go out for a walk, as this might be one of the last warm days of the year. Well, it's not that, actually. It will be wonderful for people to see the reality of our friendship instead of just reading about it or hearing about it. I want to walk between the two of you." "I thought you would never want to talk to me after what the paper did to you." "We are new friends, but that does not mean that we should be careless. It wasn't the paper that did anything to me, it was you." "Sorry, yes." "Nonetheless, we are friends because that does not depend on some kind of score card. You are my friend because, clearly, you have been 'moved'—I use the word almost ironically—by the Spirit." "I don't know whether I have been moved, but I have moved."

"People tend to want their spiritual experiences to be dramatic, which is why they use words like 'called', 'committed', and 'moved' but, in reality, our struggle to communicate with and pick up God's self-communication with us is hard and not very glamorous work. For those of us who are blessed, it results in the most wonderful moments of epiphany, and I suspect that that is what has happened to you." "I saw her." "No doubt you did, although whether that was your inner being or a technological flash is a mystery. We never have been able to work out how Perpetua's technological powers worked in practice. Bryan has been struggling with this issue for months without getting anywhere. Perhaps he never will. Anyway, I do not doubt—for all its dramatic content and my inclination for something less spectacular—that you have been moved, and the question is what we should do. I presume that your coming here together was fortuitous. I would like you to work together because of your different gifts. Our beloved brother, the former Archbishop Hawthorne, is about to produce his eagerly awaited work on a tentative doctrinal framework for Perpetuanism and it is going to need loving, understanding, and perceptive explanation. I believe you possess those qualities between you. This is a wonderful day for us. We do not mind sacrifice, but I have not enjoyed handling media relations when I know there are other things that I must do. It was all very well for the Apostles to rustle up a few Deacons, but Perpetua founded a movement with a profoundly technological and media twist. In her life and teaching she made it clear that our main purpose was to enable people to establish relationships with God, and that means a passion for communication which we must communicate. People have a passion for consumption but that is not the same thing. I think that the love affair with computers and games consoles is much better than the love affair with television, no matter how high the quality of the programmes; but choice requires communication, and taking control of your life requires creativity, contribution rather than consumption. People keep confusing the media with their purpose, as if there was something intrinsically bad about televisions, games consoles, or computers. The ultimate objective must be for people to consume intelligently so that they can produce. I need your help to shift people from being passive to active. I don't mind if people make mistakes or are initially very crude, but our purpose on earth is to reflect the creativity of God Our Parent, the compassion of Jesus My Brother, the Wisdom of My Sister the Spirit, and the assertion of personhood of Perpetua, the Sustainer. There is a paradox here, I know, between the concept of love as the creation of space for the beloved, and my rejection of the passive and advocacy of the active, but I am no theologian—or do I mean formulator of doctrine?—and this creative tension will have to be worked out. Do you want to start there?" "No thank you," said Sneer, "but I do want to understand what I am doing." "Naturally, but I am not sure how far any of us can do this. We act in accordance with what we think is the will of God, but our relationship with the Godhead is one which falls short of, and goes beyond, the idea of understanding. As I spend more time in communication with the Godhead, I find myself becoming entangled in the kind of theology, veering towards doctrine, that Perpetua claimed not to have mastered. I had hoped that her presence would reduce the need for 'dry' doctrine, but I fear that, even though she only left us a few months ago, we are going abstract. We need to capture her life and teaching before we extract its essence to make abstract propositions. The problem for Christians is that their theology diverged from their Gospels, whereas we have a great deal of evidence about the real Perpetua which can inform whatever theology we need. By the way," she said to Chris, as they were about to end, "how did you get on with the Dean of Alchester?" "Very well. He told me about his collaborative model of working with his bishop." "Yes, there will soon come a point when we need some—another of those words—ecclesiology about that, too. The Bishop and the Dean, who are both distinguished theologians, seem to have hit on a much better notion of mutual respect, trust and tolerance, without needing to justify or specify what each might do in the absence of the other. The Dean loves the historicity of Church of England worship, but feels it has something missing. The Bishop is comfortable with his tradition, but is intrigued by the new way of looking at the Godhead. I hope that neither has to choose between the two things they love for different reasons. Perhaps the greatest error of the early Christians was that they never found a way of holding the old and the new together although they claimed that was their desire. Somehow Judaism and Christianity came apart. I have to admit that I am enjoying every last moment of naive new dawn before I have to become embroiled in what may turn out to be a great deal of power playing and, please excuse me, male gamesmanship. I know that the mystery of God and the enquiry of humanity make doctrine more or less inevitable, but I just pray that there may be a short delay, that we may enjoy just a little of the innocence of faith. I think you should go down and see them."

Sneer and Smoother watched Trina as she walked away from them in the early Autumn sunset towards what she knew would be a long and difficult Winter, not so much because of external examination, but because self-examination would put them all under very great strain when they discovered that, in spite of everything that Perpetua had lived for, the same pattern which had followed the death of Jesus would be difficult to resist. She had put a generous gloss on the necessity for doctrine, but she saw a darker side which involved humanity wanting to subvert God for its own purposes. As she walked past London Minster, she saw Varnish coming out, looking tired and sad. She was profoundly sorry for him because she knew how thin the line is between being faithful and being self-deluding. As she passed within the shadow of the East Wall, she prayed that the Spirit would give her strength. Sneer and Smoother watched Varnish squint in the light of the golden setting sun, as if he were frightened of whom he might see or who might see him. Smoother did not know whether to stand his ground or tactfully—tactically—make it easy for Varnish to ignore him, but his decision to turn away came too late. Varnish adjusted his focus from the far distance of the sun to the two men, and walked steadily towards them, looking neither to the right nor the left. "Chris, I am sorry. I am tired. I hardly know what to do. I

am not really a bishop. I seem to know you from somewhere; a journalist? Perhaps I should be careful …" "Don't worry," said Sneer, almost gently, and without any attempt to mislead. "I am not up to this job. I should never have taken
it, and now my sleep is being disturbed by dreams of Perpetua. She never says
anything, she just looks serene and sad. She looks as if she is trying to lead me
somewhere." "If I were you, Archbishop, I would not question what is happening too closely. I would simply follow." "It's so difficult. I don't want to let down
the Church that has called upon me." "It is more important that you follow the
God that has called upon you than the Church." "I know, Chris, but my whole
life has been spent in the monuments of Chris. I have almost come to consider
myself as a broken monument of Christ. Beneath all of my care for buildings,
there has always been a deep commitment to Our Saviour. I simply thought that
I was so bad at prayer and theology, and so incapable of getting on God's wavelength, that I decided that serving through the physical buildings was the only
thing I could properly do. I should never have taken on this role, but now that I
have, what am I to do?" "Pray," said Smoother. "Trust in the Holy Spirit instead
of worrying about your 'prayer life', just live it from within you rather than trying to analyse it from the outside. Equally importantly, Archbishop, go home,
eat a modest dinner with a glass of wine, and sleep. You look as if you are being
overwhelmed by the Earth." Varnish moved away from them, westwards across
the park, the play of the light making his figure black and small. He seemed to
be taken up into the golden light. As he stopped to collect his tattered thoughts,
he was overwhelmed by a golden sense of well being and completeness and, for
the first time in his hard working, faithful, but combative life of service, he felt
the power of God. As the sun set, the power of the Holy Spirit was alive in the
consciousness of many who had never thought to know it, and many who had
denied it. As the last warm day gave way to a moonless night, the torn world felt
comfort beyond all reason.

17.

For a young woman who spent so much of her time handling ethical dynamite, Stacey was not given to excessive introspection. Indeed, perhaps it was
that very abstinence—among many abstinences—which enabled her to maintain such an insistent monologue, based almost entirely on the various and dis-
tilled experience and pronouncements of others. Although she felt deeply about
God and all His—and here, as in so much else in her grasp of what she received,
the gender was literal and meaningful, not metaphorical—creatures, she would

have been appalled to be told that she was a fresher in the philosophy of religion rather than being an Evangelist because she did not enjoy a personal relationship with God, but simply retailed a series of propositions. She advocated sexual abstinence without having felt any sexual desire, she lectured on the route out of addiction without ever having been entrapped by it, she preached against lying without understanding her own power of self-delusion, she proclaimed God's goodness without ever having felt it, and she expounded the truth of the Bible without ever having read most of it. Although she had not yet reached twenty, she had already preached the Lord in the Ukraine, Burkina Faso, and Brazil, so oblivious of other forms of Christianity that she did not think she was competing with them but was, rather, driving out heresy which was, although she did not know it, a very strange Papal concept for a Baptist descendant of Peter Chelcicky, Conrad Grebel & Co, Tomas Muntzer, and Roger Williams. Living in tiny overseas pieces of America, similar to its military and diplomatic establishments, with their predictable cuisine, predictable drinks, predictable television, and predictable evangelism, never faced by hardship, uncertainty, conflict or a sense of better fortune than the poor, it was her 'calling' to instruct. She was word perfect in the recitation of Psalm 23 and she was well acquainted with the blistering passages on shepherds in Jeremiah and Ezekiel. Her pastoral skill extended no further than handing out candy, and any fair-minded person would have concluded from her witness to Jesus that he had been a Pharisee rather than a shepherd. Her shallow charm and even shallower experience had brought nobody to Jesus, but it had brought many to recognise the material benefits of being associated with her sect, for in all three countries there was a keen market in the material advantages of evangelism where ancient Catholic incumbents were losing out to shinier, wealthier, less demanding 'fresh expressions'. Again, oblivious of this exercise of self-interest which, if she had known what it meant she would have characterised as cynicism, she concluded each mission with a full score card, a badge, an onward reference, an ignorance of any of the local features which characterised each country, a deep suspicion of strange cuisine, her innocence, her virginity, and an unshakeable conviction that she was doing the Lord's work. With such experience behind her, she was not altogether surprised when she received a call—rather than "the call"—to take part in the Evangelisation of England which, she was told, had fallen away from the Word of God into liberalism, corruption, and, consequently, had now fallen under "the spell" of a "witch" called Perpetua. Relieved that this assignment would not involve trying to learn a new language or trying to avoid strange cuisine, she arrived in London at the beginning of October on a morning of near-frost sunlight and was assigned to the Front Line Team, tasked with bringing the people of Grunge Park back to God. Once she had completed her acclimatisation session which consisted of digesting an impressive litany of the sins of its denizens, all of which are too familiar to list, but it might be remarked that their greatest and least obvious shortcoming was their devotion—a word decidedly too Papist—to Perpetua. Her short session had been so on point that she was not in the least fazed when the first person she met was Calib, who was at the lowest of the two points between the end of one fix and the summoning of the energy to acquire the means of obtaining the next. She offered him a small tube of M&Ms. He looked puzzled. "Is this some sort of joke?" "No. It's candy." As if from nowhere, when she heard the word, Ruthie grabbed the tube, emptied the contents into her hand, and began to cram what she could into her mouth. "It's so long since I had anything sweet," she said, looking slightly apologetic. "Greed," said Stacey, contemptuously. "Sorry! But I haven't had anything like that for what seems like years. He won't steal sweets because they don't fetch enough, and all our money goes on what he needs. I don't begrudge him any-thing. He will die if he can't get what he needs, and he looks after me as well as he can; but it doesn't run to sweets." Still mindful of the litany, and totally devoid of flexibility, Stacey's response had no give in it. She looked disgusted and hurt, but her natural resilience and training kicked in without a flicker of self-doubt. "Our God is an angry God, but he will deliver you from all your enemies." With equal facility, Calib's old learning kicked in. "So you are an Evangelist?" "Yes." "You sounded Jewish, choosing the Old Testament over the New, but Jews don't evangelise, so I am forced to the conclusion that you're a kind of Christian." "What do you mean, a kind of Christian?" "Well, when Jesus fed the 5,000 he didn't give them a lecture on gratitude or even table manners. He just gave." "Jesus!" "Well, isn't he the whole point of Christianity?" She considered this. They had naturally been taught all about Jesus, about sin and blood, and the Cross, but most of her training had been in the God of the Chosen People. She remembered a few stories, but she had never really engaged with Jesus, except on the Cross. He was a 'liberal', and there was more than half a suspicion in her sect that he had never been a man, that the incarnation was a Catholic plot, and that the Father figure had sent his 'son' to shed blood and die in order to clear the account of a highly selected group of sinners by causing them to be 'born again'. Had she been confronted with the theology of the Trinity or the Councils of Nicea and Chalcedon, she would have thought that she was being subverted by Popery. "That's got you!" said Calib, with a slightly aggressive note of satisfac-tion. "If you behave like that you will never be saved." "How do you know who will be saved and how?" "It is clear that only those who are 'born again' will be saved." "What about people who are just born, baptised, and then stay faithful?" "Popery." "I was an Anglican." "Popery! The only way to be saved is to turn to God and be baptised as a fully consenting adult." Calib was getting bored. Ruthie asked if there were any more sweets. Stacey said that she could not have any more unless she promised to turn to God. Calib said that this was the crudest and most superficial form of bribery. He muttered something about throwing sweets around in Baghdad. Stacey looked puzzled. "I get it." said Calib, "you want to sweeten us up for your angry God. Well, I would prefer to turn to sweet Jesus." Stacey was really upset. She could stand any amount of the glum acquies-cence which she had occasionally met, and she was too full of her message to notice when it was received with hypocritical joy, with an eye on the van with the food, but she had never met argument, and her only defence was to attack a caricature of Roman Catholicism (as her acclimatisation course had not differentiated between Catholic and Orthodox Christianity, in the Ukraine she had almost got into serious trouble because she thought that its old, "corrupt" religion was Roman Catholicism). Calib's energy level began to rise with the dawn of desperation. He eyed her carefully, but decided that she was not worth bothering. Her clothes were clean but achingly plain. Her handbag was thin and nondescript, and the most it could contain was a mobile phone, which was not worth an assault. He knew from his experience that she had no money. At the same time, her training told her that she would gain nothing from these two, and the aim was not to crack the difficult nuts, but to fill out her checking card and bring her allocation to God. They were interrupted by Kelvin who came to a smiling halt. "Still on that stuff?" he asked Calib, half joking. "Of course," said Calib, grumpily, "what else?" "Well, Calib, there has to be something else. Perpetua sorted you out temporarily, but you're right back. She said you could sort yourself out. She said it was in your hands. I remember. She pulled me out of nothing and gave me hope." "Are you saved?" asked Stacey. "Well, yes. I suppose I am." "Are you a Christian?" "No. I'm a Perpetuan. The Christians who brought me up did nothing but shout at me and beat me. They said I was wicked." "They would not say that unless you were." "What a silly thing to say. They beat me because they wanted me to be like them; that's power." "God is power." "True, but people are quick to claim that they are doing things in 'his' power rather than because they are working out their own nastinesses and perversions. There was an oily preacher who sexually abused me." Stacey, whose only notion of sexual abuse was encompassed by the abstract terminology of fornication and adultery, looked puzzled. "So how did this Perpetua save you?" "She gave me a purpose." "Well, any teacher or employer could do that. I don't call that 'saved.'" "I don't mind what you call it, but you asked if I was saved and I've told you. I'm no match for your sort," he said, not knowing how good a match he was, "but here's your man," he said, pointing to Father O'Helly, walking towards them, dressed in very tight black jeans and a very open-necked shirt. "He doesn't look very spiritual to me," said Stacey. "Just shows how little you can tell from appearances," said Kelvin, cheerfully walking away. "Good afternoon, miss, are you lost?" "No, I'm looking for people so that I can bring them back to the Lord." "From where?" "From their sins, from idleness, wickedness, and corruption." "That is a tall order. What is your name?" Stacey, encouraged by his openness, told him. "An American, I think? A Missionary?" She looked almost animated. "Come to save us all?" "Yes." "From, let me guess, the Devil and the Pope?" "Why, yes." "And if there were no such thing as the Pope and no such people as Roman Catholics, do you suppose that the world would suddenly become a more—how shall I put it to help you?—that's it, a more God fearing place?" "Why, of course." "So if we removed all the cardinals and bishops and priests and lay ministers and theology teachers and students, and the Catholic universities and hundreds of millions of faithful worshippers, trying to live holy lives, you think that the world would be better?" Stacey failed to see the trap. "Of course. The Pope is the Anti-Christ." "The whore of Babylon," said Joe, smiling. She blushed at the word, not her ignorance of the Book of Revelation of Saint John the Divine. "I am sorry to have led you on," he said. "It's all too easy. You say unkind and ill-judged things about my church and I retaliate by being patronising when you are trying to work for the Lord." She looked puzzled. "I am not trying to change your mind, Stacey. It isn't for me to do anything like that—only you can change it—but I think you need to start by understanding the way in which individual people bear witness to Jesus and then, when you have met hundreds, you can distill what you have found into some kind of theory. To start with a belief devoid of direct experience is always dangerous." "But it's simple." "Yes, Stacey, I'll give it that, it's simple. Like all the most elegant scientific propositions, it's simple, but simple does not mean easy. It means it's not complex, that's all." She looked puzzled. "Well, anyway, you sound like some kind of Christian," she said, grudgingly. "No, I'm not a Christian, I'm a kind of Roman Catholic, and it's well known that many of the people from your kind of background don't think that RCs are Christians, which shows a lack of history, if not judgment and generosity. I don't mean to embarrass or hurt you." She looked even more puzzled. "Come and have a cup of coffee." She followed reluctantly, hurt by his humour, but warmed by it in a way that she had never been warmed before. In truth, her upbringing had been filled with cold love, with the unflickering attention to the details of right living. "You can't give without give," he said, bringing back her coke and his coffee. "What?" "You are trying to work on behalf of the Lord to bring 'his' children back to 'him'." "Children?" "Yes, we are all God's children." She had not thought of it quite that way before. "And, as we are children, we need to be treated like children, with love, respect, encouragement, and sympathy." He was taking her out of her depth. "The people round here haven't mutinied against God. The job isn't to bring them back with threats. They weren't recruited in the first place and they wouldn't have been capable of running away. You have to go back to the beginning." "How do you know so much?" "I am a priest." "In those clothes!" He wondered whether to explain by saying, "I'm a gay priest", but the shock would have been counter-productive. Instead he said, "I was a Roman Catholic Priest, but now I am in Limbo—or would be if His Holiness hadn't abolished it a few months ago!—because I have not resigned, but I am a committed Perpetuan." The complexity was making her feel ill. He noticed immediately and was ashamed that he had taken a risk with her. "Look, Stacey, God mostly delivers messages through people to people, and so the people who deliver have to feel themselves to be rich, complex people, and with that feeling they can communicate their faith, hope, love, to other people." "But there is so much wickedness." "Yes, if you want to call it that. There is so much brokenness." "Liberal!" she said, without thinking. "Ah!" said O'Helly, and fell silent for a moment, wondering how he could save her. There was the principled way—all about the love of God—and the selfish way—all about understanding yourself—and, being a pragmatic, pastoral Priest, he started with the selfish way, knowing that it would lead to the principled or, more accurately, the sublime, way. "You look pretty prosperous to me." "Yes." "Ever been hungry?" "No." "Ever been beaten?" "No." "Ever been thrown out of school?" "No." She began to look irritated with this train of fatuous questioning. O'Helly registered the irritation. Here was a very average young lady, with average clothes, an average figure, an average face, an average intellect, and a below average capacity for imagination or enjoyment. He suspected that, although she did not know it herself, she had turned to God because she did not interest anybody else. The Church was full of people who were inadequate or felt themselves to be so—he should know—and that is how it should be. He did not like the way in which priests were supposed to learn enough theology to be more knowing than the laity. He liked hedge priests and poor priests and not very bright priests, but faithful, humble priests. If the Lord could not find a place in the Church founded by Jesus for plain people, what sort of a church was it? What he needed to do was to wean her away from expressing her religious commitment in ways which would most probably turn people away from God. "I'm sorry, this might all seem a bit obvious, but be patient, if you could, for a moment. Can you imagine what it's like to be any of those things you haven't been?" "No," she said, with the complete frankness of somebody who cannot anticipate the consequences of what they say. O'Helly's experience helped him to refrain from pouncing. "So I suppose you sometimes find it a bit difficult to put yourself in the shoes of some of the people you are with?" "Yes." "So how do you get alongside them and understand where they are coming from, and what they need?" "I don't have to understand. It isn't a question of understanding. God doesn't bargain with his people. He says what has to be, and they have to get in line." O'Helly was aware that this was going to be difficult but, at all costs, he must not quarrel with her, particularly about the nature of God. "And how do we know what God wants people to do? How can we be sure that what we tell them is not just what we want them to do because that would make them more like us?" This was a little complex. She did not have an instant reply. She was sure of the first part, but not the second. "The Bible tells us," she said and then, more falteringly, "and we all know the difference between what God wants and human sinfulness. We're all sinners." O'Helly had a surprise opening. "I know this is just a little cheeky of me, Stacey, but what sins have you committed?" She actually couldn't think of any, and frantically tried to manufacture something plausible. "I thought not. Most people don't do all that much sinning. They sit about a lot and let the few who are wicked get on with it, but there's a remarkably small amount of sin about, which is natural when you think about it, because we were made to be good. It's in our nature to be good." She looked startled. "But, at a more practical level, if you haven't sinned, it's a bit like the other things that you haven't experienced, so how can you know what it's like?" "I don't need to know what it's like. I just have to know that God doesn't like it." "You know what, Stacey, I think God is more interested in whether we really love God, than in the slips we make along the way." "But I'm not talking about slips, I'm talking about sin." O'Helly, the practical pastor, knew that it was time to administer a sharp rebuke to make Stacey think. "Stacey, you have just admitted that you can't think of a time when you have sinned, and yet you keep talking about sin. Let's face it, you don't know what you're talking about." She hardly reacted, just shifting her right foot slightly. "I know that sin is bad, and that God does not want it." "Stacey, that's a very good piece of theory. It's great ethics not to want people to do wrong, and it might even be pretty good theology, but it's quite different from the thing you really want to do, which is to bring people to God. You don't actually help people to come towards God by telling them that he thinks they're wicked when you don't know what he thinks." "They come to God because they realise they've been sinful, and they repent." "But, Stacey, they don't come to a theory or a different ethical code. You keep talking about their sin instead of about God's love." She looked shocked and almost backed off. "God's love! But he only loves those who do what he wants." "Wrong, Stacey, he is love and he loves everybody." "God of wrath! Repent!" "I'm not going to play Scriptural ping pong—I could say "Gentle Jesus"—because that's no use. If you love God and God loves you, and you recognise both of those things, then others will recognise it in you, and they will let you walk beside them. After a while they may feel so right with where they are that they will ask you to share the good news with them." "Good News!" "Well, Stacey, if it's not good news, why would you spend so much energy trying to share it. It's a very strange kind of person, perhaps a tabloid newspaper editor, who enjoys sharing bad news." She was recovering her poise. "But if you help people to avoid self-destruction, that's good news." "Yes," he said, almost laughing, "it is good news of a sort, but if you can work with people to construct holy lives, that's better. There is a kind of religion that survives on fear, but that's like taking out an insurance policy, and there is another kind which is based on love, which struggles in faith and exults in hope." He began to feel the old Catholic rhythms and knew that these would be incomprehensible, so he said, "If I were you, Stacey, I'd spend a little more time reading Saint Luke and a little less time reading the Pentateuch." "Saint Luke," she said, looking as if he had said something that had unlocked a memory. "Yes. I remember Saint Luke, and the baby, and the shepherds." He let her muse. "I will read that again, but why are you telling me so much about the way you see God when I thought you were a Perpetuan?" "I'm a bit like the Apostles—though I'm not trying to compare myself with them—who were both Jews and Christians. I'm not convinced that I have to choose and that a rift is necessary." "But aren't they heretics?" "Well, that's difficult, particularly if you're a Protestant—you are, aren't you?— because you think that Roman Catholics are, to use a Roman Catholic word, heretics." She blushed, and he covered her embarrassment by draining his coffee and leading her out into the golden sunlight. "Well, I've met some quite nice Catholics," she said, trying to put the damage right without betraying her principles, "but they have strayed." "Thank you Stacey, for warning me." "I don't wish to be rude," she said, her common politeness overcoming her theology, "but that's what we were taught." "Now we might be getting closer, might we not? It seems to me that there might be a difference between what God wants and what we're taught. After all, I was taught to be a Catholic, you were taught to be ..." "... A Baptist." "Quite so, and we both think that God wants us to be what we were taught God wants us to be." He was aware that this was a little more clever than he would have liked, but the gist was simple enough. "But God ..." "... Let's try looking at it this way. You and I were taught different ideas about history, and they are taught so early and so well that they are part of us for all our lives. It happens with faith, but God would never reject people because of what they were taught when they had no say in the matter. After all, if somebody is taught, say, that the atom can't be split because this makes teaching science easy, they can't be blamed for repeating this in front of people who know otherwise. It's not their fault. In any case, it doesn't matter what we are taught about God, as long as we stick to the single idea that God is love." "God is love," she said, and he knew that she was deeply moved because he recognised in her face the first experience of love which had ever suffused it. In that instant, the whole of her became beautiful. He felt the Holy Spirit in them as they stood in silence. "Luke," she said again. "Luke," he said, knowing that it would lead her into the paths of joy and peace. Joe knew that she could not be left like this, and he also knew that he was the wrong person for her to be with. No matter how effective the pastoral care, there is always a reaction, good or bad, which requires a different, sympathetic ear; and, just at that moment, the ear came down the street in the form of Marta. "Marta, my love, it's nice to meet another Catholic Perpetuan in limbo!" "No limbo." "All right, not literally. This young lady, Stacey, wants to hear about Saint Luke." "Good." "And perhaps she wants tea." "Luke and tea. English tea? Not good at English tea." "No, er, I would not wish to trouble you. Americans don't know about tea." "No trouble, Luke and tea. You come?" "Thank you, no." "I think you need a ladies' tea party." Stacey was not sure. She knew how to handle situations where she was calling the shots, but this was the first time it had happened the other way round since she was given her first assignment. She had not, although she would not have put it in these terms to herself, ever enjoyed an equal, ordinary, adult relationship, and she had certainly not been the recipient of gifts. Always the giver, she had never been taught how to take, and had never considered that giving would be impossible without taking. Somehow, taking was demeaning. Poor people took, unsuccessful people took. Joe watched her. "Everything we have is a gift from God. We can't be God's children if we don't know how to accept gifts." He saw the radiance intensify in her face.

Marta and Max had moved into a modest house with a small garden, bought with little Perpetua in mind, on the edge of Grunge Park. Max was paid a modest salary by the Perpetuans and Marta had been so used from her peasant childhood, to making much of little, she lived in what was for her unimaginable comfort. Not having to choose between good baby food and nice baby clothes constituted luxury. Stacey was worried about tea because she associated it with mysterious rituals, so she asked for coffee. Marta, who was not wedded to the English way, made, coffee and brought her a new, English Bible. "Look, Luke, remind us of the Nativity." Stacey read Chapters 1 and 2 with the feeling that she was reading a wondrous fairy tale. It had nothing to do with the God of her childhood—it was strange, she thought, how Christmas had not become tied up with her religion—and this meant that her main difficulty was integrating this material into her literalist pattern. She was confused by the Annunciation, and thrown completely by the Magnificat, but she felt more comfortable with the shepherds and angels. What did all this have to do with God? Well, she knew that Jesus was God, but it had never gone deep into her consciousness. Marta interrupted her puzzled wandering: "He was baby, that's the thing. Poor, hungry baby. Luke like women and babies. JesusGod baby." Marta instinctively knew where to take this trail of words and thoughts, so she took up the Bible again and said, "He's grown up now, here's what he said," and she turned to Chapter 6, then to the Good Samaritan, the Prodigal Son, the forgiveness on the Cross, and the Road to Emmaus. "Look how stories fit. Gospels are all about love. You teach Christianity, must be love. Nothing else." "So if there's nothing else, where does Perpetua fit in?" "Church forgot love, more bothered with power and structure, telling people what to do. No free will, no conscience." Stacey recognised herself and blushed. "No problem. We all do it. Perpetua came to start again, to pull down the ugly watch towers." "But she says she's God." "Look, Christians disagree about God. Some are only for the Father, some are only for the Son, some are only for the Spirit. Some believe there's only one person. Now we think there might be four instead of three. No big thing." Stacey considered the paucity of her theology and could not easily argue. She recognised that repeating her mantra about the wrath of God was not going to be an adequate response to Luke. Marta showed her how to bath the baby and they made dinner together but, as the time went by Stacey became more comfortable. Marta began to get edgy and kept on looking at her watch. Stacey pretended not to notice. Marta found as many ways as she could to delay the time when dinner would have to be served but, just after they sat down, Max came in. As soon as they saw him, they both knew that he was drunk. Stacey was horrified because she was horrified. Marta was horrified because she thought all that was behind them, that he had conquered the problem, that he could even have the occasional glass of wine without bringing back the threat." They both tried to pretend that nothing had happened, but Max said, "I'm drunk. I know I am. I know I should not be, but I am." They waited, with no strategy. "It is wrong. I know it is wrong, but I felt that I could not face my life and wanted to escape." "Escape, but you so strong with Perpetua." "It was she I wanted to escape from. I'm not a preacher, and those acts which they called 'miracles' almost blew me to pieces." Marta saw it immediately, she knew precisely what he meant. It was a perverted form of humility which had driven him back to drink. He felt it was too much. She had been fazed by the miracles, but she had read so much about miracles in her upbringing that they were not so much of a problem for her as they were for Max whose knowledge of them was limited to the Plagues of Egypt and the doings of Elijah and Elisha. Stacey had learned to say nothing, and to watch.

"Look, Max, we don't talk serious things when you drunk, it's waste, but it's all right what you have done. I see why. Do you eat?" "No thank you." "Sleep?" "Yes, I think so." "OK. You sleep. We talk tomorrow." He left the room, studiously carefully and quietly. "Shock, bad shock, but I see why." "Why?" "Power is difficult, strangeness is difficult. He alcoholic when he had no power. Now the opposite." "But you didn't holler." "Why? No good. He knew he do wrong thing before he started drinking. Why tell him what he knows? Just hurts more, needs love when gone wrong." Stacey looked at herself in a strange, neat, poky house in a faraway country, watching a Polish woman quietly understanding a drunk husband, without saying anything. "Luke," said Marta, "Luke. Max sleeping, but needs me near. You read Luke. Sleep on sofa. Talk tomorrow." Stacey read the whole of Luke, not understanding some of it, but pushing on through to the end, wondering how it had passed her by for so long. She wondered whether to plunge into something else, but was so worried at being wrong-footed in her emotions as she had only just stabilised round Luke, so she went back to the beginning, but before she had reached half way, she was asleep.

Whereas some people might have come downstairs in the morning full of apologies, or trying to pretend that nothing had happened on the previous night, Max came into the kitchen briskly and said, "I am sorry I came in drunk last night, delayed your dinner, and caused an awkward situation. There's an explanation, but no excuse. The explanation is that I used to be an alcoholic, but I pulled away from that under the influence of Perpetua, but I have been seriously disoriented by a call to preach and by my apparent agency in acts which people call 'miracles'. It has made me feel powerful and powerless at the same time." "Gifts," said Stacey, remembering Joe. "Gifts." "What?" "Oh yes, gifts," said Marta, "in Saint Paul, gifts." Stacey warmed even more at the prospect that Saint Paul, who was, if anything, more important in her sect than Jesus, was in favour of gifts. She was also startled to see the effect she had had on Max, whose demeanour changed from solemnity almost to levity. "Gifts," he said, sounding like Rex Harrison on a rising inflection, "Gifts! how stupid of me to be frightened of gifts. I must hurry, I must give thanks, I must get on with the work." Marta smiled at Stacey and the baby as she hugged Max. "Drunk not disaster," she said as he went out. Stacey went soon afterwards, promising to come again. She was walking briskly towards the station when she again encountered Father O'Helly, looking clerical. "It was a long tea party. You must have learned a great deal." "I learned about Luke and I saw a man being drunk, understood why, and didn't preach." "That is an astounding amount of learning for one evening. I wish it had happened so quickly to me, but I always had to struggle for my theology. What are you going to do now?" "Resign my assignment, hope they don't put me on the next plane, and study this Jesus and Perpetua. I am worried that I like it too much when we were taught to be suspicious of things we like, but I will try. Why are you dressed like that?" "Summoned by the Bishop; it's the Dies Irae. I hope to see you again." "Marta will know where to find me."

About the Dies Irae, he could not have been more wrong. Cardinal Podric, who lived in threadbare splendour, was an emphatic example of the general rule concerning Roman Catholicism, that the individual wisdom of many of its leading churchmen exceeds its collective wisdom by a goodly margin. "Let's make this easy, Joe," he said, affably, "for we've known each other now since Seminary, but we need to get one piece of business out of the way before I can talk to you as a man rather than as a Catholic Priest which, as you know, is a totally different proposition. Of course, it should not be, so we'll get back to that once we've completed the formalities. Am I correct in thinking that you now believe that Perpetua is part of the Godhead?" "Yes, Podric—er Cardinal." "Podric will do. So you are in disagreement with an article of the Creed?" "I suppose I am." "I suppose you are too. Let's think of it like contemporary, pragmatic, English divorce law." Joe looked puzzled that his boss would use such an odd illustration. "You see, Joe, it isn't cruelty or adultery or anything like that, it's just an irretrievable breakdown." "I thought I could be like the Apostles—only in this one thing—that I could be a Christian and a Perpetuan." "Nice one, Joe. Under John XXIII it might just have been possible, but not under this fella. He's got to prove his orthodoxy, following on from that—if you'll forgive me—charlatan Polish clown we had before." Joe looked shocked. He had never heard Podric talking like this. "You see Joe, under the rules, you can't be both, so you're not a Catholic Priest, so I can talk to you like a man. Old JP II was splendid for the world, good for inter-faith dialogue, average on ecumenism, and a disaster for the Church. All he wanted was media attention and the quick fix. He had no interest in the real church with all its pastoral and priestly dilemmas. By the way, talking about priestly dilemmas, what might you do?" "I'm not really sure, but I hope to be useful to Perpetuanism." "I am sure you will be. She was a wonderful woman who made Mother Theresa look quite flat-footed. Calling herself God was a bit of a liberty, but it might turn out that way. I am about to speak my mind to Archbishop Varnish. The days of the big congregations are over, so she was right to focus on house churches, and that means far more priests celebrating the Eucharist in houses and, therefore, Priests who are sensitive and spiritual, but not stuffed up to the eyeballs with theology and mumbo jumbo, so you will certainly find yourself back as a priest pretty soon I think. Are you really sure that it's the doctrine that took you, or the other thing?" "Other thing?" "Look, Joe, right from Seminary we were worried that your repression would damage you. There were some who said that the priesthood would save you from sodomy and others who said that the price of that would be your early death. I have known all along where your inclinations lay and, although I admire you for staying faithful, I only wish as your Bishop that I could have told you to loosen up." "But you couldn't." "No, and that's why this Church of ours is in such a mess. It can't distinguish between big things and small things. Love is big, but rules are small." "So how do you survive, Podric?" "I survive because institutional coherence requires a good deal of hypocrisy, and without it we are all lost. I am sorry to say that Perpetuanism will find that out soon enough but, in the meantime, enjoy the innocence. Come and see me quietly now and again to cheer me up.

Goodbye forever, Father Joe, but goodbye for now Joe." "Goodbye for now, Podric."

The Cardinal looked out of his study window onto a blackened brick, Westminster wall and wondered where it would all end. Because he was a man of humble origins who had stuck at his vocation without expecting anything other than the frugal and sometimes bitter, lonely life of a Parish Priest, he might have let himself go when he first became a bishop, and then the Cardinal Archbishop, but his preferment had made him, if anything, more frugal, but much less lonely. That very same humble upbringing which had steered him towards the pastoral and away from the theological had also given him a profoundly person centred view of the Church. What he cared for was the spiritual health of the people and their awareness of the presence of God and how this was described by theologians was therefore of less concern to him. It was, he reflected realistically, more a matter of his limited intellectual abilities than anything else which caused him to withdraw from more abstract discussions, a reticence which was tolerated at home because of his graceful manners and in the Vatican because of his quiet loyalty. Recent events had engaged him and he could see with the clarity of an administrator what he could not yet see with the ingenuity of a theologian, that Christianity was in a state of irreversible decline and that what he did could only marginally speed that up or slow it down. Like an opposition politician who sees the terrible polls, but goes on playing the game, he dedicated himself, yet again, to doing his duty as long as he had strength. He recollected, looking at his watch, part of that duty would be to shore up the disintegrating Church of England, for it was one of those ironies only appreciated by insiders that, in spite of its external presence and its established position, the Church of England could not survive without Evangelical energy and Roman Catholic steadfastness.

Not being an insider, Varnish did not understand this dynamic, and thought that he was simply paying a courtesy call on the Cardinal. Podric poured the strong, coarse tea and handed Varnish a plate of curiously mis-named rich tea biscuits. "So, have you managed to come to grips with the Perpetuan movement?" "To tell you the truth, we have hit something of a crisis. My bishops seem to be broadly in favour of Affirming Orthodoxy, but they, quite illogically, then go on to say that that should not be the doctrinal gold standard, and that there must be room for other views. To complicate matters, I feel myself moving towards her. It's the visions." "That's Anglicanism for you, Archbishop—not the visions—the true inheritor of Medieval diversity before printing and absolutism set in." Varnish looked puzzled. "Anglicanism is today what Catholicism was before the Papacy got hold of it. I should say in confidence that you would do well to hang onto what you've got. It might not save you—it probably won't—but it will give you more time to do what you must do—what we all must do—and that is to gather up the bits and pieces we have and integrate them into the new way." Varnish looked puzzled, and then shocked. "Do you mean what I think you mean, that we need to throw in the towel and all sign up to Perpetuanism?" "Not quite, Archbishop. If you remember what happened with Jesus, Judaism survived but in a different form, while the sect that grew out of it became a world power. The choice we have to make is whether to speed up a mutation of our own institutions and make them fit for a new role and a greatly simplified structure, or whether we wish to throw our lot in with the winners. The first course might, as it turns out, leave us much nearer to Perpetuanism than we are now. If we go for small churches and house groups we will be following a parallel strategy. Knowing what I do about your interests, I don't like to say this to you, but I believe that we have reached the end of the era of mass, regular church attendance, and that the Perpetuans are correct when they say that we will need fewer buildings. You have the heritage problem, we have the problem of churches built on the cheap from the sacrifices of the poor. We will need to reach a national settlement on what we want to keep, and arrange to share. If I want Mass in the cathedral once a month, and you want Eucharist, and the Perpetuans want their Sacrament of Union, and we all believe in one God and are only divided about some of the theology, where is the harm?" "But the Pope?" "Look, Archbishop, I'm sorry to be a little direct here, but we have a perfectly well understood arrangement in England. The established church acts as the locomotive and, sooner or later, we link on behind." Varnish looked uncomfortable. "But not even Liverpool and Everton can agree on sharing a ground, even though it would save them money." "That only goes to show that the tribal loyalties in football are more rigid and less subtle than the theological loyalties and subtleties in Christianity." Varnish tried not to meet the Cardinal's eye. "So I go back to my bishops, and abandon Affirming Orthodoxy, and open talks with the Perpetuans and, sooner or later, you come along and fall into line?" "Not quite, Archbishop. You declare your support for Affirming Orthodoxy and make that the core of your church, which allows conservatives of both wings to coexist, bringing you new perspectives, new energy (and paying you for the privilege). Then you don't make much noise about it, but allow the liberals who haven't gone over to Perpetua. Then, although I recognise it's against your nature, you tell the Government that you are no longer prepared to act as the country's chief heritage financier and curator. Then you make worship deals but no theological deals, with the Perpetuans. Then—much later, I fear, because that is how Rome works—we will join in the arrangement." That struck Varnish as a profoundly perverse, if not unjust, set of proposals, but it was not correct procedure to accuse an ecumenical partner of cynicism. "I'm not being cynical," said Podric. "I am just explaining to you how I see it. I have very little freedom of movement, whereas you have a great deal of room. I am taking a practical approach to ensure that God's people have the help they need during a period of turbulence. Look, Archbishop, if people won't go to church to experience corporate communion with God, we can't force them. There is nothing historically sacrosanct about regular Sunday worship. I know this must sound odd, even Protestant, coming from a Catholic, but we need to focus on people and their relationship with God. I know this is becoming repetitious, and even boring, but I firmly believe that Vatican conservatism, and the failure to distinguish between what is important and what is not is not only seriously damaging the structure of the Church, which is important but, much more seriously, it is damaging the Church's ability to sustain its faithful people. Look at it this way. While we have all been going on—forgive the looseness of the designation—about clerical celibacy, women clerics, gay clergy, divorce and re-marriage, promiscuity, and the pill, we have, at the same time, developed a cardre of clergy with the strangest, abnormal profile. We have a disproportionate number of child abusers, and you have a disproportionate number of gays. For what it's worth, I would prefer to be in your position than mine. The Vatican's near indifference to child abuse, but its obsession with the rules of consensual sex, is nothing short of a scandal. Anyway, I am sorry to have diverged so far from what we were supposed to be talking about but, while we have been involved in all of this, our faithful people have been fighting the most terrible, insidious, ingratiating, inviting onslaught of materialism in history. Nothing, not the rage for tulips nor the South Sea Bubble, the recklessness of canals, or the Icarian romance with railways, comes anywhere close to today's irrational worship of wealth. The high minded may say that we need to combat this, the pastorally minded will say that our people will need protection when it all goes wrong, as it surely will. Then we will see how Christianity and Perpetuanism turn out. In the meantime, Archbishop, if I were you, I would talk to Granville Brompton. He may be out of office now, but he will help you to make the first moves to scaling down your real estate holdings. As for the visions, it's good Christian practice to take notice." Varnish was again deeply shocked. "It would hurt so much, it would destroy what I came to save." "I know," said Podric, his pastoral heart replacing his administrative hand, "but the reality is that it's only the hard liners who can ever deliver the deals. Only you can deliver the buildings deal and the credibility of visions. What's more, if you do that you will be surprised at what will happen. Perhaps your keen interest in building has been a way of avoiding the Spirit. Let us bless one another, Archbishop. Some people think that you are only a buildings man. God and Perpetua know better."

Varnish went to see Granville Brompton who was comparing the entries on Handel in a series of Groves Dictionaries. "They rise and they fall," he said, as Varnish looked over his shoulder to admire the typesetting of the earlier editions. "Even Bach was out of favour at one time, and in your field, of course, schools of architecture have come and gone, even though it is much easier to establish a new fashion in something 'portable' like music than it is to do the same in something solid like buildings. Podric had a word with me after your talk, so let us see how I might help." "The trouble is, he is advising me to do the last thing I would want to do." "That's why you're the person to do it." "Precisely what he said." "Let me—sorry for the cliché—put my cards on the table. As you know, I'm a Perpetuan, but I will try to look at matters from an impartial point of view. Where is our civilisation going? It might sound like a very grand question, but it is, in fact, not grand at all. We have passed from absolute monarchy, through an era of state corporatism, into a situation of volatile global individualism. This means that when we hold onto huge pieces of historical baggage which go with the two previous periods, we are indulging in disproportionate nostalgia. When the crash comes—and it is only a matter of when rather than whether—we will all have to decide what it is that we really want to keep. The rules will change, and many institutions which we thought were timeless will disintegrate. Governments will go back to insuring people against individual and collective disaster as the institution of last resort, but, in exchange for that under-writing of our individualism, selfish or altruistic, it will shed most of what it gathered between the beginning of the welfare movement and the end of the corporate consensus, say between 1910 and 1979. The one area where people will try to hold it to its traditional role will be in climate change, but it will not work. Only collective private action can save the planet now. Governments will be far too concerned with holding the system together, enabling us to go on being prudent or prodigal. It was always going to be the case that, sooner or later, somebody would have to put a floor under our wildnesses. The only body big enough is our collective sacrifice of minimal sovereignty. It's the eighteenth century all over again, Archbishop," he said, looking down affectionately at Handel. "So how does that play out in the Church?" "I won't lecture you on the death of church corporatism, as I know Podric will have had his say, but let me just sketch the implications. Big church is out—except for great occasions, festivals, corporate affirmations—and small church is in, house groups like we Perpetuans have got. The Christian church's mistake—other than the big Constantinian sell-out, which was probably inevitable—was to split family and community spirituality from Holy Communion. It is crazy that there are wonderful spiritual leaders faithfully leading house groups, week in, week out, who can't preside at the Eucharist, quite shocking. Anyway, the churches stock is too great for all of us: Perpetuans want a few worship-days, and Christians of all kinds want a few. We can't go on as we are. Property prices are already beginning to fall. Fortunately, there are not that many locations with a glut of churches, so the mass sale won't push the price down because they'll all be in different places, but we need to unload quickly, before the market begins to look even more sick. There will be no government bail-out of churches if there has to be a bail-out of banks. Everybody is in denial at the moment, it's toxic pass-the-parcel but, before long, the music will stop and the parcel will explode all over the place. You just can't image where bits of it will end up. No, it's a bad metaphor because actually its angeographic or, as they say today, 'viral', but you get the point." Varnish did not look as if he did. "I know this is particularly hard for you, but the building thing is over. Christianity, in England at least, has to choose between heritage and the Gospel. It will be tough, just as it was at the beginning of the eighteenth century when the intellectual, commercial, and scientific spheres changed out of all recognition. That change started here in the 1970s with postmodernism, neo-liberalism, and digital technology. Now there's climate change, and it always takes Christianity too much time to adjust. There's something deeply significant, touching even, about small groups of affirming Christians crouching in dark corners of unheated churches like Catacumens. That is how it will be unless we enable the ambient spirituality that is looking for a home. We might do this separately as Christians or Perpetuans for a while, but a difference of one person in the Godhead is hardly significant compared with the fundamental issues." Granville, the old hand, knew exactly how much to say, so he stopped and turned his attention to Handel to allow Varnish to turn over what he had said without feeling pressured or under surveillance. "It's my life," he said and, at that point, Granville knew it would be all right because when people reduce a massive issue to their own loss you know they have taken the important decision. "I know," said Granville, "I have followed your campaigns with interest, and have sometimes been able to do just a little to push things along. We both know that there's no real progress without sacrifice, and you are being asked to make a very large and noble sacrifice." Varnish could not yet feel the extent of it. He was not, in his own mind, making a sacrifice for God, and he wasn't making a grand theological gesture. He saw the ruin of his ambition and, being a realist, he saw now that that ruin had been inevitable. He did not want to be unworthy, no matter how he had arrived where he was. He was, as Saint Paul had put it, what he was, the office, not the man. There was something heroic about sacrifice. "What are the practicalities?" "Nothing moves very quickly in Government or real estate and, as this combines the two, we can expect some delay, but the time is right. I would offer to help you sort this out with Max Silver, but both of us are Perpetuans and you will rightly feel that you need somebody from your own patch. I know that there may have been some differences between you, but there is no better man for this business than the Dean of Alchester." "Yes, we have had our recent differences, but I trust you, Granville, and that's what counts in situations like this. He's open and clear. Nothing will be overlooked and nothing will be hidden, and now, much as I would like to stay to enjoy some more of your time, I fear that I must go to work out what I need to say to my people. No doubt it will be characterised as a 'climb down'—as nobody is allowed to change their minds about anything—but that is a small price to pay for doing the right thing." As Varnish turned to go, Granville Brompton permitted himself a slight smile. In a conversation with Strider when Varnish was chosen, the Junior Minister had said that he was a makeweight whereas Granville had maintained that nobody would persist in the way that Varnish had done without there being a depth of character and a steadiness of temperament. "Just because he was concerned with solid matter within a spiritual church does not diminish the man. We are far too often misled by what people do rather than how they do it. Look at the number of Polish university graduates working on hotel reception desks. Varnish has stuck to his task, in and out of fashion, seeking nothing for himself. He will, of course, take some time to learn, just as our new Prime Minister will take a full calendar year to come to grips with being Prime Minister. It's very easy for those who come in for the first time after a General Election because they are on honeymoon—particularly in an era where the party of the Government changes so rarely—but it is always tough for mid-term novices." He watched Varnish leave his room and could not help following him. "I know it's customary for you to bless me and pray for me, Archbishop, but I just want to say, 'Bless You', and that I will pray for you." Varnish, who had begun to understand humility since he took on his new job, bowed his head and then, straightening, said, "God Bless you, too, Granville. We will pray for each other." He walked out into an almost perfect Georgian Square with its sedate street lighting dimmed by the brightness of a full, white, moon, and he felt a huge wave of relief and affirmation. He felt the presence of God, the power of the Holy Spirit, and the humility of Jesus, break into his troubled heart. He did not know from where he had picked this up, but he heard Perpetua telling him that he was in control of what he did for God, that he had to make his own choices. He stopped to look at the bust of Handel framed by shining leaves. "How beautiful are the feet," he said, and walked slowly home, happier than he had been at any time in his life.

The reception of Sneer at the god4u offices for the commencement of his official duties was as cordial as that received by Saint Paul on his first visit to the elders of the church at Jerusalem, except on the part of Max whose easy manners smoothed out the initial difficulties. "I know," said Sneer to Brian who had ostentatiously turned his back, "I quite understand, but if you believe, as you necessarily must, in redemption and forgiveness, I'm your test case." Brian continued to look grim, but Max remained mildly encouraging. "I think we need to look at the future, not the past. It's the Torans who are always looking into people's pasts, telling them what they have done wrong, whereas our form of mission is encouragement, looking to the future." "I want to say sorry," said Brian. "I was being rude and ungenerous." "It is me that should say sorry for all the discomfort I have caused you all." Trina heard his last words as she came to welcome him. "I will not deny that you have—that would be wrong—but I must rise above that—er, what's your first name? I've never known— and welcome you." "I never use it because it's some sort of Trollopian joke, but because my surname is so ghastly, my parents called me Quintus. That explains why I've kept my name out of the papers. But, more to the point, I was persuaded by Chris—whom I suppose to be a Barnabas—to meet you. What zeal was turned against you can now be used in your favour." "The Holy Spirit seems to be moving at such a very sharp pace at the moment," said Trina, "that I can hardly keep up. What do you think, Max?" "I think that we need the skills of Q and Chris to build a media department with Bryan. What do you say?" "Well, it's difficult to change my mind as rapidly as you have, but I have to admit that Sneer was brilliant on the TT and it will be a coup to have him here. I'm not a journalist, I'm a techie, really, not so good with content, and since Perpetua went from us we've been running a lot of Perpetua historical footage, though the amount is, sadly, decreasing. People need to know how the work is growing." "And we can afford it," said Max. "Not the kind of salary that you were picking up, Q, but certainly in the range of what Chris was earning." "Contrary to some stories that I printed, most journalists like me live frugally. They might pay us quite a lot, but we never have time to spend it. I even dislike holidays because they detach me from my 'drip'. What's the first thing to do?" "Well, there's a story from Wayne at Stumpy Knoll that might ring some bells."

It was the half term holiday, and the youth of Stumpy Knoll were bored with hanging around the dilapidated Cedar shopping mall. Wayne, Jim and some of the local followers decided on the Friday to see if they could help the week to end on a high note. When they made contact with the loungers, there were a few homophobic comments from the boys who fancied themselves to be Members of the National League—although they knew nothing at all about politics or the history of National Socialism—but the other boys told them to shut up, that being gay was not, if you thought about it—which the jeerers did not—anything to do with nationalism. It was not un-English to be gay." They were all so bored that even Wayne and Jim were slightly interesting, and Jim's playing attracted an increasing audience so that the small group was swelled by an increasing number of teenagers, alerted by text messages. By late morning, there were a couple of thousand people listening to Jim and the other musicians, generally waiting for something to happen. The followers soon had everything hooked up so that Jim's flute and backing group were nicely integrated. Then Wayne began, "I am unable to guess what we thought we were coming out here for, perhaps just some music in the open air, but it seems to me that we need to think about ourselves just a bit. All the reports and comments since I arrived here at Stumpy Knoll say that the population suffers from multiple deprivation, lack of stimulation, and abnormally high levels of addiction and criminality with a tendency, reports add, for people to fall into a state of permanent victimhood. Well, we all know that the poor have had a raw deal from society, so what is new? But we are all God's people. I know the idea of God is a difficult one, that many of us have hardly heard of God, even as a theory, so let me say a bit about what Perpetua said about God. We may not have heard about God, she said, but God has heard about us. God is not an idea like well-being or peace. God is not a crazy creator who makes things for fun. God does not gamble. Neither is God a super mechanic who wound the world up and let it go. Nor is God simply an explanation for how things are that we can choose to believe in or not. This last point was very important for Perpetua because, for hundreds of years now, God has not been understood as the source of all love. God has been belittled as one of a number of explanations for why we are here now, and that explanation has lost out to much more down to earth ideas from science. We believed that science can answer every question, but it has failed. It cannot answer questions like: why is there something rather than nothing; why do we try to reach beyond ourselves; and why are we all so sad? This stuff is a bit complicated, but I respect your ability to understand difficult ideas, and talking to you like this is an expression of trust. If we treat each other like adults, we will behave like adults. God is not a scientific theory. Perpetua said, "God is love". The universal, all-encompassing 'person' that is the source of love. God feels like the day you wake up in the morning and know that everything is perfect, and that it will go on being perfect. The complete clarity of the air, the sharpness of the atmosphere, the detail of every blade of grass, every dew drop on every petal, and every set of reflections in glass. Most reality is a poor shadow of our imagination, our fantasy, but God is the opposite. God is infinitely better than anything we can imagine. God is the massive relief when we have been frightened and find that we are safe. God is the lights coming on after a storm and the fog clearing after a terrible muddle. All of these ideas push us towards the central ideas that we are loved, that we are not alone, that there is hope, that we can reach levels beyond our imagining, and that we can reach these levels through a combination of our searching and our listening, of moving and staying still. We cannot live if we think we have to do everything, but neither can we live if we think we can do nothing. Here we are, said Perpetua, caught between these two wildly unrealistic ideas, everything and nothing. We are neither everything nor are we nothing. We are something, and what makes us what we are is being part of God's universal goodness. We can find our way to God through our own route as long as we keep in touch with others. It is like climbing a steep rock face and being on a rope, doing what we have to do, but in tune with the others in the party. As long as we work together, stick together, and work to be respected for what we do, it is possible to find a new way of living. God is beautiful, God is elegance and trouble, God is Grace and conflict. But right at the centre, God is constant, like a nucleus. We can learn to see God in everybody, particularly people we dislike; but it is equally important to listen for God. If anything, listening is more difficult than doing. That is what Perpetua said. Some of you were probably there, some of you may remember what she said, and some of you will have forgotten, but we are here to keep alive what she said so that it will make a difference to your lives." People were beginning to get restless. Trina looked anxious. Wayne asked Jim and the band to start playing again, but people showed signs of drifting away when a young girl with a shopping bag came up to Wayne and asked him if he wanted a drink. Jim saw the sky fill with golden light. Wayne said he would be very grateful, and he dipped his hand in the bag and pulled out a can of soft drink. He put his hand in the bag again, and pulled out another can, then a burger, then another can, then a burger, then another can, and so it went on. The girl looked stunned as her bag produced an endless supply of food and drink for all the people who were there. When everybody was eating and drinking, Wayne started speaking again. "I could never have imagined that this would happen today, but Perpetua is still with us. Last time you all went away after you were fed and you didn't give it a second thought, but this time you have to. It's no coincidence, you have been fed by the God who loves you, the God I was talking about earlier. Where do you think all that food and drink came from? Do you see unloaded lorries? Do you see cartons? You only see that Hypo bag that this girl was carrying. Perpetua believed when she performed her mighty acts that it was not the time for her to explain them, but she has left us to explain. She came to bring us the good news that it is in our power to make the world a better place for others and ourselves. During this week, most of us have hung around doing nothing, grumbling about school, but secretly waiting to go back to relieve the monotony. We are free to love God and each other. This meal that we have shared together is a sign that we need to work together and be together." There was a closing shot of people walking away while Wayne and his followers worked with some of the audience to clear away the cans, packaging, and leftovers. "What do you do with that?" asked Sneer, incredulous. "I've got to ask, just for the record, and I'm really sorry, but was there something funny going on there?" "No. It was a near replica of Perpetua's last day in Stumpy Knoll on her first visit. Uncanny. The problem for the contemporary journalist—and I know this from working for so long on Church and State—is that people don't take kindly to words like 'miracle.'" "No, but there are things that happen in the world for which there are no explanations. We use the word 'fantastic' or 'incredible'. All we need to do here is to turn the language round and say that something that looks fantastic or incredible has a perfectly simple explanation. Perpetua's power is still with us. If they believe in the Astonishing Astrologer they will certainly give Perpetua a chance." Thus it was that the power of the Spirit, invoked in the name of Perpetua, caused a mighty act to be performed by a follower, and it further happened, through that Spirit, that Sneer and Smoother combined to give the event wide coverage in the British media so that almost everyone knew what had happened. People were split about what this meant. The rich and educated in particular were deeply sceptical, while the poor and needy found new hope. Every day, Perpetuanism was drawing thousands to its cause while the established churches continued to fragment, but most of the people who came to Perpetua's followers had never been religious and, except for baptisms, weddings, and funerals, had never been inside a Christian church. There was a new moral seriousness in the public culture, and self-help groups began to spring up in the most deprived area. Wherever there was an awakening, there was a house group to support what was going on.

Stacey looked upon this great awakening with wonder. She had never imagined a god of Coke and burgers so near, compared with the God of wrath. They all came down to London from Stumpy Knoll filled with joy. God was doing wonderful things, and they felt that a new age was dawning. There was a gathering of all the different groups to consider their next steps. Hawthorne was about to produce his report on Perpetuan doctrine, and they would need to study this and learn how to take the message out to the country and the world. Stacey was assigned to Kylie, and they laid their hands on her, making her a full member of the leadership. She could not have imagined anything so fulfilling, as she knelt in the centre of the circle. God had come home, from the distant, vengeful skies into her heart. The vision of practical affirmation and hope, which Perpetua had come to bring, was vibrant among them. This was a time of complete joy but Max, diffidently participating, knew that this was a moment of strengthening for a mission which would test them all.

Next day, he met with the Dean and Granville to discuss the arrangements for using church buildings. Granville looked from the Dean to Max and back again. "Simon," he said, hesitantly, "one curious thing about you is that everybody calls you 'The Dean' without ever using your surname. Why might that be?" The Dean looked embarrassed, but this was no time for holding back. "I was given up by my impoverished parents for fostering. There were just too many of us at home, and my mother was on the verge of a nervous breakdown. My foster parents were very good. They brought me up as an Anglican, and they gave me their name, Prior. So I am properly called Dean Prior. I was always uncomfortable because I did not want to deny the reality of my real parents." "So what was your original name, Simon?" The Dean looked directly at Max. "It was Silver." Max looked steadily back at the Dean. Granville took his time. "So might you be brothers?" "I think it is almost certain," said Max. "When we began to deal with each other, I looked up the history of the Dean on the internet, and it began to ring bells, but I was reluctant to draw any conclusions. There is so much speculation and half-baked information out there, but I truly hoped that we were brothers. I hoped so much that I dared not put it to the test. I was happier with the thought that we were than the possible reality that we were not." The two brothers looked at each other, and Granville, their cousin, quietly withdrew. "Perpetua has brought us together," said Simon Silver. "We shall never be separated."

18.

Like a sailor with the sea, a racing driver with his car, or an athlete with her own body, Hawthorne had a profoundly ambivalent relationship with theology. It sustained him, but on the very edge of catastrophe, and the harder he pushed it towards perfection, the greater was the danger that it would take him over the edge. It was no use, he saw, as a pedestrian pursuit—a sailor that never left harbour, a racing driver who never got up to full speed, or an athlete that ended a race with breath to spare—but only came into its own at the boundaries of possibility and articulacy, where what can be thought and said become almost unified. This very extremity of necessity had led him to be misunderstood by those whose theology was pedestrian, who accused him of being a showman, by those who confused doctrine with theology, who thought he was flirting with 'heresy', by those who wanted their religion 'plain', who thought he was obscurantist; and, above all, by those who mistrusted him, who thought that his use of words was "slippery". He was relatively immune from the pain of these charges because theology was his way of trying to approach God. Whereas others practised meditation or deep contemplation, immersed themselves in the details of liturgy, took refuge in the familiar comfort of the Bible, identified with the Gentle Jesus, propounded the social justice of Saint Luke, became passionate about Church reports on doctrine, or simply felt themselves to be 'born again', his way was the way of the ocean-going yachtsman, the grand prix driver, or the Olympic long distance runner, risking, probing, stretching, and, like all of these, the public purple passages, represented by the publication of his books, were the fruit of endless trial and error, represented by articles, sermons, lectures and seminars. These were, because of the global news networks, frequently misrepresented, as if an athlete's practice runs could be equated with the real performance. Not that his relationship with God was exclusively theological for, in the end, a sailor, a racing driver, or an athlete are not simply defined by their pursuit. His profession might be theology, but his life was in the profound mystery of the incarnation for, being what he was, he knew better than those who did not push themselves how far he could be pushed and where his striving must cease. There was a small area between his comfort zone and the impossible which he faithfully and meticulously inhabited in his work, the area of possibility—of hours for the sailor, of tenths of a second for the racing driver or athlete—but, because it was so small, he was profoundly aware of the impossible in a way that eluded the glib. So the great theologian's spiritual vigour was fed by God's mystery in creation, God's being with us in incarnate history, and our incarnational perception through Our Sister the Spirit within us. He was sometimes 'accused' of flirting with the obscure but, although it was possible that he might disagree with Vogelin, Girard, Zizioulas, Charles Taylor, Rahner, Barth, von Balthasar, Kung, Millbank, or Hauerwas, his more customary responses were constructive engagement, elaboration, refinement, lateral connectivity, or eccentric illumination. In combination, these cast previously unimagined light and shadow on what had been perceived to be a familiar object admitting no new perspectives. He was of the comradeship of the extremists, the sailors who understand the despair of a competitor, the drivers who understand the vagaries of a crash, the athletes who have come so near to breakdown that they can imagine it in their greatest rival with an almost unbearable degree of empathy. For the Sunday supplements and the religious press, theology might be something of a bun fight, but for Hawthorne and his most distinguished colleagues, the races were simply the necessary public manifestations of their striving and, to alter the metaphor, they were all, like golfers, playing against themselves, no matter how frequently they were drawn into commentary on the 'performance' of another player. Yet theology is profoundly different from the metaphors of endurance in this, that a practitioner is comforted by the mystery on which he can only marginally impinge. Whereas the competitor works in a narrow range of possibility, and never thinks of the far beyond, the theologian works in the same narrow area, drawing strength from the far beyond. For humanity, probing the mystery of God, is doing God's work, behaving as it was created to behave, giving God pleasure through using human faculties, creating space, making choices, understanding the limits of humanity and the infinite goodness of its creator. In doing God's work, it feels God's Grace—the Spirit within it—as it probes and speculates and risks. In Hawthorne's case, this creative life morphed into prayer and caring in a way that made him wonder at his own completeness.

Such was Hawthorne's coherence of being that he had been remarkably unshaken by the epiphany of Perpetua. He had been 'professionally' concerned with the Godhead for so long that her claims revived a consideration of possibilities which had simply lain dormant. Because he had struggled with the GodMan issue, wrestled with the noun/verb problem of Trinity, and tangled with the concepts of difference and incommensurability, the prospect that the Trinity itself might be a construct capable of improvement did not strike him as scandalous. It had to be considered and prayed about in the same way that he would 'handle' any other piece of theological material; the prospect of God's incarnation being iterative on earth or distributed in the cosmos was, in God's own terms, a relatively trivial 'problem' that raised some critical issues for the relatively recent manifestation of the Christian church, relating to the way it arrives at a collective understanding of the Godhead: were the Councils "wrong" when they declared the immutability of Trinity? Was the sacrifice of Jesus really "final"? Again, as he considered these questions, the very provisionality of theology struck him, as it always did at critical junctures. Had he cared about our metaphors, he would have thought about Magellan, Fanjio, and Bannister, and seen how provisional had been their achievements. He was therefore not automatically prejudiced in favour of the defensive or the conservative. Today's conservatism is yesterday's radicalism, not least in the cases of Nicea and Chalcedon and he therefore took Perpetua's own 'arguments' seriously when she said that she was God's Sacred Vessel, or Sustainer, because in what way she might be was a matter of relationship, as it had been with Jesus. That the sacrifice of Jesus was full but not final—which was simply a matter of how God intersects with time which—after the incarnation, is relatively 'trivial'. This left the question of the mechanism by which the Church could make up its mind. On this last question Hawthorne, as Archbishop, had been fearlessly radical. He thought that all theology was, if it had to be given a grammatic formulation, a question and, because it was a metaphorical question, there was not much point in posturing. The Church might apply collective wisdom to refine the question, but it could do no more than that which meant, by extension, that he thought that the Vatican methodology was devoid of humility. Nonetheless, he recognised the human need for doctrine and so he had agreed, at some personal cost to himself, to undertake the work for the Perpetuans. Along with the metaphors of voyage and endurance he also often thought, thanks to Margaret Boden, of the different kinds of creativity. He might, crudely, think of doctrine's relationship to theology as approximately the same as the relationship between legislation and philosophy but, at a more usefully general level, he thought that theology, at its best, was transformative, whereas doctrine, at its best, was a set of variations on a theme. It would all come down, however, in the end, not to the doctrinal derivatives of theology, but to the nature of authority about which he was profoundly ambivalent. Having rejected both the Vatican and the Congregationalist model, he was left with the uncomfortable reality that had faced the Church of England since the Reformation, but which now confronted Perpetuans in an even more radical form, both because they had no corporate memory and because the claims they were making had not not been tested. "In the end," he thought, as he looked at the final document, "all that doctrine does is try to articulate what I have perceived, just in the way that a music critic gives shape to my profound love of music. I experience the music but the critic teaches me sonata form. The difference is in this, that in God there is only one music, and theologians try to flex it differently, and doctrine gives new flexings shape." He looked for a final time at the manuscript. The problem with print was that it could never be re-called. It could be revised, but never withdrawn. People had made the lives of others miserable, and even killed, for doctrine. He only hoped that what he had to say would do more good than harm. It was the best for which he could hope, not because he was a pessimist about people, but because they were optimists about doctrine, hoping that it would spare them the effort of establishing a personal relationship with the Godhead.

Introduction

In writing this provisional summary of the witness of those who believe that Perpetua is the 'fourth person of the Godhead' (and I will be forced repeatedly to use inner quotation marks as a sign that we are dealing with metaphor), I am deeply aware of the Jewish and Christian traditions out of which we have come to flourish, but equally aware of our historical fallibility in thinking that an enterprise is complete when nothing in human affairs is ever complete. Indeed, it is the essence of who we are to be incomplete, for in that very incompleteness lies the source of our striving, our exercise of choice, based on incompleteness, which enables us freely to give God pleasure, to 'love'. I am also deeply aware that there will be many who will place more emphasis on what we are able to put into words than is warranted. We are creatures in search of the meaning of the mystery of our creation and our creator, and what distinguishes us from our forebears is simply that we believe that there is no limit on how the Godhead may wish to be with us. We believe in the Creator God of the Jews, and the Incarnate Redeemer God of the Christians, recognised through the power of the Sanctifier, but we also believe that God was incarnate again in Perpetua, the Sacred Vessel or Sustainer, who we recognise through the same Spirit. Nothing that we can write is absolute; everything that we can say of the Godhead is profoundly provisional. Doctrine only satisfies a human need, but we exist in a position of profound privilege, to satisfy the divine need for us to love God, and that means that what matters most is prayer and our commitment to love God through treating all humanity as divine.

1. The Godhead. We believe that God Our Parent is humanity's way of 'accounting' for its own existence. This is not to say that God is a human construct but that the language of humanity, which is a God-given, but human, construct, formulates the idea of God in order to acknowledge our creatureliness as the result of a Creator. There are those who describe the reality of Godhead as, "The explana-

*tion of why there is something rather than nothing", but that is a purely philosoph-
ical approach, as opposed to a theological understanding which seeks to account
for God's creative acts by asking why it is that a totally self-sufficient God might
want to create. The only plausible answer is that God wishes for the pleasure of
being loved as a voluntary act and that, in what might appear to be a paradoxical
act, God created humanity's incompleteness as the most exalted form of creation.
We are placed in an environment which contains uncertainty (weather, natural
disasters) and ostensible unfairness (young children dying of cancer) so that we
might exercise our choice. Thus we have a deep obligation to suffering because
without it we could not fulfil our purpose. God is, therefore, an intelligent phenomenon ('being') who self-communicates with us in love—the limitless capacity for
creating possibility—and wishes us to choose to self-communicate, not 'in return',
for our relationship with God is only metaphorically reciprocal, but because it is
the essence of our creatureliness that we communicate with God. This is why we
were made. It is who we are; it is our quest to mitigate our incompleteness, to narrow the 'gap' between creatures and the Creator, to seek an 'understanding' of the
divinity into which we will be enfolded when our human life ends. Because God
has intervened in history—in our space and time—and taken on human form in
the persons of Jesus Christ and Perpetua, whose 'membership' of the Godhead we
recognise through the power of the Holy Spirit within us, through incarnational
perception, we acknowledge that our understanding of God is profoundly provisional as there may be further manifestations of the Godhead to us or to other created phenomena. We therefore acknowledge that the Godhead is manifest in four
forms: God Our Parent and the Creator of all, Jesus and Perpetua, the incarnate
manifestations of the Godhead, and Our Sister the Spirit whose presence within us
enables us to contemplate their unified and individual four-fold mystery.*

2. Incarnation. *We believe that, as far as can be known from tradition and
records—given ultimate significance by Our Sister the Spirit—having created human history, God has twice 'chosen' to intervene in that history by manifesting the
Godhead in human form in the God/Human beings of Jesus Christ and Perpetua.
In respect of Jesus, we accept the formulations on his single person and two natures
set out in the Councils of Nicea (325) and Chalcedon (451) subject to the usual
caveat that these formulations are capable of improvement. In respect of Perpetua,
we accept what she said of herself and therefore 'classify' her in an identical 'class'
with Jesus. We believe that both of these manifestations of the Godhead were di-
vinely ordained and created through the human agency of sexual love (therefore
denying the Christian doctrine of "the Virgin Birth") and that any other fulfillment of the divine will would lead to a form of gnosticism or dualism, which both
Christians and perpetuans deny. We further affirm that the purpose of both Jesus
and Perpetua was to articulate the universality and depth of God's love for us such
that when we torture and kill them, and therefore do violence to the Godhead, God
nonetheless continues to love all humanity, constant in purpose, showing that there
is nothing that humanity can do in making wrong choices which is capable of affecting God's loving purpose. We find some Christian explanations of the 'purpose'*

of the death of Jesus—to propitiate God Our Parent, to pay our debts to the God of wrath—are disrespectful to and demeaning of God's existence as pure love. We acknowledge that as the necessary consequence of our created imperfection and the 'tests' to which we are put in the natural world, that we will make wrong choices, deliberately denying what we know in the light of the lives and teachings of Jesus and Perpetua, to be the choice which would fulfil our human purpose as loving children of God Our Parent. Yet we know that the direct contact of God Our Parent with the Chosen People gradually lost its impact which 'caused' the incarnation of Jesus. We know that the Church, which he founded, steadily fell away from his ideal which 'explains' why God sent Perpetua. We acknowledge the unique blessedness of the mystery of incarnation, but do not presume to say that God can only be 'allowed' to 'act' in this way for a number of occasions defined by us.

3. Love. *When we say that "God is love" we mean that God our parent has created us as creatures capable of choosing. In its purest, receiving or hospitable, form, love is the creation of space by the lover in which the beloved can exercise unconditional choice. The degree to which the exercise of this choice accords with the loving purpose of God Our Parent is a matter completely reserved to God. In its less pure, giving or prescriptive, form, love is the active individual and collective exercise of benevolence, often at personal and collective cost, in order to enhance the life chances and choices of the beloved or to mitigate other forms of inequality and injustice. Thus, the opposite of hospitable love is power and the opposite of prescriptive love is selfishness. Because we believe that God Our Parent self-communicates with every member of humanity. It is in our created nature to attempt, no matter how imperfectly, to communicate with God, and because God would not frustrate the purposes for which we were created, we believe that every human being will be enfolded back into the perfect love of God Our Parent from which we came. We therefore reject any notion of divine punishment or "hell", accepting that each personal relationship between the Creator and each Creature is unique and likewise that no loving God would punish us for failing in an environment of difficult choices 'deliberately' made for us.*

4. Manifestations after Death. *We believe that both Jesus and Perpetua manifested themselves to humanity after they had each been cruelly tortured and killed by us as a means of demonstrating to humanity that there is nothing it can do to curtail God's self-giving directly to us, through the concrete example of Jesus and Perpetua, and through the presence within us of Our Sister the Spirit. We accept the Christian theology of Resurrection without being certain of the form in which Jesus appeared to his followers after his death—we do not believe that a theology of Resurrection requires an 'empty tomb' or that Jesus took a form which included flesh and bones—and we necessarily accept that the same theology encompasses the post death manifestations of Perpetua which are, unlike the case of Jesus, graphically clear to us as recent events. We believe that, having fulfilled their purpose and manifested themselves to us after death, they have abandoned their human natures and are 'now' enfolded within the perfect love of God Our Parent as we all shall be when we abandon our human natures and are enfolded into the* *divine. We therefore believe that the notion, adhered to by some Christians, of divine judgment is profoundly at odds with God's loving purposes for humanity. Thus, to the extent that we might colloquially say that judgment is reserved to God, the upshot of this reservation is that God will not judge us as this is simply an anthropomorphising of the nature of divinity. On the two occasions that the Godhead has revealed itself in human form, in Jesus and Perpetua, even in possessing their human natures they have signally failed to judge.*

5. Our Sister the Spirit. *We believe that Our Sister the Spirit is God within us which enables us to 'be connected' with the Godhead by being in tune with its self-communication and, in turn, enables us to recognise our obligations of creatureliness to our Creator. Whereas Christians believe that the Spirit was 'sent' after the death and Resurrection of Jesus, we believe that the Spirit is always with humanity, but that it was easier for us, through the Spirit, to communicate with the Godhead after the Resurrection of Jesus. It is again now, because of the freshness of humanity's experience of incarnate Godhead in Perpetua. Thus the Godhead, 'aware' of humanity's tendency to be distracted from its purpose, 'revives the apprehension' of the Spirit within us which, in turn, sharpens our incarnational perception. The assignment of Sisterhood to the Spirit is a conscious counterbalance, based on the proclamation of Perpetua, to the tendency to imagine God Our Parent as male. Thus, in the current understanding of the Godhead, God Our Parent, Our Sister the Spirit, Jesus, and Perpetua are 'symmetrical'. The mystery of the Godhead within us, enabling us to communicate with the Godhead beyond us through the consciousness of the lives and teachings, deaths and re-manifestations of Jesus and Perpetua, is the most profound of all the sacred mysteries, of the one Godhead apart, incarnate, and within us.*

6. Scripture. *We believe that the Holy Bible of the Jewish Old Testament and the Christian New Testament are a record of the spiritual dialogue between the Godhead and humanity, but that because it is a 'library' of works of many genres, it must be 'understood' through the means of God-given intelligence, which is able to identify the purpose of the Godhead acting through the agency of the author. To treat the whole Bible as a compendium of instruction, a work of literature, or simply a collection of books of spiritual wisdom is to estimate it at much less than its worth. It is all of these, but it is quintessentially an account of theology in action which, supremely, contains the nearest humanity has possessed until the life of Perpetua to an account of the life, teaching, death, and re-manifestation of the Incarnate Godhead, in the person of Jesus. We are committed to assembling a true and reliable collection of the accounts of the life, teaching, death, and re-manifestation of Perpetua which, we maintain, should, as the most complete and authentic account of the Incarnate God, take priority over all other scripture in its articulation of the divine love for us. We further affirm that the priority where Scriptural texts conflict should be: Perpetua over the Gospels, the Gospels over Paul, Paul over Pastoral Letters, and all of these over Revelation. We affirm the superiority of Christianity's New Testament over the Old Testament of the Chosen People, but we affirm the reverence in which we hold the Prophets and the record of encounter between* *the Godhead and the Chosen People. While those books and portions of books referring to ritual are essential to the religious life of Jews, we deem them not to be so for Perpetuans, and we further confirm that the relegation by some Christians of the Apocrypha to an inferior position is not based on any sound theological basis, but is the result of historical prejudice. In summary, we commend the reading of Holy Scriptures on a regular basis, summoning the power of Our Sister the Spirit and exercising the intelligent faculties given to us by the Godhead so that we might better understand God's love for us and our often faithless reaction to it. Most of all, our reading should enliven us to the incalculable gift we have received in the Incarnations of Jesus and Perpetua.*

*7. **Religion.** We believe that the Godhead, creating all of humanity in love so that it might give pleasure by freely choosing to love, would not 'wish' to frustrate the purpose of creation by 'refusing' to re-enfold all human beings back into perfect love when their human lives end. We therefore affirm that Perpetuans do not possess the sole means to 'eternal life', but we do say that those whose lives have been touched by the wonder of incarnation are better able to fulfill their purpose as creatures. This is not because they are 'better' people, but because they have better means. We therefore commend Christianity as the soil from which Perpetuanism grew, as we also recognise the fundamental role played in our incarnational history by the Jewish religion. Our commendation of Perpetuanism as the surest means to an effective personal relationship with the Godhead is purely based on the pragmatic consideration that she represents the freshest, most fully expressed, and recorded incarnational manifestation. We commend and respect all those of every religion and none who strive to develop a personal relationship with the Godhead and in affirming what we believe to be the most effective means, we are simply imposing on ourselves an extra responsibility which is concomitant with the gift of incarnational perception. We acknowledge that humanity is fundamentally good and that countless people of non-incarnational religions, or of no religion, strive to do their best to live holy and moral lives. We regret that to be blessed by incarnational perception is no guarantee of either a holy or a moral life, and that making wrong choices in this context is a greater denial of the Godhead than the wrong choices made by non-believers. We are therefore specially blessed, specially commissioned, and specially vulnerable.*

*8. **Theology.** We believe that the study of theology is the most exalted pursuit of humanity as it seeks to maintain and strengthen its capacity to form personal relationships with the Godhead, individually and corporately through the mutual support of other believers. Theology is necessarily both risky and tentative, seeking as it does to express the mystery that is the Godhead of perfect love in the imperfect language which is one of the many gifts from our Creator. Theology is, therefore, the science of metaphor, in its pursuit of a precision of comprehension and exposition, given depth and richness through the art of expressive imagination. Because it deals in metaphor, theology should be the subject of respectful and constructive criticism. It should be used to clear away obscurities, pitfalls, and even mines, but should not be used as ammunition. We are saddened by the perception that* *much Christian theological dispute has arisen from political and selfish motives and bears no relationship to a reverent consideration of the nature of the mystery of the Godhead. We affirm that the practice of theology must be distinguished from the study of the philosophy of religion, in that theology as the active pursuit of the articulation of our faith in the Godhead and thankfulness for our incarnational perception, is distinct from a dispassionate and non-committed commentary on our theological task. There are wide areas of enquiry where we should fruitfully collaborate with others whose lives are informed by God's self-communication and incarnational perception. Because theology is by far the most difficult and risky enterprise on which we embark, we should be able to look to each other for support in its pursuit and we should treat all holy and reverent speculation with the honour it deserves, regardless of our personal perceptions. Theology is a necessary precondition for the establishment of settled, although still provisional, language which can inform our personal lives and our religious dialogue. We stress, finally, that all theology is metaphor and is therefore provisional and capable of improvement. As such it must be encouraged and not suppressed.*

9. Authority. *Authority is the enemy of theology and we believe that there is no earthly structure which is fit to exercise authority in matters of our understanding of the self-Communication with the Godhead and our response. Neither do we believe that any institution possesses a monopoly of authority or 'access' to the Godhead. We accept that for us to conduct constructive dialogue with respect to the mystery of God and in order to provide each other with the mutual support we require both to make difficult choices and, to maintain our stance on the nature of love, the need for a common theological language which should be deliberatively, prayerfully, and collectively cultivated and maintained through prayer and study. Language will always be negotiable and complex, but we believe that the Christian approach is too structured, rigid, confrontational, and unforgiving to provide a helpful model for our understanding of God's incarnational purposes. We believe in dispersed theological authority, which should rest with the whole community of believers who participate in the development of ways of supporting each other so that we may continue to grow and speculate. There will be occasions on which we find ourselves in serious dispute and on such occasions we must exercise extreme forebearance, recognising that all who accept the basic principles of our faith (Clause 17) should be counted among us. Nobody should have the authority to expel a person from being a Perpetuan because accepting the responsibility for creatureliness is a supremely personal choice, but those who do not accept the basic principles should not take part in the few, but necessary, formal processes which enable the movement to support its adherents.*

10. The Church. *We believe that the Church exists for no other purpose than to support and encourage the flourishing of personal relationships between the Creator and creatures. We affirm the importance of corporate worship, study, and mutual support, but insist that these are means to the ultimate end of being with God while on earth. We accept that there are times when major activities of corporate worship are not only appropriate, but essential—particularly in respect of the cele-*

bration of the Sacraments—but we believe that the most frequent form of corporate life in the Godhead should be through deliberately diverse small groups, praying and studying together, alive to incarnation and wary of hierarchy and structure. Yet we wish to stress that it is important that Perpetuans do not generalise in their criticism of Christianity. It has much to teach us about Sacrament, ritual, and the holy life, but it stands as a warning in areas such as the exercise of power and the imposition of hierarchy. Above all, we are sensitive to the risk in the paradox that a church ostensibly exists to support individual piety, but that humanity was created in order to recognise patterns and tends to seek to impose these on chaos and, by extension, others. So ingrained in our thought processes, ergonomics, and language is the urge to discern and create patterns that the Perpetuan vision will be—as the Christian vision was before it and, in some places, still is—a continual goad to the established and the authoritarian. The movement (or church) must not exercise authority over the way in which individual creatures understand and live their relationships with the Creator. We believe that it should only exercise any collective function over those who accept such a function. We do not accept that Perpetuanism should work on the majoritarian principle, that minorities must 'fall into line'. To be a Perpetuan means to be a willing adherent. Nonetheless, we believe that it is extremely difficult to live the holy life of a Perpetuan in isolation from the affirmation and comfort of fellow believers. To be a Perpetuan alone is to deny oneself the warmth and support which are almost indispensable to a person committed to making difficult choices and to living a life where the concept of love is so demanding. For the sake of clarity, then, we believe that Perpetuanism is a Movement and that to call it a Church would lead to misunderstanding.

11. The Sacraments. The Sacraments of the Perpetuan Movement are living continuations of the incarnational reality of Jesus and Perpetua. We acknowledge our huge debt to Christianity's faithful crystallisation of the fundamental concept of sacramentality as the physical manifestation of divine reality and we are therefore able to maintain, in this most difficult area of theological endeavour, that in a profound sense the whole earth is the sacrament of the Creator, that our incarnational life is the sacrament of Jesus and Perpetua, and that our endeavour to establish our individual personal relationships with the Godhead is the sacrament of Our Sister the Spirit. In this we are overjoyed to affirm that Jesus and Perpetua took on our human form and that we are made in the divine image. We are also indebted to the Christian tradition for its formulation of sacramental practice which was reformed by Perpetua to bring it closer to human needs and to emphasise more sharply the reality of the human/divine intersection in Sacrament. We affirm our contemporary acceptance of four sacraments, as set out for us, by Perpetua in her teaching, acknowledging that there is always room for development and that there are an infinite number of individual, sacramental experiences:

11.a Reception. We owe a great debt to Christianity for its identification of the ancient custom of Baptism as possessing a sacramental quality, but whereas Christianity has largely perceived its Sacrament of Baptism as an initiation into a "Church", we believe that it is an initiation into the conscious, deliberative pursuit *of a personal relationship with the Godhead: to study and listen to God and to worship and communicate with God. Initiation, however, is not a human initiative to 'choose' God, but is a divine initiative to bless creatureliness. Whereas some Christians maintain that those who are not baptised cannot be the object of God's self-communication and cannot therefore be enfolded back into God's perfect love (heaven), we believe that initiation is a celebration of constructive human nature that enhances the ability of those who persevere both to hear (inner quotation marks deliberately not used) God and to self-communicate 'in return'. We do not go so far as to say that nobody can be a follower of Perpetua without celebrating Initiation—anyone can follow any figure in a casual, non-directed way—but we cannot understand how any genuine follower would wish to make the journey more difficult than need be. Should Perpetuanism be forced by the world in which we live to conduct any consultative or voting procedures, only those who have received its Initiation or formally declared their Christian Baptism to have been translated to following Perpetua, will be able to make a formal submission and/or vote. Initiation should be celebrated by any Perpetuan who has completed a course supervised by a Guide. The Celebrant should be flanked by four people who have shared a simple course in the basics of Perpetuanism. The Christian custom of choosing God Parents who are not instructed in their faith and have no intention of instilling that faith in the person to be baptised is to be deplored. There is no Perpetuan rule about the age at which a person is initiated, but we recommend that it should be undertaken as the first step, at approximately age five, on the road to the reception of the Sacrament of Union and the first episode of Affirmation.*

11.b Union. *The Sacrament of the Mysterious Union of the Divine and Human combines what Christians call Reconciliation (Confession) and Holy Communion (Eucharist). We believe that our reconciliation with God should be an iterative, deeply deliberative, and unfailingly honest pursuit which will frequently cause discomfort and pain. This 'upward' movement of our spirit, primed by Our Sister the Spirit as God within us is symmetrical with the divine reconciliation with us in the sharing in the real presence of the Godhead in our offerings. We accept the form of the Christian Eucharist as a Sacramental rite in respect of the presence of Jesus with us;, but we equally accept celebrations in similar mode but with more diverse offerings, as the celebration of the real presence of Jesus and/or Perpetua with us. While we accept the general proposition of the omnipresence of God, we believe that this does not abridge the special presence of our God of mystery both within us in Our Sister the Spirit and given to us in the Sacrament of Union with Jesus and Perpetua. The Sacrament of Union can only take place if both parts are accomplished. The first part is an individual act on the part of the person seeking reconciliation, the second part must be celebrated by a person who has both been chosen by the celebrating group and has undertaken a course approved by a Guide. The Sacrament of Union is the core form of worship and chief source of sustenance for God's people and it is one of the few activities which justify the existence of a church-like structure as a means to enhance the relationship between the Creator and creatures. We believe that all Perpetuans should be admitted to the Sacrament* *of Union as soon as each is able to grasp the significance of the celebration and, therefore, as shortly after Initiation as is appropriate. We recommend that all those who are present at a celebration of the Sacrament of Union should participate in receiving the transformed offerings so that they may be fed with the food of life, but if they receive without reconciliation, their sacramental experience will be incomplete. Union is the appropriate Sacrament within which to integrate special prayers for a person who has died as the major focus of such an event will be the enfolding of the deceased back into the limitless love of the Godhead. Unlike some Christian traditions which affirm that we cannot know whether an individual has "gone to God" because of their "sins", we are certain that all human beings are enfolded back, that the notion of God's "judgment" is an anthropocentric encroachment and an insult to God's loving purpose.*

11.c Affirmation. *The Sacrament of Affirmation is an iterative celebration which should take place at key stages in the life of a Perpetuan once he/she has celebrated Initiation and Union. We do not regard Affirmation as a precondition for Union (such as Christians affirm when their Sacrament of Confirmation precedes participation in their Sacrament of the Eucharist) but, rather, we do not see how a person can make a commitment in Affirmation without the nourishment of Union. Affirmation is, therefore, a Sacrament of chronological significance and does not rank the commitments which people make to each other and through each other to the Godhead. As a matter of rhetoric and tradition, Christianity has ranked its Sacrament of Holy Orders above Holy Matrimony, but we regard this as a wholly misled proceeding which is dangerously close to dualism and a contemporary form of Gnosticism. Every Perpetuan should consider participating in the Sacrament of Affirmation on becoming an adult and on entering a special relationship with another adult. It should also be considered at the termination of important relationships and at the commencement of critical life events, including the undertaking to be a Perpetuan Guide, and at junctures such as the onset of a serious illness. Affirmation is also the appropriate Sacrament for those facing death. Affirmation is a public event during which each person affirms themselves in faithfulness to God Our Parent and specifies the form of that affirmation in a declaration offered in the presence of the people and sealed in turn at the Sacrament of Union, which should always follow on from a celebration of the sacrament of Affirmation. The only limit on the way in which Affirmation is conducted is that when a person is presented to be a Guide, the Affirmation must be in the presence of the three Guides who bless the commitment and in the presence of those who put the candidate forward. Finally, by way of reinforcement of our general commitment, we wish to re-affirm that all forms of Affirmation are equal in the sight of God Our Parent and must be treated with equal respect and seriousness by all Perpetuans. It may be as onerous for one person to commit to daily prayer as it is for another to commit to serve as a full time Guide, and it will often be the case that a commitment to live in harmony with another person, physically, emotionally, and practically, is more onerous than being a Guide. We are wary of the clericalist bias which distorted Christianity and we must do all in our power to prevent this* *recurring; it was this distortion, we believe, that was one of the primary 'reasons' why the Godhead 'felt it necessary' to send Perpetua to us.*

11.d Response. *We believe that the initiation of the sacrament of Response is one of the most important contributions made by Perpetua to build on Christian Sacramentality. In her own words it, "Takes disparate elements from creation, from our lives, and makes of them a whole which we offer in love to each other and the Creator, God Our Parent. It is the Sacrament of healing and self-healing, of affirmation in our creative power, the affirmation that we are free to choose to love. You will remember how I celebrated it with broken glass at the beginning of my ministry." It is therefore a Sacrament which celebrates the bringing together of disparate elements and offering them to God in a constructed format, celebrating the idea that the whole is more than the sum of the parts. Once having offered the constructed whole to God, we each take away a piece of what has been offered. In this we both give and receive, share what we have and share all our burdens together. It may be offered in a 'gentle' form with soft materials, particularly as a way of introducing children, but it should also be celebrated by adults in its 'sharp form' where broken glass or other uncomfortable objects may be used. The celebration of Response calls for a particular kind of creative talent that is able to mould together all the offered elements into a whole which uplifts. This will consist of physical objects, but we also encourage the use of words, images, and music to enhance the occasion so that all of humanity's creative powers may be fused together in thanks and praise. We would normally recommend that a Guide presides at such a celebration, but he/she may identify another person with a more appropriate combination of gifts.*

12. Guides. *While we are extremely reluctant to replicate the Christian mistake of instituting a series of arrangements to replicate political governance, we recognise the importance of maintaining the integrity of our movement. We believe that the best form of insurance is that the whole movement is responsible for assessing our own corporate spiritual health, but we are also conscious that we require a small, but vital, element of cohesion and administration. We therefore propose that the leaders of our Movement, who were with Perpetua and those who have since been chosen by the laying on of hands, should make arrangements to Affirm an appropriate number of us to be Guides. These will affirm succeeding Guides, design and teach courses connected with the Sacraments and the teachings of Jesus and Perpetua, provide pastoral care for House Groups and their Leaders, design and celebrate major acts of worship with public significance—e.g. Affirmation and Response—and supervise the community and hospitality obligations of Guide Centres. Although it is difficult to define our proposals in relation to Christianity, we see Guides as being closer to Bishops than Priests. Where we differ radically from Christianity is in believing that the function of the leader and teacher should be close to the people. We further affirm our commitment to a 'hierarchically flat movement' where Guides are distinguished by their function, but not considered to be 'higher' because of it. We totally reject the Christian notion of 'Discernment', in which a hierarchical procedure can be invoked in the name of Our Sister the*

Spirit to question whether a person is "called" to serve God; rather, we affirm that a persona's calling must be presumed to be genuine and it must be 'tested' by peers. It may be that the individual calling is not matched with an opportunity, but if people make Affirmations, Perpetuans must do their best to help each person to achieve what he or she has affirmed. This clause is highly provisional.

13. House Groups. *As the basic unit of society is the family, so the basic unit of the Perpetuan Movement is the House Group or assembled family. House Groups are established to study and discuss the formation and maintenance of individual relationships with God Our parent, reinforce each other in living lives of love where space is created for the beloved, celebrate the Sacrament of Union, promote social justice, and seek to reconcile Perpetuan living with our civil and political cultures. House Groups may appoint whatever leadership they think fit, subject to any leader having completed the appropriate course approved by a Guide, and subject to the prudential rule that no one person should lead a Group for more than two years unless a Guide specifically recommends that this is more beneficial than harmful. If the primary reason for this decision is the lack of a replacement leader, it is the Group's responsibility to identify new leadership in the power of Our Sister the Spirit. Although we cannot lay down specific rules, we pray that each Group will, in the spirit and practice of Perpetua, contain people of different backgrounds and economic, intellectual, and social status. Any Group that is exclusively from one identifiable sector, or which practises tokenism, will be behaving in a manner contrary to the life and teaching of Perpetua. In saying this we are particularly conscious of our role in bringing the poor and ignorant to a better understanding of the Godhead so that they may receive comfort through the most exalted of relationships. In this we recognise our highest obligation, even higher than that of ensuring that through our lives, love and advocacy, all our citizens have more opportunities to exercise their God given choice. House Groups which claim to be Perpetuan must be attached to a Guide so that they can receive guidance and teaching. We respect self-regulation, but recognise that, as we are human beings, necessarily imperfect, each of us requires encouragement and objectivity from other friends than those to whom we naturally turn. Guides have facilitating functions in order to maintain integrity of teaching and practice, but they only have a jurisdictional role in respect of voluntary adhesion to them. Nonetheless, we hope that most Groups will be able to attach themselves to their nearest Guide so that there is a degree of local coherence and mutual support.*

14. Freedom. *We believe that the purpose of created humanity is to exercise the freedom to love God in direct relationship and through treating each other as images of the Godhead, brothers and sisters of Christ and Perpetua dwellings of Our Sister the Spirit. As such, our existence is utterly dependent upon the other who provides the space in which we exercise our freedom to choose. We are, therefore, non-existent as human beings created by the Godhead unless we are in a relationship in which we create space in which the beloved (all humanity is our beloved) can exercise freedom. Likewise, our exercise of choice depends upon the other. The exercise of freedom, therefore, is a social and not a private activity which is gov-*

erned by an culture which values taking as much as giving, but does not exercise choice in what to take. It is therefore to be distinguished both from the exercise of freedom by an individual in pursuit of his or her own preference and from the exercise of supererogation which is a duty rather than the exercise of the freedom to love. In the life of the Perpetuan the exercise of the freedom to love and its facilitation in others is the highest calling, but this does not free us from the duty of social justice where we are required not only to accord with redistributive legislation, but in conditions where it is absent or inadequate we are required to undertake supererogatory redistribution to the utmost degree of sacrifice excepting: the exercise of prudence to honour commitments we have made to those for whom we are responsible; the use of our goods such that the least well off benefit from what we retain, e.g. the creation of employment; the use of our goods for our own spiritual benefit and that of others, e.g. in the ownership of books, music and artistic objects. The honouring of the requirements of social justice must at all times reflect our belief that all human beings are children of God Our Parent. Perpetuans must interpret these principles individually in the most generous manner so that those with fewer intellectual, emotional, or physical means can exerciser the greatest possible control over their own lives.

*   **15. Civil Powers.** *Perpetuans are required to be fully active citizens and to support and promote all those initiatives which allow other citizens to be fully active, particularly those who are disadvantaged in such areas as income, wealth, intelligence, self-confidence, and opportunity. We are particularly committed to freeing drug and alcohol abusers from the trap into which their self-perception of hopelessness has led them, and we are committed to mitigating the culture of victimhood. We believe that every human being must exercise whatever choice they have, no matter how small. We believe that the civil powers are the necessary consequence of our createdness in imperfection and that they should be respected and obeyed as long as they do their best, in the face of that imperfection, to provide as much freedom of individual and collective action as is possible. Only in the most extreme circumstances should Perpetuans withdraw from the sphere of the civil powers, for in the majority of places for most of the time the Perpetuan will be involved in a constant tension between the need to create space in which freedom can operate and the temptation to preserve the freedom of the many by curtailing the freedom of the few whose conduct damages social coherence. It is these very people, those who are alienated and violent, which most require the assistance of the civil powers and Perpetuans in realising their freedom to choose. Thus, we particularly abhor the use of the criminal justice system to punish those who have made wrong choices, particularly when their conduct results from profound personal maltreatment and suffering, alienation, and a feeling of helplessness. In all but the most extreme of cases, once the judicial process has reached its verdict, the process should come to an end. We affirm the centrality of restorative justice, and we support schemes of voluntary compensation. We believe that those who do require special custodial treatment because of the extremity of their actions should be regarded as suffering from illness and be treated accordingly, so that they are helped to maximise their*

own life choices and so that the public is not threatened by their freedom. As the civil powers operate in a state of imperfection, we warn against opting out of the political process because the process produces decisions with which we disagree. Conversely, we reject the affixation of the term Perpetuan to any particular political ideology or methodology, and we reject the notion that the Godhead mimics our formulation of the civic polity.

16. Imperfection. *We believe that imperfection is a necessary precondition for exercising choice and that it therefore constitutes the defining characteristic of humanity. It therefore follows that, apart from the very nature of God Our Parent who created us out of love so that we might choose freely to love, it is illogical to hold that we should in some way be ashamed of or punished for our imperfection either by God or by each other. We therefore reject the Christian notion of 'the fall' or 'original sin' which characterise humanity as once perfect and now imperfect. If that were so—and there is some Biblical evidence that the Jews believed it to be—then the transformation from perfection to imperfection was not a 'fall', but a raising up of humanity to its 'God-given purpose. To compare creatures to the Creator and draw an unfavourable comparison is a form of blasphemy. We are not imperfect versions of the Godhead, we are created by the Godhead out of love to exercise the choice to love before we are enfolded back into the perfect love from which we came. Likewise, we affirm the rightness of God's creation, including natural disaster, illness, and a differential distribution of talents and aptitudes as part of the theatre in which our freedom is acted out. We must never forget that the unfortunate are God's special children because it is only through their existence that we can exercise our freedom to choose.*

17. Creed. *On the above basis, we set out the Perpetuan Creed, based on the teachings of Perpetua, but adding appropriate adjustments as she worked on her Creed before the events of her own death and re-manifestation:*

We affirm the mysteries: that God who is love created everything out of love and created humanity as imperfect so that we might freely love God in a personal relationship and love each other; that in love, God Our Parent sent a Son, Jesus Christ, and the Sacred Vessel, Perpetua, as God to share our humanity; by such sharing they brought new hope, but that their perfection was too much for humanity to bear and so we killed them; that they absorbed all humanity's wrong choices and gave it new resources to love through our consciousness of our Sister the Spirit who is God within us, who gives us Incarnational Perception and attunes us more closely to God's self-communication in love; that by their re-manifestation Jesus and Perpetua confirmed that, because no wrong choice, including killing them, will limit God's limitless love, all humanity will be enfolded back into the Godhead from which we came.

We affirm the mysteries: of our earthly purpose of living a Sacramental life of physical encounter with the divine through the life with each other and accept the privileged responsibility inherent in that encounter to bring the news to all humanity that it will be re-united in God.

Hawthorne put the manuscript down, saved his file, and breathed a deep sigh of sadness. He looked out of the window and saw the unseasonal golden roses glisteningly pale in the almost faded light. He felt no relief that such a difficult task was completed. He felt no joy. He felt like winter, the promise of darkness, the promise of cold and damp. He knew that humanity could create light and joy in the dark through the inestimable gifts of God, but he wished that poor humanity were not pressed quite so hard. He had always loved God's children more than they seemed to love themselves and, therefore, each other. He had done his best, but all he could see was struggle and even conflict. If only humanity could get by with theology and not have to descend into doctrine. He had done as he had been asked, however, and could not turn back.

He arrived when Trina, Max, Pluto, Annie, and Granville were finishing a meeting on the Hypo experiment. They asked Trina if they could stay and listen to Hawthorne and she said that she was happy to receive any advice they wished to offer. Hawthorne said, "I have done what you asked me to do, but I come with a heavy heart. As you know, I have been a student of theology and am rather diffident about doctrine in general because it wrings most of the God out of theology and makes it too close to law. It stops people struggling to hear and respond in self-communication to God's self-communication, it makes people think that they have the answer when even the best theology is a question, but, worse, I think that doctrine divides people because it presents a false prospect of unity. Everybody who thinks about it knows that theology is divisive, it must be because it is ultimately an individual enterprise which loses something in its need for corporate communication. In this particular case, however, there is the problem of speed. If doctrine is to work at all, it must follow a long way behind the speculations of theology so that it is founded on a settled position. It was more than 600 years after the supposed events of the Exodus that Jews began to work out what it meant, it was more than 400 years after the death of Jesus before Christians could work out what that was all about, and more than 400 years after the Reformation we have still not managed to settle on a doctrine which accounts for the Crucifixion. Yet, within months of the death of Perpetua I have produced a draft document, much against my personal judgment." "We thank you for it even more fervently because of your personal feelings," said Trina, looking worried. "What do you say, Pluto, with your external—if I can put it that way—perspective?" "I don't like rushed legislation, and doctrine is a kind of legislation, isn't it? It's turning ideas into some sort of rule. I would wait a while." "Max?" "I think the whole tenor of what is on offer—and it's a very good document, don't get me wrong—is against what Perpetua would have wanted. She did work with people to refine the Creed on one of her missions, and I know she occasionally held retreats to help followers focus, but I have not heard that she actually wanted to establish an organisation with a doctrine. She could have done it if that's what she had wanted, just as Jesus could have chosen lawyers and theologians as Apostles instead of fishermen." "Granville?" "Well, perhaps because of my Government experience you would expect me to say that it's difficult to keep any organisation together—I deliberately do not use the phrase "run" an organisation—so perhaps I am tempted towards doctrine, but at this stage I wonder whether we would not be better off with a 'light touch'. We could either put this excellent document out for consultation, or we could issue it as tentative, or perhaps we could just issue the Creed and request our Guides to promote its use during celebrations." "Yes," said Hawthorne, "although I am worried about my own work and the problems it could cause. I know that people celebrating would like to have a Creed as they have a problem with the current words. I know this Creed could cause problems but we have to strike a balance. Celebrants will also want some words for the Sacrament of Union." These proposals went down very well. Trina agreed that they should issue the Creed and some advice on words for the Sacrament of Union, but that they would hold onto the major doctrinal statement and see how it stood the test of time. Hawthorne was relieved. He did not begrudge the time he had spent; better his work should be shelved than a wrong decision be taken. "And now," he said, "I don't want to seem ponderous or self-important, but I would like to go. I am a fervent follower of Perpetua, but the best way I can serve you is not as an ex-Archbishop. If you would like me to be a Guide I would be happy to do this in some—not obscure, exactly, but in a not very prominent area—which will leave me time to do my theology which, I think, is how I can serve God and you best."

Granville and Hawthorne walked westwards into the setting sun on the South Bank promenade. "How do you feel now?" "Just a little sad. I know that I should be full of new life because of the wonderful times that I have lived through, seeing a church that was almost dead being revived by a second Incarnation, but it never quite looks like that. I often used to wonder how people did ordinary things while we were fighting the Second World War. I am sad at myself because I worry about the small things during a period when such a huge things have happened to us, but human beings need to be preoccupied for some of the time with things they can control. They cannot always be self-subjected to endless theological agonising. There is the ordinary to celebrate, and my sadness results from the feeling that I have lost some control of the ordinary. It isn't the Palace or even the liturgy, although I love that so much; it isn't even the price you pay for your theology which, in my case, involves some change in the liturgy. It's the sense that we will be doing our religion in the spiritual equivalent of a Portakabin; that's possibly the best way to do it. Perhaps our churches have made us too comfortable, but it's difficult." "I know, in spite of the flux that goes on all around us, we manage to make politics comfortable. It all looks very messy from the outside, but we have our routines. Of course we can fall from power in an instant, but that's no worse than a builder falling off the scaffolding. At least while we are in power we are indoors and comfortable. That is why Government reform is always on the agenda, because it's always in the future." "Well, that was true of Church reform until this latest upheaval. I despaired of getting anywhere and, now that I have been rescued and deposed at the same time, I am foolishly miserable. I genuinely prefer being rescued and deposed rather than being captive and in situ, but it just doesn't feel like that at the moment." "What will you do now?" "I know it will be theology or I would not have said so, but the task is to find a way of helping us to get away from the profoundly heretical—in the classical sense—the idea that God wanted the person who called him Father to die to atone for our sins. Even liberals like me can't get ourselves away from the rhetoric. Prayer books and hymnals are full of it. One of the attractions of Perpetuanism is that it takes the focus off that temporarily, but it will return because people will ask whether she died for our sins to please the Godhead. There is the rather arcane question of whether they could both have, to which her answer and my answer is no. Even though it is rather more historical than many topics, I want to think about it because it seems to me that this heresy is at the root of Christian ideas about powerlessness, of keeping religion separate from politics. And what about you?" "I want to spend more time listening to music and writing some retrospective work—not memoirs—on the changes I have seen in my lifetime. I'm not greatly philosophical. If I were I would probably never have been a politician." "And do you know anything more about the situation of churches?" "No. Everything has come to a standstill while we—or, rather, they—work out how to react to Southern Gem. The impression being given is that this is a one-off, but there will be others, and if they don't get the first one right, there will be bigger mistakes in the future. To the outsider, it's strange how the different parts of Government continue to function when there is a crisis—as you said people went on living their lives during the War—but big decisions get stacked up, and although the churches issue is not big economically, it is big in terms of the way we look after our built heritage. Max and I think that Anglicans, Methodists, and Perpetuans will need about three-quarters of the current stock of churches, including all the major cathedrals and Abbeys, as we can harness their resources so that they break even. The Catholics won't share anything. That leaves one-quarter of country churches and chapels with no purpose. The heritage lobby has been so comfortable with its position of having the right to insist that other people spend their money on what it wants that the new situation is causing shock and the heritage people are systemically endemic. Before the down-turn it would have been possible to get rid of many of these lovely buildings but the market is falling and they have to be repaired constantly to retain their viability. Even Varnish sees that the game's up. I think what the Government will do is to say to local authorities, the tourist people, and the heritage lobby, take what you want." "I thought it would come to that. Thank God I will be doing theology rather than trying to handle these building issues."

As they came towards Culture Park Bridge, the two stopped to look at its elegant arc. "I doubt we will meet again, Granville, I am going to try to stay out of public life as much as I can. God Bless you." Granville watched him walk Westwards, bronze in the setting sun. "In the Spirit," he said to himself. "In the Spirit."

19.

Granville Brompton was, as he said, not a romantic in any sense of the word. It was not just that he refused to see more good in people or things than there really was—he would have thought of that not as unromantic, but as unsentimental—nor was it simply that he was a deeply sceptical person—although he never crossed the line into cynicism—nor even that he had never formed a deep, romantic attachment—for in this sphere he felt that he had sold himself short—the essence of his outlook, profoundly against contemporary culture, was that he did not hold that powerful ideas powerfully and emotionally expressed would make much difference to society. If there was a quotation which he particularly disliked, it was Shelly's claim that poets were moral legislators. He loved ideas for their own sake, and that was the clue to his personality. He loved music of all the arts and sciences because it possessed the most powerful ideas and the least capacity for changing society, and even in music he greatly preferred the baroque depiction of tragedy to the romantic, the musical gesture rather than the self-indulgent piling on of power and pathos. There was no comparison in his mind between Purcell's *Dido and Aeneas* and Berlioz's *Trojans*, or between Rameau's *Hypolite and Aricie* and Ravel's *Daphnis and Chloe*. He only wished that Handel had spent some time setting Shakespeare's great plays, as they might have given an account as sublime as that of his setting of the Bible. Romantic music and poetry were far too didactic under the pretence of being liberating, whereas baroque music and poetry, in spite of their well regulated structures and deliberate under-statement, provided the listener with space. Most of all, baroque sensibility was collective and concerned with duty, whereas romantic sensibility was, ultimately, selfish, even pornographic, in Paul Kahn's sense of the word. By temperament, then, Granville was a man of deep feeling which sprang from within himself rather than as an ephemeral reaction to external influences. He cared about poor people, not because he saw television documentaries, but because of his commitment to justice. He cared about government over-reaching itself, not because of the howling media which was suspicious of all power save its own, but because he was suspicious of all power. He cared about words, not out of pedantry, but because he believed they were God's greatest gift—even greater than music—to humanity. He cared about proportion, not because he was fastidious—although, indeed, in many matters, he was—but because of his dislike, almost amounting to loathing, of excess. As he sat at his work table listening to a new Rameau recording and making notes on the current church buildings situation, he tried to account for his warm reception of Perpetuanism, and his answer was that it was proportionate, suspicious of power, anxious to avoid excess, supportive of social justice and modestly optimistic about people. Its weakness was that it might easily become too optimistic about people, but it had tried to balance freedom and structure in a much more attractive way than that which was on offer from either the civil or the religious institutions. It was precisely these virtues which had propelled him into New Labour and which had so recently ejected him from it. The media storm had become ever more intense in the past decade in a way that Jim Callaghan could not have imagined, but the switch to being suspicious of people and substituting criminal and governance measures for social justice was difficult for him to take. The massive volume of legislation showed a want of proportionality. It might be the last act of the central state drama, it might be that the country would soon revert to its 'natural' mercantile state, with grand ideas and small government, but it had not come in time to keep him committed. He had, too, found himself drifting away, not because he was not appreciated nor because his intellect was under-rated, but because his point of view was barely understood, and certainly not enough to make any criticism credible. Politicians were supposed to be competent, but most of them had second rate intellects and they were deeply suspicious of people like Granville who wrote serious essays and interested themselves in the long-term issues of the past and future. Perhaps most critical of all, however, was his refusal to be flurried by events. He recognised that short-term crises affected the lives of real people but he knew that nothing the Government did could have very much effect on serious crises, and he proportionately valued his own worth modestly. He turned back to his papers, forcing himself to understand the detail—since he had come out of Government harness he had almost immediately turned to grand themes—but then the door bell rang and Pluto came in. "I'm sorry to disturb you, but I wanted your advice on our experiment." "Delighted. You don't mind the music, do you?" "No, although I've always been a little suspicious of it as it landed me with my silly name." "You might be grateful that your parents only knew The Planets rather than the Biblical and classical material on which Handel based his works. You might have got a very odd name indeed. Anyway, how can I help you?" "I want to put before you very briefly what we have done, with a view to establishing whether it might be applied more widely, and possibly receive Government attention and support." "I will try but I am getting so used again to my comfortable ways that I will probably not find this at all easy and the results may not be at all reliable. While I try to be rigorous I think I am often more governed by sentiment than I care to admit." "I remember feeling like that when the old grocery stores gave way to supermarkets—I thought of many reasons for the old ways but most of them turned out not to be reasons at all—but we have something to learn," said Sir Pluto, briskly, trying to get back to his central point. "The principal way in which cultures try to avoid repeated setbacks is by learning from their mistakes, but I have always advocated learning from successes. One of the very great successes in the second half of the twentieth century was supermarket shopping. Now I know that some people can get very sniffy about it, and there are some people who genuinely prefer local, small shops—although, not infrequently their stated preference is at odds with their behaviour—but supermarket shopping has succeeded because it has given people manageable choice. The old-fashioned grocery store gave them a certain degree of synthetic deference, but you always knew that the shop was being run for the staff not the customer, and manipulating customer purchase was so easy. In spite of the fact that the self-service model, with the range of choice and the kind of product organisation which has been achieved, is often criticised for being inferior to the good old days of the family grocer, it gives people a form of control that they can manage. The ecology project is proving to be a most fascinating experiment. We have recruited a team of advisers who tell people how they can reduce their weekly shop without radically changing their eating and cleaning habits, and without the need to come back after five days because they have run out of something. It is all very practical. Take a person who regularly goes to Hypo every Friday. We have designed a new line of basic products called 'Seven Days' which, naturally, contain seven units of product that people use every day, such as breakfast cereal, but we have actually discovered that almost everyone we know only eats breakfast cereal for five or six days per week, so the "Seven Days' model is not good enough, although it's better than the packets which don't correspond to any known behaviour. Weights and measures are logical but not rational. This approach is even more critical in fruit and vegetables. We ask people what they are likely to eat. Some don't know, but surprisingly many have a very clear idea. In term times, for example, we help with lunch box planning for school children, and that means a pack of five treats—crisps, chocolate bars, and so on—which means that there is no point in a child asking for two treats one day because the consequence will be no treats on another day. It's a form of rational rationing." "What about your profits?" "They are going to be down about 5% in the first year and we might go 'down' even further." "So what about the staff?" "We would have to lose a few, but for the parallel scheme where we ask those who save on their bills to make a donation to keeping the jobs of the lowest paid." "So what are they doing?" "Talking to shoppers about what they do and what they really want. No clip boards and surveys, just walking round with old people, being a second pair of eyes and hands, helping mothers who come with children, picking up valuable information." "It sounds like a kind of dream world where things are too good to be true." "Nothing is too good to be true. We have found a way to reduce consumption without increasing unemployment. The model may not be sustainable over the long term—perhaps we won't be able to go on cutting consumption and learning indefinitely what people want when we have found out more or less all there is to know—but it will work for now. Our projections show that we should pick up some market share which will mean the same profits spread over more customers which is a cost, but not a very big one which might raise the number of people we need again. If we want a steady model of consumption in bad times and good this model may be better than one which is based on luxury consumption. We will have to see." Granville looked at him keenly. "I think there's something more than pragmatism, something even more than principle, here, Pluto." "Yes, Granville, I'm in love, with the experiment and the manager of the experiment." "I share your enthusiasm. It looks good to me, Pluto, and the Government ought to be interested in it.

Although I am now out of power, it is amazing how often people come to ask where the skeletons have been hidden. They are threatening to send me to the Lords, but I probably won't go. I will, however, do my best for the scheme although, if I am honest, you probably have far more clout in Government circles than an ex-middle ranking Cabinet Minister. The great thing that this has in its favour is that there is about to be an economic down-turn and if this kind of enlightened austerity can be harnessed there may be something in it." The door bell rang again and Varnish came in. "Archbishop. You are still archbishop?" "Yes, I'm staying until we resolve the churches issue." "I don't want to load you with any more than you have," said Pluto, "but I wonder if you have ever looked at supermarkets to see if the Church can learn anything from them." Varnish looked puzzled. "Well, look at it this way. There isn't much difference between those who manage supermarkets and those who shop in them. The independence, the self-expression of the consumer, is assisted by massive consumer information and celebrity chefs. Maybe you should concentrate on getting a more informed church membership and getting a few charismatic clergy. The Roman Catholics have rather hemmed themselves in and Anglicans seem to have opted deliberately for a non-charismatic clergy. Look at the Muslims; any male who knows the ropes can lead the prayers and all their other big positions are awarded on merit." "I don't know how to respond in detail, but we are going to have to be a different kind of Church. I accept the analysis that the clergy monopoly, which we deny, but which we know exists, has to come to an end. We have to 'be church' more than we are now and be less of a church." "I suppose I would now call myself a Perpetuan, but we are very keen on the reform of traditional Christianity so that it gives people the spiritual support they need. Christians have tended to be somewhat sniffy about 'new age' spirituality and have responded with rather condescending 'Fresh Expressions' which give people a form of spiritual support which the promoters would not accept as good enough for themselves. I won't sell anything in Hypo that I couldn't buy. Anyway, I've pressed you too far too fast, I can see," said Pluto, softening as he saw Varnish's self-confidence waver. "It is rather curious," said Granville, "but Perpetuans want to see Christianity do well, to see it adjusting to the needs of the twenty-first century. We have a different—how did Hawthorne put it?—'Incarnational Perception', but we should learn from early Christianity. The rift which grew up between Christians and Jews was a terribly costly mistake. At the time they could not have known how costly, but we know now. I think that it will soon be time to found a Christian/Perpetuan Commission, but at the moment there are many in the Anglican Church who are understandably defensive. Talking of which, Archbishop, where are you with Affirming Orthodoxy?" "I think I was precipitate, if I might say so, perhaps trying too hard to be a thinking Archbishop after being dismissed as a buildings Archbishop. It isn't wise to be what you are not. I want to settle the buildings issue and move on, leaving theology to my successor." "Very wise," said Granville. "The world would be a much better place if people did what you have done, admitting over-reach and confining oneself to playing to personal strengths. Of course there are times when people must get outside their competence zone, but not often." "Is there any way I can help smooth the buildings settlement?" asked Pluto, with as little force as he could. "My hope is that we can hand the properties over to a maintenance company that can then sell them off when the market is better and share the profits between the holding company and the Church." "I could help there. I want to sell some of my interests and concentrate more on what really needs my attention. I think that the Shanghai Tower, Cape Town Gold Holdings, Oklahoma Futures, and dozens like them, don't really need me and I don't really need them. I want to concentrate on the new Hypo and on helping the Church and the Movement to grow and work together. If I have learned one thing from all the concerns I have been involved with, it is that society cannot function without basic, simple goodness. There are millions, billions of amoral freeloaders who can only survive because good people create social capital, make sacrifices, hold things together. It's been fashionable to maintain that people only do things if they have incentives and, to a limited extent, that's true, but what we have found recently, watching our staff working on the new experimental model, is what I think we have all known, deep down, that we can only survive on the overtime and enthusiasm we don't pay for, which is given because people believe in doing good. I take great comfort from that. Managing by fear, the use of violence in personal relationships, systematic exploitation, are not only immoral, they simply don't work. That is, if I might say so, Archbishop, where Christianity has got it wrong. It should not look for growth on the basis that it can right the wrong but, rather, that it can grow the right. Behaving badly is the symptom of something else. We all know all of this in our hearts. You just have to look at the low percentage of soldiers on the battlefield who aim to kill the enemy, in spite of their fear, to know how good we are." Granville smiled broadly. "I agree with you, Pluto, but it hardly ever looks like that. If you are correct, we should have enlightened government forever instead of selfish government most of the time." "I suspect that, to a considerable degree, people who are good, but not necessarily very strong behave according to the way they are described. We care more than we like to admit about peer opinion. The trick, surely, is to generate mutually supportive peer groups which encourage virtue." "That is the point of Perpetuan house groups," said Pluto, who had begun attending a new Group on the edge of Grunge Park. Granville, looking sideways at his pile of manuscript, stood up smoothly indicating, without needing to say anything, that he wanted to get on with his work. Varnish and Pluto automatically responded and left him. As they walked across the square Pluto said, "I have rarely seen two people change as you and I have changed in the past few months." "It's the Spirit," said Varnish. "Yes," said Pluto, "The Spirit."

Pluto looked at his wall maps and began to examine the dots on his world map. He made a list of the companies whose value was still at a reasonable level and another of companies which were under-valued. Having made his calculations, he called his Chief of Staff. "Adam, I'm going to reduce my interests, but don't worry because that is as bad as it will get. All the rest of the news is good. I am going to sell my interests in a large number of foreign and international companies. It will mean a few posts will not be needed here, but I want to absorb all of these by expanding my Hypo experiment and by founding a new organisation to promote virtue—I know, it's a bit odd, but I mean it. There are quite enough organisations opposing virtue—and this will mean moving people around. There will be enough people who want to move out of commerce into the new organisation and I think there will also be some new posts in an second organisation we are considering to foster Christian/Perpetuan relations. There's a third organisation which might act as a holding company for a portfolio of Church property." Adam took notes. Apart from his slight start at the virtue enterprise he was so used to Sir Pluto's ways that very little surprised him. "We will also need to lose some floor space. I love my big room with the picture windows, but I think we should do without it." When Adam left Pluto looked out of the window. It was more than farewell to a vista. It was farewell to an illusion. He had enjoyed the view, but now he knew that he would concentrate his energy on improving the view within.

Sneer had never spent a more intense few days than those after his 'conversion', focusing relentlessly on the view within. The first phase of his reflections generated a sense of self-loathing so intense that he hardly slept. Thousands of lurid images of naked flesh, broken lives, wild promises, pained disillusion and gratuitous cruelty passed before his eyes and assaulted his ears, and then, as the flow of images and sounds slowed down from a torrent to clearer vignettes, his guilt became more forensic. He thought of a campaign to damage the Government by using flawed research to attack one of its health programmes which had resulted in the deaths of seventeen children. He thought of pictures of a teenage girl which had almost certainly resulted in her being stalked, raped, and murdered. He thought of a sales drive based on frightening old people by grossly distorting crime figures. Worst of all, he thought of his real pleasure in the disappearance of little Phil Mac. He thought how careful he had been to separate his own family from all those families who read his paper. How he would never want them to read what he published, and he recognised the callousness of his approach. He also recognised that he had not been entirely honest with himself in his relations with Poppy and that prompted him to think of Chris. In a way that he could not rationalise, he knew that the person who could untangle him was Chris himself, so he met him on a frosty November evening. "The problem," said Chris, when he had heard a litany of Sneer's hauntings, "is that your culture is pulling you into guilt. That won't help the people you feel you have harmed and it won't help you. It may well be that you can 'fix' the lives of some of those people whose lives you believe you have 'broken', but a resolution not to break any more lives and to build up weak lives will do far more good. There is something profoundly indulgent and egotistical about guilt because, in spite of the damage you might have done, all the focus in guilt is on the perpetrator. Frankly, the last thing anybody wants, including you, is your guilt." "But we live in a society that demands retribution." "Yes, that puts a different gloss on Pluto's belief that most people are good because it seems that many are obsessed with retribution. I think the answer to this apparent dichotomy is that people are fundamentally good but uncertainty coarsens their social responses. There seems to be nothing more uncertain than serious crime except, of course, that most crime follows highly predictable patterns. If you are at fault for one thing, then, it is for giving the impression that most serious crime can happen to anyone at any time with an even statistical probability. If you have done anything wrong, it is to generate the uncertainty that demands retribution, but, as I said, guilt isn't enough." "At the moment, I find it impossible to make the next step." "I don't want to be harsh, but that sounds like self-indulgence. Your pain won't mend anyone's broken heart. I think you probably need a session with Father Bill who is the Perpetuan 'Agony Aunt'. He will no doubt behave in his usual, gentle way, which will—although he doesn't intend this—hurt you even more than a good telling-off. I suspect you are all right at handling the hard stuff, because you can give as good as you get, but I doubt you will be up to the soft stuff. In the meantime, we have some difficult work to do. Snarle, your successor at the TT, is running a campaign against the Hypo experiment." "Ah yes, Pluto gone Pious!" "Old dogs and new tricks!" "Sorry, but it's all right for people like him to recant, there's no price tag." "We can't know about other people's price tags. One of our faults as journalists is to think we know more than we do by simply extrapolating our own experience. Anyway, we need to hit back." "I daresay we do, but tabloids aren't very interested in do-gooders who 'hit back' at our vitriolic onslaughts. I would take a leaf out of your own book. Don't hit back, get your positive message published wherever you can. Any riposte you send to Snarle will be twisted in evidence and used against you. We allow short term market considerations to cloud the longer view. People may be taken in, taken up, taken apart, or taken down by short-term considerations registering on a spectrum from hysteria to chronic, low-level anxiety, but over a medium-term period all this 'noise' cancels out so effectively that the brain discounts it. It used to be called telling the wood from the trees, but what matters in this context is that you establish a narrative over a period. Tabloid journalism survives on small but dramatic movements of sentiment, but long term messages always achieve salience if they are in tune with the people. So, although this may not seem very exciting, forget everything you ever knew about my career, and concentrate on essentials." "It's all very well for you to say that," said Smoother, a trifle wearily, "but your indexing was based on the premise that there is no such thing as ranking issues or impacts. It's all hyperbole." "True, but the psychology of popular journalism is to create turbulence that never threatens. We don't lure people out of their marina of comfort into the open sea, we simply set up a wave machine in their swimming pool. For a few minutes the water swills over the edge, but nothing really terrible happens. They just have little stories to tell about how the freak storm almost destroyed their digital camera." "All right," said Smoother, clearly exasperated, "so how do we get back to reality?" "There is no such thing as reality," said Sneer. "There is a difficult area between reality and perception, and the difference between the two depends not upon evidence, but upon perceptual momentum. The more volatile the populace, the less likely it is to accept any explanation grounded in evidence. Perception is the interpretation of the novel or the unstable." "All right," said Smoother, even more exasperated, "so where does this get us?" "In order to transform tabloid generated perception, you need a steady narrative. If you can show how what you propose actually benefits people, that is even better, but it's not essential. People don't mind being told that something you propose will actually harm their self-interest as long as you are consistent. After a while people, like markets, build negatives into their expectations. Tabloids generate volatility and anxiety to sell papers, but good communicators build narratives." "So what is the response to the TT attacks?" "Lower consumption, with some of the savings redistributed to the poorest, is good for everyone. You can save money, help save the planet, and reduce poverty all at the same time. That is what Annie Price has been saying for weeks now at Hypo and people in the local store believe her. You just have to go on saying it."

Sneer felt better for giving what he thought was sound and moral advice so he was not quite so downcast when he went to see Father Bill as he might otherwise have been. "I was going to tell you that I feel guilt-ridden about my past bad behaviour, but I don't feel quite so guilty as I did." "Guilt is a strange thing," said Bill, "because people think that it is a proper response to wrong doing, but it is totally improper. It's self-indulgent, it's part of the wrong doing not a reaction to it. So you have given up guilt, have you?" "I am not sure I have given it up for good, I mean, altogether." "For good will do." "But trying to solve a problem seemed to wipe quite a lot away." "Solving problems always does. The whole point about retribution, like love, is that it is sequential, not reciprocal or retrospective. Mothers love their children not to be loved back, but so that their children will in turn love their children. The true measure of penitence is not what you do for those you once hurt but, what you do the next time you are faced with a similar situation to the last time when you made a wrong choice. You can't mend the broken heart, you can't fix the broken life. You can say how badly you feel about what you have done, but you can't undo it. Only the person you hurt can mend her heart or fix her life. It's so amazing that people still hang on to the idea that they can fix what they have broken. I suppose it is because of what they have been told about our relationships with God. People are told that if they 'offend' God they have to say sorry and, in doing so, they have put it right, but that is nonsense. If anybody puts it right, it's God. If you hurt me, it's my relationship with God that mends me, not your retribution. People do wrong things, and they should say sorry, but that is nothing to do with putting any-thing right, it's just a recognition of truth. It shows empathy." "So do you mean that there is nothing that people can do about the harm they have caused?" "That is precisely what I mean. The idea that you can fix that harm is one of the most damaging illusions in our society. It misleads people into thinking that all they have to do is 'say sorry' and the situation reverts to where it was before they made the wrong choice. It's a kind of moral laziness. If you are really sorry, you can learn from the parents whose child dies of a terrible disease who react by setting up an organisation to try to discover the causes of it. They know they cannot bring the child back but they are determined to deal with their own misfortune by trying to ensure it does not happen to others. In the case of the individual, then, we can only react to wrong choices by doing our best in future to make right choices, and what should sustain us in our determination is the memory of the consequences of all the wrong choices which we have made, and have not been able to reverse. You should, quite properly, be haunted by what you have done, but your reaction to that needs to be positive and not self-indulgent. Good deeds drive away bad dreams."

Sneer went away determined, but Bill, left with his own thoughts, felt the beginnings of depression because he knew that he could not live up to the advice he so readily gave. His doctor had told him that depression was a medical condition, and nothing to be ashamed of, but he thought that he was suffering from the calm of the empty man. He had been puzzled from his early childhood by the Vicar who preached every Sunday on the sinfulness of humanity when he had not seen anything that amounted to more than the occasional fit of irrationality and bad temper. Later, he had read about terrible wickedness, but, based on his experience, he held to the view that most people were 'good' most of the time, and what they needed was encouragement to be better. It was that very 'flat' perception that was now beginning to cause him to doubt the value of his own life. He had never knowingly done any harm, he had never been sorely tempted nor badly treated, he had never faced a problem that caused him a serious dilemma, he had never been set a challenge which was too difficult for him, and so now he felt in desperate need of something difficult or dramatic to reaffirm his life. People were always coming to him for advice, which he found easy to dispense, but he longed to find himself in a situation where he needed advice. The ennui of the modest soul was upon him, and he could see no escape. Looking out of the window at a light fall of snow which had transformed his tiny garden from a scrubby patch into a microcosm of enchantment, his spirits lifted. Did he really want to be challenged? Was he tempting God by asking to be put to the test? Should he not be thankful that he had been spared to do modest good? His calm might bore him, but it served others. He wondered how different it would have been if he had fallen in love, but concluded that, had he been lucky in that direction, it would have disqualified him from helping so many people—there was something in the Roman Catholic theory of celibacy even if it was terribly distorted in practice—because the person in love only understands other people in love through his own personal experience of it. The one experience above all others that you cannot distill, bottle, and pick up off a shelf, is love. He saw Stacey carefully closing the garden gate. "How lovely the snow is," she said. "At home there's so much snow that it becomes a problem to be overcome, but these light dustings make everything look so different." "How can I help you?" said Bill, automatically. "Well, I don't want to sound arrogant in any way, but you can't help me, well, not in the ordinary sense. Where's Jim?" "Practising with the music group." "I have watched you carefully and whenever anybody comes up to you, it is not long before you ask how you can help. It's admirable, but you can't live your life with the sole purpose of helping people because, in the end, there isn't enough of your own life to draw on." "Those are weighty words for somebody as young as you." "Well, you always act older than you are so maybe I am imitating you just a little, but that isn't why I came." She looked out of the window at the snow as if to gain strength from it. Bill waited. He was used to waiting; it was what he did. He had to stop himself asking again how he could help, and then he was transformed by the ravishing repose of her profile, lit by the unusual brightness of fallen snow. Before she turned, he knew what she was going to say and, in character, waited, not wanting to be first. "I love you." He almost said, "I know" but, instead, he said nothing. The Holy Spirit played in the flakes which began to fall as she turned, and he wondered how anybody—he knew it was possible but, in that instant, he could not imagine it—could understand the Godhead unless they had experience of intense human love. He wondered about the value of everything he had ever said, perceiving that whatever he said from now on would be incommensurably richer. He thought that he could not have been more wrong when he thought that being in love invalidated any understanding of how others loved. Although we could not distil or bottle an essence from the thousand flowers that bloom, what we can do is use our own understanding of our growth to encourage others to grow. She was in no hurry. She did not need him to say anything. She knew. The Spirit was with them.

After a struggle which had preoccupied him for weeks, Gregg finally made his decision. It would either make or break him, but he had to get closer to the Perpetuan movement. No matter how hard he tried to pull away, it pulled harder. He used every mental device he could to avoid the pull, drawing on all the strength of feeling he had inherited and nurtured as an Evangelical Christian and all the discipline and self-discipline of the under-cover agent. He felt like a traitor, but he could not avoid what was happening to him. Unlike Saint Paul, he had not been struck down on the road to Damascus. Had that been the case, he could have changed allegiance with some justification, but nothing of significance had happened since the day he had seen Dexter. He had not been to a Perpetuan celebration. He had not even tuned into god4u or visited the web site. If anything, he had tried to avoid anything to do with Perpetuanism because it always subjected him to such violent inner conflict. His strict fundamentalist upbringing had held him back for weeks, but here he was, waiting to talk to Max Silver. "I know you," said Max. "I know we have met," said Gregg. "No, I don't mean that. We met at the Embassy and on the plane, but I have this strange feeling that I've met you before that, but I don't know where." "I think I have a fairly ordinary face," said Gregg, anxious to get off the point. "Well, I wouldn't say that. It puzzled me the two other times I saw you, but never mind. What can I do for you?" "As you know, I work in the American Diplomatic Service, in security, intelligence, that kind of thing. My stint in Immigration was simply to help with a temporary staff shortage." "I remember you saying so." "Well, I'm fed up with working for the Service. It isn't just the current regime, although that's got a lot to do with it. I believed in Bush because, as an Evangelical, I believed he would deliver." "What, precisely?" "Well, pro life, you know?" "Not really. I know the slogan, but I've never understood why 'Pro Life' people are in favour of capital punishment. Never mind. I should not have interrupted you." "Well, anyway, I wondered whether I could be of any use to you either here or in the United States. I don't expect much money and I'm not interested in status. I live alone and have no family responsibilities. I just feel that what you are doing is so important, a genuine religious revival, instead of all the fakes we've been through in America." "With all the expanding activity, we could do with a reliable pair of hands, and your American connections might come in handy. It won't be very glamorous—nothing like James Bond—but, as you say, you are not interested at the moment in anything special. I know as Perpetuans that we believe in trusting people, but I'm afraid I will have to take references and check you out, particularly as you're not an EU citizen." "Fair enough." Max duly checked. Gregg's record seemed simple enough. There were large gaps in his chronology but, then, one would expect that of somebody in intelligence, and although this seemed a little outlandish to a European, a gun licence was nothing out of the ordinary for an American.

Gregg was a necessary but tiny detail in Max's life. His major preoccupations were building settlement, foundation finance for Guides, American plans ,and protecting Trina from administrative and media demands. It often seemed to him that he was not running a movement, but a religious organisation and, paradoxically, it was he who kept protesting about the bureaucracy and pleading for simplicity and more time for prayer and his mission to the City. There were even times when he walked into his office and was reminded of his bank. The movement was less than a year old, but it had already become part of the 'networked' establishment in email and snail mail lists for office supplies, the Social Cohesion Forum, Inter Faith Dialogue, Pro Life and Pro Choice, Flight Discounts, Robes, and New Age Bulletin. It was in daily receipt of scores of press releases and was invited to comment on a wide variety of Government Consultation documents. Because Trina had spent nine months looking after Perpetua and was known to be "good for a quote" she was expected to comment on anything and everything that was popular, fashionable, critical, or gloomy. It was precisely because of this pressure that Max pressed Trina into taking a long Christmas break. "I know you want to take the opportunity at Christmas to lay the ground work for more house groups, but I think we can manage that. You need time for yourself. I know you were thinking of bringing us all together for a major Christmas celebration, but let that be a week before Christmas Day so that you can go away quietly, and the rest of us can disperse to our assigned locations over the Christmas and New Year period." "I accept what you say, but I feel responsible." "Which means that you don't really accept what I say. You and I should not quarrel. It would be terrible, but I am very frightened that we are becoming an organisation concerned with maintaining itself. If you don't have inner resources which you can then share with us, we will grow stiff and become useless. The one thing everybody remembers about Perpetua is how lively she was, and you need to be a lively presence among us." "I am sorry, Max, of course I do." What Max did not tell her—but he guessed that she knew—was how much work this would impose on him. Marta was patient and he now had Gregg working for him. "Have you thought any more about the 'Christmas crisis' we are facing over how to integrate Perpetua?" "Yes, I think that we should take matters very slowly. We don't want people to think we're attacking their Christmas when, in fact, we are not. At some point we will need a special day for Perpetua so that people can celebrate her birth, life, and death but, for the time being at least, it is important that we take our time. I have asked Annie Price to arrange for Hypo crib sets to include a Perpetua figure. I have taken advice, and most people seem to think that this is appropriate. There will also be separate Perpetua figures in a variety of sizes and materials available standing or kneeling. One of Sir Pluto's tiny interests is SLA—stereoscopic lithographic apparatus or rapid prototyping equipment—and so we have been able to make absolutely authentic three-dimensional virtual images of Perpetua. Of course, we have then added her clothes to the computer images: jeans, sandals, and t-shirt. Although the technology is new it is not very complex to operate and we have been using house-bound people to dress the figures. They are going very well at Hypo and I hope this is a sign of things to come." "Marta will be delighted." "It's just the gentle start we wanted. Who's that? I'm sure I've seen him somewhere before." Max and Gregg both started. "Funny," said Max when Gregg had hurried off. "That is precisely what I said when I first saw him. It's Gregg. He's an American who's working in my office to share the load." "It was only a fleeting impression."

It did not matter that the size of the Church of England had perhaps critically diminished during the year, with the strong possibility that it would disintegrate before another year had passed, nor that it had lost more than one-third of its bishops and priests, nor that there was a cash flow crisis, it was part of the Church's tradition to invite all its chief dignitaries, and a wide variety of its supporters and detractors, to a Carol Service at London Minster, followed by mulled wine and mince pies. As the Church had not yet reached the critical point of having to decide whether it still existed, its dignitaries were remarkably sanguine, exchanging cheerful small talk about new appointments, nativity play howlers and what they were likely to do with their rest period after the big day. Their parents had managed the decline of the Empire, and their siblings and cousins were managing the decline of political coherence, and so it did not seem so extraordinary to them that they were managing the decline of the Church. Indeed, they had been managing it for so long—lowering expectations, closing churches, cutting budgets, launching revivals to keep up their spirits, almost pleading that numbers did not count—that the latest episode, although it had been more traumatic than the usual steady falling off, had not called them to the lifeboats. They had been so long awaiting the emergency that they were not capable of seeing that it had arrived. There was a conspiracy of silence, nobody wanted to mention it first lest they be subsequently blamed for the final collapse of the rotten edifice. The 'Bishops' Revolt' had been skillfully damped down by Alchester and Dean Prior, Varnish was approaching a satisfactory conclusion with the Treasury, there seemed to be something of a religious revival in some dioceses, and others were very busy with their 'Fresh Expressions', the number of ordinands in training was up, and there was still the issue of women bishops and openly gay clergy to be fought over. The Church might be somewhat smaller—nobody cared to specify the extent of the shrinkage—but it was still the same recognisable institution. Bishop Reginald Crowther, the bookies' favourite (which only went to show that people would gamble on anything) to succeed Varnish, scanned the room to ensure that he had a word with anybody of influence. It would not do to be direct, but nothing should be left to chance. The Holy Spirit did not make good the idleness of the faithful. Crowther, a good media and political operator with the knack of saying the right thing without saying anything very definite, was never entirely sure of his ground as his high risk strategy of trying to please everyone occasionally threatened to please no-one. On the Perpetua issue he had followed the consensus, maintaining that there should be an orthodox core within a very loose framework, which looked as if it would see him through—the extremists of both wings were too busy hoovering up the fragments at the periphery of their spheres of influence in preparation for a fresh campaign, alongside or against each other, nobody knew—but he still needed to be careful. "Mr Dean," he said, with the professional warmth of the pastorally glib, "I am not sure that they should have allowed you in." "I'm Bishop James's invited guest. How's the campaign going?" Crowther blushed, horrified. "Oh Simon, you always were a bit of a card. How can you ask such a thing?" "The answer, Reggie, is that we may be somewhat 'effete' in the eyes of such a robust South Yorkshireman as yourself, but we are stubborn in our own way. If I am asked—and that really is quite unlikely—I would have to say that you're the best man for the job, and I daresay you'll get it, given the amount of time you've spent on it." Again, Crowther blushed, and looked genuinely shocked. "And, you will be pleased to know, I only have one piece of advice—I'm not one for giving advice—and that advice is not to pick a fight with the Perpetuans. You will be told to strike while we are doctrinally immature, strategically unprepared, and financially weak, but Christianity must not duplicate the mistake of the Jerusalem Jewish leaders. It's coalition or bust, Reggie. They are the only two options open to us." Reginald was very glad to get away. The Dean had always been full of himself and it was an insult to the Archbishop for him to wear a god4u pin. He looked round again and saw Theodore Schuhorn, the Prime Minister's Appointments Secretary, in deep conversation with somebody he did not recognise. Crowther knew better than anybody that the Secretary had taken the extraordinary step of taking soundings before Varnish had formally announced his intention to resign because everybody knew that he would go as soon as he had secured an ecclesiastical heritage settlement. The Prime Minister had announced that he was going to change the patronage rules but, in view of his recent loss of touch, nobody was sure of anything. Crowther, who did not want to be seen to be ignorant, tried to get close enough to read the stranger's name badge but, whoever it was, had managed to elude the registrariat. Schuhorn, hardly moving a muscle, summoned him with the slightest gesture. "Bishop Crowther, meet Max Silver, my guest for the evening. He told me he was far too busy advancing the cause of Perpetuanism to spare the time, but I told him that he must meet 'the opposition' or, to put it another way, the wider constituency to which the Working Party on ecclesiastical Heritage will have to sell its proposals. I was telling Silver that in this regard there is no-one so uniquely placed as you to give him sound advice." Not expecting to find any, Crowther nonetheless could not help searching for irony. Schuhorn, behaving totally out of character, was very close to making this a dangerous conversation. Crowther knew that it meant that he was either safe or sorry. The Secretary would never have made such a remark had the issue still been in play. "What do you say, Silver?" "I say, coalition or bust." "Just what the Dean just said to me." "As we work closely together, that's hardly surprising. What is your view of coalition?" "As long as it's a loose association of some kind—but no merger—that is fine. We just could not accept a takeover." "That's what they all say," said Max, when Crowther had hurriedly moved away as if scorched by his contact with the Secretary. "They care far more about the composition of the board and the language of the deal than they do about the reality of the shareholders or consumers. I expect something better of a religious organisation, but I'm learning. Even our own new movement is showing disturbing signs of corporatism." "Still, it will be a while, I think, before we have either Archbishop Trina or Lady Trina," quipped the Secretary, to show both that he was phenomenally in touch and not lacking in wit. "Frankly," said Max, "the sooner this is over the better. On the surface, it looks as if we are in no hurry while the Established Church is in desperate need of a settlement, but all the behaviour indicates precisely the opposite. The Church of England seems to have indulged in the language of consensus and non-commitment for so long that it cannot out-culturate. It's a form of deep denial betrayed by linguistic flaccidity." "Steady on, Max. Not the sort of image they like." "Sorry, I am trying to be both calm and generous, but I want this out of the way so that we can get back to where we were." "I doubt you ever will; your Constantine moment has come perilously early. Good luck, Max. You are going to need it." Crowther, industrious and sharp-eyed, continued to hoover up fragments of influence, agreeing to officiate, committing to speak at meetings, promising an article, offering a word at a committee. The prize might not be what it had been, but it was still a prize. Had he been able to start a third time he might have chosen differently but, his political career having been de-railed by New Labour, the Church was his only viable second option. As he boarded the last train North, the Appointments Secretary inserted an additional comment in Crowther's file and ranked his two names, pending the resignation of Varnish;

Crowther would be staying where he was.

Jim enjoyed playing in the shopping malls during the Christmas build-up. He did not buy the conventional, religious idea that Christmas shopping was wicked. Granted, there was an element of greed in it, but what he noticed was the generosity, and even sacrifice. He liked to see the faces of old people as they came out of toy shops with big parcels; he liked to see faces. He had been born with the special gift of being able to see things, to see past artificial expressions, and even past the boring normality of the everyday. His world was full of light and movement, only occasionally darkened by the shadows of real wickedness. Most of the time his world was joyful, amply compensating for the Downs Syndrome for which so many people he met felt sorry. His chief source of sadness, then, was not that he did not have what he wanted, but that he could not translate his visions into anything useful for others. He watched a knot of grannies emerging from the toy shop, smiling, all except for one who said, "I think the man persuaded me to pay more than I could really afford". Another said, "We'll buy you lunch, Violet, which will save you a bit." Jim smiled at Violet who, in spite of her worry, was fishing in her purse for a coin. "We don't collect," said Jim. "Perhaps we should collect for the poor but there are so many other calls on generosity at this time of year." Violet was still looking as if she had not heard him. "Listen, girls!" she said excitedly. "I've found a £20 note I didn't know I had, so there's no worry, and I can pay for my own lunch, but thank you for offering." Jim smiled, as he had done so often that week, realising that Perpetua had given him power to make things right, but part of his cheerfulness was a cover for a deeper foreboding which he could not pin down. Somewhere, on the margin of his consciousness, like a dark tornado, he saw an indefinable danger. He was not quite sure when it had started, but it grew so intense when he went to the new headquarters building that he tried to avoid it as often as he could which made him sad because he loved the people there and was particularly grateful for the level of unquestioned acceptance he enjoyed. He had to make excuses which he knew were lame, but which others seemed to accept. He had thought of telling Bill about it because he knew that Bill would understand. He had never questioned Jim's accounts of his visions not only because of what Perpetua said, but also because he was that kind of person. Perhaps connected with this, Jim's perception both of light and contrasting dark had sharpened, which posed some difficult moral questions. As he looked now, for example, he saw a couple of girls coming out of a boutique and knew that they had been shop lifting. He was being constantly paralysed by incidents such as this which contrasted with his visions of goodness. As for the powers he seemed to have acquired for doing good, he accepted these as a natural gift. The one characteristic of Perpetua that he had always loved was her refusal to get entangled in discussions of mechanics, of how things happened; to her, and to him, they just happened. As the shops began to close they packed up and Jim found a small cafe. He knew that Bill and Stacey would not mind if he went home to eat, but he knew that they liked being alone so he left them, pleased for their happiness, sad that he would never find a girl friend. He knew that there would be plenty to eat at the party, but he didn't want to reach the headquarters any sooner than he needed to so he spun the time out with a coffee and a sticky bun. He walked from the shopping mall across the new, bouncy bridge, to the new god4u headquarters.

On their way to the Christmas celebration Bill and Stacey went to pray at Saint Simple's. "I know we only use this for special celebrations now that we study and worship in our house groups, but this is a special time for us and I did want you to see where She danced and where She lay. Part of me wants to turn this church into a memorial to Her where people will come and be inspired, but part of me just wants to leave it as it is. One of the curiosities of Christianity was that its beginnings were so obscure that it literally had to make up a lot of its history. I often wonder whether it would have been different if it had had its own resident historians interested in personalities and architecture. So I wonder now whether we want a recorded architectural heritage or whether we should simply develop our spiritual tradition. I feel slightly embarrassed saying, 'This is where she prayed in the moments before she went to her death', or, 'This is where she lay before her body was taken up'. It has an element of spiritual tourism about it, but I wonder whether I am being a purist. People like pilgrimages." "One of the strange things about America is that we go on all kinds of pilgrimages, but we don't have a credible place for religious pilgrimage. There is something strange and wonderful about being in places where Jesus was, and I think that it is important for people to gain inspiration from being where Perpetua was. I know how reticent you are, Bill, but Jesus and Perpetua were incarnate precisely so that they would be a part of our history, and so we should respect that dimension of their mission as well as what they said and did. 'Where' is important as well as 'what, when, and why'." Bill walked down the aisle, relieved. Sometimes his scruples were too exacting, and he knew it. "How do you feel about getting married here?" "That illustrates my point. I cannot imagine a more wonderful spot to be married than that where perpetua prayed before she consciously went to her death for us. My only worry is that I will be so preoccupied with her that I don't give you enough attention. I won't mind that. We are marrying as part of our love for God Our Parent. I have recently been reading what Perpetua said about sex and how it is a kind of reflection of the Godhead." "I would be more definite than 'kind of', but it's a good starting point. When I was being trained to be a Priest, we were warned against the evils of sex. It was regarded by my teachers as a second-rate option, a 'necessary evil', and I suppose its excesses today have frightened some people even more than they were frightened in the 1950s, but we have to reclaim sex as the central human way of honouring God." "That's a bit extreme." "Yes. We are not finding it easy to formulate precisely the right language, but the point is that I take seriously what we say to each other in our vows. I don't think that our love for each other is somehow separate from, or even inferior to, our love of God." After they had knelt for a while in front of the altar they went into the vestry and knelt there and Bill said a prayer, remembering that he was uniquely blessed in having laid her there, and found her risen, but he was sorry that Jim was not with them. They walked through the streets which became better lit as they came nearer to the centre of the city. "Christmas will never be the same again," said Stacey as they passed a huge, civic Christmas tree. "I know, I have been agonising over what to do about the crib."

"Where have you been?" asked Bill, kindly, when Jim came in. "We expected you home for a meal before coming here for the party." "I didn't have enough time," said Jim, hurriedly. "I lose any sense of time when I'm playing." Bill looked relieved. "You look nervous." "I don't want to hide it from you. There is something wrong. I don't know what, where, or when, but something's wrong." They gathered in the open plan room at the top of the building. The initial proposal from the resource planners was that if they must have a worship space it should be in the basement, with the offices of the key figures on the top floor, but they completely reversed this so that they were now able to look out over the lights of London on a clear evening in mid-December. They had all been given their Christmas assignments and were anxious to be on the move once they had shared an evening of mutual support. They sat at a table, beautifully laid with glinting glasses, gleaming crockery, sparkling cutlery, crisp linen, and holly and ivy, setting off platters of food arranged as much for the contrast of its colours as for its flavours. "Somewhat unusual," said Sir Pluto who had come with Annie. "Where I was brought up, the church table was very sparsely decorated." "That is because the Christian Eucharist is no longer made up of two elements," said Fidel. "There was the consecration and the meal, but the first element ultimately swamped the second. The 'magic' of changing bread into flesh and wine into blood, the jargon of transubstantiation, and the Protestant reaction to it, meant that we forgot that Eucharist began as, and was always intended to be, a meal. It's a Roman Catholic thing, the changing bread and wine into body and blood. What if it's the other way round and, at the Last Supper, Jesus actually turned his body and blood into bread and wine? So let's say that God offers himself every time Eucharist is celebrated, but the Priest doesn't change anything into anything, no magic. Eucharist might then be what it is, a symbol, a sacrament. Perpetua was particularly anxious that we should get back to the notion of 'fellowship' expressed in the meal, of which the consecration is only a very small part. Jesus brought himself to us and brings himself again. I don't think I believe that any priest can bring Perpetua to us. She brings herself in the food we offer. Anyway, the important element is the sharing." When they were all seated, Trina led the prayers, and after they had eaten she took fruit and wine and blessed them, saying, "This flesh and blood, this very being of Jesus and Perpetua, they have brought for you in the love of Our Sister the Spirit." She handed the plate, and then the jug, to Max, who took fruit and handed it on, then sipped wine and handed it on. It was very quiet, and very joyful. They were at peace on the night set aside to remember the two Incarnate presences of God among them. Trina was still struggling with the theology of Jesus and Perpetua being with them particularly, and God being everywhere, but she was more comfortable with the idea that Jesus and Perpetua gave themselves in the elements rather than thinking that anything she could do made them present. As she said the words, Jim saw a golden and red light shining above the table and gasped at its wonder and beauty. In this light his life was fulfilled, he was where he needed to be. At the end of the celebration, Trina moved to the far corner of the room. "Now for the unveiling of the crib." She pulled back a curtain, and there was the baby Jesus, lying in his manger, with Mary at his head, Joseph at his feet and Perpetua kneeling between them. Annie smiled at Pluto. They had sourced a beautiful set of dies from a craft co-operative in Benin. Jim saw a faint golden light over the figures, but then everything went dark. "What's wrong?" asked Bill. "There is a terrible presence." "Why, nothing has changed except that Gregg, who must have been working late, has come in with some papers for Max to sign." Jim raised his customarily gentle voice so that the room fell silent. "There is a terrible presence among us which will seek to destroy all that Perpetua has done in the name of God Our Parent, revitalising all that Jesus did before. There is danger of a terrible catastrophe. Be careful, or everything will be lost." Bill and Trina tried to comfort him. It was difficult not to mention that this might be a symptom of his disability when they actually knew hardly anything about it. "Be careful, be careful. Where I saw a wonderful golden and red light, I now see blood, tending into blackness. Not the blood of the victim, but the blood of the murderer." "But you can't have a victim without a murderer," said Max, almost without thinking. "But we all are responsible," said Kylie. "Yes, I know. I am no theologian, and I can only say what I see. What I see is a figure who wants to take power, to conquer through force and not through love, through argument and not through listening. I see a terrible split between the loving and the powerful. Everything that Perpetua came to change is in danger."

He pointed at Gregg, lowered his head to the table, and died.

Gregg was the first to move, pulling out his mobile phone to dial for an ambulance, but Bill said, "No need, Gregg, he's dead, and it was meant to be." Gregg, terribly shaken by what he had heard, just needed to do anything to distract attention, but he could think of nothing. He wanted to argue with what Jim had said, but this was no time to quarrel with the so recently deceased. He was an outsider, an American, and he had been named by one of the inner circle who had then died. His Perpetuan mission was probably over. "Is there anything I can do?" he asked Bill, quietly, having come round the table. "I don't think so, and I'm sorry he died with such terrible words on his lips. He was always going to die relatively young, but he was such a cheerful person, particularly after Perpetua changed his life. I am sorry for what he said, but you need to settle such matters with Trina and Max. I'm so sorry it happened." Trina and Max stood together as the body of Jim was carried into a neighbouring room and placed on a sofa. Max rang the medical service and Trina began to formulate some prayers. So many of those who had followed Perpetua were already dead. She thought of Miles, Dexter, and the strange hand of the assassin. They had never had any idea why the murders had taken place, but there clearly was an opposing force which Jim had identified in some way before he, too, was struck down. There was nothing tangible to link the deaths. Perhaps she was being fanciful and there was no link at all, but only a deranged and motiveless man with a gun and something inside Jim that had finally broken. Yet she could not so easily dismiss what he had said. Jim had always been their seer. He had seen Perpetua's dance before she went to her death, he had seen the light where her body had been laid, and she had told Bill of his special powers. There Bill was, praying silently at Jim's feet. For a few moments they prayed together but their tranquility was broken by the arrival of a paramedic team. Gregg left as he let them in, and was going downstairs as quickly as he could without seeming to panic, when his way was blocked by Stacey. "I thought it was you." "Me?" "Yes, you. I wanted to stay with Trina, Jim, and Bill, but something told me that after Jim talked about you that you would do something shifty." "I have just let the paramedic team in, and was going out for a breath of fresh air. It was getting very stuffy in there." "With a large briefcase? What is in there? I suspect it's Perpetuan property. I have wondered about you ever since you came. Max thinks there is something mysterious about you, but he cannot pin it down. Nor can I, but there's something." "Nonsense." Standing on the landing four steps below him, she dived at his knees so that he pitched forward and fell on top of her, which cushioned the impact so that he was not knocked out when his head hit the marble. As if he had bounced, he was immediately on his feet, but the brief case had fallen into the corner of the landing, protected by Stacey, as she got up tentatively, hurt and worried that he might hit her. Instead, he turned sharply and ran down the remaining flight of stairs with a memory stick in his pocket. The brief case had been an unnecessary backup.

20.

Like Father Mark, violet Smythe had a radical head but a conservative heart, although in her case the struggle was more rationally conducted—largely through the construction of lists of pros and cons—and, consequently, the head was far more often victorious, although not without sacrifice, for she loved the tradition and gained more inner comfort from it than she ever got from the changes which promised so much. She had given up the BCP and the AV for the ASB and NRSV, knowing that the new words, although less noble, were more authentic, but this had removed a candle from her heart. She had accepted the introduction of new hymns that children would have found easy to sing if they had come to church, but the reduction of the use of her beloved NEH had removed another candle from her heart. She understood the need for more rigourous priests who could help people face up to a complex, modern world, but she still loved the old vicars with their comfortable ways and when Mark had come with his liberal catholicism she had accepted him, and would not have dreamed—in spite of her tendency to be slightly outspoken—of saying anything against him, but another candle went out in her heart. So although she was faithful to the cause of radicalism and rationalism, she paid a price in the steady bleakening of her life and the reduced capacity of her religious belief to bring her any comfort. She stood in the church on the Friday evening before the First Sunday of Advent making sure that the wreath, with its three purple and one rose candle equally distributed at the circumference and the white candle at the intersection of the two diagonals, was hanging true. She checked that the latest deterioration in the fabric did not cause any drafts which would affect the even burning of the candles, and she ensured that the box with the lighter and taper were handy, but not obvious. At least if her heart had fewer candles she could ensure that the wreath received the care it deserved. She looked at the chancel stalls and, even without consciously thinking about it, she knew who had been on cleaning duty that week because of how the quality of the finish varied (Clement used bees wax but Harriet used a chemical spray). She could not help taking a duster from her pocket and gave a few of her favourite surfaces an extra polish. As long as she was alone she could do what she liked. She did not want to be seen working, particularly if it might be interpreted as interference with or disapproval of the work of others. She therefore put her duster away hurriedly as she heard the outer door open. It was Ronald, looking equally furtive for he, too, hated people knowing how much he did for the church and preferred to do his odd jobs in secret, but between Violet and Ronald there were no secrets. At least, that is what they told themselves. So close were they that newcomers in the Parish wondered why they had never married, but Violet had only considered it once, feeling naturally comfortable as she was from her late teens, and that was when Ronald had been so moved by a passionate desire that when the girl left him for a younger, richer man, weeks before they were to announce their engagement, Violet hoped he would ask her for her comfort, but he had felt so vulnerable that he had never recovered. They often asked themselves and each other whether their life in the church was an escape from the real world, but they both concluded, to each other, that Jesus had wanted to comfort the lonely, and they were in need of comfort. "Another Advent," he said, repeating a script that they both knew by heart. "It soon comes round," she replied, "but at least Christmas Day is on a different day of the week each year so that we don't quite get into a rut. It's always comforting to see the wreath put up. There are so few candles in church today. Electric lights are much less enticing, although more effective, and so we only really enjoy our candles at Advent and Easter Eve, and very occasionally at Candlemas." "We should enjoy them while we can," he said. "We are not getting any younger, but as long as I have the strength to do little jobs for the Church until I am taken, I will not mind. It's the thought of being able to do nothing that worries me." "You will outlast me, Ronald, I'm sure." "On the contrary, Violet, I think you will outlast me." They smiled at each other, knowing that they had gone through the compulsory dialogue. "However," said Violet, thereby introducing a deeply significant shift in their conversation from the routine to the novel, "I wonder how long Advent and Christmas will stay as they are." "What do you mean?" "Well, we are going to have to find a slot for the birth of Perpetua and that might radically alter the calendar. You've seen that she's been put in the Creed and the Eucharistic Prayer?" "Yes. I suppose it was inevitable." "So we can't go on just focusing on the Baby Jesus without thinking about the Baby Perpetua." "It could take a long time. After all, the story about the Annunciation, the stable, the shepherds and the Presentation in Luke, and the Kings in Matthew, came decades after the death of Jesus." "We can't just think up traditions overnight," said Violet, coming as near as she ever did to making a joke. "Mark is going to want to do something, and I think it will be something small but significant. He wants to honour the change, but he does not want to disrupt people. Like me, he wants the outside to be the same even though his brain tells him that it can't be." "I wondered whether we might put a picture of Perpetua next to the crib, but it would look wrong. I seem to remember that Perpetua put nails in the crib straw so maybe we should put a syringe in the crib straw, but that would never do. People would be scandalised, and it might hurt a child." "Mark is good at this sort of thing; it will be all right." They smiled. They knew that, in spite of their niggles with Mark, that out of his radical/conservative tension there usually emerged a brilliantly simple synthesis. They supposed that was what prayer did in a Priest. They heard the door and tried to look welcoming but it was Mark, not a stranger. "Talk of the devil," said Violet, again getting close to a joke. "We were just talking about you, Mark, as we wonder what you will do about altering Christmas to celebrate the birth of Perpetua." "She's in the Eucharistic Prayer and the creed, so we can't ignore her, even if we wanted to—which, of course, we don't—and so I thought that we would show her alongside the shepherds, with the baby in her arms, and explain that she always called him Jesus My Brother." "People will wonder, you know," said Violet. "Well, as long as they wonder out loud we can help them. If they only wonder to themselves there is only a limited amount we can do. I will preach on Jesus and Perpetua." "The traditionalists won't like a new, strange, black figure in the crib," said Ronald. "Well, the kings are strange, and often one of them is black. People soon get used to novelty as long as it does not affect them directly. Today's reform is tomorrow's stagnation. In a few years, if I took Perpetua out, I would be asked why as, 'we always have Perpetua in the crib at our church.'" Mark was in danger of becoming over ironic and Violet skillfully moved to stem the flow: "The baby is the wrong shape for being picked up. It won't look right, and we don't have a figure of Perpetua." "I know somebody who's got rapid prototyping equipment. If we can get the mother and child we want in a computer design we can make a model, and then it will have to be painted. It's getting the bones and the clothes right. Perpetua has to be black, well, brown actually, but her bones have to be right. The baby, too, shouldn't be blonde and European-featured, so we can sort that problem out at the same time." Violet looked uncertain but Ronald sent her the tiniest of signals. Another candle went out, but she pulled herself together. She had been the mistress of the crib for almost 50 years, replacing figures, buying a new set, collecting straw; she had done everything. It wasn't that she wasn't a convinced Perpetuan, and she certainly wasn't racially prejudiced—intellectually, at least, though her contact with other races in a rural village had been minimal—but Perpetua holding Jesus in her arms with an empty manger and an onlooking Mary wasn't at all right. Mark sensed the hurt. "There may be other ways, Violet, let's think, but we have to do something to include Perpetua." She knew she must not suggest anything that would alienate Mark. He was a good man, but you only got one chance. She said, as tentatively as she could, "Might she kneel and put her hand on the baby? Say the shepherds had their back to the opening of the cave and she was facing outwards with her hand holding the baby's little hand?" "Good," said Mark. "Much better than my proposal. We can even keep the baby we've got. I'm sure people will understand. There are some models of Perpetua, but they're all a bit stylised. We will find the right thing." He stopped. "No. Just because it's more difficult than usual, Viiolet, it doesn't mean we should change our ways. You find the right figure of Perpetua to kneel at the side of the manger. You might need some money, but we'll deal with that. You find Perpetua for us." Ronald smiled encouragingly, and Violet's tension relaxed. That last candle had not quite gone out. Mark, thankful that he had avoided another mistake, relaxed, but then tensed again. Ronald, who had been watching him carefully and knew his every twitch, usually kept his own counsel, but Mark looked so tense that he decided to risk the question, "What's worrying you, Mark? You look tense." "It's the problem of our Patronal status," said Mark. "We're named after the Holy Trinity, but I am now a Perpetuan Guide and it does not seem quite right not to reflect the new doctrine of the Godhead. It is the actual change in the name that will worry people more than what I say from the pulpit about the new Creed. After all, they have swallowed a succession of different translations of the Creed and a new prayer will only cause temporary grumbling, but name changes are always difficult. Intellectuals tend to say that it isn't the name that matters but the substance. I take the view that one of humanity's greatest powers, since Genesis, is the power to name. People are fully aware that in religion what is on the tin must be what is in the tin but, as they don't bother too much with the doctrine—yes, I ought to be careful a la Hawthorne to distinguish doctrine from theology—they will concentrate on the label. I don't think people would fancy calling it the Holy Quartet, but that, in any case, would not reflect the true doctrine. A quartet is four very separate players, even if they gel. The Holy Quarternity would just sound ugly." "But I suppose that Holy Trinity sounded pretty ugly to the Jews," said Violet, trying to soften the blow. "Yes. In some ways Perpetua, being a copy—or, perhaps an isomorphism—of Jesus, isn't quite so radical to us as was Jesus to the Jews. All the same, we don't want to upset people unduly." "What about reverting to our name before we became Holy Trinity?" asked Ronald. "What a brilliant idea," said Mark, visibly relaxing.

"We could go back to being Saint Damian. Everybody would understand that. It would bring us in line with the School and the Carnival, and there's no sign that Perpetuans want to deny the early Saints and Martyrs." Marie came in to prepare for choir practice. "I've got a draft of the Carol Service," she said, slightly nervously, as Mark was deeply ambivalent about her role; he recognised that she did all the work and that she was absolutely reliable, but he still held onto the fiction that Scott was the Choir Leader. He wanted to keep control over choosing the music even if—and he recognised this in his more lucid moments—Marie actually knew what the choir could and could not sing. "I didn't know whether you wanted to find room for a Perpetuan Reading, and whether we could match this with a 'neutral' carol, like Tavener's The Lamb or something else that doesn't mention Christmas." "Very thoughtful," said Mark, again relaxing after his initial tension. "I was thinking of putting in a Perpetuan Reading just to get people used to the idea, but I had not got as far as the musical implications. It would perhaps be best if you put in something that was a Carol without being specifically Christmasy; The Lamb is a very good idea." Marie was relieved. She had avoided a dispute with Mark and would not have to get into a discussion with choir members who used her as a proxy to criticise Mark. Choir practice went smoothly, with the mixture of old favourites, last year's repeats and new repertoire. People seemed not to mind what they were asked to do for Christmas. They put up with Rutter, whose music they would have ridiculed out of the Festive Season, they accepted Latin instead of groaning, they enjoyed crunchy chords which would have been discords during Summer, and they were happy to repeat material. They also insisted, with a radical break from the rest of the year, that the solos were 'owned' by choristers to whom they had been handed down. Clement had received the third verse of Darke's In the Bleak from a long departed atheist called Bernard and Marie had received the first verse from her predecessor as Head Choir Girl (a euphemistic title). Nigel always sang the solo in Three Kings from Persian Lands, which he had also inherited from the atheist and which was always referred to eponymously as the "Three Bernies" and, predictably, the opening solo of Once In Royal David's City was always given to a child, copying the King's College tradition which particularly irritated Mark. Afterwards, as they enjoyed their over-catered bring and share at Helen and Clement's, they talked briefly about the changes in the Parish. "I wonder whether people felt like this at the Reformation?" asked Scott. "They certainly felt deeply disrupted for a number of decades," replied Clement. "By comparison, this feels a much more modest kind of change, even though it is doctrinally revolutionary. After all, in the English Reformation, which is what I am thinking of, the language of the liturgy changed, and that was massive, but the doctrine didn't change all that much. The clergy—or, anyway, the few thinking clergy—might have been exercised by transubstantiation and consubstantiation but I doubt most people cared. Even those faithful to Rome did not care all that much. The Eucharistic 'obsession', even in the Roman Catholic church, is relatively modern. It was, largely a religion of fear, the fear of going to hell." "So what is the difference between then and now?" "I think that people are much more affected by liturgy than doctrine, and they don't really believe in hell. Look at how Marie is criticised for the choice of hymns, and look at how much fuss Marianne makes about the Authorised Version and the Book of Common Prayer. Think how little fuss there has been about introducing, if that's the right word, a fourth person to the Godhead. Mark cares and, as an amateur theologian, I suppose I care." "And I care," said Meg, "because Kylie cured my mother." "I don't think it is cynical to say that people care most about language and about the concrete benefits of religion and are not very exercised about 'higher' things. Frankly, I am not surprised that most people have taken the change so calmly. I hope it indicates that what matters is the personal relationships we have with God resulting from doing theology in our own private ways, but I am more inclined to think that religion provides people with a degree of comfort and that, therefore, people resent being made uncomfortable. After all, are we more concerned by changing our furniture or having to do something to the roof? The roof matters in a fundamental way—we know that and pay up reluctantly—but we are passionate about colours and fabrics." As if to confirm this analysis, conversation soon drifted away from the changes. From their 'professional' standpoint as choristers with an interest in liturgy, nothing much had happened that had not happened a quarter of a century ago with the change of prayer book. There was much more interest, on the other hand, in the nationalisation of Southern Gem, even though nobody round the table had any money in it. The division of opinion was clearly and strictly ideological, with no room for compromise. "Well at least," thought Clement, "we are not behaving in the same extreme way about doctrine", and he wondered whether the bloodshed of the sixteenth century resulted from faith in the ultimate power of God or the need for political stability. When they were washing up, Helen said, "It struck me when we were talking about change that we have not yet taken up Perpetua's primary recommendation, which was to see church-going as an occasional celebratory activity, with the staple of our witness being the house group." "I know," said Clement, "but as the leader of the healthiest house group in the parish, I'm precisely the wrong person to raise the matter with Mark, who will be very sensitive. He, more than anyone, will be aware of the gap between what he does and what he should be trying to do. He loves church and he isn't very fond of house groups, but we are all so bad at reaching the people in the social housing." "We might start simply by reaching more of our own who are lonely." "I know, there is a terrible danger in house groups like ours of being cosy, but until now I have worried about what we would do if the group got too big. You can't force some people to go away. I suppose we would have to draw lots." "Well, whatever the consequences for our own group, we will have to do something about it after Christmas."

Kylie and Stacey were sitting in Mark's study. "Whatever else you do," said Kylie, "you will have to do something about house groups after Christmas." Mark looked nervous. "Don't be nervous, there are hundreds of people in your situation who are willing to go outside their comfort zones, but don't know how.

After all, Mark, I'm outside my comfort zone being some kind of Perpetuan leader. I never imagined being here and I certainly never imagined advising Guides—former Parish Priests—what they should be doing. If it were not for Our Sister the Spirit, I would be out of it, and there's the clue. We just have to go out and have faith. The first time I came here I talked to some really nice people who found it difficult to come to church and, you will remember, we were thinking about a new house group then. I am sure we can start again after Christmas, but use the Christmas period to advertise what we are going to do." "We?" "Yes, Stacey and I have been assigned to help you and other former Parishes in Alchester to put a network of house groups together. We are particularly aware of the need for relatively prosperous communities to knit with the pockets of deprivation which tend to be overlooked. If we can't crack the problem in places like Walmbury, how are we going to manage in big cities? It was all right in Grunge Park because the deprived and more prosperous areas are in a sociological and geographical spectrum, but there are places, literally separated by the railway lines, where the division is so sharp that we wonder whether we will be able to live out the ideal of mutual support." "I have to admit that, while I have always been an idealist—I think I still call myself a socialist when I'm talking to myself—I've never really got on with poor people. Well, I meet them at pastoral occasions, but I socialise with people who are like myself." "That's natural, but it cuts you off from so many people. It can also make your socialisation routine and rather meaningless." "I had never thought of it that way." "Think of the amount of time you say the same things to the same people over and over again, without the flexing of the mind which gives it strength." "I can relate to that," said Stacey, "but in a different way. Far from sticking with the folks I knew, I went to strange places, but all I did was talk at people, I never talked with them. I wonder whether that is how we deal with the poor and the strange." "The point is," said Kylie, "that we have to trust Our Sister the Spirit. I have been thinking a lot about her since the former Archbishop gave his talk on Incarnational Perception." Mark looked interested. "Never mind the doctrine," said Kylie, "let us just agree to get on with it early in the new year." Mark looked relieved. He had been putting off this moment for months, and every time he put it off, his discomfort increased. He felt like a child who has finally been found out, and is relieved of his 'naughty' secret. He knew that his comfort zone was the church building and its familiar liturgies, but he also knew that he would have to moderate his behaviour. He trusted in the Spirit, but he had been too cautious, and not trusted enough. Perhaps that was his greatest weakness. He had to let go of all the props he had collected. Kylie said, as if in tune with this thought, "And this will mean that some of the people we walk with will be chosen by their groups to celebrate the Sacrament of Union." Mark visibly flinched. "I know that is difficult, Mark, but you have to think of yourself from now on as a Guide to a collective priesthood. You've been saying those words about a 'Royal Priesthood' long enough, now you have to live them. One of your jobs will be to teach people what they need to know to be good celebrants, not just holy, but also joyful. I don't really know how Christianity managed to separate the two ideas so radically." Mark looked puzzled. "I know that you are fundamentally happy with yourself and what you do, but it comes across in a rather joyless way. I'm sorry to be so direct, Mark, but we are here to share the Good News, and we so often conduct ourselves as if we were here to share, well, not always Bad News but, in any event, difficult news." "I suppose that means allowing Clement to celebrate." "I have little doubt that Clement will celebrate, Mark, but it is not a matter of 'allowing' him. If his house group want him to celebrate, the only thing that is lacking is a certificate from you to show that he is competent. His calling from his group comes from God and belongs to God, not to you. Again, I am sorry to be so direct, but the Church of England has talked for so long about collaborative ministry; maybe the intensity of the talk is in inverse proportion to the commitment, but this is the time for a change. Guides provide guidance and, on occasions, leadership, as well as service. But the greatest thing you can do for your people is to bring out their talents so that they are primed to give and to receive. You will have to prime yourself to receive. You have worn yourself almost to death in giving. A human being is not fully human unless it gives, but also takes. A person is only a person in community, but neither are we fully human if we only take or only give. If we only give, part of us gets over-used and part of it gets under-used, so we become unbalanced. That's why so many 'good people' are actually unbalanced. They don't see the goodness in receiving. Anyway, that's quite enough of that. It's equally true that people should balance talking and listening." As always, Mark was gracious once he saw the truth of what he was being told. His immediate reactions were usually emotional and hostile, but he had learned self-control through the deployment of his intellect. The best way of gaining a little time was to ask an apparently simple question: "How do we do this?" "Clement's Group has split into two or three. Others will have to do the same. I think we should tell the new groups what they may do in the first instance but, after that, they can make up their own minds, subject to you as Guide. We don't want a batch of celebrants. It doesn't happen that way." "I don't think I need to design a course for Clement. If his house group want him, as I am sure they do, then I will encourage him, and give him the required certificate." "You are so generous. It is difficult for me to understand the depth of the sacrifice you are making. It must be very difficult to give up what you have worked so hard for, but I hope the Spirit will help you to see that you have given up nothing. Clement is your gift to us."

On the last wednesday before Christmas, Clement's House Group was accustomed to share a meal, celebrate a special Compline he had written, and light the last of the three purple candles on the advent wreath. This year the three house groups that had grown from the original, met together. "We will do things slightly differently this year," he said, "as I think we should worship first." He handed out sheets of paper. "I just need to say," he said, "for the record, that Father Mark gave me a certificate today without requiring me to take a course. So, knowing how difficult that must have been and, therefore, how generous he is, let us all think of him while we celebrate." When it came to the Great Prayer, Clement took mince pies and offered them and gave them to everyone, and then he took mulled wine and did the same. Helen was filled with a happiness she had never felt before. This was Clement finally doing what he had been born to do. "Look," she said, in a whisper, directing everyone's gaze to the wreath. It was bathed in golden light, as if it were on fire. "From the burning bush, through the first Christian Pentecost, to this blessed night," said Clement. "The Spirit is with us." Later Clement said, "I hope what happened earlier this evening will give us the strength we need. Some of us have been together almost three years and, at last, we now know that all our work, prayer and trust have been for a wider purpose than mutual building up. We will have to go out into the community and be the seeds for new growth." "We can't leave each other, and we certainly can't leave you," said Yvonne. "Remember the power of the Spirit. We were sent a message, like the Moses message and the Pentecost message. We were told to go out. The most painful part has been accomplished, so I think we must now give thanks instead of being cautious." Like all such reunions, there was a tendency for the original house group to talk about how things were before it split into three to take on new people in its widened mission. Clement was deeply conscious of the problem of shutting out the newcomers who were, quite naturally, daunted by the unfamiliar. None of them had ever seen an Advent calendar before, but whereas Clement was conscious of the problem in an analytical way, Helen was unceasingly practical, making sure that people were included in conversations and were clear about the significance of what had happened. After they had finished the Sacrament of Union, they drank a toast, sang a hymn and then enjoyed their meal. "Next time we all meet," said Helen, "we will have to have a buffet." With some effort, everybody smiled. It would not be easy, but they had been called by the Spirit to spread the Good News, and that was what they must do. It was a wonder to them that they had this power, thinking for so long that it lay exclusively with the clergy. After they had gone, Clement looked in wonder at the wreath on the rustic, solid oak table: "It was an amazing glow, so amazing that nobody commented." "It has made the house very special." "I feel affirmed. I feel that this is where the whole of my life is leading. I know that I am hopeless at mixing with people who show an indifference to anything but their sadly meagre earthly comforts, but I know that the Spirit will be with us. We have to hold on to that." "I wonder where all this will leave Sunday worship?" "I think the question we are really discussing is a 'when' rather than a 'whether'. People have been drifting away from regular Sunday worship for more than 200 years. I don't think we can have our cake and eat it. It seems to me that Perpetua wanted to replace regular church with regular theology, only supplemented by corporate celebration. It will be really hard for Mark because his reason for living is the Sunday Eucharist." "It will be difficult, but not impossible. Firstly, people have amazing adjustment mechanisms which enable them to explain to themselves why they have voluntarily opted for a change which has actually been forced on them. Secondly, we must not look at what is going to happen from a purely pragmatic standpoint, discounting the Holy Spirit." Helen smiled, and looked at the wreath. "Christmas never will be quite the same again, will it? I wonder how long it will be before there is a Perpetua birth narrative, and how it will be altered through time. We all know that Luke is a wonderful tale, but we suspend belief in the way that we do over Father Christmas. I know about the doctrine, but I still want my baby and my shepherds and kings at the Nativity Service with hundreds of children as angels and shepherds. Even a donkey if you're lucky! There will not be the same scope for imagination—what you probably think of as theology—if the media start unearthing the real facts about Perpetua's birth and upbringing, but I suppose that means that whatever happens to the doctrine, we will keep our Christmas." "It will never be the same again, and there are aspects of that which make me slightly sad, but they are all connected with nostalgia. Christmas is one of the things that happens to us every year from childhood—more predictable and dramatic, more collective, than a birthday—and so we can mark the changes in our world and our lives by observing it closely. The escalation in present giving, the decline in carol singing, the falling chance of falling snow, the loss of occasion because we live so well all year round, the decline of crepe paper decorations, and yes, the commercialisation although there's no seller without a buyer. What we are really thinking about when we look back is that we have come closer to dying." They held hands as they looked at the wreath on the table. "The Spirit is with us," said Helen, and kissed Clement.

Bishop James, although much less engaged by Christmas than by Easter, enjoyed the routine, even though the pressure on him was intense, and although his enjoyment in recent years had been tempered by internal conflict. At least, from his perspective, matters were surprisingly calm in spite of the year's upheavals. He enjoyed a warm, even creative, relationship with the Dean. Castlegate and Aleford had calmed down wonderfully, and Doris had seemed to come back towards him after a period of some distance, almost coldness. He was therefore looking forward with more eagerness than for some time to the small supper party after Compline in his private chapel. By custom, the Bishops, the Dean, and their partners prayed and then celebrated together, but only James had a partner and so Doris only stayed for part of the time, allowing the men to talk confidentially if they felt the need. "Crowther was putting himself about at the big party yesterday," said the Bishop. "It won't make any difference," said the Dean. "He's not on the short list of two. Neither, for that matter, is Mwanga. Crowther made the mistake of failing to re-write his CV, and there it all is on the OpenBook site for everyone to see: Crowther, Tory Party Agent and Parliamentary aspirant. As for poor Mwanga, it doesn't matter how good he is, this just isn't the time for a black Archbishop of Canterbury. It might be precisely the right thing for the Anglican Communion, and even for the Church of England, but no Government in trouble is going to take any risk, no matter how small— and in national political terms the appointment of an Archbishop of Canterbury is very small indeed—and the upshot will therefore be a 'safe pair of hands.'" "It's not the right time for safety," said James. "I would prefer somebody I seriously disagree with, if he's decisive. Deciding to do nothing is the worst possible decision. We need to reach a spiritual as well as an architectural agreement with the Perpetuans, because this issue puts all our previous concerns into context." "I recognise that," said Aleford. "Talking about women bishops today sounds like talking about the Berlin Wall." Castlegate nodded. "It's the same with the gay issue." "It's good to hear us speaking like that," said James. "We have to get back, as Perpetua reminds us, to the primacy of the personal relationship with God; and, in that context, I am beginning to wonder whether the clergy are not doing more harm than good, acting as arbiters instead of facilitators. Just look at the rows we have had that most ordinary believers are not interested in, and if they are, then they're being interested in the wrong thing." "True, in an ideal sense," said the Dean "but people like things that they can handle, such as liturgy and ethics, rather than having to struggle at the theological coal face. In one sense, we have made 'religion' too easy by reducing it to creeds and prayers. We have always been suspicious of mysticism, for example, because we can't control it, but you can't control love. That's the whole point of it. That's why ugly boys mate with pretty girls. It's beyond the logic of modernists like us. We can't get to grips with postmodernist experiential unlogic." Doris, coming in with mince pies and another bottle of port, grimaced. "That's all a bit modernist, Mr Dean!" James smiled at her joke. "Anyway," Doris went on, "the thing that is worrying the Perpetuans at the moment is not such an abstruse issue as you might imagine. They are worried about crib design. Until they have a special day for the Birth of Perpetua, they have to slot her into the crib." "Oh dear," said James, "it sounds as though they are already descending from their glorious heights into the kind of naughty world we inhabit—at least that's an area where we can help them, but what I was going to go on to say—I know it's Christmas and we are expected to be trivial, but this is the first time for so long that we have been able to talk so warmly together—is that we need to have a very open-minded look at what we mean by priesthood and church, and to see how far apart we really are from the Perpetuans. I keep thinking of the terrible consequences of the Jewish-Christian split and what the 'winners' did to the 'losers'. If it turns out that the Perpetuans are the 'winners', they will succumb to power. That is not a criticism of individuals but an Actonism. In a paradoxical way, it may be that our mission is to warn them against the dangers from which we have suffered, but I am beginning to think that the best solution is for us to see how different we really are, and whether we can see them as a 'legitimate' continuation of us." Doris smiled as she slipped away again. She had been hard pressed to maintain her warmth for James for, although she loved him in her heart and knew how deserving he was of that love—always remembering that 'deserving' was a poor word—not least because he would not jump to conclusions, she had found it difficult to be warm towards him while he had been going through his 'orthodoxy' period from which he now, thankfully, seemed to be emerging. The party lasted longer than tradition allowed and, as the Dean and the two suffragans walked, slightly unsteadily, across the Palace Green, they looked like the oldest and best of friends. When they had gone, James and Doris cleared up before enjoying a quiet night-cap. "Where does this leave us all, I wonder?" "Better off than we were a year ago. I know we were almost ignorant of Perpetua then, but we did not think that matters could go on as they were. I have noticed the tension ebbing out of you in spite of the apparent upheavals of Perpetuanism. Truly, James, you were much more stressed about gay clergy and women bishops than you seem to be about fundamental doctrine." "I admit it. This theme, I think initially suggested by the Dean, keeps coming up. We argue over what we can 'control' which is discipline, whereas the arguments about fundamental theology are things we have to re-solve personally. I know that Perpetuanism raises serious doctrinal issues, but doctrine is—as Hawthorne says—a long way downstream from theology. Be-cause I 'do' theology every day—a verb I don't like—it doesn't seem stressful to do just a little more, but administration and discipline are exhausting because there's no grace or energy in them. If everything goes well, you have just done your job properly, and if they don't go well, you haven't. As to your question, I don't know what is going to happen, but I am enormously lucky to have the Dean. I was terribly misled during our disagreements because I made the mis-take—particularly bad for a Bishop—of not seeing past the issue to the man. I know this is all personal relations 101, but we forget the fundamental principles in the heat of the controversy." "I am so glad, James. I thought for a time that we would never be able to talk about Simon and his complex story, which once in-volved me." "Intellectually, I have always maintained—and it's so easy intellectu-ally—that a person in a relationship can't 'own' the other's life, let alone past life, but I must admit that I have found it difficult at times. You can't help wondering if the spark is still there." "You've missed it, James. The spark has never died. We were terribly hurt during the height of the controversy, when Bruce and Hilary were pushing you into conflict with Simon, but he told me to stay calm. He was correct, but not in a forced way because, when we think about it carefully, none of us thinks that the Dean and I have to pretend that we don't love each other, our memories, and what we have in common, just because I came to love you as you loved me. I know there are contemporary theologians who liken sexual rela-tions to the Trinity, but I am not one of them, as you know." "Still, jealousy is so easy to let in and so difficult to expel." "But what of the future, James?" "Well, the Dean has kept me out of the Roman Catholic Church, and I thank him for that as I now see clearly that the 'unholy' alliance between the Petrans and Torans will end in complete disaster. The Roman Catholics and Petrans are about to sacrifice the centrality of the Eucharist for the centrality of the male priesthood, and the Torans are about to sacrifice Priestly worth because of their daft ideas about Male Headship. You put those two pieces together and the result is mess. It will not even be a clean, adversarial, single-issue struggle but a guerrilla war. Strangely, perhaps, Perpetuanism, for all its novelty, is probably where I need to be for my people and for myself. All that you can ask a Bishop to do, in the end, is to do theology, to convey what he can, and to love and encourage his flock.

You can't force feed religion. If only the Torans and Petrans could see that you can't. Shepherds take their flocks to familiar pastures until there is a drought and then they go to new pastures. Well, it seems to me that we were in a state of drought when Perpetua came among us, so we're moving on; probably not forever. If religious history follows its usual pattern we will soon be back where we were, with a different set of labels. Honestly, Doris, as long as people find some way of hearing and talking to God, I don't really mind. At least I learned that from Hawthorne. I just allowed myself to get caught up." They looked out over the frost-sparkling green. The whiteness seemed to intensify until there was only pure light. "The Holy Spirit," said James, as they embraced.

Perpetuan though he was, Clement could not resist the enjoyment of every last traditional Christmas ritual. On the morning of Christmas Eve, he read Isaiah III and Chapter 1 of Luke and, although it was only a few steps, he prepared to collect the turkey from the butcher with deliberate ceremony. He picked up the orders from the greengrocer and delicatessen, returning each "Happy Christmas!" with "Merry Christmas and a happy new year!". he lamented the lack of snow and, only on this day, the absence of a brass band. He 'popped' into church to have a cheerful word with the flower arrangers, and ran a duster over the choir stalls even though he knew his alternate on the rota must have been in. At home, he unpacked and stored as carefully as a naval quartermaster, using his wine cupboard-cum-cellar as a temporary larder, changed the soap and towels, talked to the Christmas tree as if it were human (he loved it because he had only been allowed an artificial tree as a casualty of his mother's obsession with tidiness) and now he was sitting in his customary chair with a glass of Christmas Ale and a service sheet, waiting for the start of the Carols from Kings (which no longer seemed to be called "Nine Lessons with Carols"), which he had only missed twice since he was eight. As always, he sang the Hymns, followed the readings as if they were new texts, and listened critically to the new carols and new arrangements to see if they might be sung by the choir next year. He could not help wincing slightly at the Cleobury arrangements which had not been part of his childhood. Whether the rituals were really about the birth of Jesus or his own childhood was a conundrum he could not honestly disentangle. As soon as the reverberation had died at the end of Hark The Herald, he put his jacket on, closing the door while the organ played its first recessional, and hurried down to church. One event that had not been part of his childhood was the Crib Service. There had been a Nativity Play in school and, on Christmas Eve, carols at the foot of the civic Christmas tree, near the market, with the town's brass band, as it went dark. Then there was Midnight Mass; the Church made no concessions to childhood. He threaded candles into cardboard holders and piled them in a re-cycling bin and, once the tide of children and their parents began to flow in, he could hardly keep up. Sunday church attendance might be going down and attendance at adult Christmas services was also decreasing, but the Crib Service was becoming more popular every year. He tried not to be ungenerous, pushing away the thought that this was the least demanding service for the adults, and one which allowed them to put their children on display—there were plenty of video cameras—but he also recognised that it provided a participative narrative in a way that the Sunday Eucharist should, but did not, provide. He wished that a strategy could be found to convert all this transitional attendance into something more permanent. He never could find the right balance between action and acceptance, good works and faith in the power of the Holy Spirit. As people passed him collecting their candle and service booklet, he noticed that all the hostilities of the previous nine months had been temporarily suspended. There were traditionalists, Petrans, Torans, middle-of-the-roaders, liberals, Affirming Orthodox, Strict Anglicans, Perpetuans, Methodists, Baptists, Roman Catholics and people who could not care less. Perhaps the Church needed to provide such opportunities, and the Spirit would do the rest. The Service itself was identical to that for the previous year. Mark said that it was liturgically authentic and that, until Perpetuan teaching developed, he was happy to leave things as they were. There had been no Perpetuan pressure to change anything. It was such a good story on so many levels that it could not be faulted, and its familiarity robbed it of none of its wonder. Perhaps it was the only piece of wonder that most contemporary children would carry into their old age. Most would certainly not carry the wonder of Easter, but Clement hoped they would one day carry the wonder of Perpetua and the second Easter. For many of them, too, this was the nearest they would get, outside their sexual relationships, to Sacrament, for this play in which they took part was a real drama about a real spiritual event, so different from the digital fantasies they would increasingly inhabit. He tried not to be pessimistic about what he could not fully understand, but he could not help thinking that avatars were no substitute for physical experience, friendship was better than on-line contact, and real communities, with all their oddities and challenges, were better than virtual communities where people could avoid everything they did not like, and 'wallow' in everything they did like. It was not that he particularly valued physical hardship, but he still valued the physical sensation. He was sceptical of those who had said, forty years ago, that television would kill "the art of conversation", and he equally suspected those who said that internet addiction was driving children into a kind of autism, but he had noticed a rapid decline both in lexicography and the ability to deliver speech effectively and pleasingly. It was not just that teenagers did not know what to say, they had very little idea of how to say it, even those who aspired to drama school. His love of texture was an apparent oddity, and although there had never been more television cookery programmes and higher sales of cookery books, it seemed to him to be a kind of pornography, as so few people knew anything about how to prepare and how to eat food and drink wine. Methodically, he removed the candles from their holders, discarding stumps and torn card, calculating the replacement stock requirement, while Helen ran the Hoover over the aisle carpet and a couple of helpers tidied the pews. Mark and Violet made final arrangements for the crib completion at the Midnight Mass, and then they all went to Paul and Jennifer Swayne's traditional Christmas Eve party. Paul was a mild-mannered, vaguely Toran, hard-working member of the parish who steered clear of committees in favour of practical work with children and youth. Although Mark and he would have disagreed if they had opted for a doctrinal dialogue, they were both far too sensible to embark on one. Paul knew that it would only make him more unhappy if the implicit was made explicit, and Mark valued Paul's work accepting, again without being explicit, that liberal catholics, like their Petran cousins, were pretty hopeless with children and youth and that, without Torans there would not be a Sunday School, a creche at the back of church, or any spark of religious enthusiasm at the school. "Where do you stand, then?" asked Clement, who thought he was gentler in his theological probings than Mark would have been, so he was not afraid to pitch in. "I thought it was going to be much worse than it is. I suppose we always think it's going to be much worse." "I have these two maxims: it was never as good as they say it was; and it will never be as bad as they say it will." "Very good, Clement. I wish I had thought that way all my life, it would have given me a much smoother time, instead of which I am terribly prone to pessimism and, as you say, it never turns out that bad. I thought that Perpetuanism was going to wreck Christianity and, in a way, it might, but the kids just love her. The problem with Jesus is that he comes tonight after a tremendous build-up which has nothing much to do with him, and then he's gone with the Christmas present wrapping paper. Even with no apparent digital recordings of Perpetua—and that is a massive puzzle—there are still pictures and speeches. I have to be honest, I think that some people would be put off without thinking, simply because she's not white, but to the kids, who don't care about race the way we do, a pretty girl with braids, wearing jeans and a t-shirt and saying she's God, is fabulously cool. They have been asking whether they can put a baby Afro girl in the crib!" "I can't see anything wrong with it," said Clement. "Only non-believers get worked up when we tell them that the Luke and Matthew stories are pretty unlikely. Sorry, Paul, that was tactless of me." "It's all right, just because I'm a mild sort of Toran doesn't mean that I haven't got an open mind! But how would Mark react?" asked Paul, cautiously, a little afraid of the answer. "I don't think he would be bothered at all, but he would be rattled if you did it without asking. That's the problem. People are so frightened to ask him anything, but he only gets angry when they do things without asking. I'll ask him for you next year. I'd leave it for now. The children will, I am sorry to say, very soon lose interest in the crib." "But what about the bigger picture?" "I think I am caught between two factors which I want to fuse, but they never do. I want to stick to the orthodox Biblical position; but I want the children to grow up to love God and neighbour, and the tradition that we've got just doesn't do that. My upbringing said it would do that, but I know that it won't. If you're a Toran, at the very least you have to read the Bible—and I have— but a great deal of it is pretty useless, and even some of the stuff that's useful is obscure. I don't suppose, when I try to be objective, that any loving God would have confined us to such an unhelpful set of texts as the Bible, and such a warped institution as the Church of England. I mean, I love all the people here, which is why they are here, and I love the Parish, which is why I like doing things in it, but I don't think, when I am honest, that it has much to do with God. Somehow we need God to live among us and if the children think Perpetua did that through her own life or a kind of regeneration of the Spirit, then I have to think about it. My own beliefs are probably more hereditary than self-experienced—you'd call it mimetic, Clement—yes I want to be good because other people are good, but in the end, I can't quite get my head round whether God helps me to be good or whether being good helps me towards God. I just want the children to live good and happy, and what some people call 'holy', lives. I thought Toran practice would see me through, but it hasn't, Clement, not really. I daren't say this too clearly to myself, and certainly not even to Jennifer." "That's a pity, Paul, because until you've said it to Jennifer, you haven't really said it, have you? The easy way to stick to something is to affix honour to it, and that means saying it in front of people you care about. Then they want to know why you have changed and, later, why you've gone back. So much stuff about ethics is self-delusion. I was thinking of what you said about being good and God. The only reply I can make is that it's in our nature to love God and each other. If there was a 'fall' then it was not a failure to do the right thing but a failure to do the loving thing, which isn't quite the same thing. We've got so hung up on love against the odds, love as endurance, love as sacrifice, love in death—so many operas are about unconsummated love—whereas most of us can only manage the deprivations, sacrifices, disappointments, because we have a massive store of fulfilled desire, requited love, to draw on. Look at the children you work with. It's the unloved ones that are going to be the problem, and much of their lack of love is because their environment is harsh and coarse. It is that way because we—I'm afraid I'm going to put my foot in it, Paul, but there we are—we, us middle class people, just won't give up enough of what we've got to get it shunted to poorer people." Helen, who agreed with Clement, but knew that this was dangerous territory, pulled the conversation back. "So how are you going to tackle the Perpetuan Question at Sunday School, Paul?" "I don't think we're going to be explicit. If we can handle questions about the virgin birth, we can handle Perpetua for a while without getting too adventurous. I suspect, however, that Perpetuanism won't go away, so we will have to face it sooner or later, not least because Mark is now formally committed and this is—although it's an anomalous expression—a Perpetuan parish." Unfortunately, Mark heard this last expression, and was about to become pedantic, when Helen diverted his attention by asking about Iris. "I gave her food for the journey early today, and am waiting for Meg to phone if I am needed." "What do Meg and Iris think her cure was for, then?" asked Clement. "They think it served its purpose. They are not resentful, bless them. They never are. In them I see the patience of the poor. They put up with so much. Meg, without complaining, tells me how often she gets paid late for house cleaning by people on hundreds of thousands a year." Mark's phone rang. He listened, and rang off. "Iris is dead. They did not ask me to go because they thought I was busy—always so humble—and they had Kylie with them. Iris was comfortable, and just wanted the three of them to be together when she went. 'A sign that served its purpose'; she used that phrase again. They were so grateful to be a part of what happened. They said the Spirit was with them." "Will you go?" "No. Meg said that she will phone people, and she insists on coming to Midnight Mass to say thanks. I wish we could all keep it that simple."

Clement and Helen walked through the village High Street, quiet except for evening festivities in the pubs. "I don't feel any different about Christmas," said Helen. "Nor do I, although my theological self says I should. I think it will take some catching up to knit Perpetua with the baby Jesus." "I think I'm more with Paul than you when he says it's all about people being good and not so much about them believing the right things." "I know, but that only works on a very short-term basis. What makes people behave in a certain way depends on their nature, our nature. Either we help people to go with their nature or against it, just as we do with plants. Nowhere is that clearer than in the religious impulse to control sex, as if there must be something fundamentally difficult about the very basis on which we were created. Religions that believe in a creator God don't seem to have very much faith in him. The real difference between Perpetua and modern Christianity is that she believes that people are fundamentally good, and should take control of their own human destinies. If Christianity did believe this at one time—and it's difficult to know—it certainly hasn't since Constantine, possibly Paul. So if you believe that people are good, and that it is in their nature to be good, you damage their prospects by inflicting the toxin of intrinsic corruption." "Yes, but at a practical level, will the Perpetuan movement make the world better or worse?" "If you mean will we make fewer wrong choices, I doubt it, but it's impossible to say. We can't say how Europe would have been without Christianity. These are the kind of massive questions that invite unhelpful generalisations. Millions of people have been moved to be good in the name of Christ; one only wishes as many had been moved to be happy. I would like to think that the world will be a happier place because Perpetua gave us a way back to our intrinsic goodness." They talked on as they made a simple supper; they always had white fish and vegetables on Christmas Eve, in anticipation of the richness of the following days. Afterwards, Clement read Luke's story and played a Bach Cantata for the Fourth Sunday of Advent, but instead of sitting in his usual corner in the study, he wanted to be near the tree. "Wise child," thought Helen, affectionately. "He's so easy to love, but so difficult to live with. So predictable, but so predictably fastidious. I just wish sometimes he could let some things pass, but he can't. He doesn't like it in Mark, but he can't stop it in himself. Nonetheless, he's both good and happy, and I have had a part in both." Clement, putting his book down, looked across at her as she hung up the last of the Christmas cards. "So good, but not so happy as I would like. She is much less self-contained than me. Always a worry about a child or a grandchild. Still, I have made her happier than she otherwise would have been." They looked at each other across the four lit candles, three purple, and a pink. The Spirit was with them.

Nigel Bourne didn't like The Oak on Christmas Eve because it was even worse than Fridays, full of noisy people who made comfortable conversation more difficult. "So where's your Perpetua now?" asked Tom Smiley, maliciously. "She isn't mine," he said, a trifle irritably. "But your vicar's gone over to her, hasn't he?" "I suppose he has." "So where does that leave Christmas, then?" "Exactly where it is. Even if you believe in Perpetua, you don't stop believing in Jesus." "Don't you now? So how many more Gods are you going to have? No wonder the Muslims think we're all daft." "I don't think this is the right time to start discussing the theology of the Godhead." "I should think not. The Christian church has made a fool of itself, taking on a woman so-called God; and she's black." "What difference does that make?" "Well, I know there's all this political correctness about us all being the same, but we're not." "Jesus was Semitic, but he's been whitened up by tradition." "Well, it will be a long time before they can do the same thing for Perpetua. In my view, it's a disgrace. The Church should have stuck to its orthodox position." "Which is what?" "Well, I wouldn't know." "As you don't go to church, of course you wouldn't, so why are you in favour of something you don't know about?" "I'm always in favour of what's orthodox." "Always supposing you know what that might mean. Nothing is naturally orthodox, some things just become orthodox over time. You're just a stick in the mud Tory." "You shouldn't mix religion and politics." "That's the stupidest thing you have said all evening." "If you're going to use insulting language ..." "... Oh come off it, Tom Smiley, you know you don't know what you're talking about. Have another pint to show there's no ill feeling." "Still, you can't argue," said Tom, after a grateful pull on his fresh pint, "that it's not going to make Christmas complicated. I mean, if you take Christmas away there's nothing left for Christianity to hang onto." "I take the point that you can't have Easter without Christmas." "No, I don't mean that. It's just that you get crowds at Christmas, and without that you couldn't claim to be very meaningful." "I don't think I'm claiming anything, Tom. People who want to criticise religion usually make exaggerated guesses about what we're claiming and then proceed to knock down what they've built up. The trouble is that the world is split into two kinds of subjects, those which people admit require expertise and those which don't, and the division between the two is arbitrary. For example, people think that they can pontificate about religion, education, and economics, without knowing a thing." Rather than being forced into buying Tom another pint for his inuendo of ignorance, Nigel rapidly downed the remainder of his and went home to feed the sheep and see that everything was all right for the night before going to Midnight Mass. After a couple of blessed days of clear skies and hard frost it had turned windy and wet. "Glory be to God in the highest," he said, as he walked across the yard. "Goodwill to all men. Little lamb, who made thee?" he asked, wondering how it had become a favourite carol. "Behold, the lamb of God!" he said, as he distributed the last of the food. "It doesn't matter in the long run. I've seen some changes, but so did they in the Reformation, and seemed to get over it. Of course it will never be the same again. It never was, but we have to keep something alive for the grandchildren, and they seem to look up to Perpetua as one of them. Bless Angie, she's coming up thirteen and she would have gone clean off religion without Perpetua. What's my liturgical stuffiness to that? Behold, the lamb of God! And as for Perpetua, behold another lamb of God, but black! Who said there was something wrong with black sheep? I like black sheep, so there. Behold the lambs of God!"

Mark went over to church early to enjoy sole possession of it for half an hour: pottering, rather than following a routine, got out the wine and counted the wafers, opened a new packet of candles, straightened the Advent wreath, put out the Midnight Mass booklets, checked the hymn boards, unlocked the organ, admired the flowers and greenery, switched on the sound system, put the readings on the lectern, and inserted marker tapes in his book. Content that all was as it should be, he was left with a quarter of an hour for his prayers. He focused on the birth of the child, not as a sentimental event, but as the centre of his existence. Atheists and sceptics just did not confront it but, then, neither did most Christians who were still Arians, but he embraced the concept of incarnation with immense pleasure. He was really pleased, in an emotional as well as a spiritual way, that Jesus had been a real flesh and blood man, and he was even more pleased now that Perpetua had been a real, flesh and blood woman. It was a piece of human frailty to want a gender balance, but God was obviously alive to human frailty. He thought of the Holy Spirit and Mary, wondered yet again how he could recite the passage in the Creed about the 'virgin birth', but recognised, in the clearest insight so far, that it did not matter. Ultimately, the human need for mechanical explanation was just that, a human need. He thought of Mary's labour, of Jesus being cold, of Joseph, solicitous and bewildered, but he kept coming back to this novel, twin incarnational image. Joseph and Mary short and squat compared with the fresh, young, braided Afro-Caribbean girl who, in the pride of twenty-first century nutrition, looked down at her brother. His reverie was broken by Marie who came in to prepare for Scott and the choir. He knew he must hide his irritation, she was only doing her job, and he could not expect to have the church to himself whenever he wanted it. Everything went ahead as it had in all his previous celebrations of Midnight Mass until his sermon, when he preached on the subject of incarnation, focusing in Jesus, but not failing to mention Perpetua. He recognised a few people, including Marianne Gowers, who had initially been hostile but habit, although hostile to novelty, makes compromises with it to ensure its own survival. After the blessing the choir sang the first verse of O Come, All Ye Faithful and then formed at the top of the chancel steps to watch the placing of the infant Jesus in the crib which was set on a platform below the nave altar table. Mark said a prayer and placed the figure of Jesus in the manger, and then placed a figure of the kneeling Perpetua beside it so that her hand rested on the baby's hand. Violet smiled. The simplicity and sharpness of this novel gesture deepened the silence. Usually at this point, Mark would signal to Scott to get on with the rest of the hymn, but he could not move. Everyone was looking at the baby and his sister. Then a golden light spread from their touching hands, filling the crib, and then the whole church and, filled with Christmas joy, Mark said, "The Spirit is with us."

EU GPSR Authorized Representative:

LOGOS EUROPE, 9 rue Nicolas Poussin, 17000 La Rochelle, France

contact@logoseurope.eu